THE TWELFTH TRANSFORMING

"EXCITING READING... HISTORICAL FIC-
TION AT ITS BEST... A VALUABLE BOOK
... Gedge makes ancient Egypt come alive."
The Daily Oklahoman

"The golden sweep of empire, the settings of
barbarian splendor, the tale of personalities set
against an alien panorama... Miss Gedge's familiarity with ancient Egypt makes that remote
time come alive."
The Kansas City Star

"There's a pervasive ambiance of antiquity, dy-
namic beings struggle within giant destinies—
and a centuries-old mystery is pursued with unobtrusive scholarship and industrious fictional
constructs... a stimulating novel of period pa-
geantry and royal conflict."
The Kirkus Reviews

The Twelfth Transforming

Pauline Gedge

IVY BOOKS • NEW YORK

Ivy Books
Published by Ballantine Books
Copyright © 1984 by Pauline A. Gedge

Library of Congress Catalog Card Number: 84–47570

ISBN 0–8041–0130–2

This edition published by arrangement with Harper & Row Publishers,
Inc.

Manufactured in the United States of America

First Ivy Books Edition: April 1987

For my sons, Simon and Roger.
With love.

BOOK
ONE

1

THE EMPRESS TIYE LEFT HER QUARTERS ESCORTED BY FOUR
Followers of His Majesty and her chief herald. Beneath the
torches that lined the passage between her chamber and the
garden doors stood the palace guards, scimitars sheathed in
leather scabbards, white kilts and blue and white leather helmets
cool and startling against brown skin. As she passed, spears
were thrust forward and heads bowed. The garden lay unlit,
the smothering darkness untouched by the desert stars that
flared overhead. The little company paced the paths briskly,
paused, were admitted through the dividing wall into Pharaoh's
own acres, and passed along the rear wall of the palace.

Outside the tall double doors from which Pharaoh often
issued to walk in his garden or stand and gaze at the western
hills, Tiye ordered her escort to wait, and she and the herald
plunged into the passageway beyond. As she walked, her glance,
always drawn to the confusion of painted images on the walls,
moved up to the frieze under the line of the ceiling. Pharaoh's
throne name, inscribed in gold leaf set in fragrant cedar from
Amki, was repeated continuously. *Nebmaatra: The Lord of
Truth is Ra*. There was nowhere in all the acres the palace
covered where one could go to escape from the words.

Tiye came to a halt, and Pharaoh's steward, Surero, rose
from his seat by the door and prostrated himself.

"Surero, please announce to His Majesty that the Goddess
of the Two Lands is waiting," her herald said, and Surero
disappeared, emerging moments later to bow Tiye into the
room. Her herald settled on the floor of the passage, and the
doors were closed behind her as she walked forward.

Pharaoh Amunhotep III, Lord of All the World, sat on a
chair beside his lion couch, naked but for a wisp of fine linen

3

draped across his loins and a soft blue bag wig surmounted by a golden cobra. The gentle yellow light from the dozens of lamps in stands or on the low tables scattered about the chamber slid like costly oils over his broad shoulders, the loose swell of his belly, the thick paleness of his massive thighs. His face was unpainted. The once square, forceful jaw was now lost in folds of sagging flesh, the cheeks sunken and drawn, evidence of the lost teeth and gum disease that plagued him. His nose had flattened as he had aged, balancing the decay of his lower face, and only the high, tight forehead and the black eyes that still dominated even without kohl told of the handsome, florid youth he had been. One foot rested on a stool while a slave, cosmetic box open beside him and brush in hand, knelt to paint the royal sole with red henna.

Tiye glanced about. The room smelt of stale sweat, heavy Syrian incense, and wilting flowers. Though a slave was moving quietly from one lamp to another, trimming their wicks, the flames gave off a gray miasma that stung her throat and left the room so dusky that Tiye could barely make out the giant figures of Bes, god of love, music, and the dance, that gyrated silently and clumsily around the walls. Now and then a flicker would illuminate an extended red tongue or a silver navel on the dwarf deity's swollen belly or would run rapidly along the leonine ears, but tonight Bes was largely an unseen presence. Tiye's eyes returned to the couch, rumpled and strewn with crisp mandrake leaves and bruised lotus, and now noticed a small black-haired form lying under the sheet, breathing quietly in sleep.

"Well, Tiye, you have taken an inordinate amount of trouble with your appearance tonight," Amunhotep said, his voice echoing sullenly against the invisible ceiling. "Have you come to seduce me all over again? I remember perfectly well that you wore blue and forget-me-nots the first night you came to this room."

Tiye smiled and went swiftly to kneel before him, kissing his feet. "The courtiers would die of horror if I wore such an unfashionable thing today," she teased, rising to stand, perfectly composed, before him. "How is Pharaoh's health today?"

"Pharaoh's health has been better, as you well know. My mouth aches, my head aches, my back aches. All day the magicians have droned outside the door, and I have suffered them because I owe Egypt every opportunity to cure me, but the fools sing to hear the sound of their voices. They have finally gone to swill their well-earned beer and rifle through their scrolls of spells. Do you think I have a demon in me, Tiye?"

"You have had a demon in you all your life, my husband," she retorted. "This you know very well. Is that wine in the jug?"

"No, it is a mandrake infusion, black and foul-tasting. I prescribed it for myself. I have found that it not only acts as an aphrodisiac, something every boy knows by the time he is twelve, but it also surprises me by deadening my pain." He looked at her slyly, and they both laughed.

"Princess Tadukhipa is bringing Ishtar from Mitanni with her, to cure you," Tiye said lightly. "The goddess cured you before, do you remember? Tushratta was very pleased."

"Of course that greedy Mitanni king was pleased. I sent him back his precious Ishtar coated with gold, and a mountain of ingots as well. I am making him rich again, this time for his daughter. I hope she is worth all the expense." He pulled his foot away from the servant. "The henna is dry, and the other sole is done. Go. You also!" he shouted at the lamp trimmer. When they had backed down the expanse of tessellated floor and the doors had closed silently behind them, Amunhotep sobered. "Well, my Tiye, what is on your mind? You did not come here to make love to a fat old god with rotting teeth."

She quickly suppressed the moment of anxiety such talk from him always brought to her. He was shrewd and cold, this man, extracting a pitiless amusement out of every human failing, even his own, and he better than any other knew the irony in his description of himself. For at Soleb, in Nubia, his priest worshipped him with incense and song night and day, and a thousand candles burned before a colossal statue of Amunhotep, the living god, a likeness that neither aged nor sickened.

"I want to talk to you privately, Horus." She indicated the boy. "Please send him away."

Amunhotep's eyebrows rose. He heaved himself out of the chair and moved to the couch with surprising agility, folding back the sheet and gently stroking the sleeping child's naked flank. "Wake and go," he said. "The queen is here."

The boy groaned, turned onto his back, and opened dark, kohl-circled eyes. Seeing Tiye, he slid from Pharaoh's hand onto the floor, bent his knee, and without a word strode away.

"He is older than he looks," Amunhotep remarked without a trace of defensiveness. "He is thirteen."

Tiye sat on the edge of the couch, regarding him coolly. "Nonetheless, you know very well that he is forbidden. This, of all the ancient laws, is the harshest, and the man who brings such a curse on his house is rewarded with death; he and his lover both."

Amunhotep shrugged. "I am the law today. Besides, Tiye, why should this infraction worry you? Between us, you and I have broken every law in the empire."

Including the one against murder, Tiye thought. Aloud she said, "It is the superstitious gossip that worries me. Your appetites are legendary, and the rumors over the years have only served to enhance you in the eyes of your subjects and your foreign vassals. But this . . . this will bring ugly whispers, the rubbing of amulets, hostility toward you where there was only adoration and fear."

"I care nothing for them, any of them. Why should I? I am the most powerful god the world has ever seen. I speak, and men live or die. I do as I please. And you, Great One of Double Plumes, lady of unlimited power, you sphinx with breasts and claws, why do you frown over this small indiscretion?"

"I neither frown nor smile. I simply tell you the temper of your people. While the courtiers do not care, all others will."

"To Sebek with them, then." He lowered himself onto the couch and leaned back, breathing heavily. "I have made you in the image of the man I might have been. I did not want to be that man. You govern while I am content to pursue, well, whatever it is I am still hungry for and have not caught. Immortality in a jug of wine, perhaps. The latent fertility in a woman's body. The essence of my own manhood in that boy. The gods do not have it, and neither does Egypt. Whatever it is."

"I know," she said softly, and for a moment he smiled back. They regarded each other in a comfortable, intimate glance born of years of perfect understanding, Tiye disregarding all but the unpredictable man behind the ruin of the body, a man she would always love. Finally she sighed and handed him the cup of mandrake juice, weighing her next words carefully in the seconds the small gesture gave her.

"The Son of Hapu has been dead for a long time," she said.

He drank, grimaced, and then began to laugh. "The only

death that ever shocked me. He was already so old when I came to the throne that I believed he had compelled the gods to give him immortality. Their magic had preserved him through two reigns before mine. No seer since the dawn of Egypt had such visions, such dreams."

"He was a peasant from a hovel in the Delta. He had no right to control such weighty matters as the succession."

"Why not? As sphinx oracle and mouthpiece of Amun he was as qualified as anyone else. And his predictions came true for nearly eighty years."

"All but one, Amunhotep."

Pharaoh's mouth set in a thin line, and he moved restlessly against the withered leaves, the rotting flowers. "While I still live I continue to be in danger; therefore, no, before you ask, I will not release that boy."

"Why can you not call him your son?"

"My son is dead," he snapped. "Thothmes the hunter, the handsome wielder of the scimitar. Nine years ago the chariot wheel that broke and flung him to his death destroyed direct succession in Egypt."

"You are a stubborn man, still worshipping what might have been," she forced herself to retort, knowing that he would react with contempt to any hint of agitation in her voice. "It is not like you to hold a grudge against fate. Or is it a grudge against the Son of Hapu for failing to predict Thothmes' end?" She leaned toward him. "Amunhotep, why has your grief not abated? Why can you not admit that the young man in the harem is your son and mine, the last male of our line, and thus entitled to the throne of Egypt when you die?"

Amunhotep cradled the mandrake cup in both hands, not looking at her. "I wanted to kill him when the oracle told me what he saw in the Anubis cup. That day is burned into my memory, Tiye. I can still smell the wet lotus that had been gathered and laid under my throne, and see the Son of Hapu standing there at my feet, the Eye of Horus glittering on his chest. I was afraid. The Son of Hapu himself advised me to have the child strangled, and indeed I had already given the order when something stayed my hand. Perhaps I did not feel threatened enough. *How can this son, this three-day-old tiny worm, possibly do me harm?* I thought. 'I have twice looked into the cup and read the omens,' Hapu objected. 'There is no doubt. He will grow up to murder you, O Mighty Bull.'"

Amunhotep gingerly fingered his swollen cheeks and winced. "But I relented. I locked him in the harem instead."

"Where he was kept safely, but only until Thothmes was killed."

Amunhotep's eyebrows rose. He put the cup back on the table and swung his legs over the edge of the couch. Tiye felt his soft thigh settle against hers. "I knew it was you who foiled that attempt," he whispered, eyes suddenly alight. "But try as they might, my spies could never be entirely sure. Just as I could not discover for certain that it was you who poisoned Nebet-nuhe."

Tiye did not flinch. "I understood your panic when Thothmes died," she said as matter-of-factly as she could. "You allowed the Son of Hapu to convince you that it was a deliberate plot on the part of a ten-year-old boy who had never stepped outside the harem, whose guards were changed every week, and who had never been allowed a single male friend. But there was no conspiracy. Hapu was simply asserting his power over you."

"No. He was trying once again to persuade me to do what I had been too weak to do before."

Tiye laid her head against his arm. "If you had seriously wanted to kill your son, you would have gone on trying until you had succeeded. But deep in your heart, O God of Egypt, no matter how you despise the boy, you recognize your own flesh. He will be king when your end comes, and I would rather see you proclaim him crown prince now and send him to serve his time in Memphis than face the battle that will come to me if you die without an official heir. If he had been married to his sister as soon as Thothmes had been beautified, the transition upon your death would be smooth and my mind would now be at rest."

He sat perfectly still. Only his heavy, labored breathing disturbed the thick stillness of the room. Somewhere in the dimness a lamp crackled and went out, and the cloying stench of perfumed oil intensified. "But I wanted Sitamun. And I took her. Thothmes had trained his sister well, and at sixteen she was a prize too glorious to resist."

"But there is now no unmarried royal daughter left, and only one son. And your days are numbered."

He reached over and stroked her face. "I taught you to lie with ease to everyone but me," he murmured. "Now I find your honesty a terror. Yet I do not delude myself. Supposing

I do order the release of that . . . that effiminate eunuch I spawned, and the Son of Hapu was right, and he uses his freedom to kill me?"

Tiye swiftly decided to gamble. "Then you would have the satisfaction of knowing that the oracle was right, though how such a gentle and inoffensive young man as your son could ever conceive of murder, let alone the murder of his own father, is beyond me. Besides, my husband, if by some desperate chance the prince did succeed in killing you, what then? The gods would merely welcome you into the Barque of Ra a little sooner. Your son will be pharaoh whatever you do."

"Unless I have him executed immediately and put an end to this wrangling once and for all."

He spoke coldly. His face had fallen into an expression of polite repose, and Tiye could not tell whether he was angry or simply taunting her with a reminder of his omnipotence.

"Very well," she said cheerfully, aware that her hands were suddenly icy. "Speak the pharaonic word, Majesty. I will see that the order is carried out myself. I am a loyal subject. I know how to obey. Then, when you die in your turn, I will retire to my private estates with a clear conscience, having done my duty. What will it matter that the settling of the succession will be left to lesser men who will shower Egypt with each other's blood in their scramble for the Horus Throne? I shall certainly not care that the Mighty Bull left no kingly seed behind!"

He stared at her for a long time before nodding slowly. "The crowning argument," he muttered, "and behold, my arrogant Tiye, at last I listen. Do not press my face against the bitter mingling of my pride and loss any longer. In Thothmes' death the gods exacted a harsh payment for the wealth and power I have possessed all my life." He smiled faintly. "They should be laboring for me in the royal Treasury. I now concede. Have him released. I have done it all, had it all, and whether I am extinguished by sickness or an assassin's knife, I must pass. I can at least spare you the annoyance of a ring of jackals barking in your face if I die without an official heir. But do not think that you can give him Sitamun. I need her."

Weak with a relief she dared not show, Tiye blurted, "I was thinking of Nefertiti."

Once again, startlingly, he laughed aloud. Turning, he reached for her throat, kneading and squeezing her. The gold chain holding up the sphinx pectoral pressed painfully into her skin, but she knew better than either to show fear or to resist. "A family tradition," he wheezed, shaking her, his grip tight. "Once again you secure the throne on behalf of a bunch of Mitanni adventurers. For that is what you are, all of you. Loyal servants of the crown, earners of every reward, but may the gods have pity on any pharaoh who gets in your way."

"For three generations my family has served Egypt self-lessly. Horus, you are unjust," she choked. "My father did not force you to make me empress. He did not have that kind of power. You raised me to divinity yourself."

Suddenly he released her, and she tried to catch her breath quietly. "I loved Yuya. I trusted him. I love and trust you also, Tiye. It is the pain. Sometimes I cannot bear it. Cassia, oil of cloves, the mandrake, nothing really helps."

"I know," she said, rising to stand between his legs. "There is only this." Placing her hands on his shoulders, she bent and kissed him. He sighed gently, drawing her down onto his knee, his mouth soon leaving hers to seek her painted nipple. *So much has changed, Amunhotep, but not this,* she thought, passive with pleasure for a moment. *In spite of everything I still adore and worship you.* "Nefertiti?" she whispered, then cried out as he bit her. "If you will," he replied, a quiver of amusement in his voice. He pulled the wig from her head and plunged both hands into her own long tresses.

Just before dawn she left him sleeping peacefully, free of pain for a few hours. She wanted to stay and sing to him softly, cradle and rock him, but instead she gathered up her wig, fastened the sphinx once more about her bruised neck and went out, closing the doors slowly behind her. Surero and her herald slept, the one bowed on the stool, the other huddled against the wall. The torches lining the long passage had gone out, and the guards had changed, the new faces heavy with the need for rest but with eyes alert. Into the ephemeral cool of a summer night a faint gray light was pooling. Tiye had raised a sandaled foot to stir her herald when she heard a movement and turned.

Sitamun had stepped into the corridor and was standing uncertainly, white linen floating around her, a gossamer-thin pleated short cloak around her slim shoulders. She was wigless, her own brown hair frothing about her face, one silver circlet resting on her forehead. Amulets of silver clasped her arms, and silver scarabs and sphinxes hung across her breasts. Tiye, exhausted and satiated, had the chilling impression that she was gazing back through the years at a vision of herself, and for a second was frozen with fear and an aching longing for what had been, what could never come again. Then she began to walk toward her daughter. "He does not need your presence tonight, Sitamun," she called, and at the sound of her voice her herald scrambled to his feet. "He is asleep now."

Watching jealousy and disappointment flit across her daughter's imperious face, Tiye quelled a spurt of purely feminine triumph. *It is not worthy of me to take pleasure in thwarting Sitamun*, she thought contritely as the young woman hesitated. *Such pettiness belongs to aging concubines in large harems, not to an empress.* She smiled warmly. Sitamun did not respond. After a while she bowed stiffly and disappeared into the somnolent shadows.

Back in her own apartments, Tiye ate to the music of the lute and harp players that woke her every morning and then sent for Neb-Amun. He was waiting for the summons and came quickly, a plump, graceful man in a full-length scribe's gown, his head shaved bare, his face impeccably painted. He laid down his burden of scrolls and bowed, arms extended.

"Greetings, Neb-Amun," she said. "It is too hot to receive you on my throne; therefore I shall lie down." She did so, settling her neck against the cool curve of her ivory headrest as Piha covered her with a sheet and her fan-bearer began to wave the blue feathers over her. "I shall also close my eyes, but my ears shall remain open. Sit."

He took the chair beside the couch while Piha retired to her corner. "There is not a great deal for Your Majesty's attention," Neb-Amun said, shuffling through his papers. "From Arzawa the usual grumbles over encroachments made by the Khatti, and of course a letter from the Khatti protesting an Arzawa raid across the mutual border. I myself can answer that. From Karduniash a demand for more gold, after the usual greetings. I do not advise that Great Horus send them anything. They have received much from us already, and beneath the demands are veiled threats that treaties will be concluded with either the Kassites or the Assyrians if Pharaoh does not continue to show his friendship."

"Pharaoh will arrange military maneuvers to the east," Tiye

murmured. "That should be enough. Is there anything from Mitanni?"

"Yes. Tushratta is withholding the dowry until the city of Misrianne is officially his, that is, until the scroll of ownership reaches him. He has received the gold and silver. Princess Tadukhipa has arrived at Memphis. Word came this morning."

Tiye's eyes flew open, then closed again. "So there really is to be an addition to the harem," she muttered. "After all the haggling and kidnapping of ambassadors and empty promises and insults, little Tadukhipa is in Egypt." *I would like to see Mitanni just once*, she thought suddenly. *The home of my ancestors. Who knows but that this new king, Tushratta, might be a distant relative of mine. How strange!* "Is there anything else?"

Neb-Amun paused. "There is no official confirmation yet, Majesty, but it is rumored that a new prince has arisen in the land of the Khatti, who is pulling the people together. It seems that the Khatti will recover from the sacking of Boghaz-keuoi after all."

"Perhaps, although an enemy that can penetrate to the capital city of a country is not likely to be repulsed quickly. Particularly if it is being secretly armed and victualed." Tiye turned her head and looked at Neb-Amun, but her gaze was unfocused. She frowned. "We know that Tushratta has been taking advantage of the chaos among the Khatti to strengthen his own position by aiding Khatti's rebellious vassal states. The balance of power between Mitanni, Egypt, and the Khatti was delicate, and is now upset."

"Khatti is now very weak."

"And a weak Khatti means a much stronger Mitanni. We must watch the situation carefully. We cannot have Mitanni become too swollen, but neither can we allow the Khatti to grow too arrogant. We have treaties with the Khatti?"

Neb-Amun nodded. "Yes, but they are old."

"We can dredge them out of storage if necessary. Is there word on the character of this prince? What is his name?"

"The desert police are saying that he is young and vigorous, and ruthless enough to take the risks necessary to become ruler of the Khatti. He won a palace insurrection, Majesty. His name is Suppiluliumas."

Tiye laughed. "Barbarian! Egypt will deal with him easily if necessary. Diplomatically, of course. What next?"

There was little else for the day. Cargo from Alashia, new oxen from Asia, gold from the Nubian mines, and a consignment of vases from Keftiu. "Send me one later. I want to see the quality," Tiye said. "You can go now, Neb-Amun. Pharaoh will see to the sealing of any scroll that is necessary." He gathered up his papers at once and bowed himself out.

After being bathed and dressed in fresh linen, Tiye sent for a herald. "Summon my guard. We are going into the harem."

They emerged under the high roof of the palace terrace, Tiye with soldiers before and behind, her fanbearers and whisk carrier to either side. Although noon was hours away, the forecourt was already crowded with children leaping in and out of the fountains. Slaves and attendants, seeing her pass, went down on their faces. The wide paved square leading to Amunhotep's public audience hall was likewise crowded with the staff of the foreign embassies whose quarters dotted the palace compound and who waited until such time as Pharaoh or his ministers might receive them. They, too, hearing the herald's warning cry, bent in reverence as Tiye paced through their midst. Once the heavily guarded door between the public domain and the harem water steps was closed, the noise faded. As the little group turned left under the pillared entrance to the women's quarters, Tiye's chief steward and Keeper of the Harem Door, Kheruef, came forward, his short linens fluttering in the draught that blew through the open doors of the gardens at the rear of the buildings. Tiye held out a hand.

"You will have another apartment to furnish and slaves to buy," she told him as he kissed the tips of her fingers. "The foreign princess Tadukhipa arrives within days."

Kheruef smiled politely. "Princess Gilupkhipa will be overjoyed, Majesty. Since the murder of her father and the rise of her brother to power, she has been frantic for news from Mitanni. Tadukhipa is her niece and will bring a breath of familiarity into Gilupkhipa's rooms."

"Considering that Gilupkhipa has been a royal wife for almost as long as I have, I find it hard to understand why she still pines for the discomforts and dangers of an uncivilized country," Tiye remarked dryly. "But I do not want to discuss Pharaoh's Mitanni women. I have come to see the prince."

"He has just risen and is in the garden by the lake, Majesty."

"Good. See that we are not disturbed."

Alone, Tiye walked through the precious breezes of the

corridor. To right and left, doors stood open. She passed the little reception halls, where the women received their stewards and members of their family, and the smaller, more intimate rooms where on winter evenings they gathered around the braziers to gossip. Leading from the main passage were other corridors lined with granite statues of the goddesses Mut, Hathor, Sekhmet, Ta-Urt, the deities before whom the women would stand and burn incense, muttering prayers for beauty, fertility, the continuance of their youth, the health of their children. These led to the apartments of Pharaoh's wives, who lived in the same wing deep within the palace complex. The concubines had their quarters throughout the sprawling harem, and as Tiye passed, she was gradually embraced by its peculiarly stifling atmosphere. Laughter and shrill chatter echoed all around. There was the clatter of bronze anklets, the tinkle of silver ornaments, the flash of yellow, scarlet, and blue linen vanishing around a corner. Somewhere, at the end of the passage leading to the nurseries, a sick child was wailing. Incense billowed suddenly into her face from a half-closed door, and the musical cadence of foreign prayers, Syrian perhaps, or Babylonian, came with it. Through another door she saw a naked body, arms extended, and heard the wail of a pipe.

I hate the harem, Tiye thought for the thousandth time as she broke out into dazzling sunlight and began to cross to the women's lake. *The months I spent here as a frightened, determined child of twelve, a wife like all the other wives, were the most frustrating of my life. Having my mother here as a Royal Ornament did not help, either. She ruled the other women as a divisional commander does his troops, with a whip and a curse, and she hated to see me run across these lawns in the early mornings naked, without paint, when the other women were still deep in their perfumed dreams. If Amunhotep had not fallen in love with me, I should have taken poison.*

She pushed aside her thoughts for she now saw him, her last living son, sitting cross-legged on a papyrus mat at the verge of the lake, shaded by a small canopy. He was alone and motionless, both hands lying in the lap of his white kilt, his eyes fixed on the constant white flicker and dance of the light on the little waves. Not far from him a group of trees cast a dappled shade, but he had chosen to have his canopy erected in the glare of the full sunlight. Tiye approached him steadily, but only at the last moment did he look up and see her. Rising, he prostrated himself in the grass, and then he resumed his position.

Tiye settled gracefully beside him. He did not look at her but seemed wrapped in a quiet self-absorption as his eyes continued to watch the surface of the water. As always when she visited him a feeling of puzzlement and alienation stole over her. She had never seen him behave other than passively, but after his nineteen years of life she still could not decide whether his self-possession was the confidence of a supreme arrogance or a stoic acceptance of his fate or the mark of a guileless man. She knew that the harem women treated him with a mixture of affection and disdain, like an unwanted pet, and had wondered more than once over the years whether her husband knew how slowly corrupting such influences could be on the young man. But of course he knew. The degradation of humanity was a well-charted, familiar course to him.

"Amunhotep?"

Slowly he turned mild, liquid eyes upon her, and his thick lips curved into a smile, relieving for a moment the jutting, downward plunge of the unnaturally long chin. He was an ugly man. Only his thin, aquiline nose saved him from unredeemed homeliness.

"Mother? You are looking tired today. Everyone is looking tired. It is the heat." His voice was high and light, like a child's.

She did not want to chatter, but for a moment the news she had brought him overwhelmed her, and she found she could not select the words to present it to him gently. Hesitating only briefly, she said, "For many years I have dreamed of telling you this. I want you to instruct your steward and your servants to pack everything you want to take away with you. You are leaving the harem."

The smile did not falter, but the long brown fingers resting against the shining linen tightened. "Where am I going?"

"To Memphis. You are to be appointed high priest of Ptah."

"Is Pharaoh dead?" The tone was enquiring, nothing more.

"No. But he is ill and knows that he must name you as his heir. An heir apparent always serves as high priest in Memphis."

"Then he is dying." His eyes left her and fixed themselves on the sky. "Memphis is quite close to On, is it not?"

"Yes, very close. And you will see the mighty tombs of the ancestors and the city of the dead at Saqqara, and Memphis itself is a marvel. You will live at Pharaoh's summer palace. Does that please you?"

"Of course. May I take my musicians and my pets with me?"

"Anything you like." She was mildly irritated by his lack of reaction and decided that he did not yet fully understand how complete the change in his circumstances would be. "I'd suggest you empty your apartments here," she went on crisply. "You will not be returning to them, and besides, as Horus-Fledgling in Egypt you must marry, and you can hardly expect a future queen of Egypt to inhabit less than a palace of her own."

For the first time, she had moved him. His head whipped around, and for a fleeting second she read a gleam of satisfaction in his eyes. "I am to have Sitamun?"

"No. Pharaoh reserves the right to keep her."

"But she is a fully royal sister." His mouth was pursed, his brow furrowed. *Is he pleased or disappointed that he cannot have her?* Tiye wondered. "My son, the days when the succession went only to a man who married fully royal blood have passed. Now the choice is made either by Pharaoh himself or by the Amun oracle."

Amunhotep's lip curled in a sneer. "I am the last choice the Son of Hapu could have made. I am glad he is dead. I hated him. It is you, Mother, who have forced this upon Pharaoh, is it not?" His hands left his lap and went to the white leather helmet he wore, pulling at its wings reflectively. "I want Nefertiti."

Tiye was taken aback. "Nefertiti is my choice also. She is your cousin and will make a good consort."

"She comes to see me sometimes and brings Uncle's baboons. She visited the library on my behalf and brought me scrolls to study. We talk of the gods."

So Nefertiti is deeper than I imagined, Tiye thought. "That was good of her," she said aloud. "You will serve at Memphis for one year. Afterward you will return to Thebes and be married and set up your own palace. I will help you, Amunhotep. I know it will not be easy for you, after so many years of captivity."

He reached for her hand and stroked it. "I love you, my mother. I owe this to you." His gentle fingers caressed her wrist. "Will Pharaoh wish to see me before I go?"

"I do not think so. His health is precarious."

"But his fear of me is vital enough! So be it. When do I leave?"

"In a few days." She rose, he with her, and on impulse she leaned forward and kissed his smooth cheek. "Will Prince Amunhotep want to begin a harem of his own?"

"Eventually," he responded solemnly. "But I shall select my women myself, when I am ready. I shall be busy in Memphis."

"I will leave you to give your instructions, then. May thy name live forever, Amunhotep."

He bowed. When she glanced back at him a moment later, he was still standing where she had left him, and she could not read his expression.

Before she began the official acts of the afternoon, Tiye sent a message to her brother Ay, requesting that he leave his own duties to his assistants and wait for her in his house. Then she sat restlessly through two audiences, heard the daily report from the Overseer of the Royal Treasury, and absently refused the fruit Piha offered during a brief lull in the proceedings. Her mind revolved around the changing fortunes of her son and the burden of new responsibility his freedom would lay upon her, and she was impatient to discuss it all with Ay. Before the last minister had bowed himself from her audience chamber, she had left her throne and was brusquely ordering out her litter.

Her brother's house lay a mile north of the palace, along the river road. He was waiting for her, and as the bearers lowered her litter and she stepped into the thin shade of his garden, he knelt on the grass. "Stay by the gate until I call," she commanded her servants and then walked forward to receive Ay's kiss on her feet before seating herself on the chair set ready. Ay resumed his own.

"I know I look tired." She smiled, seeing his expression. "I had little opportunity for sleep last night. But I will take some of that watered wine and rest here with you. This place never changes, Ay. The house ages gracefully, the same flowers that I loved as a child still bloom, the trees are as willfully ragged as ever. You and I have solved many mysteries together here through the years."

He motioned, and a servant filled her cup and retreated. "May I assume from Your Majesty's cheerfulness that you found Pharaoh in good humor?" he enquired, smiling.

Tiye set the cup back on the table and met his eye. "It is done," she said. "He will release the prince. My final victory over the Son of Hapu, may Sebek grind his bones! I still cannot believe he is really dead. So many courtiers were so sure that he was sustained by the gods themselves and was immortal."

Ay picked up his jeweled whisk and began to flick at the swarm of flies that hovered over his damp skin. "You and I discussed often enough the possibility of forcibly proving them wrong," he murmured dryly. "When is Amunhotep to be released?"

"As soon as possible. I want you to be ready with a detachment of your soldiers from the Division of Ptah to escort him to Memphis when I send word. You had better arrange for Horemheb to take charge. He is young but very capable."

"And he will be overjoyed to return to Memphis. Anyone would. Thebes is a stinking hole full of beggars, peasants, and thieves. At this time of year the stench from across the river wafts past my sycamores and wilts the flowers. Very well, Tiye, I will handpick the men. I am very pleased. The world is waiting to do homage to your son."

"May the gods grant him recompense for the wasted years," she said softly. "Pharaoh is also willing to seal the marriage contract between Amunhotep and Nefertiti. He will not give up Sitamun. I did not expect he would, and it does not matter. I have kept my pledge to the family. I have maintained our influence, and your daughter and my son will do the same. We have not done badly for the spawn of a Mitanni Maryannu warrior brought to Egypt as booty by Osiris Thothmes III."

They sat for a moment in a companionable silence. In the days of her childhood, when she had been promised but not yet delivered to Pharaoh, Ay had been her mentor, teaching her what to wear, what to say, how to keep the interest of the boy who was destined to be her husband. He told her of the king's likes and dislikes, his foibles, his preferences in women, reminding her night and day that she could not hope to retain her hold on a man with her body alone. The chain must be forged of intelligence and humor, a quick mind and a crafty heart. When at the age of twelve she finally stood before Amunhotep, wigged and painted, she had met his black eyes and found something that had not entered into her brother's calculations. They had fallen in love. Amunhotep had raised her to the position of empress, and long after he had ceased to take her alone to his bed, the bond remained. She had not failed him. She came of sturdy stock imbued with a thrust for power and domination that had not abated for generations, so that her family, commoners without a drop of royal blood in their veins, had succeeded in becoming the power behind every throne since the days of Osiris Thothmes III. Each Pharaoh since had been carefully evaluated by the family, his strengths probed, his weaknesses compensated for and exploited. Tiye's own father had been Lieutenant of Chariotry, Master of the King's Horse, and chief instructor in the martial arts to the young Amunhotep, a task he used to bind the boy to him. Her mother had been a confidante of Mutemwiya the queen, and Chief Lady of the Harem of Amun. Land, wealth, and prestige had accumulated year after year like deposits of rich Nile silt, but such preferments could be whisked away to leave them all shivering in the cold blast of penury and royal disapproval. Therefore nothing was taken for granted, and each step required a cautious testing.

"Nefertiti is sulky, restless, and very willful," Ay said after a while. "But none of her faults is noticed because she is so extraordinarily beautiful, and she has been spoiled by everyone from her nurses and tutors to my own cavalry officers. Whether she is also ambitious remains to be seen. At eighteen she blames me that she is not already married and a mother."

"You may tell her that she will soon be both. Surely she strikes out at everyone now because she is bored and anxious. She will quickly learn discipline in the palace."

"Do not expect it," Ay said shortly. "She is my daughter, and I love her, but my love is not blind. Perhaps if her mother had lived, if I had not been so busy . . ."

"It is not important," Tiye broke in. "The faults of a queen are hidden by paint, jewels, and protocol." She lifted the wet, salty linen away from her skin and began to fan herself. "If Isis does not begin to weep soon, I am going to die of this heat. I am a goddess. Surely I can send a priest to her shrine to threaten her."

The soft slap of bare feet on the cool tiling of the terrace interrupted her, and she turned. Mutnodjme, Ay's younger daughter and Nefertiti's half sister, emerged from the darkness of her father's reception hall and came sauntering toward them, naked but for a gold circlet around her throat and a scarlet ribbon trailing from her youth lock. In one hand she held a bunch of black grapes and in the other a small whip. Behind her, her two dwarfs scuttled, also naked, one dragging towels, the other a red ostrich fan. They stopped when they saw the queen and began to mutter agitatedly to each other, but scowling comically. Mutnodjme came up to Tiye and prostrated herself and then rose to plant an offhand kiss on Ay's cheek.

"The afternoon is well advanced," Tiye chided, noting the girl's swollen lids and flushed face. "Have you been asleep all morning?"

Mutnodjme lifted the grapes and bit into them, wiping the juice from the corners of her mouth with the back of one hennaed hand. "There was a party last evening at May and Werel's house, and after that we went boating, and after that we took torches and litters and roamed around Thebes. Before I knew it, it was dawn." She chewed reflectively. "The whores along the street of brothels have started wearing necklaces of many tiny clay rings painted different colors. I think it will be the next fashion at court. I must get some made. Are you well, Majesty Aunt?"

"I am," Tiye said, hiding her amusement.

"Then Egypt is fortunate. I am going to bathe before my skin turns to leather in this heat. Gods! Ra is pitiless this summer!" She tossed the rest of the grapes onto the table, flicked the whip languidly at the dwarfs, and walked away. Tiye watched her pass from shade into glaring sunlight, the muscles under the curvaceous hips flowing. The dwarfs trotted after her, exclaiming in shrill voices and swatting at each other.

"I pity the man who marries that one," Tiye observed. "He will need to be heavy-handed."

"She should have been married by now," Ay responded. "In any case, when Nefertiti marries the heir, Mutnodjme will be too close to the throne to give to anyone whose loyalty to the family might be suspect. Her own loyalties go to whoever can amuse her."

"Horemheb would be able to contain her very well," Tiye said thoughtfully. "I wonder if he could be induced to marry her. I would be loath to force him. He is a good commander and takes his bribes openly, not underhandedly, as a minister of the crown should."

"It would be better to hold her in reserve until Nefertiti and the prince are safely wed," Ay objected. "There is still Sitamun,

I know, but Pharaoh will not let her go until he is dead. She is his link with Thothmes, his son, and with his own past."

Tiye silently acknowledged his insight, and his hardness. "You speak too disrespectfully of my husband," she chided quietly.

He did not apologize. "I speak of political necessity, without malice," he replied. "We both know that if the prince were allowed to choose Sitamun over Nefertiti for chief wife, Sitamun's jealousy of you and her lack of political acumen would relegate you to the powerless position of dowager once Pharaoh dies. Sitamun would not allow you near the ministers and would not bother with them herself. If Amunhotep later wants to marry his sister, he may, but not until Nefertiti is chief wife."

There was a moment of silence as Tiye rolled his words around in her mind. She and Ay had often engaged in this discussion, and it had always seemed like a mental exercise, a defense against the boredom of scorching summer afternoons, but now the considerations were all too real, the alternatives vital. She watched Ay's baboons where they squatted in the dry grass at the other end of the garden. They yawned and chittered desultorily to one another, scratching under their jeweled collars or grooming each other's fur in search of lice.

At length he said, "If anything should happen to Nefertiti before a marriage contract is sealed, I would rather see Mutnodjme take her place with my son than Sitamun. But we will wait and try not to be anxious. I wish you could persuade her to remove her youth lock and let the rest of her hair grow. She has been a woman now for four years."

Ay grinned ruefully. "I've given up that fight. Mutnodjme likes to be different. She likes to shock her inferiors and titillate her equals. She is the arbiter of all that is fashionable in Thebes."

"And while she remains concerned with fashion she will not be playing more dangerous games." Rising, Tiye clapped her hands, and immediately Ay came to his feet. A host of servants poured from the quiet dimness of the house. Tiye received her brother's obeisance, holding out both hands for his kiss. "I will send Kheruef to you when I am ready. May your name live forever, Ay."

"Yours also, Majesty."

In spite of the outward confidence I have always shown, I did not really believe this day would ever come, Tiye thought as she walked to the gate where her litter bearers were rising to bow to her. *Amunhotep is free. Egypt has a crown prince, and the rest is a matter of mere detail. This is my greatest victory, and I am happy.*

2

TIYE'S BREATH OF COMMAND BLEW THROUGH THE PALACE AND the military barracks like a desert wind, so that three days after she had broken the good news of his release to her son, Amunhotep was able to leave for Memphis surrounded by the full pomp due an heir. During those three days the men who measured the height of the river had reported a tiny rise in its level, and it was both a relieved and an excited crowd that gathered on the palace water steps to catch a glimpse of the prince who was to appear among them like a rumor sprung to life. Tiye sat on her ebony throne, jeweled sun canopy over her, fans waving languidly before her. Sitamun was beside her, dressed in yellow, the plumed crown she was entitled to wear as chief wife quivering as she breathed. Ay paced between the gilded barge *Aten Gleams* and the contingent of soldiers standing sweating in formation, waiting for the prince to board. Mutnodjme, swathed in white linen and heavily painted against the sun, flicked her whip dispiritedly at the date palms above her while her dwarfs panted at her feet, too hot to quarrel.

A small group of priests from Karnak led by Si-Mut, Amun's Second Prophet, stood ready with incense and systra to speed the prince on his way with prayers. Tiye, glancing at Si-Mut's solemn, sweat-streaked face out of the corner of her eye, felt a pang of longing for her brother Anen, who had been Amun's Second Prophet only a year earlier, before the fever had consumed him. "Give me the whisk," she snapped at her whisk carrier and began to flick irritably at the flies that crawled over her slick neck and fought to suck up the salt around her mouth and kohled eyes.

Ay came to her and bowed. "Majesty, I have instructed Horemheb to open his house in Memphis to the prince until every servant and official in the palace there has been investigated. It is not likely, now that Pharaoh has decreed this move officially, but there may still be some who would wish to do him a favor by trying to harm Amunhotep."

"Or he himself may regret his decision," she answered in a low voice. "I shall be anxious until the statutory year is over and he is once more under my eye here at Malkatta. Stand aside, Ay."

A buzz of excited talk was followed by deep silence as the soldiers and their charge approached. Horemheb came striding up to the throne, the silver arm bands that proclaimed him Commander of a Hundred flashing as he moved, the blue helmet he was entitled to wear as a charioteer framing a handsome face that, though young, was already marked by the early maturity the career he had chosen had thrust upon him. As Ay's protégé he was destined to go far in the army and at court, and he knew it, but he had not relied on his mentor's favor alone. The men under him had learned that although his discipline was swift and harsh, his judgment was fair. He knelt to kiss the queen's feet.

"You understand the gravity of this responsibility, Horemheb," Tiye said as she waved him to his feet. "I expect clearly dictated and regular reports from you."

He inclined his head but did not reply.

She turned to her son, rising and stepping down to embrace him, and realized with surprise that Nefertiti stood beside him, tall and feminine in yellow, the waist-length ringlets of her wig wound with forget-me-nots made of lapis lazuli, the color of the hair of the gods. "Send me word of your doings as often as you can," Tiye said as her arms went around Amunhotep. He nodded against her cheek and pulled away smiling, and then Tiye saw his gaze lift over her shoulder to the palace behind them. All at once a mask seemed to drop over the long, sallow features, and he turned abruptly. Tiye stole a glance backward. Half-hidden by one of the fluted lotus columns that fronted the reception hall and attended by only his body servant, her husband was watching. A murmur of surprise went through the crowd, and Tiye's head jerked around again in time to see her son press his lips against Nefertiti's scarlet mouth. "May your name live forever, Cousin," he said loudly, playing with one glistening ringlet as she grinned at him, eyes screwed against the sun. "Come and visit me if your father will allow

it. I shall miss our conversations." Outraged at the breach of
good manners, Tiye glared at Ay.

"May the soles of your feet be firm, Prince," Nefertiti answered Amunhotep boldly, and he turned and walked up the
ramp, disappearing into the shade of the little cabin. Horemheb
gave an order, and the hangings were lowered. Si-Mut began
to chant, the incense rose, and the soldiers took up their positions along the railing. Oars were run out. The timekeeper
began to shout his rhythm, and the barge with its little blue
and white pennants moved lightly away from the steps and
across the lake, heading for the canal and the freedom of the
river.

As the boat dwindled from sight, Tiye clutched the fly whisk
tightly, wanting to slash it across her niece's flowerlike little
face, but instead plying it vigorously against her own legs.
Before the girl could edge away, she made a quick decision.
"Nefertiti, you will have your belongings packed and moved
into my palace as soon as possible," she snapped. "Leave your
staff with your father, or send them all to Akhmin, or sell them,
I don't care. I will provide servants for you. It is time you
learned how to behave like a wife, not a simpering concubine."

"I am neither yet, Majesty Aunt," Nefertiti replied, un-
cowed. "Amunhotep kissed me. I did not kiss him."

"You know very well that you should have taken a step back
and gone down on one knee to show that you were both honored
by his attention and embarrassed by his public display. What
is the matter with you?" *And what is the matter with me?* she
demanded of herself. *Why am I so annoyed at this tiny slip on
the part of my son, who is today surely filled with an exultation
that must be hard to repress? Am I afraid that my influence
over Amunhotep will be weakened now that he is no longer
wholly dependent on me for affection?* She managed a cold
smile to Nefertiti and felt the jealousy fade.

"I know what I should have done," Nefertiti replied half-
defiantly, half-apologetically, "but my cousin took me by surprise. It was a gesture of great favor, and I am honored."

The priests had moved to the edge of the lake, and Si-Mut
was throwing flowers upon the water as the crowd began to
disperse. Mutnodjme had come up to Tiye and was listening
to the exchange with interest.

"So you should be," Tiye said grudgingly. "We will forget
it. You might as well begin to assume some of the responsi-

bilities of a princess, Nefertiti. Envoys from this upstart Khatti prince arrived yesterday, and tonight Pharaoh is giving them a taste of Egyptian hospitality. You are all expected to attend. It is a pity Tey is still at Akhmin. I want to see her."

"Mother cannot bear Thebes in the summer, Majesty Aunt," Mutnodjme broke in. "She only feels at home on the old family estates. But I shall be there. May Nefertiti and I be dismissed?"

Tiye nodded, and both girls bowed. Mutnodjme's whip cracked over the heads of the drowsy dwarfs, and they jumped to their feet with squeals of wrath. Running one hennaed palm over her shaven head and tossing her ribboned youth lock over her shoulder, she made off in the direction of Ay's barge, moored under the sycamores at the far end of the water steps. Nefertiti beckoned to her train of women and followed. Tiye, turning back to the palace with an inaudible sigh, noted that the pillar that had sheltered the silent bulk of her husband was empty.

The excitement caused by Amunhotep's departure was soon overshadowed by the arrival of Princess Tadukhipa. The river had by now deepened and was flowing swiftly, tugging at its banks like an unruly horse, and though it had not yet begun to spill over onto the parched fields, the thorny acacias whose roots overhung the bank were already tinged with a green flush. The air had thickened but was no cooler. Breathing required an almost conscious effort, and every task was defeated by the enervating atmosphere. Sickness had broken out in the harem among the children.

Tiye watched the princess's disembarkation seated on her ebony throne, beside her husband. Though her canopy shed a thin shade and scarlet ostrich fans moved ceaselessly over her, Tiye's linens were drenched in sweat, and the pink and black marble paving under her feet scorched through her soft sandals. Amunhotep sat motionless, crook, flail, and scimitar in his lap, sweat gathering under the rim of the Double Crown and trickling unchecked down his temples. Tiye thought he might be dozing. Directly before her, cool, dark water lapped seductively against the steps. Across the river, the noise from Thebes was subdued, smothered in the heat, the thousands lining the east bank seeming to merge into one shimmering mirage. Around her, Pharaoh's court waited in their glistening wigs and dazzling white linen, flicking their jeweled whisks idly and exchanging desultory conversation. Tiye felt sick and faint. Off to her left, Ptahhotep, Si-Mut, and the other priests from Karnak stood bunched under their own canopy, thin streams of incense clouding them and adding to their discomfort. The harem wives, Gilupkhipa among them, sat off to the right in the grass under the shadow of the palace wall, their servants moving among them with cool drinks and dishes of sweetmeats, their cats and monkeys darting among them.

At last a lookout shouted, and Tiye raised her eyes, slitting them against the glare. *Aten Gleams*, homing after its trip to Memphis, had turned into the canal and was beating carefully to the steps, sail furled, oars dipping and rising in a ponderous rhythm. Now that it had passed beyond the inquisitive eyes of the Theban populace, the silk curtains of the cabin had been looped back. The court musicians rolled their drums and began to tinkle and pluck. The boat jostled the steps, the imperial flags limp, its wet, sun-burnished golden sides reflecting yellow on the paving. Slaves rushed to run out the ramp, a stir was visible in the shadow of the cabin, and Tadukhipa emerged. As soon as she left the shelter of the cabin, the women with her raised a canopy over her head, a curious, stiff curved structure of white satin topped by the grinning head of some barbaric god. Amunhotep, wheezing with the effort, struggled to his feet, gathered up the symbols of his kingship, and waited.

Tiye studied the princess. She had a tiny, swarthy face with darting black eyes topped by a soft cap of gold cloth whose tassels swung to her neck. Little brocade slippers were on her feet, hardly visible beneath a heavy skirt of many garish colors fringed in gold, and a loose shawl of the same material hid all but her arms. Six other boats had come to a halt, disgorging a chattering flock of gaudy women, the princess's retinue.

Tadukhipa minced forward, knelt to kiss her husband's feet, hesitated, gave a timid yet interested glance at Tiye, and then kissed her feet also. Despite her small swaying canopy she was obviously instantly sickened by the heat beating up at her, and Tiye saw sweat break out on her face.

Amunhotep nodded frigidly at his herald. "In the name of Amun the Almighty and Aten the All-Beautiful, I, Nebmaatra Hek-Waset, god of this land, welcome you, Tadukhipa, princess of Mitanni and daughter of my friend and brother the Lord Tushratta, to Thebes," the man shouted, his staff of office held out before him. "May this marriage be a sign of the good relations between us."

Amunhotep rose. Then, leaning down, he lifted Tadukhipa to her feet, a gesture that cost him much. Tiye had risen with him. All at once she felt his elbow slide along her arm, and knowing instantly what he wanted, she unobtrusively took his weight upon herself.

"My father sends his heartfelt greetings," Tadukhipa said haltingly in a heavily accented Egyptian. "He places me with complete confidence in your august hands. He also sends the goddess Ishtar to you because he weeps over your illness. Ishtar is pleased to visit again the land she loves." Turning, she crooked a finger at the slave behind her, and a black pall slid from the object he was holding, revealing a small golden statue. The assembly bowed. Tadukhipa passed it to Amunhotep with trembling hands.

He does not believe but wishes, in spite of himself, that Ishtar might hold the power he seeks, Tiye thought, watching him hand the crook, flail, and scimitar to the Keeper of the Royal Regalia and run gentle fingers over the goddess. *I wish it, too.* Her own fingers tightened on his arm, a gesture of possession and fear. *I do not want it to end*, she thought in despair. *Today he strives to regain his youth like a blind man rubbing ashes on his eyes. This is no diplomatic marriage. It is the last throw of dice against death. Ah, Amunhotep! All the fresh promise of our youth has come to this. An old god trembling under the glare of a pitiless eternity and an aging goddess shorn at last of every illusion.*

"Ptahhotep!" Pharaoh croaked, and the high priest came forward swiftly to take Ishtar. "Set the goddess in the shrine in my bedchamber and see that she is offered food, wine, and incense. Let us now make our thanks to Amun for my wife's safe arrival."

A portable altar had been set up before the terrace, and beside it a huge stone bowl in which flames writhed, almost invisible in the noon sun. Amunhotep, with Tiye still at his side and Tadukhipa on his left, processed slowly behind the priests while the whole court fell in behind the Followers of His Majesty bringing up the rear. A bull, already trussed, lay on the altar, moaning through the restraining muzzle, its black eyes rolling. Cymbals clashed, and the systra began to rattle. For a moment Amunhotep had to stand and endure the chant

rising from the gathered priests, and Tiye, feeling his distress
through her fingers, prayed that he would not collapse.

Ptahhotep lifted the knife. A drum began to roll. As a cry
issued from a thousand mouths, the knife arced down, and
blood spurted, steaming, into the pitcher set below the beast's
throat. Even before it had ceased to twitch, acolytes slit its
belly, and the intestines rippled out to fall into the trough prepared for them. The crowd began to applaud and shriek. Other
priests expertly cut the sacrifice into the correct portions, and
Amunhotep, gathering himself for this last effort, grasped each
one and flung it into the fire. Dancers began to sway.

"Let Ptahhotep burn the antelopes and geese," Tiye whispered to Amunhotep under cover of the uproar. "It is permitted.
Let Kheruef take the girl to the harem. You must rest."

He nodded. Taking Tadukhipa's hand, he smiled at her,
careful not to open his mouth and betray his rotted teeth in the
unmerciful brightness of full daylight. "The Keeper of the Harem Door will delight in pleasing you," he said, "and your aunt
Gilupkhipa has been waiting for a long time to speak with you.
Go."

He did not wait to see her leave. Leaning on Tiye, he went
slowly along the terrace and into the blessed obscurity of the
audience hall. Behind him was a concerted rush and screams
of delight as the courtiers fought to reach the bull's blood being
proffered to them. With red fingers they annointed foreheads,
breasts, and feet, for a thanksgiving sacrifice brought much
good luck.

That night a formal welcoming feast was held for Tadukhipa.
She sat beside Pharaoh on the dais of the banqueting hall, a
stiff, heavily painted doll that only spoke when it was addressed, enduring timidly the frankly assessing stares of the
hundreds of courtiers and guests who filled the vast room. On
Amunhotep's right, regal in horned crown with the double
plumes, Tiye watched the servants carefully to see that Tadukhipa was not neglected, but her concern was more for her
husband, who slumped in his chair, eyes often closed, breathing
heavily and rousing himself with effort to pass polite remarks
to his new wife. Beside Tiye, Sitamun's fingers flashed over
the little gilded table piled with flowers. She was eating and
drinking with a steady concentration, pausing only to lean across
her mother and offer some dainty morsel to Amunhotep. A
fitful breeze gusted between the pillars from the dark surface

of the lake, but the air remained stale, laden with the odors of food and the perfumed oil that dribbled from the melting cones tied to the wigs of the feasters.

Between the tables crowded on the floor of the hall naked dancers dipped and swayed, their anklets clashing, the silver weights woven into their hair shining as they passed under the torches. Gracefully they bent to gather the trinkets, pieces of gold, scribbled offers of employment, or propositions that were flung at them by the company, whose ribald shouts fought with the drums and harps of Pharaoh's court musicians. Tiye, momentarily diverted, saw Princess Tia-Ha rise from her cushions where she sat among Pharaoh's wives and, shedding the long blue sheath that enveloped her, slide naked to the foot of the dais. Amunhotep grunted. Tia-Ha bowed to him, blowing a kiss and tossing back her hair as her body loosened and began to undulate with the swift rhythm of the music. "That woman will never die," he said admiringly. "She is too full of Hathor's fertile vitality. Do you like to dance, Princess?"

Tadukhipa turned shy, startled eyes upon her lord while below her the assembly began to whistle and clap for Tia-Ha. "I have been taught the temple dances for Savriti the Many-Armed," she said. "If Your Majesty wishes it, I will dance for him."

"Tonight, Tadukhipa," he replied kindly, seeing her distress, "you have the fragile beauty of a spring cornflower, too delicate for the eyes of these drunken bees." He patted her arm and turned his attention to Tiye. "Suppiluliumas lost no time in sending representation to me," he said, "but the upstart Khatti prince's ambassador is uncouth, obviously nothing but an adventuring soldier." He nodded to where the man sat among the other foreign dignitaries, his unshod feet propped on his table, his arms around two dancers he had captured, his long, tangled hair and bushy beard flying as he talked rapidly to Ay, who was perched on a cushion beside him, listening politely.

"The Khatti have never cared for social skills," Tiye responded, her own eyes thoughtfully on the laughing soldier, "and they have barely learned the rules of rudimentary diplomacy. Their arrogance and their raw strength make them dangerous. Let this man be entertained by Ay, soldier to soldier. Ay speaks the language of the barracks and will discover quickly what this Suppiluliumas wants of Egypt. Apart from gold, of course. It would be wise to give audience to the ambassador from Mitanni tomorrow and learn what Tushratta thinks of them. He is directly involved."

Sitamun leaned forward, patting her red lips with a square of linen. "The Khatti live for war," she offered. "Invasions keep them healthy. Palace insurrections are a cause for celebration, and killing gives them a hearty appetite. It is no wonder that they have no time for cultural pursuits. The Babylonians can at least be reasoned with and are sophisticated enough to enjoy the game of politics, but not these people. They understand only the language of the spear."

To a renewed burst of applause, Tia-Ha swayed back to her cushions and coolly shrugged into her sheath before sitting and calling for wine.

"It is often the bully who can be cowed with threats and encouraged with vague promises," Tiye answered her daughter. "Ay will bring me a report when he is ready. Until then we must see that the foreigner is given all that he desires."

Sitamun smiled and dabbled her fingers in the wine. "Give him Mutnodjme," she drawled. "They are two of a kind. Is my lord retiring?"

Amunhotep had pulled himself to his feet, and at once the revelry in the hall died to a ripple of whispers. The Keeper of the Royal Regalia rose also, lifting the precious emblems from the box he carried everywhere with him and raising them high above his head. Pharaoh nodded at his herald.

"Mani, come forward!" the man called.

Egypt's ambassador to Mitanni left his cushions and strode to the foot of the dais, a thin, dignified man with white hair and stooped shoulders. He prostrated himself with ease and remained with his face to the cool tiling, and Tiye felt in her own body the drawing in of her husband's frail resources before he spoke.

"Mani, lover of the gods and true servant of Egypt," he said at last, forcing his voice to ring out, deep and commanding, over the company. "For the skill and devotion with which you have carried out your duties, and as a sign of our continued approval, I award to you the Gold of Favors. Rise."

Mani did so, holding out his hands as Pharaoh began to strip himself of the jewelry that bedecked him, tossing each piece to the unsmiling man. Bracelets, rings, earrings, the heavy gold pectoral showered onto the tiles, clinking and rattling. Mani bowed. The people began to shout. Amunhotep disinterestedly signaled to his servants and left the dais. Tiye nodded at Kheruef, who approached Tadukhipa with smiles and a firm indication that she should also leave.

"Have you had word yet from Memphis?" Sitamun asked.

Tiye tore her eyes from the sight of her husband striving to remain erect as he shuffled through the doors of the hall. "No, only a communication from the Nile patrol to the effect that Horemheb and the prince arrived safely."

Sitamun emptied her goblet and, wiping a hand across her oil-smeared breasts, pulled down a ringlet from her wig and began to work the oil into it. "I think that when the river begins to sink, I will accompany Nefertiti to Memphis," she said, not looking at her mother. "It will be a pleasant change. I always try to be close to my estates when the grapes begin to bud so that I may have some idea of what harvest to expect. One cannot trust even one's stewards, as you know. In any case, I have three ships being built in the Memphis shipyard, and I want to be present when they are launched."

Tiye leaned slowly toward Sitamun, and the younger woman's blue eyes swiveled to meet hers. "No, Sitamun, you will not," Tiye said emphatically. "Your brother is not for you. You are to stay away from him. When Pharaoh dies, I will assess the situation, and if Ay and I consider it necessary, Amunhotep can have you, but until then you will devote yourself to your father. Your power is already great enough."

Sitamun's eyebrows rose and she shrugged. "It is difficult to devote myself to a man who makes love all night to that boy and spends his days drinking," she said crossly, her full lips drawn down in the pout that often mirrored Tiye's own. "My life is incredibly boring. By the time you were my age, Mother, you had been empress and the most powerful woman in the world for a long time."

Tiye watched the light glint on flecks of gold dust caught in the damp curls falling on Sitamun's forehead. Faint tracks of discontent showed through the rouge on her daughter's round, burnished cheeks, and the strong black-painted brows were pulled together in a frown. *Was my face already falling into lines of willfulness when I was her age?* Tiye wondered. She rose and again the noise died away. "I would not like to have you disciplined, Sitamun, so be patient. Nefertiti will be empress, but it is possible that you will become second wife."

"I am already a second wife to one pharaoh and do not wish

to spend the rest of my life being second wife to another. I have earned the position of empress. And do not think that you can discipline me in the harem as you did Princess Nebet-nuhe, Mother. I have a food taster in my pay."

Tiye gripped Sitamun's stiff, bare shoulder. "I was a child, acting out a child's groundless panic," she spat. "You are too sophisticated to view this situation with such naïveté, Sitamun. Now go to bed. Herald! Tell Tia-Ha to join me in the garden if she is sober enough. I want to swim. Sleep well, Daughter." She left the hall through the rear doors, not glancing back at the sea of bent heads, and as the doorkeepers closed them behind her, she heard Mutnodjme's whip slash the air and one of the dwarfs howl in pain. The rest was swallowed in music and drunken laughter.

Tiye woke suddenly in the late night, drenched in sweat. A shaded lamp hovered by her couch and Piha's respectful hand touched her hair. "Kheruef waits without," the servant whispered. "Horus has sent for you, Majesty."

Groaning, Tiye swung her legs onto the floor, reaching automatically for the cup of cool water that was kept on the little bedside table. Piha held her gown while she slipped it on, and combed the sticky brown tresses. "I was dreaming of the moon on the water at Akhmin," she murmured drowsily. "Ay was a boy, and my father stood in the boat with his throwing stick poised. Does such a dream have meaning, Piha?"

"I do not know, Majesty. Shall I wash you?"

"No, I am too tired. I drank too much wine, I think. Wait up for me, and raise the hangings on the windows. I can hardly breathe in here."

Outside the door, Kheruef bowed without speaking, and the harem guards swung into formation behind and before her. In silence they walked the deserted corridors, crossed Tiye's own private garden, and entered Pharaoh's quarters through the connecting gate in the wall. As they approached the harem garden, Tiye, her feet soundless on the springing grass, became aware of a thousand soft murmurings rising and falling over the wall, and the plaintive trill of a single harp string bewitched the night. Glancing up at the roof of the building, she saw its even silhouette broken by vague humps and moving shadows, for the women had taken to the roof in the heat, lying on their cushions to catch the faintest breeze out of the north. Down where flower beds and lawns gave way to paved water steps and clusters of palms, the river was running swiftly, its passing a constant, soporific gurgle and slap in the backwaters where it darkly, slowly had begun to lick at its banks, and where frogs croaked harshly. The night air was humid but cooler than the day, and Tiye inhaled it deeply as she turned back into the palace, feeling the last vestiges of sleep drain away.

Within the dim labyrinth of Splendor of the Aten, Pharaoh's private quarters, the scorching night breath of Ra still hung, fetid and merciless. Her escort halted and drew back. The guards opened the doors, the herald announced her, and she walked into Pharaoh's bedchamber.

He was propped up with cushions, his mouth half-open, his eyes puffy and slitted against what little light came from the few alabaster lamps that glowed warmly around him. Flies buzzed and stumbled over his flabby, naked body, but he seemed not to notice them. A jar of wine, its broken seal lying crumbled beside it, stood next to his hand, and his cup lay on the floor, empty. Tiye came swiftly up to the couch and bowed.

"Horus, where is the bearer of the whisk?" she said, distressed, picking the instrument from among the sheets and plying it gently.

He smiled and rallied at the mild sting of the horsehair, and the flies rose in an angry cloud. "Shall I deny the flies of Egypt the right to feast off their god?" he said lightly, hoarsely. "They are as predatory and glutted as the rest of my citizens. Truly, my Tiye, I did not notice them. I sent the servants away hours ago. Even their tread annoyed me."

"Shall I send for water and fresh linen, and perhaps some fruit?" She glanced about the room, but there was no sign of the boy.

"No. When you leave." He spoke abruptly, sighing, his mind only half on her words, and she waited for him to tell her why he had sent for her. Presently he rolled over on the couch and buried his shaven skull among the pillows. "There is oil in a dish, somewhere on the table," he said, his voice muffled. "Massage me, Tiye. I cannot bear the touch of a slave tonight."

Obediently she pulled off her rings, shrugged out of the loose robe, and taking the dish, knelt on the sheets beside him. Pouring a little oil into her palm, she spread it over his wide back and began to work it into the yielding flesh, kneading and stroking, feeling the muscles tight with pain under her fingers.

For a long time there was no sound but that of Pharaoh's heavy
breathing. The sweet, cloying scent of the oil rose in Tiye's
nostrils, bringing back to her visions of nights that the past had
already embalmed, and, as if he had read her thoughts, he said,
"No one else could ever do this the way you do, Tiye. Do you
remember our first years together, when I would send for you
every night and the oil would be waiting? Tonight my mind is
full of that time. For a while I forgot, when your body ceased
to surprise and I turned to others, but I have such a hunger for
you again."

His words puzzled her, but she was touched by them. Though
her back was beginning to ache and her wrists to protest, she
forced her hands to keep sliding up over the massive shoulders,
down the straight spine, her eyes on the glistening warmth of
him, the familiar, bold lines of his body. "The little princess
did her best to please me," he went on after a pause, and Tiye's
heartbeat quickened at the odd, deprecatory tone of his voice.
"She danced most prettily in nothing but her jewels. She sang
me the native songs of her country. She kissed and caressed
me, but she went away carrying nothing inside her but a tale
of my own impotence to spread abroad in the harem. I tried,
but tonight I am like Osiris, maimed and dismembered. Her
youth and innocence did not excite me. It caused me to break
out in a sudden sweat of fear." With a grunt he heaved himself
over to face her, and in his dark eyes she read something she
had never seen before, the vulnerability of a sacrificial beast
pleading with her. For a second the knowledge of her own
power over him rose like a hot tide of triumph, but it soon
receded to leave her aching with sympathy.

"She has been raised as a royal child," she replied softly.
"She will know that there is a limit to the amount of gossip
she may indulge in, in the harem, and she will abide within
it. Would you like me to find the boy?"

His eyes lit with sardonic amusement. "No, I don't think
so. I have had enough of the blood of youth for one day. Your
hands have magic in them. I feel better."

The words could have been a dismissal, but she knew they
were not. He lay there waiting, begging silently to be redeemed,
and she lowered herself upon him with a smile.

3

AN AIR OF CALLOUS EXPECTANCY HUNG OVER THE PALACE IN
the months that followed, for in spite of Tiye's reassuring
words, it had not been long before every courtier knew that
Amunhotep had been unable to consummate his marriage to
the tiny Mitanni princess. This, more than any other sign,
convinced them that their god had not long to live, for his
sexual appetite was legendary. Yet, although his days were a
torment of pain and fever, the foul decoctions of worried physicians, and the endless droning of magicians, he clung to life
and found the strength to watch the gradual decay of his body
with a cutting black humor. He did not send for Tadukhipa
again, and she nursed what she saw as a personal failure in a
dignified, shy silence. His boy, his wife, and his wife-daughter
filled his nights. The river overflowed and once again gave life
to the land, sinking into the parched soil, loosening and stirring
the fertile ground. Disease also returned to the land, and in the
harem, in the hovels of the poor in the city, and on the farms,
women wailed as the coffins of the blind, the crippled, and
those wasted with plagues were carried into the tombs.

Letters finally began to arrive from Memphis, and Tiye,
sitting on her throne beside Pharaoh's empty chair, chin in
painted palm and eyes on her own gold-sandaled feet, listened
carefully to the scrolls read aloud to her by her personal scribe.
Her son's missives were short, adulatory, and reassuring. He
was well and hoped that his eternally beautiful mother was well
also. He loved the cosmopolitan life of Memphis, particularly
the variety of religious thought to be found there. He was
carrying out his duties in the temple of Ptah with gravity and
attention. Beneath the words, Tiye often fancied that she sensed
a strange loneliness, a wistful desire to be back in the familiar
surroundings of the harem but considered it natural that a young
man, gaining his freedom for the first time in nineteen years,
might sometimes yearn for the security of such a womb. Nor

did she fail to note the fact that Amunhotep never asked about his father's health. The one breath of human affection that rose from the stiff yellow papyrus, apart from that directed to Tiye herself and the occasional enquiry about Nefertiti, was for Horemheb. Eagerly Amunhotep described the young commander's kindnesses toward him. Tiye found the protestations pathetic and alarming, for her son mentioned no other friends.

She turned from his letters to the more informal detailed scrolls that arrived regularly from Horemheb himself, describing vividly how the prince had settled into his new life. Horemheb did not equivocate and would describe how his royal friend delighted in being driven about the city in a golden chariot so that people would bow to him. Amunhotep had visited On twice, worshiping in the temples of Ra-Harakhti and the Aten and sitting with the priests of the sun, arguing religion with them long into the cool nights. The priests of Ptah were suppressing their irritation with him, for he carried out his duties in their own temple absently and was always ready to find fault with them. He had taken up the lute and was composing his own songs, which he sang for Horemheb and his concubines. His voice was light but true.

Tiye heard, sifted, pondered. She had the letters passed on to Ay, in his office in the palace grounds, where he supervised the care of Pharaoh's horses and oversaw the Division of Splendor of the Aten. She had the letters Amunhotep sent to Nefertiti intercepted, and read them before they were resealed and delivered to the girl, but learned little that was new. His words to his betrothed varied only slightly from his words to his mother, apart from allusions to several conversations concerning the worship of Amun and his place as protector of Thebes that he and Nefertiti had evidently had while he still lived in the harem.

Nefertiti had moved into a suite of rooms in the palace that adjoined Tiye's own. She did not seem to mind that her own servants had been dismissed and her slaves sold. With those who now saw to her comfort she was a harsh mistress, obsessed with detail and brooking no mistakes, and no day passed without tears shed in the servants' quarters. Her niece's petulance did not concern Tiye, for it was Nefertiti's ability to govern that interested her. But the girl was haughty and did not learn easily. Following her aunt from audience to formal reception to the warm winds of the military reviewing ground, her staff of women, fanbearers, and cosmeticians behind, she listened much and volunteered nothing. With her gleaming black hair, pale gray, almond-shaped eyes, dark satin skin, and sensual mouth, she knew she was without physical peer at court. Her whisk bearer also carried a small copper mirror into whose burnished depths Nefertiti would gaze at odd moments throughout the day in order to reassure herself, Tiye often thought with annoyance, that a wrinkle had not appeared since the last swift application of face paint.

Tiye had known her niece since she was born. Nefertiti's mother, Ay's first wife, had died giving birth to her, and Nefertiti had been raised lovingly but rather absentmindedly by Tey, Ay's second wife and mother to Mutnodjme. Tey, a vague, nervous, but strikingly beautiful woman, preferred life on the family estates at Akhmin to the demanding task of disciplining two girls and entertaining for her powerful husband, though in her own way she loved them all. At Akhmin she designed jewelry, dictated long, rambling letters to her family, and flirted harmlessly with the male members of her staff. It was a pity, Tiye found herself thinking more than once as she walked beside Nefertiti's pure, immobile profile, that neither she nor Mutnodjme had inherited their father's strengths. But at least Nefertiti was diligent in dictating replies to her future husband's letters, and when she spoke of him, which was not often, she used extravagant words of affection and longing.

On a day full of a lush new greenness, when buds everywhere in Pharaoh's vast acres were bursting into flower, the women of the harem took to their boats and drifted, with much laughter and loud chatter, up and down the Nile in the windy sunshine. Tiye lay on her couch, longing to join them but submitting impatiently to the impersonal touch of her physician. She had reluctantly summoned him after several bouts of nausea and a dragging fatigue but now regretted it, chafing at the time being wasted. At last he completed his examination and drew back, smiling. "Your Majesty is not ill, but with child."

Tiye sat up, blood draining from her face, hands clutching the sheet. "Pregnant? No! You must be mistaken. It is too late, I am too old! Tell me you have made a mistake!"

The man bowed, edging toward the door. "There is no mistake. I have attended Your Majesty at the birth of every royal child."

"Get out!"

When the doors had closed behind him, she flung herself from the couch, overturning the ivory table, kicking at the shrine beside it. "I will not tolerate this, no!" she shouted at her cowering attendants. "I am too old! Too old..." She sat on a cushion on the floor, now limp and sullen, her breast still heaving, her limbs trembling. "I wonder," she muttered acidly, "what Pharaoh will say."

Amunhotep said nothing. He laughed until he had to cling to his swollen belly and tears streaked kohl down his cheeks, laughed at the irony of the news and from a secret, wholly masculine pride. "So there is yet life in my divine seed!" he chortled while Tiye looked down on him, unwillingly amused at his mirth. "And a spring fertility in that winter body of yours. The gods must also be laughing." With a surge of new strength he swung himself from his couch, tossing the sheets aside and standing beside her. She had forgotten how much taller he was than she. She lifted her head to meet his still-streaming eyes. "Are you pleased, my Tiye?"

"No, I am not pleased at all."

He cupped her face with his hands. "What a prolific pharaoh I am! We must consult the sphinx oracle immediately as to the future of the child." All at once his features became cunning. "What if it is a boy? Healthy and vigorous? I might then have second thoughts about the succession."

Tiye jerked her head from his touch. "I think the oracle ought not to be approached until the birth," she snapped, "and any haggling over the succession can wait also."

"I like to make you angry." He grinned boyishly. "I feel better today than I have in months. Let us order out *Aten Gleams* and join the harem women on the river. I shall sit in the sun, and you can curse me and flick at the flies."

Tiye did consult an oracle, but on her own behalf, not for the child in her womb. She stood before the seer in the little sphinx temple set high above the western cliffs, gifts in her hands, while the man bent over the water in the black Anubis cup. Watching his hesitancy, she found herself wishing for the first time that the Son of Hapu were still alive. While she had hated him as a rival in Pharaoh's affections, a maker of policies that she had fought to oppose, he was matchless as an oracle. He had been an impartial arbiter of the mysteries, interpreting what the gods showed him with complete disregard for his personal safety. His visions had made him great. Tiye could see him now, in this same little sanctuary, a palace made unquiet by the constant moaning of the desert winds, his handsome head inclined over the cup in complete concentration, his arrogant face hidden by the falling locks of the strange, long-ringleted female wig he always wore. When he straightened to give his pronouncements there was never admiration or subservience for her in his eyes. *Perhaps that was one reason I disliked him so,* she mused, restless and uncomfortable in the continuing stillness. *He could reduce me to the level of the lowest peasant with his glance, and it was worse because I knew he did not do so intentionally.*

The oracle covered the cup and turned, waving to his acolytes, and the boys sprang to roll up the mats that had shut out the sun. Light flooded the room, and Tiye blinked at the brilliant blue of the sky, the beige of the cliffs shimmering hot and vibrant. "Well?" she barked impatiently.

"Your Majesty has nothing to fear," he said, eyes downcast. "The birth will be normal and your life long."

"A normal birth can be hard and long or short and easy. What do you mean?"

"I mean that you will birth without complication."

"Is that all? What of the sex of the child? Did the gods show you?"

He shrugged, holding out his hands, fleshy palms up. "No, Divine One."

Though she wanted to throw them at him, Tiye placed the gifts carefully at his feet. She left the temple without a word, her retinue behind her, striding out into the bird-clouded afternoon. Pausing only to gaze for a moment at the sphinx whose calm eyes looked out over the dusty houses of the dead and the brown expanse of the river far below, she stepped onto her litter for the long ride down the path that meandered to the valley floor. *The Son of Hapu would not have been so craven,* she brooded, blind to the invigorating, dry desert wind that lifted the silver-shot linen from her legs and whipped the ringlets of her wig to tangle in her cobra coronet. *He would have given me the color of the child's eyes as well as its sex and told me how many counts would go by before it uttered its first cry. I have just sacrificed three gold circlets and an amethyst bracelet to a man who, whatever happens, cannot be proved wrong. I wonder if Amunhotep fares better when he calls the*

*Amun oracle from Karnak and demands to know how much
longer he will live.*

The queen's unexpected pregnancy caused little stir in Thebes.
In the streets the beggars ceased to importune passersby and
sat in the shade of the buildings taking bets on whether Egypt
would have a new prince or princess. There were many citizens
ready to put money into their scabrous hands, but the majority
of Thebans simply shrugged and forgot the matter. The royalty
who inhabited the brown sprawl of buildings across the river
were of no concern. Malkatta was simply another tomb like
those surrounding it, a tomb for living but never glimpsed gods.
Only Pharaoh's ministers with their perfumed linens and painted
faces directly touched the fortunes of the populace, moving
among them like screeching vultures intent on plunder. It was
impossible to evince any interest in the birth of a child most
of them would never see, to a woman who represented nothing
against which the Thebans could measure their own experi-
ences.

In the palace, however, the subject was pounced upon,
chewed, and spat out by the gossiping courtiers. The eyes of
those who had turned speculatively toward a new king and a
new administration were returned briefly to a pharaoh who had
rallied with the promise of new life and a goddess who could
yet surprise them. The court became sentimental. The worship
of Mut, goddess mother of Khonsu and Amun's consort, enjoyed a new vogue. Sculptors found themselves employment
in carving coy representations of the infant Horus sucking at
the breast of his mother, Isis, for rich patrons who wanted to
share vicariously in their ruler's return to youth. Jewelers sold
hundreds of amulets to women who hoped that their own fertility might be stimulated.

Hearing the reports of these doings from her spies, who
riddled the harem and the offices of administration, Tiye was
disgusted though amused. Yet she could not deny her husband's
improving health, his new interest in affairs of state, or her
own feeling of well-being. Optimism reigned. The air was full
of the smell of the crops ripening rapidly toward the harvest
and the luxuriant blooming of the flowers of summer, whose
heady perfume hung night and day in the warm draughts of
the palace. Only in the chill hours before dawn, when sleep
ceased to be rest and became a drug, did Tiye's earlier mis-

givings return, and she found herself waking suddenly, the baby restless in her. Then she would lie watching the pattern of red light and deep shadow the brazier cast on her ceiling, listening to the howl of the jackals out on the desert, the occasional frenetic braying of a donkey, and once the voice of an anonymous woman screaming and sobbing, the sound carried fitfully on the wind like an echo of another Egypt, dark and brimming with a mysterious sadness. In those moments, as slow-moving and borderless as eternity itself, the mood of cheerfulness prevailing at court seemed a flimsy artificial thing, ready to be blown away in an instant. Firmly Tiye tried to battle the despair that would creep over her as she huddled beneath the blankets, but it had no discernible source and clung to her until she dropped once more into a sodden slumber.

Tiye gave birth to a boy on a hot, late afternoon. Her labor was short, the delivery easy. It was as though the fragrant explosion of fruitfulness of the Egyptian harvest had overflowed into the palace, sharing its abundance with her. At the child's first lusty cry a murmur of approbation and relief filled the bedchamber, and Tiye, exhausted and satisfied, waited to be told the baby's sex. From the back of the small crowd Ay pushed his way past her physician, whispering, "You have a boy. Well done," and she felt his lips brush her wet cheeks. Feeling for his hand, she pulled him down onto the couch, clinging to him as one by one the privileged came to pay their respects. He sat impassively, watching the line of bodies bend and straighten, his hand curled around hers, though long before the last courtier had bowed himself out, she had fallen asleep.

After much fussy deliberation the oracles decreed that the royal son should bear the name Smenkhara. Pharaoh approved and came in person to tell Tiye so. He sat in the chair beside her couch, gingerly sucking on green figs and washing them down with wine. "It is fitting that this child, this symbol of a new beginning, should bear a name never held before by my house," he said. "And, of course, highly appropriate that he should be dedicated to Ra, seeing that the sun is worshiped universally. I wonder what the next child will be called." He glanced teasingly at her, picking out a fig seed from between gray teeth with one long, red nail.

"Horus, your amaze me!" She laughed, caught up in his enthusiasm, relieved of her fears, ready to believe the unbelievable. "Either the presence of Ishtar or your new son has given you back your youth."

He smiled happily. "Both, I think. I have decided to move the court to Memphis next month for the worst of the summer, as I used to do. Leave the baby to the ministrations of the nurses, Tiye, and come with me."

"Memphis." She lay back and closed her eyes. "How I love it. You and I on cushions under the date palms, watching the bees and playing Dogs and Jackals. I wonder if the ambassadors will want to move also."

"Give them all messages to carry to their little kings and get rid of them for a while. Dictate messages that will require much deliberation, so that they stay away for as long as possible."

"What a truly wonderful idea." Tiye, drowsy and content, did not open her eyes. "It has been years since we have indulged ourselves so shamelessly. But forgive me, Horus, I must sleep first."

He heaved himself out of the chair and bent to kiss her cheek. "Heal quickly, Tiye, and we will go to Memphis and sit on the steps of the palace, looking out over the green forest under a kindlier Ra."

She waited for him to mention their son's presence in Memphis, but he only placed a hand on her forehead, a surprisingly gentle touch for such a large man, and then Piha opened the doors and he was gone. She listened to the warning calls of the herald as he paced the corridor, the sound growing fainter until it merged with the twitter of birds beyond the window, and smiled at the memory of his fingers, cool on her brow. *Oh, let it be*, she thought, for one moment suspending common sense, looking only into her heart and his and finding two breathless children intoxicated by the limitless power fate had placed in their hands, and by a love as yet untested by deceit or unchanged by familiarity.

The burst of vigor and excitement that had filled the court at Smenkhara's birth soon faded, for it appeared that Pharaoh had garnered in the last harvest of his ruined body and his indomitable will. A month later he was again ravaged by fever, and an abscess on his gum broke, causing him unbearable anguish. Tiye did not see him at his own request for many days, though she called his physicians to her and listened to their veiled, polite reports. He was holding to life with all he had, lying on his couch in a dimness that became progressively suffocating as the season of Shemu drew slowly to a close in an intensifying heat.

The boy lay beside him through the long nights, still and silent while his lover tossed and muttered about people who had died before he was born and events that had already passed into history. Amunhotep would not let him go, although he lacked the strength to touch him. This Tiye surmised while she listened to the physicians, bitter because of the hopes she and her husband had shared, and guilty because his joy over his new son had caused him to live briefly and gloriously beyond his strength.

There was another source of guilt also, one she ruefully acknowledged. Each evening she would stand before her tall copper mirror when the sinking sun flushed the room red and tinged her skin an unearthly bronze, and would marvel at the new hold on life little Smenkhara had given her. She knew that she had never had her niece's cold, unapproachable beauty, and not for many years had she cared. Her attraction lay in her vitality, her earthy, forthright sensuality. Carefully she inspected her body, short and unremarkable, the hips well-formed, the waist small but not unusually so, the breasts neither small nor large yet definitely beginning to lose their elasticity. Her neck was long and graceful. It was a thing to take pride in, but Tiye no longer took pride in a body that was useful, that gave her pleasure, but that could not compete with the pleasures of a quick, devious brain. Critically she surveyed her face. *Here,* she thought, *I show my age. My eyelids are too hooded. The lines that score my cheeks from inner eyes to chin could have been grooved by the vengeful sphinx I wear between my breasts. My mouth, that Amunhotep calls voluptuous and loves so much, is too big and, when I do not smile, turns down most unbecomingly. Yet . . .* She smiled at the image softly reflected back at her like melting gold. *I feel reborn while my pharaoh struggles to keep death at bay.* Her eyes slid from the mirror. "Take it away!" she barked at Piha. "Tell the musicians to come, and the male dancers. I am not weary enough for sleep."

She had hoped for diversion but found none. The musicians played, the young men danced faultlessly, yet Tiye knew that nothing could distract her from the distance growing between her and her husband.

The month of Mesore passed, pitilessly hot. New Year's Day approached, signaling the beginning of the month of Thoth, god of wisdom, when Amun left his sanctuary at Karnak and traveled in his golden barque to his southern temple at Luxor, which Amunhotep had been building for the last thirty years. It was customary for Pharaoh to accompany the god to Luxor and during the fourteen days of festival to assume Amun's identity and beget another incarnation.

With the feast two weeks away Tiye summoned Ptahhotep and Surero.

"Surero, the Feast of Opet comes. You are Pharaoh's steward, with him every day. Will he be able to travel to Luxor?"

Surero hesitated. "He sits by his couch and takes nourishment. Yesterday he walked a little in his garden."

"That is not an answer. Ptahhotep, I know you spent a long time with him this morning. What do you think?" She did not trouble to hide her disdain. The high priest did not like her, she knew. He was a dour, practical man who jealously guarded the fortunes of his god and all his life he had suspected the levity with which Amunhotep had regarded Amun behind the solemn rites and masks of tradition. A devout consort would have been able to change that, but Tiye recognized that he considered her a commoner, no matter how rich and influential her family, and a foreign commoner at that, and so did not expect her to understand the ties that bound Amun to Pharaoh. Worse, she had supported Pharaoh in his bid to raise Ra and his physical manifestation on earth, the Aten, to a position of greater prominence. Tiye had tried to explain to Ptahhotep that the policy would mean nothing to the majority of the Egyptian people, for the worshippers of Ra as the Visible Disk consisted only of a small cult of sophisticated priests and a few courtiers. It was intended, rather, as a shrewd political move, designed to promote a feeling of unity among the empire's vassal states and subject nations. All men, whatever their allegiance, worshiped the sun. To promote the Aten would ensure warmer relations between Egypt and the independent foreign kings and make them more amenable to talk of trade and treaty. While the threat to Amun that Ptahhotep had so clearly dreaded had not come about, the general loosening of religious morals and the frivolous irreverence of a bored court had deepened his disapproval. More peasants than nobility came to Karnak now, and the offerings were correspondingly vulgar. She watched icily as the high priest drew himself up to answer her question.

"The Divine Incarnation was cheerful this morning, Majesty. He is talking of his jubilee."

He had taken her off guard. Tiye's hands, lying along the arms of the throne, tightened over the huge sphinxes' grinning mouths. "The plans for yet another celebration of his successful reign were discarded when my husband became ill some months ago. He has already blessed Egypt with two jubilees. That is surely enough."

Ptahhotep was obviously enjoying his queen's surprise. "Pharaoh ordered me to find the correct rites that were gathered for his first jubilee and placed in the library," he answered with solemn glee. "He wishes to celebrate it at the Feast of Opet."

If my brother Anen had lived, I would have known of this long ago, Tiye thought, annoyed. *I would have been prepared.* "Surero, is this true? Tell me honestly, will it tax his strength too far?"

"He has set his heart on it, Majesty. He is sure that this time he will fully recover. He wishes to make a public show to his subjects, and his foreign dominions."

Ah, Tiye thought again. *He is ahead of me.* "Ptahhotep, you are dismissed," she said shortly, and the man prostrated himself glumly and backed away. When he had gone, Tiye relaxed and sat back. "Does Amunhotep believe that his prolonged illness has made his royal brothers in other parts of the empire nervous, or perhaps greedy, Surero? Is that why he orders a jubilee?"

"I think so, Majesty. Matters of state are none of my affair, as I tend only to matters of the palace. Yet Pharaoh talks often of the need for continuing stability, the denial of weakness, so that his son may inherit a firm foundation."

"His infant son, I presume."

Surero looked uncomfortable. "I believe so, Divine Goddess."

"Very well. Do not allow the high priest to complicate the rites unnecessarily. I think Pharaoh overestimates his strength." *No wonder he will not allow me to see him*, she thought, her mind racing under her words. *Oh, wily Pharaoh! So it begins again!*

"Majesty, I have no authority over the high priest. Only Pharaoh and the oracle may order him."

"True, but you are perfectly able to make tactful suggestions to Ptahhotep. He would not like it noised about that he is deliberately weakening the health of his king. Refresh my memory, Surero. Is it not required for a jubilee that if there is a declared Horus-in-the-Nest, he must officiate with Pharaoh?"

"Yes, it is so."

"Will Pharaoh take the air today?"

"He will sit in the garden at the setting of Ra."

"Good. You are dismissed."

It does not matter, she told herself as she moved from audience hall to private reception rooms to the offices of her ministers, asking questions, making pronouncements, giving judgments, with Nefertiti and her pet monkey walking three paces behind her. *Long before little Smenkhara reaches an age where his ambitions might have a coherent shape, Pharaoh will be dead, and Amunhotep will be king. Why am I so distressed? Let him have his jubilee, let him enjoy the game of manipulating the future. He knows as well as I that it will come to nothing. No, it is my own future that causes me pain. My baby is an unknown force. But my elder son is a pliable reed that bends to my breath.*

"Majesty Aunt, is it wise to send gold to the Assyrian Eriba-Adad, seeing that Assyria is threatened by Kadashman-Enlil with whom we have treaties of friendship? Will not the Babylonians become angry and threaten us in turn?"

Tiye forced her mind into the present to answer Nefertiti's question. The girl had been trying to pick her bewildered way through the maze of foreign policy and Tiye did her best to honor that effort. "No, Highness. Without our gold, Assyria might be defeated, and the Babylonian kingdom would emerge dangerously powerful. If we sent soldiers to Eriba-Adad, then we would be fighting Kadashman-Enlil directly. This way Assyria can buy mercenaries and arms, and Babylonia will not be insulted by us. Do you see?" Without waiting for a reply she took Nefertiti's arm, and they halted. "Here is Menna's office. We have come to discuss the flooding of more land for Pharaoh next year and the payment to the Keftiu for the glass vases Surero ordered. I will leave this to you. Ordinarily I would not bother with such details but would leave them to Menna as Overseer of Crown Lands, and the Vizier of the North, but if you are to be consort, you must know all."

"But Majesty, you have stewards who report to you daily on such transactions."

"True. Yet those men are continually bribed. That I do not mind, but it is important to be able to distinguish a totally corrupt transaction from an acceptably twisted one, and that you cannot do unless you have spent time yourself in direct conversation with the ministers. Let us go in. I will not speak."

After Nefertiti had acquitted herself with cool though bored efficiency, Tiye took her to bathe in her private lake. It was noon, and Ra stood at his zenith, pouring a blazing white light over the surface of the water. Both women lowered themselves gratefully into the lily-clogged greenness. For a while they floated and splashed while their servants waited on the grassy verge with towels and canopies ready and the monkey ran back and forth gibbering. Tiye swam, glorying in the silken flow of water over her shoulders and against her mouth, but Nefertiti lay on her back with eyes closed, rocking in Tiye's small swell, her hands moving like copper fish just beneath the surface.

Later they sat side by side under Tiye's canopy, hair plastered to their backs, water beading on their brown skins and running down their spines.

"It will be a good Feast of Opet this year," Nefertiti said, delicately picking dried grass from her wet thigh. "In a little over two months the prince will be returning from Memphis."

"He seems fond of you," Tiye replied. "You must be careful how you approach him, Nefertiti. His affection for you gives you great power over him. The marriage contracts are ready for Pharaoh's seal."

The gray eyes, now paled to a soft dove color under the glare of the sun, squinted into Tiye's own. "And I am ready to be to Amunhotep what you, Majesty Aunt, have been to the Mighty Bull." She smiled with great sweetness, showing small white teeth, and began whistling at the monkey, who rushed forward and began to lick her damp arms.

"Indeed!" Tiye retorted tartly. "Such a promise of selfless devotion does you credit. Your father will be delighted." Nefertiti shot her a level look from beneath dark, feathered brows, and Tiye knew that she had been understood. "There is feasting tonight for the mayor of Nefrusi," she went on. "He is to receive the Gold of Favors at my command. His city lies just within our border with Syria, and he has done good work in helping Horemheb to keep the border quiet. I want you to honor him in my place, Nefertiti, so that I may spend the evening with Pharaoh. Your father and Sitamun will share the dais with you."

Nefertiti merely nodded without comment. The monkey had fallen asleep, sprawled across her knees. "Is Horemheb to be recalled to Thebes when the prince returns?"

"Why?" Tiye asked sharply.

The girl shrugged. "It is just that he and the prince have become friends. Amunhotep might be lonely without him."

So you are not as sure of your power over my son as I had thought, Tiye mused, *but you are clever enough to see it. Shall Horemheb come or not?*

"If I think there is a need to recall the commander with my son, I shall do so," she said aloud. "Take my advice, Nefertiti. Never try to influence a man through his friends. Either he will misunderstand and become jealous, or you will fail to win their confidence and so earn their scorn. Men are not like women. It is always better to approach them directly."

Nefertiti flushed, biting her lip, and Tiye relented. "Amunhotep has great affection for you," she finished gently. "You do not need Horemheb for a go-between."

She bade Nefertiti go and sleep and herself made her way to the nursery, where Smenkhara lay naked in his cot, guarded by two Followers of His Majesty, his tiny limbs loose on the sheet, his nostrils quivering as he slept. Tiye questioned the men and the wet nurse briefly, bent to kiss the fuzz of black hair beaded with the sweat of the afternoon, and went to her own couch. *Sitamun must be watched closely*, she thought drowsily as she turned on her side and prepared to slide into unconsciousness. *She will make no move until Pharaoh is dead, but her claim upon the prince as a fully royal daughter is very strong. She is devious enough to resort to all the ancient laws of precedence if given the chance.*

Pharaoh was sitting beside his ornamental lake, throwing crumbs to a flock of raucous ducks, as Tiye walked across the garden later that day. The sun had already sun behind the wall that sheltered the rear of the palace from the sand and cliffs of the western desert and the dead who crowded the land between. Shafts of red light lay across the lawns, still suffused with a heat that beat against her shins and splashed flame up her abdomen. Surero knelt at Pharaoh's feet, while Apuia, his butler, was bending over his shoulder under the rhythmic swish of the ostrich fans. Tiye could see the glitter of water being poured into the cup Amunhotep held out to him.

Several paces away the boy lay outstretched on his stomach, chin resting on both braceleted wrists, the smooth curve of his naked spine drenched in pink light. As Tiye came closer, she saw that he was watching the slow, arduous passage of a golden scarab beetle through the dense grass.

Slaves and servants crowded behind Pharaoh's chair. At her herald's cry they turned and went down on their faces. Amunhotep waved her forward, and Kheruef motioned for her own chair to be unfolded next to his. She smiled at Pharaoh and lowered herself under the canopy.

"Yes, I am better, before you ask," he said, flinging the last of the stale bread at the jostling birds and drinking his water. "See, I am not even sweating. Ra has sunk kindly into my bones today. Surero told me he thought you would appear. Do not try to dissuade me from my jubilee, Tiye. I will have it."

The boy had groped for a stick and was now teasing the scarab, pushing it from behind so that it stumbled and rolled onto its back.

"I am glad to see you so well, my husband," she responded. "I have no intention of trying to dissuade you from the jubilee. It will be a fine diplomatic move. I merely wish to remind you that you now have a legal heir who must be present at the rites."

He smiled at her politely. "Of course. He will be carried beside me in a basket."

"Amunhotep, the decree has been made. Let it stand. If you make Smenkhara your legal heir and you die in his infancy, there will be a long regency in Egypt, with all the problems that will entail."

He shrugged and then grinned at her wickedly. "Poor Tiye! So completely incapable of being a regent! My heart is heavy within me for your sake!"

In spite of herself she laughed. "Then imagine that, I, too, die before the baby reaches his majority."

"You?" He waved away the dish of sweetmeats Apuia proffered. "You feed on adulation and power. As long as there is something to manipulate, you will not die."

"Then consider that you will be giving Amunhotep yet another reason for hating you."

"Ah! Now we come to the point! But why should I care about the love or the hatred of any man? I am pharaoh. I am the god of Soleb, the god of Thebes, the god of the whole world. Even the other gods do me homage. That eunuch is no son of mine, let alone an embryonic god."

"I can see," Tiye hissed at him in a low voice that only he could hear, "that with your returning health has come a returning fear. Very well. Do what you will. But the decree stands."

"Of course it stands. I cannot be bothered to unmake it. You did not bother to find out what the oracle said about the baby, did you?" He placed a puffy hand on her saffron-clad knee. "He will be pharaoh. There is no doubt."

"Nor is there any doubt that the successor of the Son of Hapu is too much concerned with pleasing his royal master and not concerned enough to speak the truth!" Tiye retorted.

A shriek of rage caused them both to turn to the boy. The scarab had finally managed to evade the offending stick and, cracking open its iridescent carapace, had taken to the air. The boy scrambled after it, tossing the stick aside and snatching vainly above him. Tiye and Amunhotep watched the erratic flight of the huge insect until suddenly it wobbled, swooped, and alighted clumsily on the green sphinx lying between Tiye's breasts. The boy came tumbling toward it, oblivious for a moment to the company he was in, and Tiye's pent-up fury found its target. Her hand flew, administering a stinging slap to the bronze cheek, and the boy reeled back. "How dare you fall upon my royal person!" she shouted. "Prostrate yourself!" She read venom in the round black eyes as he fell to the grass.

Amunhotep chortled. "The sun seeks refuge from a female sphinx," he observed dryly. "Interesting. I must enquire of the oracles what it means."

"It means," Tiye said sharply as the insect sailed away, "that Ra is not particularly looking forward to sharing his Holy Barque with you, oh, my recalcitrant husband. Get up, you foolish boy." She stood, and her fanbearers jumped to flank her. Planting a kiss on Pharaoh's helmeted forehead as his retinue did her reverence, she left him.

For an hour she paced her audience hall, her scribe cross-legged on the floor beside her throne, reed pen poised over the papyrus while she tried to compose a letter to Horemheb that would keep her son at Memphis without wounding his feelings. The task proved impossible, and in the end she instructed the commander simply to explain to Amunhotep that his chance at the throne might be endangered if he appeared at Malkatta.

After all, she thought as the scribe printed rapidly, *he is not a child. He is quite capable of understanding his father's fears.* When the scroll had been rolled and sealed with her ring and the scribe and herald had gone, she slumped on a chair, all at once tired. Piha and Kheruef waited patiently in the deepening shadows for fresh orders, but she remained seated, letting her eyes wander around the room. The sound of the feast at which Nefertiti was doubtless presiding with graceful aplomb, regally pretending to ignore the admiring glances that always came her way, reached Tiye's ears in bursts of music and laughter as the parched night breeze flowed from the banqueting hall, through the gardens, and to Tiye's own domain. *I wonder if Pharaoh will bother to intercept the letter*, she thought. *Probably not. I have few secrets from him, and he knows what they are. I wish Ay were here. I would like to summon him from the feast, sit on the floor of my bedchamber and drink cheap beer with him, make him tell me the outrageous jokes he used to spread when I was younger and he was still active in Pharaoh's char-ioteers.*

A glimmer of light showed at the door, and with a start Tiye realized how dark it had become. Huya, Kheruef's assistant in the harem, bowed his way in preceded by his torchbearer. "Speak," she said absently.

"Majesty, I seek Kheruef. Two of Great Horus' Babylonian wives are fighting. If they were Tehen-Aten, I could lay hands on them, but they are above my station. I fear they will harm each other."

Tiye nodded at Khereuf. "I do not care if they murder each other, but perhaps you should go, Kheruef. Piha, bring light. I might as well walk a little by the lake before I sleep." She had hoped for peace but did not find it. The roar of the feast dogged her, and when the guests began to spill, drunken and amorous, into the gardens beyond her wall, bringing the noise with them, she retreated to the refuge of her own apartments.

4

THE FEAST OF OPET, WHICH BEGAN ON NEW YEAR'S DAY, and Pharaoh's third jubilee were celebrated with due ritual and solemnity. On the seventh day of the feast Amun left his sanctuary at Karnak, coming out into the sunlight to the frenzied shouts of the people, resting in his golden shrine and carried in the golden barque, his white-robed priests purifying the ground before him with milk and libations of wine which ran together and flowed pink between the flagstones. Quivering ostrich fans shaded the god from the glare of day, and as the we'eb priests sweated and groaned under their burden, staggering toward the Holy Barque that rocked against the temple water steps, other priests sang Amun's praises. He was still mighty, benign, Egypt's pride, the god who had led the great warrior Thothmes III into the wilderness outside the borders and had blessed him, causing him to make an empire, filling his hands with riches. Proud foreign princes abased themselves before his incarnation, Amunhotep, and the thousands who had gathered to watch him travel the two miles to his other home at Luxor stamped and shouted his praise.

As Amun was slowly lowered into his gold-sheathed boat, the slaves on the bank lifted the tow ropes, and in midstream the imperial flagship also took the strain. At a shouted command the barque began ponderously to cleave the water, the pennants of Amun on the four tall flagstaffs fronting the miniature temple rippling audibly in the wind, the sun glancing off the golden statue of Pharaoh with his oar, symbolically rowing the god to Luxor. The crowds lining the riverbank dispersed and began to push forward, running to keep up with the boat, throwing garlands in the hope that one might fall neatly around the neck of Amun-Ra in his ancient guise of a ram's head, a pair of which reared, horns curved under golden chins, at prow and stern. Dozens of little skiffs circled in the water, full of excited Thebans calling for blessings, waving goose feathers or holding

up goose heads so that the god, wombed in linen hangings
from the profane uproar around him, might know the fervor
of his worshipers.

Behind the god's barge came smaller boats carrying his wife,
Mut, and son, Khonsu. Many court women had taken ship to
escort the fashionable goddess. The drums rolled continuously,
the musicians played, and the temple chanters began to sing.
The hawkers on the bank, standing behind their makeshift stalls,
shook charms and amulets and screamed encouragement to the
undecided and abuse at those who shook their heads impatiently
and passed by. Food and drink merchants fared better, for many
in the throng had traveled far to stand for hours in favored
positions by the water and were parched and hungry.

The water steps at Luxor were crowded also, but with a
dignified, silent throng of officials and senior priests. Pharaoh
himself watched the jewel-laden boat labor closer from his
shaded throne. He was clad today in a high priest's leopard
skin with the symbol of his own divinity, the leopard's tail,
falling between his thighs. If he was bored, he gave no sign
of it, though Tiye, seated beside him and watching his face
out of the corner of her eye, saw the muscles of his jaw tense
with either a yawn or a spasm of pain. The Holy Barque grazed
the steps and more we'eb priests rushed to lift the shrine. Once
again the milk splashed pale on the stone, and the wine dribbled, rich and tantalizing, into the grass. Amunhotep lifted his
feet, and his sandal bearer knelt to remove his footwear so that
he would not contaminate the sanctuary with any impurities.

Inside the temple precincts, beyond the harmonious porch
of over fifty papyrus columns that the Son of Hapu had designed
to Pharaoh's specifications and that led into the sanctuary,
Amunhotep, ritually supported by Ptahhotep and Si-Mut, made
the blood thanksgiving. He chanted the prayers with suitable
decorum and later, stripped of all but the Double Crown and
a loincloth, wove unsteadily the stately and mysterious dance
ordained by centuries of tradition. Tiye watched, torn between
anxiety lest he should collapse and admiration for his grim will
power. It was with relief that she sat beside him to eat the feast
in Amun's presence, although the battering of the noise of the
crowds gathered outside and the stench of hot blood robbed
her of her appetite.

"I have done my duty for another year," he said to her, still
panting and sweating as he gulped his wine. "Tomorrow we

begin the jubilee celebrations while Amun simply sits here."
He jerked an elbow behind them to the god who now occupied
the throne that was vacant for most of the year. Amun's golden
feet were buried in flowers, food, and incense, and smoke
wreathed about his faintly smiling face, the two plumes of his
crown glinting in the light of the torches. "How I pity his harem!
Poor little wives and dancers! They all die virgin." It was no
secret that Pharaoh could seldom be bothered with the god's
women, secreted away here and at Karnak. "I shall enjoy sitting
beside you on the royal barge, dear Tiye, in the rosy splendor
of the sunrise."

She endured his teasing with pleasure. "And I shall enjoy
watching you raise the djed-pillars in the jubilee hall."

They grinned at each other. Tiye hated sunrises, and Amunhotep the undignified though largely symbolic task of hauling
on the ropes.

It was not Tiye who waited in the darkness of Luxor's
sanctuary for the ritual bestowal of the royal seed by Pharaoh
in the guise of the god. A bored Sitamun lay at the foot of the
statue, unconcernedly eating slices of melon dipped in honey
while her father struggled against the wave of sickness that had
seized him in the antechamber and his physician fed him sips
of the mandrake infusion he had hurriedly brewed.

In the summer dawn of the following morning, Amunhotep
and Tiye were towed to Karnak in the barge *Aten Gleams*. The
Feast of Opet was over, and the jubilee was beginning. Painted
and heavy with jewels, they sat side by side unspeaking, he
because his teeth were clamped against the shivering of the
fever stirring again in his ravaged body, she still half-somno-
lent. The journey they were making symbolized every pharaoh's movement toward incarnation and birth as god and was
reenacted at each jubilee. *Which of my sons can be considered
the incarnation of the god?* Tiye wondered hazily as Ra rimmed
the horizon, shimmering, already mercilessly prepared to de-
vour the land. "Please have no more jubilees," she whispered
aloud in Amunhotep's ear so that the priests accompanying
them could not hear. "I need my sleep. This is torture." He
grunted but did not reply. Suddenly she felt her hand enclosed
in his, which was shaking and slippery with sweat.

Later, in the magnificent hall he had built for his first jubilee
within the confines of Malkatta, his coronation was also reenacted. The goddesses of the south and north, Nekhbet and Buto,

raised the white and red crowns over his head. Ptahhotep placed once again the flail, crook, and scimitar into his hands. The assembled courtiers' foreign embassies watched in proper awe as the deed to Egypt and all its subject nations was given to him. Yet Tiye could take no pleasure in the sight of the baby Smenkhara, borne in his basket by a discomfited priest. Amunhotep was clearly in distress. His labored breath rasped in the ears of all present. The dignitaries, their expressionless eyes following his every stumbling move, whispered among themselves. Like royal jackals, Tiye thought in a flush of protective fury. Like pale sem-priests waiting eagerly to be handed a body to disembowel. She sat beside her lord, under the gilded baldachin with its frieze of sun-bearing uraei, its sphinxes, its bound and dying enemies of Egypt under her, her body tense with his suffering as hour by hour the speeches were made, the gifts brought by men who crawled to kiss Pharaoh's feet and display their offerings with their assurances that he would live for ever and ever. If Pharaoh had not been so stubborn, young Amunhotep would be standing beside him, receiving the trinkets, smoothing the moments for him, she thought, her own head aching from the weight of the great horned disk of Hathor and the solid silver plumes that rose above the copper feathers of her crown. She felt the eyes of the assembly dart from Pharaoh to her, cold, speculating, assessing eyes, and more than one noble rose from Pharaoh's feet to press fervently his lips to her own. The gesture was more than politeness. It was an acknowledgment of her position as ruler in Egypt, a promise of future loyalty to the link with the next administration.

Pharaoh did not leave his throne when toward the end of the ritual the time came for the djed-pillars to be raised. At his signal it was Ptahhotep on his behalf who strained on the ropes to raise the tall wooden spires with their three crosspieces into place. The company shouted "Stability!" and bent to do homage to the symbols of an unchanging way of life, but the voices lacked conviction, and the night wind gusting through the hall seemed to bring with it the threatening chill of the unknown.

After the strain of presiding at the two festivals Pharaoh took to his bed in the now-familiar grip of fevers and dental pain, and when Tiye received a letter from Memphis announcing that Amunhotep the younger would be returning within the month, she decided not to plan a formal welcome for him. She

knew only too well that a great public ceremony for an heir
could turn into a surge of hysterical acclamation on the part of
a court grown weary of a Horus who would not die. She had
arranged a small reception—herself, Ay, and Nefertiti—on
the palace water steps when word was brought to her that her
son's barge would soon dock, but her greeting was delayed.
For the prince first sailed directly to the crowded Theban quays
and did not cross the river until he had first mounted his chariot
and been driven slowly through the narrow, dung-filled streets
of the city. Tiye listened, astounded and disturbed, to Horemheb's report after she had at last risen from her chair to
receive her son's kiss and had sent him with Nefertiti to inspect
the wing of the palace that had been reserved for him. Her
equanimity had been further shaken by the sight of Mutnodjme
coolly stepping from the boat behind Amunhotep, white ribbons
on her youth lock fluttering, whip wound around one supple
forearm, her earrings swinging.

"You should not have allowed it!" she shouted angrily at
the young commander as he faced her in her audience chamber.
"What demon possessed him, that he should parade himself
before commoners like a whore and, worse, endanger his royal
person?"

Horemheb opened his mouth to reply, the scar on his chin
standing out livid against the dull flush of embarrassment on
his face, but Ay smoothly interposed. "Majesty, it is rather
difficult for a simple commander to gainsay a prince of the
blood, particularly when no whisper of the prince's determination to ride through Thebes had come to him until Amunhotep
ordered the captain to steer to the eastern shore. He did not
have time either to dissuade my nephew or to prevent him by
more devious means. He is not at fault."

"Of course he is at fault!" Tiye spat at her brother, but the
face so like her own remained calm.

"Let him speak, Tiye."

Tiye blew out her lips and nodded frostily at Horemheb.
The young man spread his ringed hands.

"Majesty, it was either waste precious time trying to change
His Highness's mind, and I have known him long enough to
appreciate that that task is beyond the power of any living
creature, or spend the minutes deciding how best to deploy my
soldiers around him so that he should have the greatest protection."

"That I see. Go on."

"I protected him as best I could. I called out the retainers stationed by the warehouses and commandeered what chariots there were. But the prince refused a guard. I drove him myself. He insisted on being seen as clearly as possible."

"Was he recognized?" Ay asked quietly.

"Not until his herald strode ahead holding the white staff and calling his titles. But the people were strangely quiet. They fell back and averted their eyes, of course, but once he had passed, they did not cheer him."

"I am not surprised. It is the first time in a hundred years that any member of royalty has been so foolhardy. He rode through all of Thebes?"

"Yes, every cubit." Horemheb's slim shoulders slumped, and Tiye realized that he was very tired. But her ire still simmered.

"I can see that discipline around my son has been culpably lax," she said waspishly. "I understand your impotence, Horemheb, but did you not stop to remember that my son's anger is not as important as your responsibility to me, your queen? And what of Mutnodjme? That was the last act of madness."

Horemheb straightened and came closer to the throne. "Majesty, you do not appreciate how the prince has been occupying his time in Memphis. I allowed Mutnodjme to entertain him in the hope that his attention might be diverted from the people of On, who follow him everywhere. No one is less interested in matters of religion than your niece. The prince has enjoyed the antics of her dwarfs and her skill with the whip."

"I have a good mind to let her use it on you. Do not smile. I warned you before you left that if your reports were not full and truthful, you would be punished. Why was all this information not included in the scrolls you sent me?"

"I tried to be plain, Majesty, but it was difficult. The prince had set up his own informers, and I believe that my letters to you were read regularly by him before being resealed. My seal does not have the authority of yours. Nor did I trust a message by word of mouth."

Tiye fell to tapping the arms of the throne. "Tell me of the people of On."

"The prince has gathered around him many priests from the sun temples. They debate religion from dawn until dark. Your son is most sophisticated in these matters and already speaks with authority. He has invited many of them to Thebes."

"And what has been the reaction of the priests of Ptah?"

"Naturally they are angered."

Tiye studied Horemheb for a moment. "Does the prince trust you?" she asked at last.

"Yes, he does."

"Then you may keep your position as his bodyguard, but you will report to me every day. Ay, send May to take temporary command of the border patrols instead of Horemheb. Werel will be perfectly happy to transport her family to Memphis. Horemheb, get out." He bowed and backed through the doors, and when they were closed, Tiye sighed, a gust of frustration and annoyance, and slid from the throne. "Talk to me, Ay. Why this senseless parade through the streets of a dangerous city? Why the gaggle of priests he has dragged to Malkatta? And is Horemheb playing some game of his own?"

Ay folded his arms and began to pace, eyes hooded and suddenly sleepy, broad brow furrowed under the rim of his yellow helmet. "If you had not been so preoccupied with Pharaoh's condition, you would be able to answer those questions yourself. Pharaoh has always feared death at the hands of his son, and you have pondered the matter like a dog worrying a piece of meat from a bone. But you forget that the prince has also gone in daily terror of his life, and until his father dies, he will not be safe from the caprices of an old man who has lived his whole life under the sway of the most powerful sooth-sayer the world has known, and who may still turn and accuse his son of causing his illness with spells. Amunhotep's mad journey through Thebes was a way of making Egypt aware of his existence, of insisting on his right to live, the right to vengeance if he dies."

"Pah! You speak in silly riddles! I think it is the taste of impending power, sweet in his mouth, that has prompted it. He will become as arrogant as his uncle."

Ay stopped pacing, and his arms loosened. The wide mouth parted in a smile of complicity. "It is unfortunate that you have no royal blood in your veins, Tiye. You and I should have been man and wife."

"A fully royal woman legitimizing the claim of her brother, as in the old days? You fancy yourself in the Double Crown?"

He grimaced, still smiling. "Only in moments of extreme boredom."

"What of Horemheb?" Tiye turned from her brother's warm gaze. "He did not handle himself well."

"On the contrary, he behaved with the instinctive good sense of the born soldier when he dismissed the impossible solution and concentrated on the possible. And I think you ought to take note of his reasons for admitting Mutnodjme so freely into the prisoner's presence. In any event, she has already returned home. Her cousin has failed to hold her interest. My daughter has no ambitions, unless they are to keep her life as full of variety and comfort as possible."

Tiye's hand went to the ankhs hanging from her bracelet. "Words, words," she said softly. "And under them all is a great happiness that my son has come home. You and I have become too much like mice immobilized by fear of hawks circling above that we cannot see. It is time to relax and fix our gaze on the abundance of the fields around us."

"A pretty speech," he murmured dryly, and she laughed at her own pomposity and dismissed him.

In the evening she took her attendants and went in search of her son. His sumptuous apartments were still in chaos as his servants hurried to unpack the chests and boxes that had accompanied him from Memphis and the palace craftsmen delivered the furniture Tiye had ordered. After one glance inside the silver doors opening to his reception hall, she went out into the garden and finally found him sitting in the grass by the edge of the lake, just as she had always seen him in the harem, his legs tucked under him, a crowd sitting or lying with him. She scanned them quickly as her herald ordered them to make their obeisances. Nefertiti had had her arm linked with his before she knelt to bow to her aunt, and Sitamun had been reclining very prettily on one elbow, her scarlet linen pulled tight over the suggestive mounding of one hip. Amunhotep rose and came forward smiling, arms outstretched, taking her hands and kissing her gently on the mouth.

"Tell me who these men are with their faces in the dirt," she said good-humoredly as Piha unfolded her chair. "Sitamun, you should not be publicly lolling among the flowers like some little concubine. Piha, send for another chair."

Sitamun gave her a look of mortification as she came to her

feet and pulled the gossamer-thin blue cloak across her breasts with both nervous hands.

"But the grass has just been watered," Amunhotep said in his high, lilting voice. "Sitamun was enjoying it." He waved an arm over the company. "Majesty Mother, these are my friends. Pentu, priest of the temple of Ra-Harakhti at On. Panhesy, also priest of the sun, whom I have made my chief steward. Tutu, who has so diligently written down my words and whose hand you saw in my letters to you. Kenofer, Ranefer..." One by one the men left the ground and kissed her feet, looking up at her with a mixture of reverence and challenge. With few exceptions they were distinctive for the shaven skulls and long white kilts of their priesthood. Around their necks or emblazoned on their forearms were the emblems of the God of the Horizon, the hawk with the disk.

"Mahu," she said as one man raised kohled eyes to hers. "What are you doing here? Have you lost your headship of the Mazoi?" *So this is my son's spy*, she thought. *Chief of the Memphis city police.*

Mahu smiled ruefully. "No, indeed, Majesty, but the prince has seen fit to include me, a humble soldier, in his circle of friends."

A humble soldier with a not-so-humble liking for the secrets of your queen, Tiye thought again. "And you, Apy? Are you neglecting Pharaoh's interests in order to sit in the grass at Thebes?"

"Certainly not, Divine One," the man replied swiftly, bent double before her. "I simply accompanied the prince on his journey and will take this opportunity to report to the Overseer of the Royal Estates directly on the condition of Pharaoh's holdings in Memphis before returning home."

Tiye sat, and the company relaxed. Amunhotep sank to the grass, pulling his feet in under him, and immediately Nefertiti went down with him, knee to knee. Tiye wondered what she had interrupted, having noticed several scrolls scattered in the grass, together with dishes containing the remains of pastries and cups half full of wine. She became aware of her son's placid yet steady gaze on her and turned to him. "What did you think of Thebes, Amunhotep?"

He considered the question with a seriousness it did not deserve. "The streets are filthy," he said at last, "and the common people smell."

The little crowd burst out laughing, and Tiye heard the familiar note of a fawning sycophancy in the sound. Amunhotep did not even smile but continued to hold his gaze on her. She was suddenly aware that he was assessing her, weighing her against the balance on some scale whose meaning was a mystery to her. It made her embarrassed and suddenly aware of her age among this gathering of the young.

"Did you feel that you had to see it, after Mutnodjme's tales?" she asked politely.

He dropped his eyes. "Perhaps."

"I prefer Memphis also"—she smiled—"but I try to remember that without the princes of Thebes in the ancient days, our country would still be under the yoke of foreigners. Besides, Thebes is Amun's home. Under all that filth and decay is a noble, proud city." Several of the young men glanced at each other. Amunhotep studied his hands.

"What you say is true, Majesty Aunt," Nefertiti responded, "but let us all appreciate Thebes with the river flowing between us and the city." Tiye could not fail to note the girl's animation, the sparkle in the gray eyes, the exaggeratedly graceful gestures. "Tell me, Great One, what do you think of the new Khatti ambassador and his train? What wildmen!"

At the new subject of conversation the little group loosened and began to chatter. For a while longer Tiye sat and talked with them of inconsequential things. Sitamun was still sulking. Her responses were monosyllabic but polite. In the end Tiye left them, feeling as she did so that directly her back was turned, they would continue with the discussion that she had interrupted. Putting them out of her mind, she went to Pharaoh's bedchamber. For once the painted mats that covered the windows had been raised, and as the lamps had not yet been lit, the evening shadows lay gently across the tiled floor. Apuia was serving the king his meal, and Surero stood ready to assist. Servants crossed and recrossed the room with silent purpose, and in a corner a single harp player fingered a plaintive melody. There was no sign of the boy, but as she approached the couch and bowed, Tiye heard laughter outside in the garden and glanced out the window in time to see him go racing by, Pharaoh's greyhounds in pursuit.

"See, I am eating," Amunhotep said good-naturedly. "The fever is down, and my teeth have stopped trembling in my gums. Come and sit on the couch. Tia-Ha was here last night, bearing me quinces and plenty of gossip. So the eunuch has returned."

Tiye settled herself beside his feet, shaking her head at the dishes immediately offered but accepting wine from Surero. "The measure of a man should not be taken only when he draws a bow or throws a spear, as you have told me often enough," she retorted, sipping the cool red liquid with relish. "Your son has no love of military arts, though he can drive a chariot well enough. I presume when you call him eunuch, you are not denigrating his religious or musical pursuits."

"Well, he looks like a eunuch," Pharaoh grumbled, swallowing delicately. "With that thick mouth and the stooped shoulders. I suppose you want my seal on the marriage contract."

"It is time, Amunhotep."

"Then we shall see what kind of a eunuch you eunuch is." He raised his cup to her, and his eyes twinkled mischievously over the rim as he drank. "I have read the scroll."

"It is a perfectly ordinary contract."

"Return it to me tomorrow. I will affix my seal. Have you given any thought to a contract for little Smenkhara?"

"No, but I daresay you have. By the time he is of marriageable age, Sitamun will be too old to produce heirs with fully divine blood in their veins."

"But not too old to give Smenkhara as strong a claim to the throne as our present heir if he marries her." He waved away the ruins of his meal and leaned back. In spite of his forced cheerfulness Tiye saw that one side of his face was swollen, and that a thin film of sweat had broken out across his upper lip.

"In that case there could be civil war if Smenkhara pressed a claim, and there would certainly be no children," she said crossly. "Your son and Nefertiti will produce dozens of royal children. The game palls, Amunhotep."

"Yes," he agreed unexpectedly, his eyes closed. "It does. Surero, bring in the Syrian acrobats and have the lamps lit. Are you going, Tiye?"

The question was petulant, and she stood and looked down on him with sympathy, for he was seldom a whiner. "I must feast tonight with the Alashian delegation," she explained. "The contract will be before you tomorrow, Horus. May your name live forever."

He opened his eyes, surprised at the formal farewell. "Yours also. Give my condolences to Nefertiti."

He always manages to have the last word, she thought with inward laughter as she swept out.

5

AS PHARAOH HAD PROMISED, THE CONTRACT WAS SEALED AND delivered into the palace archives, and Nefertiti became a princess and his son's wife with the pressing of his ring into the warm wax. Amunhotep listened to Surero's minute account of the celebratory feasting that would be held for the pair with a lack of attention, finally ordering Smenkhara to be brought to him and playing with the baby throughout the rest of Surero's report.

Pharaoh did not attend the simple rite of royal marriage that took place a few days later at Karnak, but Tiye was not concerned. She knew that it was the ratifying of the contract that had been important. Commoners did not regard marriage as a religious undertaking, and it was only royal gods who sought the blessing of Amun on the unions that would produce more divine beings. Nevertheless, Tiye took a delight in seeing her son and Nefertiti, resplendent in silver and dressed in blue and white, the imperial colors, standing solemnly with hands joined before Amun's mighty sanctuary. When it was over, there was a feast that was open to all, but Tiye, suddenly exhausted, left it as soon as she could. *I have accomplished a great deal in a short time*, she thought as Piha slipped the yellow gown from her shoulders and bowed her into her sleeping robe. *Now I am tired. I need time in which to do absolutely nothing.*

She decided to visit her private estates at Djarukha, a journey she had not made in years. The season was making her restless in a way she understood only too well. The river had risen, turning the country into a vast, calm lake. Idle peasants flocked to Pharaoh's building projects at Luxor, Soleb, and the Delta, and work went on in his tomb, its gaping entrance now lapped by the waters of the Inundation. The sowing had begun and soon new crops would thrust against the wet, black soil, while persea and date palms spread tender green leaves to a Ra become beneficent and forgiving. Fish teemed in the river and the canals, eggs hatched in the nests along the banks, and Tiye's own body made her feverish with the vitality of spring.

"Come with me, Ay," she urged him as they sat side by side on the roof of her audience hall. Shaded by her canopy, they were enjoying the scented breezes and the glitter of sun on the water beyond the lushly waving crops that spread between the dun cliffs at their back and the snaking Nile. "We will stop at Akhmin for a few days and persuade Tey to come, too. I have nothing to do. No foreign crises, no policies to determine, and Pharaoh's health is stable. I am beginning to fancy that I can smell Thebes, and I can certainly hear it. I want the quiet of the little house Amunhotep built for me all those years ago."

Ay glanced at her and then away, knowing as well as she what had prompted the sudden urge to travel. "If you like, Majesty," he offered noncommitally. "But are you sure that you do not also need to get away from them?" He indicated the little group gathered in the shade of the prince's apartment wall. From where he and Tiye sat, the prince himself could be clearly seen, cross-legged on the grass as usual, short white kilt rumpled above thin knees, white helmet bobbing as he gesticulated at the listening crowd. His words did not reach Ay and Tiye, but there was no mistaking the authority in the abrupt movements of the hands, the confidence in the uplifted face.

Tiye clicked her tongue. "Look at him!" she said. "He drifts about his apartments with Nefertiti on one arm and that gaggle of priests all around him, arguing, arguing while the sun pours down outside. His nights are spent plucking on his lute and dictating songs. What is the matter with him? He should be splashing in the water with her, running naked under the sycamores, lying with her under the stars. What is he saying to them with such passion?"

"Why don't you ask him?"

She turned her head to look at him. "I am not sure I want to know," she replied simply. "His presence here has already changed the mood of the palace, but I cannot say how. I wait for a word of Nefertiti's first pregnancy, but that word does not come. Only silly servants' rumors that I ignore."

"You have never ignored a rumor in your life," he objected. "Nor have you shrunk from the truth, however painful that may be. Why do you want to run away?"

"Because I am beginning to wonder if the game I have played with Pharaoh has gone too far and I am unable to undo a mistake. It is not a game anymore. There sits the future lord of the greatest empire in the world, with more power latent in his hands than the gods themselves have. What kind of pharaoh am I forcing on Egypt in order to vindicate my hatred of a dead man and show my hold over a living one?"

"You are being too complicated," he chided her gently. "The throne is his by right. It is the prospect of letting go that terrifies you, the rumors of his impotence that titillate you with a vision of Egypt remaining in your hands forever. Summon him and ask him what he teaches these hangers-on of his. Summon my daughter and ask her if she is still a virgin. Why do you shrink?"

"I shall go to Djarukha with all my musicians and friends," she snapped. "There I shall bathe alone and take long sleeps in the heat of the day and think about what you have said. I shall get drunk at sunset and laugh immoderately over nothing. Oh, smell the wind, Ay, so full of flowers!" She stretched luxuriously. "The season of Peret always wakens memories in me, good memories. I find myself dreaming of how it was when Father and Mother were alive and we were all at Akhmin, or the many summers Pharaoh and I spent at the palace in Memphis, drunk with each other."

"I know," he responded quietly. "This is the only time of the year that I fancy I hear Nefertiti's mother laughing among the women. I love Tey dearly and do not want to relive the past, but it lies in waiting every spring."

They went on talking desultorily of the past, but their eyes were drawn to the group on the grass, and finally their conversation died away.

Tiye sailed to Djarukha on a river that had regained its banks, stopping at Akhmin to sweep Tey and her servants into the royal entourage. As Thebes receded and they left the green, landscaped estates of the nobles behind, Tiye allowed herself to surrender to the atmosphere of rural Egypt. She, Ay, and Tey sat under awnings on the deck watching the tiny mud-brick villages slip by, set in the hectic green of the new crops. The river itself was busy with native and foreign craft plying between Memphis and Thebes, but Tiye, dozing with eyes half-closed as her slave whisked at the flies around her, let her thoughts meander across the palm-delineated fields to the sheltering cliffs and the desert beyond, to an Egypt redolent with Ma'at, unchanging and peaceful, under the superficial shouts and cries of commerce.

"Already I feel calmer," she remarked to her brother and Tey one violet evening as they sat replete after the last meal, listening to the soft wailing of pipes from the stern and turning their faces to the pungent night breeze. "Malkatta is the heart of Egypt, but it is all too easy to forget that the country is the body. When we do leave the palace, it is to scurry to Memphis with curtains drawn against the eyes of the fellahin. Our idea of beauty becomes the formality of royal lakes and flower beds ranked like a military division on display."

"Perhaps Your Majesty would like to call a scribe and dictate a poem," Ay murmured dryly. "Something extolling the virtues of a simple life. The fellahin would be gratified to know that the soil they water with their sweat is beautiful."

"Oh, I don't think they would," Tey said, her hands moving nervously in the chaos of cosmetics, bits of jewelry, small tools, and uncut stones that traveled with her everywhere. "They have no conception of beauty, and it would only upset them to try and teach them anything. Look at this piece of jasper, Ay." She held up a red stone against whose surface the sunset was sullenly etched. "I polished it myself for days. Artificial flowers are coming into vogue, and I thought I would try my hand at reproducing the red karkadeh, but there's a small brown flaw in the upper corner. It didn't show at first. I was desolate."

Ay took the stone from his wife's rough, blunt fingers. "I was not serious, Tey," he said, rolling it between forefinger and thumb.

"Oh." She snatched the jasper back good-naturedly and tossed it into the leather bag in her rumpled lap. "I must press some grape flowers when we get to Djarukha. I was thinking of a circlet done in gold and carnelian, or perhaps even ivory, for Nefertiti. But she seems to want nothing but lapis lazuli these days."

Tiye glanced across at her sharply, but as usual Tey had spoken out of an absentminded innocence. The little head in its straight, stark, old-fashioned wig was bent over the restless hands. Tiye's eyes sought her brother's, but Ay was watching his wife with an indulgent smile. *There is no point in trying to discuss Nefertiti with Tey*, Tiye mused. *I will put them all out of my mind. Besides, where is the harm in Nefertiti's decking herself with the precious stone from which the hair of deities is fashioned? It is only a matter of time before she herself is deified, and she knows it. The crowns that adorn the likenesses of myself are rimmed in lapis lazuli.*

At Djarukha the three of them swam, ate immoderately, and spent the evenings in wine and reminiscences. While Tey laid her collection of flowers under papyrus sheets and wandered the riverbank with her young bodyguard, Tiye and Ay sat in the coolness of the reception hall, sometimes talking, more often than not simply lost in their own thoughts. Ay was anxious to return to his responsibilities in Thebes, Tiye knew, but she herself was content to explore the illusion that she was again a young goddess for whom a pharaoh in the flower of an arrogant maturity waited in the new palace on the west bank. She slept long and deeply in the room that looked out over her own verdant acres, her own orchards and grapevines, and none of her pretty copper mirrors left their cases.

They returned to Thebes a month later, leaving Tey at Akhmin on the way home. Once back at Malkatta, Ay vanished into his offices, and Tiye entered the harem in search of Tia-Ha to hear the latest news. The distance she had just placed between the court and herself, however briefly, had served to heighten her awareness of change, and as she paced the gleaming, echoing corridors, she knew that a new wind was blowing. White-kilted priests bowed to her as she swept by them. Strange, youthful faces bearing the arm bands of the royal scribes and temple overseers turned to her in respectful awe. Rounding a corner, she found herself face to face with a burly soldier, who swiftly covered his face and knelt, his own surprise evident in his clumsy obeisance. He was dressed in a short linen kilt and an unadorned white helmet, and his broad chest was bare but for a gold pectoral of Ra-Harakhti, falcon-headed sun god. From his belt there hung a small scimitar, and in one hand he clutched a spear. *What is a temple soldier from On doing here?* she wondered, passing him with barely a glance, and the guards on the harem doors opened for her. Kheruef came hurrying to meet her, his staff of office held negligently under one arm, his headcloth wound loosely around his shaved scalp. Enquiring for Tia-Ha, she also ordered him to have Ay in her audience hall at sundown.

Inside the cells of the women it was cool and murmurous with whispers and soft footfalls. The door to Tia-Ha's apartment stood open, and a gush of perfumed air funneled out to greet Tiye as she entered. Bent over a low ebony table covered with tiny, unsealed alabaster pots was Tia-Ha's cosmetician, a spoon in each hand. He and his mistress went to the floor, and Tiye waved them to their feet. The stench of myrrh, lotus, and unnameable essences was overpowering.

"What are you doing," Tiye asked curiously, coming forward. "The smell is making me quite dizzy."

"I am trying to select a suitable perfume, Majesty," Tia-Ha replied, stirring in a pot with one hennaed finger and holding it up to her nose. "I am tired of myrrh and aloes and persea. I am hoping also to sell some of these. My cosmeticians say it is a good year for rich oils. Some of these come from a cargo of goods I have had shipped to me from the Great Green Sea in exchange for linen. You can go," she said, nodding to the man, who laid down his tools and bowed himself out.

"Send some to my own cosmeticians," Tiye said, "but not the myrrh. The palace is already too full of the whiff of religion."

Tia-Ha raised both carefully plucked eyebrows, clapped her hands for refreshments, and sank onto the cushions littering the floor as Tiye herself went down.

"But it wafts without bringing pleasure, My Goddess," she retorted. "A puff of great seriousness and no frivolity. Is Djarukha so far away that your spies have not reached you?"

"I did not wish to see them. Tell me the gossip, Princess."

Tia-Ha rolled her sooty eyes. "The harem gossip is always dripping with juices but not much fruit. And the body servants of royalty are very close-mouthed."

"But we are old friends"—Tiye smiled—"and you will tell me all."

Tia-Ha sighed. Her slave came quietly offering dates and wine. "We see almost as much of the prince as we did in the days when he lived in the apartment next to this. He and the princess, the priests, and the queen."

"Sitamun?" Tiye came alert. "Tia-Ha, are there any whispers about Amunhotep and his sister? She will end up dead by royal decree if she is not cautious."

"There are whispers, of course, but Her Majesty is never alone with the prince. She is too clever for that."

"Have you seen Pharaoh while I was away? Does he know there is gossip about her?"

"Majesty," Tia-Ha said gently, pulling a sticky black date from the dish and staring at it thoughtfully, "these are the questions of a novice, a child. Even little Tadukhipa, who walks the passage with one shoulder against the wall and will converse with no one but her aunt, knows the answers. Are you well?"

No, Tiye thought despairingly. *I am suddenly old and tired and do not wish to summon the strength to face a new administration.* She rose. "Perhaps I wish to be a novice and a child again," she snapped brusquely. "Your perfumes have given me a headache, Princess."

"If you want me to spy for you, I will," Tia-Ha responded equably, "but Kheruef's women do it better. I prefer to evaluate that which is already known." She nibbled at the date and then reached for her goblet. "Princess Henut, she of the daunting dignity, came to blows a few days ago with one of the Babylonians. Henut belongs to a fading breed, Majesty. She has always clung to a proper reverence for Amun-Ra, and the incense in her apartment would choke a priest. The Babylonian had been putting on airs. It seems that the prince visited her and burned some incense of his own to the Babylonian's god. The woman was boasting in front of Henut. Henut struck her with a fly whisk. The Babylonian was foolish enough to slap the princess's solemn face. Kheruef had her whipped."

Tiye stared at the beautiful, plump mouth against which a few strands of Tia-Ha's long black hair had become caught with date juice. "Are you saying that a harem fight was precipitated by . . . by *religion*?"

"I am. It seems that Amun still has his champions."

"I cannot believe it!"

"I must say one more thing." Tia-Ha rose and met the empress's eye. "The prince sent a pair of gold earrings to the Babylonian when he heard of her punishment."

Tiye groaned. "Oh, gods." The hierarchy within the harem was rigid, and by tradition it was Pharaoh's Keeper of the Harem Door who meted out punishments and rewards. To flout the custom was not only unwise, it was dangerous. If the women thought they could woo anyone other than the one man set over them, there would be a scramble to bribe, cajole, or threaten, and the harem would become an undisciplined rabble. *Amunhotep has lived in it all his life*, Tiye thought, incredulous. *He must know the unwritten rules. Did he feel that the Babylonian woman was part of his family and must be protected?* She turned on her heel and left without another word.

The prince was sitting at an open window, one elbow resting on the sill, his eyes on the bright garden bathed in late afternoon sun below him. At his feet a scribe sat cross-legged, a scroll unrolled under his hands, reading aloud. Tiye had been able to hear the soporific drone long before she made out any words. The gloom in the chamber was cool but for small splashes of white light pouring from the slits beneath the roof. Three or four tiny monkeys in jeweled collars loped and grinned at each other as they eluded the grasp of their keepers, their shrieks echoing against the lines of wooden pillars that fluted up to the dusky blue ceiling. Half-woven lotus wreaths, negligently piled on the prince's stepped throne, lay quivering and wilting under the lazy batting of a large mottled cat. At Tiye's herald's call, Amunhotep swung from the window, and the scribe ceased to read and bowed.

"Majesty Mother! So you have returned! Was Djarukha beautiful? Is all well there?"

She took the outstretched hands, cold and moist to her touch, and then realized with a shock that he was wearing a priest's pleated kilt slung low under his softly swelling belly, and that his full lips had been stained with henna like a girl's. She stepped back, tossing her head at the scribe who hurriedly rolled up his scroll and scurried away.

"Djarukha was indeed beautiful, but I return with many questions for you, my son." As always when she was with him she did not want to make polite conversation. She recoiled from the things she knew she must hear, yet the sincere, defenseless eyes precluded the empty chatter of the courtier.

"I have missed you, Majesty. The palace is not the same without the chance of meeting you around some corner or in the gardens."

She smiled noncommittally. "Amunhotep, I met a strange soldier today, a guard from On if I am not mistaken. There are no religious ceremonies to bring him from the temple there. Any changes in palace servants should be discussed with Pharaoh or myself, or with the overseer in my absence. I presume this soldier is your man."

"A contingent arrived a while ago, to guard the priests who are my friends," he replied without embarrassment.

"Why do the priests need protection here, in a god's own domain?"

He took her arm and drew her to the window. "Such a lovely day," he said dreamily. "See the ducks fluffing their feathers and dipping their beaks into the lake. And the way the water cascades from the buckets of the gardeners like melted silver. My priests sometimes make the priests of Karnak angry, Mother, because we have been teaching the supremacy of Ra. They wanted their own guards beside them."

Tiye felt her spine loosen in relief. She draped both braceleted arms over the sill. "So that is what you have been discussing, huddled together! The supremacy of Ra. Foolish one! The priests of Amun are not going to give such playing with words a second thought. It is commendable that you are seriously trying to continue your father's policy of encouraging a universal religion in Egypt. It has worked rather well in dealing with foreigners. Amun's servants are used to the politics of religion, and the great God himself is not threatened by such expediency."

Amunhotep moved closer to her until his thin shoulder brushed hers. "Amun is of a new order," he said quickly. "He has risen to great power in Egypt, but he is not the first power. When Thebes was nothing but a collection of mud huts and Amun only the Great Cackler, a nothing, a local deity chained to a village, the sun in his visible glory as Aten ruled all Egypt. The Aten must rule all Egypt again." The childlike voice had acquired purpose and strength. Tiye did not dare turn her head for the confusion churning in her. "Where did you learn all this?" she managed.

"I know. I have known since I was born. But even if I had begun my life in error, the scrolls drawn up from ancient writings for Pharaoh's first jubilee would have enlightened me. Ma'at has become perverted. I am delegated to restore it to its former fullness."

"And of course the priests of Ra are most eager to see Ma'at restored."

He did not hear, or pretended not to hear, the sarcasm in her voice. "Of course," he pressed earnestly.

"Amunhotep," she said, turning at last to face him, "your father is Ma'at, in his body, in his person, as pharaoh of the empire. Wherever he is, there is truth, the rightness of things, custom and tradition and law."

"So you say." His full lips suddenly twisted into the semblance of a smile, and anger flooded her for a moment.

"Don't patronize me, Amunhotep! Be careful how you encourage the sun priests! You are the Horus-in-the Nest and will soon be the incarnation of Amun in Egypt. Karnak is as much your home as Malkatta, and the priests of On must realize this sooner or later. Pursue this religious hobby if you wish, but remember that when Pharaoh dies, the priests must go home!"

"You have not understood." Suddenly he gripped her hands and, bending his head, began to kiss them with such fervor that she was taken aback. "But you will. Great Mother, Divine Woman, one day your eyes will be opened." As quickly as the odd fit took him, it was gone. He placed her hands back on the sill, straightening her rings one by one and smiling sweetly at her. She was so dumbfounded that she could only stare at him, trying to gather her wits.

"Amunhotep, I want you to stay out of your father's harem," Tiye managed. "You are free; you can begin to acquire women of your own. You need no longer feel drawn to what was both home and prison for you. I have been told what happened between Henut and the Babylonian."

He sighed. "Majesty, you do not yet understand why I prayed with the Babylonian, do you?"

There was a moment of strained silence. Behind them the monkeys squealed, their claws making little ticking noises against the smooth tile of the floor. The servants chatted among themselves, their eyes on the royal pair, waiting for a summons. The patches of sunlight had shifted position, and the cat, having abandoned the bruised lotus wreaths, lay supple and boneless in sleep.

Tiye shrugged, annoyed. "I understand only what I see, and that is all that can be expected," she said. "I expect obedience from you as a prince, Amunhotep. Is Nefertiti not pleasing to you? Why have you not begun to buy concubines?"

"I do not want Tehen-Aten," he replied, and although his long face remained calm, his shrill voice cracked with emotion. "When Pharaoh dies, I will take over his harem."

"This is Sitamun's doing!" Tiye felt her legs stiffen and her hands curl in upon themselves with rage. "The queen has been putting ideas into that innocent head of yours. I will not have it!"

"But she is my sister and of royal blood and mine by right."

Tiye thrust her face close to his. "She is also strong and wily and will try to control you. Don't you see? She wishes to be chief wife eventually, to supplant Nefertiti."

"Your eyes are so blue, like a cold sky, like the goddess Nut when she opens her mouth to swallow Ra at evening," he said gently. "I like them. I like Sitamun, too. She has put all her staff at my disposal. She worships me."

"Nefertiti worships you also and is beautiful. Get Egypt a son on her, Amunhotep, and if you must have Sitamun when Pharaoh is gone, then take her simply as Royal Wife." *Then see how adoring she is*, Tiye thought.

The young man's gaze fell once more onto the slowly bronzing light filling the garden. He leaned out the window, and Tiye could not tell whether it was a flush of embarrassment spreading under his pale skin or the touch of the westering sun that turned his face dark pink. "A god does not beget children lightly."

"But you are not yet a god. Let your body play, my son, and your mind lie fallow for a while. Send the priests away."

He did not answer, and she pressed him no longer. Signaling to her herald, she departed.

Shortly afterward, hungry and unsettled after her odd conversation with her son, Tiye sat on the throne in the middle of her reception hall and told Ay what had passed between herself and the prince. "How many of these soldiers are now in the palace?" she asked him.

"A hundred, Majesty. But the priests outnumber them."

"A hundred!" The headache that had begun in Tia-Ha's airless apartment intensified, making her wince. "Well, we must hope that this foolishness will run its course, and that before long the prince will lose interest in matters that belong to childhood awe and not to the noon of maturity. I do not want to atagonize him or hurt his feelings by ordering them home. But those priests anger me. They are fawning on a boy who means well, using him. It goes beyond simple bribery."

"A report from Memphis was waiting for me in my office. It seems that the prince has made a substantial gift to the temple of the sun. But he has also sent grain and honey to Karnak."

Tiye relaxed. "Then he is simply trying his wings. Poor Horus-Fledgling! Tomorrow I will talk to Nefertiti, but now, dear Ay, I want to sit on the dais among the flowers and eat and watch the entertainments."

"Pharaoh?" The question was soft, guarded.

"He is apparently no worse. I do not want to face him tonight. I will instruct Kheruef to send him Tia-Ha."

"Horemheb tells me that Pharaoh has doubled the number of Followers of His Majesty around him."

"So! Even now the Son of Hapu controls him!"

"He is not foolish. He is aware that the eyes of the courtiers are turning to Amunhotep, and he does not know his son. Besides, royal sons and fathers have murdered each other before now. Amunhotep himself dismissed all Followers appointed to guard him and now uses only the soldiers from On."

"Has Amunhotep approached any of the army commanders apart from Horemheb?"

"No. He would be foolish to do so, this early. The army clings to what is, not what will be. He will have command of it soon enough."

"Good." She got up, reaching for his arm. "Eat with me tonight in Pharaoh's place. Is little Smenkhara well guarded?"

"Certainly, though I do not think Amunhotep knows enough yet to smell a rival. Everything is under control, Tiye."

Tiye was not so sure, but tonight did not care. She felt as empty as a new corpse waiting to be beautified.

6

AS DAY FOLLOWED DAY, THE COURTIERS GREW ACCUSTOMED to the presence of the Ra priests drifting quietly around them. Changes in religious fashion were frequent at court, and while the omnipotence of Amun, his consort, Mut, and their son, Khonsu, was taken for granted, the lesser deities, and sometimes foreign ones as well, enjoyed brief vogues before falling out of favor before new gods to be wooed and importuned.

It relieved Tiye to see that Amunhotep, having made his gesture of childish rebellion, was now accepting his place. He seldom went into the harem any longer, and when he did, it was merely to visit those of his father's older women who had been kind to him. If his glance strayed to Tadukhipa or Pharaoh's other young wives, he quickly allowed himself to be diverted to safer pursuits. He was politely loving to Tiye, and she often wondered if the imperceptible distance that had developed between them dated from their odd conversation, if indeed he had been trying to tell her something she had missed and that had put him on his guard. Often in the dark quiet hours before dawn when she would come awake suddenly and lie unable to fall asleep again, she would feel his soft mouth pressed against the backs of her hands with an urgency that, try as she might, she could not decipher.

Through the anxious months of harvest and the hot, dead days of the season of Shemu, Tiye saw the administration settle into a rhythm of government that differed little from the current that had flowed under her since the days of her youth. Pharaoh lingered in the twilight world of the chronic invalid, no longer emerging to feast or enjoy his garden, dealing only halfheartedly with the few official documents that could not be sealed by his wife, and returning tiredly to his boy, his sorcerers, and his naked dancers. He was drinking steadily, with the determination of the fatalist to muffle all but the present, and on her more and more infrequent visits Tiye almost always found him bloated, feverish, and lazily incoherent.

She herself was spending much of her time in the Office of Foreign Correspondence, wrestling with matters of diplomacy, for Eriba-Adad, king of Assyria, had died, and both the Khatti and Mitanni were eyeing the Assyrians with feral greed and Egypt with wary flattery. She and Ay spent long hours discussing the letters she dictated to Suppululiumas and Tushratta, blending veiled threats with bribery and allusions to Egypt's military supremacy, a pursuit Tiye had always enjoyed. She also made her annual state pilgrimage upriver to Soleb in Nubia, beyond the second cataract, and stood arrayed in the disk and double plumes, cobra, and horns of her divinity in the temple her husband had built for her there. Her own colossal image stared coldly back at her through the thin blue fog of incense, and her priests lay supine around her like a flock of wingless white birds.

The journey south had always delighted her, and until now the solemn yearly repetition of ritual had not blunted the pleasure she took in watching her superiority confirmed. But this year the listlessness of yet another blistering summer smothered her every nerve in fatigue, and she returned uninspired to Malkatta to endure the remainder of the season.

One welcome break in its tedium was an announcement from the princess's herald that Nefertiti was pregnant. Amunhotep received the formal congratulations of the court and the delighted bows of his family with grace, and Nefertiti preened before her excited women and spent much time fingering the little gifts showered on her by the inhabitants of the harem. Pharaoh lent her the services of his personal magician so that the spells of protection could be prepared properly, and Tiye gave her a lucky amulet she herself had worn while carrying Amunhotep.

But the excitement soon paled for Tiye, and she withdrew from the happy furor. It was too hot to remain in a state of delight. Sometimes she sent for Smenkhara and his cooing nurses, smiling at him as he lazily batted at her necklaces. But she was not a woman who gloried in her motherhood and instead found herself speculating on him as a grown man, a prince of Egypt. Would he become a threat to his brother, Amunhotep? Perhaps Nefertiti's child would be female, a suitable wife for him if no royal son appeared. But if her child was male, Smenkhara would stay a prince forever.

Yet whether pacing the halls of Malkatta, sitting on her throne to hear the dispatches and reports, or presiding over the endless feasting where below her on the floor of the banqueting chamber a dozen strange languages filled the air, Tiye was increasingly coming to view the country, the empire, even herself, poised on the brink between a judgment and its results, as though Anubis had lowered all hearts onto the holy scales in the dark hall where the spirits of the dead were scrutinized. She could discern no outward reason for this recurring impression, but with the experience of twenty years of active rule she did not dismiss it.

One morning just before the month of Thoth began, Tiye was pondering the difficulties of celebrating a new Feast of Opet without a pharaoh competent enough to perform the ceremonies when the Second Prophet of Amun was announced.

Piha draped a scarlet sheath around her, and Tiye, surprised by the visit, indicated that the prophet should be admitted. Si-Mut entered bent almost double, his shaved skull gleaming with beads of sweat, his priestly ribbons stuck to his forehead.

"Stand and speak," she said, going to sit at her cosmetic table. "But I remind you, Si-Mut, that I do not customarily give audience in my bedchamber." The cosmetician opened his box and began to brush the yellow paint over her cheeks.

"I apologize, Goddess, and realize that my news is perhaps known to you already, but seeing you have not been to Karnak for many months, I humbly take the chance that it is not."

Tiye closed her eyes while the manservant smoothed the green eye paint over her lids. "If I had wanted to go to Karnak, I would not have hired a priest to perform my duties there. What is the matter?"

"Prince Amunhotep yesterday stretched the white cords for his new temple to the Aten within the sacred precincts."

Tiye felt the kohl brush against her temples. "I know that. He and his architects have been fussing over the plans to extend the Aten shrine at Karnak for months. It is a harmless building project and makes him happy." She opened her eyes and picked up the mirror as the cosmetician dabbed a fresh brush into the red henna. Behind her own bronze reflection she could see the face of the young priest, hunched and anxious.

"This morning, Majesty, Princess Nefertiti is performing the same ceremony."

"What of it? I presume you mean in preparation for the new palace my son has commissioned on the east bank."

Si-Mut took a deep breath. "No, Majesty, I do not."

With difficulty Tiye controlled her lips while the brush moved softly over them, her eyes narrowed as she watched Si-Mut struggle to hide his own anxiety. She set the mirror down, and the cosmetician began to tidy away his pots. Her hairdresser stood waiting nearby, the black-ringleted wig held in both hands. Tiye swung around. "Do you mean to say that Nefertiti is laying the foundations for another Aten temple?"

"Yes, Holy One."

"Leave me. And send Nen immediately."

Si-Mut immediately bowed and, arms outstretched, backed out the door. The hairdresser settled the heavy wig carefully onto the thick reddish curls and began to touch the tresses with perfumed oil. Tiye sat very still, her mind working furiously.

When Nen was announced, she rose and spoke before he had finished his obeisance.

"You are responsible for keeping me informed on matters relating to Karnak. It seems you have used your time to swill wine at my table and lie in your boat on the river."

At her soft tone he whitened. His glance flew fearfully to her hands, lying deceptively loose at her sides.

"Majesty, if I am accused of negligence, I wish to know my accuser."

"I am your accuser! You brought me no word of the princess's plans for Karnak."

He kept his eyes on her hands and said in a puzzled voice, "I made a report to you of the plans both the prince and the princess had for building a temple."

"You did not indicate that the princess was building her own temple. Her architects must have wandered the sacred precincts, there must have been rumors. I do not like to be uninformed. You are dismissed from my service, and my patronage is withdrawn. Go home to Memphis."

The moment when she might have struck him had passed, and with obvious relief he raised his head. "Majesty, Princess Nefertiti allows no one near her but those servants chosen for her by the prince. The ones you hired for her have been relegated to the second circle. It is very difficult to get word of her doings. It is true that her architects have been busy at Karnak, but always in the company of the prince's men. They have all been using the project offices of Queen Sitamun."

Sitamun knows my men, Tiye thought. *It would not be hard for her to keep knowledge from them. She is begging to be disciplined, but then, Sitamun has always been a gambler, and her timing has always been bad. Can she not see that it is too soon to be obvious? How could Pharaoh and I have bred such a fool?*

"Leave me. And Malkatta. Immediately." When he had slunk away, Tiye turned to Piha.

"The onyx earrings and the royal coronet today. Hang an Eye of Horus and an ankh beside the sphinx on my pectoral, and I will wear the new clay rings around my neck also. When you have finished dressing me, order the royal barge, fanbearers, and my herald. I am going across the river."

The day was like a giant crucible, feeding heat through the curtains of her litter as she was carried to her barge, and it intensified as Tiye disembarked at the Karnak water steps. Ptahhotep and Si-Mut waited to kiss the burning pavement before her. It had always seemed to her that Thebes was hotter in summer than the west bank, more fetid in the time of humidity, noisier during the tumultuous weeks of Opet. She had made no effort to conquer her distaste for the city and no longer felt uneasy that Malkatta had been built in such close proximity to the houses of the dead. Over the welcoming chants of Amun's priests and the rattle of the systra held in their immaculate hands, she could hear the grind of Theban daily life. Peddlers screamed raucously in the streets. Donkeys brayed, carts rumbled, street musicians set up a harsh jangle, men and women argued, and children shrieked. The odor of the city drifted over Karnak's sheltering walls and through the sacred gardens, a mixture of rotting offal and cooking spices that caused Tiye to lift a lock of her lotus-drenched wig to her nose. Behind her *Aten Gleams* rocked invitingly on the low tide of the river, which added its own stench of mud and wet vegetation. She sighed inwardly and stepped onto her litter, ignoring the clustered priests. "Take me to Princess Nefertiti," she commanded before letting the damask curtains fall closed. Sweat welled from under the tight band of her wig, trickled down her scarlet-covered spine, and prickled uncomfortably beneath her arms.

She lay still as the litter swayed along the paved paths crisscrossing the city within a city that was the home of every powerful deity Egypt wooed. At length the bearers lowered her gently to the ground. Tiye raised the curtain onto a group of startled men and women, who watched her step forth in a hushed silence. Her fanbearers sprang to cover her. The assembly went down onto the churned earth. In one sweeping glance Tiye took in the silver dish full of white paint held in the arms of an Aten priest, the pile of thin cords at her feet, the bull standing stolid and uncomplaining as it waited for the knife, and the dry, black soil turned over when the trenches for the foundations had been dug. Beyond, the bulk of the temple of Mut cast a thin shade, and to right and left colonnades, pylons, and avenues lined with statues shimmered in the heat. *Let them lie*, Tiye thought grimly, looking down on the group from under the wide-tasseled canopy. "The princess," she said tersely to her herald and watched him walk to Nefertiti, who was crouched but not resting on the fiery ground. In the moment of quiet, the whisks made a pleasing susurration, and the flies hung like black dust in the air. Nefertiti rose and glided toward Tiye with a grace unaltered by her distended belly, her eyes squinting against the glare. Tiye dismissed her fanbearers and motioned the girl in under her own sunshade.

"This is Karnak, Nefertiti," she said without preamble. "Why are you building a new temple to the Aten here when your husband is enlarging the shrine that already exists?"

Nefertiti looked at her coolly. "Because it is right that I make a ben-ben of my own where I can worship the god by myself."

"Tradition forbids the erection of a temple for a mere woman."

"But I will soon be a goddess, Majesty Aunt. Amunhotep is eager to see me performing my own obeisances in a temple my zeal has caused me to build." She paused, then added, caustically, "Remember, you have a temple all to yourself at Soleb."

"I am worshiped at Soleb as the divinity Pharaoh commanded that I should be! You are still only a princess and may never achieve that degree of immortality. Not only are the Amun priests made anxious by this show of preference for the Aten, they are offended by your lack of discrimination."

"Do not lecture me on matters of religious taste, Majesty Aunt," Nefertiti said quietly. "You hardly ever set foot inside Karnak except for the unavoidable observances. You have a predilection for being worshiped rather than worshiping."

"But this"—Tiye waved contemptuously at the rough site— "could ultimately affect the stability of Ma'at in Egypt."

"I do not think so. Amunhotep is also building for Amun, in a small way."

"A placatory gesture?"

"Perhaps. But at least my husband shows more reverence for the gods than his father did when he built Malkatta on the west bank and removed his divine person from all that is holy. Amunhotep's new palace on the outskirts of Karnak grows every day."

Their eyes met, and Tiye thought she caught the glint of sarcasm in Nefertiti's limpid gaze. *I understand my son's desire to remove himself completely from memories that are bitter to him*, she mused as she scanned the oval purity of Nefertiti's painted face, *and it is true that he builds for both Amun and Ra-Harakhti. Then why am I cold with unease?*

"Your devotion to the things of the gods does you credit,

Nefertiti," she said aloud, "but never forget that matters of state come first. You would be better occupied with the concerns of diplomacy."

"I am."

For the first time Nefertiti smiled, and a wave of anger flushed along Tiye's veins. "If you cannot love my son, the least you can do is have respect for his kindness and innocence," she said icily. "You are a child playing silly games with him. See that you do not use him."

"You insult me, Majesty," Nefertiti replied, and Tiye struggled to hold her anger in check.

It will not do for me to lose my temper with Nefertiti in public, Tiye thought. *However unwise I consider her behavior, I must not provide the court with material for gossip about dissension in my family.* "I think this temple is foolish and possibly dangerous," she said after a moment, "but if Amunhotep desires it, I will let you proceed. Ptahhotep and the other priests will accept it eventually if you are tactful. Don't stand out in the heat too long, child. You need rest and quiet." She signaled to her litter bearers and walked stiffly toward them, moving to recline on the cushions and pull the curtains closed with deliberate dignity. "Back to my barge!" she shouted and then closed her eyes as she felt herself lifted. *Everything infuriates me these days*, she thought. *I must try to be reasonable with Sitamun.*

Tiye found her daughter lying on the cool marble slab of her private bathhouse, taking a massage. The room was dim, the floor pleasingly damp underfoot, and the tingle and splash of running water gave an illusion of winter coolness. Sitamun rested on her stomach, chin propped against her folded hands while her body servant pressed and kneaded her firm flesh. She greeted her mother sleepily. "I am honored, Majesty."

Tiye nodded but made no reply. She watched the respectful hands work the oils into skin that gleamed dully like satin under moonlight. Sitamun often annoyed her, sometimes amused her, sometimes brought a flood of love rising like a pure spring, but occasionally shook Tiye with jealousy. Today the jealousy was there unbidden, an emotion fully formed as she saw the slave brush aside the wealth of dark hair to massage the long neck, the graceful spine, the pleasing curve of the naked buttocks. Sitamun murmured in contentment, turning her head to one side with Tiye's own slow gesture, smiling slightly with Tiye's own generous mouth, a woman of dewy freshness.

"I know why you are here, Mother," Sitamun said, eyes half-closed, "so you need not repeat your warnings. I was happy to lend my architects to my brother and Nefertiti while their new palace was being built. I daresay I shall move into it myself."

"I could not care less whether you supplied Amunhotep with architects," Tiye retorted, stepping closer. "Did you know about Nefertiti's temple?"

Sitamun lifted her head. "Yes, of course. My men were ordered to keep me informed on every aspect of the building projects."

"Why did you not tell me about it?"

Sitamun looked up lazily. "I presumed everyone knew. Nefertiti's pomposity is a good subject for gossip. Did you expect me to rush to you outraged at the news and then to protest to her? That would hardly be the way to stay in Amunhotep's good graces."

Tiye clenched her jaw. "Is that more important to you than my displeasure?" she said coldly.

"Yes, it is. I am trying to make myself indispensable to him." She turned onto her back, and Tiye averted her eyes from the hollow belly, the sliding breasts. Sitamun's hair fell almost to Tiye's gold-sandaled feet. "I have been a Royal Wife, a queen, for nine years, learning to please a capricious, insatiable man. Oh, I know that Pharaoh took me to his bed because I reminded him of you, but it has been my own skill that has kept me there. Put yourself in my place, Majesty. When Pharaoh dies, I will be relegated to the harem for the rest of my life. You would not accept such a fate, and neither will I. There is no great harm in what I am doing. I quite like my brother." She flexed one long leg as the masseuse's fingers dug into her thigh. "He will declare me a queen. Perhaps even empress."

"How can you underestimate Nefertiti so blithely? Don't you see that her ambition is as strong as your own?"

Sitamun's blue eyes swiveled upward to meet Tiye's. "Certainly. But she is younger and less experienced. You would like to see us at each other's throats, wouldn't you, Goddess? You want to control Amunhotep yourself, but you are too proud to compete with Nefertiti and me, for you know you would lose. You have only the power of political acumen to throw against youth and beauty, and Amunhotep is greatly affected by beauty."

"Do you not fear me, Sitamun?" The question was almost inaudible.

"Yes, I do," Sitamun replied drowsily, "but while my father lives, you dare not touch me, and when he dies, I will have a new pharaoh's protection. In any case, I do not think you will harm me. You are not that insecure. If you were going to murder me, you would have done it a long time ago, when you and I were rivals."

Tiye laughed harshly. "We were rivals only in your conceited mind, Sitamun. At least use your influence over the prince to keep these sun priests in their place. I do not like his religious direction. You can care nothing for this Aten nonsense."

Sitamun slowly closed her eyes and smiled. "No, but Amunhotep does. Oh, Mother, you have been Egypt's first minister for too long. You see dark problems where there are none. He is amusing himself, that is all. We are all amusing ourselves." She sat up, signaling her attendant for a towel, and Tiye knew there was no point in arguing further. With a frigid nod she took her leave.

I suppose there is some truth in what she says, Tiye thought as she walked back to her own apartments. *It is all too easy to forget how to laugh, to dally, to be foolish for the sake of being foolish. And she is certainly speaking more than a suspicion when she accuses me of jealousy. I do wish to control my son, to be admitted to his circle of friends, to have him defer to me. And I will. She is wrong in imagining otherwise.*

In the weeks that followed, Tiye kept careful watch over the frenetic building going on at Karnak, observing that her son paid full reverence to Amun while his temple to the Aten rose pink and new amid the awesome towers of an older order. Sometimes it seemed to her that Amunhotep was laughing under the rituals that he made deliberately ornate, not in the way his father laughed, with the good-humored scorn of the sophisticate, but with the cold secrecy of an initiate into deeper mysteries.

She endeavored to spend more time with him, walking with him and Nefertiti, Sitamun, and his hangers-on while they fed the ducks that thronged the royal lakes or picked flowers to weave into necklaces or ate an evening meal in pretty simplicity on the grass while watching Ra sink into the mouth of Nut. Amunhotep spoke seldom then of religious matters, but she could not tell if it was because he was inhibited by her presence or not. He talked a great deal, with charming hesitancy, of the glories and attractions of nature, and it was obvious that animals trusted him. He was followed by monkeys, cats, and his father's greyhounds, and when he inspected his division of charioteers, the horses in the stables came up to him without fear and nuzzled him gently. Tiye was at once repelled and fascinated by a guilelessness that seemed too studied to be authentic, a frankness that seemed to ridicule mere honesty. Yet she was touched by the deference he showed her. He wrote songs for her that he sang himself, playing the lute he had mastered with such skill. He drew her arm through his own as they strolled the gardens or held her hand like a little boy.

The court began to affect a simpering naturalness. Artificial flowers of amethyst, jasper, and turquoise set in gold appeared on necklaces and belts and in red-painted earlobes or were woven into the hair of wigs that hung to the waists of both men and women. No courtier with social aspirations paraded in the gardens without a monkey perched on one shoulder, a dog or goose at his heels, and a servant or two carrying kittens in baskets. Their women congregated on the lawns to share dainty sips of local beer and discuss the relative abilities of their respective gardeners. The harem acres, usually deserted until midmorning, were suddenly full of sleepy-eyed concubines who stumbled from their silken couches at dawn to breathe and exclaim over the new air. The trade in unperfumed oil began to soar.

Tiye watched the courtiers transform Malkatta into an expensive imitation of a wealthy townsman's summer retreat while her son moved oblivious at the center of the new diversion. She hoped it would not last long. Her eyes followed Amunhotep as he nuzzled his cats, rolled on the grass with his monkeys, and ran laughing after the tame ducks that waddled out of his way, and for the first time seriously tried to imagine the Double Crown on his strangely malformed head. It alarmed her that she could not. *But this is part of childhood*, she told herself, *the freedom to be gay and artless with one's friends. When did Amunhotep ever have that opportunity before? He will tire of it soon. He must.*

* * *

Nefertiti was finally brought to bed in Tiye's own quarters and gave birth to a girl with an ease and speed her slimness had belied. After the furor that had broken out among the privileged spectators died away and they had left to continue their rejoicing with wine, Amunhotep took his daughter in his arms.

"I shall call her Meritaten," he said, holding her closely while she flailed her tiny arms and began to cry. "Beloved of the Aten is a good name. She is my flesh."

"Do you not wish to consult an oracle before naming her?" Tiye asked.

"I am the chief servitor of the Aten and know the god's mind," he replied solemnly. "Meritaten is a name that pleases him very much."

"Will you send an official message to your father?"

Ignoring her, he handed Meritaten to the wet nurse and sat beside Nefertiti. "I told you it would be easy," he said to her, running a finger down her damp cheek, "and before long you will have your beautiful body back. That will please you."

Nefertiti pulled away politely from his hand. "If it will please you also, Amunhotep," she said. "May I sleep now? I am weary."

He stood immediately. "Sleep then, fortunate one." He turned to Tiye. "Majesty, share a cup with me."

Tiye nodded, and they went through to the little private reception hall beyond. As servants hurried to light the lamps and Kheruef poured wine for them both, Tiye slipped into her chair, and Amunhotep took the stool at her side.

"Pharaoh should hear this news from one of your heralds," she said mildly. "Can you not put aside your hatred on this occasion?"

He picked up his cup and began running a finger around the rim. His silver rings shone. "Mother the sphinx," he said slowly. "Mother the unknowable, the all powerful."

"Your talk is foolish. Your father is a sick man, and this news is great."

Amunhotep's thick lips curled. Suddenly he drank, draining the cup, and held it out to Kheruef to be refilled. His brown eyes were full of merriment. "Your husband is indeed sick. He is a man, nothing but a man. He will die. Go to him yourself with my news."

"You are cruel and pitiless! Is there no forgiveness in you?" she cried out, shocked.

He gazed into his wine without replying. Presently she said more calmly, "A daughter is good, Amunhotep. She will be queen for Smenkhara."

"Unless I have a son." He came to life and eyed her kindly. "Are sons harder to deliver than daughters, Majesty?"

Tiye laughed. "It makes no difference to a woman."

"But Smenkhara gave you pain."

"That is because I am no longer young."

For a long time he regarded her, his eyes moving from her face to the sphinx hanging from her neck and back again. Then he said, "You are wrong. You are immortal."

Does he somehow truly believe that because I am a goddess I will live forever? Tiye wondered. *Does the thought please him, or is he wishing instead that I would die so that the last of the old administration could be swept away?* She watched as he emptied his second cup and set it on the table. "I am of course immortal in my godhead," she agreed conversationally, "but my body is all too mortal!" He did not smile and seemed all at once to sink into a dark trance, his eyes steady on her face.

"I remember Thothmes," he burst out suddenly.

The name shocked her. "Your brother?"

"You brought him to visit me. He came once, with reluctance. He stood in my room with his arm around your shoulders, smiling, not meeting my eye. He was very brown and smelled of horses and sunlight, and he had the dust of the training ground on his sandals. He said . . ."

"I know what he said." Tiye swallowed, unprepared for the vividness of the memory. Her elder son, so tall, the touch of his firm hand on her shoulders in a protective gesture, his breath warm on her cheek, white teeth . . . Thothmes was always laughing, like his father. Always striding, shooting, thundering by in his chariot, a prince full of the magic of godship and command. Life had been simpler then. Thothmes was a mighty Hawk-in-the-Nest, and Sitamun was his princess. *I should have known*, Tiye thought passionately, *that it would not last*. "He said, 'Little brother, when you grow up, I will take you lion hunting.'"

"I dreamed of it for days," Amunhotep said, and as always the only evidence of his distress was the cracking of his childish voice. "I would wake every morning excited before my eyes had even opened, thinking, *Today he will come. Today I will ride in his chariot and see the desert and really look at a lion.* But he never came."

"He was not a reflective young man," Tiye objected gently. "He knew you were a prisoner and thought it ridiculous and simply said whatever came into his mind because he was embarrassed."

"And then he died." Amunhotep slid from the stool and stood swaying, the wine he had drunk so quickly going to his head. "It was my destiny to live in spite of everything, to become pharaoh. I am as indestructible as you."

"You have a beautiful daughter, a loving wife, a kingdom waiting to honor you," Tiye pointed out, mystified and shaken. "The past is embalmed, my son."

"Yes." Suddenly his head went down. He put a hand on the table to keep his balance, and then with a short bow he lumbered across the lamplit floor, his step clumsy, his soft hips swaying like a woman's. The servants sprang to open the doors, their faces impassive. In the dimness beyond, his herald raised his staff of office, and his On bodyguard fell in behind him.

Pity and scorn washed over Tiye, eclipsing for a moment the protective love she had always felt for him. *He is like a witless beggar*, she thought as she ordered an escort and began to make her way to her husband's quarters. *Why memories of Thothmes now? I saved his life, yet he is not grateful. He wished to be reborn from the harem in triumphant strength like Ra, to be like Thothmes.* But her irritation faded as she glided through the torchlit passages full of the busy slap of servants' feet and the lazy laughter of courtiers bent on a night of diversion, and only love and puzzlement remained, like the bitter residue of a tart wine on her tongue.

Pharaoh's quarters were full of yellow light as she was announced, and the great double doors swung ponderously closed behind her. The boy, naked and glistening with warm oil, crouched in the middle of the floor, a Dogs and Jackals board between him and a little Syrian dancer with fresh lotus flowers in her hair. Other dancers sprawled together or sat giggling, heads close. Musicians stood by an unlit brazier, and the ding of finger cymbals and lutes wove in and out of the sounds of conversation. At the foot of the couch three physicians were consulting quietly, ignoring the noise. Tiye's spirits rose at the cheerful babble. *He is better*, she thought as she crossed the room, but as she neared the couch and saw him, her buoyance left her. Amunhotep lay on his back, breathing harshly. His skin was gray and transparent, giving an illusion of tightness to his flabby cheeks, and Tiye fancied that she could see the large bones lying just beneath the surface of his flesh. His mouth was slightly parted, revealing black teeth punctuated by several gaps. She bent to kiss him, and her nostrils were assailed by a faint, sweetish odor that turned her blood to ice. She had not smelled it often but now recognized it immediately as a harbinger of death.

"Amunhotep?" she whispered.

He opened one eye and tried to smile. "I know," he managed, the breath whistling through his lips. "Our latest god has become a father. At least, someone has become a father." His pupil was dilated, unfocused, and Tiye wondered how drugged he was.

"It was a girl," she said, leaning close to his ear. "Nefertiti is well."

"Nefertiti has done her duty nobly. Is the eunuch pleased?"

Tiye laughed briefly. "You are a terrible man, Mighty Bull," she whispered, her lips moving against his temple. "I love you very much. I can see that I must waste no sympathy on you. I think your son is pleased. He has gone to his quarters to get drunk."

"Lucky Amunhotep. Make them turn me on my side, Tiye, so that I can see you."

She signaled, and his body servants came running, easing his bulk over, pressing the pillow away from his face. Now he opened both eyes, and Tiye, as always, became dominated by a gaze in whose depths, drug-glazed as they were, a steady glint of vitality still showed.

"Why do you allow all this noise?" she asked. "You need sleep. Send them away."

"No. These are the things I have lived for. I drink the physicians' filth and the pain lessens, and I watch the bodies stretch and whirl, and the music rubs against my skin, and I find myself drifting, dreaming of red wine flowing into jeweled cups and blue eyes speaking of endless lust..." The words degenerated into incoherence and then ceased.

Tiye did not take his hand, soothe him, comfort him. She knew he would not have wanted it. She sat looking into his eyes, the cacophony of a banqueting hall all around them, until she became aware that he no longer saw her. She rose and beckoned the physicians. "What is his condition?"

Their spokesman raised his eyebrows and shrugged. "He is ravaged by fevers. His gums are riddled with abscesses. Yesterday he lost two more teeth. For five years, Majesty, I have been coming to you with the same words: His will to live is not human."

"Of course it is not!" she snapped pettishly. "You speak of Amun himself. Give him everything he wants and continue to report to me." She left the chamber, hearing the doors swing to behind her with relief, the cheerful noise giving way to the brooding silence of the corridor. She was exhausted, and as she walked, she fancied that she carried the odor of death with her, clinging to the folds of her sheath like pollen from some monstrous flower.

News of the seriousness of Pharaoh's condition spread quickly, and the silence of expectation fell over Malkatta. Foreign embassies presented no credentials. Ministers with arms full of scrolls stood in the corridors outside their offices as though unwilling to enter. Bored courtiers strolled in the gardens, unwilling to gossip, faces turning occasionally to the intermittent sounds of Amunhotep's painful dying. Tiye, eyes swollen and mind numbed from lack of sleep, passed from her quarters to the relative quiet of her gardens, bracing herself for more hours of lying in darkness listening, as the whole of Malkatta listened, to the macabre shrieks and laughter that came distorted and sinister through her windows. Once she ordered her own musicians to perform, but at their first wails she turned from them in disgust, their ghoulish melodies making her an accomplice in the orgy of Pharaoh's dying. In the end she stopped trying to sleep, sitting rigid beside her couch while her scribe read to her at her feet.

But the summons came eventually, and Tiye knew that this time it would be the last. Her only emotion was one of relief. For years the court had gone about its daily business against a backdrop of tension and the expectancy of bad news from Pharaoh's quarters. The ministers had become used to dealing with him through Tiye. For months at a time his place at the feasts was empty. When he did appear, the courtiers were shocked, sometimes resentful. Few could remember the time

when Amunhotep's voice and physical presence pervaded Malkatta's precincts. For too long he had been an atmosphere
brooding over them, an invisible god. *His death will bring
more than grief,* Tiye mused as she sent her herald to wake
her son and made her way quickly through the dream-heavy
dimness of the palace. *There will be disbelief as well.* The
noise in the royal apartment crescendoed to a burst of clamor
as the doors were flung open for her. For a moment she halted
and then turned to the Followers of His Majesty behind her.
"Throw them all out."

She waited, tight-lipped, while the soldiers dispersed the
astonished crowd. The music trailed away, and the musicians
fled past her, bowing hastily. The dancers and attendants followed, a stumbling, wild-eyed mob of sweat-slick bodies that
veered past her, some falling to their knees as they recognized
her, others backing out, until the soldiers had herded them all
into the passage.

Tiye looked around in the new stillness. The floor was
littered with empty wine jars, torn flower wreaths, dancers'
baubles, a discarded yellow cloak, and even a broken pot of
kohl whose contents oozed, black and sticky, over the dusty
blue tiling. The boy rose in one fluid movement from the corner
where he had been squatting and came toward her warily, one
hand clutched tightly around something that glinted through
his curled fingers. He fell to the floor. Mutely she nodded at
the soldier beside her, and he ordered the boy to rise.

"Show me," Tiye barked.

The boy turned cold, impudent eyes upon her. "He gave it
to me." The small hand unfolded, and on the palm lay a gold
ring surmounted by Pharaoh's royal cartouche picked out in
turquoise. The soldier deftly took it, and the boy glared at him
furiously. "He gave it to me!"

Swift footfalls sounded in the passage, and Ay came striding
in, with Horemheb a moment behind. Tiye nodded at their
bows and turned to Horemheb. "Take this boy. Ship him to the
Delta immediately and have him sworn into one of your border
patrols. Put him under a captain who will see that he does not
run away."

"If he does, it will be the five wounds and a swift be-
heading," Horemheb said grimly. The boy began to scream
obscenities and flew at him, long nails reaching for Horemheb's
eyes and bare feet flailing, but the Follower in attendance

intervened smoothly and, after fetching him a stunning blow to the temple, picked him up from the floor and vanished into the half-light beyond the door.

"Leave us also, Horemheb," Tiye ordered quietly. She was trembling. He bowed immediately and left.

Only now did Tiye summon the courage to look down the long room, through the ominously silent shadows, to the massive couch beside which a stone lamp glowed. The physicians stood behind it, stooped and resigned. With Ay beside her she crossed the expanse of floor, and as they came up to Pharaoh, the door opened again and Amunhotep and Sitamun slipped inside. Tiye did not even glance at them as they stopped at the foot of the couch. Her eyes were on her unconscious husband, who tossed and muttered.

"Well?" she addressed the physicians.

"We have done all we can," one of them said in the monotone of complete exhaustion, "and he refused to have the spells sung over him."

"Very well. You can leave."

They did not stop to pack the welter of herbs, amulets, and unguents that had spilled over the table, but left as quickly as good manners allowed, and Tiye could not blame them. The last weeks in attendance on Pharaoh must have been a nightmare they would never forget. Placing a hand on her husband's drenched forehead, she murmured his name, but even in his unconscious state he felt the pain of her touch and pulled away. His entire face was swollen, his mouth rimed in dried foam, his closed eyes weeping yellowish tears that clotted on his lashes. Tiye withdrew her hand.

For a long time the four of them remained motionless in the tomblike silence of the room, and Tiye realized with despair that Pharaoh would die as he had lived, self-contained, apart, with an arrogant denial of everything beyond his control and a contempt for all who would offer to fulfill his needs. He did not recover consciousness. His restlessness grew more spasmodic, his muttered, disjointed sentences fainter and fewer. A servant approached Tiye on noiseless feet and spoke with eyes averted. "The high priest and his acolytes are without, Majesty. They bring prayers and incense for the passing of the god."

"Let them come."

The room filled slowly with silent white-robed men bearing long incense holders that glowed and smoked. Ptahhotep approached the couch and knelt, taking Pharaoh's limp hand to kiss it while a low, tuneful singing began. *I wonder if he is aware of this*, Tiye thought. *I think he would prefer the loud riot I expelled, but he would understand my reasons for what I did. God you are, and god you will always be, Amunhotep.* She stole a glance at her son but could read nothing on his face. In the flickering light his jaw looked longer and narrower than ever, his nose sharper, his thick lips looser. Sitamun's eyes darted from her father to the clustered priests, and Tiye thought she saw impatience in the long fingers linked together before her.

Gradually the room filled with throat-catching, sweet smoke that wisped into every corner, driving out the lingering odor of stale wine, perfume, and sweat. Pale light began to filter through the shutters. Somewhere beyond the lawns and flower beds the distant rattle of a tambourine sounded, and the faint ululation of a morning song, a servant on her way to her daily duties in kitchen or harem.

At that moment Tiye suddenly realized that she was gazing down on a body. Pharaoh had gone, but such was the spell he cast that for minutes she said and did nothing, waiting for the eyes to flick open and seek her own. "May the soles of your feet be firm, Osiris One," she finally murmured. "May your name live forever. Raise the hangings, open the shutters," she said to the servants. "Dawn comes." They moved to obey her, and Sitamun fell stiffly to her knees. Tiye had supposed the girl would pay the body some mark of respect, but she prostrated herself before her brother, pressing her mouth fervently against his feet.

The light had strengthened as Ra fought urgently to be born. Without pause the priests began the Song of Praise that Pharaoh had not cared to hear for many years, their eyes going to the young man whose gaze had turned to the window. Sitamun rose and walked away. One by one the priests came to kneel and do homage to their new ruler, and when the hymn was over, they, too, left. Ay knelt swiftly to kiss the now divine feet, and Tiye did so last, hardly aware of her actions. Amunhotep took no notice of them but stared out into the garden, where dawn was over and the light was changing from pink to white.

"How very winsomely Ra completes his final transforming," he said cheerfully.

"I will send out the heralds at once," Ay said to Tiye, "and if you wish, I will instruct the Scribe of Foreign Correspondence to prepare dispatches to those kingdoms with whom we have relations. Your presence is not required for that."

Tiye nodded. "Send for the sem-priests to take him away," she said. "And for his servants to gather his goods." Ay took her arm, but she gently shook him off. "I will go to Tia-Ha," she said. "I am not grieving, Ay, not yet. I simply cannot believe that a god whose ka pervaded the whole of the empire for so long is gone. I will tell Kheruef."

The door clicked softly, and she and Ay glanced toward it, startled. Amunhotep had left.

By the time Tiye entered her friend's apartment, the shrieks of mourning had begun in the harem. The women were flocking to the garden, tearing their gowns as they went, rushing to grasp handfuls of earth to sift over their heads. Tia-Ha rose from her cosmetics table, still in her voluminous sleeping gown, and the familiar, comfortable disorder of the room melted Tiye. Her stiff limbs loosened and began to shake. Before Tia-Ha could kneel, Tiye reached for her hands, pulling her forward, and Tia-Ha's arms went around her. "Bring warm wine and be quick," she snapped at her slave. "Sit on my couch, Majesty. How cold you are!" Within moments she had placed a woolen cloak around Tiye's shoulders and pushed warm wine into her unresisting hands. Tiye drank gratefully.

"It is the shock, Tia-Ha," she said as the alcohol reached her stomach and spread warmth through her limbs. "For so long we have expected it. We ought to have been ready."

"How can anyone be ready for the death of a Horus such as he? Cry if you wish, Majesty. My quarters are a good and private place. Listen to them! The harem women have had no such excitement since Princess Henut attacked the Babylonian. Amunhotep goes to the Holy Barque on a tide of delicious sorrow."

Tiye smiled wanly. "He would laugh to hear you. But no, Tia-Ha, I will not cry. I think I have forgotten how. Pharaoh did not like tears. He regarded them as a weakness."

"And for a queen, they are. You will have your hands full, organizing a new administration for your son and seeing to the comfort of the delegations that will arrive for the funeral." She fell silent and sat cupping her goblet in both hands.

"You have fulfilled your duty as a Royal Wife with great

devotion," Tiye said to the lowered, tousled head. "Would you like me to arrange with my son to have you released from the harem, Tia-Ha? You could retire to your estates in the Delta. I care nothing for the other women, but you have been my cherished friend."

"Retire?" Tia-Ha's sultry eyes sparkled. "Oh, the lush delights of the Delta! The orchards, the odorous vineyards, the lusty young slaves pressing the grapes with such a panting, such a rippling of muscles. It would be an interesting retirement. But I think not. I would like to be free to come and go farther than the Theban markets, but my life has been spent here, and I would miss the gossip, the fights, the whiffs of power that come curling through those double doors. Thank you, Goddess, but no."

Tiye nodded, relaxing under Tia-Ha's lilting voice, and a healthy fatigue stole over her. She felt no guilt as she recognized relief pooling out from under her grief and tension. Egypt had been preparing itself for this day for a long time. "I think I will sleep now," she said. "It was good to come to you, Tia-Ha." Tiye rose, this time waiting for the other's obeisance before leaving the harem. Pacing slowly to her own quarters, she ignored the tumultuous expressions of formal grief all around her. *We did well, you and I*, she thought as she swung her legs onto her couch and sleep rushed to claim her. *Life has been sweet.*

BOOK
TWO

7

DURING THE SEVENTY DAYS OF MOURNING FOR PHARAOH
Amunhotep III, while his body was beautified under the hands
of the sem-priests and his magnificent tomb was prepared,
Malkatta filled with foreign dignitaries from every corner of
the empire, all bearing words of condolence for Empress Tiye
and assurance of everlasting brotherhood for her son. Amunhotep sat solemnly on a throne, but the royal regalia rested in
the arms of their keeper on the dais steps, for the new pharaoh
was not entitled to wear them until his coronation. He attended
graciously to every smooth word and replied politely, yet those
present had the impression that his thoughts were far away.
When he was not in Pharaoh's audience chamber, he could be
found in the nursery, bent over little Meritaten's cot, or sitting
with his wife by the lake, saying little, listening to his scribe
read to him from the ancient writings. Tiye waited for him to
dismiss the sun priests, soothe the men of Amun, and visit his
ministries, but he did not. She wondered if by continuing to
behave like a prince he was defending himself against the
possibility of even now losing the kingship.

Nefertiti had no such fears. She sent for the cobra coronet
and spent an afternoon examining it while its keeper stood by
in silence, anxious lest she should offend it by some precipitous
act. But she did not dare to place it on her head. The girl passed
long hours watching the construction of the palace Amunhotep
had commissioned just outside the Karnak complex, although
the architects and master craftsmen dreaded her coming, for
she was never satisfied. To her husband she was as loving and
thoughtful as ever, but to those watching, Nefertiti's shows of
extravagant affection rang hollow.

Some weeks before her father was to be dragged on the

ritual sledges to his tomb, Sitamun sought out the new pharaoh, walking gracefully across his lawn, the transparent blue robes of mourning floating becomingly around her in the soft breeze. The river had reached its full height and was now receding, and the bare earth was already covered in thin, green shoots of new crops. Optimism was in the air, and the court was almost jubilant at the prospect of fresh intrigues, new commissions to be handed out, an untried face staring down on them from beneath the weight of the Double Crown. Sitamun had dressed carefully and wore four loops of gaily painted and gilded clay rings about her neck. Her wig was festooned with turquoise and lapis lazuli cornflowers, and a single huge jasper hung on her brown forehead. The ribbons holding the blue sheath under her painted breasts fluttered to her gold-sandaled feet, and around her shoulders she had draped a short red-bordered cloak. Bracelets tinkled on her arms, and her rings flashed as she greeted her brother, arms outstretched, head bent. Behind her, her retinue wafted like bright petals.

Amunhotep smiled as she straightened. "Mourning suits you, Sitamun. It matches the blue of your eyes."

"My pharaoh, my dear brother," she said, smiling back encouragingly, "by right I should have waited to give you your coronation gift, but I wanted you to have it in peace so that selfishly I might enjoy your pleasure. Will you walk to the canal with me?" Without waiting for an answer her arm slid through his, and they began to make their way to the forecourt. "The Aten temple is still a long way from dedication," she went on, "and the princess's own rises slowly also. Does the delay make you impatient?" He warmed to her, answering her questions easily, feeling her other hand cover his own. "And Princess Meritaten does well, I hear," Sitamun continued as they began to cross the white dazzle above the water steps. The crowds always drifting about went down before them.

"She does. And she is already very beautiful. I think she will have Nefertiti's foreign eyes."

They had come to the edge of the private canal that separated the palace and river, and strolled under the shade of the date palms and sycamores that lined it. At the point where the water steps angled and finally ended, a small barge took the gentle swell, a blue and white damask sail folded neatly against its mast. It was made of cedar, and Amunhotep could smell the scent of the exotic wood. Its sides were inlaid with gold that gleamed dully under the trees. On the prow a giant, rayed sun had been overlaid in silver, and on the stern a silver Eye of Horus regarded them dispassionately. In the center of the deck a cabin had been built, its furnishings of Babylonian brocade, Nubian leather, and silk from Asia, its appointments all worked in blue and white, the imperial colors. Small folding chairs of cedar inlaid with ivory were scattered about the deck. A golden canopy was folded back against the front wall of the cabin. Slaves kilted and head-clothed in blue and white stood lining the rail, and as Amunhotep stepped forward, they knelt on the deck.

Sitamun waved one bejeweled arm. "This is my gift to you, Horus. I have caused the Aten to be emblazoned upon it. Accept it with my humble homage and love."

Their servants set up a buzz of admiration behind them. Amunhotep's grave gaze swiveled to his sister.

"I accept with amazement," he said. "It is strongly built. A magnificent gift. The steward of your estates must be sweating in fear."

All laughed dutifully at the timid joke, and Sitamun smiled into his eyes. "I am richer than any woman save our mother," she said coolly. "Therefore I can give with munificence. The crew and slaves are yours also."

Amunhotep turned and embraced her warmly. "We will take a little journey immediately," he said. "The day is perfect." At his nod slaves sprang to motion, running out the ramp and untying the sail. Pharaoh swayed into the cabin, with Sitamun following. The servants scrambled after them, spilling over the deck and settling under the awning. "Just to the great bend," Amunhotep ordered, and the little craft left the steps and began to glide down the canal. Amunhotep lay back on the cushions. "Nothing is more pleasant than a day spent on the river," he said dreamily. "If you look carefully, Sitamun, you can see the nests of birds almost hidden by the palm branches. I love to drift past the flocks of heron and ibis, such dazzling whiteness, such thin, delicate legs! Truly, life is a wondrous thing."

Sitamun, reclining beside him, allowed her blue linen to flutter away from her legs in the warm wind that blew through the cabin. "Look, Amunhotep," she said, pointing to the bank, "a crocodile." They watched as the silent beast slid into the water. "They like to wait close to Thebes. Sometimes bodies end up in the Nile. How terrible, to die without being beautified, to have no place in the next world."

"The fate of the body is not important," Amunhotep said kindly. "By the Aten's power we are born, and by that same power the ka survives."

Oh, no, Sitamun thought. *If I must listen to one more discourse on the power of the sun, I shall fall asleep.* But Pharaoh did not speak further, and when Sitamun glanced up, she found him staring at her.

"What will you do now that your royal husband is dead?" he asked, his voice high and quick, his bovine eyes moving over her body with an appraisal that was too obvious to be insulting.

Sitamun lifted the ringlets away from her breasts and began to play with her necklaces. "What can I do, Horus? I belong to the harem. I am a widow. But even if I could leave, I would not. I wish to serve you as faithfully as I served Osiris Amunhotep. I have been a princess, a consort of an heir, a queen. If my long experience of court life could be useful to you, I am yours to dispose of as you see fit."

He nodded sagely. "You have been kind to me, Sitamun. Your advice in matters of rule would be useful, if mother cannot supply the answers, of course. Have the hangings dropped, and we will discuss it."

Sitamun gave a short order, and a servant hurried to untie the heavy curtains. As they were enclosed in the warm darkness, it seemed to Sitamun that her brother's eyes grew more feverishly bright. His languid, long-boned hands had begun to fidget, passing over his soft belly, stroking each other, plucking slowly at the ankle-length kilt he wore. "In this dimness your mouth melts into an undefinable age," he murmured, his voice breaking. "I have a mind to make you a Great Royal Wife. Such beauty should not be wasted."

Senses suddenly alert, Sitamun felt his palm move to her body, plucking at the ribbons that held her sheath in place, passing gently over her breasts. He lifted her wig, and her own hair tumbled over her shoulders. The sight of it seemed to fill him with sudden energy, and his thick, heart-shaped lips descended to enclose her own. For a moment her body rebelled, repulsed by his sheer ugliness, but she closed her eyes, summoning the courage and skill she had used time and again with her father, and found the task more pleasurable than she had imagined it would be.

Afterward he gently replaced her wig and called for the

curtains to be raised. On the deck the servants still chattered and giggled, and water slapped against the golden sides of the craft. Amunhotep regarded his sister. "I enjoyed that," he said. "You know more about making love than Nefertiti. Perhaps you could teach her."

Incredulous, Sitamun struggled to keep her expression non-committal, not knowing whether he joked or was indulging a fit of spite against his wife. She realized that neither was true, and that he was simply speaking his thoughts aloud. In that respect, Sitamun decided as she tied up her sheath and clapped her hands for something to quench her thirst, he was dangerous.

The news of Sitamun's gift to her brother, their pleasure trip, and the time they had spent secluded from their staff went from mouth to greedy mouth at Malkatta, where the seventy days of mourning for the dead pharaoh had left the court eager to return to its normal affairs. Within two days Nefertiti was brooding over the rumors, and on the third night she confronted Amunhotep in his bedchamber. The air was chill, and two braziers smoked at either end of the capacious room. The doors to Amunhotep's golden Aten shrine stood open, and the incense he had burned while he said his prayers still smoldered. He himself was sitting propped up on his couch, knees to chin, arms folded loosely across them, lost in the trance he so often entered after he had held his daily conversation with the god. His head was bare, and Nefertiti, approaching him swiftly, was struck yet again by its curious shape. She was too accustomed to it to feel distaste and found, rather, that the more she saw of her husband, the more drawn to him she was. She understood him no better now than she had when the marriage contract was sealed, but her need to protect his odd innocence had grown. Coming up to him, she lifted his limp hand and kissed it gently. He raised his head, blinking, and swung his legs over the edge of the couch.

"Horus, you look tired," she said.

He nodded. "I dislike the dark hours, Nefertiti. I feel safe only under the heat of Ra, the light that reveals every hidden thing. Night is full of whispers unless I am able to sleep it away."

Nefertiti clenched her fists under the cover of her sleeping robe. "And did you feel safe behind the curtains of the sumptuous barge Queen Sitamun gave you?"

"Oh, very. Sitamun is not a part of the darkness. She cannot hurt me."

"Pharaoh, your father is dead. No one can hurt you now. But you can be used. Can you not see that Sitamun wishes to use you to become empress?"

He rose abruptly and began to wander about the room, and Nefertiti noticed that he stayed always within the border of light cast by the dozens of lamps in stands around the walls and flaring on every table.

"Sitamun has a right to become a reigning queen with you," he said almost sulkily. "I love you, Nefertiti. You are beautiful, and you were good to me long before Mother had me released from the harem. But Sitamun is my own blood, my sister, my wife by right."

"But a pharaoh has not been obliged to wed fully royal blood for hentis! The way of choosing an heir has changed!"

"That is not the point." He picked up a green glass vase from Keftiu and absently began to trace the outline of the sea urchin etched onto it. "As the chief of a chosen and holy family I must keep that family united. Darkness hosts against it. We must lock arms. We must love each other strongly."

He had sometimes spoken to her in this vein before, and she was terrified that she was beginning to understand fully his implications. She asked brusquely, "Is that why you made love to Sitamun behind the hangings of her barge?"

"My barge, Nefertiti." He frowned over the vase and then, setting it down, came toward the couch, hands linked behind his back, short sleeping kilt sagging under his loose belly. "That is partly why. But she is also beautiful."

"How is it, Pharaoh, that Sitamun's beauty can excite you so, and yet my own has roused you so little?" She was aware of being on dangerous ground but was close to tears of jealousy. His periodic impotence was a secret she had kept more out of pride than loyalty. She had cast about in her mind many times for its cause, for when he did come to her full of desire, he was as passionate as any woman could wish.

He sat beside her, draping an arm across her shoulders. "Dear Nefertiti!" he said. "What is flesh but a vehicle for the ka? How can you care about Sitamun's flesh when you and I share the communion of our kas? You are my wife, my cousin, my friend. It is enough."

It is not enough if it means that my position as future empress is in jeopardy, Nefertiti thought furiously. Turning to him, she began to kiss him, wrapping her arms tightly around his neck, but his lips remained cool and unresponsive, and finally she drew away. "Do not marry Sitamun, I beg you," she whispered. "If you must have her, put her in your harem."

"But I have already decided." He spoke mildly. "She is to be queen, with you. She is my sister." He emphasized his last words, and Nefertiti suddenly saw the truth of the issue she was confronting. "Your sister—and your father's wife," she said slowly, her heart pounding. "Of course. That is why she excites you. That is why you make no move to fill your own harem. Will you acquire all your father's women, Amunhotep?"

For the first time she saw him angry. "Don't say that!" he shouted, full lips drawn back trembling over his teeth, hands clasped together. "You are disrespectful!" Amazed, she saw his eyes fill with tears. "That man was not my father! Go away!" He jerked at her with his elbow, and she slid speechlessly to her feet. Bowing, she turned to leave, but he called to her, his shrill voice muffled, "Lower, Nefertiti! Bow to the ground! You know who my father is. All of you know. Put your face to the floor!"

She did as he commanded and then, rising, fled from the room. In her own bedchamber her body servant was lighting the lamps. "You should have done that by now!" she shrieked and, striding to the girl, slapped her twice with all the force she could muster. "And why is my sheet not turned down, my gown laid out?" The girl ran, and Nefertiti flung herself onto the couch. Bunching the sheet in both hands, her body rigid, she surrendered to her rage for fear she should have to face the darker thing beneath it.

The day of Amunhotep's funeral dawned pearl-clear and cool, and Tiye shivered as she stood in her tiring room while Piha and her other slaves draped her in blue and the Keeper of the Royal Regalia waited in the anteroom with her crowns. *Today I will sacrifice to my husband*, she thought determinedly. *I shall look back down the years with gratitude*. She knew that the procession was already forming on the road that led behind the valley where every pharaoh had been buried since the time of Thothmes I, Egypt's Restorer. The harem women would be milling about, gossiping and adjusting their robes. The foreign delegations, swathed in their barbaric costumes, would be anx-

iously watching the Overseer of Protocol and his scribes. The
ministers and other courtiers were doubtless whiling away the
time by gambling or picking at the sweetmeats their servants
carried.

Kheruef appeared at her doors himself, wearing a floor-
length kilt of mourning blue, his headcloth a strip of gold-shot
blue linen. "It is time, Majesty. All is in order."

"I do not want to wait while the women are sorted out."

"They are ready, and Queen Sitamun is on her litter."

The horde fell silent as Tiye stepped under the pylon that
divided Malkatta from the environs of the dead and made her
way to her litter. Although it galled her that tradition demanded
that she be carried beside her daughter, she gave no sign of it,
and greeting Sitamun politely, she reclined on the litter. Her
husband's coffin already waited far ahead, propped against the
rocky wall of the tomb, guarded by a thousand priests from
Karnak, who had accompanied it in the early hours and had
watched it being dragged on the sledge by the red oxen of
custom to its resting place. Beside it stood the four canopic
jars of white alabaster topped by the heads of the sons of Horus.
The temple dancers were also there, sitting silently under their
canopy.

At Tiye's signal the cortege began to straggle along the road
as the sun gained strength. From far back in the procession,
behind the family members and the army commanders, the
harem women began to shriek, scooping earth out of the baskets
they carried and sprinkling it on their glistening wigs. Following them were the kitchen slaves and overseers of the burial
feast that would take place outside the tomb when the ceremony
was concluded.

The temple of the Son of Hapu loomed on Tiye's left, the
vast granite statue of her old enemy staring serenely and, Tiye
thought, smugly over her head to the river beyond. This day
he was unattended, for his priests walked in the procession.
She averted her eyes and briefly toyed with the idea of having
the temple razed. Some excuse could be found, perhaps that
the stone was needed elsewhere. She herself would smash the
nose from the statue so that Hapu could no longer smell, and
pick at the eyes so that he could not see. But she quickly
discarded the idea, for the common people had already taken
to gathering in his forecourt, their arms full of flowers or bread
or cheap blue beads, bringing their blind children to be healed.

How ironic, she thought, that a misguided seer should cure the blind.

To her right her husband's own mighty temple was drawing slowly closer, its columns towering agaist the blue of the sky, and beyond it, well into the strip of fertile land that was flooded each year, the two sentinels that the Son of Hapu himself had designed. Each was a likeness of Amunhotep over ten times taller than a man, and both gazed with omnipotence across the Nile to teeming Thebes and Karnak. The Son of Hapu had selected red quartzite for their sculpting, answering those who dared to ask him why he should concern himself with an engineer's business with a secretive smile. When the monuments had been erected and dedicated, the reason became clear, for the statues sang at dawn, a clear, ringing note of purest quality. None knew what magic the Son of Hapu had performed to make the rock live, but even Tiye had been awed. Her own masons and engineers could give no answers to her irritated questions. Members of the court who could drag themselves from their couches before Ra to this day stood in the grass at their feet to hear the magic.

The litter swayed on. Beneath the keening of the women conversations had started. Sitamun was eating a quince, holding the fruit away from her spotless linen so that the juice should not dribble onto it. Tiye allowed her thoughts to run on of their own accord until the procession halted for refreshment. When the canopies were folded away, those unfortunate enough to continue on foot began to sweat as Ra neared his zenith.

Tiye looked once again to the left, where a broad avenue of sphinxes led to a fine mortuary temple whose white terraces mounted gracefully to three shrines hewn out of the cliff itself. It had been built by Thothmes III, who had also erected another, smaller version that lacked this breathtaking symmetry. Few worshipers paced the avenue any longer, and the forest of myrrh trees that had been brought from some mysterious place and planted there were often neglected. It was sometimes said that Osiris Thothmes had not built the temple at all, that a woman pharaoh had raised it before her reign ended in confusion, but Tiye gave no credence to the legend.

The procession swung right, into the shade of the cliffs, and emerged again into blazing sunlight, where the priests were already waiting. Incense spiraled into the limpid air. The painted coffin stood prepared. Tiye stepped from her litter, and together with Sitamun and Amunhotep approached it. The ceremonies began.

For several days the courtiers camped in varying degrees of comfort in whatever shade they could find, whiling away the time. Some went hunting out on the desert. Some dictated letters, sampled foreign wines, or made love while the Amun priests chanted on. Interest was stirred when it came time to Open the Mouth, for all knew of their new pharaoh's antipathy toward his father. The more superstitious among them waited for some manifestation from the dead god as his son approached with the knife in his hand, performing the rite as heir with a polite indifference. A surge of sympathy went out to Tiye, who swung open the coffin and was the first to kiss the bandaged feet. Pharaoh's other wives followed suit, tears watering the sem-priests' careful handiwork, but Amunhotep remained standing under his canopy, arms folded across his scrawny chest, eyes vacantly staring at the surrounding rocks.

It was with a feeling of universal relief that the coffin was at last carried into the damp hole to be swallowed by the darkness. Tiye and Sitamun followed it bearing flowers and watched as it was nestled into its five sarcophagi. The golden nails were driven in, and the flowers laid. All around, the torchlight gleamed on Pharaoh's belongings, the gold and silver, jewels and precious woods.

Evening came, violet and dark blue, and Pharaoh's last feast was set on blue cloths that carpeted the ground. Cushions were strewn, torches lit, and while the guardians of the dead sealed the tomb and pressed the jackal over the nine captives into the wet mud, the company fell upon the food and wine.

The funeral feast went on all night, until the valley resounded with the shrieks of the drunken guests, and dawn revealed a welter of bones, crumbs, half-eaten fruit, broken pots, and the sprawled bodies of the unconscious. Tiye had eaten and drunk little, retiring to her tent only to lie sleeplessly listening to the uproar. Just before dawn she ordered out her litter and with relief returned to Malkatta, going straight to the Office of Foreign Correspondence. The business of government would go on, and until her son's coronation it was her duty to keep her hands on the reins. She could not predict his course, for he had shown little interest in the affairs of state. *Perhaps*, she mused, automatically correcting her scribe while her thoughts ran on, *he will be content merely to wear the crown, and my usefulness will not be at an end. It will be Nefertiti and Sitamun, two fledgling sphinxes, who will press for an active role for my son. I will take each day as it comes.*

A month later Tiye performed her own homage to her dead husband. In Karnak she dedicated an offering table to him, standing barefooted, wine and meat in her hands, while Ptahhotep poured cleansing water over the great stone slab. A fire was lit, and Tiye watched, a lump rising in her throat and her vision blurring, as the sacrificial meat was consumed. Carved on the table's side were her own cartouches, the insignia of a monarch still reigning, and the words she had chosen to commemorate publicly Amunhotep: *The principal Royal Wife. She made it as her monument for her beloved husband, Nebmaatra.*

"For thy ka, Osiris Nebmaatra," she whispered as the tears at last ran down her painted cheeks. "Forgive me for this show of weakness, but surely tears are no weaker than love, and I loved you." She turned to the wooden stela that she had also commissioned, on which she and he were locked in each other's arms forever, both young and handsome, with life spread out like Egypt herself for their pleasure. The fire spat and crackled, and Ptahhotep sang to the dead god. Tiye allowed herself the luxury of the grief from which she had been guarding her own ka. Now it consumed her, bringing with it the stark promise of loneliness, and she let it feed. She did not cry for him again.

8

AMUNHOTEP'S CORONATION TOOK PLACE TOWARD THE END OF the month of Phamenat. As was customary, he first received the homage of the northern gods in the temple of Ptah at Memphis before returning to Thebes to be crowned. Like his ancestors, he sat on the great stepped throne in Amun's pillared inner court at Karnak, the lotus of the south and papyrus of the north beneath it, to be purified with water and crowned with the red and white crowns of a united country. The ancient jeweled cloak was laid around his frail shoulders, and the crook, flail, and scimitar were placed in his hands. He seemed to submit to it all with the same vague meekness he had exhibited at the funeral, allowing himself to be guided through the ceremonies almost as if he were a sacrificial animal. The only emotion he showed came at the reading of the titles by his herald. They were many, including not only the traditional Mighty Bull of Ma'at and Exalted One of Double Plumes, but also the titles he himself had added: High Priest of Ra-Harakhti the Exalted One in the Horizon in His Name of Shu Who Is in His Disk, and Great in His Duration. At the end of the ceremonies the Keeper of the Royal Regalia placed the cobra coronet on Nefertiti's head, but the disk and plumes of an empress remained in their satin-lined box.

Nor did Amunhotep show much interest in the presentation of gifts and the feasting that went on the next day at Malkatta. He accepted the costly trinkets and prostrations expressionlessly, while Nefertiti and Sitamun exclaimed over the pile of precious objects that grew higher as evening approached. Immediately following the coronation feast a new pharaoh traditionally appointed new ministers, the young broom sweeping out the dust left by the old, but to Tiye's surprise no officials were retired, and the devotion of the young men who had taken up residence in the palace with her son when he returned from Memphis went unrewarded. Sitting with Amunhotep on the dais of the hall his father had built for his first jubilee, she asked him, as the feast drew to an end, why he had made no changes.

"Because my palace at Thebes is not yet fit to live in, my Aten temple is not ready for my holy feet, and I am not clear in my mind what to do," he replied over the loud babble of a thousand conversations and the click of the dancers' finger cymbals. "Egypt runs perfectly well under your hand."

Tiye put down her cup and turned to him slowly. "Do I understand that you are asking me to serve you as regent?"

He laughed, a sound as rarely heard as his father's loud guffaw, but Amunhotep's mirth was a choked squeak. "Yes, my royal mother, until such time as I wish to govern by myself. That *is* what you were hoping I would do, is it not?"

Tiye's ringed fingers closed over his, and they smiled into each other's eyes.

"Of course, dear Amunhotep, but I was quite prepared to

do nothing more than retire and offer you advice when you needed it."

"Were you indeed?"

Tiye had never seen him so happy. She kissed him on his flushed cheek. "Pharaoh Amunhotep IV," she said admiringly. "The throne was ordained for you after all. We will do great things together, you and I."

The mood of elation was still with her when she was at last able to lower herself thankfully onto her couch in the small hours of the morning. The palace was now quiet. She lay basking in the triumph and satisfaction of the day while dawn filtered slowly between the slats of the window hangings. She had been ready to keep her hands on the reins of government only indirectly, through subtle pressures and tactful manipulations, but Amunhotep himself had removed that necessity. *I am to go on ruling*, she thought. *What joy that knowledge brings! I had not realized until tonight how daunting the prospect of relinquishing power to my son was.*

Within days Amunhotep embarked on the customary journey down the Nile to visit every accessible shrine and to have his kingship confirmed by each local deity. Remembering his lack of interest in the other rituals of his coronation, Tiye suspected that he was undertaking the trip solely to see On again. He left Malkatta in the barge Sitamun had given him, the barges of his entourage strung out behind like golden beads on a silver thread. Sitamun and Nefertiti accompanied him, and Tiye did not fail to notice that he also took little Tadukhipa and several of his father's younger wives. *He is wasting no time in appropriating the harem women who appeal to him*, she reflected as she watched him go, and she wondered at the uneasiness that that thought raised.

In Amunhotep's absence the court relaxed into its comfortable routine of sybaritic indulgence. The ministers and underlings no longer had to flounder on a sea of spiritual double meanings, afraid of giving offense through sheer ignorance. Tiye, too, returned to the routine of many years with peace. Since Amunhotep had refused to move into the pharaonic apartments, preferring to stay in the wing he had occupied as prince until his fine new palace on the east bank was ready, she decided to take them over herself, leaving her old apartments for Nefertiti or Sitamun, whichever woman could inveigle Pharaoh into giving her the sumptuous rooms of empress. Lying on the couch she had moved from her own quarters to her husband's luxurious bedchamber, she wished for the man she had loved an eternal continuation of such joys in the land the gods inhabited.

Tiye also took advantage of the lull in court affairs to look into family matters she had been neglecting. Now that the continuance of the family's material well-being and position as first nobility in Egypt was assured with Nefertiti's marriage and proven fruitfulness, Tiye decided to deal with the nagging problem of Mutnodjme. The girl was almost seventeen, well past the age of bethrothal, and as notorious at court for her familiarity with the young charioteers as she was in Thebes itself. Mutnodjme was not to be found for several days, but when she finally appeared, striding loosely across the blue water tiles of the royal bedchamber, slapping the pillars negligently as she approached, she made her reverence with the customary cool self-possession. Tiye bade her rise and take the chair prepared for her. For a while Tiye assessed her. The brown scalp was still closely shaven but for the defiant youth lock, now grown past the girl's slim waist and wound with red ribbons. The shapely legs were unusually long, the waist cinched in as tightly as ever with a belt hung with tiny gold bells. Large jasper-studded hoops hung from her ears, and her wrists were circled by snake bracelets with red jasper eyes. Her own huge almond eyes were heavily kohled under dark green lids, while the full lips, a hallmark of the family, were hennaed orange. She was wearing a heavily pleated sheath barely touching her knees and had casually flung a cloak across her breasts.

"You look naked without your whip," Tiye said.

Mutnodjme smiled. "That fool at the door took it from me," she drawled. "Majesty Aunt, I am sorry for answering your summons three days late. Depet and I went to a party at Bek's house. He was commissioned to do part of Pharaoh's new temple, you know, and had to leave for the quarries at Assuan the next day. Depet and I decided to go, too. We commandeered some junior minister's fishing boat, as well as his staff and most of the wine from his kitchens. We did not get as far as Assuan."

"I am not surprised. The boats of private individuals can only be seized by officials of Pharaoh on vital business and are supposed to be paid for later, you know."

"I know, but everyone does it. The poor little wretch was paid, never fear."

"With gold?"

Mutnodjme grinned engagingly. "No."

Tiye indicated the jumble of scrolls on the table. "I have just been reading two years of reports on your behavior, Mutnodjme. My spies tell me that you have been selling yourself in the brothels in Thebes."

"Then you are paying them for the wrong information. I have not been selling myself. I have been giving my services for nothing. What would I do with more money? Besides, to take payment would reflect badly on the family."

Tiye pretended a gravity she did not feel, mastering the desire to laugh while Mutnodjme's elegantly sandaled foot began to swing back and forth. "It is a serious matter, for your behavior now reflects on Pharaoh. You are the sister of a queen. I have decided to give you in marriage to Horemheb."

Mutnodjme shrugged. "I daresay he is a wise choice. He does his best to keep me out of the barracks. He is a very good soldier, Majesty Aunt, a respected commander. I respect him also. As long as he does not demand instant obedience from me, I suppose we shall learn to like one another. I shall devote myself to handling the servants and buying fashionable clothes."

Now Tiye did laugh. She had expected no other response from her niece. "Then I will have the contract drawn up and will approach Horemheb. Tell me, Mutnodjme," she said, changing the subject on impulse. "How is Thebes speaking of its new pharaoh?"

Mutnodjme uncurled and leaned back in her chair. "The people are relieved, I think. The rumors of the boy my uncle took into his bed shocked and angered them. They live by the old laws, the peasants. They worship the old gods—Osiris, Isis, Horus—and the Declaration of Innocence is more to them than a piece of parchment to be waved self-righteously under the noses of the gods when they die. A pharaoh who breaks a law of the gods brings down a curse upon his subjects."

"They believe that such a curse has been averted by my husband's death?"

"I don't know. But they do expect a return to piety with my cousin's accession. Besides, since when has a pharaoh had to fear the opinions of an ignorant rabble?" Mudnodjme stifled a yawn, and Tiye saw that the turn the conversation had taken was boring her. Good-naturedly she dismissed her, regretting as Mudnodjme glided out that in giving her to Horemheb she was losing what might have been the best spy available in Thebes.

The entire court gathered to greet Amunhotep when he disembarked at the Malkatta water steps some weeks later, looking wan but excited. Speeches were made and incense burned, but Tiye's attention was drawn to Nefertiti and Sitamun. The former was pale and silent, the latter more vivacious than ever, her loud, musical voice commanding attention, her gestures charmingly pretty. Amunhotep smiled fondly upon her, often patting her arm and once even kissing her unexpectedly on the lips, but no murmur of surprise arose from a court already growing accustomed to Pharaoh's inexplicable public displays of affection. Tiye caught her brother's eye, and he raised his dark eyebrows knowingly.

The formal welcome soon broke into smaller groups of people who drifted toward the feast that had been prepared by the fountains in the forecourt. Tiye, walking to the tables behind Amunhotep, heard the voices of her niece and her daughter raised above the level of conversations going on around them. Their servants were standing with faces averted in embarrassment, and several courtiers had stopped to hear what was being said. Tiye halted.

"Majesty, you shriek and gibber like one of the palace monkeys, but your silly posturings will be in vain," Nefertiti was hissing. "You have not only reached the end of your youth, but you are barren."

Sitamun was smiling complacently. "And you, Majesty, are an arrogant upstart. The disk and plumes are mine. Accept your place and try and produce a few more girls to keep you busy. Or take up weaving to help pass the hours you will be spending in the harem." It was a deliberate insult, for only men wove cloth, just as only men baked bread. An audible gasp went up from those listening. Sitamun came to herself, glared at them all, and swept past the fountains to take her place beside an oblivious Amunhotep. Nefertiti stood biting her lip, her gray eyes glinting. When she became aware of Tiye's thoughtful gaze, she managed a polite smile, turned, and glided to her cushions on Pharaoh's left with as much dignity as she could muster. The interested assembly quickly scattered, darting apprehensive looks at Tiye, but she kept her shock to herself as Amunhotep beckoned her, and the musicians began to play.

But that display of public animosity between two women was not the last. As the days went by, they ceased to be seen together, to dine in each other's company and finally even to speak to each other, and soon their growing animosity spread to their household staffs. Although Pharaoh had made no move to put into formal writing his decision to award Sitamun the status of empress, Tiye successfully urged Amunhotep to order the Keeper of the Royal Regalia to deliver the empress's crown to her. Tiye, long past the stage of caring more for the trappings of power than power itself, saw Sitamun flaunt the glittering, heavy thing with increasing anxiety.

Pharaoh himself seemed to be oblivious to the charged air around him, spending his time drifting from architects' offices to lake to dining hall, stopping often to feed ducks and other birds from the baskets of dried bread he insisted his servants have ready wherever he was. He did occasionally join Tiye in the Office of Foreign Correspondence, and one morning after a particularly ugly quarrel between the two queens' stewards, she decided to warn him about the dangerous situation he was fostering. He had taken a seat beside a large desk, and in a patch of sun that pooled into the room through the high windows was feeding nuts to a pair of tiny monkeys that scampered among the scrolls. He still favored a white helmet, leather or linen as the season demanded, but today only the royal uraeus, the king-protecting cobra and vulture, reared golden above his high forehead. He was dressed in the gown of a vizier, a long, unpleated sheath held up by one strip of linen around his neck. His pectoral consisted of rows of carnelian scarabs rolling silver suns across a turquoise sky, and his fingers were heavy with his cartouches. His brown eyes were rimmed with an unusual shade of kohl, a blue so dark that they seemed like the centers of blue-rimmed daisies. A droplet of gold shimmered from one ear, and the other lobe was painted blue. He tutted and clucked at the monkeys, who snatched the food from him until, having become glutted, they began to throw it onto the floor. He smiled at them indulgently.

"Is it true that the pharaoh before me promised to send gold statues to Tushratta?" he asked, referring to the scroll Tiye held, "and that they were never sent?"

"Yes, I think so. I must ask that the files be searched.

Tushratta has written me a letter also, reminding me of Pharaoh's promise, and has sent with it a quantity of very good oil. Relations between Egypt and Mitanni have always been good, Majesty, although over the matter of women there have been some misunderstandings. Mitanni has withheld wives from both your father and grandfather, forcing them to make requests several times and to offer higher payments each time. Your father enjoyed the game. But this matter of the statues should be attended to. It is as well that the goddess Ishtar be returned."

"I will send Tushratta two statues, but of cedar overlaid with gold," Amunhotep said, stroking the monkey that had leaped onto his shoulder and was patting his cheek, "because I do not know if statues of solid gold were promised. But I do not like to think that he is a king without truth."

"He will be insulted."

"No. He will know that I send them in good faith, and if I err, he will write again."

"Here is a letter from Alashia announcing shipments of copper to Egypt and asking for silver and papyrus in return. My son"—Tiye tossed the scrolls on the desk—"I can no longer concentrate on the correspondence. Are you ready to end the foolishness that has gripped the palace, and formally name Sitamun your empress? Are you aware that members of the court are now taking sides? Malkatta has become a quarrelsome place."

He glanced at her in mild surprise. "I told her she could be empress, and I ordered the regalia delivered to her. That is surely enough."

"You know as well as I that such gestures mean nothing unless they are backed by written proclamation. If I call for scribes and papyrus, will you dictate these things and seal them and give them to your heralds to proclaim? Then perhaps all the fuss will die away. And while we are on the subject of edicts and documents, Kheruef tells me that you have sealed a marriage contract with Tadukhipa. Is that true?"

He smiled. "Little Kia. That is what I call her. Yes, it is true. But I have called none of them to my bed lately."

"Why?"

He looked away and busied himself with the monkey, scratching its ears, pulling its paws. Tiye had to bend forward to hear his answer. "I do not know," he whispered. "If you wish, Mother, I will make Sitamun empress."

Tiye shouted, and a scribe hurried in, sinking to the floor and setting his palette across his knees. "Is it what *you* wish, Amunhotep?"

Again his head sank over the animal's ruffled fur. "I think so."

Quickly she dictated the document while Amunhotep lowered the monkey to the floor and seemed to withdraw into himself, his body stilled, his hands loose on the desk. When the scribe had finished, she did not wait for him to copy it into hieroglyphs for fear Pharaoh would wander away and forget the matter. She took the papyrus and laid it before him. "Your seal, Amunhotep." He drew the ring from his finger and pressed it into the wax and then rose and was gone before she could collect herself enough to bow to him. "Give this to the heralds," she ordered. "They will know what to do with it." The scribe bowed himself out, and Tiye slumped in the still-warm chair with a sigh of relief. Perhaps now there would be peace.

The formal ratification of Pharaoh's decision in fact brought a surprising change in Nefertiti. With all the graciousness of which she was capable when it suited her, she made it known that she was now content. She took Meritaten to visit the empress in her apartments, bearing grapes new-picked from her father's estates at Akhmin and expensive containers of the year's most sought-after wines. In the flush of conquest Sitamun was magnanimous, and before the afternoon was over, she and Nefertiti were laughing together over the sennet board while Meritaten lay in the grass kicking and gurgling.

Tiye, while pleased to see the hostilities at an end, could not still the small pulse of caution in her mind. "It is a clever act," Ay said bluntly. "Nefertiti is, after all, a member of our family, and we do not readily accept defeat. Sitamun should not trust her."

"It is hard not to trust Nefertiti when she exerts all her charm," Tiye replied, "and my daughter is in many ways a simple woman. She will accept Nefertiti's peace."

And I will deal with Sitamun myself if she tries to interfere in government, Tiye thought. *She will be easier to handle than a Nefertiti eager to assume active power would be. But I am sorry. I would have preferred to leave Egypt to Nefertiti when I am gone.*

The season of Shemu had brought the heat, and Nefertiti and Sitamun had taken to the roof of the empress's quarters, lying under the pale shade of the great canopy. Their backs were against the curve of the wind catcher that was set to funnel any breeze out of the north into the bedchamber below them, their limbs sprawled on the linen sheets. Pieces of the sennet game they had been playing lay scattered around them, together with dishes of fruit, ribbons, and their sandals and cloaks. Beside them their servants wielded great ostrich fans that barely stirred the stifling air. Sitamun plunged both hands into the bowl of water between her legs and tossed the water up over her unpainted face.

"I wish Pharaoh had decided to go north," she complained, closing her eyes as the shining droplets trickled down onto her bare breasts. "Half the court has vanished to the Delta, and here we sit, panting. His Aten temple will be built whether he is present or not."

"I think he will eventually go," Nefertiti replied, "but he wants to see the expanded sanctuary finished and the forecourt paved before he does. The workmen ought to have had that done by now, but I suppose the heat slows down everything." She motioned, and a slave wrung out a cloth and gently wiped her face. "If Tiye pressed him, he would take us all to Memphis, but she says she is too busy at the moment. Mutnodjme sent me a letter. She said that even as she was dictating, it was raining. Rain in Memphis. So rare! And we are missing it."

Sitamun shrugged down until she lay on her back. "Osiris Amunhotep used to move the whole court on the first day of Shemu and did not return to Thebes until New Year's Day," she said. "I remember how once a shower began while we were still in the barges, a day from the docks. Everyone crowded to kiss Pharaoh's feet in thanksgiving, and then, after we all had our sheaths and kilts removed, we stood naked, washed by the rain. It was a good omen. It heralded a happy summer. All we get in Thebes are dust storms and an occasional khamsin to relieve the boredom."

Nefertiti's glittering gray eyes flicked over Sitamun's voluptuous body and off to the heat-hazed cliffs dancing in the distance. "I am arranging a party tonight in the harem gardens," she said. "For the women only. No one sleeps, anyway. We will bathe in the lake and watch the fire walkers by torchlight. Will you come, Majesty?"

Sitamun turned her head languidly. "If Pharaoh does not require me."

Nefertiti suppressed the response that had risen to her lips, knowing very well that Pharaoh spent his nights surrounded by hundreds of lamps and a dozen weary servants, poring over his architects' plans for the Aten temple, praying, or composing songs. The furnace heat of Shemu had seemed to cauterize all sexual desire in him.

"Good. The older children will come, too. Smenkhara is walking now, did you know? He follows Meritaten's nurse as she carries my little one about. There does not seem to be as much sickness in the nursery this year. Many fevers, but no sign of a plague."

Sitamun answered her in a bored, lazy monotone, and the afternoon ended in silence as both women finally succumbed to the heat and fell asleep.

Nefertiti's party began as the horns were blaring midnight. The darkness had not brought coolness, and while slaves spread mats on the verge of the lake in the guttering orange flames of the huge torches, the women ran to the water with shrieks and laughter. Tadukhipa, her long black hair bound decorously on top of her little head, stood quietly in the shallows while her servants drenched her, for she was afraid of water. Tia-Ha sat in the shallows, submerged to her chin, having her slave wash her hair and feed her sips of wine. Tiye, arriving late with her retinue, had her chair placed a little apart.

As the musicians began to play, the women left the water, dripping and panting, and flung themselves onto the mats to be served food and to have wreaths of flowers and blue beads draped over them. Nefertiti had spared no expense. Far out on the lake a pool of yellow light was growing as an enormous raft was poled toward the bank. When it came to a halt just out of a swimmer's distance, the naked male slaves who had been guiding it stood up and began to dance, golden rattles in their hands, water lilies bound on their foreheads. Torchlight glimmered on the black water. The men completed their gyrations and dove into the darkness. Suddenly horns blared, and women dressed in shimmering silver fishnets rose from the water. Climbing gracefully onto the raft, they began to fling showers of gold dust in the air, where it hung in a yellow mist. Harem servants moved among the guests with wine jugs. Now little wooden boats painted gold appeared on the lake, carrying men with golden fishing rods. As they approached the women on the raft, they began to cast toward them, the thin lines of the rods cutting the night like spiders' webs in the torchlight surrounding the women. The guests lounging on the bank shouted encouragement and applauded. One by one the fishnetted women were hooked, dragged with mock struggles to the edge of the raft, and pulled under the water, only to reappear seconds later in the boats.

"This was a good idea," Sitamun said to Nefertiti. "Oh, look! There are the men placing stones on the fire for the Nubian walkers."

Nefertiti motioned to a slave, and Sitamun's cup was quietly refilled. "Do you like the wine, Majesty?" she enquired softly.

Sitamun nodded and drank. "It is magnificent. Where on earth did you find it?"

"It comes from your father's estate in the Delta. An excellent vintage. Rames, his steward, had it shipped to me especially for tonight."

"You have gone to much trouble."

Nefertiti smiled gently, noting the flush the wine had brought to Sitamun's cheeks, the slight, drunken hesitation in the words. "Nothing is too much trouble for my friends," she said. "Besides, we all need some compensation for having to languish here through Shemu. This helps to pass the time."

Her chief steward, Meryra, came and bowed. "The food is ready, Majesty."

"Then serve us. I trust you are hungry, Empress."

While Nefertiti picked at the food on her plate, Sitamun ate with relish. Out on the lake the fishermen had now drawn silver knives and, making a show of gutting the pliant female fish they had caught, danced to the clashing harmonies of pipe and drums.

"It will be some time before the stones are hot enough for the walkers," Nefertiti said. "Come for another swim with me, Majesty."

Sitamun looked to the lake, where many of the women had returned and were screaming with drunken mirth. Those still on the bank were occupied in eating and talking. The surface of the dark water riffled suddenly as a stray breeze stirred it. Sitamun, flushed and sweating, agreed. They shed their light robes and walked hand in hand to the lily-clogged bank, picking their way through revelers too intoxicated to reverence them. Twice Sitamun stumbled, but Nefertiti caught her elbow, guiding her. Once in the water, Sitamun revived.

"Let us swim out toward the raft," Nefertiti called, pushing wet hair away from her face. "But stop when you leave your depth, Sitamun. You have had a lot of wine."

Instant defiance curled Sitamun's full mouth. "You only caution me because I am the better swimmer and will show you up!" she taunted. "Oh, how cool this is. Come!" She spun in the water and began to swim, cutting skillfully across the reflection of the torches. Nefertiti followed more slowly. As they moved farther away from the verge, the torchlight became fainter until they finally reached the blackness between the light on the bank and the torches illuminating the entertainment far out on the lake. Nefertiti slowed her stroke, stopped, and began to tread water. Sitamun swam on, but her own stroke had by now become feeble, her movements looser. Nefertiti watched her disappear into the band of darkness, turned quietly, and began to swim leisurely back to the shore.

I will not be the one to call a halt, Sitamun thought, her arms flailing, her legs tiring. *I have bested Nefertiti in every other way, and if she thinks to prove her superiority in the water, she will lose again. My heart is pounding. I drank too much wine.* Taking a shuddering breath, she glanced over her shoulder but did not see Nefertiti's silhouette against the flaring torches. Fighting for more air, Sitamun looked ahead. Nefertiti was not there, either. The raft had emptied, its torches burning low and beginning to gutter. In the little boats circling it, the women, fishnets artfully slit by the knives of the men, were gracefully dying. The men themselves were diving into the water one by one, and vigorous applause reached Sitamun's ringing ears from the bank. She let her legs drift down through the water, and though her feet groped for the bottom, they could not find it. Panic stabbed her, but she quickly mastered it. *Very well*, she thought. *I will float here and get my breath and then paddle back. What game is Nefertiti playing? She must have seen that I would win, or simply run out of strength and turned back.* Gasping, one hand against her laboring heart, she began to tread water, looking around her.

She was in a circle of darkness bounded by torches that seemed infinitely far away. Black water lapped against her, much colder at this depth than the sun-warmed shallows. Above her, the moon swayed in the night as she tried to focus on it. She closed her eyes as nausea gripped her stomach. *Too much wine*, she thought again. *I wonder what is below my feet, hidden in the cold slime, the darkness.* Cramp lanced her calf, and she drew in her knees, reaching to massage her leg. She again became aware of the distance between herself and the warm gaiety of the women, a vista of rippling black water that fed a chill into her veins. All at once she vomited, a stream of sour wine and undigested food, and immediately felt better but began to shiver. *I must get back*, she thought dully, digging at the cramp with stiff fingers as it attacked again. *Then I will have to take a hot bath and a massage, or I shall become ill.*

She turned toward the lights on the bank and was gathering her strength when a faint splash off to her right startled her. She saw a white disturbance on the surface of the lake, and in a moment its wake was slapping against her body. Panicking again, she arced forward but had done no more than lean into the water when she felt arms encircle her thighs. She screamed, kicking frantically, fingers scrabbling at the grip. Something pressed against the small of her back, and she realized it was a human head.

Shocked and suddenly sober, Sitamun began to fight, her cries lost in a burst of cheering from the bank where the fire walkers had begun their show. Her desperate hands found hair, and she pulled with all her might. The arms loosened, and she quickly raised her knee, aiming it at her attacker's chin. But she had been enervated even before she and Nefertiti walked into the water, and her blow merely grazed a cold cheek. She felt her wrists encircled, forcing her fingers away from the floating tangle of hair, and as the head tore free, the surface of the lake was abruptly broken directly in front of her. She glimpsed an open, gasping mouth, two hollow eyes, a battered water lily entwined in the wet, matted hair. She dug both feet into the man's stomach, pushing as hard as she could. The hands left her wrists, and for one moment she was free, but before she could gather herself to swim away, the fingers closed with a confident force around her neck. Sitamun felt herself being forced under the water. Now she fought with maniacal strength, nails raking the smooth skin, feet kicking out, lungs stretched and bursting, heart racing unevenly. Once she was able to break into the air and had time for one mouthful of the breeze that rustled like silk across her lips, but her spasm of frantic strength was over. The man knelt on her shoulders, his hands splayed on the top of her head, his own breath short but steady as he looked toward the lights along the verge. Sitamun's last touch was as soft and light as a lover's. Her fingers strayed downward along his thighs and came to rest trustingly beside his knees. He thrust the body deeper with both feet and quickly swam away.

Tia-Ha smothered a yawn. "A wonderful way to spend a hot summer night," she said, "but if Your Majesty will dismiss me, I think I will seek my couch." Tiye nodded, smiling, and the princess rose, stretching luxuriously. Her servants began to roll up her mat and gather her trinkets. The moon had shrunk to a brilliant point in the dry sky. The torches were smoking as they burned themselves out. The women were drifting back to their quarters, some with their arms around each other, some supported by their servants, others moving rapturously but unsteadily on their own. Tiye scanned the lake. At its edge sat Nefertiti, still deep in conversation with Tadukhipa. The raft bobbed, all but one of the torches that had been fastened to it extinguished. The boats had left much earlier. Then Tiye noticed something rising and falling with the lake's small wash, lit faintly and intermittently from the shore. Tia-Ha had seen it, too. She turned to Tiye as Tiye came to her feet. "I cannot make it out," she remarked. "I wonder if one of the entertainers dropped something into the water."

"Kheruef," Tiye said over her shoulder, "send a boat out and bring in whatever it is."

Kheruef hurried away, and the two women walked to the place where Nefertiti and Tadukhipa had been hooking water lilies to make the frogs jump away. At Tiye's approach they rose and bowed. "Majesty Aunt, why is that boat going out?" Nefertiti frowned. "My dancers have retired, and the raft will be recovered in the morning."

Premonition swept over Tiye as she watched the boat cut across the lake, the pole rising and falling under the slave's expert thrust, drawing nearer to the gently moving debris, and she could not answer. A shout came from the boat as one of the slaves reached over, drew back, and pulled his companion to the edge. The two of them lifted something shapeless and obviously heavy and began to return to the shore with the uncoordinated speed of distress.

"It is a body!" Tadukhipa whispered, eyes wide. "One of the dancers has drowned!"

Nefertiti shrugged and turned away, but Tiye, her knees suddenly weak, grasped her niece's arm. Kheruef and two of his underlings waded out and helped to drag the boat onto the grass. Still Tiye could not move. Only when the men laid the body on its stomach and Kheruef began to run toward her did she force her legs to obey her.

"Stay with me," Tia-Ha snapped at Tadukhipa, her eyes on Tiye's white face. She sank to the mat, taking the little princess down with her. Tadukhipa's hand stole into her own. Kheruef came up to Tiye and fell at her feet, his face ashen, his hands closing over his head in a gesture of terrified submission. Tiye walked past him, still holding Nefertiti.

The naked woman was sprawled like an ungainly animal, one knee bent, one arm curving to encircle the head with its ropes of dark, sopping hair. "Bring a torch," Tiye said in a level voice. One of the male slaves raced to obey and reappeared with lights. "Kheruef. Kheruef! Get up, you old fool. Turn her over." He left the ground, weeping, and with clumsy, trembling hands grasped a shoulder, the soft hill of a hip. Tiye released Nefertiti. The girl was staring, lower lip between her teeth, every muscle tense. The body rolled sluggishly, and then Sitamun gazed past them at the sky. Water dribbled from one corner of her parted mouth, and her hair lay across her throat like a ragged scarf. Tiye found herself in the grass smoothing the cold cheeks with both frantic, disbelieving hands. A babble of screams and excited, frightened talk broke out. "Bring Commander Ay," Kheruef ordered tersely, "and then a physician. Notify Pharaoh, but not before Ay."

Tiye lifted the unresisting head and cradled it in her arms. Nefertiti had begun to wail, her own arms outstretched. *Why is she making that foolish noise?* Tiye thought irritably. *Sitamun is asleep. She has floated on the water and fallen asleep.* "Sitamun," she choked, mouth moving against the white forehead. Then warm hands lifted her, and Ay's arms went around her. New torches flickered in the hands of the soldiers he had brought. She felt someone settle a cloak over her shoulders and suddenly came to herself. Ay was squatting beside Sitamun, his hands busy lifting, probing, his eyes sharp. A physician crouched beside him, exchanging low words with Ay she could not catch. Tia-Ha appeared before her, and wine slipped down her throat. Nefertiti had fallen silent, but Tiye saw her swallowing convulsively. Ay rose. "It is too late to do anything for her," he said, and something in his voice made Tiye stare at him, sluggish senses alert. "She is dead."

Out of the corner of her eye Tiye saw a look flash between Nefertiti and her steward Meryra, standing stolidly beside her. It happened so quickly that she wondered if she had imagined it but noticed that Ay had seen it, too, and watched him assimilate and interpret the signal in the second it took him to recover. He turned and barked orders at his men. "Gather all servants, slaves, and dancers who were here tonight. Majesty, may I question the women?"

Tiye nodded faintly. "But it would be better to wait until morning," she objected, surprised to hear her voice so calm. "Most of them are unfit to speak. Kheruef will help you."

There was a stir beyond the torches' harsh flare, and someone whispered, "Horus comes!" Already the crowd was prone in the grass, faces pressed into the earth, and Tiye realized immediately that she could not bear to witness her son's shock. She took a last look at the waxen face, the glazed eyes that leaped with a semblance of life under the torches' light, and turned away.

Tiye paced her apartments for most of the night, too distraught to rest. She expected Ay to request an audience, but the day turned into afternoon and the afternoon into the stale breathlessness of a summer night, and he did not come. She made no effort to summon him, knowing that he would appear when he was ready. She choked down some food and allowed Piha to see to her bathing, dressing, and painting, but refused to receive either Tia-Ha, who came to her at noon, or Nefertiti, who asked to be admitted in the evening. She walked from reception hall to bedchamber and back repeatedly, her mind taking refuge in the exercise of the solving of a puzzle. Sitamun was an excellent swimmer. Drunk or sober, the lake represented no threat to a woman who had been a fearless worshiper of river and lake since she had been old enough to walk. Sitamun was empress, and Nefertiti's swift acceptance of a race lost had been too facile, too eager. Or had it? *Am I misreading my niece's character through the wavering vision of my own grief? Sitamun was very drunk, and so were most of the other women. Was Nefertiti sober? The party was Nefertiti's idea. A perfect setting.* Tiye placed both hands over her burning eyes and groaned aloud. *I wish you would come, Ay,* she thought as she stopped by her couch and heard Piha moving quietly behind her, lighting the lamps. *My daughter lies under the knives of the royal sem-priests. My son has shut himself away in his own chambers, and his sobs can be heard outside those heavy double doors.*

Ay was finally announced an hour later and, ordering her servants out, closed the doors behind them himself. His eyes were filmed and sunken under the protective kohl, and for the first time Tiye saw the sharp military set of his shoulders curved in anguish. They eyed each other over the soft glow of the lamps until Tiye motioned him to sit and herself sank nervously to the edge of her couch. Although he did not often observe the strict protocol surrounding an audience with royalty, he now waited for her to speak first, and she was forced to take a deep breath.

"I do not think I want to know," she said harshly.

"You know already. So do I. Every slave and servant in the palace has been cajoled, threatened, or beaten. Every one of Osiris Amunhotep's wives and Tehen-Aten has been questioned. Only Princess Tadukhipa had anything useful to say."

"And what was that?"

"She saw Nefertiti and Sitamun enter the water together sometime before the fire walking began." He put out a hand to forestall Tiye's shocked outburst. "No," he said grimly. "My daughter did not perform the deed with her own delicate hands. The princess saw her not long afterward, being dried by her body servant."

"Did you caution Tadukhipa?"

"I told her never to speak of what she had seen because it would embarrass Queen Nefertiti. It was a long time before the little one understood."

Tiye looked down on the hands that had twisted together painfully in her lap. Carefully she loosened them. "There is always some doubt."

"Of course. But only the shadow of a shadow. The desert police found a man wandering behind the desert hills this morning. His tongue had been cut out. It was a wonder that he had not drowned in his own blood. Needless to say, he could not read or write. He was a palace slave, that much is certain from the softness of his skin and hands. He was scratched about the arms and stomach. I saw him myself."

Their eyes met. "She cannot be punished," Tiye whispered.

"Of course not. Even if her guilt could be proved, which it

cannot, she is a queen, and as such her person is above the common law. We cannot even arrest the steward Meryra. That would be tantamount to admitting that we believe Nefertiti is at least implicated."

"I would like to see both of them flayed until the flesh falls from their bones!" she cried out bitterly. "What can I tell Amunhotep?"

"There is no point in telling him anything, Majesty. Only he can discipline in this matter, and I do not think he will do anything but be distressed. Besides . . ."

"Besides, we are all guilty of similar acts of jealousy and fear," she finished for him hoarsely. "Nefertiti will learn discretion, as we did. Let me rest against you, Ay. I am sick at heart and so tired that I cannot think anymore. I want to grieve like any mother, and with you I can lay my divinity aside."

He came and sat beside her. Her head slid against his chest with the ease of long familiarity, and he put both arms around her neck, as he had so many times in their childhood. The steady beat of his heart comforted her, and for the first time since she had glanced out over the lake the previous evening, she felt her body relax and her eyes grow heavy. Ay kissed her and, laying her carefully down, drew the sheet over her.

"Sleep now," he said. "I will send Piha and your fanbearers. Do not feel guilt, Tiye, over the thought that you might have prevented this by plotting to keep a balance between my daughter and yours. If Sitamun had been more wily and less sure of herself, it might be Nefertiti who was awaiting beautification in the House of the Dead."

She murmured, eyes closed, and heard him go out and call to her servants. *Of all the children born to Amunhotep and me, only Sitamun and my son grew to adulthood*, she thought dimly, already half-asleep. *Now Sitamun is gone. Oh, my husband, is it possible that all our fruit will wither and fall? So much love over the years, without living trace? I wish you were here in my arms.*

9

Pharaoh did not appear in public during the seventy days of mourning for Sitamun, and it seemed to the court as though he were once again in a prison, this time of his own choosing. The forbidding double doors leading to his reception hall remained closed. He was not seen in the garden or on his building sites, though Tiye received word that he had ordered new quarries opened at Gebel Silsileh to provide sandstone for the masons. His butler, Parennefer, and his chief steward, Panhesy, passed through the palace corridors unobtrusively, seeing to the wants of their lord. Tiye questioned them occasionally, anxious for news of her son, and they assured her that Pharaoh was well, that his grief was almost spent, and that he was purifying himself in coarse linen and incense ash before his Aten shrine.

"Why is it necessary for him to be purified?" Tiye asked Panhesy, puzzled. "And if that is his desire, surely only Ptahhotep has the authority to perform such rites."

Dropping his earnest gaze, the young man bowed low to her and answered with his face hidden between his outstretched, silver-laden arms. "It is Pharaoh the man who cleanses himself, not Pharaoh the god on behalf of Egypt," he said diffidently, and with that Tiye had to be content.

Like her husband Nefertiti was staying away from active involvement in court life. She was sometimes seen walking decorously in her gardens dressed only in white linen, her black hair sleekly shining, her arms bare of jewels. Tiye noted grimly, on the few occasions when she caught a glimpse of the slim, straight figure, that Nefertiti's beauty was only enhanced by the naturalness she had affected. Tiye herself bore no ill will to the girl. She understood Nefertiti's vicious act with the wisdom of a ruler for whom an uncompromising line between virtue and dark necessity did not exist.

Any royal death precipitated rumor and excited gossip, par-

ticularly among the harem women. Tia-Ha told Tiye that conjecture was running rife, but the women were tolerant. They
believed that both queen and empress had been in love with
Pharaoh, and Nefertiti had been driven to destroy a rival by
jealousy and passion. Such affairs of the heart were common-
place. The inhabitants of the harem understood such things,
and the talk was kindly. The only detail that caused them unease
was the discovery of the mutilated servant. It was usual for them
to pursue their intrigues through subordinates, but to torture
the instrument of one's freedom instead of rewarding him vi-
olated one of the harem's unwritten laws. They approved of
Tiye's decision to have the man nursed back to health and taken
into her service, and regarded her action as the only real proof
that the queen was guilty.

Tiye listened carefully to her friend's words. She knew that
once Sitamun was buried, the gossip would wither. It was a
matter of waiting through the slow days of mourning.

The empress's funeral was a restrained tribute to a woman
who had run second in almost every race she had attempted.
Still young at her death, she had nevertheless belonged to the
old administration. After only a few brief years in the arms of
her popular brother, Thothmes, she had been forced, when he
died suddenly, to please an aging, unpredictable man. Since
then she had walked in the shadow of her mother, less intel-
ligent, less vital, less powerful than Tiye. Even the winning
of the empress's crown, her one bid for self-determination, had
brought her merely a momentary vindication.

Only those ministers and courtiers obliged to attend royal
interments formed the cortege, together with the official mourners. Pharaoh emerged from his period of meditation looking
ungainly and alarmingly vague and took his place silently with
Ay, Tiye, and Nefertiti. They rode on their litters without exchanging a word, the procession strung out behind them along
the same route to Amunhotep III's tomb they had taken such
a short time ago.

The rituals were performed in the same mood of dignified
simplicity. Tiye had dreaded the moment when she would pass
her husband's possessions to reach the chamber adjacent to
him, where Sitamun was to lie. But when the time came for
her to walk through the tomb behind her daughter's coffin, she
found that all trace of him had already been rendered anonymous by the events in Malkatta since his death. Time had

moved the living forward. The thrones he had filled with his
regal bulk, the glittering chests closed upon his thousands of
gowns, the boxes hiding his many jewels could have belonged
to one of the ancients. *I wonder if the darkness will stir when
I leave this place*, she thought as she stepped forward to lay
flowers over Sitamun, *if currents will flow between father and
daughter through the magic eyes of their sarcophagi. One of
your queens has come to you, my husband. How long will it
be before I, too, share these damp rooms?*

The feast that brought the days-long ceremony to an end
was conducted with quiet decorum, and as soon as good manners allowed, the courtiers drifted to their litters and vanished
back to Malkatta.

Tiye rode back to the palace beside Pharaoh. He had wept
over Sitamun's remains quietly and with a dignity that surprised
them all, and he did not talk to Tiye as they swayed along
under Ra's blind ferocity. They passed through the city of the
death, Thothmes III's magnificent beige funerary temple shimmering like a paradisiacal mirage on their right, and were almost in sight of the palace walls when Amunhotep gave an
abrupt order, and both his litter and Tiye's swung left. His
father's great temple began to overshadow them, bars of shade
alternating with white sand, but the litters did not turn onto the
ram-lined avenue that would have led to its pillared forecourt.
The two colossi loomed ahead, their shadows short in the noon
sun. Amunhotep spoke again, and the litters came to a halt.
He stepped down, inviting Tiye to do the same, and she followed him as he walked up to the nearer statue. For a second
he craned his head, his gaze traveling its awesome height, and
then he took her arm politely and drew her into the pale shade.

"Majesty Mother," he said, his voice still thick with the
tears he had spent, his eyes under swollen lids resting on her
face with a look that was almost an apology. "For seventy days
I have prayed and wept in my rooms, beating my breast and
rubbing my forehead with ashes from my shrine, because I
could have saved the life of my sister and did not."

"Amunhotep," she protested, touching him gently, "her death
was not the fault of Pharaoh. Why do you reproach yourself?"
His sincerity, so genuine but misdirected, disarmed her. She
touched the corner of his mouth with one hennaed finger, as
she had often done when he was a child, a sign of affectionate
disagreement. He kissed it and drew away.

"I have heard it said that Sitamun was a victim of her own ambition, but it is not so. She died because I was a coward. I did wrong in the sight of the god."

"How can that be? You are Amun-Ra's incarnation."

"I knew what I was obliged to do but quailed. The eyes of Egypt are blind, her ears stopped with deceit. She would have shouted against me. But I am braver now. I am ready."

Tiye suppressed the sigh that rose to her lips. "You frighten people with your riddles," she chided gently. "A king must speak clearly so that his people may obey as one."

"It is yet two months to the end of Shemu and the celebration of New Year's Day," he said. "I want us to go north to Memphis, just you and I and our servants. Can you leave the court for that long?"

His request sent a tide of uneasiness flooding through her. Turning away from him, she let her gaze wander the cracked brownness of the fields that spread from her feet to the line of dusty palms that traced the Nile. *Why do I suddenly cringe?* she thought. *It is natural that he should want to distance himself from the pain of loss for a time. But just the two of us? Does he have something serious to discuss with me? It is the prospect of him and me alone together that alarms me. Why?* Behind her, Amunhotep's breath was warm on her naked back, and she felt his hand settle pleadingly on her shoulder. "I suppose that Nefertiti can take my place for a while," Tiye said without turning. "There is always a lull at this time of year, and it is true, I would like to see Memphis again. It has been a long time. Not since your father and I. . . ." Her voice trailed away, but then she resumed. "Very well, my son. I would like that very much." It was the truth. More than anything she wanted to escape the miasma of death that had for so long drifted through the palace, the whispers and innuendoes, the strain of trying to see beyond men's eyes to their hidden thoughts.

"Good. In three days then, Tiye."

She turned to bow to him but saw only his back, the counterpoise of his pectoral sparkling between his stooped shoulders, his soft linen brushing his pale calves. When his litter was out of sight, she laid her cheek against the pedestal of her husband's immobile image and closed her eyes.

They left Malkatta on the morning of the third day in the boat that Sitamun had presented to Amunhotep. He had decided to call it *Kha-em-Ma'at*, another form of his title Living in Truth, and had had his artisans engrave its name on its graceful hull. A disgruntled crowd of courtiers assembled at the water steps to see them depart. Nefertiti sat under her scarlet fans. Now that the funeral was over, she had begun to hint that the empress's crown should be hers, but her husband had turned a deaf ear. Smenkhara and Meritaten dabbled in the water that lapped the steps, Smenkhara with a timid fascination, the baby gasping and chuckling as her nurse dipped her into the coolness. Prayers for the safety of Pharaoh were chanted, the courtiers made a sullen obeisance, and the flotilla of royalty, servants, priests, and soldiers slid along the canal and out onto the river.

The prevailing summer wind, when it could summon the energy to blow through the thick heat, was from the north, so each barge bristled with oars. Tiye leaned over the side of *Kha-em-Ma'at*, listening to the shouts of Pasi, the captain, the swift patter of bare feet as the sailors answered his orders, the gurgle of the oars as they made eddies in the muddy water. Behind her, fruit, scented water, and wine waited under the open canopy for her appetite to rise. Her son sat drowsily on cushions beside the low table, fly whisk in his fingers, humming to himself. The banks were deserted, slipping by like the edge of an arid nightmare, the mud villages empty of life. The fields were brown, the leaves of the palms withered. Even the sky was vacant, the smaller birds having sought the shade of the growth along the river. Only the hawks seemed inured to the heat. They glided, wings flung out to catch the slightest breath of moving air, screaming occasionally as their sharp eyes scanned the barren ground for prey. Tiye's fanbearers struggled to hold shade over her as she leaned out farther, mesmerized by the brown water slipping turgidly under her gaze. *In a day or two it will be blue*, she thought. *The first sign that the sterility of Upper Egypt is behind us. Ah, fair Memphis! Crown of the world.*

On the evening of the fourth day out from Thebes, as the royal barge was being tethered against the bank, Pasi came to the canopy and bowed before Amunhotep. "I had hoped that we might tie up a little farther downriver, where there is a village and some vegetation, Mighty Horus," he apologized, "but I had underestimated the sluggishness of the current and the strength of the wind. Forgive me for requesting that you spend the night in this place."

Amunhotep smiled and dismissed him, walking with Tiye to watch the other barges tie up and the servants flock ashore to set up the tents, carpet the sand, light torches, and prepare the evening meal. "It is a lonely place but somehow beautiful," he said to her, scanning the view. "I do not remember passing it on my way either to or from Memphis."

"That is probably because the captain of the barge you were traveling in contrived very hard not to incur your wrath by stopping here," Tiye retorted. "Gods! I can almost hear my thoughts echo against those frowning cliffs. It looks as though not even peasants have been foolish enough to settle here."

"Peaceful," her son murmured.

They were ramped to one side of a huge area of virgin sand, through which the river wound in a slow curve. At either bend cliffs met the water, but here they drew back, rising in a ragged sweep on the west side but broken on the east into long mysterious gullies, fingers of rock into whose shadows night had already crept. The sun was almost gone, its red rim limning the black cliff top, its last rays pouring onto the unsullied sand. Beyond the cheerful human bustle on the bank, the dead silence was palpable, pressing against the intruders with a weighty impatience.

"A terrible heat must beat in here during the day," Tiye said. "How great a distance do you think it is from one end of the valley and the other, Majesty?"

"So pure," he sighed, pulling himself from his contemplation. "Nothing but sharp rock and blinding sand, a giant cup to hold the daily gold of Ra."

Out on the bank a group of servants suddenly began laughing. The sound left their mouths only to be returned to them a hundredfold, as if an invisible army hidden in the cliffs were mocking them. Tiye's flesh crawled. At the bottom of the ramp stood her maimed, tongueless servant, a huge pot of lamp fuel in both arms as her understeward shouted some order at him. Tiye turned back into the cabin, letting the curtains fall as she went.

Within another day the haunted silence of the valley was a memory, and in another three they were tying up at Memphis to a tumult of welcome. Thousands lined the bank, some scrambling to the roofs of the warehouses or plunging into the water to catch a glimpse of the royal visitors. Amunhotep smiled indulgently at them, raising the crook and flail high as he descended the ramp and lowered himself onto the waiting litter. Tiye ordered her own litter to be brought aboard and secured her curtains tightly before allowing herself to be carried ashore, for she did not believe that the faces of living gods should be exposed to the rude gaze of peasants. She remained secluded until she was set down safely behind the walls of the palace, when she went onto the roof immediately, Amunhotep close behind. "I had forgotten how beautiful it is!" she breathed. "What a fine view the palace commands. So many trees, Amunhotep, and such a profusion of untended flowers. Look at the sun on the lake the ancients built. I see the Syrian temple to Reshep has been given a new roof—you can just glimpse it through the foliage. Our trade with Syria must be lucrative for them. I think there are a few women still in the harem here. Will you visit them?"

He smiled noncommittally. "I do not think so. But I will go into the temples as I used to when I was high priest of Ptah. Would you like a barge ride into the papyrus swamps of the Delta tomorrow? It is only a half-day away."

"Your father and I used to hunt wildfowl in those swamps, many years ago," she said dreamily. "I would like that very much. Have you noticed how different the noise of Memphis is from the irritating clamor of Thebes? I . . ."

He had turned away from her and was squinting up at the sun, his attention no longer on her words. *I suppose I must not mention his father*, she thought crossly. *Well, I will try not to, seeing he has invited me here, but he must conquer a hatred that no longer has validity.*

For a month she and her son went their own ways. Pharaoh spent much time being carried in and out of the myriad temples of the foreigners who now called Memphis their home, and although he received a delegation from the temple of Ptah, he made no official visit there. Tiye herself met the mayor of Memphis and the commanders of her border patrols, whose soldiers were stationed in the city when they were standing down. She also received many of the wealthy merchants and foreign diplomats whose business kept them headquartered in Memphis, feasting in the gracious reception hall her husband had loved to decorate. She visited the harem, finding it a well run but melancholy place, half-empty and quiet.

But when their duties were done, Tiye and Amunhotep began to enjoy wandering the cool rooms of the empty palace

THE TWELFTH TRANSFORMING   133

or aimlessly pacing the winding garden paths together. In the hot afternoons they separated, lulled to sleep by the swish of fans and the muted plucking of harps. They spent a day being poled through the shoulder-high, rustling papyrus swamps. Amunhotep, though he could drive a chariot well and shoot a bow after a fashion, resolutely refused to hunt. Tiye's own fingers itched to hold a throwing stick as clouds of geese, ducks, and other water birds rose unchallenged around them, but it was good nonetheless to lie in the little hunting punt, watching the feathery papyrus fronds meeting over her head against the deep blue of a sky that bore no trace of the angry bronze tinge of a southern summer.

Time flowed as sweetly as the wine poured into the cups they raised. Tiye could not decide whether it was the influence of the bittersweet memories that came stealing from every corner of the palace or the lazy pattern of carefree days that were wiping all signs of tension from her face.

One twilight, as they sat together on the terrace looking down into the scented garden, Amunhotep turned in his chair and quietly gave an order to the servant behind him. The man went away and returned with the Keeper of the Royal Regalia. He carried a heavy chest Tiye recognized only too well.

"Greetings, Channa!" she said, surprised. "I did not know that you had accompanied us."

He bowed, murmuring a respectful reply. Amunhotep ordered him to place the chest on the table and then commanded both Channa and the butler who had been in attendance to depart. The terrace was soon empty but for the two of them.

Amunhotep leaned over and poured her wine himself. She kept her eyes on the chest, her heart suddenly painfully active, her throat dry. Picking up her cup, she drank quickly to hide her agitation. Pharaoh began to speak, haltingly at first, but with increasing courage as the night deepened and concealed his face.

"At the feet of Osiris Amunhotep I told you that Sitamun's death was my fault," he said, and Tiye, incredulous, realized that she heard him pronounce his father's name for the first time. "Now I will tell you why. I knew deep in my heart that the god did not wish me to make her empress. I should have married her and allowed her to remain only a queen. She was my sister, and I had a right and a duty to marry her, but another's blood call was stronger. The god punished me for my cowardice by destroying her. If I had done what I knew was proper, she would still be alive. No," he said softly as she tried to speak, "I am not thinking of dear Nefertiti."

He reached forward and, lifting back the lid of the chest, drew forth the empress's crown. The great polished disk gleamed darkly, and the silver horns of Hathor curving round it glittered in the starlight. Its two plumes quivered under his nervous hands as he positioned it on his bare knees. "I knew I should have offered it to you, not Sitamun," he went on, "but I mistrusted the will of the god. I shall not do so again. The crown is yours."

Tiye felt herself go rigid in the chair. Her hands gripped the armrests. "My son," she managed when she felt she could trust her voice, "Sitamun died because of the rivalry for the crown that existed between her and Nefertiti. You bear no responsibility. You chose one woman over another, exercising your right as Pharaoh."

"I have heard the rumors," he cut in simply. "Human hands destroyed Sitamun, but it was the god who decreed that she should suffer. I must have you, Tiye."

Tiye began to tremble and clung more tightly to the chair. "Let me try to understand you," she said. "You wish a marriage contract drawn up between us? You wish me to be chief wife and empress in Egypt?"

"I do. The document can be written and sealed here, before we return to Malkatta."

"Nefertiti should hold the titles." She could not breathe, for her throat had swelled, and her words came almost as a croak.

"No. I love my cousin, but she is not of my blood." Gently he placed the crown on the table between them. Tiye kept her eyes on the dusky garden below, but all her inner attention was fixed on the heavy thing. It was a challenge, a prize, a doombringer.

"You are, of course, proposing a marriage of formality only." She forced her hands away from the arms of the chair, folding them in her lap, and turned to look at him.

"No." He swung to face her, encircling the crown with his arms. The lamp set on the table illuminated only one side of his face, leaving the other plunged in shadow like a half-carved monolith. "So much has puzzled me since I became old enough to take command of my thoughts," he said quietly. "I did not know why I had been born, why the Son of Hapu prophesied against me, why I was left to the ministrations of the harem women. When I was a child, I cried often. I had strange dreams. I grew older and sat in the harem garden watching the flowers open like butterflies' wings, the butterflies flicking over the grass like untethered flowers." He passed both hands over his face, and though Tiye had never before heard him speak with such calm deliberation, his pale fingers shook. "I walked the passages of the women's quarters, listening to the prayers of the foreign wives, watching their prostrations to the gods they had brought with them from every corner of the empire. I began to realize that under every name—Savriti, Reshep, Baal—they were worshiping one god. I asked for scrolls from the palace and temple and began to read, but not until Pharaoh's first jubilee did I understand." His voice cracked suddenly, and he paused, swallowing and searching for words. "Many thousands of hentis ago, the kings of Egypt were not the incarnations of Amun. They came from the sun. They ruled as Ra on earth. After the princes of Thebes drove the Hyksos rulers from Egypt, they took their local god Amun for their totem, and as Thebes grew in power and riches, so did Amun. But the pharaohs have since forgotten that only Ra gives life to all the world, and that Amun's power is bounded by Thebes. Your husband glimpsed the truth, but it was as a flash of weak light in a dark room. He tried to give the Aten greater prominence, but only for a show." He leaned closer, meeting her gaze. "Mother, I am the incarnation of Ra. I was born to restore power to the sun in Egypt. My father is Ra-Harakhti, God of the Horizon in His Dawning. In choosing your body to bear me, he has brought a new age, a glorious age, to Egypt."

"Your father was Osiris Amunhotep, Amun's incarnation on earth!" Tiye almost shouted the words.

He smiled kindly, almost condescendingly at her. "No, he was only a man, like my brother Thothmes. It was necessary that Thothmes should die. My destiny was to become pharaoh against all odds so that the sun might be glorified."

Tiye could not think. A tangle of emotions struggled within her: shock, fear, fascination, dread. The fluttering of her heart was paining her, and she placed one stiff hand under her breast. "I do not see the necessity for making me your wife," she choked.

He leaned over the crown, his eyes changing from brown to yellow as they neared the lamp and took its light. "Amun has grown rich and strong," he whispered. "My magic must be even stronger. They are all around me, the evil ones, the devils, thronging me in the night, buffeting me in the day. I learned much from the women who opened shrines to foreign gods. Incantations, spells I can use to protect myself. But the greatest protection of all is the joining of a son's body to that of his mother. Such a union is considered holy by the sun people beyond the Great Bend of Naharin, in Khatti, in Karduniash. I have spoken to the foreign women. I know. It is not only holy, but for me, the sun's incarnation, it is imperative. From your body I came. It is your body that I must possess."

A moth had fluttered into the glowing lamp. Tiye could hear it struggling, its wings singed, its soft black eyes blinded, beating against the alabaster, consumed by a deadly intoxication. The moon was rising, a cold silver disk whose light irradiated the terrace. Tiye saw it lying colorless across her feet, a weightless shroud. *Think!* she berated herself fiercely. *Think. Ay, what have we done? This is the child for whose survival I fought grimly and secretly, for whose birthright I risked the wrath of Pharaoh, this fanatic, this man who is now confirmed in a position of power. Can such madness be controlled, contained?* But something far back in her mind whispered, *What if the Son of Hapu foresaw this, but its enormity was too great to be understood by a pharaoh who cared nothing for religious matters? The Son of Hapu wanted my son destroyed. He was the oracle of Amun. Is that why he predicted that the boy would grow up to murder his father? Did he mean his father Amun? What must I do?*

She attempted to speak, but her voice would not obey her. Waiting a moment, she tried again, struggling for a soothing tone. "Amunhotep," she said, "for a royal prince to wed his sister is proper and right, for the seed of a god must not pass to commoners. It is acceptable for a pharaoh to wed his daughters for the same reason. Such unions were once considered necessary when royal women held the right of succession in their blood. But now the succession is a matter for the oracles, and Amun bestows divinity according to their pronouncements. Marriages between brother and sister or father and daughter are now arranged only for dynastic reasons or for the purifying of royal blood." Her voice had risen and thinned. "Under the law of Ma'at there are two couplings that bring down curses and punishments and are not allowed. One is between two men, and the other is between a man and his mother. What you are proposing to me would shake the foundations of Ma'at in Egypt and incur the disapproval of everyone from courtiers and priests to the fellahin in the fields."

"Ra is omnipotent," he reminded her, "and overshadows not only Amun but Ma'at as well. Ma'at must be restored to its ancient simplicity. Ra's family is small, and his power must be preserved and shared within it, must be made to grow stronger to provide a spell that neither man nor greedy god can break. As Ra's incarnation I look to his laws, which override the laws of a Ma'at that has become perverted. Your husband bedded with a boy, and your courtiers break the laws of Ma'at every day. But those who obey me, the sun's chosen emissary, cannot err, and the family of the holy can only enhance Ma'at." Eagerly he pushed the crown toward her. "You are already a chosen one. I need you."

"And if I refuse?"

"You will not. How can you? The circle of power around me is not yet closed, and the darkness seeps through to me. You can close it, Tiye. You and I will make children of the sun."

She rose, cramped and drained, and had to hold to the arm of the chair with both hands to prevent herself from falling. "I will think about all you have said," she murmured, "but now I must sleep."

"You are shivering. Piha! Bring the goddess a cloak!" He rose also, and coming around the table, he kissed her on the neck with his customary gentleness. "Sleep then, Empress. Ra will chase all doubts away with his dawning." He was exultant, feverish with relief and anticipation, and he walked buoyantly across the moon-splashed terrace as though a great weight had rolled from him.

Tiye went to her bedchamber, scarcely aware of where she was. She stood mute and withdrawn as Piha and her other body servants undressed her, removed the paint from her face, palms and feet, extinguished all but the night lamp by the couch, and held the sheet back for her. She slid beneath it woodenly, and they bowed themselves out. Piha curled up on her mat in the corner and was soon breathing heavily in sleep. Outside the door, her bodyguard shuffled and coughed once quietly. Tiye sat up and let her forehead droop to her bent knees. *Very well*, she thought. *What alternatives do I have? It seems that Egypt*

*is in no danger from my son, for he speaks only of restoring
her to some former pristine grandeur. If he is mad, then it is
a madness that does not threaten the military or diplomatic
supremacy of the empire. I am regent. I control that supremacy,
and if I become his empress, I can go on controlling it. He
has little interest in the administration and would be free to
pursue his religious insanity quite harmlessly while I keep this
country safe. There would be an uproar, of course. Every priest
would curse me, every citizen cry out. How long would it last?
How long did Thebes and the court remain scandalized by my
husband's boy? Not long. But this would be different. It would
not be a royal indiscretion, kept in the dimness of the king's
apartments. I would be flaunting a broken law of Ma'at in the
halls of audience, with the crown on my head, every day. The
foreign delegations would think nothing of it. It is true what
he says, that foreign nobles and royalty often marry their moth-
ers. It is Egypt that would seethe. Better to refuse, to insist
that Nefertiti wear the horned disk. But what if he is right?
How long has it been since any pharaoh really believed in his
heart that he was Amun, god of Thebes? So many times Osiris
Amunhotep and I joked about our divinity, believing only in
our power to make ourselves gods. My son's life has been
strange, even as he said. Is it possible that Thothmes died by
the hand of Ra? That the Son of Hapu was terrified by what
he saw in the Anubis cup? Perhaps this is not just a question
of grasping at a chance to continue wielding the power my
husband gave me, but something more awesome. If I decide
wrongly, will Ra's anger fall upon me?*

She drew the sheet around her and, sliding from the couch,
crept to the window. Cool air blew into her face. The garden
was hushed and dark save for the occasional torch of a soldier
or a servant hurrying on some errand. She considered his words
over and over again, and as she did so, the pure white flame
of his conviction began to touch an answering spark of somber
light buried deep within her. She knew she was a jaded woman,
with sensitivities blunted by a lifetime of intrigues, decadence,
and the corruption attendant upon the practice of absolute power.
She had never heard matters of the spirit spoken of with such
transparent conviction, and under the layers of cynicism, the
corroding armor of questionable decisions made in the interests
of political necessity or social stability, Amunhotep's earnest
certainty touched a chord. *What if he is truly the harbinger of*

a jealous god, come to restore the balance of a Ma'at corrupted by centuries of error?

She fell asleep kneeling against the window, her head on the sill. Sometime toward morning she woke with a start, feeling Piha's solicitous hand on her shoulder, and staggering to her couch, she fell once more into a dreamless slumber.

For three days she wrestled with herself, and Amunhotep did not approach her. He had himself rowed to On, to worship his god in the temple of the sun, and spent much time kneeling before his portable shrine and playing with his monkeys and cats. When he joined Tiye for the formal evening meal, he did so in full regalia, the Double Crown on his head, the crook and flail laid at his feet, the leopard's tail and pharaonic beard fastened in place. He said little, and Tiye was disinclined to speak either. She watched her son out of the corner of her eye as he ate slowly, lifting the fruit and vegetables delicately to his large mouth, his eyes liquid with his own far thoughts, his shallow chest rising and falling with his breath, the falcon-headed sun god Ra-Harakhti that he always wore around his thin neck shooting glancing rays of reflected light into her face.

She woke on the fourth day with a decision already firm in her mind. Once dressed and painted, she summoned her herald and bodyguard and found her son at the foot of the terrace, throwing bread to the birds that wheeled and piped over his head. Sitting on the step beside him, his scribe was reading a letter aloud, which she soon realized was from Nefertiti. Tiye descended to him alone, and hearing her sandals on the white stone, he turned and smiled.

"I will take the crown," she said without preamble, "providing the agreement is put into writing and sealed with the pharaonic seal. Do it now, Amunhotep." *Or I shall change my mind,* she thought.

He made as if to embrace her, but seeing her stiff face, he faltered, and his arms fell to his sides. "Take fresh papyrus," he said solemnly to the scribe. "Write what I shall tell you."

He began to dictate, and suddenly Tiye could not bear to stand there motionless, listening to the shrill, childlike voice. The sun on her head was already too hot, the stone beneath her feet too chill. With a short bow she left him, shouting as she went for Piha and her canopy bearers. She was almost running by the time she reached the ornamental lake, pulling off her bracelets, tearing the necklaces from her throat, tugging the wig from her head and flinging it aside. With a cry she dove into the water, pulling from the bottom, letting it fill her mouth, her ears, her open eyes. When she could hold her breath no longer, she broke the surface and began to swim. *What have I done?* she thought. *What?* She left the lake only when her limbs refused to obey her, and lay spent on the verge under the canopy, rubbing the droplets of water into her skin.

Amunhotep came to her that night, announced by his herald, who then ordered her own servants out of her apartments and withdrew. She slid from the couch, sinking to the floor to kiss the naked feet that came to rest before her. He bade her rise, and for a moment they stared at each other. He was a head taller than she, as tall as his father, she thought. He had been drinking perfumed wine, and she could smell gusts of lotus essence on his breath. His mouth was hennaed, his eyes heavily kohled. The loose folds of his soft white bag wig rested against his neck.

"Are you afraid?" he asked kindly, taking her hand, and as she looked at his long fingers playing against her own, Tiye knew she was not. She shook her head. He removed his wig, placing it carefully on her table and running his other hand over his shaven skull. His long, slanted jaw and almond eyes seemed to leap into prominence, giving him a feral look, but his glance was mild. Under the diaphanous white cloak he now discarded he was naked, pale full hips swelling, round thighs quivering in the lamplight. Tiye was both repelled by his strangeness and drawn to that part of him that was herself. *The god I loved is in this man*, she thought, *as well as my own blood*.

She sat on the couch, and he perched beside her. Taking her face in both hands he turned her head, and now in his eyes a feverish light burned, a spark of vitality that left a flush along his high cheekbones. "Sitamun would have had those cruel grooves in her face within a very few years," he whispered, his breath coming short, "but her eyes would never have acquired the deep steadiness of yours. I love you, my mother. Put your arms around me."

A sense of unreality began to steal over her as she embraced him. It was as though she were asleep in another place, a different time, dreaming this vision of another self, living vicariously through it while she watched from a vantage of safety. He made love not with his father's controlled passion, but with a stubborn persistence she recognized as her own. He did not seem to mind that she was passive with foreboding, still asking herself, even as he entered her, what madness she had committed. Her flesh recoiled even before he had ceased to move in her, and with the quick intuition of which he was sometimes capable he withdrew and lay beside her, breathing deeply.

"No harm will come to you, Tiye," he said as though he had read her thoughts. "No god will presume to judge you. You are under my protection."

During the following week, their last in Memphis, he came to her each night, making love with the same endearing yet curiously passionless tenderness, and with familiarity a similar response came from Tiye. Her body craved the knowing, expert touch of her dead husband, and often his face rose before her inward eye as she and Amunhotep moved together, but then she had never received from him the solicitous gentleness her son showed to her. Often she would not speak a single word to him, as though speech would confirm her crime, bring into the harsh focus of reality a situation to which a dreamlike quality still clung, and he either understood or preferred her silence.

During the days, they would stroll quietly arm in arm in the gardens or play board games under the trees. Amunhotep paid a final visit to On, but did not ask her to join him, by which she was relieved. The new, silent efficiency of her servants had not escaped her notice as they began to pack her belongings for the return to Malkatta.

Most of the trip back was made under sail, and they arrived at the palace water steps three days before the Feast of Opet was to begin. Word of their coming had been sent ahead, and Tiye, almost fainting in the heat that she had left behind nearly two months earlier, saw from the deck that the whole forecourt and both sides of the canal were lined with courtiers. Nefertiti, the two children, and her brother sat in reverent isolation under a canopy. Ptahhotep, Si-Mut, and a small group of Amun priests clustered under their own sunshade. Horemheb stood with his soldiers where the ramp would be run out, but Mutnodjme swaggered impatiently, plucking crisp leaves from the trees with her whip while her dwarfs waded, fat and naked, in the canal.

No shouts of welcome greeted the barge as it floated along

the canal and bumped the water steps. Pasi's command to dock
echoed lonely and clear against the pillars of the audience hall
beyond the crowded courtyard. Pharaoh began to descend the
ramp, Tiye behind him with head high, the disk and plumes
glittering. The crush of people swayed and went to the ground,
still in an ominous silence. Ay and Nefertiti bowed and stood
waiting. Meeting her niece's eye, Tiye read gray hatred in them.
Steadily she approached, determined to see Nefertiti give way,
and she had the satisfaction of seeing the girl's gaze falter and
drop. Tiye had known that this second would set the pattern
of their relationship, and breathed an inward sigh of relief.
Pharaoh was looking about with a benign, vague smile. "You
may all rise," he called shrilly. "Nefertiti, let me hold Meritaten. My little baby has grown since I have been away." He
cuddled the child and moved on, his retinue forming around
him, his monkeys gibbering with pleasure and leaping for the
trees, his cats, released from their cages, bolting for the shade.
Tiye felt a twinge of jealousy as he smilingly beckoned Nefertiti
to walk with him, but she suppressed it quickly as she turned
away and signaled Ptahhotep.

"High Priest, attend me in my hall in one hour." She turned
to Ay. "Come with me."

Trailed by the Keeper of the Royal Regalia, her fanbearers,
and other members of her retinue, she walked into her husband's private quarters. Taking the crown from her head, she
handed it to the keeper and ordered the servants out and then
strode briskly to the throne and mounted it. Ay stood in a
hostile silence until the last servant had backed away and closed
the doors. When Tiye motioned for him to speak, he almost
ran to the foot of the throne.

"Have you taken leave of your senses?" he said through
clenched teeth, arms clamped to his sides. "Have you gone
mad? Is it true?"

She regarded him coldly. "Yes, it is true."

"The whole palace erupted when the edict was read. People
falling over one another in the halls, shouting the news from
office to office . . . Why, Tiye, why? Ptahhotep has boated across
from Karnak every day, almost incoherent with worry."

"I will deal with Ptahhotep shortly. Do not shout at me, Ay.
I stopped being your little sister a long time ago. I wouldn't
care to answer for what Pharaoh's actions would have been
had I not accepted the crown."

"You could have taken some discreet princeling to your bed," he sneered. "The court would have thought nothing of it. But your own son..."

"If you do not stop shouting at me, I will have you whipped! I am empress! I am goddess! I will not be addressed in this fashion!"

He glared at her, breathing hard, then bowed shortly. "I am sorry." But he did not look sorry. Tiye saw how color had leaped into his cheeks, and his large hands clenched as he tried to control himself.

"Nothing will be gained if we shout at each other," she said crisply. "I need your acumen, Ay, not your ridiculous judgment. In a few days the court's outrage will have turned to titillation, as it did over my husband's boy."

"I hope you are right. You risk loss of face over this, and with it will go a dangerous weakening of power."

"I believed I had to take the chance." She told him what had happened at Memphis, and Ay, his anger forgotten, listened thoughtfully.

"All the same," he said when she had finished, "it was an irreparable act carried out in haste. You could have waited until you returned, discussed it with me."

"Perhaps. But I did consider this carefully. If Amunhotep is wrong, or merely deluded, then all I will have done is to scandalize the palace, distress the priests, and break a law of Ma'at. Scandal is soon forgotten. But if I had refused him, and his claims are justified..."

"Our first concerns have always been our own security and the safety of the empire, in that order," he broke in. "Both are bound up in the person of Pharaoh. It is becoming obvious that Amunhotep will not rule unless his religious needs are satisfied, and if he does not rule well, we and the empire will suffer."

Tiye was offended. "Do you think that I am one of his religious needs?"

Ay smiled at her sadly. "I think so, Tiye. More is involved, of course, but that is his main reason for this marriage. For Egypt's sake and your own, I hope you remember that."

"I will try," she said sarcastically and dismissed him.

For the rest of the morning she gave audience to Ptahhotep, striving to reassure him that a transgression against Ma'at did not threaten and never had threatened the stability of the country or the supremacy of Amun. She dwelt on her own long rule with a pharaoh who had pursued his pleasures and had left Egypt in her hands, giving Ptahhotep the deliberate impression that under her son's kingship nothing had changed. She knew better than to flatter or fawn on him, and when he left, he was mollified. *I would do well to believe my own words*, she thought as she walked to her bedchamber to rest during the unbearable early afternoon hours. *I have exchanged one pharaoh for another. I am still ruler and empress.*

But as she lay under the moving fans in her darkened room, her mind filled with images of her son's mouth closing over her own, kissing her body with gentle purpose, his eyes meeting hers as he mounted her, and she could not sleep. When Piha came to raise the hangings and the late sun, still hot and stifling, flooded the room, she sent for Kheruef.

"Go across the river into the city," she ordered. "Buy me a Declaration of Innocence. Do not send a servant, Kheruef. Do this yourself."

"Majesty," he told her, his face impassive, "may I have the temerity to remind you that you are counted as one among the gods, and the gods do not need the declaration."

"Kheruef, I have never in my life left anything to chance. You are my steward. Do as you are told." He bowed and went out. She had intended to busy herself with other matters until he returned but could settle down to nothing. *This guilt is different from the guilt I felt over the murder of Nebet-nuhe*, she thought, standing in the middle of the bedchamber with arms folded and head down, *different from the guilt I used to feel over the manipulations of the audience chamber, the whippings, banishments, and punishments I have decreed. Why?*

Kheruef did not return until sunset, and although he had obviously taken the time to retire to his own quarters and hurriedly wash and change his linen, a smudge of dust still clung to his cheek. Tiye smiled tightly at him.

"You are still dirty, Kheruef."

"I wrapped myself in the coarse apparel of the fellahin and went into the public forecourts on foot, Majesty," he replied primly. "I did not think you would wish to pay as much for the declaration as a man in fine linen and smelling of the gods would be forced to pay."

"That is why you are my steward," she answered. "Read it to me."

He unrolled the scroll and, sinking to the floor in the attitude of the scribe he had once been, began to read, "Hail Usekh-nemtet Long of Strides, I have not done iniquity. Hail Hept-seshet Embraced by Flame, I have not robbed with violence. Hail Neha-hra Foul of Face, I have slain neither man nor woman. Hail Ta-ret Fiery Foot, I have not eaten my heart. Hail Hetch-abehu Shining of Teeth, I have invaded no man's land. Hail Am-senef, Eater of Blood, I have not slaughtered animals which are the possessions of the god." His voice droned on in the quiet singsong monotone reserved for prayers, spells, and the conjuring of spirits, and Tiye listened without betraying her agitation. "Hail Seshet-kheru, Orderer of Speech, I have not made myself deaf unto the words of right and truth." *No*, Tiye thought, *I have not done that. I am trying not to do that, but the question remains: Does Amunhotep speak the words of right and truth, or not?* "Hail Maa-ant-f, Seer of What Is Brought to Him, I have not lain with the wife of a man. Hail Tututef, I have not committed fornication, I have not committed so-domy, I have not turned back the generative power." As Kher-uef's voice momentarily faltered, Tiye felt the words insinuate themselves under her skin and run gentle, accusatory fingers along the back of her neck. *"I have not turned back the gen-erative power."* *But surely*, she reasoned, *these things do not apply to those responsible for matters of state, to whom the breaking of laws is often a necessity.*

She heard Kheruef through to the end, not facing him until the scroll rustled shut. "Give me pen and ink," she said. "I will sign it myself." He set a palette and the scroll on the table by the bed, placed a wet pen in her hand, and indicated the place reserved for a signature. Twice she inscribed her names and all her titles. Then she let the scroll roll up and tucked it under her headrest. "That is all, you can go," she said, handing him the pen.

He took it, replaced it on the palette and, hesitating, fell to his knees before her, grasping her feet with both hands and kissing them.

Tiye stepped back. "What is it, Kheruef?" she asked, astonished. "Get up!"

Although he straightened, he remained on his knees. "Majesty Goddess, I ask you humbly to relieve me of my duties to you and to the harem. I wish to retire."

"Nonsense! Why?"

"I have grown old in your service. My children are strangers to me, my wives are lonely." His eyes refused to meet hers.

"You liar, Kheruef," she said evenly. "You are my eyes and ears, my mouth in the harem, and my rod among the servants. I know you better than I know myself. If you insult me so, I will become angry."

"Very well." He took a deep breath. "Majesty, this thing that you have done with Pharaoh is evil, a pollution. I cannot serve you any longer because of it."

"How do you know that we have not simply made a political arrangement?"

He managed a smile. "Am I not your eyes, your ears? Is it not my duty to bring you every rumor? The servants of Memphis are not tongueless."

"I do not understand this sudden self-righteousness." Her tone was biting. "You came from Akhmin with me when I entered the harem as a child. You have carried out every command without question." Their eyes met, and she knew that her reference to the poisoning of Nebet-nuhe had not been lost on him.

"This is different," he resisted quietly.

"How?" She lashed out at him bitterly, already mourning him.

"I cannot say, Divine One."

" 'Foolish as the words of a woman,' " she said, quoting the ancient proverb to him sarcastically, and then capitulated quickly for fear she should begin to beg. "I will accept your resignation. You have earned my gratitude. Give Huya your badge and staff of office and go home, Kheruef."

He rose without joy. "I love you, my queen, my goddess."

"I love you also. My father did right when he gave you to me. May your name live forever."

"Dismiss me." He was crying.

"Go."

But my dear Tiye, the gods do not suffer hurt, she heard the mocking voice of her husband say as she listened to Kheruef's footsteps recede down the passage. *Well, it will not hurt for long*, she told herself determinedly. *I am no stranger to betrayal*. She called for Piha to bring wine and music, and sat by the couch as the quick melodies filled the room and wafted out over the darkening garden.

Amunhotep came to her that night, painted and dressed in

transparent blue linen, and she met his mild lust with a passion she had not felt since the Mighty Bull had died. *It is what I want*, she vowed silently as they threshed and muttered together, *and I will show my omnipotence to the world*.

10

As Tiye had predicted, the scandal of her marriage soon became an item of conversation only for courtiers too bored to discuss anything else. The resistance of the priests gradually relaxed when they saw Pharaoh perform, albeit carelessly, the duties Amun required of him. Tiye looked back on the anguish of her decision at Memphis with an indulgent inner smile. She had been right to trust her instincts. Had not the governing of the country, the life at court, the relationships within the royal family fallen into perfectly acceptable patterns? A new pharaoh always faced a period of difficult adjustments.

As though to emphasize the return to normalcy, the river began to rise on the day the priests of Isis had predicted, and with it men's spirits. At Malkatta the feeling was generally that a new age was under way, and the most visible symbol of rebirth was Pharaoh himself. His coupling with Tiye seemed to release Amunhotep from his spiritual prison. The impotence that had plagued him had disappeared, and while he would never have the complex sexual appetites of his father, he no longer spent his nights cowering in a bedchamber bright with lamps and torches. The dark hours were shared with his empress or his queen, and even secondary wife Tadukhipa at last left the years of her virginity behind.

It was during this period also that Amunhotep began his Teaching. What had started years earlier as religious discussions between himself and the priests from On in the garden now became an almost daily discourse in Pharaoh's public audience hall. He would sit on the throne, sometimes in the white helmets he used to prefer but more often in loose bag wigs, the crook and the flail in his wide lap, his voice carrying thin and high over the restless crowd. The On priests and guards sat around him under the gold baldachin, watching the listeners. Nefertiti was always there, her small face haughty under the crystal glitter of the cobra coronet, and little Kia often had her chair placed at his feet. Although his audience was initially made up of only his own household staff and a few curious courtiers, before long those same courtiers made it understood in the palace that the favor of Pharaoh depended on one's attendance in the hall to hear him speak.

Amunhotep beamed on the ever-enlarging crowds, speaking with a kind condescension of the universal supremacy of Ra as manifested in his visible shape as the Aten Disk. He never mentioned Amun, and Tiye, who came to listen to him occasionally when she was not busy with more pressing matters wondered whether the omission was deliberate or whether her son simply regarded Amun as so insignificant that he forgot to mention the god at all. The content of these speeches inevitably bored Tiye, but she often remained for their duration, held in her place by the note of confidence in her son's voice that was never present at any other time. His eyes would light, and his long hands would take on life as they gesticulated gracefully. To her surprise, his words struck answering chords in some courtiers, and speaking to them later, jealously alert for any indication of insincerity, she saw nothing but the dawning of speculation in their eyes. She and Ay sometimes discussed the possible consequences of Amunhotep's strange convictions taking hold at Malkatta and decided they would be insignificant. The days when religious belief was a living force in the lives of the nobles were long gone, and little but the outward manifestations of piety—household shrines, incense, and token observance—remained.

Her complacency regarding the harmlessness of the Teaching was shaken one day, however, when Ptahhotep appeared at the hour of formal audience with one of his young priests. She had earlier caught sight of him waiting far back in the hall, and something in his stance, arms tensely folded over the priestly leopard skin that hung across his chest, shaven head lowered, made her uneasy. The young priest beside him was fidgeting, moving from one leather-sandaled foot to the other, fingering the white ribbons that encircled his head. *Not a we'eb*, she thought. *Perhaps a Master of Mysteries, but I cannot see his arm band*. She had to wait through three more ministerial speeches, her scribe's pen scratching diligently at her feet, before Ptahhotep and the younger priest approached the throne and made their reverence. The hall was now almost empty, and Tiye's stomach reminded her that it was past the time of the noon meal.

Ptahhotep came closer, hesitated, and Tiye motioned her herald and bodyguard out of his way.

"You may speak, High Priest."

He stepped to the foot of the throne. "Majesty and Goddess, I do not know how to put this carefully. Since Great Horus began his Teaching, there has been increasing unrest at Karnak. No priest had neglected his daily observances, but among the younger men there have been arguments, discussions, even quarrels, and the peace and orderliness of the cells is threatened. My phylarchs tell me that the young priests do not always sleep at night. They creep into one another's cells, they take scrolls from the temple library, suddenly little animosities are breaking out. Everywhere but in the holiest of holiest itself, the priests whisper of Ra-Harakhti. Others even question the omnipotence of Amun himself. Myself, Si-Mut, the older men know that this is but a small eddy soon dissipated, but others are not so patient."

"We have discussed this before. Pharaoh means no disrespect to Amun. Has he not ordered you to continue to make the sacrifices each day on his behalf? Control your priests yourself, Ptahhotep, and do not look to me to do it."

"Majesty, the question is not one of my control," he replied, offended, "but of this priest." He indicated the shamefaced young man at his elbow. "He has requested permission to leave Amun's service and join the ranks of the Aten priests preparing to serve in Pharaoh's new temple. If I let him go, will there be others? Do I discipline him, command him to go home to his family in disgrace, command him to stay?"

"Really, Ptahhotep, I . . ." Tiye began but then stopped herself. The decision was not an easy one. Several courtiers had recently closed their Amun shrines, ordering new shrines to the Aten from their goldsmiths, but for them it was a new game to play. Before her now was the first stirring of something deeper, the first priest with the conviction to act. Tiye had sometimes seen priestly linens among those who gathered to hear Pharaoh teach. If she ordered Ptahhotep to discipline this man or to send him home, it would be admitting that his priests served under coercion. If he were released to the Aten, he might start a mass desertion. "You," she said, turning to the young priest, "what is your name and station?"

The young man bowed. "I am Meryra, Master of Mysteries in the House of the Ben-Ben of Amun."

"What do you want?"

"I want to be released from the service of Amun. He is a great god, Egypt's salvation in the days of Hyksos domination, but I no longer believe that he is almighty. It is the Aten who shines on all the world."

"Why can you not serve both gods?"

"I can worship Amun, but I can only serve the Aten. I wish no harm to any man. I am pure of speech and have never caused offense either with my body or my words. Majesty, I only wish to leave Karnak quietly and join the Aten temple staff."

"Does Pharaoh know of this?"

"Yes. But he will allow it only with the permission of my superior."

At least Amunhotep has been diplomatic in this, Tiye thought. *I can see why Ptahhotep did not go to Pharaoh with his complaint.* "It is pointless to keep men against their will," she said to the high priest. "They will serve Amun only grudgingly and will make trouble. Let this man go. But, Meryra, you leave having forfeited all you have to the god you are deserting. Do you understand?"

The clear eyes met hers without flinching. "Yes, Majesty."

"Ptahhotep, I suggest you make it known at Karnak that any priest who leaves on behalf of the Aten immediately impoverishes himself. Thus only the most fervent will go, and the waverers will stay. Is there anything more?"

"Your Majesty is gracious."

"Go, then. I want my food."

It would have been dangerously foolish to hold that young man against his will, she thought as she and her entourage walked toward the banqueting hall. *I only hope that my son has the good sense not to reward Amun's traitors openly, or we will have a veritable river of greedy priests flowing from one temple to the other at Karnak. Well, to Sebek with them all. Today I want beer with my bread.*

In the weeks that followed, Tiye's judgment proved to be less effective than she had anticipated. While the abandonment of Amun's temples that she had feared did not take place, there were enough dissatisfied priests who were encouraged by Ptah- hotep's announcement to shift their allegiance to the Aten. She knew how important it would be to keep a diligent eye on all religious activity and held regular conferences with her spies in priests' dormitories, hoping that any similar problems could be forestalled.

The few minor disturbances that did occur were promptly dealt with, and Tiye had again begun to feel that she was gaining control over the situation when she received a visit from a visibly disturbed Ay. It was Shemu, when the Inundation still seemed an eternity away, and the scalding wrath of Ra's breath spread fever and violence through the land.

She had just risen from her afternoon sleep feeling enervated and still exhausted and was sitting on the edge of her couch when her brother was announced. She nodded for him to speak.

"Tiye, I want you to come across the river with me. Pha- raoh's Aten temple is almost complete. There has been much talk of the statues that line the forecourt, and we should see them before the temple is dedicated and we cannot walk where we will."

Tiye rose listlessly, and Piha draped her in a white gown, fastening jewels around her neck, wrist, and ankles. "I have heard the rumors also. Amunhotep has been trying to persuade me to inspect his craftsmen's work, but truthfully, Ay, I have not been able to find the interest." She sat before her cosmetics table and picked up the mirror. It showed her a heavy, puffed face and sallow skin. She put it down again as the cosmetician began to open his pots.

"Find it today. *Aten Gleams* is waiting to ferry us. There might be some air stirring on the river."

"Don't taunt me. My eyes are watering, Nebmehy, so be careful with the kohl. I have not seen Mutnodjme for a long time, Ay. Where is she?"

"She and Horemheb have gone north to Memphis, and then to Hnes to visit Horemheb's father. The marriage seems a good one, Tiye. Depet and Werel's parties are not the same without my daughter."

"Your other daughter is not so retiring. Her hostility puts me off my food every evening. Huya tells me that she is preg- nant again." Her Keeper of Wigs set the one she had absently selected on her head, tucking her own auburn hair out of the way, and her Keeper of Jewels draped the hairpiece with a golden, carnelian-studded net. After the Keeper of the Royal Regalia had placed the queen's cobra coronet on her brow, Tiye picked up the mirror again and this time managed a smile.

"So her steward told me." Ay laughed. "She has paid fortunes to every seer and oracle around to promise her a boy, and she has even bought spells from the Anubis ones."

"I know. Call for a litter, Ay. I want to ride to the water steps. It is too hot to walk."

They gossiped as they were ferried across the river, and Tiye was revived by a small puff of wind that stirred out of the north. At the Karnak water steps they were met by a litter and a covering contingent of guards who escorted them past Nefertiti's Aten temple. Tiye, who had been letting her gaze wander idly as they glided past the temple's first pylon, suddenly called a stop. "Step down, Ay, and come here. I think my eyes have sand in them." Obediently he walked to her litter, and the fanbearers rushed to shade them. Tiye felt rage and bewilderment as they came to a halt and craned their necks upward.

The stone pylon towered over them. On each of its supports, incised deeply into the stone and painted vividly in blue and gold, a giant Nefertiti strode across the bodies of dead Nubians and vile Asiatics. The scene was an approximation of one that ran around Tiye's own throne. But in that carving Tiye was represented as a clawed and breasted sphinx with enemies beneath her. Here Nefertiti was portrayed in a male's short kilt, and her pose, now frozen in the stone, was one in which no one but a ruling pharaoh had ever been depicted. Raised in one vengeful hand was the royal scimitar, with the flail lowered in the other. The figure had no breasts, and on the head was a tall, flat-topped crown fronted by a cobra. Only the face was recognizably feminine, unmistakably Nefertiti's.

Tiye and Ay looked at each other. "The days when I knew what was happening in my dominion before it came to pass are over," Tiye muttered between clenched teeth. "How dare she do this? It is sacrilege! What is she trying to prove?"

"She is saying in stone those things she cannot say with her mouth," Ay replied shortly. "I trust Your Majesty has honest food tasters and incorruptible guards."

"She would not!"

Ay turned back to the litters. "She has struck before without warning. This is a warning."

I was stupid to ignore the building here, Tiye thought, sick with anger. *I have the feeling that the cords that bound Egypt to me alone are being unpicked by Nefertiti's deft little fingers.* Stiffly she got back onto the litter, and Ay ordered the procession to move on. He was brooding and had little to say as they approached Amunhotep's temple.

They left the litters beneath the first pylon leading to the huge flagged court and, sheltered beneath a sunshade, walked toward the private inner court. Groups of Aten priests, regal in white linen, turned from their conversations and bowed profoundly. Sweating stonemasons laid aside their tools and prostrated themselves on the hot stone. Several pillars that marked the outer walls were already in place, but between them were still only pits where the others would be sunk.

Tiye and Ay came to the second pylon, taller and wider than the first. Flagstaffs holding aloft the blue and white emblems of royalty stood before it. Once the temple had been dedicated, priest-guards would stand at either side of the entrance to prevent the common people from entering the inner court, but today the pylon was deserted, sending waves of heat that beat out at them as they passed. Tiye had expected some manner of a roof under which worshipers could stand in comfort, but there was none. The sun poured into the vast space without pity.

She stopped just inside the entrance. Hundreds of offering tables spread before her in seemingly endless rows, each set on a small dais of two steps, filling the court with just enough room between them for processions to pass. The wall of the court was marked at regular intervals by pillars only three-quarters freed from the stone of the wall itself. On each pillar was an image of Pharaoh—hundreds of identical images of Amunhotep staring down into the holy place. Ay touched Tiye's arm. "Come and look at them." They made their way around the offering tables to the wall and gazed upward.

The likenesses were immense but well executed, conveying perfectly the calm infallibility inherent in Pharaoh's godhead. The cobra and vulture rose together from the winged helmet. Amunhotep's eyes were canted downward, giving a slightly forbidding, judgmental cast to the otherwise serene face. The nose was beautifully delicate, the full lips closed and faintly smiling, the pharaonic beard jutting to where the crook and flail—it was already well known that Amunhotep disdained the scimitar—were crossed on the smooth chest. The stone hands grasped the regalia firmly, and carved on bracelets around each wrist and upper arm were the king's cartouches. The figures were unpainted. Tiye stepped back and looked along at the others, an infinity of motionless images of her son staring down on the tables from which the flames of offerings to his god would rise.

Then, as her eyes moved lower, she saw that Pharaoh's full belly curved down into hips and upper thighs that in turn became the bottom half of each pillar. Apart from the helmets, the statues were naked, and as no kilt had been carved to hide them, it was obvious that not one of the figures had genitals. The thighs of each lay tightly together, like a woman's. Tiye began to walk beneath the walls, eyes on the statues passing slowly above her. As she paced, a deep spiritual disturbance began to afflict her, emanating from the massive things above, an invisible aura that flowed toward her, surrounded her, until she began to believe that her eyes were deceiving her, that the carved mouths were crying out some tormented truth that only they could feel, filling the temple with the eddies of their inner torture. She came to the end of the wall and turned, shocked and faint.

"Where is the ben-ben?" she whispered.

"There is no ben-ben," Ay said soberly. "No god, no pyramid, no holy stone. The Aten is not present in this temple."

"Ay, I am afraid. There is great evil in this place, and I feel like a child stumbling upon living terrors in some deserted valley. My son knows that Pharaoh is the Mighty Bull, the symbol of fertility in Egypt, ensurer of the vital seed of man and crops alike. To have himself portrayed without the organ of regeneration is to invite sterility for all of Egypt." Walking to the nearest offering table, she leaned against it. "But that is not the worst transgression. Pharaoh's essence inhabits every carving of himself, every painting, every place his name is written within the cartouche. He is fully present wherever these things are placed, casting his virile, ageless magic over all, as the god he is, and long after his death he protects and nurtures his people. What protection for Egypt is there in these misshapen things?"

"I know these truths, Tiye," Ay reminded her gently. "But

perhaps Pharaoh is trying to state other truths. He believes he is Ra's incarnation, Aten the Visible Disk, and unlike Amun, the Aten has no sex. I think he believes Egypt has nothing to fear from these representations of himself because the magic they cast is stronger than Amun's magic. He talks a great deal about how he and everyone else must live in truth. The images are an example."

"But it is Nefertiti who will draw the approval and recognition of the gods by the blasphemous portraits of herself we saw a moment ago! They will believe that she is pharaoh, and my son nothing but a vulnerable man!" She had paled.

Ay stepped to her side. "Let us leave," he said. "It will be different here when the tables are heaped with food and flowers and a priest stands with incense rising on each dais. Unfinished building sites often have an air of forbidding about them." His voice rang hollow.

"Not like this." She met his eyes. "Ay, I am pregnant. I have not felt resentful or afraid about it, merely resigned. But now I sink under the knowledge. I did my best to prevent this, but when it happened, I was glad for Amunhotep, and yes, I gloated a little when I thought of Nefertiti's reaction. Now I could wish myself back in Memphis with a denial for my son on my lips." She spoke with great bitterness. Putting his arm around her, Ay led her out to where the litter bearers lounged in the shade of the pylon. Her skin was cold.

When Amunhotep came to her that night, she still had not shaken her mood. He smiled at her, talked of small things, and made love to her with, she fancied, a willing mind but an unexpectedly reluctant body. She could not respond. Her visit to the Aten temple had changed her perception of him, and now it was as though she was seeing him for the first time. His innocuous words seemed sinister to her, the movements of his deformed flesh in the lamplight an unspoken threat. Though she wanted to, she did not dare to question him.

Next day she paid a visit to Tia-Ha, hoping that her friend's cheerful common sense would restore her anxiety to a proper perspective. The princess was sorting through her gowns with the aid of her body servant, and her apartment was even more chaotic than usual. Tiye greeted her, received her reverence, and picked a way through the disorderly piles of bright linens to the cushions that had been flung out of the way against a wall.

"You are always in such a muddle, Tia-Ha," Tiye said, sinking onto the pillows and settling back. "You have more servants than anyone else in the harem, yet your visitors can hardly get through the door."

"I am not well organized," Tia-Ha answered, waving the girl out. "I promise myself that I will become neater, and I dictate long lists of things to be done, but before my servants can carry out the instructions, someone brings me a new board game to try, or I receive an invitation to a party and must make myself beautiful, and my women and I end up playing together or dabbling with cosmetics." She lowered herself onto a chair facing Tiye, kicking aside the gowns that littered the floor. "Today is a good example," she went on. "I decide to get rid of my old gowns, give them to my servants, and what happens? Scarcely have we begun when the empress comes to see me! It is of course my greatest pleasure to gossip with you, dear Tiye. You are looking well. So is Pharaoh, if I may say so."

"Yes, I suppose he is," Tiye replied noncommittally, her eyes on Tia-Ha's sandaled feet. "Tell me, Princess, have you by chance been across the river to see the sanctuary of Amunhotep's Aten temple? It will soon be finished and closed to the populace."

Tia-Ha laughed. Swinging her legs up onto the couch, she shrugged deep into the cushions and began to pull the rings from her plump fingers, dropping them one by one with a tinkle into a glass bowl on the floor. "By chance, Majesty? When the courtiers in their hundreds have been trotting like sheep into their barges to be poled across the river solely to look at their naked pharaoh in stone? No, not by chance. I, too, followed my curiosity and went to see what all the fuss was about." The last ring rattled into the bowl, and Tia-Ha began to massage her knuckles.

"And what did you think?"

"I was prepared to see some grave violation of Ma'at," Tia-Ha explained, "but the images offend only my concept of good taste. Why, Majesty, you are upset!"

Tiye had transferred her gaze to her own hands clasped in her lap. "Art is a sacred pursuit," she said faintly. "A king may not cause his true physical likeness to be copied. Any statue or painting is to represent only the king as Divine Incarnation, without human flaws."

"But Pharaoh's predecessor did it. Do you remember the

delight our husband took in unveiling that little stela that showed him slumped on a chair with his body wrapped in thin feminine linen?"

Tiye's heart lightened. She smiled gratefully at the princess. "I remember. But that stela stands in the palace. Temple art is different."

"Not very. Besides, there is no god in Pharaoh's new temple to see his body, so what does it matter? Shall we have some shat cakes?" Tiye nodded. Tia-Ha clapped sharply, and a servant appeared immediately, listened to her order, and went away. "What amuses me is the way the courtiers are rushing to have themselves portrayed as little copies of your husband. In the Teaching, he tells them that Ra has given him a unique body as a mark of especial favor, so they hurry to their craftsmen with instructions to cover the walls of their houses and tombs with distorted images of themselves. If there is benevolent magic in such ugliness, they want to share it. But how on earth the gods are expected to recognize the overseers, stewards, generals, and commanders from such grotesqueness, I do not know! Even the two mighty viziers are slavishly following the fashion. Everyone wants to ingratiate themselves with Pharaoh. That is the way it has always been."

"So you believe it is all a fashionable diversion and will pass?" Tia-Ha's servant had returned with a dish of shat cakes, and Tiye, suddenly hungry, took two.

"Of course I do." Tia-Ha was hesitating over her choice of the sweet concoctions, her head on one side. "Now, with Your Majesty's permission, I would like to change the subject." She darted a shrewd glance at Tiye and began an involved account of the boating party she had attended the evening before, and soon Tiye was laughing as she ate, her misgivings forgotten for a while.

In the middle of the season of Akhet, as the river was rising and the air was relieved by a slight cooling, Tiye gave birth, with difficulty, to a girl. She had successfully hidden a fear for her life that had increased with the swelling of her body, knowing that in the veiled glances of the courtiers was an expectation of punishment for her flaunting of a forbidden relationship. In the face of Pharaoh's disapproval she had set statues of Ta-Urt, goddess of the childbed, about her chambers, and when her labor began, she had ordered magicians into her bedchamber with amulets and chanted spells. Their voices and her groans were the only sounds in the crowded room, for the few courtiers who were privileged to watch a royal birth only looked on in an anticipatory silence. Defenseless and drowned in pain, Tiye felt their hostility. There were no murmurs when the birth was announced, and the small audience filed out in the same accusatory silence in which they had stood. Amunhotep held the child proudly to his shallow chest.

"Sister-Daughter," he said, looking down on the tiny, sleeping face, "you, above all, are the proof of my piety. I shall call you Beketaten, Servant of the Aten. And you, Tiye, most favored Great Lady, your fears were ungrounded."

Tiye half-opened eyes that felt weighted with every year she had lived. Her husband stood beside the couch, a blurred, stooping figure, his bag wig hanging loosely over his bony shoulders. She murmured but did not have the strength to make a coherent reply. Yet some fleeting impression had impinged itself upon her consciousness, and though sleep prowled the fringes of her mind, she held it at bay, searching hazily. She heard Amunhotep give the baby to the nurse, exchange words with her, and pad to the door. She felt the physician's hand on her forehead. The doors opened, Ay's voice asked a question, the doors closed. It had something to do with the baby held against her husband's chest. No, not the baby, the chest itself. The pectoral. Electrum, no jewels, just fine-linked chain holding . . . A stab of foreboding slashed through her drowsiness. Holding the Aten, symbol of Ra-Harakhti of the Horizon, but it was not right. Where was the falcon-headed god? Only the disk remained, circled by royal uraei and sun rays ending in hands. Ankhs hung from the Aten's neck. *I must tell Ay,* she thought dimly. *What does it mean?* But before she could think about the matter, she fell asleep.

11

THE YEAR THAT FOLLOWED WAS OUTWARDLY A TIME OF OP-
timism. In the harem nurseries the royal children throve. Some
weeks after Tiye, Nefertiti also gave birth to a girl, and
Amunhotep named her Meketaten, Protected by the Aten. It
did not seem to worry him that as yet he had fathered no royal
son. Nefertiti recovered quickly, buoyed by the relief she felt
that Tiye also had produced a girl and there would be no
precipitate scrambling to name an heir. But Tiye's body knitted
slowly, and through the weeks of the Inundation she rested,
conducting what business was necessary from her couch, content to drift in a somnolent placidity. Perhaps that was why she
felt more affection for the baby Beketaten than she had for any
other of her children save her first son, Thothmes. The love
she had felt for Amunhotep as a child was a fierce, irrational
protectiveness in the face of his mortal danger, but as she
fondled and watched Beketaten, her strength growing slowly
with the baby's own growth, a genuine bond was forged. She
did not peer coolly into her daughter's future as a consort for
her son Smenkhara. She held the tiny sleeping weight against
her own warm body, and the present was enough.

Smenkhara himself was now almost four, a quiet little boy
given to bursts of volubility, with the natural grace of his dead
brother Thothmes. He began his official schooling in the harem
under the watchful eyes of Huya, an event that caused him
distress, for Meritaten was still only two, too young for education, and the two had become inseparable. She was a tiny,
doll-like child with Nefertiti's gray eyes and her father's aquiline nose, a creature that belonged to the fluttering soft linens,
the jewels, the ribbons and perfumes with which she was surrounded. She would stand outside the schoolroom where
Smenkhara and the young children of Pharaoh's ministers droned
their lessons, her gray eyes fixed with a serious patience on
the door, ignoring the sighs and shufflings of her attendants.

When she heard the prayer to Amun and the brief chant to the Aten which signaled the end of classes for the day, her fragile body would tense in anticipation until Smenkhara emerged. Shaking himself free of the excited horde of shouting boys, he would run to her to receive with the calm assurance of undoubted affection whatever she had brought—a flower, a glittering dead scarab beetle, a piece of broken pottery. They held no long conversations through the hot afternoons but would play at whatever took their fancy in a separate but completely companionable silence.

Nefertiti was pleased with the harmony between them, seeing it as a basis for future negotiations, but Tiye simply listened to the daily reports from the schoolroom and nursery and stored the information in the back of her mind. Love had nothing to do with dynastic necessity.

Tiye herself sat easily on the pinnacle of power during this year, secure in Amunhotep's continued affection. Nefertiti's jealousy appeared to subside to a sullen smolder, dampened not only by the fact that they had both produced girls but also by the recurrence of Pharaoh's impotence. If he was unable to make love to her, she also knew from her spies in Tiye's apartments that he did not bed Tiye either. The fire that consumed him was the invisible flame of religious fervor.

Amunhotep often prowled his still-unfinished temple, watching his artists chisel the Aten's name enclosed in the cartouches of a reigning monarch under the new symbol he had adopted for it. Long into the nights he prayed in his brightly illumined bedchamber, standing before the Aten shrine in the pleated female gowns he had begun to wear, golden incense holders smoking in both hands. To the crowds who filled the audience halls to hear his Teaching he often shouted, his shrill voice rising as he leaned over them from the throne on the dais, the sweat of his enthusiasm staining the gown that folded over his painted feet. After the Teaching he would retire to his couch and fall into a deep, exhausted sleep while the listeners dispersed, some hurrying to more congenial pursuits but an increasing number drifting slowly onto the forecourt or into the gardens, arguing furiously. Under the regal panoply of daily government, the palace was charged with petty animosities, and at its center Pharaoh walked with his attendant monkeys, a gowned and moving reflection of the grotesque representations of himself that had begun to adorn Malkatta's richly painted walls. As the atmosphere at court became testier, Tiye took refuge in the voluminous foreign correspondence that never seemed to decrease, and spent much time with courtiers of her own generation who could share her memories of her first husband.

One day Tiye was passing with her servants and bodyguard along the road that led from Amunhotep III's funerary temple to Malkatta. She had been offering sacrifices to her dead husband, bringing food and flowers to lay at the feet of his likeness while she whispered prayers for the well-being of his ka. It was a rite she liked to perform, for with the closing of the sanctuary doors behind her she was transported back through the years. Amunhotep's mocking, warm personality seemed to fill the vast, pillared room, bringing to her a feeling of security. In the presence of her son, in his arms, she was always uneasy with the dread of some future judgment against her despite her acknowledged divinity and sometimes longed for the turbulent though uncomplicated relationship she had shared with his father. A faint echo of it existed here, in the temple built for his worshipers, and Tiye sipped at it judiciously. She knew better than to indulge in fanciful longings for what was past but took comfort from it nonetheless.

The party had reached the bisecting path that was traveled by an increasing stream of supplicants on their way to the temple of the Son of Hapu. Where the temple itself cast a deep shade across the road, she suddenly heard curses being shouted, and the grunts of angry men. Curious, she raised the curtain of the litter and ordered the bearers to halt. She was about to send a Follower to investigate when there was an abrupt silence, followed by an agonized scream, and a man burst upon the cavalcade. He stopped, terror leaping into his eyes as he saw royalty on the otherwise deserted road, hesitated, and then turned to run. Tiye nodded at her captain, and he and several other soldiers raced after the man, disappearing around the corner of the temple. Sun beat up from the dust of the road, and Tiye heard her bearers passing the water jug between them. The soldiers left behind shuffled uneasily until the captain and his men reappeared, the fugitive held firmly in their midst. Two of them were carrying a second man, and even from a distance Tiye could tell from the limp limbs, the lolling head, that this man was dead. Her soldiers moved to surround her as she stepped from the litter, and servants unfolded her canopy. From its shade she watched as the body was laid on the road.

"He is not long dead, Majesty," the captain said. "The blood still flows."

Tiye glanced at the battered head, the shaven skull smeared with dark blood, the smashed lips, the bruises on the neck. She looked away. The other man, panting and perspiring, was also badly bruised. His white linen hung in tatters, but the blood splashed on his arms and smearing one cheek was not his. As he saw her gaze swivel to him, he gave an inarticulate cry and tried to prostrate himself, struggling to free his arms from the burly Followers on either side. It was then that Tiye noticed his armbands, emblazoned with the Aten's glyph. Startled, she looked at the corpse. Its armbands were etched with Amun's double plumes.

"It is not possible!" she almost shouted. "Stand straight, priest. What is this?"

He struggled to speak, his eyes on the blood pooling on the road, already sinking into the dust. Flies had begun to gather, buzzing greedily around the battered head, and a soldier pulled his fly whisk from his belt and beat them away.

"Pity, Majesty," the man croaked, swallowing convulsively. "I did not mean to kill him. We met on the road, and I was hot and thirsty. He had water and bread. We stopped to talk. He shared his food with me, and when we had finished, we should have parted but..." He closed his eyes. Tiye waited impassively. "We began to talk and then to argue. He flung the water carrier at me, and rage coursed through me. I hit him. We fought. I had him on the ground, but he struggled and cursed me. I picked up a rock and..."

Contemptuously Tiye waved him to silence and turned to her captain. "Take him to the palace cells and guard him. Pharaoh must judge this. Deliver the corpse to Ptahhotep. Priests fighting. I cannot believe it!" She swung to the litter. Before she twitched the curtains shut, she caught a trace of the odor of new blood, and from nowhere a vulture had appeared, circling clumsily but with chilling tenacity.

Once returned to the palace, she went straight to her son. He was stepping from his bathing slab, arms outstretched so that his body servant could dry him, and he welcomed her with his usual winsome smile.

"It will be a good feast tonight, Tiye. Pupri and Puzzi will be relieved to be returning to Mitanni after so long."

For once she had no interest in the machinations that had kept the Mitanni ambassadors in Egypt since Osiris Amunhotep's funeral. Quickly and tersely she told him what had happened on the road, watching his face for any reaction, but he only listened with mild warmth in his large brown eyes. When she had finished, he ushered her into his bedchamber, standing while red linen was draped around him, fingering the thin cloth admiringly. He sat to have the soles of his feet painted red, and finally sighed gently.

"I will speak with the Aten priest," he said. "They still have so much to learn. The Aten does not need a violent defense. It is a life-giver. Do you like these bracelets, dear mother? Kenofer presented them to me."

She ignored the outstretched, painted palms from which gold spilled. Going to his chair, she squatted, looking up into his face. "Amunhotep, a man has died, and not just any man. A priest of Amun has been carried to the House of the Dead, slain by the sun men. If his murderer is not executed, you will be condoning a violent resolution to all the silly squabbling that is going on, as well as showing favoritism to the Aten."

He raised both plucked eyebrows and smiled. "You are skilled in matters of state, my Tiye, and I seldom argue with your decisions. But since I commune directly with the god, I am better equipped to deal with matters of religion than any man." The body servant juggled the gold bracelets over his long fingers. "The priest was misguided in his zeal, that is all. I will warn him and release him."

"If you do so, the Amun priests will go in fear of their lives! They will be bitter and resentful."

"But their god will protect them."

She could not tell whether under his benign tone she heard a true naïveté or sarcasm.

"If you let him go, will you at least appear at Karnak for several days afterward to perform the mourning rites in person?"

"I do not think so." Politely he turned away to face his mirror, and she rose to her feet. His cosmetician dabbled a brush into the blue eye paint. "I have no quarrel with Amun; and it is only a matter of time before the Aten priests see that there is no real threat in his insignificance. Then both factions will withdraw, and there will be peace."

She argued no further. Kissing him on his smooth brow as though he were a prattling child, she left him, taking a litter to her brother's house through the warm twilight.

Ay was drinking wine in his garden with a few of his officers. Behind them the first lamplight gleamed out through the little frontal pillars, and the laughter and movement of his servants and concubines mingled with the rich odors of hot food. Ay's baboons lay in the dark grass, clustered together and grunting softly. Night already hung thick in the trees that sheltered the garden from the river, but between their trunks the serrated gray line of the little water steps could still be glimpsed. Conversation died away as Tiye's herald called her titles, and the men prostrated themselves. Bidding them rise, she motioned for Ay to accompany her, and together they strolled past the placid animals along the path that led to the quiet water.

"Pharaoh is to release a priest held in the palace cells," she told him. "I want him killed. See that it is done quietly but make certain that the body can be easily found and that the badges of his priestly rank are left on him."

Ay nodded. "Very well. Do you wish to tell me why?"

When she had finished speaking, he drew her in under the rustling sycamores. Now the river was visible, a silver ribbon with the new stars pricked out on its surface. Ay's barge was a dark bulk tethered to the steps, and the footfalls of the servants who patrolled the perimeters of his home grew and faded. It was a peaceful night. Thebes was no more than a fitful mutter on the other bank.

"If this religious fanaticism spills over into the palace, we could be facing a very serious situation," he said. "I can't believe that Pharaoh is blind to the possibility. Is he hoping for this to happen?"

"I do not know. Sometimes it seems a small matter to me, a game we allow him to play to keep him occupied, but then I look back and see just how much things have changed, how turbulent life at court has become. I did not ever think that I would have to try to influence him in matters other than those of government, and I fear my influence is not enough."

"What would happen if you simply told those responsible for this priest's fate to disregard Pharaoh's order, and issued one of your own?" His face hovered, pale and indistinct, opposite her own. His wine-scented breath was warm.

"I am afraid to consider. Pharaoh's word is law. Often his word is really that of his advisors or myself, though it comes from his mouth, but either way it is just as sacred. If he then reversed *my* order, my power would be diminished."

Ay laughed, a short, harsh bark. "It is as foolishly intriguing as a Dogs and Jackals game. He is Pharaoh, but you are still ruler of Egypt, and Nefertiti keeps the family's fortunes high. Our blood becomes less foreign and more royal. If Amunhotep's reign continues to be one religious crisis after another, the Amun oracle will be only too happy to appoint an heir that we suggest to him. We still occupy a position of great strength, Tiye."

"What you say is true, but under the rock is sand. And it is shifting. At the moment the balance between Amun's and Aten's adherents at court is even, but what if Amun's worshipers dwindle?"

"What worshipers? Only the priests are true worshipers. I will do as you ask, Empress. Stop fretting."

But power rests in continual fretting, she thought as she felt his reassuring hand descend on her shoulder, *in worrying about the past intruding on the present, present decisions stretching into an unknown future*. "Your officers will be ready to dine, and I am already late for Pharaoh's feast," she said, laying her cheek briefly against his hand and stepping away. "Bring me word when it is carried out. Have you received any word from Tey lately?"

They walked back toward the torches which now flared over the garden, talking of small family matters, and Tiye left Ay to his guests. A burst of hearty masculine laughter followed her through the gate, warming the empty reaches of the moonlit path that crunched under her litter bearers' feet, and a fit of loneliness swept over her. She would rather be sharing food in the informality of Ay's garden than be sitting beside Pharaoh under the gilded baldachin, with the heavy disk and plumes on her head.

The priest's body was discovered out on the desert behind the western cliffs, close to a winding path used by nomad caravans. The man had been stabbed cleanly, through the heart, but the weapon had been removed. By the time he was found, he had already begun to wither, his juices sucked up by the sand and the moisture-hungry air, and the Aten armbands rested loosely on his upper arms. Relief and a new reverence for the empress swept through Karnak. The story of the two priests' quarrel and the murder of the Amun man had spread rapidly. Karnak seethed with indignation and apprehension, not only in Amun's temple complex but also in the cells of those who served Amun's consort, Mut, and his son, Khonsu. Murder was a frightening escalation in the rivalry between the Aten and the gods of Thebes. Some priests angrily demanded weapons from Ptahhotep, arguing that they had a right to defend themselves, but the majority limited their anxiety to long discussions in their cells and would no longer go about Karnak and the city alone. Ptahhotep knew that any violent response from the priests under him would lift the feud into a far more serious arena, where the consequences for Egypt could be disastrous. He strictly forbade retaliation of any kind, while wondering what course to follow. He saw Pharaoh's hand in the releasing of the Aten priest from prison without an interrogation and was enraged, but when the man's body was discovered the next day, his rage turned to gratitude, for he recognized the empress's summary justice in the act.

The courtiers likewise saw the hand of their empress in choosing a simple solution to a problem that was becoming more complex every day. They admired her facility for acting in such a way that Pharaoh suffered no loss of face. They had viewed the animosity between both gods' factions with alarm because it threatened to disrupt their otherwise comfortable lives, and they knew that Tiye had given them a reprieve. They waited to see what Pharaoh would do and, when he did nothing, forgot the incident.

But in the privacy of his bedchamber Nefertiti raged to her husband. "Who is Pharaoh, she or you?" she demanded, pacing the room as he lay on his couch and watched her. "I told you, Horus, that her interest in the Aten was a sham, and now she has proved it. She has killed a priest. How often have you said that the god is kind and gentle and needs no weapons? She uses you!"

"That may be," he responded mildly, "but she is my empress. I am indulgent toward her lack of understanding."

"Your indulgence is seen as weakness in the palace! Discipline her, Mighty Bull! Call her to public reprimand."

"It cannot be proved that she was responsible for the priest's death. It could have been brought about by Amun's men."

Nefertiti's delicate red lip curled, and she strode to the couch. "Even if she is not guilty, she goes about the palace as though an invisible Double Crown sat upon her head. Surely it is time to take the government from her hands. There is no longer any need for a regent. You appointed her as such because you were ignorant of the workings of power. That was nearly four years ago. I have worked with her. I can help you."

"And what would you have me do with Tiye?"

It was on the tip of Nefertiti's tongue to say "Kill her," but she restrained herself. "Retire her to Akhmin, or if that is too close, to her estates at Djarukha. She is too old to learn of new things, and in her heart Amun will always reign supreme. As long as she is seen at court, there will be trouble between the old and the new." She had perched beside him and was interspersing her words with light kisses on his eyes, his cheeks, the softness of his full mouth, but he drew away unmoved.

"I love her," he said simply.

The anger that had been dying in Nefertiti revived. "Do you not love me also?"

He placed a fraternal arm around her stiff shoulders. "You know that I do."

"But not the way you are thralled by Tiye," she said bitterly. Words were ready to tumble into the dusky stillness of the room. *She is aging, she is not as beautiful as I and her ripeness is fading, she is your own mother and Egypt is still unquiet with the fear that the gods will punish, she is ugly and wily . . .* With difficulty she forced them back. "I am your humble servant," she said huskily. "But, Amunhotep, the time will come when you wish to rule actively, and it will be too late."

He kept silent. Later they played sennet, and Nefertiti, her outburst forgotten, sang with him as he played his lute, turning upon him the full light of her loveliness, teasing and laughing with him. But as so often happened after one of their arguments over Tiye, he was unable to respond. Nefertiti was not disappointed. She knew by now that his periodic impotence was a sign that her attacks on the empress had found their target. She was content.

Tiye herself had hoped that her order for the unofficial execution of the Aten priest would result in the lessening of religious tension for a while, so she was dismayed when, several days later, she saw Ptahhotep at the rear of the hall of public audience, obviously waiting his turn to approach Amunhotep. Usually the throne to Tiye's left remained vacant, for Pharaoh seldom bothered with his ministers' complaints, but today he had taken his place directly as divine arbiter. Nefertiti sat on a cushioned stool at his feet, and the Keeper of the Royal Regalia was kneeling before him, cradling the chest containing the scimitar. The crook and flail rested loosely in his lap. He had come late to the hour of audience, trailing up to the dais with Nefertiti on his arm, but to Tiye's relief he had offered no comments on the cases she was settling, only listening attentively and nodding occasionally as she spoke. The high priest was the last. Tiye watched him come striding forward, leopard skin flung across one shoulder, his staff bearer and acolyte to either side. The prostrations were made, and Tiye bade him speak. The scribes raised their pens in anticipation. Ptahhotep was doing his best to hide embarrassment and apprehension under the cloaks of dignity and authority.

"Goddess, pardon my effrontery, but this matter concerns Pharaoh alone," he said to her, and turning to Amunhotep, he went on, "Mighty Horus, it is your prerogative alone to appoint or dismiss the First Prophet of Amun. I have served in that capacity at Karnak for over twenty years, obeying the god, the oracle of the god, and my king. The Anniversary of Appearings has come and gone four times, yet he has neither appointed a new high priest nor confirmed me in that position. I humbly beg Pharaoh today to do one or the other."

Tiye had forgotten this ancient kingly privilege. Out of the corner of her eye she saw her son's face begin to cloud with indecision, and she leaned toward him. "What do you want to do?" she whispered. "Shall I advise?" He nodded eagerly. "You understand of course," she went on in a low voice, "that if you confirm Ptahhotep in his position, you are also confirming an unresolved situation at Karnak. He is of the old order. The Aten threatens him, and he does not know what to do about it. If you let him continue as high priest, you will be telling both court and temple that in spite of all the trouble your actions have brought to Malkatta, you support Amun in the manner of your father. The Amun priests will have their confidence renewed. But I think Ptahhotep is asking to be relieved of his duties. He wishes to retire with dignity before circumstances move out of his control and result in his humiliation. Do you understand?" He was frowning in concentration, and she saw him tentatively lick his red lips. Nefertiti was openly hanging on every word, her eyes going from one to the other.

"I think I do," Amunhotep whispered back.

"Good," Tiye said. "Then let him go. My advice is to promote Si-Mut, Second Prophet of Amun, to the position of high priest as a show of willingness on your part to recognize Amun's ongoing power, but also as a sign to the Aten men that you have been unhappy with Karnak's bickering and expect a return to harmony and cooperation between the two gods under a younger, more pliable man."

Ptahhotep was standing patiently with head bowed, and the scribes were waiting to record the judgment, their eyes on Amunhotep. Tiye sat back and smiled encouragingly at Amunhotep and was relieved when she saw him begin to raise the crook and flail to announce his decision, but before he could rise, Nefertiti touched his knee and mounted the steps. She put her lips to his ear and began to murmur, but Tiye interrupted sharply, "This is the place of public audience, Majesty, not your bedchamber, and as empress I am entitled to hear any comments on this matter you may wish to make."

"That is true, dearest," Amunhotep reminded her. "I would be very pleased to hear your opinion, and I am sure Tiye is interested also. Speak out."

Tiye waited, eyebrows raised condescendingly, and after a moment of discomfiture Nefertiti put a hand on Pharaoh's arm. "Si-Mut is certainly pliable, my husband," she said quickly, "but it is to the empress that he bends. If you appoint him, the Aten will never reign supreme. This is your chance to have a high priest who not only worships you but acknowledges the universal power of the Aten also. With such a man ruling the House of Amun you can make what changes you like at Karnak, stop the priests from harassing and sneering at the Aten's servants."

"Really, Majesty," Tiye cut in coldly. "Any man who acknowledges the Aten as his sole god belongs in the temples of On, not ruling over the fortunes of Amun. The staff of Amun's temple would not submit to such a one even for a day but would come running to Pharaoh demanding a new appointee. If you have had your say, perhaps Pharaoh would render his decision and let us all retire for the afternoon."

Her mocking tone brought a gleam of anger to Nefertiti's eyes. "I am not as foolish as you imagine, Empress," she responded loudly. "Of course Pharaoh's choice should please both sides," she went on, turning to Amunhotep. "Consider Maya, Amun's Fourth Prophet. He often comes to the Teaching. He is young and adores you. He would not stubbornly insist on defending Amun at every turn and obstructing your desires for Karnak. Choose him!"

"I have not had time to consider this carefully," Amunhotep interposed, looking miserably at Tiye. "How can I choose?"

"Trust me, my son," she answered smoothly, confident that as always he would do as she wished. "I have never advised you rashly. Nefertiti is making the situation more complicated than is necessary."

He pulled his arm from Nefertiti's grip. "I wish I had not come to the audience today," he muttered. "Give me a moment."

His chin sank into his palm. Tiye waited, outwardly immobile but inwardly fuming at Nefertiti's unwarranted intrusion. *Amunhotep will, of course, take my advice*, she thought, watching the impatient shufflings and aimless glances of the courtiers. *It was naïve of Nefertiti to think that she would do anything other than confuse him.*

Moments passed, and finally Amunhotep looked up. "I approve of your idea, Nefertiti," he said with a sidelong glance at Tiye. Then he rose, and lifting the crook and flail high over Ptahhotep's head, he called, "We recognize the loyalty and service of the high priest of Amun. Let him retire with honor. The leopard skin shall pass to Maya, most blessed and fortunate servant of his lord." Relief washed over Ptahhotep's face, and Tiye saw that she had been right. A buzz of conversation broke out. Amunhotep sank back on the throne, mopping the perspiration that had broken out along his upper lip, and waved Ptahhotep away. Tiye rose stiffly, and without deigning to notice Nefertiti she said to her son, "This decision was yours alone, and I will honor it. But I believe it showed a lack of good judgment." Turning, she stalked down the steps, removed her crown, and handing it to its keeper, she left the hall.

Nefertiti accompanied her husband through the rest of the day's activities, basking in a glow of triumph. It was her first public victory over the empress, all the sweeter for having been unplanned. Tiye did not appear at the evening meal, and Nefertiti presided on the dais beside Amunhotep, animated and sparkling, her witty sallies drawing laughter from the guests privileged to be seated close to the dais. She did her best to coax a smile or a little conversation from Pharaoh, but he refused to be drawn, sitting with eyes downcast to an empty platter. Occasionally, he would mutter, and Nefertiti would turn to him immediately, only to realize that he was not addressing her at all. He was drinking steadily, holding up his cup to be refilled while his gaze remained on the table. After a while, impatient and annoyed, Nefertiti ignored him, talking across him to Tadukhipa or down to the guests, and he went on sipping the red wine and whispering to himself. Now and then he shuddered and reached for a cloth to wipe his neck, and Nefertiti became convinced that he was drunk. None of the feasters paid him the slightest attention until the entertainers had performed and it was time to leave. Then the crowd became restless, waiting for him to receive their reverences and give his permission for them to retire. In the end Nefertiti had to put her ear close to his face and pretend to be listening. Rising, she told the assembly they could make an obeisance and go. The sound of their departure seemed to rouse Amunhotep, and sluggishly he pushed back his chair, drained the last of the wine in his cup, and lurched through the rear doors without even looking at her.

But his strange behavior could not dampen her spirits. It was a long time before she was ready for sleep. Ordering musicians into her bedchamber, she listened to some peasant songs, humming the melodies with the singer, and when they had finished, she had her scribe recite love poems. Before going to her couch she stood at the window dreaming with arms folded, scarcely aware of the gentle night sounds coming faintly from the garden below. She was reluctant to see the day end but finally sought her couch, sighing with contentment as her tiring maid drew the sheet over her and vanished to her mat in the corner.

It seemed to her that she had been asleep for only moments when the sound of feet in the passage beyond her door brought her awake. Drowsily she lifted her head to listen. The first faint light of dawn showed her the servant also stirring, uncurling from her mat and rising to investigate. The girl had taken three uncertain steps when the door was flung open and

Pharaoh staggered into the room. Nefertiti watched, wide-eyed, as he rushed at the servant and with a blow toppled her into the passage, slamming the door shut behind her. He was naked. "Amunhotep, what is wrong?" she cried, struggling to sit up, but before she could fling back the sheet, he had fallen toward the couch and was tearing the linen from her grasp. She was too shocked to resist. Sinking back onto the cushions, she felt her legs pushed apart, and he forced himself into her, breathing harshly, while she lay trying to collect her wits.

There was a discreet tapping on the door, and Amunhotep shouted, "Go away!" He began to mutter, disjointed, incoherent sentences that were unintelligible to her as he moved, until with a strangled gasp he rolled to lie beside her, knees drawn up to chin. He was trembling. "Bring me water."

Wide awake now, Nefertiti slid from the couch and poured from the jug to her hand. Propping himself on one elbow, he drank, demanded more, then slumped back onto the pillows. "I have had a dream, Nefertiti, oh, such a dream," he whispered. "I hope you are not alarmed."

I am more than alarmed, she thought, watching his limbs shake with spasmodic tremors. *I am terrified.* She willed herself to take a corner of the sheet and wipe his face, half-turning to the door to shout for help, but he caught her wrist.

"In a moment. You can tell them soon, call all of them, tell them . . ." He began to laugh. "Sit here beside me." He pulled her down and released her, and Nefertiti quickly wrapped the rumpled linen around her, suddenly unwilling that he should see her naked.

"Was it a nightmare?" she asked, forcing a soothing tone. Her fear began to subside as the shudders jerking his body lessened in violence and his speech became less slurred.

His head rolled on the pillow. "No, not a nightmare—I have had a vision. I have been in the Duat, I have ridden in the night barque, the Mesektet boat, with the gods and the Osiris kings!" His voice rose, and she saw him swallow, fighting to control it. "I heard the dead weeping for light as I passed through all the Twelve Houses of Darkness, through the twelve transformings of Ra, and I was able to give them what they desired!"

"You dreamed you were in the underworld with Ra?" she said, puzzled.

Amunhotep sat up and, clasping his arms around his sweat-slicked chest, began to rock to and fro. "It was no dream, I know it. I entered the mouth of Nut at sunset as Flesh, the Ra-to-be-eaten, and I stood in the barque through all the attacks of the serpent Apophis, but that is not the greatest thing." He closed his eyes. "Ra had to take me through the Duat to make me understand. I am not Ra's incarnation, Nefertiti, I am the Aten himself. It was at the twelfth transforming of Ra that I felt myself born."

She looked in disbelief at the ecstasy on his face, wondering if he had become insane. "It was only a dream, my husband," she insisted, and at this his eyes flew open, fixing her with an intense stare.

"It was the greatest vision of my life," he corrected her. "Now my true nature has been revealed to me. As I was being expelled from the womb of Nut at dawn, I looked back expecting to see her face peering down, but I saw myself. Nefertiti, I saw myself!" He stood and began to stumble back and forth before her, fists clenched with excitement, feverishly restless. "I am so happy. At last I have been able to make you a goddess. The power no longer seeps from me when I make love to you, it is refreshed, renewed, for I am the source of all light and life!"

Nefertiti, her composure restored, began to think. He had come to her first, instinctively; he had poured out his new truth to her, not to the empress. "Is that why you are here, Pharaoh, and not in Tiye's apartments?" she queried shrewdly.

He swung round and came up to her. "Yes, yes. The god guided my steps, for now, I believe, I no longer need my mother to replenish my power. I love her, but the demons are finally vanquished. The coupling of my body with hers is no longer necessary. I am immortal."

Nefertiti smiled soothingly. "Rest now," she said. Going to the doors, she flung them open. A little group was huddled worriedly beyond. "Parennefer." She beckoned Pharaoh's butler forward. "Bring a headcloth and clean linens for your master, and some food. Ra has been pleased to give Pharaoh a great vision this night," she said to all of them. "Pharaoh is naturally exhausted, but there is no cause for alarm." Firmly she closed the doors on them. When she returned to the couch, Amunhotep was asleep, lying motionless and utterly silent. Nefertiti sat in the chair nearby and watched him.

12

WITHIN DAYS GARBLED ACCOUNTS OF PHARAOH'S VISION WERE circulating at Malkatta, passing from one courtier to another. The news was treated as deserving more attention than a piece of current gossip, however, for it was already clear that life at court was going to be divided into the time before the vision and the time after it. Pharaoh had changed. Overnight he seemed to lose the vague charm that had endeared him to some and had caused others to regard him with condescension. His orders came clearer. Topics of conversation other than religion lost interest for him. His demeanor was less mild, reflected in his straighter stance and more definite gestures. A few ministers saw this as evidence of new strength and rejoiced in the prospect of a Pharaoh with determination at last, but the majority cast downward, wary glances his way and whispered among themselves. For not only had Amunhotep decreed that he was to be approached henceforth on bended knee—a degree of reverence that even the most respectful had never before seen in Egypt— but after the night of the vision he refused admission to every Amun priest who requested an audience with him.

Tiye did not appreciate the gravity of the change in her son until she tried to confront him over the matter of the new form of obeisance. She knew that he was once again potent but would summon only Nefertiti or Kia to his bed. Firmly she pushed away the niggles of jealousy, convinced that her mercurial son would eventually tire of them and come creeping back to her at some unexpected moment. She knew she could not press openly for her conjugal rights. She had long since accepted the price she had paid for retaining the disk and plumes, a price that seemed to grow with the years, setting her apart from many at court who believed that her behavior would eventually bring a curse on the royal house. She knew also that the fellahin in the fields and the peasants and tradesmen in the cities spoke of her with increasingly open contempt. She told herself that she did not care. They were, after all, only Pharaoh's cattle to be used and herded and used again, a faceless mob without understanding. The love of her son and the freedom to rule were compensation enough. The loss of either never crossed her mind until she requested audience with Pharaoh and met an embarrassed Overseer of Protocol outside the reception hall.

"Great Goddess and Majesty," he said, eyes averted, "I must remind you that according to Pharaoh's latest pronouncement, all must go to him on their knees."

"The Empress of Egypt can hardly be included among 'all,'" she pointed out dryly. "Herald, announce me." The Overseer of Protocol retired, crimson-faced, and Tiye swept past him into the hall before the herald's last words had ceased to echo. Her son was on his throne, stiff with paint and jewels, regalia held across his chest, the Double Crown on his head. In spite of the formality of the audience hour, a time he usually regarded with bored distaste, he was wearing only a diaphanous red gown tied beneath his yellow-painted nipples. Tiye came to a halt and bowed as she always had.

He immediately turned his attention to her, beaming. "Speak, Mother," he said.

She did not return his smile. "Amunhotep," she said coolly. "It is time to cease the game of strange reverence you have been playing. It slows the performance of the court, and it is becoming painful for those who are in and out of your presence continually."

He shifted on the throne with a trace of his former insecurity, and an expression of doubt flitted across his face. "It is not a game, Empress, and you might make me angry if you call it so. How else should mere humans approach their creator?"

She opened her mouth to laugh until she saw his expression. "But, my son, surely you do not believe . . ." She flung up her hands. "Even if you do, let the edict be lifted from those in attendance on Nefertiti. She is becoming insufferable."

Again he had the grace to look fleetingly ashamed. "You have my permission to order those around you to do the same if you wish," he offered eagerly.

Tiye snorted in disgust, her dignity rapidly deserting her. "When will you learn that power does not reside in an outward show!" she said loudly. "If my ministers began crawling toward me like beasts, I would be tempted to kick them, not consult with them!"

"Do not speak to your pharaoh in that manner!" he shouted immediately, and apprehension rose in Tiye as she saw that he had begun to shake. "You are my mother, but..." His last words had tumbled out, breathless, and his voice ended on a shrill note.

"But what?" She kept her voice soothingly even. "Did the god tell you that you could make men crawl about the palace floors on all fours?" He did not deign, or did not trust himself, to answer. "Maya has been trying to obtain an audience with you for days," she went on. "He wishes to make his report on matters at Karnak. Will you not see him?"

Amunhotep began to breathe deeply. He met her eye, looked down, struggled with himself, and then, raising his head, burst out, "Maya now belongs to Amun! I will never receive the priests of Amun again. I have sworn."

"I have sworn," Tiye mimicked him, furious. "You are dividing Egypt in two, do you realize that? I gave you the throne, and I can take it away from you. I have made you what you are!"

"You are angry because I no longer summon you to my bed," he retorted shortly, gripping the crook and flail until his knuckles gleamed white. "Be thankful that you are my mother, and that the Aten is indulgent toward you. And you did not make me," he ended, his petulance destroying the impression of force he had given. "I am the Aten. I made myself."

Tiye swung on her heel, aware now of the silent, kneeling men who had been listening to every word. The scratching of the scribe's stylus could be heard against the curling papyrus. Although she walked calmly to the door and the soldiers sprang to open it for her, she felt bowed with humiliation. *I handled that like a foolish junior minister*, she thought. *It will not happen again.*

She did her best to calm anxieties at Karnak, forcing herself to meet Maya's bewildered gaze as she told him that the god who had elevated him to the most powerful priestly position in Egypt would not receive him. But she could do little to stem the turbulence brewing in Malkatta. Thousands of courtiers were forgetting their indifference and were flocking to take sides as they perceived that she was beginning to fall from favor. Many continued to voice their allegiance to her as empress, believing that the power that had kept Egypt in her hands for so many years would prevail over her son's capriciousness, but Tiye, pondering coldly, knew that they were the older generation, those of her own age who remembered her husband and the easy days of a more straightforward administration. The young bloods at court, spoiled and eager for change, for argument, even for the titillation of an outright breach between mother and son, swaggered their support of Pharaoh. Tiye had by now come to see Amunhotep's cursed vision as a river upon whose banks her people were standing, and soon the water would flow too swiftly and too deeply to cross.

Warily she began to focus her attention on Smenkhara and saw behind the potential power of the little five-year-old the dreary necessity of yet another royal death. But not yet. She was still too full of the anguish of love for Amunhotep.

A month later Tiye realized the full magnitude of her blunder, for Nefertiti, basking in Pharaoh's good graces, had persuaded him to withdraw the edict. He had made it in haste, in the first flush of spiritual exultation, and was happy to rescind it when his young wife gave him a suitable excuse. According to Tiye's steward Huya, Nefertiti had suggested to Pharaoh that the courtiers, having learned true humility, might now be allowed to leave their knees. Tiye was relieved, for the sight of so many wealthy and dignified people walking the halls with bruised knees had finally prompted the humor she had feared, and after the humor would have come contempt for a pharaoh who had already allowed too much familiarity with his sacred person. *If I had only kept my head*, Tiye mused, *and remained silent, the edict's repeal would have come to be seen as victory for me over both of them.*

But the rescinding of Amunhotep's command did not bring the expected return to the former code of reverence. Knees, backs, and heads remained bowed if Pharaoh so much as passed by. Tiye, who believed implicitly in the unalterable hierarchy that was a part of Ma'at and demanded due worship, felt the obeisance of the people turn gradually to an obsequiousness she despised. Amunhotep had designated Meryra First Prophet of Neferkheperura Wa-en-Ra, Amunhotep's throne name, and his sole duty was to worship Pharaoh continually, following him and carrying his sandals, sandal box, and white staff. Tiye bit her lip and kept silent. She and Osiris Amunhotep had also appointed priests to worship their divine images at Soleb, but she could imagine her first husband's caustic comments if she had suggested that they be trailed by a chanting priest every hour of the day.

Sometimes, watching her son and Nefertiti progress to the water steps for the short trip across the river to Karnak, accompanied by a retinue that had suddenly burgeoned to include incense-bearing acolytes, four cosmeticians to ensure that the god's and goddess's kohl did not run, a circle of soldiers to see that the royal couple were not accidentally contaminated by contact with a lesser mortal, and, of course, the fanbearers and body servants that were necessary, together with animals, trainers, and feeders, she was tempted to laugh at the silly, self-conscious spectacle of the overpainted, half-naked, misshapen king. But in spite of his flaunted physical grotesqueness, her son was developing an inward dignity that kept Tiye from coming to any conclusion about the truth of his vision. Such things were beyond the scope of her capacity to understand, and she knew it. She could only tell herself, in the long, humid nights, that the empire was still intact, there was still a pharaoh on the Stepped Throne, and she was still empress, a position Nefertiti could never wrench from her. Yet the feeling that empire, pharaoh, and her own fate lay quivering in the balance came back to haunt her, and on many nights she dreamed of the Judgment Hall and the Feather of Ma'at slowly descending onto the scales.

On a thick, hot day when a pleasant wind was blowing from the swollen river, Amunhotep, Nefertiti, and Tadukhipa stood in the shade of the first pylon leading into Pharaoh's Aten temple, their bright linens pressed against their legs by the breeze and the blue and white flags rippling on the flagstaffs high above. To right and left the fanbearers stood, quivering ostrich fans in their hands, their heads averted. Amunhotep's First Prophet was bent low, his eyes on the book of chants held before him by an acolyte, his voice snatched away by the wind. Amunhotep waved into the now paved forecourt.

"It is good to see it finished, but the workmen have been so slow," he complained. "My palace is not ready, nor the gardens and small shrines that will surround this temple. I am not satisfied." He glanced to where the temple of Mut cast a short noon shadow. At a respectful distance, a crowd of Amun priests and temple dancers had gathered, heads between outstretched arms, knees bent. "How can I worship if every day

I must be carried to the sanctuary past those charlatans?" he muttered. "I will order them out of sight when I come." His last words were drowned in a sudden burst of strident horns that erupted from every temple. Tadukhipa covered her ears, and Nefertiti grimaced.

"It is noon," Nefertiti said. "In my own temple, even before my own altars, I hear the singing and shaking of the systra wafting from Amun's precincts, not to mention the dancing that goes on endlessly in the temple of Khonsu. How can my prayers be heard?"

He smiled and, bending, kissed her on the lips. "Your prayers are heard, I assure you, Majesty."

"You are not happy with this beautiful building, Great God?" Tadukhipa glanced up at him shyly, and he drew her to him, putting an expansive arm around Nefertiti also and hugging them both to his hollow chest.

"I am happy with it, little Kia, but I wonder now whether it should have been erected at all. I commissioned this temple in the days of my imperfection. My judgment, though well-meaning, was impaired. I should have chosen a site far from Karnak, where the Aten could be worshiped in peace, but I was eager to give the god a place within the sacred confines. I no longer believe that he wants it. The closeness of Amun is an affront to him."

"You will abandon the work here?" Nefertiti asked, surprised. "Will you stop work on your palace also?"

Amunhotep gave her a speculative look. "Perhaps. I had not considered such a thing before, but it would be good to live and worship far from unfriendly eyes," he replied. "Let us make our prayers. Prophet!"

The quietly talking crowd fell silent and straightened. The litters were lowered to allow the royal trio to mount. The prophet fell to his knees and reverently removed the golden sandals from Pharaoh's feet, placing them in their box. The acolytes charged the incense holders, and while the soldiers fanned out, the litters were carried across the forecourt and into the inner sanctuary, where Amunhotep mounted the steps to the sanctuary and stood solemnly to receive the homage of the two women.

In the days that followed, the idea of a new site for an Aten temple took hold in Pharaoh's mind, and he spoke of it often in his private moments with Nefertiti.

"The Ra oracle would have to be consulted to determine a suitable site," he told her one afternoon as they walked hand in hand around the lake, "but I am sure he could find one sufficiently holy. We must plan in secret, though. I do not wish to affront the empress."

Nefertiti glanced across at his worried face. "Tiye will not be affronted by the erection of yet another temple," she pointed out. "Building projects are going on all the time. But if a site is chosen a long way from Thebes, and you decide to live as well as worship there, she will indeed be angry." Nefertiti pulled him to a halt and stepped to face him. "But it will not matter, dear Amunhotep. What will she be able to do? You are pharaoh and cannot be gainsaid. I will support you, together with all your ministers and worshipers!"

He cupped her cheeks. "My loyal Nefertiti," he said softly. "The Aten is touched by such devotion. Many courtiers are not yet ready to see in him their only god, but there are no doubts in you, are there? Can you imagine how it would be to spend our time always like this, away from the babble of Thebes, the hostility of Karnak, the judgment of our inferiors?"

"I desire it above all things," she responded, stepping into his embrace, "but if such happiness is to be, you must ask the oracle to approve a place far removed from Malkatta or you will have no reason to build a new palace at all."

They swam together, flung bread to the birds, and laughed at the antics of the monkeys, but under his good humor Nefertiti could sense her husband's preoccupation, and he soon returned to the theme of their earlier conversation. They had come to the nursery and were playing with Meketaten and Beketaten while Smenkhara sat in a corner helping Meritaten string beads. "Supposing I do set this change in motion," he said to Nefertiti under the squeals of excitement from the two princesses, to whom he was offering sticky sweetmeats. "It will mean great inconvenience for every foreign embassy quartered at Malkatta, not to mention the ministers, who will have to travel a long way to see me. It would be better . . ." He hesitated, gathering both little girls onto his knee.

"It would be better to move the whole capital of Egypt," Nefertiti finished for him. She glanced to where Smenkhara and Meritaten were absorbed in their task. "I agree."

Amunhotep gently pulled his gold necklace away from Meketaten's mouth. "I could not do it," he whispered to Nefertiti over the heads of his daughters. "My mother would refuse to speak to me."

Nefertiti beckoned to the nursery attendants who waited just out of earshot, and the princesses were lifted from their father's lap and carried, protesting, away. "You have been in awe of the empress for too long, Amunhotep," Nefertiti urged in a low voice. "She wants Egypt to stay forever under her hand. But you are the Aten, the Beautiful God. She cannot stand against you."

Amunhotep smiled wanly. "I feel so strong when I am with you, Nefertiti. Will you accompany me to the oracle?"

Nefertiti rose. "I should be honored. Now come and speak to Meritaten, who has been waiting to receive your attention."

Nefertiti shared a few pleasantries with her daughter and then stood watching as Pharaoh exclaimed politely over the necklace she and Smenkhara had made and chatted with her. *The oracle must be consulted soon, before Amunhotep's nerve begins to fail him*, Nefertiti thought, *and I must tell him that I am pregnant again. The news will bind us even closer together. It is a magnificent gamble that we are taking, but if all goes well, I will finally be able to remove him from the empress's influence. Then we shall see who rules Egypt.*

The announcement was made in the middle of the cool, color-splashed month of Phamenat, when the humming of bees in wet flowers, the armies of fresh crops rippling in the breezes, and the skittishness of newborn animals made even the most jaded courtier into an optimist. Tiye and Amunhotep sat under the gold canopy of the great baldachin at the hour of audience. Nefertiti was on a small silver throne at Pharaoh's left foot, pink quartz lotuses sewn into her waist-length wig and a vine with tiny silver leaves twining around the cobra hooded on her small forehead. There had been an unusual number of speeches to be heard and delegations to be presented, but the proceedings finally came to a close.

After a glance at Amunhotep that he did not return, Tiye had raised a hand to signal the close of the formalities when her son suddenly came to his feet. A hush fell.

"I have made two decisions that will affect you all," he said quickly, the crook and flail clutched tight and crossed on his sagging belly. "I speak as Aten the Glorious. The spirit of Ra has instructed me to choose a new name. The old one incorporates the name of a false god, and I repudiate it. From henceforth I am Neferkheperura Wa-en-Ra Akhenaten, the Spirit of the Aten. On my queen I bestow the appellation Nefer-neferu-Aten, Great Is the Beauty of the Aten, as a mark of my love for her and her devotion to our god. Heralds, scribes, and foreigners, take note." No one moved. A profound stillness had fallen on the princes and nobles assembled, and all eyes were on Pharaoh. Tiye noticed the sidelong glance he stole at her before his gaze returned to the crowd. "My second decision is likewise irrevocable. I am moving the capital of Egypt and the seat of government from Malkatta to a site the god has chosen, four days away downriver. Thebes, Karnak, Malkatta are places full of the odors of deception and false religion. The Aten desires a home that will be his alone. I leave for there tomorrow to lay the sacred cords for the boundaries." A long sigh of disbelief soughed through the hall, followed by a breathless silence until one of the sun priests began to clap. His fellows took up the gesture, laughing and singing their approval, and soon the courtiers realized the expediency of joining in. Amunhotep stood smiling. He raised the crook and flail. "Those who live in truth are welcome in my new city," he announced. "It is the dawn of a new and glorious age for Egypt. The night of lies is past." Hurriedly he stepped from the throne, and taking Nefertiti's arm, he processed through the supinely worshiping bodies and out the doors.

Tiye kept her composure until Pharaoh had gone, and then she slipped out the rear door. Grasping her herald's arm, she punctuated her words to him with vicious shakes. "Get me Ay immediately. I want him in my quarters within the hour. Send to Horemheb at Memphis. He is to leave his duties to his second-in-command and wait upon me in haste. Tell Pharaoh's ministers that on pain of death—of death, do you hear?—they are to be in their offices tomorrow morning to speak to me. Why are you standing there?"

The man bowed and ran, the marks of her nails white in his flesh. Behind her the Keeper of the Royal Regalia hovered, the damask-lined box open to receive his holy charge. Tiye tore the crown from her head and flung it at him with such force that he staggered back even as he caught it. Whispering prayers of apology to its magic, he set it lovingly in the box. "I am not ashamed to show my displeasure!" she shouted at the hapless priest. "Put the useless thing away, but remember this. On no account are you to deliver it to Queen Nefertiti until you have consulted with me first. Now take it away, before I toss it into the lake." With one horrified stare he made a quick obeisance and fled.

Ay caught up with her as she was entering the passage to her apartments. Bowing perfunctorily, he followed her into the seclusion of her reception room and waited for her to speak. For a long while she could not. Fighting to control her breath, she stood with her back to him, fists clenched and gently pounding her white-clad hips. In the end he went up to her, removing the ringleted wig and passing his hands soothingly through her long hair, massaging the rigid muscles of her neck. She pulled away from him and rounded.

"You heard?"

"Yes. I was with the Khatti ambassador at the back."

"Ingrate! Asp! Worm of Apophis! I have given him everything! Everything, Ay, even my body! Thebes was a sleepy, poverty-stricken mud village until the princes of our dynasty graced it. The people know, they will see the city sink once again into obscurity, there will be riots. Doesn't he know that he is running into madness . . ."

"Hush!" he said, halting the tirade. "You have a conveniently selective memory, Majesty, if you think that you gave him your body for any reason other than that of good policy. May I remind you also that our dynasty, as you put it, only began less than two hentis ago with our father's father arriving in Egypt a warrior prisoner. As for riots, the army is perfectly capable of quelling a few. And you hate Thebes, anyway."

"He did not tell me!"

"Ah!" He smiled sympathetically. "Of course he did not tell you. How could he? He must have suffered agonies at the thought of facing you with such news. Put your hurt pride away and look at yourself, Tiye, at me. It is time to relinquish a little, a very little, of Egypt to the next generation."

Her face was still flushed, and a vein stood out angrily on her forehead. "If he has come under the special protection of the gods, we can replace him with Smenkhara." She spoke euphemistically of the insane, whom all were forbidden to harm.

"I do not believe he is mad, although I do think that from time to time such fits come on him. In any case, it would be a difficult task to prove that claim to the people. He is not a

cruel god. He has made no wars, offended no foreign kings,
he is fertile, he worships what he calls the truth. Perhaps it is
not Ma'at, but neither is it entirely sacrilegious. Let him go,
Tiye. Thebes is too well established to wither. There will be
peace at Karnak and Malkatta with him out of the way, have
you thought of that?"

"I do not want the center of power taken from Malkatta,
from the place where I can oversee everything."

"It does not matter. The empire maintains itself under the
system your husband Osiris Amunhotep established."

"He is grotesque, an affront!" Her tone was biting, cruel.
Going to the throne, she picked up the jug always kept filled
with wine and poured for them both. By the time Ay had taken
his cup from her hand, she had drained hers and was pouring
more. "I have two courses of action open to me," she said. "I
can acquiesce to him in everything and hope that this stupidity
tires him eventually. Or I can fight him with every resource I
have."

"You would lose. Any command of yours can be overridden
by him, and you are well aware of it. Will you poison a pharaoh,
Tiye?"

She shrugged and, raising her cup, saluted him mockingly.
"Why not? I am better for Egypt than he is."

"Oh? How I admire your facility for self-justification! You
might as well know that if the court is transferred to a new
site, I have decided to go with it."

Tiye coughed and spat out her wine. "What?"

He met her shocked gaze warily. "It is not a question of
taking sides. You know that I love you, that you and I have
never kept secrets from each other. But, Tiye, I do not want
to end my life drooling impotently over past glories in a crumbling palace. I am a man of many talents, and I intend to go
on using them until I drop."

"What a pretty picture of my end you conjure!" she shot
back sarcastically. "I suppose you think that I should also pack
and follow my mad son to some forsaken rural hole?"

"Yes, I do. You underrate the influence you still have with
Amunhotep. You are a steadying force on him."

"How boring." She strode up the steps and flung herself
onto the throne. "Who would have thought, when my father
led me through the harem doors, that one day I would be

reduced to being a steadying force. Leave me alone, Ay. Can you not see that I am in pain?"

He bowed immediately and, setting his half-full cup beside the jug, strode away.

Horemheb will support me, she thought, watching Ay's straight, bare back vanish and the doors close quietly. *And Amunhotep likes him and will listen to him. He must abandon this silly scheme.* "Huya!" she yelled irritably, and the Keeper of the Harem Door entered. "I want Smenkhara and Beketaten removed from the nursery at once. I do not care where you put them. I will decide that later, and also what new tutors to hire. But they are to have nothing more to do with Nefertiti's brood." Not for the first time was she grateful that the ordering of a pharaoh's harem belonged to the chief wife.

"I understand, Goddess. It will be a blow to Princess Meritaten."

"I know that. I have no other choice. Do it."

I think I will go to my bedchamber and get drunk, she thought when he had gone. *I am not too old for that, Ay. In wine there is often inspiration as well as a sore head.* Wearily she pulled herself to her feet. *Well, why not kill him and stop pretending to a virtue I do not possess? A seat of government trundled to gods know where! Four whole days from Thebes.* Suddenly her breath caught in her throat. She knew where, but had forgotten until now. The desolation of that place where she and Amunhotep had stopped on their way to Memphis, the daunting, echoing heat of it. Oh, Amun, no, she thought as she descended the steps and crossed the floor. *It will drive them mad, my soft, spineless ministers. If he wishes to worship himself in perfect silence, let him give the throne to Smenkhara and dig himself a hole in that cursed burning waste, like the mad old priests dotting the desert outside On.*

Enraged and frightened, she came to her bedchamber. Its atmosphere welcomed her with the faint, musky whiff of her perfume, the drifting sweetness of persea and lotus blossom, a swirl of the odor of wet soil blowing through the undraped window. But it brought a less welcome element with it, and as Tiye crossed, exhausted, to the couch, her mind began to fill with images of her son as lover. "Piha, bring wine," she ordered, a lump in her throat, "and send a slave to undress me. I am going to spend the rest of the day on my couch." She knew it was cowardly, but it was also a relief to recline with

a full cup in her hand while her thoughts grew vague and her
stomach unknotted.

Sometime during the long, darkening evening she awoke
and remembered Piha's solemn face at the door, telling her that
Queen Nefertiti requested audience. She also remembered, even
through the drunken haze, the satisfaction of her reply. "Tell
Nefertiti to plunge into the Duat and stay there. I will not see
her."

13

IN SPITE OF SWOLLEN EYES AND A POUNDING HEAD, TIYE ROSE
just before dawn and submitted to her dressers and cosmeticians, scarcely able to bear their touch. As she sat squinting
with difficulty into her copper mirror, she was aware that the
court, too, was abroad early. Malkatta was murmurous with
low voices, banging doors, an occasionally sleepy curse, and
when she left her quarters with her herald and bodyguards, her
nostrils were assailed by odors of fresh-baked bread and stewing
fruit that nauseated her. The Song of Praise drifted fitfully into
the gardens with the sun's first rays, and with a wave of depres-
sion Tiye wondered at the thoughts of Amun's servants who
had to sing for a pharaoh who would always be deaf to the
adoration in the time-hallowed chant.

The building that housed the offices of ministries was also
unusually busy for the time of day. Pharaoh's civil servants
were seldom in their offices before midmorning, if at all. Many
of them, having received their sinecures as bribes or payment
for loyalty, had immediately hired capable assistants and devoted their time to the more pressing demands of fashion and
intrigue. But today, bleary-eyed and grumbling, they were all
waiting for the appearance of the empress, preferring inconvenience to punishment.

Tiye swept first into the airy cell where Bek, son of Men,
engineer and architect, worked. Men had designed brilliantly
under the Son of Hapu for Osiris Amunhotep, and his son's

talent was as great. Tiye knew that Bek had earned his position. He bowed profoundly as she was announced. She indicated that he might sit, and he lowered himself behind the sturdy desk strewn with scrolls, empty ink pots, and draughtsman's pens. Her fanbearer unfolded her stool.

"I would have thought that you were under Pharaoh's orders to accompany him to his building site," she said after a moment. "Are your servants packing, Bek?"

The young man smiled politely. "My underlings have completed a survey of the site, Majesty," he replied, "and I will visit it in person later, when I may walk it with only my scribes. Horus does not need me in order to demarcate the boundaries of the city. I am commissioned to design."

"Did your surveyors experience any difficulty with the site?"

His dark eyes dropped. "No, Goddess. The land is level. They did their work in a surprisingly short time."

"What did they say about it?"

He did not look up, but his gaze traveled over the untidy heap of scrolls on the desk. "Only that, in spite of the fact that the sand is deep, the masons and engineers will find their work easy."

"That is not what I meant." The low voice had sharpened.

Bek stiffened. "They said that even at this time of the year the heat was oppressive."

Tiye stifled a sigh. "You are a loyal servant of your king, and that is commendable, but if you truly desire Pharaoh's well-being, Bek, you will do your best to dissuade him from this plan. The survey, as you say, was done hurriedly. There may be problems that were missed."

Now his face came up. "My father took great pride in his work as glorifier and beautifier in Egypt," he said. "So do I. I will not paint over any difficulty that might arise, but neither will I carve one where it does not exist. I try to live in truth, as my lord has taught me."

"Bek," she said patiently, touched in spite of herself by his youthful trust in her son's dubious interpretation of Ma'at, "truth is not always a gentle thing. It can eventually wound and destroy. Think of that as you labor over your drawings for Pharaoh's new city. You will be helping him use a truth to destroy himself."

"Perhaps." The tone was polite, noncommittal.

Tiye rose, and he also. "Your work is very harmonious and

beautiful," she said, and Bek recognized that she was not flattering him. He bowed.

"My father taught me well. Long life to Your Majesty."

She nodded and went out.

Over the next few hours she went from office to office, conferring quietly with all Akhenaten's ministers, trying to convince them to dissuade him from his scheme. She even visited Ranefer, Ay's second-in-command, standing outside the stables on a mat unrolled for her clean, soft sandals while behind the man the horses shuffled and whickered and the pungent smell of dung made her wince. Two strong impressions had emerged for her consideration by the time she got onto her litter and was carried back to her quarters. One was the power to convince or confuse that her son's Teaching had. Each man had referred to it in some way. The other was the strength of the inadvertent bond Akhenaten and Nefertiti had forged between themselves and the young men who had surrounded them in the days of his princehood. Akhenaten had carried them with him in his rise to power, and they were still young enough to be grateful.

Her son came to bid her farewell just before noon. Politely she knelt and kissed his feet, acutely aware of her puffy eyes, her sallow complexion dulled by the wine of the night before. He raised her and returned the kiss on her gold-circled forehead. He was so transparently guilty, so eager for her approval that she bit back the arguments rising to her tongue. Perhaps, when he saw the site again, he would change his mind. Perhaps its appeal for him would have been lessened in the course of his own growth.

"I will return in fourteen days," he said. "I hope, dear mother, that you will have decided by then to move to my holy city yourself."

"The building of it will take years," she responded noncommittally. "Is Ay traveling with you?"

"He must. My horses and chariot are needed." He hesitated, clearly unable to decide whether to stay or to leave her, and seeing his distress, she put her arms around him.

"May the soles of your feet be firm, Akhenaten."

He embraced her, pathetically pleased at her use of his new name. "I love you, my mother."

It was like a return to the times that had gone to hold him thus, to feel her cheek against the thin, bowed bones of his shoulder, his breath stirring in her hair. Tears of regret and weariness blurred in her eyes. She pressed her lips against his neck. "You had better go," she said unsteadily. "My precious egg, my poor prince. Go!" He smiled warmly and departed.

The palace sighed with relief when the last of the barges in Pharaoh's party disappeared from sight. The tempo of life slowed, and Malkatta slipped briefly back into the indulgent gaiety of days past. There was a loud cheerfulness to the feasting, a casual laziness to the sun-drenched days. As if to test their freedom, the courtiers wandered across the river to Amun's temple at Karnak in greater numbers than the priests had seen in years, and prayed with a fervor that surprised both the god's servitors and the new worshipers themselves.

Tiye felt as though she were an invalid recovering from a long illness. She called her jeweler and spent a day selecting new earrings, pectorals, anklets. She ordered a dozen new gowns. Together with Smenkhara she went to her dead husband's mortuary temple, offering him food and flowers and burning incense. She saw to new apartments for Smenkhara and Beketaten and hired them new tutors from the House of Scribes at Karnak. For the first time in many months she appraised her son, seeing in him his father's full lips and almond eyes, though the boy's were paler than Pharaoh's had been. He had also inherited Amunhotep's confident, regal walk. But he was as yet too young to display any character traits she could recognize as her first husband's. His conversations were often punctuated by long periods of silent rumination, whether for pondering or simply because of loss of interest and concentration, Tiye could not tell. He could also be surly when he chose. "I want Meritaten back," he demanded one day as they rocked in Tiye's barge anchored to the shore. Smenkhara had a fishing line dangling over the edge and was holding it in one negligent hand as he half-turned to his mother on his ivory chair. "She must miss me. Doing lessons by myself is boring, and I hate Beketaten. She whines when I won't play with her."

"That is simply her age," Tiye reminded him. "She is only two, Smenkhara. Meritaten was also a whiner at that age."

"No, she wasn't, she just sulked. And anyway, how would you know what she was like? You only came into the nursery to see Beketaten, and then you hurried back to my brother the king." He dragged the line sullenly to and fro. "Pharaoh took Meritaten and Meketaten with him on his trip downriver, and I wanted to go, too, but you wouldn't let me. They are all having fun together." His lower lip stuck out mutinously, and the youth lock was flung off the brown shoulder.

Tiye pulled her bare feet into the shade of the canopy. "Well, I didn't go either," she pointed out, and he raised both elbows rudely.

"Pharaoh didn't want you, that's why."

"Is that what the servants are saying, or did you come to this conclusion by yourself? In any event, you are a nasty, spoiled little prince," she snapped. "How long is it since your teacher whipped you?"

"My teachers have never whipped me. I threaten them if they try. And I decided all by myself that Pharaoh was happy to leave you here."

"I can see that discipline in the nursery has been lax. You may be pharaoh one day, Smenkhara. You must know what it feels like to be an ordinary mortal before you taste the joys of godhood."

The precocious child swore under his breath. "I bet my new fish pendant that you were never whipped, O my mother."

"Yes, I was. Your uncle Ay whipped me once and slapped me many times because I was willful and refused to learn from him."

A long silence followed, and Tiye assumed he was ignoring her. Drowsily she half-closed her eyes, letting the breeze caress her face. But after a while he said, "That is different. You are a woman. Will I really be pharaoh one day?"

"I am empress and goddess and will not be insulted by any," she barked back. "Now fish quietly. I want to sleep."

Moodily he kicked the side of the barge and relieved his feelings by sticking out his tongue at his silent body slave. "I don't want to fish anymore. I want to swim."

"Not without your instructor. Your stroke is not strong enough yet."

"When I am pharaoh, I shall do what I like."

"Probably," Tiye replied, almost asleep. Smenkhara's bad temper was fading, and she saw he hauled in his empty line and went to sit under his own canopy to play sennet.

*   *   *

For the auspicious day marking the formal establishment of the boundaries of his new city, Akhenaten had laid aside the clinging, many-pleated female gowns he increasingly preferred to wear, and had donned a short white male kilt. His slender neck was heavy with gold circlets, and an amethyst pectoral portraying the sun disk surrounded by silver bees, hung on his breast. Above the thickly painted face rose a tall blue soft crown to which the cobra and vulture were attached. The hands that gathered up the guiding reins of the chariot were almost invisible under ring scarabs, cartouches, and the loose amulets around his wrists. Behind him Nefertiti leaned against the burnished sides of the vehicle, looking radiant in pale royal blue. Miniature crooks and flails hung from her belt, and between her blue-painted breasts a rearing lapis lazuli sphinx snarled. Her own crown was a curious conical sun god's helmet into which all her hair had been piled, accentuating the sweeping, flawless lines of her jaw and temple. The result was that her face lost some of its femininity and acquired a sternness that reflected the intractability that was beginning to appear in her character. Meritaten, blue and white ribbons in her youth lock and naked under a loose linen cloak with enameled ankhs, held her mother's ring-encrusted hand, while little Meketaten sat on the floor of the chariot, one hand tugging at her father's gold sandal and the other shaking a little bell Tiye had given her. Behind Pharaoh, other chariots waited, full of wigged and kohled dignitaries sweating under the fringed canopies attached to their vehicles. It was midmorning, and the sun's force, unchecked because the sheltering cliffs trapped all wind, beat onto the sand and was reflected up onto protesting skin.

Akhenaten took a last long look around him as he waited for Ay's signal. Water trickled along the metal band of his helmet past his jeweled ear and down his neck. His eyes scanned the unsullied run of gold-white sand spreading, shimmering, from the sparkling blue of the Nile on his right to the tumble of cliff and shadowed gullies on his left. Ahead, dancing on waves of heat, the curve of rock was consummated eight miles away in its meeting with the river, its heights sharp brown against the vivid blue of the sky. In spite of the low laughter and conversation of the waiting courtiers, the prevailing silence, ancient and mysterious, flowed over and muted mere human sound. There were those who looked about uneasily, cowed by the impression that some presence was watching the interlopers, but the majority were lighthearted, eager for the ceremony to be over so that they could return to the sumptuous tents Pharaoh had provided. Atkhenaten acknowledged his uncle's signal. Turning, he smiled at Nefertiti, who planted a kiss on his hennaed lips.

"A new beginning," she said, eyes shining. "It was ordained so." "Yes it was," he agreed as his horses strained for an instant against the sand clogging the golden chariot's spoked wheels before jerking it forward. "From this place, hallowed by my presence, the worship of the Aten will spread over the whole world." Behind him the glittering cavalcade began to roll. Meketaten squealed with delight and held her father's calf with both chubby arms. Meritaten's solemn gaze was fixed on his back.

For the rest of the day the nobles and princes of Egypt, growing hungrier and soon consumed with raging thirsts, followed their god's chariot slowly around a circuit of the cliffs. At intervals along the route, portable altars had been raised. As Akhenaten and his family arrived at each one, the attending priest lit incense and lay prostrate in the burning sand while Pharaoh dismounted and his prophet, in the chariot behind, came to make an offering to him and to the Aten who fired the sky with the same spirit imbuing Pharaoh's body. By the time the eighth and last offering had been set aflame, the sun had changed from blinding white to a rich red and was sinking over the river. Cheerful cooking fires flickered between the clustered tents and the flotilla of tethered barges. The disheveled courtiers shouted, more with an inexpressible relief than with adoration, when they saw Akhenaten whip his horses into a canter ahead of them as the chariot finally gained the firmer gray sand by the water. Already the musicians were filling the pale twilight with quick harmony, and on the carpets, beside the inviting cushions, servants waited with wine jugs that had been cooled in the river. Dismounting and handing the reins to Ay before his own tent, Akhenaten looked out to where the last offering still burned, a leaping, erratic point of red light. "Where each altar stood, I will have stelas erected," he said to Nefertiti. "I saw many secluded rifts in the rock where royal tombs might be hollowed out. Did you? I intend to move all the bodies of the Mnervis bulls from On and bury them here, and institute the care and worship of the living one here also."

"One thing at a time, my divine husband," Nefertiti teased

him, wet linen clinging to her skin and grains of sand lodged in the crevices of her neck. "I am going to swim before I eat, and drink before I swim. Nurse!" She surrendered the children hastily and disappeared into her tent, but before he went to his own anxiously waiting slaves, Akhenaten spent a moment inhaling the dry night.

Once the official ceremonies had been performed, Ay had little to do. He spent some time making sure that the horses were well watered and had sufficient shade, and then supervised the workmen under him while they performed a few minor repairs to the chariots. He could have ordered the charioteers to use their spare time practicing battle maneuvers, but he decided that it was simply too hot for much exertion. One afternoon he accompanied Pharaoh on a rigorous climb to the top of the cliffs surrounding the site, and while the litter bearers panted and struggled to make the ascent and the guards tried to maintain the correct formation on the slope, Akhenaten talked continuously of his dreams for the bleak vista they all surveyed when they reached the summit. Dizzy with heat and thirst, Ay had scarcely absorbed most of what Akhenaten had said, but over the next three days, as he visited the tents of friends to talk or gamble, or sat by the glittering river, idling away the hours under his sunshade, some of Pharaoh's excited words came back to him, and he began to ponder his future. The king had made it plain that he expected the Master of the King's Horse to take up residence in the new city, and for the first time in his life Ay felt his loyalties violently divided. As Amunhotep III's brother-in-law he had occasionally been called upon to choose, in matters of ministerial policy, between the directives of his ruler and the well-being of his family, but those choices had been small compared to the decision he now had to make. He had told his sister that, though it would be all too easy for him to remain with her in the backwater Malkatta would inevitably become, he would accompany Pharaoh, and he had meant it. He was rich, he was powerful, and he enjoyed the favor of his lord. Could Tiye blame him for being unwilling to relinquish these things in order to gamble on the chance that Pharaoh's enterprise might fail and she might be seen to be the better ruler after all? And if the breach between mother and son continued to widen, was his place not with his daughter and grandchildren? Surely their claims on him were stronger than Tiye's. *If the choice were hers*, he thought as he sat with eyes half-shut against the blinding sparkle of sun on bright water, *she would not hesitate to stand with the winning side. She knows that I am as much a realist as she. She hopes that the choice for either of us need never be made. She does not believe anything will come of this plan, but she is not here, watching the priests mark the boundaries and listening to her son's enthusiasm. Forgive me, Tiye, but I must be where Pharaoh is. I am not yet old enough to risk the possibility that his plan might fail. I will never betray you or be disloyal, but I think the balance of power has just shifted, and unless you compromise, you will never get it back.*

On the fourth evening, he was walking thoughtfully beside the river with two of his charioteers when he saw a small imperial craft approaching from the north. Turning back to the dock, he waited for it to tie up. A challenge rang out from Pharaoh's guard and was immediately answered. A ramp appeared, and a tall, blue-helmeted man bounded onto the bank, soon followed by a woman and a stream of servants. Ay ran forward to greet them. "Horemheb! What are you doing here? And Mutnodjme!"

"I could ask you the same question," Horemheb said, coming up to him. "I received an urgent summons to Malkatta and am on my way upriver. Somehow I seldom manage to escape having to berth in this accursed place when I travel. What is all this?" His braceleted arms swept over the huddle of tents, horses feeding, bursts of music, and the welcome smell of the evening's roast goose.

"You had better not refer to this sacred ground as accursed in Pharaoh's hearing," Ay retorted and quickly told him what had been happening since the last routine dispatch had been sent to him.

"I daresay you missed a messenger on the river, or you would have known. Mutnodjme, how are you?"

The girl dutifully pressed her lips to his cheek. "I survive," she drawled. "This looks like a very large party, so perhaps I shall do more than survive until I reach Thebes. Is Depet here? Give me gold, Horemheb. If she is, she will want to dice."

Her husband good-naturedly handed her a pouch.

She has not changed much, Ay thought fondly, *other than that her face is thinning, and her eyes are lazier*. "Where are your dwarfs?" he asked.

She shrugged. "One of them fell off the barge while we were having a boating party some months ago, and in the noise and laughter I did not notice," she said. "He drowned. The other one ran away. I have ordered two more from Nubia, but they are very rare. Pitch and cook over there!" she shouted at the servants. "I will be back in three hours!" She began to wander away.

"Will I be a grandfather again soon?" Ay called after her, and she yelled over her shoulder, "Certainly not!"

Horemheb grimaced, smiling. "I think she is happy, Commander, and loves me in her way. Is Pharaoh disposed to see me, do you think?"

"I am certain he is." They began to stroll along the river. "I hear you have had some trouble with the border troops."

Horemheb nodded. "Without a clear policy from Pharaoh on military matters, discipline has been difficult to maintain," he admitted. "My captains found some soldiers looting boats and cattle and terrorizing small villages. The men were bored, but that is no excuse. I had the noses of the ringleaders removed, and banished the others to Tjel. Osiris Amunhotep's lover was one of them."

Ay digested the information silently, shocked that anyone from the old administration still survived, as though it had all belonged to a time many hentis ago, in another age. So much had happened since then.

"I am surprised he has survived this long."

Horemheb laughed. "He surprised us all. He was a tough little bad-tempered peasant with a constitution hardier than I would have believed possible. But Tjel will make a man of him. It is the grimmest fortress in the empire."

Ay thought briefly of the feral face and rebellious black eyes of the child, and then he turned his attention to the larger concern. It was true that Pharaoh had shown no interest in the state of his army or the protection of his borders. *I must obtain his permission to regulate things myself,* Ay decided, stilling a brief pang of worry. *I have tried to avoid antagonizing him, but surely he will see that we cannot have unrest so close to home, for foreigners will take it as a sign of weakness.*

"Does Pharaoh know you had to discipline troops?"

"I sent a scroll to the Scribe of Recruits, and if he reads the dispatches, he must know." Horemheb gave Ay a sidelong glance. "But I worded it carefully. Pharaoh would doubtless have preferred that I strike my men with a lotus bloom and banish them to the back of the schoolroom."

Ay did not laugh, and Horemheb's tone was not light. They mae their way carefully through the groups of feasting revelers and came upon Akhenaten sitting with Nefertiti.

Pharaoh was overjoyed to see his friend, putting his arms around Horemheb's neck and kissing him fervently. "When I move my august person to my new city, you must come and live here," he insisted eagerly. "The command of the border is a small position. I will bestow some other title upon you so that I can see you every day."

"Your Majesty is gracious," Horemheb replied, bowing several times to hide the embarrassment Amunhotep's embrace had caused him, the imprint of the king's enthusiastic kiss staining his own mouth red. "But I am a serving soldier and would not be happy living in idleness."

"You always did tell me the truth without fear," Pharaoh applauded. "But my need of you is greater than your desire for happiness. It is not far from here to the Delta, if you insist on keeping your post, and I am certain that Mutnodjme would be pleased to return to court."

"There is much time in which to make such decisions, beloved," Nefertiti interposed swiftly, her arm sliding around his waist. "Your mother may wish to dispose of Horemheb's services in some other way." She smiled into Horemheb's eyes, and the commander recognized malice in her glance.

"You are right." Akhenaten nodded, kissing her. "I am too eager to reward those who love me."

"Is the breach between the god and his mother so wide, then?" Horemheb asked Ay later that night under the screech and wail of pipes and singers. "It is preposterous to think that loyal Egyptians will have to make some kind of a choice between the two."

Ay looked around at the noisy, drunken company. Servants were gliding between the flaring torches planted in the sand, removing the ruins of the feast. Dancers were swaying, yellow light sliding lazily over their naked, oiled skin. Splashes and shrieks of mirth came from the bank of the river, hidden in darkness. In the middle of the uproar a servant stood trembling, holding up a tray piled with trinkets while Mutnodjme's whip cracked perilously close to his defenseless head, deftly picking up the necklets and bracelets one by one and flicking them through the air to send them rattling into waiting laps. Her youth lock was coiled against one ear and secured by a spray of golden papyrus fronds, and she had powdered herself with gold dust. Applause and roars of approval greeted each nonchalant flick of her jewel-laden wrist.

"Her skill is remarkable," Ay said and then sighed and turned to Horemheb. "I still hope that there is no true breach, only a misunderstanding, and that it will be healed. The bonds that join my sister and Pharaoh have always been strong. But if, the gods forbid, the wedge driven between them should swell, there will be no question of divided loyalty, Horemheb. Pharaoh is Egypt."

"I know," Horemheb answered. "It is not just a matter of old and new loyalties but a question of survival." He turned on his chair to meet Ay's glance, and they regarded each other in perfect understanding. "My father was able to afford to send me to the School for Scribes at Karnak," Horemheb went on, "but he did not have the influence necessary to secure me a good position when my training was over. I might even now be sitting cross-legged on the docks at Thebes tallying shipments of grain if it had not been for the empress, who heard of my skill and made me a royal scribe." He smiled faintly, his gaze still on the loud feasting. "Yet now I really have no choice, Ay. If I wish to retain power in the army and move toward an even higher rank, I must be where Pharaoh is. He has the ultimate disposition of all troops, and that authority will, of course, move with him here. Besides, he will be rewarding those who are faithful to him, and one has to live."

It was a realistic assessment of his own position as well as Horemheb's, Ay knew. Many of the younger men who had got their start under Tiye's patronage and who still had far to climb would be brooding over similar arguments.

"It is the way of life," he muttered, absently fingering the scar on his chin. "I only wish Pharaoh had chosen a different site for his new city. I do not like this place. I am not surprised that it has remained virgin until now. I think it wants only to be left alone."

"There speaks a sorcerer, not a soldier," Ay chided, and Horemheb suddenly laughed.

"At dawn tomorrow we leave for Malkatta, and I become a soldier again. Mutnodjme wants to make offerings to Min at the shrine at Akhmin on the way, so we will carry your salutations to Tey."

"Tonight I wish I were lying with her on her couch, listening to the owls hunt in the garden," Ay said half to himself, but Horemheb had not heard, having stood to catch the blue necklet his wife had sent flying toward him.

Ay rose an hour before dawn to bid farewell to Horemheb and Mutnodjme. He watched their craft angle silently away from the beach, feeling all at once lonely, and while he waited for the rest of the camp to stir, he returned to his tent. Opening the doors of his traveling shrine, he performed his morning devotions to Amun. Later Pharaoh performed his last formal act before quitting the site, most reluctantly, himself. He and Nefertiti, a child on each lap, sat on thrones before a portable altar while the prophet burned offerings and the courtiers kissed their feet and lay in adoration on the sand. While they murmured, "Eternal life! Great is thy lifetime, O Unique One of Ra, Lord of Crowns," Akhenaten reiterated his desires. "See," he called. "This city was desired by the Aten. It shall be built as a memorial to his name in all eternity. It was the Aten, my father, who showed this site to me. I shall erect a great Aten temple here for my father. I shall erect a stone sunshade for the Great Royal Wife Nefer-neferu-Aten Nefertiti. I shall lay out estates for Pharaoh, for the Royal Wife; my tomb shall be made in the eastern mountains, and there my funeral shall be made. If I die elsewhere, let me be buried here. If the Great Royal Wife or the Princess Meritaten dies elsewhere, let them be buried here. For as the god liveth, I shall not leave this place." Longing and anticipation filled the formal, repetitive words. Meketaten had fallen asleep against her father's breast, but Meritaten listened intently.

"Mother," she hissed into Nefertiti's ear. "He did not say Smenkhara. Can Smenkhara be buried here, too?"

But Nefertiti hushed her, for the priest had begun a hymn to the Aten and her husband. Ay, having made his obeisance and being told he could rise, now stood to one side. He saw his daughter's black-kohled eyes slowly travel the prostrate forms of Pharaoh's worshipers covering the sand and wondered uneasily what she was thinking.

It was a surfeited, tired court that returned to Malkatta and scattered to scented baths and the welcoming softness of waiting couches. Tiye, dressed in cloth of gold, the disk and plumes glittering on her ringleted head, had waited with a sinking heart at the water steps to make the formal welcome. The days of peaceful self-indulgence into which she had slid had been shattered by Horemheb, to whom she had given audience only hours before. He had listened to her urgings in a respectful silence but had then resisted any suggestion that he might try to dissuade Pharaoh from his course.

"I am humbly sorry, Great One, but it is impossible," he had said forthrightly.

"Do you mean impossible for you to try or impossible for Pharaoh to be swayed?" she had countered irritably.

"Impossible for Pharaoh to be swayed, Majesty. Perhaps if he is closer to the Delta, he may appreciate more fully the problems of his army."

"Oh, so you intend to stay in favor so that you can defend Egypt's soldiers, do you?" she had snapped sarcastically. "I am not yet senile, Horemheb."

He had smiled at her with the gentle commiseration of years of friendly intimacy. "I worship you, my goddess, but your worry is like the fretting of a mother over the sex of an unborn child."

He had refused to be drawn further, and eventually she had dismissed him in frustration. Now she gloomily watched Pharaoh and his family disembark, Smenkhara and Beketaten standing with her, arrayed sumptuously for the occasion. Tiye's ill humor was slightly mollified by her son's evident delight in seeing the children. He put a finger under Smenkhara's chin, lifting the painted face to meet his own. "How handsome you are, my little brother!" he exclaimed jauntily. "And you, my sweet pretty flower. Come for a kiss." He held out his arms, and Beketaten ran into them, showering him with wet kisses. "I have missed my daughter," he went on. "How golden and rosy she grows!" He talked to her for a moment before surrendering her to her nurse. Meritaten was already at Smenkhara's side, her hand stealing into his. Tiye noticed them edging away in the direction of the fountains and let them go. Akhenaten turned to her, waiting for the deep obeisance she haughtily refused. She inclined her head.

"I have missed you also, Tiye," he said unexpectedly. "I wish you had been there to see the incense of dedication rise beside the cliffs." He kissed her gently with more self-confidence and dignity than he had in months, and Tiye, nonplussed, felt her bristling defenses give way. *Perhaps all will be well*, she thought, looking over his shoulder to where Nefertiti stood waiting alone in a pool of reverence.

Tiye was still in a mood of optimism when later that day she went to his apartments with a scroll her scribe had just finished translating for her. Akhenaten was still lying on his couch after sleep, his face pasty and drawn, his eyes bloodshot. He greeted her wanly.

"Are you ill, Horus?" she enquired, watching as his body servant placed a wet, cool cloth on his forehead.

He nodded and then winced. "I have a terrible headache," he whispered. "I can hardly bear to move. When I blink, it is like scimitars slashing into my head." She almost relented, but he waved her closer. "What is the scroll?"

"It was received by the Scribe of Foreign Correspondence yesterday, and it worries me, Akhenaten. Aziru has become prince of the Amurru."

"Why should that worry anyone? All the tribes of northern Syria are our vassals. It does not matter what little prince captains the Amurru so long as he does what Egypt tells him."

"It matters in this case because Aziru is known to be in correspondence with Suppiluliumas. He has even visited the Khatti capital, Boghaz-keuoi, on several occasions. I fear a secret alliance between them that will undermine the security of our hold on Syria."

"What would you have me do?" He cringed with pain, placing both palms against his temples and closing his eyes.

"Send to Aziru at once for reassurances of his loyalty, and for a hostage."

"What does his scroll say?"

Tiye smiled contemptuously. "He worships and adores you, calls me the lady of your house, and pledges to Egypt his undying faithfulness and devotion."

"What beautiful words! He is a son of the true Ma'at."

"He is a liar and a scoundrel!" Tiye retorted hotly, and Akhenaten struggled to sit up, crying with pain.

"If he is not telling the truth, the Aten will punish him," he managed. "Give the scroll to Tutu for a kindly reply."

"But Akhenaten!"

"Help me, Mother. I am going to be sick."

A servant rushed to the couch, kneeling and holding out a

silver bowl. Another held Pharaoh's head. Akhenaten rolled to his side and vomited. Instantly Tiye's anger vanished. Snatching the wet cloth from the sheet where it had fallen, she wiped his face and helped to lower him onto the cushions. He pulled a blanket over himself with shaking hands, and Tiye saw that he was suddenly drowsy.

"I should not have disturbed you," she said, bending to kiss his forehead. "I will return later to see if you are better." Before she reached the door, he was asleep.

In the passage she confronted Parennefer, who had risen from his stool. "Bring Pharaoh's physician at once," she said. "Perhaps the sorcerers also."

"Pharaoh is angry with his physician, Goddess," he replied awkwardly. "His illness began while he was away, and he was told that he had been under the sun too often without protection. Pharaoh said that his father would not hurt him, and sent the man away."

Annoyed, she could only answer, "If Pharaoh wishes to suffer, I suppose we must let him."

Tiye unwillingly surrendered the scroll to Tutu, instructing him to reply firmly to Aziru even though Pharaoh did not wish it, but knowing that Tutu would do as Pharaoh wanted. She had given Akhenaten her interpretation of the situation in northern Syria and advised him as to what she believed was the proper course of action, and there was little more she could do. The setting and pursuing of foreign policy was Pharaoh's prerogative alone. He was free to accept the advice of his Scribe of Foreign Correspondence and other ministers or to reject it and formulate his own relationships with vassals and allies, but his was the final word. Tiye was aware that any directive he issued to Tutu was binding, but she was annoyed that Tutu took such pleasure in seeing her overruled.

She returned to her son's quarters in the evening, hoping to persuade him to take some nourishment, and was surprised to find him bathed, dressed, and sitting between the pillars of his reception hall with Nefertiti, looking out over the dusky garden. His lute lay at his feet, and a scribe sat cross-legged behind him, writing quickly as Akhenaten dictated a song. The words came high and fast, the long-fingered hands accentuating the rhythm of the poetry with slaps against his knees, the arms of the chair, each other. He was leaning forward, his muscles tense, rocking slightly to and fro. Every so often he snatched

up the lute and plucked quickly, humming under his breath
until the words began to flow again.

"Yes, I am better, Mother, I cannot stop now or the beautiful
words will cease, do not approach me," he shouted all in one
breath, waving her away, a grimace of anxiety on his face.
Nefertiti did not bother to acknowledge her presence at all.
Tiye looked through the deepening shadows that clung to the
pillars and saw Pharaoh's retinue standing with heads lowered
in the gloom, not daring to move or make a sound. Only the
scribe was oblivious to the air of almost painful expectancy.
He was breathing heavily, and his tongue was caught between
his teeth with the effort of writing down the monotonous gush
of half-formed words. Chilled and bored, Tiye left them.

14

THE ENTIRE COURT AT MALKATTA WAS SOON INVOLVED IN
turning the desolate and inhospitable land of Pharaoh's vision
into a place worthy to be the home of the Aten. Bek, Kenofer,
Auta, and the other royal architects and craftsmen worked night
and day on the slowly complicating plans for a city that would
rise magically from nothing, a creation from chaos like the
world itself. The cynical inhabitants of Thebes watched as day
after day the Nile became increasingly choked with traffic:
huge, ponderous barges creeping carefully past them laden with
finely dressed ashlar from the Assuan quarries, rafts piled high
with golden straw to be mixed with river mud, lateen-rigged
boats bearing fortunes in precious cedar beams. Thousands of
workmen and their overseers had to be moved into the hastily
erected barracks to the north of the site. A whole village of
peasants renowned for their skill in masonry was removed from
its site west of Thebes and resettled at Pharaoh's command.
Occasionally the city dwellers, their ranks thinned by
Akhenaten's compulsory draft, would cheer derisively as flotilla after flotilla jockeyed by, but before long they had either
lost interest and gone back to their daily pursuits or sat with

their beer and bread on the bank and kept silent, hoping the hours might be enlivened by the sight of a gilded and canopied pleasure craft bearing dignitaries downstream.

Akhenaten also ordered a halt to the work still going on at Karnak. Those who had labored for years on his and Nefertiti's Aten temples were dispatched to begin their tasks again in the new city. The Amun priests waited fearfully for him to recruit their workmen also, but as usual he simply ignored them. Karnak adopted a policy of wary, deliberate inconspicuousness.

Malkatta began to hum like a great hive and, with the aid of perspiring ministers and harried officials, hauled itself from its easy, slipshod inefficiency to a level of clean organization. Pharaoh counted the days until the time when he could leave, and his time was spent hurrying from one office to another, demanding reports or endlessly discussing his vision for the most beautiful city ever built. Well-meaning and eager, he often obstructed the very ministers he sought to encourage into haste, for when he appeared, all work had to cease while the proper obeisances were performed and the correct stance maintained in his presence. Akhenaten was supremely happy, in spite of the headaches that felled him with increasing regularity and which he came to dread. They meant the loss of his frail dignity, for he always ended up vomiting with pain. The attacks were invariably followed by bursts of frenetic creative energy and religious fervor. The courtiers, ever anxious to please in ways they could understand, took to having their servants follow them about holding silver ewers into which they politely spat or, if full of wine, vomited. If the Aten caused such behavior in his blessed incarnation and holy self, then they wished to share the attention of the god.

With the shift in the government's priorities came a realignment of power, and many ministers who had flourished under Amunhotep III found themselves dispensable. Pharaoh did not openly dismiss them, but the day-to-day orders that should have come to them went to their subordinates. Sensibly they retired without demur, and their places were taken by Akhenaten's favorites.

With a sense of regret, Ay saw ever more clearly the wisdom of a shift in his personal allegiance. He liked his second-in-command, Ranefer. The young man understood horses and was respected by the charioteers, but he had been appointed to serve under Ay by Akhenaten when he had come with the prince from Memphis, and Ay anxiously watched Ranefer for any sign that he was about to be usurped. So far there had been no indication, however, that Ranefer would be made Master of the King's Horse. But Ay believed that moment would eventually come unless he took his stand without equivocation. There was no longer any doubt that Pharaoh was in control of the kingdom. He was indisputably ruling now, not, like his father, through control of Egypt's secular institutions, but with the power of the priest kings of ancient times. Nefertiti's star was also rising. In the year after the demarcation of the city she had given birth, to her chagrin, to another girl, but Akhenaten was delighted, naming her Ankhesenpaaten, Living through the Aten. Wealth and beauty cast a magnetic aura around her into which the powerful were drawn. Tiye still commanded, would always command, the awed respect due to a goddess and empress, but she was a goddess of the old order, an empress no longer fully in control of an empire. While Ay had no wish to see her further humiliated, he deliberately set out to win the confidence of Akhenaten, a task that proved not to be difficult. Ay knew that Pharaoh had always liked him, and could both rest comfortably in his presence and seek his advice without the timidity that cursed him in his mother's company. Tiye's advice had all too often been condescending or, worse, an unintentionally acid demolition of his hesitant opinions. Learning from her example, Ay did not argue but discussed with an encouraging lift of the eyebrows, always deferring to Akhenaten if Pharaoh showed signs of being adamant.

The only sport Akhenaten truly enjoyed was handling his chariot, which he did very well, and as Master of the King's Horse Ay spent much time standing behind Pharaoh's thin, bowed spine and helmeted head as he shouted gaily at the animals, his frail wrists flexing skillfully with the pull of the reins. To Ay there was something endearing and pitiful about his nephew's eager shedding of his self-consciousness. To his surprise, Ay found himself looking forward to the hours spent listening to Pharaoh's high, tuneless singing, the creak of harness, and the whip of wind against his ears.

"In spite of the fact that you are building a new chapel to Min on the family estate at Akhmin, I think you are my friend, Uncle," Akhenaten said to Ay one day as they dismounted, coated with dust, and walked stiffly to their litters. "It is more than the tie of blood, is it not?"

Ay smiled at the anxious, almost diffident question. "Of course I am your friend, Majesty," he responded diplomatically.

"You like to be with me? Nefertiti tells me that you only spend your time with me so that you can make reports to my mother." He caught Ay's arm and brought them to a halt.

Ay looked directly into the sand-rimmed, distressed black eyes. "Akhenaten, you should know that the empress is my oldest friend as well as my dear sister," he said carefully. "With her I share memories that belong to no one but the two of us. But I do not denigrate my pharaoh in anyone's presence. Queen Nefertiti is too eager to protect you from all that might hurt you."

To Ay's astonishment and dismay, the large eyes suddenly filled with tears. "Sometimes, when I am told one thing by one person and something else by another, and the Aten does not tell me who speaks the truth, I begin to hurt." The thick lips were quivering. "Sometimes I think that no one loves me at all."

Ay felt Pharaoh's body straining toward him and knew that if he opened his arms, Akhenaten would fall into them. He put his hands behind his back. It would not do for the waiting courtiers, out of earshot but watching them patiently, to see their king seeking such comfort.

"My god, my lord," he said quietly, "you have the worship of an empire, the love of Ra himself, and surely the love of such unworthy mortals as myself and your mother."

Akhenaten brushed the tears from his cheeks, biting his lip. "I love you also. I love my empress, but she is becoming sharp-tongued. Uncle, will you accept the honor of being my Fan-bearer on the Right Hand?"

Ay stared at him, quickly assimilating his nephew's words. The highest position in the land was being offered to him, not forced on him. The laughter of relief rose to his mouth, and he swallowed, kneeling on the hard-packed dirt of the parade ground and kissing Pharaoh's dusty feet. "I do not deserve this," he said, knowing that he spoke the truth, "yet I will serve you faithfully, O Spirit of the Aten."

"Good. I shall let Ranefer take over as Master of the King's Horse. You will come with me to my holy city?"

"Did you doubt it?"

"Yes. Nefertiti said you would stay here with Tiye and conspire against me."

I must have a few harsh words with Nefertiti, Ay thought. *Will she never learn discretion?* "I can only deny this and try to prove to you with my deeds that the queen is wrong."

Akhenaten touched him gently with one foot, and Ay rose. "I do not think I believe it anyway, Uncle," Pharaoh said, sniffing and straightening. "Carry my fan and show all the whisperers that they are wrong to doubt your faithfulness."

I am not yet sure myself that they are wrong, Ay thought, his gaze absently on his pharaoh's lumpish thighs as he paced toward the litters. *But you need me, Akhenaten.*

He was still not sure when he sought audience with his sister the following day. Tiye dismissed the Scribe of Assemblage as Ay prostrated himself and watched the man's bare feet pad past his face. Tiye's own leather sandals with the gold-roped stays came close. Ay raised himself on his elbows, kissed her feet, and rose.

"The Scribe of Assemblage tells me that there are now four thousand troops on the building site," she said crossly. "What is Akhenaten thinking of? One thousand would be enough to keep order among the fellahin. Sebek-hotep must wake sweating in the night when he sees the rate at which gold is being drained from the Treasury. And you, Fanbearer on the Right Hand, you must be paid for your new position."

Ay watched the wrinkled, large-veined hands, heavy with jewels, swiftly roll up the scroll and toss it onto the pile on the scribe's desk. She was wearing a diaphanous pale-blue gown whose pleats floated out from under her brown, sagging breasts. Her wrinkled nipples were painted blue and glimmered with gold dust. The blue cloak she had cast onto the stool behind her was bordered with small hollow globules of gold, each containing a pellet that would tinkle as she walked. Her own red-brown hair frothed away from her high forehead, and a girlish coronet of blue enamel forget-me-nots encircled her brow. Hanging from it were spears of green enamel leaves that brushed against cheeks beginning to be pendulous with age. The clear blue eyes were set in a nest of fine wrinkles and pouches of weariness. For the first time, Ay thought that she had dressed without taste, the fresh youthfulness of her attire emphasizing, not hiding, her advancing years. Her voice, too, had the shrill querulousness of an impatient old nurse. With a sense of shock he saw in Tiye their mother, Tuyu, Handmaid and Royal Ornament, where before he had only seen in her the strength and arrogance of their father.

"As long as tribute and foreign bribes pour into the Treasury, it is bottomless," he objected mildly. "It appears that Pharaoh believes he can keep the demons away from his city with the spears and scimitars of living men. It does not matter, Empress."

"It does matter!" Tiye snapped back. "There is trouble brewing in northern Syria. Our vassals are making overtures to a nation that might become an enemy. Any fool but Pharaoh can see it. Egypt may need every soldier she has."

"Pharaoh is aware of it."

"Oh, yes." Her tone was sarcastic. "He reads the dispatches. For him, every word glows with truth. He calls those brigands Aziru and Suppiluliumas his brothers."

"Why do you take it all to heart? Aziru and Suppiluliumas are arguing as much as agreeing with each other. If they ultimately fight one another, it is good for us. If they make war together on us, we will defeat them. Perhaps a little war will bring Akhenaten to his senses."

"You are so calm, Ay." She smiled coldly. "So clever. When I listen to you, I begin to believe that my judgment has deserted me. But I tell you that the jackals smell a weakness in my son, and their appetites are whetted."

"Then let them try to feed. Egypt is more than powerful enough to ram dry bones down their throats. You used to be able to laugh, Empress, to leave matters of state behind you when you left the ministers' offices. What is wrong?"

The soft shoulders slumped. "I do not know. You, perhaps. Fanbearer—quite an honor. I am too tired to spy on you, outthink you, brood upon my every suspicion that you are edging me toward my death. I could join my voice to Nefertiti's and whisper to Pharaoh that you curry his favor only to hold your place as first noble of the kingdom, but I do not want to hurt him, even if it is the truth."

"There is nothing wrong with following a policy of personal gain in such circumstances, as you would be the first to admit if you were in my position," Ay pointed out. There was a pause. Tiye's head was down, her eyes and fingers on the scrolls the Scribe of Assemblage had left. Then Ay said quietly, "You miss him in your bed, don't you?"

The proud chin rose, but Tiye's smile was grimly self-deprecatory. "Yes, I do. But it is Osiris Amunhotep Glorified whom I miss most of all."

"Then find someone to replace him. Your nights need not be cold."

"It is not that. It is . . ." She cast about for words, then shrugged. "It is not important. But I have decided finally that when Akhenaten moves the court, I will stay here."

He nodded. "You realize, then, that you must keep Smenkhara and Beketaten with you."

Their eyes met. "Of course," Tiye answered dryly.

In the pause that followed, her gaze dropped to the cluttered desk, and she began to move the scrolls about pensively. After a while Ay said, "Can it be that the empress of Egypt has succumbed to self-pity?" He expected a tart reply, but she raised her head and smiled at him humorlessly.

"It could. The space between us has already grown, Fanbearer. I freely admit that if our positions were reversed, I would behave no differently than you have, but I mourn the loss of your presence already. Allow me the luxury of a purely human weakness."

She came out from behind the desk, holding her arms toward him, and wordlessly they embraced. Ay knew that in the generosity of her spirit, he was forgiven.

Three months later, in the middle of the harvest, word came to Malkatta that Suppiluliumas' maneuvers had become a full-scale military campaign, and that the Khatti had indeed waged battle against Aziru in northern Syria. Tiye stood in the Office of Foreign Correspondence surrounded by scribes. Tutu, Scribe of Foreign Correspondence, hovered anxiously in the background, and her son stood pale and sullen before her, his monkeys gibbering around him.

"But we have a peace treaty with Suppiluliumas," Akhenaten protested, looking uncertainly to the embarrassed Tutu. "Tutu showed it to me. How can we march against him?"

"Majesty, I am not suggesting that we make war on the Khatti," Tiye said carefully, trying to remain calmly persuasive. "But while they bicker with Mitanni as well as the Amurru, we must visit the border states that are becoming unstable. Our native viceroys there are beginning to wonder at Egypt's inaction in the face of so much unrest and are beginning to question the advantages of continued allegiance to us. Ribbadi of Gebel in particular is frantic for word from you, and the wandering Apiru tribes are once more raiding and looting the border towns. My first husband faced a situation like this and acted promptly."

"Well, what do you want me to do?" Akhenaten asked plaintively. "I'm sick of listening to Ribbadi's letters, begging for assistance. He writes all the time. I told Tutu to send him a scroll forbidding him to bother me so often. I have written to all the viceroys reminding them of their earlier blessings at Egypt's hand."

"It is no longer enough," Tiye said gently. "Call Aziru to Egypt to explain why he tried to treaty with the Khatti in the first place. Gather your Nubian Shock Troops, your archers and charioteers, and ride north. To crush the desert tribes who harry the border would be a neutral diplomatic move, favoring no one and yet reasserting Egypt's power. It is also advisable to visit your vassals, replace the viceroys that can no longer be trusted, perhaps execute a few whose loyalties have shifted. Shower the rest with gold in person, Horus. Then choose to go hunting in the area with all your might displayed. Letters cannot replace a sight of Pharaoh in all his might."

"But what of all the treaties?" He was clearly distressed, his brow furrowed under the golden cobra, his tongue darting over his hennaed lips. One of his monkeys ran up the arm of his chair and leaped onto his shoulder. Gratefully he began to fondle it. "You speak of killing, Mother. How can I kill men whose letters are friendly, who assure me of their trust, who call me the greatest king in all the world? I will think about sending to May and asking him to quell the bandits. The Apiru never write to me."

"Well, that is a start. Tutu is here. Will you dictate right now?"

"No, not now. I promised the children that I would play with them in the nursery."

Tiye was about to beg, then thought better of it. "Would you like me to write the letter for you?"

"All right." His face brightened, and kissing the monkey's ear, he set it down and rose. Instantly the people in the room began to prostrate themselves. "But it is to be nothing more than a discipline against the Apiru. I will think about the viceroys later." He walked out, the room emptying after him.

*If I cannot persuade him of the seriousness of the situation,
perhaps Nefertiti can*, Tiye thought. *He must be made to understand.* She grasped Nefertiti's braceleted arm. "Majesty," she
said in a low voice, "you do not like me, but surely you love
Egypt. Do your best to keep these affairs before his eyes."

"I think he is right, Empress," Nefertiti hissed back. "The
longer the delays, the more likely it is that our enemies will
make war on each other and become weaker because of it."

"You are wrong." Tiye's nails bit into the young woman's
flesh. "Suppiluliumas still cannot quite believe that the greatest
power in the world chooses to remain impotent. He will work
subtly, making alliances where he sees the potential for future
gains."

Nefertiti smiled tightly at her aunt. "This is all you have
left, dear empress, the dubious ability to interpret foreign affairs
in order to try to regain some influence over the god. It will
not work. Your star is falling." She pursed her lips and sucked
soothingly at the two monkeys clinging to her gown. "I must
go. Take your fingers from my arm, Majesty. Already you have
bruised me, and I will need a massage to remove the marks."

"You need a good whipping, Nefertiti. Your father was
always too lenient with you." Tiye stepped back disgustedly,
and Nefertiti glided out. Tutu stood waiting, eyes downcast.
"And you, you venal toe-licker," Tiye spat at him, "if it was
in my power, I would have you replaced. A Scribe of Foreign
Correspondence is supposed to think for himself and offer bold
advice, but all you do is parrot my niece's words." Frustration
made her want to cry. Tutu was flinching, but his lower lip
stuck out mutinously, and Tiye knew he realized that he had
nothing to fear from her. She was tempted to push the scrolls
to the floor and walk away from the office, the sly minister,
the responsibility that had become such a desperate burden.
There would be fresh dusty grapes from her vineyards at
Djarukha set out beside her couch, and beer from this year's
barley, dark and cool. "I want a copy of this for my own
scribes," she said, "and you had better have it translated into
Akkadian and sent to Urusalim and Gebel. It will do those
cities good to know that Egypt is at least chasing the desert
bowmen. 'To the commander of the fortress troops of His
Majesty, May, greetings. It has been brought to our wise attention that . . .'" Tutu wrote quickly and as silently as he could,

and when Tiye had finished, she left without another glance at him.

Outside in the passage Huya was waiting patiently. "Have my litter and canopy brought," Tiye ordered. "I want to go to the parade ground today and watch the Division of Splendor of the Aten go through their paces." Huya looked into her face and did not demur. Tiye was carried out onto the blinding sand of the parade ground, where the captains shouted their orders and the soldiers wheeled and marched, scimitars flashing in the sun, their bare feet churning white dust. The sight did not cheer her. The army of Egypt was like a chariot without an axle, beautiful but useless. She began to long passionately for the day when Pharaoh and his minions would sail away and not come back, and Malkatta with its quiet gardens and echoing corridors would belong to her and her memories, alone.

15

IN THE FOLLOWING YEAR TIYE PERSUADED PHARAOH to dispatch another punitive expedition north, grimly aware that Egypt was merely holding up a splayed hand against the fury of a khamsin. Ribbadi's letters, reproachful, puzzled, loving, and finally panic-stricken, cut her to the quick, but she could do nothing. Abimilki of Tyre begged for troops. Other petty kings and viceroys begged for understanding, and Tiye knew that their letters required the patience and cunning of a man with the seasoned wisdom of Osiris Amunhotep to decipher. The passive simplicity of her son was no match for the wily protestations of men who had already secretly allied themselves with the greatest force ever pitted against the stability of the Egyptian empire, but whose words of wounded loyalty brought a pleased flush to Akhenaten's long face. Aziru, taking advantage of the confusing situation and carefully avoiding antagonizing Suppiluliumas, began murdering Egyptian officials in Syria and blaming his old enemies. He responded to Akhenaten's request for his presence at Malkatta, apologizing that since he was busy defending Syrian cities against the Khatti, he could not appear for at least a year. Tiye, furious, demanded that a division march into Amurru territory and execute Aziru, but Akhenaten, after vacillating between the evidence of Akkadian cipher pressed into clay that he could hold in his hands and the less physical and more uncomfortable interpretation his mother gave him, decided to believe Aziru. He granted him a year's grace. Ribbadi fled from his city of Byblos, and the Khatti flowed slowly after him. Megiddo, Lachish, Askalon, and Gezer sent letter after letter to Malkatta, screaming for money, troops and food, and while Akhenaten agonized over the truth, the vassal cities fell to marauding Apiru, now in the pay of Suppiluliumas. Many of the Canaanite vassals were forced to sue for peace to the Khatti, trading Egypt's overlordship in return for their lives.

During the following year, the eighth of Akhenaten's reign and the fourth since he had decreed the building of his city, Aziru marched against Sumer and took it with much bloodshed. His letters to Egypt remained full of protestations of loyalty, and the difficulties he was having evading Suppiluliumas. Ever the gambler, he sent similar letters to the Khatti prince himself against the day when, as he believed, Egypt and the Khatti would fight. He wrote to the defeated and harried Ribbadi, offering his asylum, and Ribbadi, his good judgment failing him, fled to the Amurru with little but his family and a few household possessions. Akhenaten did not hear from him again. Aziru once more began convoluted negotiations with Suppiluliumas.

In Malkatta day-long processions of slaves laden with boxes and chests began to move between palace and river, for after four years of construction Pharaoh's city was finally ready for occupation. He had named it Akhetaten, Horizon of the Aten. Barges slipped downstream, bright with torches at night, bearing the last possessions of the men who wandered through the empty rooms of their apartments and houses before ordering their servants to seal the doors. In the Office of Foreign Correspondence, chaos reigned as scribes covered the floor knee to knee, rapidly transcribing the more important missives from clay tables to lighter and more portable papyrus scrolls that could be taken to Tutu's new headquarters at Akhetaten while the tablets themselves were carried into storage. The daily dispatches were often lost amid the disorderly pile of older correspondence. Pharaoh, who was overwrought with excitement and anticipation, retreated to his unfinished Karnak temple, where he was soothed by the worship of his priests and the incense mingling with the prayers of Meryra, while Nefertiti snapped at the servants struggling to pack her thousands of gowns, her jewels and sandals and heavy wigs.

The only place in the palace that was free from all activity was the nursery, where Smenkhara and Beketaten, taking advantage of their tutor's frequent absences, and their mother's self-imposed seclusion, went to play with Nefertiti's three daughters.

"I will dictate a letter to you every day, telling you what lessons I am doing and how many fish I have caught and when I shoot my first lion," Smenkhara promised Meritaten as they sprawled on mats together, waiting for the fitful draughts blowing down the wind catcher from the roof. "And you must tell me in return what Pharaoh's new palace is like, and whether the hunting is good in the hills there, and what new women are bought for the harem. Meketaten, you are lying on my foot. Go and play with my sister."

"But I want to go swimming, and Beketaten only wants to tease the monkeys," the girl replied sullenly. "Don't kick me, Smenkhara! I can lie here and listen to you if I want to."

Meritaten sat up. "You!" she called to one of the slaves standing by the door. "Take these two down to the lake. Where is Ankhesenpaaten?"

"She is being washed before she sleeps, Highness," the woman said, bowing, as Meketaten jumped up, and Beketaten, across the room, began to wail with indignation.

"I don't want to swim. I'll tell Mother!"

"Tell her, then," Smenkhara said rudely. The slave bowed again and waited while the princesses came to her, Meketaten skipping, Beketaten pushing the monkeys out the window and onto the flower bed with angry reluctance. "Send someone to us with beer," Smenkhara ordered as they went out. "And hurry. It is hot, and we are thirsty." The door closed.

"I will ask my father every day to send for you," Meritaten said in a low voice, her eyes on the remaining servants fanning themselves in a cluster at the farther end of the nursery. "I will throw tantrums and scream and make myself sick until he listens."

Smenkhara wound her youth lock around his fingers and pulled her face close. "Pharaohs do not listen to eight-year-old girls, particularly your father. He is too frightened of the empress to send for me. Besides, he does not like me. He cannot afford to."

"Why not?" Meritaten jerked her hair from his grasp. "My mother is pregnant again and says that this time she will have a prince, and he will marry me, and I will be queen one day."

"Yes, you will, but only when I become pharaoh and marry you. That is why my brother the king does not like me. At least, so my mother says."

A servant approached and soundlessly knelt, placing a tray with beer and cups before them. Smenkhara emptied his cup in one drought. "I am sick of lying about in here. Put on your kilt, and we will sail on the river. You can watch me fish."

Meritaten obediently set down her cup, clapped her hands for her kilt, and waited while her slave wound it around her waist. Smenkhara watched with interest until her sandals were put on and the kohl retouched around her eyes, and he grabbed the ribbons of her youth lock and nonchalantly began to tow her toward the door.

Tiye stepped from her litter and, ordering her retinue to wait by the gate with a wave of her hand, walked toward her brother's house. The garden where she had sat so often through the years, drinking wine and laughing with him, watching his baboons scratch themselves and lumber from one patch of shade to another or listening to the hum of chatter and the babble of music, was empty and still in the oppressive heat of midafternoon. The sheltered stone quay where his barge used to rock was empty also, the water steps a painful dance of white light, the river at their foot oily and sluggish. *I always feel at home here*, Tiye thought as she came to the raised yellow- and blue-painted pillars of the shaded portico. *There are so many good memories. My father with his hooked nose and white waving hair, smiling quietly as my mother held forth on some nugget of harem gossip in her deep voice, her bracelets sliding up her brown arms and her fingers stabbing the air. Anen cross-legged on the grass, his priestly linens folded neatly in his lap, his head down as he listened, not really taking in the words. Ay himself venturing a comment or correction, always gracious, always the knowing courtier, and in the early days Tey as well, beautiful and flushed, interspersing the conversation with unfinished phrases, disconnected words, spoken flotsam drifting occasionally to her tongue from the confused river of her private thoughts. Osiris Amunhotep never came here, nor Sitamun,* Tiye thought as a single servant rose from a stool by the open doors and prostrated himself on the warm stone. *Strange that I do not place Ay's first wife here, though she must have been, or the children Nefertiti and Mutnodjme. How gently the years fall away as I wait.* A tiny movement at her feet brought her back to the present, and she bade the man rise.

"Tell my niece that I am here, and bring chairs for us," she said. She turned her back on the doors while he hurried within, allowing herself to indulge in a moment of pure nostalgia, and when she swung back to the house with a sigh, it was to find Mutnodjme bowing at her back. The young woman's youth lock was unbraided, falling in a crinkled black rope to her naked knees. She was without paint, her face pale, her eyes seeming smaller under the habitually swollen lids. She had hurriedly cast a transparent white cloak around her shoulders but otherwise was undressed. Her servant unfolded stools, served water from the barrel cooling by the wall, and then at a word from Tiye disappeared into the dim interior of the house. Mutnodjme smiled faintly and collapsed onto her stool as Tiye settled comfortably beside her.

"You have been supervising your father's move," Tiye said, and Mutnodjme nodded.

"Everything has gone, and I am exhausted, Majesty Aunt. I slept longer than usual today. Forgive me for not being up to greet you. As soon as I receive word that Father is settled and I have forgotten nothing, I, too, go north to rejoin my husband."

"Are you happy with Horemheb?"

The question startled Mutnodjme. She raised her feathered eyebrows and grinned slowly at her aunt. "Yes, I am. He makes few demands on me apart from the ones I like, and he has taught me the boundaries across which I may not venture, while keeping my respect. He is becoming quite an influential courtier, you know."

"I know," Tiye replied shortly. "Were you able to replace your dwarfs?"

"Horemheb tells me in his latest letter that two new ones are waiting for me at Akhetaten. They cost him a fortune."

"He will quickly make another." Tiye eyed the languid,

relaxed slump of the angular shoulders under the filmy linen, the long legs crossed at the ankles, the brown nipples showing where the cloak parted and fell to the ground. "Do you think you will like Pharaoh's city?"

Mutnodjme shrugged. "It is a marvel to behold, a toy of great beauty, one vast temple. I am happy wherever my friends are. It is certain that my husband has been given an estate for us, the like of which I have never seen. Pharaoh has spared no expense to assure the contentment of his courtiers. Therefore I will like living at Akhetaten."

"I hear that Tey has decided to move from Akhmin."

Mutnodjme laughed, lifted her chin, and upended her cup. Water trickled down her neck and across her navel and began to pool between her thighs. "My mother is trying once again to be a dutiful wife. It does not suit her. Even though Father has built a very secluded estate for her across the river from the city, she will become anxious and sillier than ever until the call of Akhmin is too strong to be denied. Then she will steal away."

"Ay loves her."

"And she him. That is not the point, Majesty Aunt. She only feels safe at Akhmin."

I understand, Tiye thought with a sudden spurt of sympathy for Ay's lovely, disheveled wife. "Mutnodjme, I did not come here today just to gossip. I have a task for you," she said abruptly. "It is not a divine command. You may refuse it if you wish."

Mutnodjme began to smile. "You want me to be your spy in Akhetaten, don't you, Goddess?"

Tiye smiled back wryly. She had not realized the degree of perceptiveness hidden beneath her niece's air of lazy detachment. "Yes, I do. I will pay you very well. You stand apart from the struggles for power. You care about nothing, and that is why you will be able to report exactly what you see and feel."

"Horemheb would not like it." Mutnodjme's voice was sharp. "And it is not true that I care about nothing." Her eyes had cleared, and she was watching Tiye intently. "I care about my husband. I will not put him in danger or subject him to the risk of disfavor."

"Yet your infidelities are the talk of every bored courtier."

"Pah! To while away an endless afternoon with a handsome body, what is that? I would kill for Horemheb."

Tiye hid her surprise. "Spy for me, and you would be protecting him in the long run. It is only a matter of time before those surrounding my son see the necessity of making him understand what the truth really is. Horemheb surely cannot believe either in the supremacy of the Aten or the policy of abject appeasement Akhenaten is following with regard to the empire. Pharaoh needs real friends, Mutnodjme, people who will resist him for his own good."

"Horemheb only moved to Akhetaten because Pharaoh promised him the Nubian gold monopoly the Amun priests hold at present," Mutnodjme replied, "and perhaps because he has some influence already. He likes your husband, Empress, whether he believes him right or wrong. He does not understand him, but he is prepared to be loyal."

"Horemheb used to be loyal to me!"

"He still is, but we must live, and besides, nothing could have been gained by his remaining either at an empty Malkatta or patrolling on the border, though my father wanted to send him back there." She got up and, sliding to the water barrel, drew another draught. Tiye shook her head at the proffered cup, and Mutnodjme leaned against a pillar and drank. "Do you swear, Majesty Aunt, that you are pursuing no plots that involve my husband?"

"Of course I so swear! Horemheb is the best young commander Egypt has, and I know his larger and more important loyalty is to the country itself."

"What will you pay me?"

Tiye smiled inwardly. "One hundred new slaves every year, from the country of your choice. One quarter of my profits from Alashian trade. And my permission to dike and flood an extra one hundred acres of my private estates at Djarukha, for your own cultivation."

Mutnodjme nodded. "Agreed. But I will report to you only what I wish, not necessarily what you ask, and I dictate no scrolls to be held against me later."

"I have thought of that. I will give you my tongueless slave. Speak your reports to him, and he will come to me and transcribe them in front of me. I will read and then burn them."

"Majesty, you know that I am lazy and refuse to hurry breathless from one audience to another, or hang about outside closed doors in the hope of catching some item of news. Besides, I am not sure that I can trust you."

"Then, have me spied upon." They laughed together. Mutnodjme eased down the pillar until she was squatting at its base. "I do not want reports on royal policies from you," Tiye went on after a moment. "I want the smell of the air, the tones of men's voices. You need not send to me regularly, either. I am sure that Ay will keep me informed, too."

"Majesty, Pharaoh has built a great house for you there," Mutnodjme said quietly. "Why will you stay here in the twilight? Is it because of my disagreeable half sister?"

"I am goddess," Tiye replied coolly and rose. Mutnodjme bowed perfunctorily. "May your name live forever," Tiye finished and, stepping out into the glare of the late afternoon, made her way to the gate, where her servants dozed. The garden no longer breathed sweetly of the past, but as she bent her head to shield her face from the sun, she realized that the pain she carried under her breast was not the sadness of a vanished mood. It was the sudden envy she felt toward Mutnodjme. She glanced back. The portico was empty, the stools still drawn close together, a patch of water evaporating on the stone, and Mutnodjme's cup lay forgotten on the grass where she had tossed it.

On the night before Pharaoh was due to leave Malkatta, Tiye could not sleep. She had wandered about her apartments during the day, unable to settle to anything, expecting that Akhenaten would send for her. She had called her dancers to perform, Tia-Ha to amuse her, and Piha to massage her, but her thoughts remained on the man who was both son and husband, child and lover. She refused to believe that he could go without a word to her, even though it had been months since he had wanted to spend any private time with her. He had issued no directives regarding the disposition of the old palace, left none of his own staff to provide a link to his empress. It was as if with his departure the whole huge magnificent edifice that had held the heart of Egypt for years would disappear, leaving nothing but lizards and jerboas to crouch in the foundations. Proudly Tiye had refused to approach him. If he wished to sail away without a word, as though she were already dead, then so be it. She told herself that she longed for the kind of peaceful retirement her own aunt, Queen Mutemwiya, had enjoyed in the seclusion of a sumptuous apartment in the harem. She would fight no more battles.

She had ordered her physician to prepare a sleeping draught, but Ra sailed the Duat through House after House, and she still lay tense, listening to the faint notes of Karnak's horns drifting across the river, her naked body sticky and restless under the linen sheet. Twice she roused Piha to bring her water, but its warmth nauseated her. She was so certain that sleep had eluded her that she could not believe she was waking to the dark form bending over her until it hesitantly touched her cheek. She cried out and sat up, and Akhenaten took a step away from the couch.

"I sent Piha to the servants' quarters," he whispered unnecessarily. "I wish to speak to you alone, Tiye."

The use of her name was a good omen, but she whispered back, "Does Nefertiti know you are here, Majesty?" She could not tell, in the dim light, whether it was a flush of embarrassment or simply the play of shadow on his thin neck as he craned down at her. "Or were you ashamed to bid me farewell in public?"

"Why, no," he said in a louder voice, his expression puzzled. "I supposed we would say farewell on the water steps in the morning. I could not sleep."

Relenting, Tiye patted the couch by her knees. "Neither could I. Amunhotep, it is still not too late to change your mind. Leave your city to the owls and jackals and stay here!"

"Do not call me that!" He scowled briefly, his pendulous lower lip jutting. "It is not too late for you to change your mind either, my mother. I have prepared a magnificent house for you in Akhetaten, full of pleasure gardens and other delights, as befits an empress. Please come." Under the band of the plain white linen sleeping cap, his high forehead was furrowed. Tiye laid hot fingers gently on his bare thigh.

"There is no reason for me to leave my home," she said. "You have made it obvious that you no longer need me, either as empress or as wife. I did wrong to break the law with you, Akhenaten. My judgment was impaired. I look for nothing now but peace."

"I do not understand." He picked up her hand and began to knead it. "The Aten has made us one forever. The joining of our bodies was needful. I told you."

"But it is not needful any longer." The words were spoken half as statement, half as question. "Let me go, Akhenaten."

He glanced at her sharply, distress in his face. "Does that mean you do not love me? Have I offended you?" Anxiety drove the light voice even higher. "The Aten would be angry if I offended you, Tiye."

She felt herself being unwillingly drawn once again into the maze of strong, conflicting emotions that had lain dormant in her, waiting to entangle her thoughts and direct her body whenever her son was near. Tonight she firmly denied them. "Go back to your couch," she said harshly, taking her hand away. "Yesterday you were ill. My physician told me so. You need to sleep so that you may sail tomorrow."

"How can I leave Malkatta knowing that I have disappointed you?"

Oh gods, Tiye thought wearily. "You have not disappointed me, my son. Are you not the incarnation of Ra, the Spirit of the Aten Disk? How can a god disappoint?" She spoke soothingly, but she was not mollified.

"You make me feel like a child!" he burst out, coming suddenly to his feet and beginning to sway from one to the other. "I know you do not mean what you say! You try to calm me, but you really just want me to go away!"

"You are my pharaoh," she said deliberately. "You have Nefertiti, surely the most beautiful woman who ever walked the earth. You have such power, such wealth! What more is there? Why do you make these outbursts in my presence?"

He stopped swaying and stiffened. "Because I do not have from you the adoration I have from everyone else. You know me too well."

It was a moment of great clarity she had not expected from him, and it astonished and disarmed her. "But the knowing is with love. Do not worry. You will still be pharaoh at Akhetaten, and I will still be your mother here in Malkatta."

"Will you miss me?" His hands were pressed together between his soft thighs. "Will you miss me enough not to plot against me and do me harm?"

"So Nefertiti wishes me to come to Akhetaten so that she can keep an eye on me!" Relieved, Tiye laughed. "I am flattered. Yet for your own peace of mind, you must remember that she speaks from jealousy. I only want to be left alone."

He began to fidget again, and puzzled, she saw that she had

somehow insulted him; even so, she pressed forward. "I have done my utmost to see you seated firmly on the Horus Throne, and I have no desire now to face the prospect of Nefertiti's sour complaints. Your lack of trust in me, Amunhotep, does you no credit. I have tried to be both wife and mother to you, and I have failed. I miss your father! Please leave my chamber."

For answer he came back to the couch and pushed her down. He was trembling. "I am my father, and you are my wife!" he cried out. "You love me, you know you do! Tell me, Tiye!"

"I do not want to hear it tonight," she said forcefully. "I am not easily biddable, like little Kia or one of your concubines. You have ignored me both in and out of bed for too long. Take your hands from my shoulders or I shall call for my guards."

"If you will not come, then give me your love to carry with me," he said, his voice muffled in the pillow beside her ear. "Once more, dear Tiye, to ensure my good fortune."

"I am not an amulet or a spell!" She struggled under his weight, knowing that she could easily throw him off, but she was suddenly weakened by the truth of her own words. *It has been so long, too long*, said the insidious voice in her head. She felt the familiar touch of his skin against her body, and her knees loosened, her thighs opened. Angry in spite of it, she tried to rise on her elbows, but as her face tilted, Amunhotep's mouth closed over hers, tasting of cloves and perfumed wine, the flavor she had come to associate with his father. A vision of his full, lined face was there, so real that she felt a quick wrenching in her stomach before she pulled away. Instantly her son drew back also.

"You do still love me!" He smiled happily. "I knew you did."

"I love you as my son, my god," Tiye managed, her voice thick, her limbs heavy. He lowered his head and kissed her again, more gently this time, with the soft, exploratory hesitancy she remembered so well. Her body, still vital, knew only that it had been hungry, but her thoughts recoiled even as her arms went round his neck, his movements recalling the days at Memphis, the first joy of their marriage, reminding her of the months when he had ignored her. She had forgotten the sensation of his strange, misshapen belly, his flabby thighs and boyish genitals, but the repulsion that had always hovered in her mind was still not as powerful as her physical response to him. *He is going away*, she thought dimly, listening to her own muttered words of love and encouragement, *and then it will not matter anymore.*

"That was good," he said later as she lay beside him, head turned away, the sheet bunched in one stiff hand. "It was like being born all over again, like watching myself expelled from my own womb." He stood and fastened his kilt. "At Akhetaten I will live in hope that one day you will come sailing to the wharf. Once more your body has blessed my endeavors, Tiye. The god will call you to my city."

Tiye shuddered and did not turn to see him leave. "Dawn comes, and I want to sleep" was all that she was able to reply.

When he had gone, she pushed the pillows to the floor and set a headrest under her neck. The ivory was cool, spreading comfort down her spine. Reaching under the couch, she drew out the Declaration of Innocence that had so offended Kheruef and placed it on her stomach, one hand over it protectively. She wanted to sleep. Her eyes burned, and her mouth was dry. But the realization that had come to her several hours earlier now returned. *I am not a woman to him, as Nefertiti is*, she thought. *I am an amulet, a lucky charm to keep evil at bay, something to be lifted from a chest now and then and strapped to his arm, only to be dropped back with his other trinkets when the moment of anxiety is gone.* The humiliation of it made her squeeze her eyes shut and groan softly. *You are getting old, Empress,* she told herself. *This savage blow to your pride has not even provoked anger in you, or a desire for revenge. Nothing but shame, and wonder. But perhaps it is only that he wished to reassure himself that his hold on me was as strong as ever, that my loyalty was not suspect. If I had been prepared, if I had sent him away immediately, he would have sailed to Akhetaten in doubt and misery. It is better this way. Let him feel safe, my innocent son. Let tomorrow be glorious for him.*

In the end she fell deeply, soddenly asleep, dragging herself to consciousness with difficulty when the music of pipe and lute penetrated her dreams. As she opened her eyes, Piha was raising the shades, and her musicians, their duty done, were bowing and retiring. Already the day was breathless with heat, the sky glimpsed through the window an azure blue tinged with bronze. The Declaration of Innocence was still in her hand. She pressed it to her cheek and then dropped it beneath the couch.

*　*　*

The remains of the court of Malkatta—Tiye's retinue, the few courtiers who chose to stay, and the older harem women—gathered on the water steps a scant two hours later to watch Pharaoh's departure. Tiye sat on her throne under the thin shade of a canopy, the horned disk and plumes bearing down on her sweat-slicked brow like the weight of the empire itself. From steps to river the canal was choked with craft of every description, all flying bright pennants, all crowded with laughing, jostling people. Those standing behind Tiye were silent, and it was slowly borne in upon her that more than a few paces of grass and hot stone separated her and her attendants from the excited hundreds her eyes scanned painfully. She had glimpsed the crest of an invisible wave many times since Osiris Amunhotep had died, a distant pale line of warning and melancholy, the rising tide of time itself, and now it rose around her. She turned on the throne. Everywhere there were faces touched lightly or scored heavily with approaching age, bodies loosened and folded, eyes filmed, limbs that would move heavily, and some with pain. It did not matter that those bodies held kas that would always be buoyant with the exuberance of youth. Between spirit and its yearning was aging flesh, and only the eyes around her could still show the soul undistorted. Tiye found herself gazing at Tia-Ha, a short, fat woman with too much paint on her cheeks, bowing and smiling with the girlish gestures of a coquette. Quickly she looked away only to meet Nefertiti's level regard. Tall and slim, her wig netted in golden spirals that coiled around the ringlets to her waist and then went whirling past the smooth hips to the knees, the woman was staring at her. *And she is a woman*, Tiye reflected with dismay. *Twenty-eight years old. How has it happened?* Nefertiti's new pregnancy was showing, and she seemed to symbolize all that Tiye knew she had lost forever. In the triumph of the moment Nefertiti smiled at her aunt before she vanished into the gloom of the curtained cabin.

Akhenaten stepped forward, the Double Crown gleaming, the pharaonic beard of woven gold and lapis lazuli sparkling. Fresh incense billowed upward, and the Aten priests began the prayers of worship and safe voyage. Akhenaten took Tiye's hands as she rose.

"You know that I have vowed never to return to Thebes," he said quietly. "If you wish to see me again, you must come to Akhetaten. A new age begins for our beloved Egypt, O my

mother, and ten thousand hentis from now, when the worship
of the Aten has spread throughout the world, men will have
forgotten that Thebes and its god ever existed. But they will
remember that you gave birth to me, and they will speak your
name with reverence."

She stroked his cheek once, delicately. "Your head pains
you again today."

He began to nod, squinting against the agony the small
movement caused. "Yes. Once more the god's hand is on me,
but I will be able to sleep when Thebes is out of my sight."

There was nothing more to say. Tiye sat back on her throne
as Akhenaten went to slit the throat of the bull already trussed
and waiting quietly on the portable altar, and the wine and
purifying milk were poured over the water steps. Bowls of
blood were passed among the people thronging before the palace and those already standing in the barges, but there was
none of the frantic rush to anoint that had been characteristic
of thanksgivings in previous days. Akhenaten's court had learned
sobriety.

At last Pharaoh raised a bloody hand and walked up the
ramp, disappearing into the cabin. Pasi, his captain, shouted,
and the ropes were untied. The oars hit the water with a splash,
and *Kha-em-Ma'at* pulled away from Malkatta.

Tiye did not remain, but signaling to Huya and her women,
she made her way into the palace, through the giant reception
hall, now cool and empty, through Pharaoh's private audience
hall and throne room, to the garden beyond. Here she mounted
the steps set against the outside wall of the palace and stood
at last on the roof. Beyond the line of palms waving stiffly,
the hundreds of barges were jostling for position behind the
royal boat, which had already turned north. Oars dipped and
gleamed with water. Banners and flags rippled. The islands
that dotted the Nile between Thebes and Malkatta gained def-
inition as one by one the boats separated, and water began to
glitter between them. Today there was no haze. The pylons
and towers of Karnak stood out knife-sharp against the blue
sky, and around it the horizon of the mighty city spread to right
and left seemingly without end.

"There are thousands of people lining the quays and standing
in the water," Tiye said presently to Huya. "They are even on
the roofs. Yet I cannot hear them."

"That is because they are silent, Majesty," Huya replied

dryly. "It is not a day for rejoicing. I can glimpse no Amun priests at the Karnak water steps either."

"It is a sight they do not wish to behold." Tiye shaded her eyes with one hand. The uneven brown mass of city dwellers was curiously still as well as quiet, and gradually a sense of their hostility stole over Tiye, a premonition of resentment and latent, directionless violence.

Huya felt it also and, stirring beside her, stepped back from the edge of the roof and wiped his face. "I do not think they yet understand what has happened to them," he remarked as Tiye also left the low parapet. "There will be no more purchases of food, wine, and luxuries from Thebes, for that trade has, of course, gone north to Akhetaten with the foreign ambassadors. With it has also gone the commerce that brought the majority of foreign goods to Malkatta, not to mention the grain harvests from the private estates of the nobles. And Pharaoh is no longer building in the vicinity of the city. There will be many hungry people without employment."

"They still have the priests' business," Tiye snapped. "There are upwards of twenty thousand priests at Karnak whose goods still need handling. Thebes will suffer, but it will not die. Listen to the emptiness around us, Huya! I think I will sleep the rest of the day away."

It was good to lie in the quiet, darkened room, to close her eyes and drift into sleep without tension. She did not wake until the following dawn and did not rise until she had eaten in bed and had been entertained by singers. She dressed and was painted with deliberate leisure and, taking Huya, Piha, and a handful of Followers, strolled unimpeded through the palace. Room after room greeted her with echoing aloofness. Doors stood open onto bare tiled floors splashed with sunlight. Patterns she had long failed to notice sprang out at her along walls no longer hidden by furniture, the colors and lines oddly fresh and new now that they dominated the empty rooms. Scoured passages gave back the slap of her sandals, and dust was already gathering in the formal stillness of bedchambers. The huge reception hall with its dais and friezed baldachin seemed to hold the heart of the strangeness, its perpetual gloom and awesome height redolent with memories. Appalled, Tiye ordered the sealing of all empty rooms in the palace.

In the afternoon she visited the ministers' offices, only to face the same air of abandonment. The slaves had not yet cleaned them, and it was possible to imagine that the men who had worked there might return at any moment, for scrolls, pens, empty inkpots, and bits of cheap pottery on which architecture apprentices had scribbled half-formed ideas lay piled on desks and across the floors. Tutu's office was the worst, a shambles of hasty evacuation. Tiye picked a broken tablet out of the wreckage, deciphering the language of official communication with difficulty. "To the god my king, seven times seven I fall at your feet..." The deep Akkadian characters ended in a crumbling break. Sighing, Tiye reiterated her orders for the sealing of doors and sought refuge in the harem with Tia-Ha.

When she arrived, she found the princess pacing, picking her way with unerring skill through the disorderly welter of cushions, discarded gowns, and half-eaten fruit and sweet-meats.

"Already the palace distresses me, Majesty," she told Tiye. "Now that Pharaoh has appropriated the younger women for his new harem and only we old matrons are left, Malkatta is like a friendly tomb."

"So you want to retire to the Delta after all." Tiye sat on the couch, her eyes on the play of sunlight against her shins as Tia-Ha passed back and forth in front of her.

"If my goddess will be kind enough to let me go." Tia-Ha blew out a gust of breath and threw up her hands. "I have so little time left. I had thought that it would be intriguing to observe your son's administration, but its course has been sober, predictable, and without any great scandals. Apart from your own marriage to him, of course." She cast a sidelong glance full of warmth at Tiye. "I cannot take the heat of Upper Egypt any longer. Have I permission to send my steward north to prepare my house?"

"Certainly." Tiye managed a smile. "Years ago I offered you your freedom. Your husband is dead. You are a widow. Perhaps you will marry again."

"No," Tia-Ha replied, coming to a halt and gazing out the window. "Not after Osiris Amunhotep. Diversions there will be, but not love. There is no longer anything but you to hold me here. There is nothing for you, either, Majesty. Go to Djarukha. Do not stay here. These empty apartments will begin to haunt your dreams."

"I am still empress," Tiye reminded her waspishly. "Malkatta is a more fitting home than a private estate."

"Of course." Tia-Ha turned and bowed contritely. "I spoke hastily, out of concern for you. May I dictate letters to Your Majesty, full of all the new gossip I shall uncover among the provincials?"

"Oh, Tia-Ha! How could I live without word from you! May Hathor prolong your vigor!"

"A congenial man will do better." Tia-Ha laughed. "Come, Tiye. Let us while away the evening with the sennet, and perhaps you would do me the honor of feasting with me in the garden once Ra has gone."

"I shall miss you," Tiye said by way of reply.

Tiye did not visit her friend again, and they said no formal good-byes, but a week later Huya reported that Tia-Ha's apartments were empty. Tiye went onto the roof with the news and sat through the deepening twilight of the evening, wrestling with the grief the princess's going had prompted. It was more than the loss of an old companion, for they would exchange letters and gifts in the months to come. Tiye knew that the pain welled up from the place where her past existed, where she and Tia-Ha were young, and Amunhotep her husband still lived in the vitality of his manhood. *We were so happy then*, she thought as the darkness gathered around her, and the stars began to appear. *I seldom considered my fate as the years slipped away, and when I did, I imagined that the latter part of my life would be spent surrounded by the fruits of my endeavor, a time of contentment and companionship. No presentiment of the truth ever troubled my young dreams. Now that past is over, gone like a swift glimmer of moonlight on ruffled water, and if I am to have courage, I must not look back. I am alone, the future is barren, my title of empress means nothing anymore. Yet I am still the goddess of Soleb, and there the priests still sing to my immortal likeness, and the incense fills my temple. I must remember that. Even if the years ahead hold only the unwanted peace of encroaching age, I am forever worthy to be worshiped.*

16

DURING THE FOLLOWING MONTHS, TIYE HAD CAUSE TO RE-
member Tia-Ha's warning that the empty rooms at Malkatta
would haunt her. The closed and sealed doors began to prey
on her mind. She would lie awake at night thinking of the dark
passages fronted by door after red-waxed door, and if she dared
to imagine herself going through them, it was to see other
stately rooms opening one after another, all filled with a forbidding secrecy. During the day she found herself less and less
able to pass the unguarded portals leading to Pharaoh's rooms,
the queen's suite, or the places of public audience. She began
to hold modest feasts of her own in the dining hall, inviting
her own engineers, architects, stewards, and personal ministers
to eat and enjoy her musicians and dancers, but the few hundred
attending could not dispel the larger shadows, and their merriment rang shrill and false. Tiye soon transferred her meals
to her own rooms, taking over a large portion of Nefertiti's
former apartment to accommodate her guests, so that she would
no longer see unfilled places or tall pillars casting unbroken
shadows in the yellow lamplight.

Before long messages arrived from her brother and Mutnodjme. She did not trust her scribe to read Ay's scroll to her,
so it was Huya who sank cross-legged before her. Ay had
written in his own hand, not with the hieroglyphs expected but
in the clear-flowing hieratic script used by tradesmen. "To my
dearest sister and eternal empress, greetings. May Min favor
you with youth, strength, and every blessing. Know first that
my wife, your subject Tey, is well and kisses your feet. Know
second that the Vizier of the South, Ramose, has died and has
been replaced by Nakht-pa-Aten, he that was once a priest of
Amun but who has since seen the truth of the Aten." Tiye
smiled grimly to herself as Huya paused to cough discreetly.
Nakht-pa-Aten was a pleasant enough young man but more
than ignorant of the duties of vizier. "Pharaoh immediately

made him a Person of Gold. Indeed, the Gold of Favors has been distributed with great prodigality since Pharaoh took up residence here. I myself have been fortunate enough to be showered with the Gold of Favors, and I am now the King's Own Scribe." *A little warning*, Tiye thought. *As Pharaoh's most trusted scribe, Ay will be constantly spied upon by those jealous of him and by those who are suspicious of his relationship to me and who fear for Akhenaten's safety.* "Know third that Aziru himself is once more negotiating for peace and alliance with Suppululiumas. Suppululiumas's campaign against northern Syria and our dependencies there is coming to a halt, because he has been victorious. I kiss your beautiful feet and pray before your divine image, O Goddess of Soleb. May your name live forever." Huya allowed the scroll to close with a rustle.

Tiye was silent. *It is pointless for me to worry afresh about the erosion of the empire*, she thought. *I can do no more; therefore I would be well advised to put it out of my mind. Certainly my son would never allow things to go so far that Egypt would have to fight on our own soil! Even now it is not too late to recapture some of our might and prestige. A small show of arms, a few executions . . .* She came to herself with a burst of quick laughter. "Burn the scroll in the brazier on your way out, Huya, and send the dumb servant to me." He bowed and left, pausing to thrust Ay's neat, strong handwriting into the orange flames.

Behind her the doors closed, and the dumb servant came in bowing and then fell to the floor and crawled to kiss her feet. She waved him up, going to the table and dipping a pen in ink. She held it out to him, and for a moment their eyes met. Tiye looked into the face of the man who had murdered Sitamun. She did not regret having put him to work in her kitchens and later having had him taught to write. Dumb servants were few and far between. He took the pen, waited until she had put a suitable distance between them, and then began to write. The message was not long, and Tiye took it from the table where the man had carefully placed it. *All Akhetaten is agog with the disclosure that the Great Temple here does indeed have a ben-ben, unlike the unfinished Aten temple at Karnak*, Tiye read silently. *It is a sacred stela. On it are carved the likenesses of Pharaoh, the queen, and Princess Meritaten.* The room seemed suddenly chill. Tiye held the piece of papyrus with distaste

and, striding to the brazier, cast it in. There was no doubt who
was worshiped in Akhetaten, in the holiest of holiest. Her son
was sacrificing to himself, with Nefertiti proudly elevated to
a share in his godly omnipotence. The inclusion of Meritaten
on the stela disturbed Tiye, but she could not say why. "Tell
the sender of this news that the dikes have been dug at Djarukha,
and a shipment of slaves can be expected within the month,"
she instructed the man. "Now get out."

When he had gone, Huya slipped back into the room and
stood waiting. Tiye indicated the scribe's palette on the floor.
"Take a dispatch for Pharaoh," she ordered, "and have it copied
and sent to Ay as well. Begin with the usual salutations, and
do not forget to add 'my august and all-seeing husband.'" She
waited while he penned the words, gathered her courage, and
dictated. "By the power of Your Majesty's great virility I, your
empress, am again with child..."

The pen clattered to the tiling. "Majesty!" Huya exclaimed.
Tiye clenched her fists under cover of her cloak. "Steward,
you forget yourself," she said coldly. "Have you blotted the
scroll? No? Then continue. 'I rejoice with you at the prospect
of a royal son at Malkatta and wait your word as the parched
soil awaits the life-giving wet touch of Hapi.' Finish with my
titles, and I will use my royal seal. Tell my herald to deliver
this personally, giving it to no one but my son. Ay's copy can
go with the other dispatches. Say nothing to me!" Huya closed
his lips firmly, bowed, and backed out. Tiye opened her hands
with conscious effort. *The gods do not know the meaning of
the word justice. They laugh at me. Very well. I shall hold up
my head, and not one of them shall receive the incense of
thanksgiving from me. The only satisfaction will be if my child
is born alive and is male. Nefertiti's rage will be worth seeing.*

Pharaoh soon wrote himself, expressing his delight at the
prospect of another child. Tiye listened to the words grimly,
the baby restless in her womb. She herself could feel nothing
for this child, no anticipation and certainly no pleasure, but at
least there was also no fear. At an age when she ought to have
been enjoying a placid reaping of the rewards of a lifetime as
ruler, she regarded her swelling body as grotesque, but not, as
she had while she waited for Beketaten's birth, as an instrument
of death. She had so much less to live for now and found
herself calmly fatalistic as the weeks sped by. She ate, drank,
and slept as much as she wished. Often she sought the company

of her children, growing up free and largely undisciplined in the silent palace. Beketaten, at six, was a beautiful but willful girl still given to sulks and peevishness if she did not get her way, which was seldom. Smenkhara was harboring a permanent resentment against his mother for holding him in a place that had become nothing but a backwater. He, too, could be sulky and uncommunicative, and the spoiling he received from his tutors and servants, who took their cue from Tiye's attitude toward him as an heir apparent and treated him with an unhealthy deference, did not improve his character. Tiye tried to allay his restlessness with bright stories of his future, but he listened with frowns.

"I know you open my letters to Meritaten and hers to me," he accused her one day. "You are so suspicious of everyone. What do you think we are doing, plotting against our parents? Meritaten is nearing the age of betrothal. She will soon be nine. We speak to each other of marriage, that is all."

"I know," Tiye replied mildly. "But remember that although Meritaten is almost old enough to bear children, it will be at least five years before you will be capable of fathering any. Pharaoh will not give her to you. He will wait to see if Nefertiti can produce a son, and even then, I think his plans for her immediate future are very different."

Smenkhara glanced at her distorted, thinly veiled belly. "Or he will see if you are going to give him a boy. I shall have to grow up to be very powerful and get rid of him and take Meritaten for myself."

"You are boring when you snap all the time. It is not natural for a nine-year-old boy to worry and fret about the future. You have everything you could possibly want."

"I only want Meritaten. I wrote to Pharaoh and begged him to send for me."

"I know you did. I destroyed the letter, and if you are so foolish again, I will destroy every letter from you bound for Akhetaten. Get out of my sight, Smenkhara, and enjoy your youth while you can. Go swimming and fishing. Ride in your chariot. Shoot with the soldiers. Tease the servants. Do not ruin yourself with impatience."

He flung away, and in the set of his angry shoulders Tiye saw his father. Guilt filled her. Amunhotep would have loaded the boy with lessons, put him in the army for a while, but she did not care enough. For the first time the welfare of Egypt did not concern her as much as her own comfort. *Pharaoh will give Meritaten to no one*, she thought as Smenkhara's hunched form disappeared into the dancing heat haze. *She shares the sacred stela in his temple with him. He will keep her for himself. Why should that thought worry me? My husband married Sitamun, his daughter. Why is this any different?* She could find no answer.

Early in the following year word came to Tiye that her niece had given birth to another girl, named Nefer-neferu-Aten-ta-sherit. Tiye, very close to her own time, laughed both in relief and in smug pity for Nefertiti, surely smarting under her inability to produce a royal son. Accompanying the official communication was a report from Ay. After much hesitation Pharaoh had at last taken Ay's advice, and Aziru was summoned to Akhetaten to account for his behavior. The letter granting him a year to appear had been returned by the same messenger who had taken it, and who reported that Aziru was not at home to receive it. Aziru had later written, apologizing fulsomely to Akhenaten and explaining that he had been away campaigning against Suppiluliumas in the north and so did not meet the Egyptian envoy. Pharaoh was now undecided. Should he demand Aziru's presence in Egypt again, or should he praise him for his efforts against Suppiluliumas and let him be? Of equal interest to Tiye were Mutnodjme's infrequent, often short messages that nevertheless gave a vivid picture of the state of affairs in Akhetaten. "We wallow in family affection," she sent by the dumb servant. "Pharaoh, the queen, and the girls are seen everywhere in the chariot, kissing and fondling one another in displays of what Pharaoh teaches are the truths of love. All courtiers are encouraged to follow the royal family's example. Pharaoh's health is not good." *What does she mean by that?* Tiye asked herself irritably as she made her usual walk to the brazier and watched the papyrus catch fire. *Pharaoh's health has never been good. Are his headaches worse? Or does he have a brief fever?* She mused on the vision of Akhenaten, Nefertiti, and their daughters providing such a distasteful public spectacle. *Poor Akhenaten*, she thought. *He means so well, he is so transparently eager to expound what he knows to be his truth*. Tiye wanted to gather him into her arms, to protect him from his own indiscriminate, simple tolerance. *Perhaps it is time for me to leave Malkatta*, she thought. *Not to sail into*

Akhetaten as empress, no, but to arrive as a mother wanting
to provide a haven for her son. When my baby is born, if I
survive, I will go.

For two days she seriously entertained the possibility of
sailing north, but on the third day her half-formed plan dis-
solved. She had been woken earlier in the morning than she
had wished, not by the delicate strains of music but by a dull
roar she could not at first identify. She sat up with difficulty
on her couch, and Piha rose from the corner to help her to the
window.

"It is too far away to be coming from this side of the river,"
Tiye said presently. "What do you think, Piha?"

"I do not know, Majesty. I think it is voices. I have heard
crowds shouting like that during Amun's processions."

It was indeed voices, a continuous babble rising and falling
as the wind veered. "I cannot tell if it is a crowd of happy or
angry people," Tiye murmured. "Something is happening in
Thebes. Call Huya."

Her steward presented himself but, when she questioned
him, said he did not know the reason for the uproar.

"Well, send a herald across the river to find out and see that
he has an escort. Call my bodyguards and have the commander
deploy troops along the riverbank in front of the palace, and
particularly by the canal. It is as well to be prepared."

By the time an answer came, the noise had died away to
be replaced by an ominous silence. Tiye was walking to her
reception hall when the herald met her. He was panting and
sweating. At her curt permission to speak he fought to control
his breath.

"The First Prophet of Amun is behind me," he gasped,
"together with other temple dignitaries. Half the priests from
Karnak are on barges between here and Thebes."

"Have Maya announced to me immediately."

She had scarcely seated herself and placed her feet on the
ivory footstool when the room began to fill with people. Between her officials of audience and the door a stream of white
figures flowed, bending in worship and then shuffling and
whispering together. Last came Maya, swathed in the leopard
skin, accompanied by his acolytes. Tiye spotted Si-Mut's shaven
head and distinctive bulging forehead far back in the throng.

She bade Maya approach, and as he made his obeisance,
she studied him. He was breathing shallowly. The whites of

his eyes showed, and he nervously wet his quivering lips. She nodded.

Maya's voice was measured though thready with emotion. "Majesty, at dawn many barges arrived at the temple water steps, together with soldiers from Akhetaten. The captain bore a scroll from Pharaoh. It was a directive, ordering me to open Amun's Treasury and deliver the god's possessions into the hands of the soldiers to be loaded onto the boats."

Tiye in her turn strove to remain calm. "Did Pharaoh give any reason for his directive?"

"No, Majesty, but the captain said that the wealth of Amun was needed to pay for the purer offerings to the Aten. There are thousands of altars at Akhetaten, and every day they are piled with fresh food, wine, and flowers."

There was a small silence, and then Tiye said coolly, "I trust you obeyed your Pharaoh."

Maya's eyes widened in disbelief. "Yes, Majesty, I had no choice. The soldiers were armed and the temple guards unprepared. But . . ."

Tiye leaned forward. "But what?" she shouted. "How dare you come running to me, expecting me, your pharaoh's wife and empress, to countermand his divine will! How *dare* you presume! Your words imply that if the temple guards had been ready, you would have resisted." She sat back, her heart racing, the baby struggling frantically within her. "Would you?"

Maya spread his hands. "Majesty, before the god I do not know. Everything has gone. The Treasury held so many riches that they could not be counted. Gold, silver, ebony, ivory, jewels. Sacred vessels. The offerings of thousands. All Amun's goods for trade. All his profits from his estates in the Delta. His land is also confiscated."

Fear flared like a sudden burst of fire along her veins, but she mastered it. "Maya, you know that Egypt and all within it belong ultimately to the ruling god. No pharaoh has ever before wished to strip Karnak, but each has had the power to do so."

"No pharaoh has done so because each Horus has been Amun's son," Maya replied. "But now Pharaoh repudiates the god who is Egypt's protector and clothes another with Amun's own glory! We, his priests, are in terror that Amun will curse the land. Majesty, have pity on us. Tell us what to do. The Treasury was also used to pay our servants, our cooks and architects and masons, the fellahin who tended Amun's herds and tilled his soil. These people now have no work."

"It is commendable," Tiye remarked dryly, "that you think of Amun's slaves before his priests. If the Treasury is gone, can the priests not exist on offerings alone?"

The gathering at the rear of the hall muttered quietly. Maya shook his head. "There are fewer worshipers all the time." He did not dare to explain, but everyone listening knew that rich offerings came from the wealthy, and the wealthy now carried their gold to the Aten's door. Only the flowers and loaves of the poor were left in Amun's forecourt these days.

"Majesty, there is more," Maya whispered. "Pharaoh has forbidden Amun all public processions. We may celebrate the god's feasts, but only in the privacy of Karnak itself."

Tiye stared at him. "No Beautiful Feast of the Valley? No blessing of the dead? I . . ." She came to herself. "How many priests can Karnak now support?"

"I have not yet tried to calculate, Divine One," Maya replied more confidently, the gleam of relief in his eye. "But of twenty thousand, the offerings of Theban citizens will not support more than five hundred, and that not well."

"The quality of that support is irrelevant." She pondered briefly, and then came to a decision. "Out of the love I bore my first husband, Osiris Amunhotep Glorified, I will provide gold from my own fortune to keep another five hundred in the god's service. You may decide who they will be. The rest must leave the temple and find work elsewhere." She glared at the men clustered by the door, and the whispers of protest were immediately stilled. "Understand that I do this not because I disagree with Pharaoh, who is all wise and all holy, but out of love for him who now sails in the Barque of Ra. I have spoken."

Swiftly Maya accepted his dismissal, and the delegation silently filed out.

No sound was heard once the doors were closed. Tiye's men waited in a shocked numbness. Tiye herself sat frozen, her mind working furiously. *If I had spoken otherwise, I would have laid the foundation of a civil war,* she thought grimly, *and civil war would play into that snake Suppiluliumas's hands. What madness, Pharaoh! The priests will starve, begging in the streets of a city already dealt one death blow. Is it malice against Amun, a peevishness against a city you have always hated, a new vision sent to you from the Aten? At least worship*

*may continue. What should I do? First, a protest to Pharaoh.
I must put my reasons clearly, or he will lose interest halfway
through the scroll. Did Nefertiti put him up to this? Too many
questions I cannot answer. I am blindfolded, my ears are muffled here. Yet I do not wish to leave after all. Egypt may need
me at Malkatta. Me and Smenkhara ...*

She prepared to rise, but a stab of pain and then another
caught her across the small of the back. She gasped. "Huya!
Call my physician, and send Piha to help me to my couch.
Amun's problems must wait." The men around her sprang into
life. She sat suddenly folded in upon her pain, her concentration
now only on herself. *A curse*, she thought, teeth pressed tightly
together, lips bared. *Has Amun chosen this moment to make
his displeasure known? Is the curse to begin with my death?*

Piha touched her reverentially, and she opened her eyes,
leaving the dais with her maid's support and walking slowly
to her bedchamber. "Is Huya there?" she asked. Lowering her
onto the couch, Piha nodded. "Send him after Maya. I want
priests here with incense and prayers. Bring me magicians also,
and surround the couch with amulets. I do not want to die!"

It was the last time she allowed herself to panic. Gathering
a lifetime of dignity around her, she lay waiting for the birth
of her child, her eyes straying from one anxious face to another
as the hours moved slowly past. She heard the click and rattle
of the charms being laid around her, and catching the sweet
whiff of incense, she was comforted. Sometimes the eyes regarding her were Huya's, brown and worried, but more often
it was Osiris Amunhotep bending over the couch, breathing
the odor of cloves and wine heavily into her face, his black
eyes neither sympathetic nor dismayed but merely steady and
mildly commanding. Gratefully she drew strength from his
refusal to enter into her suffering, his presumption that on her
own she would win. "But I do not want to win!" she groaned
to him once. "I want to be with you, Horus. I am lonely." "Do
not bother me with trifles, Empress," he rumbled back, smiling.
"If it does not need my seal, it does not deserve my attention."
Somehow the words took on a numinous meaning. Tiye clung
to them, repeating them to herself many times as she trod water
in the Duat, watching the Holy Barque sail slowly past with
Osiris Amunhotep unmoving among his divine predecessors.
The dead around her called piteously for light. *I am not properly
dead*, she thought. *I still feel such pain. And now the barque*

is leaving us, is entering another House. Cold water gripped her from feet to waist, numbing and impenetrable, its temperature dropping rapidly as the doors closed behind the barque, and blackness prevailed. Terror-stricken, the dead began to wail. Tiye opened her eyes wide, striving to find one glimmer of light. For an age she strained, until all at once it seemed to her that a faint grayness was suffusing the cavern. The doors were opening again. *But how can that be,* she thought, puzzled. *The barque cannot be drawn backward.*

Then startlingly her surroundings gained clarity and color, and she realized that she was lying on her couch, her head turned toward the window, whose stiff papyrus hangings were moving gently in the breeze. With difficulty she rolled her head on the pillow and found Huya smiling down on her. "Speak," she managed to whisper.

"You have a son, Majesty. But you lost much blood and have been walking in the shadow world for five days."

She was too weak to feel any emotion. "Water." Her lips moved. "My husband . . ."

He snapped his fingers, and Piha came, lifting her gently and holding a cup to her mouth. Warm milk mixed with bull's blood slipped past her throat. *I have been purified,* she thought as she tasted it. *I am clean.* "Word was sent to Pharaoh," Huya continued. "You may expect a dispatch with the chosen name within days. The baby is well-formed though as tired as you. I have chosen a wet nurse for him. Shall I bring him?"

She moved her head once, a denial. Already she was drifting into a healthy sleep. The baby did not matter as much as the mercy of Amun. Her life had been spared. It was a reprieve.

In the following year, the tenth of Akhenaten's reign, Nefertiti again gave birth to a girl, Nefer-neferu-Ra. The passage of time and the waning of competition between the two women had mellowed Tiye's dislike of her niece, and she was able to feel sympathy for a woman who craved a princely son yet could only produce girls. She wondered what the last three years had done to the queen, whether constant childbearing had sagged the tight, faultless body and disappointment put lines of petulance on the smooth face. Yet she had no desire to see Nefertiti, or her son. She sat on the roof of her apartments under a canopy, looking indifferently out over the river to the heat-distorted silhouette of a Thebes already decaying into obscurity, knowing and yet not caring that she lived in an artificial peace, in a place and state of being that existed only for her, a drop of water held in the palm of the hand. It was as if she were existing in the timeless limbo of the dead whose tombs crowded the desert around Malkatta. Like them she was still, watching time slowly break down and change everything around her while she remained immovable. Only Smenkhara and the baby linked her tenuously to the future, a future in which she had no interest.

Tiye's recovery from her son's birth had been slow, and before long she had begun to realize that she would never regain her full strength. The knowledge did not distress her, and she was soon able to walk about palace and gardens, take her meals, confer with her ministers over affairs that were nothing more than the day-to-day problems of her small household, knowing that the fatigue taking her to her couch early each evening would be with her the rest of her life. Her physician prepared tonics and prescribed massages every day, and these remedies helped, but the days of an energetic command were gone. Tutankhaten, as his father had instructed that he be called, was healthy and grew under the ministrations of his wet nurse and her staff. Akhenaten sent regular dispatches enquiring after his welfare and hinting anxiously that Tiye should bring him north, but Tiye excused herself in various ways.

Angrily and yet with a grim humor she watched herself develop the fussy ways of an old widow; complaining if her morning fruit was not cut for her in a certain way, snapping irritably at her body servants if they did not perform their duties efficiently, grieving if her sheets were not turned down precisely. With the acute self-knowledge that had always been hers, she knew she was lacking the fresh, bracing breeze of masculine company. Huya and her stewards she did not consider, for they were servants and approached her with an almost feminine servility. Accordingly she ordered that Smenkhara's lessons be read in her presence, and she required his company for larger portions of each day, hoping that his burgeoning manhood would offset her own cramped aging. He was unexpectedly kind, sensing in his mother a deep need for his companionship and responding with the careless cheerfulness she craved. But her mind still lay fallow. Smenkhara at eleven years could not have the maturity of an adult.

Late in the year she received word from Akhenaten. She sat on a chair at the foot of the wide steps that led into the hall of public audience, watching her servants gather to pass the time of day around the fountains of the forecourt, listening to a letter that, after the stilted greetings, lapsed into a jumbled informality that brought her son's voice to life. "It is not right that the mother of the sun should live secluded in a palace that belongs to a former age of darkness," he wrote. "The family of the Aten should be together. With you, dear Tiye, began Egypt's journey into truth, yet your strength is hidden under the shadow of Amun. The beauty of the Divine Ones fills Akhetaten like a circle of brightness, but as before, when you were widowed and had not yet graced my bed, the circle is weak because of your absence. Come, I beseech you, so that I may be strong again. I am building three magic sunshades in the Great Temple of the Aten, one for myself, one for you, and one for my daughter Beketaten, whom I love dearly, so that standing beneath them, we can renew our might. I do not command the one from whose body the sun has come, but I beg her to hear my words and consider well."

This cannot be Ay's idea, Tiye thought as her scribe rolled up the scroll and laid it aside. *Ay would have written me directly if he thought I was needed. Akhenaten feels threatened, but by what? Is it his health, his visions? More likely he realized that his queen will not give him a son and so wants Tutankhaten near him.* "What is next?" she said sharply.

The scribe reached down beside him. "There is another dispatch from the Fanbearer on the Right Hand."

"Good. Read it." Perhaps Ay would now explain his master's letter. Tiye leaned back, preparing as always to defend herself against the wave of homesickness Ay's words brought.

Her scribe skimmed the formal opening. "As far as I can determine, there has been a revolt in Nukhashshe against that people's chieftain, Ugarit. He has appealed to Suppiluliumas for help. It is very difficult for me to ascertain the truth. Tutu's office is always in chaos, and the man himself an ignorant ditherer who is nevertheless very zealous in his religious observances. I have tried to obtain other opinions from his staff, but Tutu jealously guards his prerogatives as Scribe of Foreign Correspondence. If the news is true, there can be no doubt that Suppiluliumas will respond to Ugarit's plea."

Tiye clenched her jaw. Nukhashshe was so close to Egypt that its rulers had always been allies, and many treaties had been signed and cemented with marriages over the years. The fact that Ugarit had not appealed to Pharaoh to quell his people's unrest spoke more eloquently than anything else could have done of Akhenaten and Egypt's spreading impotence. Suppiluliumas would send soldiers, and when the dust had cleared, he would be closer than ever to Egypt's immediate borders. It had been a long time since Tiye had thought in terms of the empire. Now it was Egypt herself that was threatened.

"Take a letter to Prince Suppiluliumas," Tiye said wearily. It would do little good, she realized, for Suppiluliumas certainly knew how little power she still had, but at least it would serve to remind him that someone in Egypt was watching his movements with eyes unclouded by his deceit.

She wrote also to Pharaoh, her words harsh, demanding to know why, when communications to her were so clear from her own men stationed in Egypt, he did not take immediate action against his enemies. She accused Tutu of misrepresentation, but resisted denouncing his behavior as treasonous. A voice of caution warned her that unless she was physically present to justify her charges, Tutu would turn his attention to discrediting her, and she would lose what little credibility she still had. She did not mention Ay, unwilling to give his enemies an opportunity to twist his dispatches to her into disloyalty to Pharaoh. The letter took her a day to compose, deleting and correcting until she was satisfied. When she had finished and was lying on her couch, she ached for her son, knowing that, in spite of her railing against poor Tutu, it would have taken a man with the genius of the Son of Hapu to unravel the tangled threads of the country's diplomatic situation. Egypt no longer possessed such men. Ay, trained and raised under the old administration, would have suited, but he was now chained and muzzled by men who no longer moved in the real world, whose inferior judgments had been warped by the atmosphere Pharaoh's fantasies and dreams had generated. *It is perhaps a passing storm, a desert khamsin under whose power we hide our faces and huddle in whatever shelter we can find,* Tiye thought. *May the gods grant that it may blow itself out! Then we will dig and sweep, wash off the sand and grit, anoint our eyes, and stand again. If we can only endure, Smenkhara will take the throne, and the empire can be rebuilt. It is not yet too late. Oh, Akhenaten, my son, my son! Hapu was right. You should have died. You did not murder your father, but you are destroying everything he held together in his august person. Per-*

haps I should give Smenkhara his heart's desire, send him to Akhetaten with the other two children, and then retire to Dja-rukha. I have always been happy there. I shall not miss the children. They, too, are part of the magic I tried to conjure and failed, and they belong to the discarded spells. Such thoughts invited the numbing blessing of wine, and the wine brought sleep, yet sunrise and a new awakening did not dispel her feeling of fatality.

As time passed, the urge to relinquish all semblances of authority grew, until finally she began to make plans to leave Malkatta to the jackals in the new year and be settled at Dja-rukha just before the crops were sown. She could have left immediately, thus avoiding the worst of the summer heat, but deep in her mind was the dim idea of a last suffering, a day-to-day enduring of an almost unendurable fire as expiation for the last ten years of her life. The gods did not demand such an action. Sacrifices were never made out of guilt, only for petition and thanksgiving, but Tiye knew it was herself, not the gods, she wished to appease.

The slow moments of a sweltering Mesore went sluggishly by, and she panted in the thin shade of the trees or dipped often in the lake, her mind as faint and beaten by Ra's ferocity as her body. She was lying on her couch one noon, trying to sleep, her swollen eyes on the bars of white light between the slats of her window hangings, when Huya was admitted. Listlessly she watched him approach, a naked, portly, once-handsome man now frequently short of breath and troubled by pains in his joints. He stopped, bowed, and she bade him speak.

"Majesty, I apologize for interrupting your rest," he said, "but your niece has arrived from Akhetaten and wishes to be admitted at once."

Tiye's heart turned over, and she sat up. "My niece? Which one, you fool!"

"Princess Mutnodjme. I have shown her into your reception hall and ordered cool water for her."

"Tell her I am coming. Piha! A loose gown, and my hair needs combing." It was loneliness that brought Tiye to her feet with a rush of gladness at the thought of seeing the girl again, and not until she was walking along the passage under the waving white ostrich fans of her attendants did she wonder what had brought Mutnodjme to Malkatta in person.

Guards opened the door to the hall, and Tiye walked through.

At the far end of the room, where pillars divided the stream
of white hot light that poured like molten metal onto the floor,
Mutnodjme stood, leaning against the wall, her dwarfs dicing
noisily at her feet, her outline black against the blinding dazzle
of the early afternoon. Hearing the herald call Tiye's titles, she
turned, and cracking her whip over the heads of the dwarfs,
so that they howled and scuttled out into the garden, she strolled
toward her aunt.

The tantalizing assurance of a pampered maturity was in
every movement of the long legs, the loose swing of the heavily
braceleted arms. The familiar face glowed with a lazy sen-
suousness. Mutnodjme's full eyelids had been oiled and then
sprinkled with gold dust. Thick kohl gleamed black around the
eyes that always held a hint of amusement in their dark depths.
The mouth that mirrored Tiye's own was slickly red. Gold with
the mauve tinge characteristic of Mitanni smiths hung from
both ears to her tanned shoulder blades, and a thin gold chain
passing around her shaven skull and under the youth lock held
a gold disk against her forehead. She wore no necklace, but
anklets tinkled on both legs. Her many-pleated sheath was
scarlet, belted in gold studs and caught across one shoulder,
leaving the other and one breast bare, its nipple circled in gold
paint. Glancing beyond the pillars as Mutnodjme knelt to kiss
her feet, Tiye caught a glimpse of her niece's retinue, a flitting,
glittering group of young men and women in drifting linens
and bright jewels, themselves thickly painted against the sun.
Mutnodjme had risen and was waiting.

"I see you have a new whip," Tiye offered, suddenly at a
loss for words, wanting to embrace Mutnodjme in a moment
of affectionate relief but instead merely touching her yellow
cheek.

Mutnodjme nodded. "White bull leather with a silver handle," she drawled. "Not taken from a white bull of course, but
stained later. I miss my old one, but it wore out. It is good to
see you, Majesty Aunt."

Something impelled Tiye to ask, "Do I look well?" and she
immediately regretted the weakness of the desire.

Mutnodjme considered, her head on one side. "Better than
I had expected after such a difficult birth. I know it was ages
ago, but everyone at Akhetaten has been anxious for your
recovery, greedy for any word from Malkatta."

"I do not believe it!" It had always seemed that those who

left the palace to go to the new city had also abandoned their memories, but Mutnodjme was telling her it was not so.

"It is true. When word came that you had given birth but would probably die, Pharaoh turned us all out to stand for hours in the forecourt of the Aten temple while he prayed within, and he was then ill for days afterward."

"But he did not come. For all his solicitude, he did not come."

"No." Mutnodjme met her eye. "He did not. The queen's atmosphere fills the city like perfume. It is heavy in our nostrils, day and night. When we are not prostrate before the Aten, we pray to her."

Tiye searched her niece's face for the sarcasm that was carefully absent from the voice, and found it. "My brother. Is he well?"

"He has aged, but his health is as good as it always has been."

"And your husband?"

Mutnodjme hesitated. "Horemheb is strong and high in favor. In the way in which you enquire, my goddess, he is well."

"So. We will have time to discuss the family later. How starved for news I have been! Your mother?"

"I do not see Tey very often. She is never at court. But she is content on the estate Ay built for her."

"And yourself, Mutnodjme? You are as beautiful as ever!"

"I know." Mutnodjme laughed. "I have become the object of every young courtier's desire. Isn't that boring? Horemheb laughs, but I do not. I am tired of hot whispers and groping fingers at Pharaoh's feasts. I tend to cling to my old friends, the men I have slept with before, the women who have shared my secrets in the past. I am twenty-eight, Majesty Aunt. The young are beginning to annoy me."

"A sober Mutnodjme? Impossible!"

Mutnodjme barked a laugh. "Certainly not. But I do not want to begin all over again. You see this gown? One bare breast, a coy titillation. It is all the rage of Akhetaten. Simpering and eyelids fluttering, silly flirting. My uncle's court here at Malkatta may have been in some measure depraved, but it was an open, robust depravity. The dissipations of Akhetaten have a paler, sick cast to them."

You always were astute, Tiye thought, *but you were never this articulate*. "Are you here out of boredom?" she enquired gently.

Mutnodjme shook her head. Clapping her hands sharply, she shouted "Hoi!" and one of her menservants came running, a small chest in his hands. At Mutnodjme's signal he placed it on the throne step and withdrew, bowing. "Be pleased to dismiss all your train, Majesty Aunt," Mutnodjme asked. "This is for your eyes alone at present."

Tiye immediately complied, and the two women stood looking at each other as the servants departed. At last the door was closed, and they were alone. Mutnodjme hesitated, one hand on the lid of the chest.

"This has no interest for me, you must understand that," she said quietly. "But it may trouble you. If it does not, I will return to Akhetaten and consider our arrangement at an end. Although I have done very well by you, Empress! If it does, my husband has instructed me to tell you that he is at your disposal."

"I understand." Curiously Tiye watched as her niece pulled back the lid and drew out what appeared to be a small carved group of monkeys. There seemed to be nothing unusual about it. Egypt worshiped many lesser monkey gods, and baboons were considered sacred. Mutnodjme placed it in her hands.

"This is a particularly expensive example, done in alabaster and carefully painted, but reproductions are available all over Akhetaten, smaller and larger, in wood or stone or, for the poorer people, in clay. They are for sale at stalls in every market." Without waiting for permission, Mutnodjme turned and sat on the throne step.

Tiye bent over the carving. There were four monkeys, graded in size. The largest half-stood, half-squatted behind the others, its pendulous breasts sagging, its fat thighs spread wide. Yet it was not female, for a disproportionately large penis jutted from beneath its swollen belly. Its tail curled up between its legs and nestled between the legs of the female monkey that knelt before it, both hands around its penis. The thick lips of the largest one were puckered toward the smaller monkey standing at its left, and its hand circled the neck and rested on a tiny breast. The other hand was thrust between the legs of the small monkey on the right. The genitals of all the animals were painted bright red; the ears, huge eyes, tails and hair, gray. The whole piece suggested flagrantly obscene sexuality, but it was not the impression it conveyed that caused Tiye to give a low cry and thrust it away. The largest monkey wore a double crown canted between its pricked ears, and the next in size a tall, cone-shaped helmet. Mutnodjme leaned over and swiftly removed it, dropping it back into the chest and flipping the lid shut.

"No one knows who began it," she said. "But even before the carvings appeared, there were rumors. Of Pharaoh copulating with his monkeys, of nights spent with the queen and both the older girls together. Lusty jokes have always abounded at court, but this is different. There is malice in it. Pharaoh has completely lost the respect of the citizens of Akhetaten, and before long those things"—she indicated the chest—"will begin to be found all over Egypt. The Thebans will love them."

Tiye swallowed and, feeling dazed, went to sit beside Mutnodjme. Her hands shook. "What does Pharaoh say? His anger, his shame . . ."

"Pharaoh feels neither," Mutnodjme said calmly. "He smiles. He says his people are only beginning to understand true affection, and when they do, the carvings will vanish. The queen is beside herself with rage, though. She has forbidden ownership of them, but of course the common people take no notice. She should have ignored them altogether."

"Yes," Tiye whispered. Nefertiti had always lacked the right instincts so necessary in a ruler. Her loves and hates were too extreme, too public. Yet Tiye had never pitied her more than she did now. Her, and her defenseless, foolhardy husband, Egypt's god. "Is it because they are shown embracing on the ben-ben in the Aten temple?"

"Partly. After all, Pharaoh and the queen do not behave like gods to be worshiped. But it is also because they have wished to display themselves as a family drowned in mutual affection, before their subjects. Forgive me, Empress. To speak so of Pharaoh has always been blasphemy, yet I believed you would want to know, and my letter bearer would not have been able to communicate the perversity of it to you. It is not just the carvings. The people cheer him in the streets, but it is the sound of derision, and he cannot hear it. Horemheb begs . . ."

Tiye held up a hand. "No more," she said quietly. "Eat with me tonight when I have rested and pondered. Leave me, Mutnodjme."

Obediently the other woman rose, bowed profoundly, and

swung down the long hall. *I did not ask that an apartment be prepared for her*, Tiye thought. *But I suppose she will open Ay's house.* The whip was snaking white behind the bare heels, and Tiye, mesmerized, watched it undulate. Long after Mutnodjme had gone, she could not wrench her eyes from the floor. Finally she summoned Piha and went back to her room.

The sun had lost a little of its fierce heat, but the air remained stifling. Tiye ordered a bath, and then tried to sleep, but Mutnodjme's voice and the image of the distorted red genitals fought for prominence in her thoughts, and her heart refused to settle to a calming rhythm. *But I wanted to go home to Djarukha!* she protested silently. *I had decided! I can do nothing, I am too old, it is too late.* With anguish she remembered how cool the lily-choked lake before the blue pillars of her portico was in the gentleness of the north, how moist the air. *I miss my mother, my father*, she thought as her control finally gave way and she began to weep quietly. *For once it is not you, Osiris Amunhotep, I long for. It is the safety of Yuya's strong arms and the smile with which Thuyu woke me every morning. Oh, stop!* she tried to berate herself. *There is nothing so pathetically ridiculous as an aging woman in tears. Let them foul the bed they have made for themselves. Let me go home!* But she already knew she would never see Djarukha again.

In the twilight she sat on the dais in the great reception hall, Mutnodjme beside her, their ministers and servants grouped around the small, flower-laden tables below. Tiye had commanded a room full of light, and hundreds of torches and lamps leaped gold in the draughts that blew between the tall columns. A procession of tray-bearing slaves came and went from the food tasters to the gilded table, and the stewards bent from time to time to fill the wine cups. Between the dais and the floor of the hall the musicians set up a wall of clamor that screened the women's conversation from the other diners, and dancers swayed between the tables. Tiye tried to eat, but the very sight of the rich food sickened her, and in the end she sat drinking and watching Mutnodjme demolish every course presented. Between mouthfuls her niece cast blank glances at Prince Smenkhara, eating at the foot of the dais with Beketaten, and Tiye smiled inwardly in spite of the turmoil in her mind. Mutnodjme was not as politically neutral as she pretended to be. Either that, or the situation at Akhetaten was so grave as to make everyone there a budding oracle. When the food had been consumed and such entertainment as Tiye had been able to gather had begun, she beckoned Mutnodjme closer.

"Did Horemheb or your father send you to me with that abominable thing?"

Mutnodjme signaled, and a servant lifted the low table away. Sighing with satisfaction, she leaned back on her cushions. "I had forgotten how tasty beef can be when a god is not peering over one's shoulder disapprovingly. We are not forbidden meat at court, but Pharaoh will not touch it, of course. In answer to your question, Goddess, I came of my own accord. Ay and Horemheb approved, though. They need your help. They could not tell you in dispatches, and indeed, one can scarcely speak of such things there are so many spies in the city, people who work for themselves in the hope of dropping gossip in Pharaoh's ear and gaining favors. My cousin is easily swayed by ideas clothed in the adoring language of Aten worship."

Mutnodjme's every word pierced Tiye's heart, and for a moment she hated her brother, Horemheb, all the sycophants trying to worm their way into a simple man's affections when their own hearts were cold. Mutnodjme's indifferent honesty was infinitely preferable. "Then tell me now what it is the great fanbearer and the mighty commander want me to do."

Mutnodjme grinned at the sardonic tone. "They want you to take up residence at Akhetaten, to see Pharaoh every day, to lend weight to their own advice. The most pressing problem is the situation beyond the borders. Tutu tells Pharaoh one thing, my husband another, and Pharaoh hesitates because he simply cannot believe in the perfidy of men."

"Nefertiti would do her best to discredit me, perhaps even have me murdered. Tutu has always resented me. Mutnodjme, I am tired. I would be going into a nest of vipers whose only wish would be to see me dead. I would also have to cope with a swarm of fawners who would immediately gather around Smenkhara. I would have no friends, no one to trust." She stopped speaking, overwhelmed at the prospects as she described them. The stabbing pains in her abdomen that always assailed her in times of stress or fatigue began without warning, and she held her breath until they had passed.

"Then go to Djarukha and wait for the summons of the gods," Mutnodjme said softly. "Majesty Aunt, I have always loved you. But do not mistake me. I am not declaring my affection for you as an offering of active support if you decide to come to Akhetaten. I know myself too well. I merely want to see you happy. You have earned the right to peace."

"I have not been happy since Osiris Amunhotep Glorified died," Tiye responded flatly. "Would I be content at Djarukha, after listening to you? I do not think so. I brought Pharaoh into the world, and it seems I have a duty to protect the world from him and him from the world if I can. How the Son of Hapu must be laughing!"

"Then you will come?"

The question angered Tiye. Pain lanced her again, and she felt sweat break out along her spine. "Of course I will come!" she managed. "How can I refuse such a challenge?"

Mutnodjme sipped thoughtfully at her wine, her eyes slowly traveling the noisy hall. Smenkhara was clapping in time to the music, his eyes on the naked dancers. Beketaten was slumped belly down on her cushions, fast asleep. The harem women, flushed with wine and excited by the unexpected break in the boredom of their existence, giggled and shrieked. There was nothing left to say. After a moment Tiye rose. Silence fell. The guests prostrated themselves. Her herald grasped his staff of office and sprang to precede her, and together with Piha and Huya she left the hall, striving to stand tall against the pain until she had gained the privacy of her apartments. Collapsing on her couch, she sent for her physician and lay waiting for him, knees drawn up, fists bunched, her muscles tense as much against the rage she felt at her fate as against the pain.

Mutnodjme sailed for Akhetaten the next day. In the afternoon Tiye dictated a letter for Pharaoh and then called for Smenkhara. For once he came promptly, his slim hips swathed in a loose kilt, his feet sandy and his legs still beaded with water from the lake. He bowed to his mother, casually kissed the hand extended to him, and turned excited eyes on her.

"We are going to Akhetaten, aren't we, Majesty?"

"Yes. How did you know?"

"The servants have been gossiping about nothing else all day. When do we leave? I cannot believe I am really going to see Meritaten again. Thank you, Mother."

"I think you will miss Malkatta when you have been in Pharaoh's new city for a while," Tiye said calmly. "You have enjoyed a freedom here that you will never see again. But you have a few more months to savor it. We will leave when the river is highest. Go and tell Beketaten." She had wanted to share his enthusiasm, but she found herself accepting his gratitude and excitement grudgingly. She watched the light die out of his eyes. He pursed his lips, gave her a perfunctory obeisance, and walked away. He had suddenly become a responsibility that already weighed heavily on her.

17

TIYE LEFT MALKATTA AT THE END OF THE FIRST MONTH OF winter. When news of her decision had reached Akhetaten, she had received an ecstatic letter from Pharaoh, guarded greetings from Ay, and nothing at all from Nefertiti. Resolutely she refused to look into the future. While her stewards strode purposefully down the passages of the palace, scrolls in their arms and frowns on their faces, and myriads of servants fetched and carried, packed and repacked, Tiye surrendered for the last time to the magic of Malkatta, allowing every memory to overtake her. Sitting under her canopy by the lake, she remembered being poled across the river, a little princess newly appointed to Pharaoh's already vast harem, to look at the unpainted rooms, the churned, stone-littered ground, the overseers with their shouts and whips, and the straining backs of the fellahin. She had stood with a slim young Tia-Ha and other princesses in the awesome grandeur of the empress's quarters, as yet untenanted, her hands behind her back, her kohled eyes on the ceiling as Kheruef described the plans Pharaoh had for his new palace. Many of the women were silent and uneasy, not wanting to consider the proximity of the dead and the nights they would have to spend with only a wall between them and those who lay stiffly in their coffins. Tiye had been silent also, but not from fear. She had been wondering why her husband had decided to move his court from its ancient and honorable site on the east bank, close to Karnak. A man with such unlimited power and wealth could do anything he pleased, yet it seemed a pointless, irrational waste of gold and effort. At that moment she had felt eyes on her back and, turning, had seen the young pharaoh staring at her, his ministers surrounding him. She ought to have instantly averted her gaze, but she found herself staring back. Though the marriage contract had been sealed and she had been in the harem for over a month, she had come no closer to her husband than a long stone's throw at official feasts. Now he was imperiously crooking a finger at her. Bravely she had walked to him, crumpling at his feet until a toe gently pushed against her ear gave her permission to rise. Behind him she caught her father's eye. He had winked solemnly at her.

"Princess Tiye, what is so interesting about the ceiling?" Pharaoh had enquired.

"Nothing at all, Divine Horus," she had replied, caught off guard. "I was not even thinking about the ceiling."

"I see. And what do little girls think about when they are gazing to the heavens with their mouths open?" His men had laughed.

Tiye flushed. *Stand your ground with him*, her father had instructed her in the days when she was being prepared to become a Royal Wife. *Do not be docile. You are not beautiful enough for that. You must display your character if you want to capture him.*

"I was wondering, Mighty Bull, why Your Majesty would want to build a palace here when you have a perfectly good one on the east bank. You are putting your women, your ministers, and all the foreign delegations to a great deal of trouble."

"So I am, and enjoying every moment of it. Kheruef!" The Keeper of the Harem Door bustled over and bowed. Amunhotep pointed into Tiye's face. "This one tonight, but you had better muzzle her. Yuya, I do not know what education you provided for her, but it must have been cheap. She is impudent."

Yet when the palace was sufficiently finished for occupation, it was Tiye who had moved into the empress's sumptuous apartments. She smiled now, hearing his voice again, feeling her own shyness and determination. If the gods willed it, Smenkhara would move back when his time of incarnation came, and perhaps Meritaten would have her chests unpacked where Tiye herself had stood as a small, defiant girl. The thought of Malkatta empty and slowly crumbling as the years went by was too painful to contemplate. Long before the day of departure came, she had drained each room dry of its memories, and she set her sandaled feet upon the barge's ramp without a backward glance.

She traveled alone, Smenkhara and Beketaten in the barge behind her and Tutankhaten with his nursery attendants farther back still. Behind the royal boats dozens of craft bearing servants and household effects strung out on the fast-flowing current. To either side were the barges of the military, carrying Tiye's bodyguards. The day was cool and bright. A sweet wind blew from the north, keeping the sails drawing and the oars flashing, and it riffled the short green crops and stirred among the fresh leaves of winter. The music and chatter of the harem women watching from the roof of their quarters soon died away to be replaced by the gurgle and slap of water against the hull and the rhythmic cry of the man who set the leisurely beat of the oarsmen. Tiye, seated comfortably on the deck under an awning, glanced to the east bank and then called Huya.

"Why are there crowds on the Theban docks? Is it a god's day? I cannot hear them shouting."

"It is no god's day, unless they celebrate a district deity," Huya replied. "They gather to watch you go, Majesty."

Tiye looked at them thoughtfully. The air was hazed with winter humidity, and her barge was favoring the west bank, so that she could not pick out individual faces, but the sullenness of the Thebans was unmistakable. A few small, weather-beaten craft were tethered to the docks, but most of the many wharves were empty, and one or two, Tiye noticed, were already rotting, leaning lazily toward the water. It had been a long time since she had ventured beyond Malkatta's sheltering walls. "Drop the cabin hangings," she ordered. "I will move within. They have no right to stare at a goddess."

But she had no sooner reclined on the cushions spread in the golden dimness than she heard a shouted challenge, and her barge came to a halt. She waited. Presently the captain spoke to her through the curtain.

"Majesty, it is a boat from Karnak. The high priest begs to see you."

"Let him come aboard." *I refuse to carry the guilt of Thebes's fate with me*, she thought resignedly as she heard the scuffles and sounds of Maya being bowed aboard. *The city will simply have to bide its time.*

A shadow fell across the hanging. "You may raise the curtain and kneel outside," she called. "Why did you not come to Malkatta, Maya? I am not pleased."

The curtain lifted, and the high priest's pale, distressed face met her gaze. "Empress, Majesty, we at Karnak could not believe that you would really desert us. If you go, then where is a divinity who will champion us? Amun surely sleeps!"

"Perhaps he needs the rest," Tiye snapped but then cursed herself for her levity. "Maya," she said gently, "Pharaoh needs me. You do not understand the complexity of the situation. All you see at present is an empty temple and a poverty-stricken Thebes. I order you to be patient and tend Amun lovingly. I do not withdraw my patronage with my presence. That is all." He bowed his head and let the curtain fall. She heard him cross into the temple barge, and then her captain's crisp order and the rocking of the cabin. But for many miles she brooded over the high priest's stricken face and the angry misery of the thousands she was leaving to a gloomy fate.

Yet she took pleasure in the sight of her beloved Egypt drifting by in the euphoric bliss of another winter. Sometimes oars were needed, but more often the current alone carried them forward swiftly, and they needed only the control of the helmsman. At night they tied up in empty bays. Torches were lit, carpets laid, and she and the children ate to the loud music of frogs crouched in mud and the far coughing of hippopotamuses in the marshes. The nights were cool. Tiye slept well in the little cabin, surrounded by Followers, piled with blankets yet breathing the crisp, unscented air. Her physician cautioned her against bathing in the winter river, so each morning she sat on deck swathed in woolen cloaks, eating her first meal of the day and watching Smenkhara gasp and splash in the shallows before he joined her. "This is how life should be," she murmured occasionally, but smiled at herself even as she said the words. By the time her barge came in sight of the first cluster of palm trees at the foot of the cliffs that almost met the river, she was longing for the luxuries Akhetaten could provide.

Beside the river, in the shade of the trees, was a small customs house with several quays sunk into the Nile mud where river traffic coming up from the south disgorged its goods. The house was not as large as the one that marked the northern extremity of the city but was nonetheless important, for here the trade from Nubia—gold, slaves, ostrich feathers, hides, ivory, and ebony—was unloaded, tallied, and stored temporarily. Here, too, were barracks for the soldiers who patrolled the southern cliffs and the narrow neck of the Nile. Tiye did not expect to be challenged, for she was flying the blue and white imperial flag, but as she glided past the stiff palms and the busy, crowded wharf, a skiff put out from the shore. A man wearing the blue helmet of a charioteer was balancing in the prow, and on both forearms, a silver commander's band glittered. It was Horemheb. At a word from Tiye, the oarsmen shipped and then sat panting. The skiff bumped alongside, and sailors ran to assist the commander over the side. He came straight to her and fell on his knees.

"Rise, Commander," she said coolly. "I trust you have something important to say to me. I am tired of water and discomfort." He got to his feet and followed her in under the shade of the awning. "Sit."

"It is an unhoped-for pleasure to see you again, Goddess," he said. "You must believe that though my wife journeyed to Malkatta under her own advisement, I would have come myself if I had found a suitable pretext."

"Oh, I believe you," Tiye said smoothly, her eyes rapidly taking in the brown, bare chest that had broadened in the years since she had seen him last, the face that had matured into a handsome decisiveness, the pleasing, masculine line of linen-covered hips and long legs. His presence, a hand's touch away, the faint scent of male sweat and mandrake perfume on him, reminded her forcibly of how long she had been surrounded by women and old men. For one delirious second she wished twenty years removed from her life. "But I am surprised you needed an excuse to visit me. Is Akhetaten a city of cowards and self-seekers only?"

He paused before replying. At a faint movement of her head Huya offered wine and withdrew out of earshot. Horemheb said, "You were right, and I was wrong, Divine One. Accept my apology."

"Oh, but you were not wrong, dear Horemheb," Tiye responded lightly. "Did you not obtain the gold monopoly from Nubia for your loyalty to my son?"

He flushed. "I deserved that. But, Majesty, I am still loyal to Pharaoh. My motive for coming to Akhetaten was not greed alone."

Tiye relented. "I know, Commander. Neither is my motive a greedy one. I will not plot against my son or intrigue to further Smenkhara's career. I am here because I, like you, recognize the threat to Egypt's security and want to help Pharaoh face it."

"He is beside himself with excitement over your arrival. The day after tomorrow is the customary day for the receiving of foreign tribute, and at the same time he will honor you. I wanted to greet you first, though, and escort you to Ay's house. It is on the west bank, opposite the palace, and as quiet as you could wish. Tey has prepared an apartment for you until you approve the estate Pharaoh has built for you. Tomorrow you will be officially welcomed."

"Where is Ay?"

Horemheb looked away. "Pharaoh demanded his presence at dawn this morning, and I have not seen him since."

A hundred questions leaped to Tiye's tongue, but she bit them back. It was better to answer them with her own observations as time went on. "Very well. Have your helmsman come aboard and take the tiller. Your skiff can be tied behind. Then come back to me and tell me what I am seeing as we pass the south end of the city."

After carrying out Tiye's orders Horemheb came to stand respectfully behind her as she leaned on the rail and looked for the first time on Akhenaten's dream city. "Alabaster quarries have been dug in the cliffs behind the customs house," he said as they swung out into midstream, "but you cannot see them from here. There are the glass and faïence workshops. Not a pretty sight, and fortunately they stretch back into the desert instead of straggling along the riverbank. Ah! Here comes the first estate. It is Panhesy's, and next to it, Ranefer's. My home is the fifth along, beside that of Thothmes the sculptor, who ought not to be living among ministers but is a favorite of the queen."

Horemheb's inflection made Tiye glance at him sharply, but he kept his eyes and his pointing finger on the bank. Tiye filed away the scrap of information and turned her attention back to the unfolding wonder of Akhetaten. She had become accustomed over the years to the filth and squalor of a Thebes growing ever more dingy and dilapidated, and now the sheer beauty of her son's city took her breath away. The nobles' estates Horemheb was pointing out to her could hardly be seen through the luxuriant forests of palms and groves of fruit trees that surrounded them. Here and there she caught a glimpse of still lake water through the profusion of green. Water steps of whitest marble ran down into the blue depths of the Nile at regular intervals, and against them, white, gilded craft rocked, dainty barges with masts from Lebanon and the Aten Disk emblazoned in glittering electrum on their sides. For perhaps two miles one house succeeded another, all fronted by artificial lakes, all buried in greenery and riotous with flowers. Then buildings ceased, but the greenery continued, lawns, orchards, and clumps of flowers. Little paths wound through it, leading occasionally to a compact paved square containing a stela and an altar. She felt the craft veer, and Horemheb cleared his throat. "See the little island?" he said. "Pharaoh had it planted with shrubs and flowers. You can make out the bridge that links it to the bank where Maru-Aten, the summer palace, is built. I cannot describe the palace to you, Majesty, but you will doubtless see it for yourself before long. It is the queen's favorite retreat. There is a royal temple there as well, two lakes fronted by pleasure buildings, decorated pavements, every delight for which Egypt is famous. We must begin to tack to the west now, but as you can see even from this distance, the gardens and treed walkways continue into the city itself."

As the barge began to move gradually away from the small island, Tiye turned her attention to the west bank. Here the only trees were the usual palms growing along the lines of the irrigation canals, and the rest of the ground was thick with crops. "No one but Ay lives on the west bank?" she asked.

"No one. Pharaoh refused permission to all but Ay. He wishes his subjects to be as close to the temple and palace as possible. When it rises here, the river floods only the west bank, so while we quickly had fertile fields to harvest for the city, it was a costly enterprise to build the dam and dig the canals necessary to protect the fanbearer's home from the fury of the flooding. Ay is grateful, though, because Tey has shown no inclination to slip back to Akhmin." He smiled, and Tiye laughed back at him. "There are the water steps. Now turn around if you will, Goddess. There is the center of Akhetaten."

Tiye had expected the same lopsided jumble of three-storied, flat-topped houses that made up the bulk of Thebes, but no houses were to be seen. The bank of the river was thick with palms and sycamores, and behind them, row upon row of tall white pillars rising from above a wall and marching away out of sight. She thought she glimpsed a wide road running toward Maru-Aten. Horemheb saw her puzzlement. "That is the Great

Palace and harem," he explained. "Farther in and across from
the Royal Road is the temple. Beyond that are the ministers'
offices and the homes of lesser nobles. And out on the desert
beyond *that*, of course, are the hovels of the poor and the
homes of foreigners. I have no doubt that Pharaoh will show
you his city himself."

Tiye had time for no more than a cursory glance at the east
bank before the barge bumped Ay's water steps. In front of
the house and filling a forecourt entirely shaded by the trees
surrounding it, Ay's servants were already prostrating themselves on the pink stone. The ramp was run out, but before
she disembarked, Tiye asked Horemheb to see to the housing
of her goods and servants. He bowed. "I will return tonight,"
he said. "Ay is having a small feast for you. A family affair.
Mutnodjme will come too, of course. Pharaoh does not want
to greet you himself until he can do it with proper formality.
Welcome to the Horizon of the Aten, Most Beautiful One."
She acknowledged his obeisance and descended the ramp.

Tey rose and bowed several times. "Majesty, I am honored,"
she said, and Tiye, touched, noticed that the woman was unusually tidily dressed and painted. Tey was wearing a soft blue
sheath, many years out of date in its slim line and covered
breasts, but flattering in its very decorum. Her wig, neck, arms,
and ankles were decorated with her own creations. Tiye had
forgotten how lovely she was.

"I am happy to see you," she said. "Be pleased to walk
with my herald, Tey, and I will follow." *My son has turned a
burning waste into a piece of the blessed Delta*, Tiye thought
as she walked between the prostrate servants. Brilliantly plum-
aged birds swooped and trilled over her head. In every direction
she saw only the green gloom of closely bunched trees whose
foliage met above her. Off to the left of the forecourt a lake
moved darkly, its surface thick with pink and white lilies.
Papyrus fronds waved silkily on its verge, with blue lotuses
buried among them. *In such a place a pharaoh might indeed
forget that there is another world outside*, Tiye thought again.
*By the power of his will Akhenaten has caused his own reality
to have life, in spite of everything. For this, I admire him*.

She found herself mounting steps that sparkled white, pink,
and black, marble of a color that could only have come from
the quarries at Assuan, but before she could pause to appreciate
their beauty, she was passing between two rows of pillars that

led into Ay's reception hall. To the right a small Aten shrine stood open, and beside it a shrine to Min. A table laden with fruit, cakes, and wine had been set out, and incense burned in a tall golden holder beside the food. Tey bowed her to a seat, and Tiye smiled.

"Sit, my dearest Tey. How good this is! I feel as though I have woken from a dream." But she realized as the words left her mouth that she had left one quiet, self-absorbed dream only to plunge deeply into another more exotic one that had the quality of a drugged state.

"I have ordered that the children be served by the lake and then taken across the river to visit the zoo," Tey said. "I hope you approve, Majesty."

Huya bent with sweetmeats, but Tiye shook her head. "Are you happy here, Tey? If I had bet on your staying, I would have thought that I would lose a lot of gold, and yet Akhmin seems to tempt you no longer."

Tey hesitated. "I do not work as well here," she said. "It is more beautiful than paradise. I have only to raise my eyes to what I want, and Ay lays it at my feet. But Akhmin is my heart. I stay here for my husband. He needs me."

His need must be great, Tiye thought, noting the soft cleanliness of the hands that had always been stained, charred, and roughened by Tey's craft, the limpid eyes that no longer seemed to hold the confused depth of a jeweler's dream. "You are fortunate to be needed so much," Tiye commented more tartly than she had intended, feeling all at once alone, but Tey replied gently. "No man ever needed me as much as Egypt needs you now, Empress. Help Ay, dear Tiye. Akhetaten is a mirage, a vision conjured by the dust devils for our destruction."

Shocked, Tiye met her sister-in-law's eye. *So much change while I drifted about Malkatta yearning for a quiet retirement at Djarukha*, she thought. *Mutnodjme, Horemheb, and now you, a woman I believed incapable of all perception save what you brought to bear on the glowing heart of the gems you worship.* "I will judge for myself," she said, unable to keep her voice from shaking. "Now, tell me what sort of crop you expect at Akhmin this year. Some of the vines are very old and cannot be producing well anymore."

Tey brightened, and they warmed to a subject of constant appeal. Before Tiye became aware of the passing hours, it was time to bathe and dress, and the sun was hanging orange over the western hills.

The family meal of welcome had been set in the walled garden opposite the lake. Darkness had fallen by the time Tiye accepted a chair on the grass and received a cup of scented wine from Huya. She sat contentedly inhaling its perfume, watching the flower-girt servants come and go. The new-risen moon was a silver sliver in the dark blue sky, its light almost overwhelmed by the torches set on the wall or held by the men who stood motionless under the trees. Flowers lay piled and quivering on the tables scattered about. At the far end of the garden, discreetly in the shadows, Ay's musicians tuned their lutes, talking and laughing quietly. The air was cool enough for Tiye to have donned a woolen cloak over the unadorned pleated gown that folded lightly over her knees and brushed the grass beside her. An intermittent breeze lifted the waves of gray-streaked auburn hair from her shoulders and caressed her brow. As Ay's concubines came one by one to kneel before her and kiss her red-painted feet before finding their own places politely out of the range of the immediate family, she watched Smenkhara and Beketaten. Smenkhara had reverted briefly to an effervescent boyhood on the journey, swimming, running, crowing, and laughing at everything, but tonight the knowledge that Meritaten was just across the river had sobered him. He sat cross-legged on the grass, his ringed hands loose in his lap, his eyes absently following the movements of the servants. Though at thirteen he was not officially a man, he had recently shaved his youth lock, and a red ribbon was now tied around his smooth skull. Tiye's glance rested on him. He looked more like his father than ever with his strong features uncluttered by wig or helmet. Beketaten was petting one of Ay's baboons while its keeper held the leash. Her high voice carried over the garden, full of assurance. Pleased, Tiye noted how compact her ten-year-old body was, how graceful at an age when girls began to be all arms and legs, ungainly as storks. Tiye sipped her wine, lost in the deep contentment of the evening. Delicious odors had begun to waft from the kitchens at the rear of the house, and the musicians were already playing little snatches of various melodies.

Over the rim of her cup she saw lights moving across the forecourt, and then Ay himself came striding over the grass, his face alight. He kissed her feet fervently, and she melted into his arms.

"Oh, Ay, I have missed you so! Many times I have longed for your smile! I feel as though we have been separated for an eternity. Let me look at you."

Good-humoredly he stepped back to oblige her. Ay had aged a lifetime since she had seen him last. His frame, always heavy, now carried too much flabby weight. His face had sagged, become slack and jowly. Unhealthy dark pouches made his eyes seem smaller.

Seeing her shock, he smiled ruefully. "I know, dear empress," he said. "There is no longer time for exercise. My cosmetician lays on the paint and kohl and clucks under his breath, but my deterioration cannot be hidden."

"Are you well?" she asked anxiously as he sank down beside her with a sigh.

"Perfectly well, though tired all the time. My physician has ordered me to keep my body cleansed by fasting twice a month instead of once, and it seems to be helping." She could see a swift assessment of her in his smiling glance. "You have aged also."

"I know. Sometimes I can hardly bear to look into my mirror. Tutankhaten has taken away what youth I had left." She spoke without bitterness.

"But I like what is left in your face," he said gently. "Flesh changes, but spirit does not. Is that young Smenkhara, plucking up my lawn so thoughtfully? He is almost a man, Tiye."

Tiye watched the familiar, somnolent expression steal over her brother's features as he looked at his nephew, and she knew he was weighing Smenkhara in dynastic scales. "Our future Horus?" she said quietly.

"May the gods grant it may be so."

"Is the situation so bad?"

"Worse than you can imagine. Be prepared for changes in your son. When we first came here, I was encouraged. Akhenaten seemed to become more his own man than ever before, once the unwholesome memories of Malkatta were left behind. But it did not last. As well as memories, he left behind every restraint. In fact it was one of his indiscretions that kept me from greeting you earlier today. Aziru arrived at dawn."

"What?"

"He finally decided to respond to Pharaoh's summons, though

I wish for Egypt's sake he had decided to flout the order. I have spent the whole day with him, Pharaoh, and Tutu, trying to soften and explain the impressions Akhenaten made. I fear he will leave Egypt laughing up his grubby brocaded sleeve, and his last apprehensions will have been dispelled. Thank Amun you came! But let us not talk of matters of state tonight." He made a visible effort to calm himself. "Here is Horemheb. I see Mutnodjme has dressed her dwarfs tonight. We will eat and drink and be foolish, will we not?"

Tiye nodded, waiting for the obeisances of the others, fighting the fatigue that always stole over her at sundown. *I must grasp strength from somewhere*, she thought as she felt Horemheb's lips touch her foot. *There will be no time for self-indulgence from now on*.

Yet the moment of gloom passed as evening folded into full night. They gossiped and reminisced while the musicians filled the air with sweetness. Before long Beketaten was taken protesting to bed, and soon a yawning Smenkhara followed. The adults sat on, Tiye and Ay in their chairs, Tey at Ay's feet, her arms wrapped around her knees, Mutnodjme and Horemheb sprawled on cushions in the grass, talking with the informality of the family gatherings that had taken place so often on Ay's estate at Malkatta. *In spite of everything we are still a close family*, Tiye thought. *Nothing has broken the ties that bind us. We are no longer Maryannu, yet the force that compelled our ancestors to hold tightly to each other against a land in which they found themselves prisoners remains. Tey and Horemheb have been drawn into the family instead of taking its members away. Tonight I am happy and safe*.

When she could no longer keep her eyes from dropping shut, she left them still conversing and went to the sheets invitingly turned down for her. She fell asleep almost at once, lulled by the rustling of leaves outside her window and the occasional hoot of a hunting owl.

In the morning she stood passively in Tey's tiring room while her servants dressed her carefully for her reunion with her son. She had chosen a white gown of a thousand tiny pleats that she had ordered altered so that it covered only one breast, conforming to the latest fashion in the city. *At least one is hidden*, she thought wryly as her body slaves draped the linen around her. *It is no longer possible to be proud of my breasts*. The gown was heavily bordered at hem and voluminous pleated sleeves with silver sphinxes and belted and hung with the same silver ornaments. She hid her graying hair under a formal wig whose ringlets fell almost to her waist, and satisfied herself as she critically studied her reflection that the dark green eye paint reduced her hooded eyelids as successfully as the kohl hid the lines radiating across her temples. Electrum bracelets, rings of amethyst and lapis lazuli, and her sphinx pectoral completed her garb, and she was ready for the Keeper of the Royal Regalia, who approached on his knees and lifted the empress's great plumed crown from its chest, setting it reverently on her head. She was already tired. She sat on a stool while her attendants sorted themselves out according to precedence in the passage outside, and did not stir until Huya announced the arrival of Pharaoh's bodyguards to escort her across the river.

She was ferried in Akhenaten's state barge to a point a little south of the city, where she disembarked and was immediately escorted to a sumptuous litter whose gold curtains were tied open, revealing a high-backed throne. Chariots of gold waited before and behind, and the Royal Road was lined with scimitar-girt, helmeted soldiers. Horemheb, arrayed in his best behind his charioteer, bowed in greeting as she mounted the throne and settled herself regally. Smenkhara and Beketaten prepared to follow the litter on foot, but Tutankhaten sat on his nurse's knee in a litter to the rear. At a nod from Tiye, and Horemheb's shouted order, the procession moved off. The day was bright. Hawks wheeled high above, spots of black against a deep azure sky, and the trees lining this portion of the road dappled the company in light and shade as they swayed in a refreshing breeze.

For some minutes the litter rocked gently along, the chariot wheels flashed in the sun, and the two children chattered gaily. Then Horemheb called a warning, and the cavalcade halted. Tiye, looking ahead, saw a company gathered on the road at the point where the trees ceased, standing in front of the first dazzling white, low buildings of Akhetaten. With beating heart she recognized the royal palanquin. Her bearers lowered her but she did not alight, and for a moment the hundreds of courtiers and soldiers stood motionless while she drew in her reserves of dignity. She saw that Nefertiti was staring at her, breathtakingly lovely but expressionless under a stiff cone crown, while the three elder princesses, painted and heavily jeweled and dressed, like their mother, in the filmiest of linens, lounged under the canopy of the palanquin, whispering to each other.

Finally Pharaoh came forward, and servants rushed to offer their shoulders for Tiye's balance as she stepped onto the road and walked to meet him. Ay paced beside Akhenaten, the scarlet ostrich fan over one shoulder. Preceding them was a priest, chanting solemnly as he carefully backed toward Tiye, sprinkling the ground before Pharaoh's feet with purifying water. Long before Akhenaten reached her, he had begun smiling. Her hands went out. He grasped and kissed them and then drew her closer, pressing his red lips into her neck, both cheeks, and finally against her mouth. "Majesty Mother. Empress, this is a great day!" he breathed, embracing her. "The whole city waits to honor you. The sun and his mother are reunited!"

"It is good to touch you again, Akhenaten," she replied, but beneath the surge of love that rose in her was a chill of apprehension. His voice had not changed but was as high and piercing as ever. Nor had the lines of his face, the beautiful, clear swoop of the nose, the mild almond eyes ringed in gleaming kohl, the long jut of the chin. But through the loose, sheer woman's gown that trailed around him she could see how stooped and sunken his frail chest had become, how long-slung and protuberant his soft belly, how much whiter and fatter his thighs. She had expected such marks of aging in him. What she had not anticipated was the development of his breasts, now unusually large, the nipples thickly painted a bright orange. Sternly she forced her gaze to leave them. She signaled, and her children came to prostrate themselves before him.

"Stand!" Akhenaten shrieked delightedly. "This cannot be my brother Smenkhara! So tall, so manly! Come, kiss your pharaoh." Smenkhara stepped dutifully into the open arms, and as Akhenaten kissed him fervently on the mouth, Tiye saw the boy go red with embarrassment under the yellow paint on his cheeks. Pharaoh turned to Beketaten. Tenderly he stroked her hands. "My own princess," he said. "You, too, have grown. You still have the sky-blue eyes of my empress. How beautiful you are!" Bending, he kissed her also, and Tiye caught her brother's eye. Ay's expression was stiffly unreadable. Tutankhaten stood unsteadily holding his nurse's hand, his round black eyes on his father. Akhenaten lifted him, and the chubby arms went around his neck, one hand reaching for Pharaoh's jasper earring. "So this is my son, the prince of my body. At last! Is he well, Tiye, is his health good? I have been thinking of betrothing him to one of his sisters. All of us, holding hands, an unbreakable circle! Let us continue on our way. It is time to receive the yearly tribute and then to feast together."

His priest rushed forward and again began to sprinkle the ground as Pharaoh turned after handing Tutankhaten back to his nurse. Tiye bowed, relieved that Akhenaten had not thought to command Nefertiti and the princesses to greet her, but she did not fail to notice the intense, joyful glance Smenkhara had exchanged with Meritaten. *One thing at a time*, she thought as she regained the throne and watched the heavy royal palanquin being smoothly hoisted onto the shoulders of Pharaoh's bearers. Smenkhara began to edge forward as Meritaten loitered behind, but at a sharp word from Tiye he sullenly fell into step with Beketaten.

On the slow walk to the palace, Tiye had ample time to observe both her son and his queen, and the sights of Akhetaten. Above the glinting gold backs of the chairs on the palanquin, the cone and the blue bag wig almost constantly drew together. She saw Akhenaten and Nefertiti kiss and gaze into each other's eyes. She saw Nefertiti's head droop becomingly and briefly onto her husband's shoulder. The princesses walked, skipped, or danced beside the palanquin, often holding hands or draping braceleted arms around one another, ignoring the tumult around them. Tiye looked about her. The Royal Road was pleasingly broad, lined with soldiers who held back a roaring multitude. She would have liked her curtains untied so that her face might not be displayed to commoners, but evidently such considerations had no place here. The crush of people struggled to lie on the stone of the road as Pharaoh passed but rose and cheered her as she was carried by. The side streets that opened off the main thoroughfare were also choked with people. Glancing over their heads, Tiye saw pleasant squares with trees and the fronts of small houses, which, while no match for estates like Horemheb's or Ay's, were still spacious and contained court-yards filled with greenery behind their high, sheltering walls. Only once did she glimpse a jarring ugliness. One street that caught her eye led, unchecked by verdure or marketplace, past several walls and gates and straight out onto the desert. Where it disappeared into the sand there was a jumble of mud shanties and a litter of offal.

The city was a marvel of flags and graceful pylons, carefully tended trees, pillars that soared blue, red, yellow, and white into the hot sky. Every surface was painted or incised with pictures representing the glories of nature in brilliant colors, but Tiye did not fail to note that the largest of the walls and pylons were adorned with immense representations of the queen. Nefertiti stood or strode throughout Akhetaten, sometimes with flail raised, sometimes making offerings to the Aten with Meritaten a very tiny figure beside her knee, but always in a simple, male kilt and the cone crown that hid all trace of her femininity. On every corner there also stood shrines, small slabs of stone with scoops for incense and offerings. By the time the party approached the center of the city, a thin, faintly perfumed haze of incense had begun to envelop Tiye. Lightheaded from its odor and deafened by the tumult around her, she tried to grasp one dominant impression of Akhetaten and could not. Later, she knew, the city would reveal its secrets, but today its citizens had flowed into its center, obscuring its heart.

The Royal Road continued to run straight on toward the north. In the distance Tiye could see that the mighty palace on the left was joined to another building on the right by a walkway high above the road, to which ramps gave access on either side. At its midpoint there was a huge window from which one could look along the road in either direction, and the top of the walkway was roofed and pillared. Beneath, two small square portals and one large one in the center permitted the passage of chariots and those on foot.

When the cavalcade reached the arches, it halted. Soldiers rushed to form a cordon around Tiye and the children as she descended and followed Horemheb through a flagged pylon until she found herself ascending one of the ramps, with Pharaoh, Nefertiti, and the princesses just ahead. Below, the crowd was filling the road, their faces turned upward. Akhenaten reached the window and leaned out, one arm around Nefertiti's shoulders. The princesses lounged against its carved lintels, waving to the people and giggling behind their painted palms.

"People of the Holy City!" Akhenaten shouted above the melee. "Today is blessed in the history of Egypt. Today the empress graces us with her august presence. Today also, as a mark yet again of my favor toward him, the noble Pentu receives the Gold of Favors from my hand. Pentu!" He waved gaily at the man who knelt reverently below with hands already extended to catch the shower of gold that would fall. "This is the third time, is it not?"

"It is indeed, Most Munificent One!"

"For your devotion to the Aten, for your sacrifices and prayers, I make you a Person of Gold!"

Nefertiti drew away as he lifted the heavy gold pectoral from his neck and shook off his gold bracelets and rings, tossing them jocularly out the window. A roar went up as Pentu bent this way and that, trying to catch them. Tiye found Ay at her elbow.

"This is the Window of Appearances," he murmured in her ear. "Every day when Pharaoh crosses from the palace on his way to the temple, he pauses here to speak to his subjects and distribute gold to any who have earned it."

"But this is a travesty!" Tiye whispered furiously. "His father only bestowed the Gold of Favors four times in his entire lifetime, and that only for superior devotion or bravery in battle! To debase the ceremony in this way is unbelievable!" Pharaoh was joking with Pentu as the man scrambled to retrieve the glittering hoard around him.

"I have received it myself but once," Ay went on, his lips against her ear. "Pharaoh is prodigal now only with those whose loyalty he wishes to buy. I find it pitiful. When Horemheb received it, he remained standing and let his servants gather the gold. See how Pentu grovels!"

"He exposes himself to the common populace *every day*?" Tiye had to swallow her rage as with a last wave and smile the royal couple turned into the shadow of the walkway, and she flinched at the cheer that went up as she herself passed the window.

Akhenaten's palace was a vision realized, a home fit for the sheltering of the lord of the entire earth. Malkatta was a polite, small reflection of this maze of lordly pylons, long pillared courts opening out into another court and another, trees forested around lakes and fountains, ramps leading to gardens and gardens to rooms whose very size caused the foot to pause in awe. The palace seemed alive with movement, for its walls were decorated with ducks swimming, bulls leaping, fish flicking through green water. The pavilion of the queen was fronted by palm frond columns inlaid with glittering glazed tiles. Between the formal terraced gardens and Pharaoh's reception hall there were over forty columns, and twenty more lined the hall that led to the royal pair's private apartments. "There is even a private temple here patterned exactly on the Great Temple across the road," Horemheb told her as she tried to maintain a sense of both proportion and direction. "It is called Hat-Aten and is forbidden to all but the royal family. There has never been a palace like this in the history of the world."

It seemed to Tiye that Pharaoh was deliberately taking the procession to the main hall in a roundabout way, flaunting his magical creation. *No wonder my son needed Amun's fortune,* Tiye thought. *No wonder he took all he could from Malkatta. How depleted is the Treasury? I must ask Apy. That all this should have been done so quickly!* She was exhausted by the time the entourage entered the audience hall and climbed to the echoing dais. Here there were three thrones, and at last she could sit and rest her weary feet on the stool provided. The guests rose from their prone positions, and she felt their eyes on her enquiringly. She looked out over them inquisitively and was reassured. It was the day of tribute, and the hall was filled with costumes and tongues from all over the empire. She had expected a melancholy ritual but was astounded to see that even the Khatti had sent representatives.

But her relief vanished soon after the payment of tribute began. Many of the delegations made elaborate speeches and kissed Akhenaten's feet repeatedly, but their hands were empty. They had come merely as observers, and Egypt could no longer compel them to bring the goods she had once demanded. Pharaoh beamed on them as they crawled to him, casting proud sidelong glances at her. He spoke to them kindly, condescendingly, while Nefertiti clasped him around the waist and occasionally kissed his cheek.

Tiye scanned the crowd more carefully and spotted Aziru, flamboyant in heavily tasseled brocade, leaning against a pillar surrounded by his ruffianly bodyguards. He caught her eye, bowed very low, and smiled at her slowly. Beside him was the Khatti ambassador, the same man who so long ago at Malkatta had set his feet impudently upon a dining table with his arms full of dancers. He was now fully mature, a man with swarthy features and the watchful eyes of a hawk. Pharaoh seemed like a caricature beside the two virile foreigners, plump, benign, and womanly. Tiye closed her eyes. *O Amunhotep Glorified,* she prayed to her dead husband. *Help me. Give me wisdom.*

The traditional vassals of Egypt, southern Syria and Nubia,

presented the customary gifts of horses, chariots, and exotic animals, ivory tusks and weapons, precious stones, and gold bars. Her trading partners, independent nations who took no part in Egypt's wars, brought slaves, vases, ostrich feathers, and other curiosities, mere symbols of the years of good trade that had existed. But as the day wore to a close, Tiye cringed in an agonized shame as she watched servants accept and catalogue such a small list of goods when in her husband's day the hall at Malkatta, the passage, the forecourt, and the treasuries had been choked with tribute.

That night a feast was held in the same hall, now echoing with music and full of the loud laughter of the celebrants. Smenkhara was at last free to talk to Meritaten, and though Tiye would have liked to watch them seated knee to knee, their tables together among the children, she found herself trying to eat under Nefertiti's frozen gaze. Akhenaten had placed Tiye in the position of honor on the dais, directly to his right, and Nefertiti at a table to herself behind him, where pharaohs usually seated secondary wives. Tiye herself had often been relegated to such a position at Malkatta when her husband was entertaining a new wife, and it had not concerned her, but Nefertiti was obviously nursing a wounded pride, and every time Tiye turned to her son, she caught her niece's baleful glare out of the corner of her eye. The gray stare served to straighten Tiye's spine, weary though she was.

The wine was flowing freely, and the noise rose as the night progressed. Throughout the feast courtiers detached themselves and approached the dais to do homage to the empress, welcoming her to Akhetaten, picking their way through the riotous groups of people, the discarded flowers and blue bead trinkets, the monkeys that leaped and gibbered from one to another with snatched morsels of food in their tiny hands. Pharaoh's favorite pets squatted beside his plate and under his chair, occasionally shrieking at one another or pulling imperiously at his gown for pieces of fruit. Cats stalked arrogantly among them, disdaining enticements of roast beef, their carnelian studded collars gleaming in the lamplight.

Once the children had eaten, they left the dais and mingled with the guests, all but Smenkhara and Meritaten, who were whispering into each other's ears and smiling happily. Tiye watched the ten-year-old Meketaten, a circlet of turquoise forget-me-nots on her forehead and the blue ribbons of her youth

lock trailing down her back, pick her way to the lively group
of harem women and stand hesitantly beside a woman whom
Tiye did not at first recognize as Tadukhipa. When the older
woman became aware of the girl's presence, she took Meketaten's hand and drew her down beside her, putting an arm
around her. She said something that brought a faint smile to
the girl's wan face. Tiye turned to her son and found him also
looking at his daughter.

"Meketaten is pale," Tiye said. "Was there much fever here
this summer?"

"The Aten protects his own," Akhenaten replied shortly.
"Meketaten is inviolable."

18

TIYE SPENT ONE LAST NIGHT IN THE PEACE OF AY'S HOME
before inspecting the house that had been built for her and
grudgingly pronouncing it suitable. It lay to the north of the
palace, with gardens that ran down to the river, but the grounds
were divided from Pharaoh's apartments only by a wall that
contained a door. Worse, it was directly across the road from
the Great Temple. Tiye had envisioned something more remote
from the life of the city, a sanctuary to which she could retire
at will, but the anxious pride with which Akhenaten led her
from room to room silenced her objections. He had obviously
seen to the furnishing and decorating himself and had tried to
have the friezes and reliefs conform as closely as possible to
the art she had loved at Malkatta. But in spite of his efforts
Tiye knew when she stepped over the threshold that she could
live here for years and never disperse the air of opulent, sinister
magic that she was increasingly coming to realize imbued all
the city.

She gave Huya orders to have her goods unpacked and then
went into the temple for the ceremonies of dedication of the
sunshades Pharaoh had built. After only two days she was
becoming used to grandeur, and the interior of the temple did

not surprise her. There was no progression of courts that diminished in size while increasing in secrecy, until a dark sanctuary held the god. While the building was of a magnitude that dwarfed and tired her, it held only a massive forecourt, filled with altars and reached through three pylons and a grove of trees, and an inner court, larger still than the outer, with hundreds more offering tables leading to the main altar in blinding white rows. Though statues of Akhenaten dominated the palace and were set all over Akhetaten, none stood here. *Of course not*, Tiye thought, sweat gathering under her wig and prickling in her armpits as she stood with Beketaten in the choking incense that rose throughout the temple. *Not when the ben-ben itself is Pharaoh and his family.* The only shelter from the sun lay under the three small kiosks that Akhenaten had erected for the renewing of his own powers and those of the empress and Beketaten, and as the first part of the ceremony came to an end, Tiye stepped under the stone with relief. Standing in the blessed shade, she watched Pharaoh, surrounded by his priests, mount the steps to the high altar and begin the afternoon prayers. Songs of praise to the Aten rose from the choirs gathered in the forecourt. Cymbals clashed, and systra rattled. Flames, almost invisible in the bright sunlight, rose from the hands of the hundreds of servers who waited by the altars to light the piles of food and flowers. *A sunshade is a solemn and holy object*, Tiye reflected as she glanced along at Beketaten, standing with wide eyes under the ornate stone of her own kiosk, *but in this place I would prefer my own canopy and a couple of fanbearers to keep the flies away.* As she watched Akhenaten raise gold-girt arms to the fierce sky and the priests cry out and sink to the hot stone around him, she was far more impressed by the dignity and nobility that always cloaked her son in moments of worship than by the austere magnificence of her surroundings.

That night, after she had for the first time been bathed and dressed under the high star-spangled ceiling of her new home and had been carried to Pharaoh's private reception hall, he presented a golden funerary shrine to her. "A tomb in the cliffs behind Akhetaten is being beautified for you, Mother," he told her eagerly. "You will lie surrounded by its protection. Look!" He walked around it and the bowed servants whose arms trembled under its weight. "I have caused your likeness to be engraved upon it, your sweet body swathed in the finest, most transparent linen, and my own royal likeness before you, to protect you from the demons after death. Here are our names, linked together."

"Akhenaten," she said in a low voice, a lump in her throat, "I thank you for this great gift, but a tomb awaits me in Thebes near my first husband. I would prefer to lie there."

"That man died trusting in a false god," he snapped back, his color rising. "I will not allow you to be contaminated by his presence!"

"As you wish," she said equably, privately resolving to issue her own edict to Huya.

Akhenaten pettishly waved the shrine away, and the servants staggered out with it. He resumed his seat beside her. "I spent a lot of time overseeing it," he complained.

She kissed his cheek, saying soothingly, "It is a great gift. I am very grateful. Drink your wine, Akhenaten. Am I not here as you wished?" But he sat gloomily slumped over the table, breathing shallowly. "The music is haunting," Tiye remarked after a while. "You have talented composers here."

"I wrote it myself," he muttered. "There are words, but they are not suitable for feasting." He straightened and began to sing softly in his thin treble, "How manifold are thy works! They are hidden before men, O sole God, beside whom there is no other. Thou didst create the earth according to thy heart while thou wast alone: even men, all herds of cattle and the antelopes; all that are upon the earth. . . ." He kept his eyes on his plate and swayed gently to the rhythm. When he had finished, Tiye saw that he was crying.

"That was beautiful," she said gently, putting an arm around his neck. "Why do you weep?"

He shook his head. "I do not know. I am the Living One of Diadems. I do not know. . . ."

He left the hall soon afterward. Tiye sat on, her wine before her on the littered table, her consciousness attuned to the gestures and quiet conversations of the few select guests who mingled informally with those of the royal family bidden by Pharaoh to be present. The air in the room had relaxed at Akhenaten's departure. Smenkhara and Meritaten, already inseparable, were engaged in an earnest discussion. Meketaten, in the middle of the bevy of young wives who were sharing harem jokes, played a string game with Tadukhipa. Nefertiti had not appeared at all, and Tiye wondered whether she had even been invited. She was sipping the last of her wine, preparing to retire, when she saw Parennefer go up to Meketaten, bow, and whisper to her. The girl inclined her head and, rising, went out. A silence fell. All eyes followed her, and Tiye, puzzled, crooked a finger at Huya.

"Send me Piha. I am ready to retire. But you see what you can find out about Princess Meketaten from the nursery servants. And send a herald to the house where Aziru is staying. Command him to present himself before me tomorrow morning." Conversation had begun again by the time Huya reached the doors. *Something is troubling my little granddaughter,* Tiye mused as she waited for Piha, *and it is serious enough to provoke a strong reaction from these people. I suppose before long I will know what it is, but now I must rest.*

Huya came to her just after dawn, when the musicians who had woken her had retired and Piha had brought her morning fruit and watered wine. She sat propped up on cushions in the disordered bed, spearing pieces of watermelon and sipping as the light strengthened in the room.

"Well," she prompted. "You work quickly, Huya. Get on with it. I have to think about what I am going to say to Aziru."

He nodded. "Princess Meketaten no longer lives in the nursery," he said. "She has an apartment in the harem. I went there, but the overseer would not let me in."

"Do you mean to tell me that the child is sharing my son's bed?" Tiye pushed the remains of the fruit away.

"I have not mingled with the staff here for long enough to ascertain the truth of the rumors, Majesty, but it appears so."

Tiye's mind suddenly filled with a vision of the grotesque statuary Mutnodjme had placed in her hands. "Did you enquire into the girl's state of health?"

"I was not given the opportunity, Divine One."

"Bring in my scribe."

When the man had settled his palette across his knees, Tiye dictated rapidly. "'To Meryra, Keeper of the Harem Door, greetings. As is my right as empress and first Royal Wife, I, Tiye, Goddess of the Two Lands, do receive into my own august hands the care and ordering of the harem of the Mighty Bull and appoint my steward Huya as Keeper of the Harem Door. Thou art retired.' Have a herald deliver it immediately, Huya. Then go to Nefertiti's apartments and request permission for me to see her later this afternoon. Is Aziru going to do as he was told?"

Huya smiled. "He will be here in two hours."

"Good. You are dismissed. Send Piha."

When the woman entered, Tiye had left the couch and was holding a mirror, peering into it and fingering her hair. "Piha, I think it is time to hide all this gray," she said. "Tell my cosmeticians to buy red henna and come and dye it tomorrow. I will wear a wig today."

Wigged, painted, and wearing the empress's disk and plumes on her head, Tiye sat enthroned beneath the baldachin in her reception room, her staff around her, when Aziru was announced. She bid him advance, his tall frame bent almost double in reverence, and held out a hand for him to kiss. His bodyguards, disarmed by her own Followers, stood to either side of the door, arms folded. The room filled gradually with the faint but unmistakable odor of goat. Aziru straightened, and Tiye's scribes picked up their pens.

"So, you are at last able to answer the summons of your lord," Tiye said dryly. "You must have brought mountains of tribute, Aziru. Either that or you travel with an enormous retinue. How many years has it been since Pharaoh summoned you?"

"Your Majesty cannot have seen the letters I sent to Pharaoh, explaining the delays caused by my campaigns against his terrible enemies," Aziru boomed in heavily accented Egyptian. "I came to him on wings of brotherly devotion as soon as it was possible." His eyes sparkled impudently into her own.

"You are wrong," Tiye responded. "I read the letters when I was still at Malkatta. And not only yours. Ribbadi had much to say, as did Abimilki."

"Those vermin . . . those treacherous dogs!" Aziru's voice trembled with emotion. "I praise the gods that Pharaoh in his infinite wisdom did not believe their lies. Their spite and jealousy was unbounded. They longed to enjoy the fruitful relationship that exists between Egypt and my people."

"Your loyalty does you credit and is equaled only by your histrionic ability," Tiye answered sarcastically.

"Your Majesty is unkind. Have I not defended Egypt at great cost to my people? Did I not give sanctuary to that whining woman Ribbadi when he could not hold his own city and had to flee?" Tiye saw that Aziru realized his tactical mistake as soon as the words had left his mouth. He fell silent, and his eyes dropped.

"I trust that our dear ally Ribbadi is enjoying the protection and peace of our brother Aziru," she said evenly, leaning forward. "I am surprised that he did not accompany you or send letters for Pharaoh with you. In days past he wrote many letters. I suppose he could have given them to our spies in Amurru, but surely his friend Aziru offered to bring them? Has Ribbadi lost the use of his mouth, his hands?" Aziru looked up and regarded her speculatively. Tiye could almost read his quick thoughts. Were there truly Egyptian spies in Amurru? What had they reported to Pharaoh? Could the empress's sharp gaze pierce the veils of deceit that had screened him from Pharaoh's mild eyes?

"Indeed, Ribbadi is at peace," he answered after a pause, and Tiye sat back grim-faced.

"And we both know what kind of peace that is. My late husband Osiris Amunhotep Glorified brought the same fate to your father, and I would strongly recommend that you, Aziru, reflect upon his end. Akhetaten is now my home. Reflect upon that also. How long do you intend to stay?"

Aziru bowed. "Pharaoh's hospitality is boundless, tempting me to prolong my visit indefinitely, Majesty."

"His hospitality may be boundless, but my patience is not. Nor is the forbearance of my country. You are dismissed."

He promptly bowed again and swaggered out, his bodyguards stamping after him. *He will not go home until he has ascertained the extent of my power over my son,* Tiye thought as the doors thudded shut. *And that is something I myself have yet to discover. But Akhenaten must now listen to me, or Aziru will stop vacillating between Suppiluliumas and Egypt, conclude binding treaties with Suppiluliumas, and desert us altogether. Once it would not have mattered, but now every ally is precious.*

In the afternoon Tiye ordered her litter and went to Nefertiti's grandiose apartments. She would have preferred to send for the queen, but she knew that the thread of family affection and negotiation was stretched to its limit, and any insistence upon her prerogatives might snap it altogether. Nefertiti was reclining on her couch, the fans moving gently above her, her musicians playing softly. Her latest pregnancy was far advanced, but she had made no effort in public or private to hide her protruding belly, donning the filmy linens that accentuated the inviting sensuality of her body. Nefertiti was thirty-two years old, glowing in a maturity that seemed to combine ripeness without incipient decay and the promise of physical pleasures. Her natural dignity was accentuated rather than diminished by the slow aging evident in her face, and the mild impression of dissatisfaction emanating from features exquisite in their regularity only served to give her worshipers a hint of dissipation that removed her from the pedestal of untouchable godhead yet held her tantalizingly just out of reach. She answered Tiye's stiff bow with a slight inclining of her head, both hands imprisoned in the respectful grasp of the cosmeticians who were working rich oils into her skin.

"Forgive me for not rising to abase myself, Majesty Aunt," she said. "My back and legs are aching, and besides, I find bowing rather difficult." The kohl-ringed gray eyes coolly challenged her.

Tiye ignored the barb. "I wish to speak with you in private," she said. "I have left my attendants in the garden. Dismiss yours also."

Nefertiti made a small grimace. "Have you almost finished?" she asked the servants bent over her long fingers. "Well, wrap my hands in linen and wait outside."

Tiye stood while the young men did as they were bid, bowed as they passed her, and slipped through the door. She walked to the couch and sank onto a chair, and for a moment the two women eyed each other. Tiye expected her niece to keep the conversation light so that she might maneuver behind pointless words, but as ever she was misled by a sophistication of face and body that did not extend to Nefertiti's mind. Her niece was as rash as Sitamun had been.

"You had no right to dismiss Meryra as Keeper of the Harem Door," she began. "He has been my steward for a long time, and I gave him the running of the harem for his efficiency. The women were content under his hand. Pharaoh likes and trusts him."

"Pharaoh likes and trusts everyone," Tiye said mildly. "While I was in Malkatta, you had the responsibility of the harem here, Majesty. But you know full well that since I am empress and first wife, it was in fact mine. I simply appointed another keeper, as is my right." She had not intended to confront her niece but had hoped to argue gently and tactfully, perhaps win her over by reducing her defensiveness, reassuring her that her jealousy was unfounded. Obviously Nefertiti intended to render such an approach impossible, and Tiye was forced to discard warmth in favor of a position Nefertiti could never mistake as appeasement.

"I cannot imagine why you bothered to do such a thing unless you still have yearnings for your son's body and want to control the parade of women to his bed. I think it is a tasteless obsession in a woman of your age, Majesty. You cannot possibly compete any longer."

Tiye smiled into the sulky face. "I have absolutely no desire to try to claim my physical rights as a wife," she said adamantly. "If you cannot imagine why I have decided so soon to take an interest in the affairs of the harem, you are more stupid than I thought. Meketaten worries me."

Nefertiti's eyes slid away from her own. "There is nothing wrong with Meketaten. A touch of fever this summer, that is all."

Tiye wanted to shake her. "I see that I must speak as clearly as though you were in your infancy. Did you not object when Pharaoh put his daughter in the harem?"

"No. Why should I have? It is his prerogative."

"Bu Meketaten is still a child, as slim and gangling as a little boy."

"No. She became a woman six months ago. Pharaoh ordered that she was to keep the youth lock. He likes it."

The implications of Nefertiti's artless words chilled Tiye. "She is your daughter, and my blood! Has it not occurred to you that if she becomes pregnant, she may die? Look at her, Nefertiti! How could such an unformed little body carry a child?"

Nefertiti began to pick at the swathes of linen on her hands. "She is pregnant already."

Now Tiye made no effort to control herself. The blow caught Nefertiti on the temple, and she muffled a scream. Tiye rubbed her knuckles and placed a hand over her pounding heart while Nefertiti moaned and rocked. "Be quiet!" Tiye hissed. "I did not strike you hard. It appears that Kia is a better friend to your daughter than you. She at least is endeavoring to comfort the girl."

Nefertiti sat motionless, and then her head fell back onto the pillow. "Meketaten understands that it is the seed of the

Aten," she snapped. "The god must bind those of his blood ever closer to himself. It is his duty."

"You do not believe that any more than I! It is the duty of a Divine Horus to father an incarnation, but not like this. Why did he not choose Meritaten?"

Nefertiti's glance was wary. "Truly, my aunt, I do not know. But you do not yet understand the consequences of arguing with your son. He cries, the demons attack his head, I can do nothing."

"You are the most beautiful woman Egypt has ever seen," Tiye said sadly. "But you have the heart of a viper."

"No," Nefertiti flashed back. "A cobra. A royal cobra, Majesty Aunt. All Egypt worships me. Do not stand in my way."

A pall of fatigue began to settle over Tiye. "You would be wise to decide now not to confront me directly in the future, Nefertiti. For all your clawing and spitting, I am more ruthless than you. I cannot be disposed of as easily as Sitamun. I came to you today to try and persuade you to help me convince Pharaoh of the immediate necessity of mounting a campaign against Syria. But now I do not persuade, I demand. Drop your own words into his ears, or you may live to see Egypt on her knees."

"Ridiculous." Nefertiti's eyes gleamed in the darkness. "No nation dares to challenge us."

"It is you who dares not challenge Pharaoh with the truth. Not his truth, but the hard glare of reality. You prefer his favor, his rich gifts. But those things will cease, and sooner than you think, if tribute and foreign loyalties continue to decline."

"You have forgotten one thing," Nefertiti said in a low, menacing voice. "Akhenaten adores me. If I choose to remain silent, you are impotent."

"Oh, I think you will do as I say. Otherwise a certain sculptor will have his beautiful throat cut."

Tiye saw, with satisfaction, the color fade from Nefertiti's fine-grained skin. It had been a chance shot, an impulsive arrow fired by the sudden memory of Horemheb's brief comment, and Tiye herself was surprised when it met its mark. "Does Pharaoh know in which direction the yearning of his perfect wife lies? Obviously not. I need not kill him, of course. It would be enough to start spreading some lively gossip. But I would prefer to murder him, dear niece, and murder I will unless you drag yourself out of your preoccupation with your own comfort."

"You demon," Nefertiti whispered. The linen wraps lay shredded on the sheet, and her oil-slick hands were shaking with rage. "You ugly, aging bitch. Sebek take you!"

Tiye rose. "You do not trust the Aten to exact a vengeance on me? How disappointed Pharaoh would be to hear of your lack of faith. Think about it, Nefertiti, when you are calmer. Enjoy what is left of your rest." She bowed and called sharply, and servants swung the door wide.

The lines are drawn, and more quickly than I really wanted, she thought as she strode away. *I hope Nefertiti is too simple to realize that she can keep the upper hand by inventing the right lies. Now I must visit Tutu. Threatening my niece and bullying a sniveling minister is a far cry from the diplomacy I delighted in and you watched with such pleasure, Amunhotep my husband. It is like the careless butchering of oxen, and I despise the necessity. How feeble the times have become!*

The Office of Foreign Correspondence at Akhetaten was situated at the end of the road that ran between the Great Temple and a smaller one, close by the maze of walled courts that sheltered the estates of the ministers who were not entitled to riverfront properties. As she was carried in her closed litter along the dusty street, her nostrils, even behind the thick curtains, continued to be assailed by the odor of incense that hung in the air, mingled with the stench of offal and other rubbish that was flung over the walls into the street. Stately chants and the tinkle of shaken systra wafted from the temple's precincts, ethereal and beautiful over the hoarse shouts of hawkers and the babble of the shrill, coarse laughter of the fellahin women passing the time of day. The tap of a drum told her that she was passing dancers. She opened the curtains slightly, expecting to see naked whores displaying their wares, but the women were temple dancers, lithe and unblemished, hung with flowers, their arms and faces raised solemnly to the sun as they moved. *Akhetaten is certainly no Thebes*, she reflected, letting the curtain drop. *And how typical of my son to design and build an Office of Foreign Correspondence so annoyingly far from the palace.*

Inside, the office was noisy with street sounds, even though it was protected from the populace by a gated wall and high slit windows and surrounded by shrubs. Bins and chests overflowed with scrolls. Scribes' palettes lay on every surface. A group of men stood arguing in one corner, and Tiye finally

saw Tutu himself leaning over a scribe's shoulder, dictating.
Tiye waited beside the silent men who held the canopy over
her head while her herald went within, calling her titles, and
by the time she herself stepped over the threshold, all were
prone on their faces. Tiye let her gaze deliberately scan the
untidy room, giving the prostrate men time to fully appreciate
her presence, and then commanded, "Kneel, Tutu!"

The young man pulled himself onto his knees, head bowed.
"I am Your Majesty's slave," he mumbled uneasily. Tiye moved
until her feet with their blood-red nails, the gilt straps of her
sandals, and the hem of her jeweled gown were within his
vision.

"Tell me," she went on smoothly, "how many times have
you been made a Person of Gold?"

Tutu's head jerked, puzzled. "Four times, Divine Goddess."

"Then you have received more than your share, for certainly
you do not need Pharaoh's gold." She laid a light emphasis on
"Pharaoh" and watched carefully for a flinch. "How much do
the foreign ambassadors pay you to keep the truth of their
depredations from coming to Pharaoh's ears? Does Aziru pay
you in slaves or silver? And Suppiluliumas must pour gold into
your hands like water in exchange for the quiet destruction of
dispatches from his enemies. I am surprised that you are not
living by the river, but I suppose it would not do to flaunt your
wealth. Is your tomb a rich one, Tutu? Answer me!" Quick as
light her foot flashed into Tutu's throat.

"Majesty, I am as filth beneath your feet!" he croaked,
swallowing convulsively. "I grovel! I am as dung!"

"That is no answer. Stand up!" Tiye looked around the office
and felt as if she might laugh. It was not Tutu's downcast face
or the frozen bodies among which he stood or Huya's quickly
hidden smile. It was perhaps the ludicrousness of her having
to resort to such childish games. "You may look at me."

Reluctantly he raised his eyes to meet hers, and she tried
to read them. Tutu looked hurt, bewildered, and embarrassed,
but not guilty.

"Now answer."

Tutu lifted both shoulders in a gesture of wounded innocence. "I worship my pharaoh. Never would I betray him. I
read him the dispatches when he visits this office."

"You do not urge them upon him if they are serious? You

read them to him without advice, without interpretation or admonition? What kind of a minister are you?"

"Goddess, I am a simple man—"

"Damn your simplicity! Someone should choke you with your gold!" She wanted to demand his immediate dismissal or at least insist that he bring all correspondence to her in the future, but both orders would have to come from Akhenaten. Despairingly she wondered what had happened to the clandestine correspondence from the spies scattered throughout the empire that his predecessor had controlled, and decided that it had probably ceased. Turning, she stepped out into the sunlight, breathing deeply and reaching for Huya's arm. "Help me onto the litter," she commanded. "I intended to speak with Horemheb tonight, but I am too tired. Have them take me to my own house, Huya, and send to Horemheb tomorrow."

She lay on the litter doubled over the dragging pain in her abdomen, fighting a sense of loneliness intensified, she knew, by sheer weariness. That night she ate alone, refusing entrance to Ay, who came to enquire after her, and had her lamps extinguished early. Huya was absent on business in the harem. *And that is something else I must do*, she thought as she drifted toward sleep. *I must speak to Tadukhipa. I should have brought her aunt from Malkatta for her. I must visit Meketaten. I have not asked after Ankhesenpaaten, either, or spoken to Meritaten, and I am simply putting off an audience alone with Akhenaten. So much to do, to try and understand before I can begin to salvage anything.*

The evening of the following day she met with her brother and Horemheb in her garden, far from the prying ears of servants. Mutnodjme had accompanied her husband and lay on her back in the grass, graceful limbs splayed and eyes halfclosed, while the others talked. Tiye knew that the young woman could be trusted, and indeed, Mutnodjme's silent presence was somehow comforting. *I disliked my own daughter and cannot bear my other niece*, Tiye thought, glancing at Mutnodjme's dusk-shrouded form, *but this young woman has my complete affection*. Horemheb was speaking softly, leaning forward on his chair, elbows on his brown knees.

"I am convinced that Pharaoh will not listen to any of us. He believes that his reign as the Aten on earth began a return to true Ma'at, not only in Egypt but in the entire world. The turbulence outside our borders he interprets as simply the struggle of others less enlightened against this knowledge. As such, he insists it will gradually die away as the Aten asserts its omnipotence. He need do nothing. The Aten will triumph as its light spreads out from Akhetaten to embrace and enlighten all men."

"I think that my daughter likes to believe it, too," Ay put in. "She is foolhardy and vindictive, but she recognizes power when she sees it, and the concept of world power embodied in the Aten has made her drunk. You tell us, Majesty, that you have threatened her with the death of Thothmes the sculptor, but Nefertiti will sacrifice him without a qualm to keep her hold on your son."

"In that case, let us not wait. There is no need at present to deprive the young man of life, but it would be advantageous to tell Pharaoh of his wife's flirtation. If Nefertiti cannot be persuaded to join her voice to ours, then the sooner a wedge is driven between her and Pharaoh the better." Tiye spoke calmly, but her heart contracted with compassion for Akhenaten. She could not deny his ineptitude as a leader, his failure to maintain the distance and dignity vital in a pharaoh, but the thought of depriving him of his trust in Nefertiti was a bitter one. In his simplicity he had bought the affection of his ministers, and even Horemheb, whom he had first befriended, had been unable to give him the blind loyalty he had wanted. *And you, Ay,* Tiye mused, looking across at her brother. *Though I love you, I think I would no longer place my life in your hands. You betrayed me when you left Malkatta, and now you consider betraying your pharaoh. In your eyes Akhenaten is nothing but a gaming piece and Egypt the board. You will sit between Akhenaten and myself, committing yourself fully to neither until you see which way the balance shifts.*

"I think such a course may be dangerous," Ay objected. "If Pharaoh's trust in Nefertiti is shattered, it will drive him even more deeply into the arms of the Aten for reassurance. The Aten has prohibited violence against any man. Aziru grasped that fact as soon as he arrived. In spite of my attempts to discredit him, he has been fawning on Akhenaten and protesting his innocence in the face of the evidence from the few loyal governors Egypt has left abroad."

"What I suggest is not such a dangerous course as you believe. I will put myself in Nefertiti's place. Surely a son will turn to his mother after such a crushing disappointment."

"Or a husband to his wife?" Ay said wryly. "Only as a mother can you now hope to sway him."

"I have no intention of entering into a sexual relationship with him again," Tiye said tiredly. "I bitterly regret my weakness in allowing him to share my bed at all."

"I think it would be better to put aside all such machinations and simply take Egypt out of his hands." The voice was Horemheb's. He was sitting back now, his expression unreadable in the darkening garden, his legs crossed, his hands curled around the arms of the chair. Tiye sensed rather than saw his tension. She and Ay turned to him in the pregnant silence that followed, and finally Tiye said quietly, "Go on, Commander."

"He is despised by the priests of every god save those at Memphis and On. He is derided by every courtier who lives on his generosity. He is mocked all over the world by the rulers of tribes who are once again finding a pride in their own military might. Your son has lost us an empire, Goddess. He must be prevented from taking our country from us also."

At Horemheb's words Tiye felt her grip on the arms of the chair become painfully tight, but somehow she could not release it. "He is the incarnation of Amun, a prince of the royal blood, true son of a pharaoh," she responded hotly, stung irrationally into a defense of her son, "whether he believes these things or not. It is a sin against Ma'at to lay hands on him."

"I do not speak of murder." Horemheb's deep voice took on a placatory tone. "Let him keep his kingship until Prince Smenkhara is ready to reign. But take from him command of the army and use it to make a war of recovery."

"And I suppose you would lead such an army?" Ay replied evenly. "Are you being deliberately naïve, Horemheb? Once victorious, could you resist the temptation to place the Double Crown on your own head? Do not forget that although we regard the omnipotence of the Aten as Pharaoh's delusion, there are many men, both in the army and among the courtiers and priests, who are genuine converts. I think in trying to wrest military might from Pharaoh we might well precipitate a civil war. We would eventually win, but at the cost of much blood. And supposing we gave the crown to Smenkhara? How long would it be before he ceased to be grateful and began to view those who brought down his predecessor with suspicion? Or, if the crown went to one of us, Smenkhara as legal heir could raise much support from the common people and war against us. We must remember, too, that whatever happens, we will remain tainted by our association with the Aten. If the country returned to its true state of Ma'at, we would be discredited. The only answer is to do what we can indirectly."

I will not forget this argument, Tiye thought. *It has the glibness of words spoken many times before, and brought out tonight to test me. I must arrange for spies in both households.* "Horemheb, how desperate is the situation beyond Syria? Is Egypt in any immediate danger?"

"Not at present," he replied unwillingly. "The foreigners make war on one another with the delight of those long kept under Egypt's peaceful thumb. They are still in awe of her and prefer in any case to kill one another to test their skill and strength. One day Suppiluliumas will march the Khatti on us, but not yet."

"Thank you," she said quietly. "You did not have to be so honest. You could have tried to impress me with an urgency that is not present."

He laughed shortly. "It would not be wise to lie to you, Majesty."

"No, it would not. Therefore, I propose that first we discredit my niece, so that I can slowly begin to turn my son around. I must add that any thought of murdering the queen would be foolish. Amunhotep would be lost to all reason if she died in suspicious circumstances. That is a divine command," she emphasized, having noticed Ay and Horemheb exchange glances in the darkness. "Ignore it at your peril. Mutnodjme, are you asleep?"

"No, Majesty Aunt." The cool voice drifted over the grass. "It has been a most interesting conversation."

"Then call your litter bearers. I want to go to my couch."

Mutnodjme rose, brushed herself off, and shouted for her servants. Horemheb also came to his feet and, pressing his lips to Tiye's hand, murmured his worship. Together they bowed and vanished into the night.

"How long has Horemheb had designs on the Horus Throne?" Tiye demanded sharply of Ay when the torches of the couple had disappeared.

Ay pulled his chair closer to hers. "I do not think he as yet has such ambitions," he replied. "But it is frustrating for a born commander to see soldiers idle year after year while their country crumbles for lack of a simple order."

"And you, Ay, have you such ambitions?"

"Tiye," he chided her gently, "the gods have blessed me with fifty-eight years. I am too old to dream the foolish and exhilarating dreams of youth. My sister is a goddess, my daughter a queen. What more could an old man desire?"

I wonder, Tiye thought when he had gone. *Ambitions that would lie safely dormant under a strong Horus must inevitably stir in times like these. I pray I may not live to see them mature.*

Tiye had to wait several days before she could speak to her son, for the excitement of her arrival had precipitated another debilitating headache, accompanied by the vomiting that had become so much a fashion at court. In the meantime she received dispatches from Thebes. Maya wrote that the emaciated bodies of starving priests had begun to be found floating in the Nile. The mayor wrote also, his letter one long complaint of violence among the jobless, desecration of the empty Amun shrines by the ignorant fellahin, and the shortages of food caused by Pharaoh's command that goods of every kind should first pass through the customs houses at Akhetaten. Tiye listened to her scribe's drone impassively. She could do nothing, and therefore anxiety would serve no purpose. She went dutifully to the Great Temple and stood under her magic sunshade twice a day, watching Nefertiti and the priest Meryra perform rites for the sick pharaoh.

While passing the time before her audience, she sent for one of the Aten priests and had him read to her from the scrolls of the Teaching. She was struck, as she had been when Akhenaten had sung to her, by the artless beauty of his religious conviction. Here was no solemn arbiter of man's fate but a god with the gentle humanity of Akhenaten himself. "Creator of the germ in woman, who makest seed into men, making alive the son in the body of his mother, soothing him that he may not weep, nurse even in the womb, giver of breath to sustain alive every one that He maketh! ... Thy rays nourish every garden; when Thou risest, they live, they grow by Thee. Thou makest the seasons in order to make develop all that Thou hast made. Winter to bring them coolness, and heat that they may taste Thee. ... Thou makest millions of forms through Thyself alone ... Thou art Aten of the day over the earth. When Thou hast gone away and all men, whose faces Thou hast fashioned in order that Thou mightest no longer see Thyself alone, have fallen asleep, so that not one seeth that which Thou hast made, yet art Thou still in my heart. . . ." Such sentiments were so unusual that Tiye wondered what had prompted them. While she and her first husband had deliberately encouraged Aten worship for diplomatic reasons, neither had had any real interest in Ra as the Visible Disk. Another small segment of Teaching, entitled simply "Revelation to the King," read: "There is no other that knoweth Thee save Thy son Akhenaten. Thou has made him wise in Thy designs and in Thy might." Here was a son she could recognize, a man deep in the toils of visions that were incomprehensible to all save himself.

It was with genuine sorrow that Tiye presented herself outside his private rooms and heard her herald announce her titles. She knew that Nefertiti was at Maru-Aten with Ankhesenpaaten, sitting for a sculpted portrait that was to be done from life, and Pharaoh would be alone at this hour. She walked through the doors confidently.

Akhenaten rushed to greet her, smiling and folding her in an exuberant embrace as her servant withdrew. She answered his kiss and stepped back, regarding him. He was pale, with dark smudges under his green-lidded eyes, but otherwise seemed well.

"I am glad you have recovered, my son," she said. "I was distressed at the thought that my arrival had made you ill."

"My excitement overcame me." He smiled back. "To have you here with me! It is wonderful. I feel safer now." He released his hands and invited her to sit, himself sinking back onto his chair and arranging the voluminous folds of his gown across his plump thighs. At the farther end of the room three monkeys sat perched on an arrangement of wooden frames that had obviously been built especially for them. Below the perch was a large golden bowl filled with overripe fruit, and the smell of the animals' droppings and the bruised fruit wafted unpleasantly around Tiye. She looked for Parennefer as Pharaoh offered her wine, but he poured for her himself. "After I have suffered the touch of the god, I like to be alone," he explained in answer to her enquiring eyebrows. "Often the god speaks to me or shows me visions, and I cannot listen properly if Parennefer or one of the others is hovering to serve me. The pain is terrible, Empress, but the rewards are great. Ah!" he rubbed his orange palms together. "To see the family united and growing larger is bliss."

"Are you speaking of little Meketaten and the child she carries?"

"Certainly. All my children must receive the blessing of the Aten through me, so that I and they might remain inviolable. But I speak also of dear Nefertiti's child, soon to be born. The Aten brings fertility to everything." His high voice was husky, almost drowned by the sudden gibbering of the monkeys who, seeing an intruder, had left their perches and were bobbing around her, hands impudently outstretched for a sweetmeat. Akhenaten tossed them each a date from the plate on the table. Tiye kept her hands around her wine cup.

"I have been studying the Teaching," she said. "It is exquisite, Akhenaten."

"I dictated the words, which came from the god," he said proudly, "but the music for it is mine alone. So much comes to me with my sickness. It is a holy gift. Yesterday while I lay weak and spent watching Meryra light the incense in the shrine by my couch, I saw your face in the smoke, young and lovely as I remember you from my childhood. It was such a happy omen!"

Tiye noticed that he had begun to sweat. His forehead under the white helmet beaded suddenly, and moisture trickled down his long neck. His hands moved constantly against each other.

"I will always be the mother who cared for you and tried to lighten your days of imprisonment," she said gently. "That is why I have come to you today. I will not see my dear one hurt."

He frowned across at her. "I remember that tone also," he said with swift perception. "You are going to tell me something I do not wish to hear. Why did you dismiss Meryra as Nefertiti's harem keeper?"

The familiar feeling of picking her way through tall reeds without a path to follow returned to Tiye. "I replaced him with Huya because he was putting his duties to his queen before his duties to you, Divine One," she said with careful emphasis. "He would not have told you that Nefertiti is seen in the company of your sculptor Thothmes too often."

He blinked rapidly. "I suppose she is," he said quickly, "but that is because Nefertiti has been commissioning many statues of herself with which to beautify Akhetaten and cheer the hearts of her subjects."

"I expect that you are right," Tiye replied. "Nevertheless,

you know it is my prerogative as chief wife to appoint whom I choose. As your harem is so very large, I decided to trust the position to Huya."

The dark, restless eyes flickered over her face. "I remember him. Kheruef left your service because he said we broke a law, you and I, but Huya remained loyal. I will give him a tomb in the northern cliffs."

"That is generous of you. Could I prevail upon your generosity yet again and ask for Tutu's dismissal? He does his work now no better than he did at Malkatta—"

"Malkatta belongs to a past I despise!" he broke in loudly. "Mother, why are you trying to turn me into a little boy again? All is well at Akhetaten. I rule justly, I love my people, I do right in the sight of the god. Tutu stays!"

"Very well." She backed down hurriedly, appalled at the sudden change in her son. Sweat now poured from him. He lifted the skirts of his gown with both trembling hands and mopped his face, uttering small whimpering noises, his breath coming fast and noisily. Then he sprang abruptly to his feet and began to pace the room, his robes floating away from his flabby body, his hands gripping his breasts before sliding to entwine about each other.

"All will be well!" he shrieked. "As long as I obey the god and harm no man, Egypt will prosper."

Alarmed, Tiye went to him, calling for Parennefer over her shoulder. The monkeys ran excitedly after her, and stumbling, she kicked them out of the way. "Akhenaten," she murmured, putting an arm around his wet, hot neck. "Forgive me for distressing you so. I love you. I only wish to help you."

"So does Tutu. He is a loyal child of the Aten, and Nefertiti is my rock, the ground on which I plant my august feet! Her breath is as the sweet lotus, her smile as the rising of the god. Her touch is pure! Now I am unhappy once more!" He shook her off and began to sob, a hoarse, dry sound that sent a thrill of terror through Tiye. The doors opened, and she saw Parennefer look quickly inside and then disappear. She forced Akhenaten over to the table and urged wine on him, steadying the cup against his red mouth. He drank in gulps, shuddering.

"Pharaoh, it may indeed be as you believe," she said urgently, "but the fact remains, Nefertiti should not be with the sculptor so frequently. She is the queen. It is not seemly."

Wine ran from the corner of his mouth. He leaned against

her, swaying, his eyes closed. "It is hard to be God," he slurred, a broken whisper. "They do not love me, any of them. I shower gold and gentle words upon them, but beneath their smiles is darkness. Only Nefertiti. Only her . . ." He slumped, and unable to hold his weight, Tiye let him slide onto the chair. Her own palms were damp, and her knees shook. The door clicked open, and she turned to see Horemheb bowing grimly to her before he directed his attention to Pharaoh.

"My dear lord," he said, kneeling and repeatedly kissing the twitching hands. "Do you remember the trip we took together to Memphis, when you first left the harem? How we would pray together in the evenings, in your beautiful tent with the river lapping outside and the piping of the marsh birds all around? We would share wine, and you would ask me of Memphis. I am still here, Akhenaten." All the time he was speaking in such a soothing tone his hands were moving, rubbing the silver-girt arms, gently massaging the still shoulders. Parennefer and Pharaoh's body servant looked on, motionless.

"I am not a child, Horemheb," Akhenaten muttered tiredly. "Is Parennefer there? I want to sleep. Forgive me, Mother. I cannot talk anymore. Perhaps tomorrow . . ." He allowed his butler to help him to his feet and his servant supported him across the long room.

Tiye grasped Horemheb's arm. "You did not warn me!" she muttered, shaken and furious.

"Your Majesty would not have believed," he answered gently. "Now you must understand why I spoke as I did in your garden. I am perhaps your son's only friend. Whether his fits are the hand of the god or intermittent madness I cannot say. I love the man I have known for so long. It is the ruler I wish to despose." The moment had stripped them both of tact.

Tiye's nails bit farther into his arm. "You know perfectly well that Pharaoh the man cannot be separated from Pharaoh the god!" she answered swiftly. "Don't make me kill you, Horemheb! I need you!"

"I am aware of that, but Egypt needs me also." He bent and kissed the hand curved like talons around his flesh. "Majesty, do what you can. I will wait."

She let go of him, looking dispassionately at the marks she had made. "How long has he been like this, so unpredictable?"

"It has grown on him slowly. He never harms anyone, but we have all learned to be careful what we say in case our words trigger what you saw. I cannot go far from him. He trusts me, and I am able to comfort him."

"Gods!" She laughed hurtfully. "He spoke the truth, then. You do not love him, any of you carrion. I will press for Nefertiti's disgrace, but no amount of incense will purify me of the deed. Take Smenkhara under your wing, Commander. It is time he stopped flitting about like a gilded butterfly and applied himself to the manly arts."

He nodded briefly and turned on his heel. Tiye stood still, listening to the monkeys snuffle and scratch, once more looking back down the years to the source of her growing guilt, the moment in the garden at Memphis when she had agreed to marry her son, while the haughty face of the Son of Hapu rose in her mind's eye. Her cup was half-empty. She drained it quickly and went away.

19

TIYE TRIED ONCE MORE TO REASON WITH NEFERTITI, bringing all her powers of persuasion to bear on the sulky woman, desperate to avoid the necessity for blackening the queen's name, but Nefertiti mouthed the same tired accusations of jealousy and spite that she had hurled at Tiye in Malkatta, and in the end Tiye gave up. Closeted with Huya, she laid out in minute detail the gossip that must spread in the harem, among Pharaoh's personal servants and, with more colorful words, in the markets of the city. If she had been younger, she would have been able to insinuate herself between husband and wife swiftly, expertly, with her body, and would have felt a great deal cleaner than she did using less direct methods. But with Nefertiti lazily encouraging Pharaoh in his disastrous policies instead of trying to sway him, with Horemheb still loyal but increasingly restless, with Ay himself disillusioned, there was no time.

Huya did his work well. He knew that rumors could feed on nothing more than a dropped word, the lift of an eyebrow, a secret smile. He had a reputation for silent efficiency and was wise enough not to jeopardize it. His soft voice was forgotten in the wave of excited conjecture that swept first the palace and then the city as a whole. The monkey sculptures had been entertaining, but the queen in a new guise as adulteress provided infinite titillation. Was it not well known that the queen had begged Pharaoh to allow Thothmes to own an estate on the river when more worthy men had to be content with walled houses behind the palace? Did she not retire almost every day to Maru-Aten, there to sit for one sculpture after another?

While the gossip spread, the queen appeared to become even more publicly affectionate to her husband, clinging to him on the double litter, caressing him as they sat together at the feasting, but no one failed to note that the empress was now seen constantly in their company, a small, very straight, aloof woman always richly and formally garbed and always wearing the glittering disk, horns, and plumes of her divine position. There were those who, bowing in adoration before the pouting mouth, the piercing blue eyes, the inscrutable face slashed with lines of petulance, wondered at the coincidence of the rumors and the empress's coming. But to most, Tiye was the shadow of older times, a reminder of a way of ruling that had disappeared more suddenly than they cared to remember.

As Nefertiti's delivery drew near, it became a source of amusement to speculate on her unborn child's paternity, and when at last she took to her couch, the buzz of gossip reached a fever pitch. Huya told Tiye that though he had not himself seen it, he believed that courtiers were placing bets on whether the baby would be another girl, and therefore presumably Pharaoh's, or whether it might be a boy. That possibility had not occurred to Tiye. But now she found herself a victim of her own lies and innuendoes. She did not want to have to contend with the possibility of Nefertiti's bearing a son. It was imperative that Akhenaten be persuaded to declare Smenkhara his heir, for she believed that if Nefertiti produced a boy, her own son by Osiris Amunhotep would probably be disinherited. *What irony that would be*, she mused grimly in the sleepless nights, *if the son of a mere sculptor should eventually receive the Double Crown. But I do not believe that Nefertiti has done more than dream romantically over her stone chipper. And can*

I blame her? The body of my poor son becomes less desirable as time goes by.

But, confounding the rumors, Nefertiti gave birth to another girl, her sixth, and those courtiers who had allowed their imaginations free rein parted with much gold. Pharaoh was as touchingly delighted as he had been at Meritaten's birth and named the child Sotpe-en-Ra, Chosen One of Ra. The gossip abated briefly, but Tiye, watching Pharaoh carefully, believed that it had done its work. She did not know what passed between the royal couple in the privacy of Akhenaten's bedchamber, but Nefertiti on more than one occasion was seen in public with red, swollen eyes while her husband stood apart from her, his arm around the fragile, distorted body of little Meketaten.

Aziru was still at court, living in ambassadorial quarters in the palace, quietly watching the minute shift in the balance of power with wary eyes. The Khatti delegation had returned to Boghaz-keuoi without Pharaoh's having made any attempt to come to terms with Suppiluliumas, a prince who was now as powerful as a pharaoh himself. Tiye was tempted at least to send warning letters to him, but decided that if she did not eventually get her way at court, such a move would only serve to further destroy Egypt's crumbling image among the Asiatics.

The New Year began with a week-long paean of praise to the Aten. Songs composed by Akhenaten were sung daily throughout the city while the royal family attended rites four times a day in the temple. Pharaoh fasted and prayed. Tiye, standing by the hour in the sanctuary, defenseless as they all were against the merciless, blinding fire of the sun, thought of Ra in his guise as sphinx, a reclining god of watchfulness, whose benignity could at any time become a bloody vengefulness. *You should beware, my son,* she thought as she watched him lift his face to the sky, eyes closed. *Ra as the Visible Disk is indeed a god of gentleness and beauty, but how, on a day like this, can you remain oblivious to the god in his guise as destroyer? I know that the sun, like Hathor, can kill in his other aspects. It would have been wise not to invite his jealousy by elevating the Aten at the expense of his other manifestations.*

At the end of the first month of the New Year, the month of Thoth, Meketaten was brought to her couch. Huya woke Tiye in the early hours of a stale, close morning, lighting her lamp and bringing her cool water as she struggled to clear her head.

"Pharaoh sent a message to Your Majesty, inviting you to the birth if it is your wish," he explained as Piha passed a cool cloth over her face and combed her hair. "He and the queen are already in attendance."

"How long until dawn?" Tiye stood while Piha draped her in a thin cloak, and then sat to have her sandals put on.

"No more than two hours."

"Where is Tadukhipa? Is she with the princess?"

"No. Pharaoh will not permit her in. He allows only the fully royal and the witnesses of tradition to be present."

Tiye's mouth tightened. "What else is a Mitanni princess but fully royal? Order her brought from the harem, Huya. I will have her admitted. If my escort waits, I am ready."

She was led, not into the harem, where Meketaten had her apartment, but through the gate into the palace grounds. The darkness was thick and smothering. Tiye would have welcomed even the hottest breath of wind, but the trees stood motionless, clusters of blackness against an inky sky sprinkled with a few pale stars. The paving beneath her feet was warm, the grass brittle. Inside the palace the wind catchers provided air that was at least fresh, and the high ceilings gave an illusion of coolness. Tiye followed the escort until they came to Pharaoh's own suite of rooms. The door to the bedchamber was ajar, and a thin haze of incense drifted out into the passage. Tiye dismissed the guard and entered.

Meketaten was lying propped up on pillows, a sennet board beside her. To one side of the couch Akhenaten sat, dressed in a pleated kilt and white scarf but little else. Nefertiti's chair was also drawn up to the couch, and she held a playing cone in one hand. The midwife was busying herself at a table nearby. Tiye bowed and as she approached, the girl lifted a pale, frightened face to her grandmother, the smile she attempted failing to hide the panic in the almond eyes. Tiye took the child's cold hand and kissed her.

"I see you are passing the time pleasantly," she said, glancing swiftly at an open Aten shrine that was pouring a choking smoke over the couch. "If you beat your mother at the sennet, I will give you a pair of golden earrings. What do you think of that?" The window was tightly draped, making the room stifling. Tiye looked for amulets, but there were none. *It would have been better*, she thought, *to have diverted the girl with Dogs and Jackals. The sennet is a magic game, portentous with predictions, charms, and curses. I hope Nefertiti has the good sense to let Meketaten win.* She bowed in front of Pharaoh. "My son, I wish to speak with you outside."

Akhenaten nodded agreeably, beamed upon his daughter, and strode into the passage, Tiye following. "It is a great day," he said. "Do you not agree?"

"Akhenaten, why are there no amulets around the couch, no priests to make spells? And do you think it wise to impede the princess's breathing with so much incense that cannot find an outlet?"

"You say you are studying the Teaching, and yet you ask such foolish questions?" He stroked her head indulgently. "The Aten blesses without the allurements of charms or the songs of priests. I am the sole arbiter before the god. All prayers are addressed to me, and I take them to the god. Meketaten understands this."

"Then at least lift the window hangings."

He shrugged lightly. "Very well."

"And I have sent for Tadukhipa. I beg you, Divine One, let her enter. The princess loves and trusts her and will be heartened by her presence."

"But my little Kia is so softhearted," he objected. "She will cry."

"I do not think so, and even if she does, it will do Meketaten much good just to see her there. Please, Akhenaten."

"Oh, very well. Have Apy put her on the scroll of witnesses." A sharp cry interrupted them, and Tiye, glacing through the door, saw the sennet board slip to the floor and Nefertiti reach for the flailing hands.

"It will be a long labor," she snapped, anger knifing through her for a second at the sight of Akhenaten's impassive face as he watched his daughter toss. "I will go back to my house now, but send a message if she asks for me, and keep me informed of her progress. Here is Tadukhipa."

The princess bowed timidly several times, her hesitant gaze slipping back and forth between Pharaoh and the empress until Akhenaten waved her within. Tiye watched as she went through the door, made her obeisance to the queen, and settled herself by the couch on a stool a servant had produced.

"Kia!" Meketaten exclaimed, the spasm already past. Tadukhipa took the small hand. "You will stay with me? I am sleepy now. Tell me another story of Mitanni while I close my eyes."

Tadukhipa glanced at Nefertiti, who nodded. Tiye turned away. Men were beginning to straggle along the passage, eyes filmed with sleep, their servants yawning around them. They carried scrolls, board games, jugs of wine, cosmetic chests, anything necessary to help pass the time they would have to spend in the room waiting for the royal birth. One by one they knelt to kiss Akhenaten's bare feet before disappearing inside. Tiye bowed to him briefly and left.

She went back to her couch, had the lamps extinguished, and tried to sleep but found she could only doze. Dawn came, and with it a hymn of praise to the Aten, sounding jaded and slightly off-key to Tiye's tired ears. Movement began in the house: the pad of naked feet, the rattle of utensils, the murmur of morning prayers chanted under the breath of busy servants. It was too soon for any news, so Tiye bathed and was dressed, and went into the garden. Already the heat of the day was unbearable to an uncovered head. She sought shade, ate a little fruit, and had her scribe read to her from the Abydos Resurrection Plays, but she could not concentrate. Piha helped her into the lake, where she stood submerged to her chin, her canopy bearers stoically holding the shade over her head.

A servant came in the afternoon to report that labor was progressing slowly, the princess was in good spirits, and Pharaoh and the queen had gone to the temple for afternoon prayers. The man assured her that princess Tadukhipa had remained with the little one. Tiye dismissed him perfunctorily. She spent the rest of the day lying on cushions under the sycamores, fanned by her sweating men, while Piha occasionally trickled water over her and brought her fresh linen.

At dusk, as she was preparing to move inside, she was surprised to see Smenkhara and Meritaten coming over the lawns surrounded by their servants. She had scarcely spoken to Akhenaten's eldest daughter, and as she watched the thirteen-year-old glide gracefully toward her, she was struck by Meritaten's likeness to her mother. It could have been Nefertiti herself, gray-eyed and lithe, who knelt in the half-light to kiss the empress's feet.

"This is a pleasure, Princess," Tiye said, patting the cushions while Smenkhara kissed her cheek cheerily and squatted beside her. Meritaten sank delicately, arranging her linens with small, pretty gestures. "I trust you are well? Huya tells me there is much fever in the nurseries, and the physicians are busy. But of course you have apartments of your own now."

"I let no one from the nurseries in," Meritaten said easily, smiling across at Smenkhara. "It was as well that you ordered Prince Tutankhaten removed. Many children have died." She pushed shoulder-length hair away from her jaw. "The demons of summer seem to have clustered in the children's quarters. You would think that Pharaoh's prophet could chant them away, seeing as he is also Controller of Demons and must constantly deal with the evil ones who wish to destroy my father and the worship of the Aten throughout the world."

"Then I am surprised Meryra is not in attendance at your sister's confinement."

"But that is a matter of the body only," Meritaten answered quickly. "My father has promised that Meketaten has the full protection of the Aten's beneficence."

Tiye turned to her son. "How are you enjoying your time with Horemheb? Do you like things military?"

He responded to her light teasing with an open grin. Since coming to Akhetaten, he had changed. The reunion with Meritaten had held at bay the capricious sullenness that had so annoyed his mother, and his face had lost its heavy, spoiled expression.

"I like the commander," he said, "but there is not much merit in straining to draw the bow or cursing as I flail around with the heavy scimitar. The chariots amuse me. I may one day be as capable behind the reins as my divine brother is." He reached for Meritaten's hand. "But, Mother, I did not come to see you to pass the time of day. I know you are preoccupied with Meketaten. Everyone is."

Except the two of you, Tiye thought. *There is an invisible union between you that shelters you from any other concern.* Smenkhara's shaven head was bare but for the blue and white ribbons bound around his forehead, and he wore a thin white kilt around his loins. *Is it my imagination or a trick of the failing light that gives him the suspicion of a swell over his belt?* she wondered and then dismissed the fancy.

"Speak, then," she urged kindly. They exchanged glances.

"We want to be betrothed," he said. "You have told me often enough that since the queen has no sons, I will sooner or later be hailed as the Horus-in-the-Nest. Meritaten is fully royal, as I am. There can be no objections to a marriage. I am fourteen. In two hears I will be legally a man, and I am already so in my body. Meritaten is old enough to bear children."

Tiye had not expected his request to be made so soon, though she had known it would come eventually. "Have you approached Pharaoh?" she asked.

"Not yet. I do not think the queen will like the idea because she hates you so, and she will try to convince Pharaoh that the match is not suitable. Therefore we ask you to press our request upon the god."

"But I am..." Tiye stopped. She had been going to say that she was convinced Pharaoh had other plans for Meritaten, that for years she had believed the princess would be married to her father as Sitamun had been married to Osiris Amunhotep. But it had been Meketaten who had been forced into the royal bed. Perhaps Akhenaten would accept a petition from her on behalf of these two. She smiled at them warmly. "I can make no promises, but I will try."

"Thank you!" Meritaten's small teeth gleamed at her in the gathering darkness. "I must go now and pray for my sister. Are you coming, Smenkhara? May we be dismissed, Majesty?"

"Go." They scrambled to their feet and were soon lost in the darkness, their arms around each other. Tiye felt strangely comforted at seeing such uncomplicated, happy affection in this place.

She slept briefly, waking to receive a message from Pharaoh's apartments that there were no new developments. *A first birth is always a long affair,* she told herself, lying with eyes open in the suffocating darkness of her room. *Longer still for a body as immature as Meketaten's.* She slept again and woke to find that dawn had passed and the sun was already two hours into the sky. Again there was no news, and again she spent a restless, preoccupied day, filling the time with unimportant details. But at sunset a herald bowed before her and told her that though Meketaten's pains were following one another with speed, the baby had moved little, and the princess was weaker. Tiye sent for Huya.

"Find a statue of Ta-Urt," she ordered. "There must be one stored somewhere among my household goods. Then get me any priest willing to pray to any god other than the Aten. I don't care whom he serves so long as he knows the prayers for women in labor."

"It will take some time, Majesty. I will have to send into the city."

"Well, send then. And hurry up."

It was fully night before he returned, bringing a small votive statue of the swollen hippopotamus goddess and a furtive priest who set up the incense cups and began his prayers with one respectful eye on Tiye, who stood beside him as he performed the brief ritual. When the man had finished, Tiye gave him gold and sent him away with friendly words and ordered Ta-Urt returned to whatever chest Huya had found her in. Then she made her way into the palace.

The crowds of servants and lesser ministers clustered around the door fell back silently as she swept past them, but those within did not acknowledge her presence. Tadukhipa sat slumped on the floor, the princess's fingers twined in her own, dozing. Pharaoh held a sleeping monkey on his lap. His head was bowed. Nefertiti was wringing out a cloth and laying it on Meketaten's forehead while the girl moaned. The atmosphere was unbearable, a mixture of the stench of incense ash, human sweat, and agony. Meketaten began to writhe, uttering muffled cries, and Tiye realized with a shock that the princess was too weak to scream aloud. She left them.

She was summoned again just before dawn and knew even before the solemn herald had finished bowing to her that Meketaten was dead. Tight-lipped with rage, she strode into the palace. Already the word was passing among the servants, and inquisitive eyes followed her along every passage. Steeling herself, she crossed the threshold.

Tadukhipa had gone. Pharaoh stood with his back to the couch, arms folded. Nefertiti was sobbing openly, kneeling by the couch. The midwife was carefully lifting a covered bundle from the bloodied sheets, and quickly Tiye averted her gaze. The nobles who had been forced to be continually present had all slipped away but for Ay and Horemheb, who sat on the floor in a far corner. The midwife bent before Tiye and departed, and Tiye moved quietly to the couch and looked down. No one had closed the bewildered eyes, or yet washed the gray, foam-flecked face. Meketaten had bitten through her bottom lip, and blood crusted on her chin and smeared the little teeth. She lay with thin arms loosely outstretched, the sheet barely covering the pitifully flat breasts, her shoulders still hunched against torment. Tiye reached down and gently pushed the lids over the staring eyes. She must have groaned aloud, for Akhenaten turned and saw her. Tears slipped down his cheeks.

"It was a boy," he whispered, forming the words so slowly and with so much difficulty that he seemed drunk. His eyes turned to Nefertiti, now wailing with arms upraised. "You brought sorrow and anger to the god," he managed, "and he has punished me. You broke the magic with the sculptor. You weakened the power of the god. You are to blame!" The last words were shrieked, and Tiye sensed rather than saw Horemheb rise to his feet. "My little daughter. Ah, Meketaten!" Parennefer hurried to his side, and Horemheb came forward, soothing words already on his tongue. They led Pharaoh away.

Gathering her resolve, Tiye went to Nefertiti. "You need rest, Majesty," she said, taking the stiff arms and lowering them firmly. "Sleep now. This outburst is not grief, but madness. Ay, take her to her apartments." She turned to the servants huddled by the door. "Is there a House of the Dead in the city? Bring sem-priests, but first have the princess washed and tidied." She shouted at them until they rallied and ran to obey. As she left the room, the new sun struck the walls like a burning fist.

The harem women were already wailing, and Tiye could hear their mindless ululations as she crossed the royal garden and went through the gate in the wall. They had mourned often of late, as one small body after another was carried from the nurseries, but this outcry was frightening in its intensity. Tiye hurried into her chambers in order to shut out the sound, but even in the sanctuary of her bedroom she could hear it. Sharply she ordered wine, though the morning had scarcely begun, and stayed on her couch until she summoned Huya in the late afternoon.

"Pharaoh resisted every effort to keep him on his couch," he said in answer to her question. "He lies before the altar in the temple with the sun beating down on him. His ministers are afraid for his health. Word of the death has gone into the city, and the shops and stalls are closed. The queen is asleep. I took the liberty of taking the news to Prince Smenkhara myself, Majesty. Princess Meritaten was with him."

"Has the body been decently removed?"

"It has."

"Meketaten," she muttered to herself once he had gone. "Such folly, such wickedness. How long will it be before the gods run out of patience with my son and truly punish him?"

The customary seventy days of mourning were decreed for the princess and her stillborn son. The funeral seemed a quiet, drab affair to Tiye, sitting on her litter under the protecting canopy and watching Pharaoh offer prayers to his god for the survival of Meketaten's ka. Her attention was diverted from the rites by the strained, shocked faces of the courtiers. It was not grief for the princess that had stirred them, Tiye decided, but a kind of fear. Many of them had almost unconsciously edged toward the place where Smenkhara and Meritaten stood, as though the young prince offered a protection they suddenly craved. *Perhaps the long dream that has held them in thrall is beginning to fade*, Tiye thought. *The Aten has failed them. From now on their faith will be tinged with doubt*. But such doubt obviously did not afflict Pharaoh. He wept and prayed earnestly, his light voice often drowned by Nefertiti's uncontrolled sobbing. There was none of the dignity of proper ritual, and Tiye was relieved to escape back to her house.

Once there, she instructed Huya. "Set up an Amun shrine in Prince Smenkhara's quarters. The worship of gods other than the Aten has not been expressly forbidden. Do it quite openly and make certain that the people of Thebes, particularly Maya and the priests, know about it. I also think it is time for Smenkhara to begin work on his tomb. He can have his engineers design here if he wishes, but it is imperative he dig in the Valley in West-of-Thebes with as much dust and noise as possible. See to it."

She wanted to approach Akhenaten immediately to secure Smenkhara and Meritaten's betrothal, but Ay warned her that Pharaoh's temper was precarious. He was closeted in his apartments, fasting and praying, seeing no one. Grudgingly she settled herself to wait, but one week went by and then another, and Pharaoh's grief showed no signs of abating.

A month after the funeral one of Ay's officers requested words with Tiye as she was about to be rowed across the river to visit Tey. He was obviously agitated and was trailed by several anxious Followers of His Majesty. "Divine Empress, your brother begs you to come at once to Pharaoh's apartments," the man said. "You are needed. Pharaoh is distressed."

Tiye nodded, looking regretfully at her little craft bobbing invitingly on the sparkling blue water. "Captain, the sailors can stand down. Huya, you had better find an escort of Horemheb's soldiers for me immediately." Within the hour she was seeking admittance to the private wing of the palace, and long before she passed through the doors of her son's reception room, she could hear him shouting, his voice shrill and hysterical. His herald barred her way politely. "Forgive me, Majesty, but arms are not permitted in Pharaoh's presence. Please tell your soldiers to wait out here with me."

She ignored him, and signaling to her bodyguards, she pushed past and entered. There was a flurry of indignation behind her, and a group of Followers pressed on the heels of the men Horemheb had provided her, scimitars drawn. She would have turned to settle the dispute, but at the sight of her Nefertiti sprang forward, pointing finger rigid, her face white and her eyes blazing. She had been weeping. Kohl smudged her cheeks and had been smeared across one temple with an unconscious hand. "It is her fault!" she cried out, mouth quivering, her beautiful face a grimace of distress. "She is responsible for the lies! You did not doubt my love until she came! Ask her the truth and see if she has the courage to deny it!"

Swiftly Tiye appraised the situation. Her son stood rocking on his heels, his arms wrapped tightly around himself as though in pain, breathing rapidly and noisily. Horemheb was beside him, grim and for once powerless. Around them Pharaoh's retinue shuffled, glancing at one another in fear and embarrassment and trying to appear inconspicuous. Ay watched from the shadows at the far end of the room. Nefertiti paced alone, her women huddled together out of her way.

"How can you speak of truth?" Akhenaten quavered. "You have deceived me, you have made me a joke before my people. I trusted you. I poured out my love for you, and all the time you were making light of my devotion." He was fighting for control of his voice, his words rendered almost unintelligible by emotion. Nefertiti thrust her face into Tiye's.

"Tell him!" she hissed. "If you love him, how can you stand to watch him in this agony? You and Huya, that sly royal tool, dripping your poison into willing ears. What can you gain by this, except the destruction of my husband?"

Tiye looked past the fierce eyes to where Akhenaten was watching her, leaning tensely toward her, his gaze nakedly begging her for reassurance. She turned to meet Ay's glance. "Stand away, Majesty," she said coldly. "The royal cobra on your brow is no match for an empress's disk. Your own lust has brought you to this moment. If I were Pharaoh, I would have you immediately disciplined."

"I knew!" The howl was from Akhenaten. Flinging out his arms, he fell to his knees and then buried his face in his trembling hands. "Meketaten died because of you. You have never been the Aten's choice for me, but I was weak and loved you and made you my queen. If Sitamun had lived to wear the crown, Meketaten would not have died. It is a judgment on my willfulness!"

Nefertiti walked to him, ashen, shocked from her rage by the pitiless words. "As my heart must be weighed against the Feather of Ma'at, Horus, I swear I loved my daughter as fiercely as you," she managed huskily. "I would never have harmed her. Meketaten died of your lust, not mine. Think about that before you pass judgment on me. I have supported you since the days of your imprisonment and deserve better from you than this public humiliation. I know that I am quick-tempered and often foolish. But if you punish me for something I have not done, you will be losing the strongest ally you have."

The room had fallen so silent that far to the west the sound of oars splashing in the river and the singing of sailors could be faintly heard. Flies circled lazily, the everyday sound strangely out of place. Pharaoh's breath rasped in the quiet air, and he made no answer. His eyes were closed, his nostrils flared. *I did not imagine anything like this when I gave Huya his instructions*, Tiye thought in horror. *I wanted a strain, a small estrangement, room between them into which I could insert my hand, not a void large enough to swallow us all. What if he orders her execution?* "Majesty," she began, but at the sound of her voice he screamed, "Be silent!" and came to his feet, every movement of his lumbering body a slow warning. Turning to Nefertiti, he whispered, "You have forfeited the right to belong to the family of the god. Leave my sight. Take your lover with you. Because the Aten is a benevolent god, I will not harm you. You are banished to the north palace."

Nefertiti's regality momentarily deserted her. Crumpling, she clung to his knees and began to sob. "Akhenaten, I have done you no harm, I have given you beautiful children, I have shared your visions. Do not cast me away, I beseech! Who will nurse you when you are ill? Who will stand with you when you rise to pray in the night? I will do anything you ask, I will cast soil upon my head, I will shave and mourn, I will have the sculptor killed if you but indicate the desire, but do not place yourself once more between the claws of the vultures who hate you."

At her first broken words Akhenaten had visibly softened, swallowing repeatedly, but Nefertiti's tactless mention of Thothmes caused him to stiffen. His gaze wandered to the window, and his ringed hand gestured impatiently at his guard. The captain came immediately, lifting the queen reverently but firmly and leading her to the door. Dazed, she did not resist until she came level with Tiye. Then she shook herself free of the restraining soldier and lifted both clenched fists under Tiye's chin. "You will die for this," she murmured so low that Tiye had to strain to hear. "And I do not care what method I devise to do it. I am already disgraced. There is nothing for me to fear any longer."

Tiye, looking into the tearstained, distorted face, put a hand on the woman's shoulder. "I am not sorry, Majesty," she replied softly, knowing that her words could be interpreted in many ways. "Go with dignity."

Nefertiti was convulsed. She launched herself on Tiye, but the empress smoothly stepped aside, the Followers sprang to her defense with practiced skill, and the doors soon closed behind the queen. Horemheb, after one glance at the king, began to shepherd the others out.

Akhenaten continued to gaze dreamily out of the window, eyebrows raised and a small smile on his lips, but his body jerked intermittently as one tense muscle after another spasmed.

Ay took his sister's elbow. "You have won, but I do not like the cost," he breathed.

Tiye rounded on him. "I have a good mind to go back to Malkatta, where I ought to have stayed in the first place, and let you all destroy yourselves," she said bitterly. She would have gone on, but feeling eyes on her back, she turned to see her son's unnaturally brilliant gaze fixed unblinkingly on her. Ay bowed and departed. Horemheb would have gone to Pharaoh, but at a violent, dumb dismissal he also bowed, lips pursed, and was gone. Tiye and Akhenaten were alone.

"Are you a vulture?" he said conversationally. "Will you pick at my entrails?" He was trying to lift a cup of wine to his mouth, but his arm thrashed so uncontrollably that the liquid was slopping onto the floor. Taking a deep breath, Tiye strode to him, guiding the cup, forcing him onto a chair. At her touch he suddenly went limp and clung to her, burying his face in her lap. "I have lost daughter and wife in the space of a few weeks," he wept. "Surely now the Aten is appeased! I am in pain, Mother! Put your arms around me. Swear you will always be with me!"

Tiye embraced him, shrinking from the frenetic clutch of his hands. He soon ceased to sob aloud, and she was able to extricate herself, urging him onto his couch and drawing the sheet over him. He pulled it up to his chin and lay with eyes open. She asked to be dismissed, but he did not answer. After a while she bowed shortly and went away.

Nefertiti had moved disdainfully into the north palace by the next day, leaving her staff to begin the task of packing her belongings. Those courtiers who fed on intrigue were disappointed to see that she left subdued and pale but with head high. Most attendants believed, however, that the rift between the queen and Pharaoh would be temporary. Nefertiti's crime had not been serious. Pharaoh had acted hastily and would regret it, and the queen would come gliding back to her quarters. The empress was too old to take the queen's place, and no amount of concubines would give Pharaoh the close relationship he had shared with the empress's beautiful niece. The court also waited for the sculptor's banishment, and several ministers tried to hint to Pharaoh that their loyal service entitled them to the river estate he had been given, but in a peculiar way Akhenaten blamed his wife, not the handsome and talented young man, for the spectacular lapse. She had been one of the enlightened ones; she should have known better. Thothmes was not even forbidden to visit the north palace. Pharaoh merely turned his back on queen and sculptor alike.

But those courtiers who expected a reconciliation after a suitable period of chastisement had not understood the subtleties of Akhenaten's religious philosophy. A member of the Aten's sacred family had turned elsewhere for the affection that made the circle of protection around Pharaoh so strong. In Akhenaten's eyes, Nefertiti's worthiness to be a magic link was now suspect. The month of Athyr passed, and Khoyak. The Nile overflowed and turned the west bank into a calm lake that mirrored the winter softness of the sky. The empress was seen in the halls of audience and in the temple every day, haughty and unapproachable, accompanying her son wherever he went, and though the royal pair smiled at each other and talked together, there was none of the extravagant display of physical affection to which the court had become accustomed. Not even Pharaoh's closest staff knew on what level mother and son communicated, and Parennefer was too much the well-trained servant to let slip the fact that pharaoh and empress did not share a bed.

At the queen's dismissal, Tutu realized how precarious his own position was and attempted to return his office to a semblance of order, but the weeks went by, and it became obvious that the empress was not going to have her way. Pharaoh's temper was unpredictable, and any pressure brought to bear on him either was studiously ignored or resulted in outbursts of passionate rhetoric. Ay, Tiye, and Horemheb finally acknowledged that Pharaoh's refusal to consider the chaos outside Egypt's borders came from his deep conviction that his god would bring order through nothing but his prayers, and they changed their policy. No day passed without the name of Smenkhara being dropped into his ear: how devout the young man was, how loyal to his pharaoh, how well he fitted in to the royal sun family. Their brotherhood was reiterated time and again, but care was taken not to mention the fact that Smenkhara's father had been the man Akhenaten still hated. Pharaoh listened, smiled indulgently, but made no comment.

Tiye had recruited fresh spies from among Horemheb's soldiers, placing them in the north palace, but it was difficult to get news. Nefertiti had withdrawn completely into herself, and her staff remained loyally silent. Traffic through the high double wall that separated the north estate from the rest of the city was slight and noted assiduously by the guards on the gate. Access was easier on the river, but even then Tiye's men ran a great risk, for the west face of the north palace rose above a series of garden terraces that climbed down to long water steps, and anyone standing at a window had a full view of all movement on the river. Tiye's spies in Horemheb's household fared better. A stream of whispered information flowed into her house, but since most of it was innocuous, she was forced to conclude that Horemheb had already spotted her men but let them alone.

Of more immediate concern were the two attempts on her life. One of her food tasters died in agony, and a steward was violently ill after surreptitiously sampling the beer that stood waiting to be carried to her bedchamber. Despite a diligent search Tiye could not track down the culprits, so that while she was fond of beer, she reluctantly kept to wine that she insisted be unsealed in her presence.

She was not afraid to die, and increasingly found herself thinking of death with longing. It was becoming harder to swing her feet to the floor each morning, to hold herself straight during the interminable days of solemn protocol, to find time simply to lie by the water and let her mind wander where it would. She knew that she was old, that rightfully she should be enjoying an increasingly eventless slide into infirmity and death, accorded the respect and rewards due to a goddess, empress, and mother of a pharaoh. But it was necessary to endure the ministrations of the man who came regularly to dye her hair, the cosmeticians who skillfully hid the ravages of her face, the dressmakers who did their best to disguise a used-up body. Appearances no longer mattered within Egypt herself, but the foreigners, knowing that Tiye still sat on the ebony throne, might pause and think twice before plunging deeper into war. They could not know, or could surmise only from garbled and suspect accounts, that she no longer wielded useful power, that she served only to hold up before the world the reminder of a happier Egypt. *I will hold on until Smenkhara's future is assured*, she told herself. *Ay is too old to depend on, but Horemheb will guide Smenkhara back to Thebes*. She began to pray, almost self-consciously, to Hathor, goddess of youth and beauty, with a fervor she had never before brought to her religious observances, asking only that she might keep her strength until she was no longer needed.

20

SMENKHARA WAITED IN THE DAILY EXPECTATION OF A SUMmons from his mother or Pharaoh to tell him that a contract of betrothal between himself and Meritaten had been approved, but time passed, and no herald came to him with the words he wanted above all else to hear. Sometimes he wondered if the shock of Meketaten's death and the queen's subsequent banishment had driven the matter of the betrothal from Tiye's mind, but knowing her as he did, he doubted it. He willed himself to believe that she was biding her time until a favorable moment to approach Pharaoh presented itself, but in his impatience he resolved a hundred times to cast all caution to the winds and go to his brother himself. He and Meritaten talked of nothing else each afternoon when they met in her private quarters, and Meritaten characteristically calmed his restlessness by pointing out that they had waited so long it would be foolish to jeopardize their happiness by a premature move. Reluctantly Smenkhara poured his energies into his lessons with Horemheb and tried to be content with seeing the princess as often as possible.

But one day, as he went to make his usual visit, her guards turned him away from her doors. Astounded, he tried to argue with them. They listened deferentially and silently, but each time he attempted to push past them, he was held back.

"You are all mad!" he shouted at them finally as he walked away. "I come here almost every day. I will demand that the princess have you replaced!"

An hour later he had found an unguarded section of the wall that sheltered her small garden, and within minutes he was walking up to where she sat listlessly beside her pond, rubbing his knees and glowering. "What is the matter with your guards, Princess?" he demanded. "They refused me admittance, and I had to climb over your wall. See how I have scraped myself." He sank onto the mat beside her, and his hand found a circlet. "This is the queen's crown," he exclaimed. "Is your mother

here?" He glanced swiftly around the garden. "Has the banishment been lifted?"

Deftly she took it from him. "No," she said shortly. "My
father had it brought to me early this morning. Go away,
Smenkhara."

He edged closer, pulling her hair so that she had to look at
him. "What a foul mood you are in! I thought we might go
fishing in the sunset. The fish will be biting well, and the
breezes on the river will be pleasant. I deserve a little time to
myself. I have been drawing bow all day with Horemheb. Why,
Meritaten, what is the matter?"

She jerked her head viciously so that he had to release her
hair. "You may no longer call me by my name," she said coldly,
though her mouth quivered. "To you I am Majesty, Great Royal
Wife. But you are still only a prince, Smenkhara."

For a moment he did not understand. Then with a curse he
pulled her to him roughly, speaking into her mouth. "Pharaoh
has made you queen, hasn't he? I do not believe it. My mother
promised! Tell me it is in name only!"

Her lips moved, cold against his own. "No. It is not." She
moved back. "Yesterday my father took me to Maru-Aten. We
walked in the gardens there. He offered me the queen's crown,
and when I refused it, because of you, he said I had no choice."
Her voice was even, her gaze steady on his face. "He said that
unlike my mother, I am a fully royal sun child, worthier than
she to wear the cobra. I am to move into my mother's apartments tomorrow. I obey the will of the Disk."

For answer he kissed her, rage stiffening his mouth and
blinding him to all but the surge of hurt and betrayal he felt.
She struggled against him and, freeing herself, exclaimed,
"Don't! You have bruised me!" He pushed her away. Gingerly
she felt her lips. "If you do that again, you can be executed,"
she said. "I ordered my soldiers to keep you away from me.
Do not come to me again."

"How calm you are!" he sneered. "I did not realize what
ambitions you hid beneath that winning smile. I hope the glory
of being omnipotent will compensate you for your father's
flabby touch. But perhaps you enjoyed it. Queen of Egypt!
Queen either way, as your father's wife, or later as mine, if all
had gone well. In my innocence I misjudged you, Majesty."
He threw as much scorn and sarcasm into the last word as he
could.

Meritaten flinched, head down, and as he rose and turned to leave, she screamed, "Smenkhara!" He turned back contemptuously, but seeing her face, he knelt and flung wide his arms. She fell into them, and for a long time they held each other fiercely, rocking back and forth until her tears ceased. Then they sat hand in hand, not looking at each other.

"Egypt would bless me for killing him," Smenkhara whispered, and she squeezed his hand, shaking her head.

"He is my father, and I love him," she replied. "You had better go. The Aten tells him things. The god might tell him about you and me, here today. Good-bye, Smenkhara." She fumbled for the coronet and set it on her brow. The cobra's crystal eyes glittered dangerously at him. He bowed to it respectfully and fled.

Passing that same evening behind the banqueting hall with a slave who was carrying a jar of sealed wine for the empress, Huya saw the prince slip through the back entrance into a passage that allowed kitchen slaves to take food to Pharaoh's private rooms. Once having delivered the wine safely into his mistress's presence, he retraced his steps, calling several of Tiye's guards to him on the way, and found Smenkhara standing in the shadows just out of sight of the guards at Pharaoh's door. He bowed.

"I am happy to have found you, Highness," he said smoothly. "Your mother wishes you to wait upon her in her quarters."

Smenkhara sighed. "Very well. But she will be feasting for hours yet. I will come later."

"Your pardon, Prince, but she will not want to be kept waiting. I have asked these Followers to escort you to her apartments."

A resigned understanding spread over Smenkhara's face. "You are a meddlesome old woman, Huya. Here. Take it." He drew a small scimitar from his belt and tossed it to the steward. Huya caught it impassively, and it disappeared into the voluminous folds of his linen.

"I suggest that Your Highess pass the time with these men in discussing the current state of defense in Akhetaten," he said. "The empress will be with you presently."

Huya needed no more than a few tactful words with Tiye as she left the hall and wearily made her way to her own sanctum. Once her wig and jewels had been removed and she had been draped in her sleeping robe, she ordered Smenkhara's admittance and Piha and her women out. Her son entered and bowed and then stood sheepishly with his hands behind his back. Tiye looked at him resignedly. "It is a good thing Huya has sharp eyes, or you would be dead by now," she snapped. "Such behavior is incredibly childish. Why is it that you have never been able to see beyond the moment?"

"You told me I could have Meritaten!" he flashed back at her. "You said I was to be patient! I have been as patient as anyone could wish, and what use was it? I left my future in your hands, where it crumbled away."

"I did not tell you that you could have Meritaten," she reminded him coldly. "I said that one day you would probably be pharaoh and as such could then marry her. Think, Smenkhara! Your uncle and Horemheb and myself are daily singing your praises to Pharaoh. Time will smile on you yet. Then you will have the princess, and everything else you desire."

He clenched his fists and glared at her mutinously. "I don't want to wait!" he shouted. "I don't want to listen to you anymore when you prate of patience! I have lost her, and it is your fault!"

Tiye stepped forward and, taking him by the shoulders, shook him violently. "Well then, see if you can get close enough to Pharaoh to kill him!" she shouted back. "You are a whining, spoiled brat, and your royal father would turn his back on you if he could hear you now. I do not talk to you for the sake of hearing my own voice. I am sick of you. Egypt deserves better than a sulky child who cannot wait to be thrown a sweetmeat. Go, and see how quickly Pharaoh's guards can slit open your belly, and good riddance to you!"

He shrugged her off. "I hate you because you are always right," he spat back. "You are right, and you are cold. Does my pain mean nothing to you?"

"Of course it means something to me." She turned from him exhausted and slumped onto the couch. "But you will not have achieved manhood until you are able to hide every hurt, master every disappointment, and continue to walk the path that was chosen. The gods do not trust a slave."

"You should have been a priest." His lip curled. "Dismiss me."

"Go, you fool."

She did not wait until the doors closed behind him but with

a sigh lowered her aching body directly onto the couch and felt her muscles slowly loosen. The blow had been hers, too. The news of Akhenaten's decision to marry his daughter had come as a bitter shock, but she, unlike Smenkhara, understood that, in the long run, it meant nothing. Of far greater importance was the naming of an heir, and Tiye knew that she must concentrate her waning powers on that task and no other.

Meritaten quickly accommodated herself to the cobra coronet and the new responsibilities and privileges that went with it. More mature than the young man she loved, she buried her feelings for him deep under the pleasure she was learning to take in ruling. Now it was father and daughter who kissed and caressed, clung to each other and whispered into each other's ears while standing in the chariot or sitting under the canopy of the double palanquin. Meritaten stood beside him at the Window of Appearances, a slighter, more youthful version of Nefertiti, smiling and waving at the city crowds while Akhenaten made his pronouncements, expressed his love for his people, and showered the Gold of Favors onto whatever minister had recently praised him. The possession of Meritaten seemed to bring to him a precarious peace. His health improved, and in the temple he publicly thanked the Aten for a returning zest.

No such change was apparent in Meritaten. Outwardly she remained a beautiful, cheerful girl, attentive to her father-husband, imperious to her staff, and gracious to the members of the court, and only her closest servants knew that she babbled in her sleep and often woke weeping. Tiye was told by a spy that the deposed queen in the northern palace had laughed hysterically at the news that she had been supplanted by her daughter, and had given thanks that the empress was not having everything her own way. Tiye kept that precious piece of gossip to herself. She looked upon the situation as temporary. Like so many others, she believed that eventually Akhenaten would relent and release the queen, relegating Meritaten to the place in the harem that her sister Meketaten had suffered.

Yet one day as she was crossing the Royal Road on her litter, being carried to her sunshade in the temple with Beketaten beside her, she heard the thud of hammer on stone. Her bearers slowed, and impatiently she lifted the curtains to shout at them to hurry, only to see that they and the escorting soldiers were trying to force their way through a large press of city dwellers. White stone dust rose over them in a choking cloud. Beketaten sneezed and covered her mouth daintily, but Tiye was too curious to care about the discomfort.

"Captain, turn this rabble away so that I can see what is happening," she ordered and, letting the curtain fall, waited in the privacy of her daughter's company, listening to the shouts and blows of the soldiers. By the time Huya raised the litter's curtains, the road was clear. The dust hung like pale mist, and through it the stonemasons could be seen, oblivious of her presence, their great hammers rising and falling, their naked backs white with dust that clung to their sweat. Beside them several men were working more delicately with chisels and small hammers, pausing now and then to cough. With a wave Tiye stopped her herald from ordering them all onto their faces. "Go and ask the overseer what they are doing," she commanded. She watched as her spotlessly clad servant picked his way unwillingly through the stone chips, a corner of his kilt held against his face. The overseer bowed profoundly several times, words were exchanged, and the herald minced back and knelt before her. "Pharaoh issued a directive this morning," he explained, "that every image of Queen Nefertiti in Akhetaten is to be removed, and her name is to be effaced from every inscription. When this has been carried out, Queen Meritaten's name and titles are to be incised in their place."

Tiye stared at him. "Very well. Move on." She leaned back onto her cushions as the litter was lifted, oblivious to the jolt as her bearers started forward.

Beketaten pouted. "Lucky Meritaten," she said. "Do you think that one day Pharaoh may marry me and put my face all over Akhetaten?"

"Don't be stupid!" Tiye snapped, not really listening. This was not only a mark of great favor to his daughter, she thought swiftly, but a final humiliation for Nefertiti, an attempt not only to express a savage grudge against her but also, in effect to take away her life. A name had magic! If a name survived death, the gods would grant its bearer life in the next world. *Pharaoh must realize that he cannot obliterate every appearance of her name*, Tiye thought. *It has been sunk into stone too many times in too many different places. It is the act of a disappointed child, or a cowardly and dangerous man.*

"I do not want to say my prayers today," Beketaten complained. "Ankhesenpaaten has a new cat and a whole box of toy crocodiles that she wants to show me. The crocodiles snap their jaws when you pull them along."

"How very pleasant," Tiye murmured absently. A new and horrifying possibility had occurred to her. What if, behind the impenetrable wall separating the north palace from the life of the city, Nefertiti was already dead? With the sound of the mighty hammers still ringing in her ears, Tiye suddenly believed that in the name of his god her son would be capable of anything.

She could hardly bear the slow passing of the hours until her brother and Horemheb could be summoned, and it was full night before they made their obeisances to her in the privacy of her garden. Once they were all settled, she voiced her fear.

Immediately Horemheb shook his head vigorously. "No. The queen lives."

"So you have been in correspondence with her, perhaps have even seen her," Tiye said sharply. "You have just made a tactical error, Commander."

"And your spies are doing a bad job, Empress," he responded. "She summoned me secretly."

"For what purpose? You must be willing to tell me, or you would not have revealed yourself like this."

"She wanted assurances of my loyalty to her. She asked my opinion of the possibility of a successful palace revolt."

Startled and angry, Tiye looked at Ay's face, a pale, unfocused circle in the half-light of the distant torches. "Did you know about this?"

"No, Tiye," he said calmly. "But I expected it."

"I suppose I did also. What would her aim be, Horemheb? The Double Crown for Smenkhara? For little Tutankhaten, though that is unlikely? Supreme power for herself, or perhaps even for you? That woman's nearsighted stupidity has no bounds!"

Horemheb laughed mirthlessly. "Power for her august self, through me. She does not like either of your sons by Osiris Amunhotep, Majesty, and would probably wish to eliminate them both. She would marry either me or Tutankhaten."

The idea was so preposterous that Tiye was tempted to laugh. "Did you dissuade her?"

"As best I could, using the arguments we aired together many weeks ago. I think she is beginning to see the results of her husband's disastrous policies, but she will never cooperate with you or her father. She has much time in which to brood. She is a bitter woman."

"And it is her own fault. Palace revolt, indeed! The time for change will not come until Pharaoh dies. I have become convinced of that. Any new administration concerned with returning Egypt to her former strength will need the trust and cooperation of the Amun priests."

"I know." Horemheb's voice was even. "I have pondered the whole matter most carefully and have come to the same conclusion."

They talked a little more, without enthusiasm, and then separated. Tiye sat on in the fragrant darkness. *I am angry because I should have planned and executed a revolt myself*, she thought. *Nefertiti does not have the courage to bring it to a successful conclusion. It is that weakness that gives Horemheb pause in allying himself with her. But I cannot harm my son. There are too many memories.*

The weeks that followed were dreary for Tiye. Resigned to the knowledge that her influence in all important spheres of government had shrunk to the level of unheeded suggestions, she brooded on past mistakes and her present impotence. It was not in her nature, she knew, to give herself up entirely to defeat, but she came close to despair when she opened her eyes each morning on hours that lay waiting to be filled by whatever she could devise. Sometimes she visited Tey, but her sister-in-law's self-absorption and lack of concern for events outside the boundaries she had erected for herself made her poor company. Tiye dictated many letters to her old friend Tia-Ha, whose scrolls full of vivid descriptions of life on her drowsy estate in the Delta arrived regularly, and tried to close her mind to the large concerns of Egypt about which she could do nothing, but her frustration could not be allayed.

One of the events that only served to sharpen Tiye's discouragement was Aziru's departure from Akhetaten. Pharaoh gave him a magnificent farewell feast at which dancers, singers, acrobats, and trained animals entertained hour after hour while one succulent steaming course followed another, accompanied by the best vintage wines. Akhenaten had invited Aziru to sit on the dais on his left hand, a singular honor. Meritaten, resplendent in yellow linen and heavy with gold, sat on his right, and Tiye was relegated to a position behind him, where she listened to the conversation between the foreigner and her son with increasing dismay. *Aziru ought not to have been allowed the privilege of a seat on the dais*, Tiye thought, *but should have been placed with the other ambassadors on the floor of the hall, from where Pharaoh appears aloof and powerful in his jewels and the regal luster of the Double Crown. He should have been subjected to a coolly dignified audience at which Pharaoh could press for the renewal of the treaty between them and hint at retribution if Aziru indulged in any further warmongering.* But for most of the night Akhenaten merely fawned upon his new queen, described with relish his building projects, and expounded on the Aten's wish that all men might live in universal peace. Tiye had been praying that the subject would not come up, but Meritaten herself had precipitated it. "I trust you have enjoyed the peace of your stay in Egypt," she said politely. "The prospect of a return to a part of the empire stricken with famine and war must be difficult."

Aziru turned expressionless eyes on her. "The peacefulness of life in Egypt is a blessing indeed," he answered. "A citizen of this favored land, living in quiet contentment, might never know the conflagration of fire and scimitar that rages all around."

How bold and impudent he is, Tiye thought. *He feels quite safe in reminding Pharaoh of the state of the empire.*

"But then Egypt has the finest army in the world," Aziru went on smoothly. "What could she have to fear?"

"I dream of the day when the army will be disbanded," Akhenaten interjected eagerly, "and the peace of the Aten will rule the world with Egypt as its fountainhead. The god who gives life to all does not have commerce with death. Listen, Aziru, to the words he has given me on this matter. 'The eyes of men see beauty until Thou settest. All labor is put away when Thou settest in the west. When Thou risest again, Thou makest every hand to flourish for the king, and prosperity in every foot, since Thou didst establish the world, and raise them up for Thy son, who came forth from Thy flesh. . . .'"

Meritaten watched her husband with a smile, and Tiye listened stiffly, her eyes on Aziru's sharp profile. He was nodding politely, even warmly, but Tiye could imagine the scornful thoughts that filled the dark head. Shame coursed hotly through her.

"The words are full of loveliness," Aziru said when Akhenaten had finished and was waiting expectantly for a comment. "You have the gift of poetry, Divine One. Are these sentiments read to your soldiers as well as to the members of your court?"

Tiye groaned inwardly as Akhenaten nodded. "Of course. All Egypt shares in the revelations the Aten gives me. Would you like to take an Aten priest back to Amurru with you in order to instruct your people?"

Determinedly Tiye refused to attend to the rest of the conversation, and a little later she excused herself and went to her couch. She did not arrange an audience with Aziru before he left, nor was she on the water steps to bid him farewell. Nothing she could say to him now would matter, for he had already made his decision. He had observed her arrival in Akhetaten, seen Nefertiti disgraced, pondered over the rising of Meritaten's star instead of Tiye's son, and drawn his conclusions. Pharaoh bade him farewell with many rich presents and the tearful embrace of a brother. *I would have put a spear through his black heart and sent his mangled body to Suppiluliumas*, Tiye thought. *The time when Egypt might have won Aziru back as an ally is long gone.*

Tiye and Meritaten had had little to do with each other since the girl's marriage to Pharaoh and had met only in the temple or occasionally at the feasting, so Tiye was surprised when in the middle of the month of Phamenat the queen's herald presented a request that was in fact a royal command. Taking Huya, Tiye made her way to the queen's apartments. She had not been there since her acrimonious interview with Nefertiti, and the memory of that meeting came back in all its frustration. Meritaten accepted Tiye's polite bow with a smile and, coming forward, kissed her grandmother on the cheek. She looked fresh and pretty in white linen and turquoise earrings and necklet. The queen's coronet sat on her straight black hair, and from it hung a fine-woven gold net set with more tiny turquoises that capped her head. Tiye thought that Meritaten was going to be even more beautiful than her mother, for the faultless little face glowed with a mildness and gentleness that was unknown to Nefertiti. As she looked around the room, she was mystified to see, set up beside Meritaten's throne, a plain desk covered with scrolls arranged neatly in rows, and several scribes either busy copying or waiting with pens raised for the queen's orders. The queen indicated a chair, and Tiye sat.

"How is Prince Smenkhara?" was Meritaten's first question,

and Tiye saw the passionate interest that the girl was trying to hide.

"He is well and keeps busy," she answered. "His studies remain difficult for him, and I do not think he will ever have much skill with weapons, but he likes horses and drives his chariot out on the desert behind the city every morning."

"I know," Meritaten said and then flushed. "Thank you, Majesty, for not condemning the urgency behind my question. Everyone knows my feelings for him. It would be foolish to try to hide them. But although the courtiers also know my loyalty to my father, many consider my affection for Smenkhara unseemly now I am queen."

"You have great courage, Majesty."

"I have no choice," Meritaten retorted ruefully. "But I did not require your presence in order to pass the time of day. You have been ill?"

Tiye smiled. "Not ill, but feeling the effects of my age. Suddenly everything ached. But a week on my couch with massage every day and a short fast has restored my health." It was not entirely true. She had forgotten what it felt like to wake alert and vigorous every morning, but worse was the knowledge that those days would never come again.

"Praise the Disk!" Meritaten said politely. At a gesture her chief scribe unfolded from his position on the floor by her throne and handed her a scroll. "As you know, Majesty, my mother had some responsibility for the handling of foreign correspondence. She heard it and composed answers and, if it was a serious matter, conferred with Tutu and presented it to my husband for judgment. Because he has no interest in the scrolls that pour into Tutu's office every day, I am trying to make sense of them myself so that I may serve Pharaoh better. I need your help, Grandmother."

Tiye's eyes widened, and a tide of excitement began to rise in her. Here, unlooked-for, was a weapon, a chance to pierce Pharaoh's stubborn, willful ignorance. "Meritaten, you know that Pharaoh will not listen to reason when it is a matter of the empire's affairs, that your mother did not care to risk his displeasure and either told him simply what he wanted to hear or herself refused to listen to the dispatches. Are you prepared to disturb and anger him?"

"I had not thought about that. I am simply bewildered by

the flood of scrolls Tutu puts into my hands and do not know what to do with them. But surely the truth is all-important."

Tiye realized suddenly that she was looking at the best and purest result of her son's Teaching. Meritaten, raised and schooled under no god but the Aten, her thoughts and actions steeped in her father's constant revelations, was free from his own struggles, the doubts that beset all of those who had grown up under Amun and Egypt's myriad gods. She was a symbol newly born, the promise of what could be. *What could have been*, Tiye corrected herself. *The odor of failure clung to my poor son even before this city rose magically from the desert*.

"Yes, it is," she agreed thoughtfully. "I will do what I can. What do you have there?"

Meritaten handed her the scroll. It was a copy of a tablet received from Aziru, already translated from Akkadian. Tiye read it swiftly. Gone were the fulsome words of flattery, the groveling phrases calculated to soften an emperor. "In order to protect my people, I have today concluded a treaty with Prince Suppiluliumas," Aziru wrote. "The arm of Egypt no longer extends in might over the world. The words of her king are empty as wind among the reeds, and her promises less than the lightest words of love." With an exclamation of disgust Tiye flung it on the table.

"That is not all," Meritaten said, handing her another. "This came today from Rethennu."

It was short, a simple statement of fact without embellishment. Aziru, doubtless with the full knowledge and permission of his new overlord, had attacked Egypt's vassal, the Amki.

"Majesty, if I take these scrolls to Pharaoh, will you come with me and give me your support?" Tiye asked.

Meritaten nodded. "He will not wish to cause me distress," she said, averting her face. "I am with child."

She could scarcely form the words, and with a rush of pity Tiye saw the shadow of Meketaten pass over the dainty features. "That is good news for Egypt," she said. Beckoning to Huya, who helped her out of the chair, she went to stand close to the girl. "You have nothing to fear, Majesty," she said in a low voice. "You are thirteen years old. Your body is stronger and better formed than your sister's was. You will live."

"But I do not want this baby," Meritaten answered urgently, her face still turned away. "It is not Smenkhara's."

Tiye could not urge patience on her as she had on Smenkhara. She could not speak of the probability of Akhenaten's early death, the possibility that one day the queen would receive her heart's desire. Putting a respectful hand on Meritaten's arm, she kissed the red lips. "I am your friend as well as your grandmother," she said gently. "Remember that, Goddess."

Tiye wanted to strike at her son while the memory of Aziru's stay was still fresh. As Ay was, of course, in attendance on him constantly, she called the next morning for Horemheb, and together with Meritaten they waited on Akhenaten, the two scrolls carried by Meritaten's chief scribe. Pharaoh greeted them all gaily. He had just returned from the temple, and his skin and linens were imbued with the lingering smell of incense and flowers. The prophet Meryra was purifying the room as he did every day, sprinkling wine and milk on the floor and walls, and his soft chanting punctuated Akhenaten's conversation.

"This is a happy occasion!" he exclaimed. "All my dear ones do homage to me together. Meritaten, my beauty, come and kiss me. Did you rest well?" He reached for her, enfolding her and kissing her on the mouth with an unselfconscious thoroughness. Keeping one arm around her, he bestowed a light, warm kiss on Tiye and waited while Horemheb prostrated himself. Ay stood nearby, the fan over his shoulder. "What favor can I grant you all today?" Akhenaten went on teasingly. "A little trip on the river? A time to renew our friendship?"

Under the geniality Tiye sensed his rising unease. His kohled eyes darted from one to the other. She said nothing. The words must come from Meritaten if there was the slightest chance of Pharaoh's listening. She nodded imperceptibly at the girl, who gently freed herself and took the scrolls, placing them reverently in Akhenaten's hands.

"I beseech you, my husband and god, to read these," she said. "And know that we, your family, are justly indignant at their contents. Remember as you read that I am your dutiful daughter and loyal wife and will do nothing to harm or discredit you or your own mighty father, the Disk."

He frowned at her as he unrolled the papyrus, his lower lip extending in both puzzlement and defense, and retreating to the throne, he draped himself over it. Ay signaled unobtrusively, and immediately a chair was set for Tiye, which she sank onto gratefully. The room fell silent but for Meryra's drone. Akhenaten read the scrolls once, snapped at the priest to be quiet, and then read them again. When he had finished, he let them tumble from his lap. Already he was breathing heavily. His gaze swiveled from face to waiting face, and all at once he closed one eye and winced, but the spasm passed.

"How can Aziru do this?" he asked plaintively. "Did he learn nothing during his months here? When he left, I embraced him like a brother, I wept tears of love in his arms! Yet while the slaves are still cleansing the house I provided for him, he turns to the Khatti." He covered his mouth with one hand, and his long features twisted with anguish.

Meritaten went to him and gently pulled the fingers away, kissing them and enfolding them in her own. "Father, in spite of your great faith, the world does not understand your ways," she said. "Perhaps it never will. Aziru cannot see the incarnation of the Disk. He sees only a ruler who was once a mighty protector but is now a lover of peace when only war will save the Amurru from the depredations of the Khatti. You must not blame him."

"Can he have stood in the temple and not heard the voice of the Aten speaking through my holy lips? It is a judgment on me. Once more I have offended the god, and I do not know how!" The last words rang out, laden with guilt. Akhenaten pulled himself upright on the throne and then bent over, elbows on flaccid knees, face buried in one hennaed palm. Meritaten glanced uncertainly at Tiye.

"If I may, Majesty, I think I can tell you how," Tiye said. "You have stayed your hand because you have been unwilling to bring harm to any living thing under the Aten, but in so doing you have endangered the home of the god itself. A pack of hungry lions stalks to and fro, and soon they will leap the border and come here, to Akhetaten. If Egypt falls the light of the Disk is extinguished. This is not a time for peace. The god now desires his preservation!"

"No!" Akhenaten sat back and pulled his hand from his daughter's grasp. His fingers went to the pectoral draped over his shallow chest and began to tug and twist the golden ropes. "It is Nefertiti. I sent her away cruelly, in haste. I must recall her, restore her, I was wrong . . ."

"Divine One, you were not wrong." Horemheb stepped forward. "Listen to your empress, the goddess who all your life has lent you her wisdom. Aziru is invading the Amki, doubtless with men and arms supplied by Suppiluliumas, that implacable enemy of all true religion. Between Egypt herself and the Amki there is only Rethennu. For the sake of the god who has honored Egypt with his first revelations, who has deigned to sit bodily upon the Horus Throne, do not let foreigners desecrate this land!"

"Egypt still has the power," Ay's deep, cultured voice added. "Our soldiers have grown fat and lazy, but within months they could be ready to march. There are still officers capable of leading them. Send no message to Aziru, Horus! Strike now, unexpectedly. Give the animals a taste of real war."

Meritaten put her head against his arm. "Listen to them, my husband! You are hearing the truth."

His arms went around her, and he buried his face in her neck. "I am so tired," he said, his voice muffled but his torment nakedly clear to those who listened. "At night my dreams are full of horror. Death comes to me, the demons of revenge, of the terrible darkness of the Duat. Nefertiti's face bends over me, and I reach for her and wake trembling with fear. In the day I see the bent backs of my worshipers. Their faces are hidden, but I know that if I surprised them before they had composed themselves to rise, I would see that I am surrounded by creatures without hearts in their bodies, without features. If I fail the god, I will not live long."

"Then do not fail him." Tiye forced her voice to remain detached as she watched Meritaten's childlike attempts to comfort her father. "Wake, Akhenaten. Wield the scimitar."

"I do not know how!"

"Horemheb will do it for you. Give him the order."

He writhed. "I cannot!"

"Dear nephew, you must," Ay said emphatically. "Please."

"Go away, all of you. I will ponder it. Go! Meritaten, bring the physician!"

Horemheb shrugged. Tiye let out her breath in a long sigh and struggled to her feet. They would try again and again mercilessly now that Meritaten held his affections, and eventually they would win. If the gods gave them enough time.

21

IN THE FIRST MONTH OF THE NEW YEAR, THE FOURTEENTH OF Akhenaten's reign, Meritaten gave birth to a girl. Pharaoh named her Meritaten-ta-sherit, Meritaten the Younger, and celebrated her and her mother's safety with great ceremonies in temple and palace. Meritaten soon left her couch and appeared once more beside Pharaoh, but some of the sparkle had left her. She was wan and thoughtful, given to sudden fits of irritability that would end in tears, and she showed no interest in her daughter. The baby was healthy, plump, and with her own even features, but Meritaten turned from her calmly after appointing whatever nursery staff was necessary. She was once again sharing Pharaoh's bed, and Tiye, watching her carefully at the evening meal while Akhenaten covered her with kisses and pushed fruit into her sullen mouth, wondered if Meritaten had somehow imagined that the birth of the child would signal the end of her conjugal duties.

Soon after Meritaten's confinement, the Office of Foreign Correspondence received word that Suppiluliumas had signed a treaty of friendship with Mattiwaza, Tushratta's successor in Mitanni, and was at present quiet, resting, no doubt, in the satisfaction of yet another conquest. He could afford to wait, to plan his moves carefully. Yet Tiye felt that Akhenaten was weakening. Though he railed at them, accused them of treason, retreated behind increasingly debilitating headaches and fits of nausea, she, Meritaten, Horemheb, and Ay had wrung from him permission to bring the army up to full strength. The border troops still maintained constant patrols, but the divisions of regular troops had long since been thinned. Horemheb ordered a conscription, the building of new barracks, and the refurbishing of weapons and chariots, and his officers were soon able to begin drilling the new recruits. Tiye, delighted, knew that word of Egypt's stirring would quickly reach Suppiluliumas's keen ears.

Like the echo of a long-dead voice, letters came for her from Thebes asking for personal confirmation of the army's reorganization. Tiye listened to the dispatches with a feeling approaching awe. Malkatta seemed not only far away but already buried in a stagnant past. *I, too, have been seduced by the strange magic that imbues Akhetaten*, she realized. *How long has it been since I have bothered to enquire into the health of other cities? Time seems suspended here, but what is happening in Akhmin, at Djarukha, Memphis? The spell that ends at the line where grass gives way to hostile desert keeps me a prisoner with distorted vision and deaf ears. I had intended to visit the Treasury and never did. I was anxious at the mere trickle of tribute that has since dried up altogether. What happened to my concern?* Holding the scrolls that had been sealed with Amun's imprint made her feel like a spirit. She sent for the Treasurer at once.

"The Treasury is depleted but by no means empty," the man responded huffily to her sharp question. "Trade still exists between Egypt and the islands of the Great Green Sea."

"Only there? What of Nubia and Rethennu?"

"Majesty, our hold on Nubia is rather weak at present, as you must know."

"No, I did not know. Nubia is not a vassal; it is a part of Egypt. Why is our hold weak?"

"That is not my affair. I merely keep the tallies in my lord's storehouses. But I believe that the Nubian tribes have been restless of late, and several Egyptian tribute collectors have vanished."

"Well, what of the mines in Nubia? The gold routes?"

"Commander Horemheb has a monopoly on the taxes derived from Nubian gold, Goddess. Forgive me, but in this case you should address your questions to him."

"I will. Rethennu?"

"There has been nothing from Kadesh for a year."

"Then why is the Treasury not depleted?"

"Pharaoh has raised taxes substantially every year, particularly on the fellahin, and of course all offerings in Egypt that are made to other gods now come directly to Akhetaten."

When she had dismissed him, she sat gnawing her lip and thinking furiously. The fellahin were cattle, but useful cattle without whom the country could not survive. If they were being taxed to their limit and probably beyond, Egypt could be brought

down by any disaster that further threatened their survival—
if war was declared and ran too long, if the Delta cattle became
diseased, if the grape crop failed, if Isis did not cry. *Our stability
is as fragile as a reed stem*, she told herself. *The gold that
showers these streets, the jewels with which the courtiers deck
themselves, the delicacies, the exotic food, the constant stream
of new dresses, not to mention the entertainers brought from
beyond the Delta, all as solid as a puff of sand-laden wind.
How can we pay for a war?* She sent for Horemheb, but at her
terse questions he regarded her as though she were already
senile.

"Certainly the flow of gold has abated a little," he replied.
"I lose miners every day from death, but lately they have also
been escaping. The gold route has become rather dangerous,
so I pay for soldiers to stand guard at the mines and escort the
gold to Thebes, from where it comes north by barge."

"Your own soldiers? Paid with the gold they guard?"

"Certainly."

"Horemheb, do you remember when the mines were guarded
by a few overseers, when the gold traveled to Thebes unhin-
dered and the Medjay did little more than check on its progress?"

"No, Majesty." He was uneasy and genuinely did not understand her sudden panic. Aware of the uselessness of questioning
him further, she dismissed him.

The New Year was celebrated at Akhetaten with the customary burst of optimism. Because Pharaoh had shrunk from
issuing the order for mobilization Tiye had so desperately
wanted, the rumor of war sank temporarily to a whisper. Akhenaten's health had improved, and weak but smiling, he distributed the Gold of Favors to his physicians and other lesser
officials in person from the garlanded Window of Appearances
with Meritaten at his side. All settled down to wait for the Aten
to decree the rising of the Nile, their thoughts on the sacks of
seed in their storehouses, ready for the sowing.

But the Inundation was late. The month of Thoth passed,
and the river remained a thin ribbon of muddy water flowing
deep below the level of the dusty, cracked banks. There was
some concern but no alarm, for the flood had been late before.
The Aten was all-powerful and would not fail its obedient son.
In anticipation of an answer to the prayers for a flood, worship

intensified at Akhetaten. Crowds milled about the Great Temple's forecourt and gathered three deep around the little shrines on the street corners, placatory gifts in their hands.

Paophi came and went, and still the level of the Nile did not change. The disgruntled courtiers had their pleasure craft hoisted onto land, for the river had begun to smell. The officials responsible for reporting on the speed and plenitude of the annual flooding sat under their canopies beside the nilometers, eyes fixed on the stone markers sunk in the banks, but the oily, stinking water still lapped below the first notches. Athyr passed. Khoyak, the month that had always marked the time of the river's highest level, saw a drop in it instead as the dry air lifted moisture from the surface. The air became fetid and full of stinging insects. Dismayed, the fellahin dug into their meager stores. Standing on the edge of their villages, they watched the cracks in their fields widen into gaping miniature ravines, the baked soil around them too hot to walk on. The trees did not leaf. The brown spears of the palm trees hung stiff and brittle, and the branches of the sycamores cracked off at the slightest touch.

At the beginning of Mekhir, when the peasants ought to have been ankle deep in black mud, strewing seeds, snakes began to invade Akhetaten, and scorpions sought the coolness of the rifts appearing everywhere in the ground. Morning and evening Tiye had her house searched by servants with sticks, and forbade milk to be left on the floors for the house snakes.

By the end of Pharmuti all accepted the fact that there would be no flood that year. Water steps all along the riverfront at Akhetaten hung stained and dry, feet above the thick, refuse-filled water. The shadufs that fed water to the gardeners brought up mud that seemed alive with unnameable worms and repulsive water insects. Pharaoh ordered servants to take their buckets into skiffs and lift water bodily from the river for the gardens, and gave permission for the lakes to be emptied. Tiye, stting on the roof of her house and looking across the hollow valley where the river now trickled to the brown desert on the other side, thought that the gardens should also have been sacrificed to provide enough water for the fields opposite to grow a small crop for the palace. But Akhenaten refused, still believing that water would come.

"It is a test," he told Tiye as they sat in his audience hall. "Our faith is being tried." Sweat ran from them both. The

swish of the fly whisks filled the room, a soft, wearying susurration of sound. Flies hung in thin clouds along the ceiling
and crawled over salty flesh. No early fruit had come to Akhetaten from the Delta, and the salads so greedily enjoyed at
this time of the year were sparse and tasted of mud. *Everything
tastes of mud, smells of mud*, Tiye thought, feeling her scalp
prickle with the heat. She glanced beyond the shade of the
entrance pillars to the dead brown lawn already showing patches
of dry soil. "Have you sent north for grain?" she asked. "Rethennu should be willing to sell us something." She longed to
rub her skin. Water no longer cascaded clean and cool in her
bathing room. The liquid Piha trickled carefully over her was
as brown as her own skin and full of grit.

"There is no need," he replied. "Our granaries are full of
last year's harvest."

"But, Akhenaten, what of Thebes, the villages, the rest of
the population? The tax collectors have been taking everything.
The people have nothing stored. Soon they will begin to starve."

"I care nothing for Thebes," he said. "As for the fellahin,
they must simply wait. The god will yet prove his power."

"If the fellahin die, there will be no crop sown next year at
all," Tiye muttered darkly. "The only reason this country has
survived other droughts is that each pharaoh has been careful
to maintain stores of extra grain in every city. Your collectors
emptied those granaries a long time ago."

Suddenly Akhenaten began to retch. Bending over with one
hand on his stomach, he signaled frantically, and a servant
carrying a bowl rushed to his side. He vomited and then sat
back gasping. Another slave knelt, proffering a damp cloth.
Pharaoh wiped his lips. "That always hurts," he said, still short
of breath, "but the pain does not last long." He handed back
the cloth and straightened slowly. "Have you seen the terraces
of the north palace, Empress? Still so lushly green? Nefertiti
does not suffer the withering of *her* garden."

She divined his thought. "No, Akhenaten, the fertility of
her domain is not due to Nefertiti's enjoying the protection of
the god," she said. "Water from her lake can be poured onto
the upper terrace and then simply trickles down over the others."

"It is time to pray." He rose, pulling the wet linen away
from his legs, and Meryra stepped forward, incense already
smoking in his hand. "Mother, did you know that in the city

the people have opened shrines to Isis? If the Aten sees such lack of faith, he will punish them even further."

"They are afraid," she suggested, watching a little color creep back into his gaunt face. "They want Isis to cry."

"There is no Isis," he snapped impatiently. "I will talk to them from the Window of Appearances on my way to the temple. Come with me. Where is Meritaten?"

He turned to her querulously, like an old man, as she hurried forward. They left the hall, crossed the wide forecourt, and approached the ramp. Beyond the wall, the Royal Road was strangely silent. The sun attacked them with blind ferocity, drying their lips, making their eyes water, burning up through their sandals. The air was full of dust. Breezes were no longer welcome, for the slightest stir out behind the city lifted the sand and sent it blowing down the streets to mingle with the powdery topsoil already suspended, breathed into dry lungs, clinging to moist skin, insinuating under linen to add to the torment. Tiye, squinting against the sudden glare, saw Akhenaten's arm slide through his queen's, his other hand rise to brush away the flies crawling over his neck. *There are no people to adore him today*, she thought as they walked up the ramp and under the slight shadow of the roofed window. *They are lying in their homes dreaming of water*. She was taken aback when the royal group stopped and turned to look down, for the road was filled from wall to wall with a silent crowd. Akhenaten raised a hand. There was a slight swaying below, and heads were bent, but the people did not sink to the hot ground.

"Foolish ones!" Pharaoh called, his voice kindly. "Do you come with guilt in your hearts? I have heard how you turn from your true protector at the first testing of your faith and mutter prayers to another, while the Disk blazes overhead, watching your every motion. Have no fear. I, and I alone, stand between you and the god. I will petition the Aten, and he will hear his son and send the flood. I, Akhenaten, promise you."

There was no answering cheer. Tiye, snatching linen from Huya and wiping her neck, saw doubt and distress in the up-turned faces.

"Bring water, Pharaoh!" someone shouted indignantly. "You are a god! Make the river rise!"

Akhenaten lifted the crook and flail over the people, but the muttering continued. As he stepped into the shadow and began to move toward the temple, the cry was taken up by the entire crowd. "Make water, Pharaoh!" they shouted, derision unmistakable in their voices. "Make water, Divine Incarnation!" Meritaten stiffened beside him in shame, hurrying him forward until they were beneath the stiff trees of the temple garden and walking to the pylon. Passing beside it, he abruptly stopped and, leaning against its rough stone, doubled over. Once again a servant with a bowl came to his assistance, but the spasm passed. Akhenaten straightened, his face drawn in pain, and continued into the temple.

Tiye watched from the privileged shade of her kiosk as Meritaten stood alone in the vast expanse of the sanctuary, a small black head crowned with the golden cobra above a field of offering tables, bowed against the insufferable heat, swaying a little while her husband mounted the steps to the raised altar and began to pray. His words, though unintelligible, echoed anguished and pleading against the tall walls. He prostrated himself, then knelt, gripping the sides of the food-laden table, his forehead pressed against the stone. Meryra circled him with the incense and poured oil on his head. His groans rang out. Beyond the altar the ben-ben rose, and on it his likeness smiled. The oil slipped lazily down his neck and trickled along his spine, glistening in the harsh light. In the forecourt the temple singers' voices rose and fell. To Tiye there was something anciently barbaric about the scene, the twisting, tortured man, the rows of smoking slabs, the priests unnaturally motionless in white, the slight, gorgeously arrayed queen swaying faint and sick, alone in the huge expanse, and floating over all, like the compelling, emotionless voices of demons, the disembodied singing. The ferocity of the sun was almost unendurable, and the sudden fancy took Tiye that the Aten, feeding for years on the frenetic worship of his son, had grown bloated with it and yet insatiable, his growing strength at last overcoming the life-giving gentleness Akhenaten had taught, and being unleashed in its full horror over Egypt. The more Pharaoh moaned and prayed, the more the heat seemed to intensify. Tiye, with aching legs and paining back, sank onto the stool she had ordered placed in the sunshade. Meritaten turned around at the small movement, her face pale. Tiye beckoned, but after a moment's hesitation, Meritaten shook her head, not daring to offend her father or the god by seeking shelter.

Glancing back at her son, Tiye froze. He was lying before

the altar, but face up, his limbs rigid. His head was canted back at an impossible angle, and strangled cries were coming out of his mouth. Meryra stood at his feet, waving an incense holder over him. Tiye did not hesitate but strode into the glare, shouting at the priests as she went. Hurrying up the steps, Meritaten behind her, she bent over Pharaoh.

"Bring a litter quickly," she ordered, "but a canopy first. Majesty, find Panhesy and have him send for the physicians."

"But Empress," Meryra protested. "Litter bearers cannot come into the sanctuary! It is forbidden!"

She ignored him. Other priests were rushing to obey her, and already Pharaoh's litter was moving along one of the aisles. Akhenaten's teeth were now clenched, his eyes open wide and unseeing. Vomit dribbled from the corner of his mouth. "Go and tell those women in the forecourt to be silent!" Tiye shouted at Meryra. "It is too hot to sing!" Ashen and cowed, he went away, and presently the chanting faltered and stopped. Gently the litter bearers lifted Pharaoh, and the canopy was unfolded over him. Tiye followed as he was carried to his apartments.

By the time he was laid on his couch, the rigidity had gone out of his body, and he had begun to mutter and occasionally shout words of prayers, snatches of love songs, and long, incoherent speeches. She left him to the physicians and waited with Meritaten in the passage outside, where Parennefer, Panhesy, and other members of the staff were clustered anxiously. Several minutes later one of the physicians stepped from the room and bowed.

"What is the matter with him?" Tiye demanded.

"It seems to have been some kind of fit, Majesty," he explained. "Pharaoh is already much improved, but weak."

"Are you able to treat him?"

The man hunted for words. "No," he said at last. "If Pharaoh were a common man and not a god, I would say that either the demons had him in their grip or that he suffered from a madness that under the law ensures a man complete protection. But as Pharaoh is divine . . ." Wisely he did not finish. Tiye dismissed him and, gesturing for Meritaten to follow, went into the room.

Akhenaten was propped up on pillows. Tiny shudders shook him intermittently, and his face was still gray from the violence of the attack, but his eyes were clear. Meritaten knelt to kiss his hand, and Tiye bowed, sitting on the couch beside his knees.

"They have ordered me to stay out of the sun," he said. One hand crept into Tiye's and clung to it tightly.

"Then you must obey, my son," she answered, a sudden thought coming to her. "Did the god speak to you? You have been ill like this before, but never with such violence."

The hooded eyes dropped. "No, the god did not speak. No vision came."

Tiye stroked the long fingers. "Pharaoh, I want you to consider what will happen if someday the god visits a bout of illness upon you from which you do not recover, if the dreams in which he causes you to walk have no end. I do not speak of death," she said hurriedly, seeing his expression harden. "But it is time to appoint an heir."

"I have been thinking about it," he said slowly, much to her surprise. "It would have to be a child of my holy loins. Tutankhaten is the only candidate." He spoke the words clearly and sensibly, as though the fit had purified his mind. Tiye battled the desire to let her sheer astonishment at this turn of events show on her face, afraid that any reaction at all might deflect his train of thought.

"I think not," she disagreed gently. "Tutankhaten is too young. He would become the prey of unscrupulous men who through him would seek to undo all you have done for the Disk."

"You could be regent," he offered, blinking up at her.

Tiye smiled into the simple, confident face. "Akhenaten, I am not going to live forever. Neither are you. Smenkhara is now sixteen, and a man. He would need no regent, only advisors. He is not your son but is of my body and your brother. Declare for him so that I may sleep in peace." She watched him carefully for the telltale signs of distress, but he remained calm, lying loosely under the thin sheet, only the fingers warm in her grasp betraying any reaction. His face held an expression of sad dignity. Meritaten had gone suddenly still, her eyes fixed unblinkingly on Tiye.

"I would have to make him a full member of the family of the Disk," he said musingly, "but perhaps it is ordained. He looks very like me, Mother, have you noticed? The same shape to his head." Akhenaten gently removed his hand from hers and placed it on his breast. "I understood the things the people did not speak today," he went on. "I pretended not to, but I did. They ask in vain. The Aten will not give us water. I know it. The sin must be mine, that the god does not hear my prayers. Perhaps he tires of his son, and his eyes have turned to a new incarnation." His voice was full of defeat and a genuine sorrow. "Very well. Have the scroll prepared, and I shall sign and seal it, but not today." The light voice was thick with fatigue. "I must sleep. Meritaten, stay with me. I am afraid."

Hardly daring to acknowledge her victory, Tiye ordered a scribe to her own quarters and dictated the document giving Smenkhara the right to wear the Double Crown upon his brother's death. She kept it with her, determined to waste no time and acquire Pharaoh's seal as soon as possible the next day. Then she sent for Smenkhara. He did not appear for hours, and when at last he bowed before her, he was drowsy with wine.

"If I cannot swim or be with Meritaten, I might as well drink," he said sulkily in answer to her sarcastic comment. "My friends and I were at Maru-Aten. There is not much foliage left, but the pavilion is cool."

She threw the scroll at him. "Read that."

Listlessly he unrolled it, leaning against the wall. When he had finished, he dropped it on the couch. "Well, it is about time," he said, "but it means little now. Pharaoh could live on for many years while Meritaten grows old and fat and I waste away with boredom."

"What have I done that the gods should have punished me with such a surly, ignorant, selfish, ungrateful son?" Tiye stormed. "I have just obtained Egypt for you, yet you still complain. Listen to me. From now on, Pharaoh will watch you closely. You must be dutiful in the temple. Close your Amun shrine. Do not spend too much time with your friends. We do not wish to suggest that you are planning to take the crown before it comes to you legitimately. It hurts me, Smenkhara, but I do not think that Pharaoh has long to live. You should think about what you will do with Egypt when he has gone."

Smenkhara shrugged, and Tiye, watching him relaxed against the wall, seeing the slouching, thin shoulders and small swell under his belt, felt a pang of real fear go through her. "I like Akhetaten," he replied. "You kept me from it long enough. I shall stay here and let Malkatta rot. I shall marry Meritaten and enjoy my rights as pharaoh."

"It does not matter where you live as long as you take steps to stabilize our foreign dominion and restore the worship of Amun."

"That sounds very uninteresting. I suppose I ought to think about sending out ambassadors. Have you any wine here, Mother?"

"No. Think about what you will do, but remember that you are not pharaoh yet. If you appear too eager, Pharaoh might change his mind."

"What mind?" Smenkhara laughed.

To her astonishment, Tiye felt her eyes fill with tears. "It is a mind filled with the kind of dreams no god would even deign to show you," she said thickly. "I refuse to let you make fun of him, and I order you to shut the blasphemous mouths of your so-called friends. He is my son, and I love him. Get out of my sight."

"He was your husband, too, as long as you had use for him," Smenkhara said rudely, pulling himself away from the wall, bowing perfunctorily, and sauntering to the door. "Do not think, Empress, that you can use me also. When the Double Crown is on my head and Meritaten is in my bed, I will be grateful, but not until then." He did not wait for a retort or a dismissal, and the door slammed shut behind him.

Tiye lay back and let the tears come. They were not solely for Akhenaten but also for herself, the sudden, hopeless weeping of the old, for whom self-pity is an inviting indulgence. Smenkhara was a callous, self-seeking man who was not yet aware that in looking with such scorn upon his brother he was seeing himself.

Pharaoh ratified the document of succession the next day, as he had promised. A ripple of relief went through the palace, and the more naïve courtiers and large numbers of the city dwellers went to the river, watching the dribble of water the river had now become and expecting the Aten to signal his pleasure by releasing the flood. But others were too preoccupied to care what Horus might be in the nest, for news had arrived from the Delta that disease was beginning to spread among the herds, whose grazing land was becoming bare. Frantic dispatches were exchanged between courtiers and their stewards on the Delta estates, but all knew there was nothing to be done.

Djarukha was faring less badly than other estates. Two large lakes were maintained on Tiye's property and at her order were

being used to at least sprinkle the fields so that some grass
might be available for her cattle. She also kept a store of grain
there that her steward opened for the villages that housed her
workers. She did not intend to be faced with dead fellahin, no
one to work when the Nile did rise again. Ay was attempting
to relieve those on the family estate at Akhmin with the same
measures, but the slaves of other nobles were not so fortunate.

Pakhons and Payni dragged slowly by, and now the emaciated bodies of peasants began to be found cast against the
banks beneath the water steps in Akhetaten itself, mingled with
the bodies of oxen and decomposing goats. The courtiers were
shocked and indignant, and Ay commissioned soldiers to patrol
the river near the southern customs house at all times so that
they might hook the bodies out of the water before they drifted
within sight of the city. But they could not snare every one,
and the nobles kept as far from the Nile as they could so that
they might not see or smell Egypt's agony. Pharaoh supplied
the favored of the city with grain. Akhetaten was magic, was
holy, was the seat of the god and his chosen family, and in it,
no citizen was allowed to go hungry. The dwellers of the city
sat down to bread and last year's wine while the fire of Shemu
consumed the land and Egypt lay like a barren desert, filled
only with the wails and keening of mourners.

Nefertiti's lush terraces began to wither. Whether the deposed queen refused all contact with the city, immuring herself
in wounded pride, or Pharaoh himself had ordered that no
communication take place, Tiye did not know, but she sent
Huya to the north palace to make certain her niece was in good
health. He returned with only his own impressions. The lake
had dried up. Nefertiti was well, although there was sickness
among her staff.

"The queen is very silent," he said, "and sharp-tongued
when she does speak. She has put on a little weight, but it only
adds to her loveliness. Her face is becoming very sorrowful."

Tiye was reassured to know that Nefertiti was well and
seemed to be ruling her own little kingdom capably. She resolved to secure her release if Smenkhara became Pharaoh in
her lifetime. Nefertiti would no longer be in a position to cause
much harm in government.

The sickness in the north palace soon invaded the central
city as well. Hardest struck in the royal palace were the nurseries and the older women on the harem staff. Huya, worried

and harassed as he tried to organize the comings and goings
of physicians, isolate the dying from the healthy, and see to
the removal of bodies, advised Tiye to remove Tutankhaten
and Beketaten from the palace entirely. Tiye immediately arranged for the children to stay across the river with Tey. Pharaoh, buoyed by the certainty that in making Smenkhara his
heir he had placated the Disk, was convinced that the sickness
would soon die away. Although high summer had come, he
paraded through the harem apartments preceded by a worshipping Meryra, rebuking the ill and dying for their lack of faith
and promising them that soon the river would flood and their
bodies would be cleansed. But looking up at their king's wet,
red mouth, the trembling of his hands, the feverish gleam in
his eyes, the stricken saw death grinning at them over his
shoulder.

The sem-priests and employees of the palace House of the
Dead worked steadily to prepare those who had died within
Pharaoh's domain for burial, but the place of embalming for
the ordinary citizens of Akhetaten soon became so choked with
rotting corpses that a special edict was issued from the temple
Office of Physicians allowing bodies to receive a rudimentary
embalming before being buried immediately in the desert. Be-
reaved families found themselves observing the obligatory seventy days of mourning for relatives who had already been
placed in the sand. Worse still, many of the dead decomposed
so rapidly that by the time the hard-pressed embalmers came
to examine them, they were no longer able to be preserved.

The stench of death hung over palace and city while the
disease ran its course. Tiye kept to her quarters, having her
servants burn perfumed oil to mask the odor, but it could not
be entirely erased. Every day she sent a herald across to Ay's
house with orders to bring back a full report on the welfare of
Beketaten and Tutankhaten, waiting anxiously until he had
returned to reassure her that the children were not ill. Five
times she received thankfully the same message, but on the
sixth morning the herald reported sickness among Tey's servants and the grim news that princess Beketaten was suffering
from a cold. Immediately Tiye began to arrange for the children
to be sent north to her estate at Djarukha.

She had almost completed the preparations for the journey
by noon of the next day when Huya came to her, his face grave.

"Majesty"—he bowed—"Princess Tey begs your presence, together with your physician. Beketaten is too ill to be moved."

Tiye's heart sank, but she fought against the dread stealing over her. "Very well. Send Piha to dress me and have my barge ready. Is Tutankhaten well?"

"Yes. But two of Tey's tiring women died yesterday."

Tiye had been resting. She swung her legs over the edge of the couch, her heart suddenly pounding, sweat breaking out all over her body. The heat was unendurable. "Go and inform Pharaoh."

"Majesty, the god has been vomiting all morning, and his physicians will not let him rise."

"Well, then, tell Panhesy."

She let Piha drape her in thin linen but could not bear either the touch of paint on her aching face or the weight of a wig on her head. *In one more month it will be New Year's Day,* she thought as she walked slowly into the sunlight, *and in another, the river will begin to rise. Winter will be here again. Isis, I have prayed to you every day to turn your anger away from us. Soften your heart and let the tears flow.* She went slowly, one hand on Piha's shoulder to steady herself, dizzy and frail. *Beketaten, I loved you as a child,* her thoughts ran on painfully, *but I have ignored you of late. Have you been lonely?* But under that new source of guilt an older one flowed dark and inevitable. *She is her father's sister. The gods are finally punishing me. Beketaten will die.*

The river was so low that the boatman had to pole against jagged, half-submerged trees and even rocks that jutted ominously above the surface. Tiye, in the cabin with curtains raised to catch any breeze, saw the bloated body of a huge crocodile go by, circling lazily under the poleman's quick thrust. She looked away; it was a bad omen. When they reached the west bank, the ramp was run out, canated upward to reach the first water step, and Tiye needed her captain's arm to stop herself from falling as she crossed. The odor of the milky water was like a physical blow, and she raised her perfumed linen to her nose and hurried through the brittle garden toward the shade of the portico. Tutankhaten came running to meet her, and before steeling herself to go within she bent and hugged him, all at once terrified for his safety. *It is no use sending him to Djarukha,* she thought, feeling his sturdy arms around her neck. *There is plague everywhere. Perhaps Nefertiti would take him.*

The sickness in her palace seems to be slight. Warning him to stay close to his own apartment, she kissed him and plunged into the stifling house.

Tey had had the good sense to raise the window hangings on the west side of Beketaten's room and to station fanbearers beside the window to waft air within. Beketaten lay on her side, wracked by shivers. On touching her Tiye recoiled, for the girl's skin was dry, and as hot as a brazier. *The Aten is consuming her. Her own father is eating her up,* she thought hysterically, and then immediately mastered herself. Bowls of river water stood on the table by the couch, and a physician washed the girl continually. At a nod from Tiye, her own physician made a swift examination, but Beketaten was unaware of his touch. She was muttering and occasionally calling out in delirium. Both physicians consulted while Tiye stood overwhelmed, looking down on the thirteen-year-old fruit of herself and Pharaoh.

"There is a boil on the princess's lower spine that is not ready to be lanced," her physician said quietly. "It must be causing her great pain. As you know, Majesty, nothing can be done for the fever. It must run its course. Spells might be efficacious."

Spells. Tiye closed her eyes. *Do I have any right to obstruct the anger of the gods? Yes, I do, for their wrath ought to be directed at me, not my child.* She turned to Tey, hovering anxiously in the background. "Is it too much to hope that there are magicians in Akhetaten who know the old chants against fever demons, Tey?"

Tey looked thoughtful. "My artisans would know. I will ask at once." As she went out, Beketaten began to shriek, and the physicians ran to her. Her body had begun to convulse, her spine arching, her legs stiff, and the men needed all their strength to hold her against the mattress. When the fit was over, Tiye bent to comfort her, but though her eyes were open, consciousness had not yet returned to the girl.

In Tey's pretty reception room Tiye accepted wine and some dried fruit from the previous year's crop, chewing and swallowing with distaste. She had scarcely finished when Tey bowed, three swarthy, awed workmen in coarse kilts and bare feet behind her. They hurried to prostrate themselves.

"These men are employed in my workshops, Majesty," Tey explained apologetically. "I do not think any priest-magicians of the old order reside at Akhetaten, and in any case, finding them would take too long. My men are not priests but know the spells. Fever is a constant companion of the workman."

Tiye looked down on the sturdy backs and untidy black heads at her feet. It was true, there was no time. *What has Egypt come to*, she thought resignedly, *when a royal princess must endure the presence of three fellahin such as these?* "Get up," she said unwillingly. They struggled to their feet and stood awkwardly with eyes averted. "You will sing against the demon in my daughter's body. You will keep your backs turned to her couch. When all is finished, I will reward you with one month's supply of grain. Come with me."

She took them to Beketaten. The girl was crying now without tears, a whimper on every outward breath that stabbed Tiye to the heart. As carefully as they could, the men went to the far wall and faced it, clearing their throats, humming until they found the tone they wanted. They began to sing, a rough, uncouth sound that nevertheless brought back to those listening a distorted reflection of the past. There was a small flurry behind Tiye, and she swung round to find a herald on his knees. "Well?"

He held out a scroll. "Pharaoh is very distressed for his daughter," the man whispered. "He commands that this be laid on her breast. He cannot come himself."

"What is it?"

"It contains a prayer of healing to the Aten."

"Go." When he had been ushered out, she unrolled the scroll and deliberately ripped it in two. Dropping the pieces on the floor, she stalked after him. The workmen would sing until the fever abated or the princess died. There was nothing more that Tiye could do.

Beketaten died four hours later, weakened not only by the fever but also by the convulsions that had not been prevented by the physicians' attempts to cool her. Huya arrived, and Tiye gave him instructions for the disposition of the small body. She did not go to look at her daughter herself. She could not bear the sight of another corpse, another lifeless husk, even one to which her own body had given form. "Take her quickly to my embalmers," she ordered. "By the time her father issues his own directives, her beautification will have begun. I would send her to Karnak for proper burial if I could. I will stay here with Tey for another night, Huya. I do not wish to go back into the city just yet."

Huya hesitated. "Majesty, while I was preparing to come, a letter arrived for you from the Delta, from the estate of the Princess Tia-Ha."

Tiye did not need to be told its contents. Her judgment had begun, and from now on nothing would halt the pitiless revenge of the gods. "She is dead, then?"

Huya nodded. "In her sleep, Majesty. She left certain pieces of jewelry to you, and a promise that she will speak favorably of you to the gods."

A goddess did not need the pleadings of a mere human, Tiye knew, but Tia-Ha understood the needs of her empress. *The strongest link with my past has been broken*, she thought as she made her way unsteadily to the chamber Tey had set aside for her. *My dear friend, my cheerful companion, I have not laughed since we parted. There is no loneliness as poignant as this. I cannot grieve for my own daughter as intensely as I mourn for you, the one who shared my life since girlhood and who has taken its memories with you.* She lay on her couch, watching the sunset paint the walls red before washing them with darkness, aware, with the dying of the light, that to be left alive after all she had cared for was gone was punishment enough for any sin.

22

BEKETATEN'S FUNERAL WAS CONDUCTED IN THE BLAZING height of summer without so much as a single flower to lay upon the nest of gilded coffins. The hand of the god lay heavy on those who stood outside the rock tomb, listening to Meryra and his priests recite from the Teaching. Nowhere in the beautiful words was there a suggestion of punishment or retribution, yet Egypt panted, shrunken and dying in the grip of famine and disease. No feast took place afterward, and the participants parted quietly, seeking a solace that no longer existed in the palace.

New Year's Day was celebrated in a continuation of the fatalistic mood that had surrounded the funeral; it was more like a gathering of outcasts or a drawing together of the wounded for comfort than a demonstration of Egyptian power. No foreign delegations waited to pay homage to Pharaoh and present rich gifts. Few courtiers could summon the optimism to flaunt new fashions on a day when traditionally every important official displayed his power and the climbers made themselves eagerly obvious. No mayors presented the good wishes and bounty of their cities, and one by one they sent apologies for their absence. They were all trying to cope with fresh crops of bodies in their streets every morning; epidemics of disease, blindness, and paralysis; and outbreaks of violence between the fellahin, who had left the land that held only death, and the townspeople, who had little and did not wish to share what they had. Even Horemheb was not present, having been called urgently to Memphis to deal with a mutiny in the barracks there. Mutnodjme, as unruffled and indifferent as ever, kissed Pharaoh's feet and laid the artificial flowers of custom across them. Meritaten sat beside her father in glittering gold and blue eye paint, but she was withdrawn. Tiye did not attend. After the news of Tia-Ha's death she had suffered a collapse, a small fever accompanied by throbbing joints and a recurrence of abdominal pain that kept her on her couch. Ay held the fan by his lord's right knee, as outwardly confident as ever, but he would meet no one's eye.

The feast that followed, though it featured many entertainers, was sparsely attended, and the laughter of the guests was more dutiful than gay. By midnight Pharaoh was alone on the dais amid the ruins of the meal, and the great hall was empty but for Smenkhara, who sat cross-legged before his little table, head sunk onto one palm, picking moodily at the dry bread remaining on his plate. Servants stood motionless in the shadows that drowned the walls, out of reach of the few torches that still guttered. The queen had excused herself much earlier, pleading a faintness in the close heat. Behind Akhenaten his fanbearers, steward, and butler waited patiently for him to leave, but he made no move, his mouth parting occasionally, as though he were going to speak. The cloying stench of dis-

carded perfume cones hung in the unmoving air, mixing with
the odor of stale food.

Smenkhara was sunk in some gloomy reverie of his own,
only his fingers moving among the crumbs and shreds of black
bread. At first he did not hear his name, but Pharaoh called
again, and Smenkhara looked up, startled.

"Majesty?"

"Come up here, Prince."

Obediently, Smenkhara rose and mounted the dais, bowing
low several times. Akhenaten indicated Meritaten's vacant chair,
eyeing him expressionlessly for several seconds, and then smiled
slowly.

"Smenkhara," he whispered, "what has happened to the
most favored nation under heaven? Everywhere I look there is
pain and death. Even here, in the place the Aten chose for his
own abode, there is evil. I am used up, I am become as a
discarded pot. My prayers do not leave my mouth and taste of
famine. My breath is as the khamsin; it blows only death." He
stopped and swallowed, and Smenkhara could still hear the
emotion Pharaoh was trying to control. "I, the one who stood
between the god and the people, do not know what to do. My
intercessions are not heard. The god no longer gives me direction." The full, orange-painted lips shook as his gold-draped
shoulders hunched. "I had thought when I made you my heir,
the god would be satisfied, but it is not so. It was not enough."
He pressed both palms together, and Smenkhara watched the
fastidious fingers knit around one another with the slow tight-
ening of extreme agony. "For some reason that I do not understand, my divine father has repudiated me. He no longer loves
me. My immortal task must go to you." Behind him Smenkhara
heard a sharp intake of breath and thought it must be Ay.

"Majesty," he said, "I do not know what you mean."

"I must pass my powers to you. Already the Aten is changing
your body, fashioning it after the pattern he most desired in
me. You will officiate in the temple and make known the god's
will to the people."

"But, Horus, I do not want to!" Smenkhara stuttered, suddenly cold. "The god has not indicated anything of the sort to
me! I am only a prince, a Horus-Fledgling. I know nothing of
the Teaching!"

"Neither did I until the god chose to enlighten me." Akhenaten's voice was muffled, his eyes big with tears. "In another

month the river should begin to rise if I have done right in the sight of the Disk."

Smenkhara stared at him. "You are giving me the Horus Throne? You are descending the Holy Steps? A pharaoh cannot relinquish his divinity to another except by death!"

"No, I will remain the ruler upon the throne, Divine Incarnation in Egypt. I do not give you power to rule, only to pray. One day you will be the Aten's incarnation, but he wishes to bring you into his family now. His ears will be open only to you. Keeper, take the crown and regalia. Parennefer, clear the passages. We will go to my chamber." He unlocked his fingers and drew them down Smenkhara's cheek, and something in the suddenly languid almond eyes made the young man draw back quickly. "Come, Smenkhara," Pharaoh urged as the keeper removed the crown and replaced it with a white linen scarf, laying the crook and flail beside the scimitar in the gold chest. "I will bestow on you true membership in the royal family."

"But I am royal already!" Smenkhara blurted, now frightened. "My mother is empress, my father . . ." His words trailed away as he caught Ay's stern glance over Akhenaten's shoulder. The warning was unmistakable. For a second Smenkhara almost flung himself from the dais to seek the sanctuary of his own quarters, but instead he shakily rose with Pharaoh. Akhenaten put an arm around his shoulders, pulling him close. His breath was coming hard, and his nails stroked Smenkhara's oil-streaked bare flesh. The herald began to call a warning to all who might meet the Lord of All Life.

Pharaoh did not relinquish his hold on the prince until they were behind the closed doors of the royal bedchamber, and then it was only to wave his body servants out. He seemed to have recovered from his solemn mood. His smile was indulgent, encouraging, his eyes sparkling. Pouring wine, he held it out to Smenkhara, who snatched it and drank deeply, the silver rim of the cup chattering against his teeth. He was beginning to sweat. Akhenaten came close, slipping the blue and white ribbons from the young man's head and running his hands over the smooth skull, down the cheeks, across the cold mouth. "You are very handsome," he said. Smenkhara could not meet his eye. He stood trembling, with head hanging like that of a sacrificial ox. Akhenaten lifted away his necklaces, removed his bracelets, and took his rings, kissing each finger as he did so. He was panting, the thin breast rapidly rising and falling.

He began to dabble and then to knead his fingers in the perfumed oil that had melted from Smenkhara's cone and now smeared his chest. Smenkhara squeezed his eyes shut, trying frantically to escape in his mind: to Meritaten and the balmy days together at Malkatta, giggling and drinking beer in the garden. To his barge on a full-flowing river, fishing rod in his hands. To his new friends, who flocked after him with small gifts and called him Highness.

But he could not shut out the revulsion he felt at Pharaoh's touch. The hands were now on his neck. Akhenaten's perfumed breath was in his nostrils. He opened his eyes to see the long face coming close, the thick mouth slightly parted. *I must not flee*, he thought grimly. *If I do, I may lose my chance to sit on the throne. If I displease him, Pharaoh might even choose Tutankhaten over me for an heir, and I would stay a prince forever and never have Meritaten.*

The lips met his own, withdrew, and returned with more assurance as he was pulled against the god's soft body. Pharaoh's questing hands slid down Smenkhara's straight back, met the edge of the kilt and, loosening it, let it fall. The oil-slick fingers dug into the firm buttocks, the mouth moved down Smenkhara's neck. In spite of himself, the young man felt his bowels loosen. "Be brave, Prince," Akhenaten murmured, drawing away and smiling sleepily. "This is necessary." He sat on the edge of the couch and drew Smenkhara toward him.

Later he lay with his arm around his brother, Smenkhara's head pillowed on his shoulder. A wind had risen, and puffs of dust blew in through the slits under the ceiling and drifted around the window hangings. It was almost dawn, but apart from the light of one somber yellow lamp the room was dark.

"You are a good man, very willing," Pharaoh said. "You can be assured of the Aten's favor. You already have mine. Let me give you a present, Smenkhara. What would you like?"

I would like to run to the river and plunge in and wash and wash, Smenkhara thought bitterly, full of shame and humiliation. But an idea came to him, and he raised himself on one elbow, looking down through the dimness onto the calm face.

"If I have pleased you, Majesty Brother, if you love me and truly want to reward me, give me Meritaten."

Akhenaten's features froze. "That is not possible."

"Why? You have the authority. I am now your heir. Have you forgotten how your predecessor refused you Queen Sitamun, your own sister, how he made you wait until he was dead? Do not make me wait thus for Meritaten." The underlying threat was obvious, as Smenkhara intended: *If you make me wait, I shall despise you as you despised Osiris Amunhotep.* Smenkhara, watching him closely, saw the battle between Pharaoh's hatred of his father and his own sense of ownership reflected in the wide eyes. Tensely he waited until finally Pharaoh sighed.

"I have not forgotten. How could I? Very well, Smenkhara, we will share her. After all, we are one family."

"No! No, Majesty, you have me now, and I will be dutiful and obedient, I swear. But as I am the next incarnation, Meritaten is mine alone, by right. Beketaten is dead."

"There is Ankhesenpaaten."

Smenkhara unscrupulously threw the winning dice. "True," he whispered, "but the Aten has already shown me that I am your successor. He came to me in a dream last night and told me that you would give Meritaten to me."

Akhenaten lay very still. Slowly an expression of great sadness softened his face, and he looked up beseechingly. "The god spoke to you? Ah, Smenkhara, how fortunate you are! I long for the voice I used to hear. Very well. If it is the will of the Disk, I will give her to you."

Smenkhara's eyes widened. He could not believe that Pharaoh had capitulated so easily. "Thank you," he said, unable to keep the joy out of his voice.

Akhenaten smiled. "If you are truly grateful, then kiss me."

For a moment Smenkhara regarded Pharaoh's expectantly parted lips, but then, stiffening his resolve, he lowered his head and kissed them.

Akhenaten made no effort to keep his relationship with his brother a secret; indeed, he would have considered it unnatural to do so. He made it known that he had consecrated Smenkhara to the service of the god with his body, conferring power on him in the only way he thought acceptable. Akhetaten and the court were past caring. After one disillusioned glance at the couple who paraded through the palace arm in arm, caressed each other, and were seen with mouths and bodies pressed together at every opportunity, their anxious eyes returned to the river. The time of Inundation had come and gone once again, but the level did not change, and by now it was actually shrinking, the water gradually evaporating into the dry, hot air.

Akhenaten continued to be unconcerned. "Soon the floods will come," he assured everyone. "Smenkhara is communing with the god." In the long, arid nights Smenkhara would make love to his lord with proper attention and afterward lie increasingly glibly as Akhenaten questioned him about the Aten's desires and pronouncements. There would be a flood, Smenkhara told him with desperation, but it would be late. Egypt had to learn patience.

Akhenaten soon began to call his brother by the affectionate title once bestowed on Nefertiti, Nefer-neferu-Aten, Great Is the Beauty of the Aten, and Smenkhara allowed himself to be also addressed as "Beloved of Akhenaten," for Pharaoh was pouring out all his love on the young man. Akhenaten had even commissioned two statues from the artists Kenofer and Auta, one showing the king with his left arm around the prince and his right hand caressing Smenkhara's chin, the other, never finished, portraying them kissing. Both statues showed the royal bodies as grossly deformed. Smenkhara watched them emerge from the stone with an ominous horror. He did not like to be reminded of his slowly elongating skull, the layer of fat building on his belly that no amount of exercise seemed to control. To Pharaoh such physical changes were a sign of the god's favor. To Smenkhara they were a terrifying vision of the future that drove him to seek ever more fervently the pleasures of the present.

Khoyak, Tybi, and Mekhir came and went. The momentary hope that this year an Inundation would occur, which had brought a semblance of official bustle to the court, began to die. Pharaoh still paraded to and from the temple, Smenkhara on his arm, stopping at the Window of Appearances to smile and encourage the few city dwellers who gathered to catch a glimpse of him. He still played with his children, sat in public audience, and presided over the feasts, but it was as though he suffered from some inner blindness, unable to see the reality pressing ever more inexorably around him. The view from the Window of Appearances itself was stark. The myriads of trees were dead, the beautiful lawns were disappearing under the encroaching desert sand, and the people, though still lining up at the palace granaries every day, were thinner and silent. The city smelled of disease and excrement. Pharaoh's daughters greeted him in a quiet, half-empty nursery. His audiences were held for ghosts. All the foreign delegations had left Akhetaten.

But some official acts were still performed. Pharaoh, by now anxious to do anything that would lift the Aten's curse from Egypt, at last dictated and sealed a contract of marriage between Smenkhara and Meritaten. On the night when the young man was to receive his wife, he waited for her in his quarters. He was very calm, almost cold, the time long gone when excitement could have touched him. Even when he saw her standing in the doorway, her servants retreating and his own door slaves bowing low before closing behind her, his heart did not falter. She had dressed simply in a yellow pleated gown caught over one shoulder. A golden fillet lay over her straight black hair, and thin gold links went around her wrists and one ankle. Smenkhara watched her come gliding over the dusty floor. He felt nothing, only a formless sadness that welled up where his great love for her had been. For a long time they stood looking at each other. Finally he spread his arms wide, and she stepped into his embrace. He was content to hold her, burying his face in her hair, inhaling the warmth and perfume of her firm young body, his eyes closed against the anguish that caught in his throat and threatened to spill over in tears. She pulled away and attempted to smile at him, her mouth trembling, her own tears running down her painted cheeks. With a cry he kissed them away and then sought her mouth. She had not changed much. Childbearing had widened her hips a little. Her breasts were fuller, her eyes steadier. Yet although he went on kissing her, he continued to feel nothing. Even tenderness had gone. There was only the terrible, aching sadness. Gently he drew her down onto the couch, pushing aside her linens, telling himself that now finally he was free to touch her wherever he wanted. He had waited and won her. She was his. She lay quietly, one arm loosely around his neck, watching him, still crying. After some minutes he flung away. "I cannot!" he choked. "Amun help me, I cannot!" He sat staring down at his hands. "It is useless. We are not the same."

She turned her head away. "No," she whispered. "We are not the same."

Akhenaten went into Ankhesenpaaten's apartment. His third daughter had left the nursery the year before, having become a woman and proudly performed the rite of passage. Her youth lock had been removed and her hair allowed to grow, so that now it lay at chin length, glossy and black, framing a big-eyed, pretty little face. With her new status had come her own suite of rooms in the palace, together with her own staff. She was a happy, uncomplicated child with her father's love of nature. As she heard him announced, she left the floor where she had been sorting her trinkets and ran into his arms. He hugged her fondly.

"You look very fresh today," he said. "I see you are wearing the circlet of onyx flowers I sent you. You are like a flower yourself, Ankhesenpaaten. Are your women looking after you properly?"

"Of course they are! Grandfather was here earlier, bringing me these bracelets. Tey made them. What do you think?" She scooped them off the floor and dribbled them into his hands.

"They are lovely, but I wish it had been possible to bring you real lotus blossoms." Akhenaten handed them back. "Even a water lily would be a wonder."

"Do not worry." She touched his check. "The Aten has promised Prince Smenkhara that his anger is almost over. We have not fared too badly, have we, Father? Egypt is strong!"

"You are right. Now, dear one, order your women out. I wish to speak with you alone."

Ankhesenpaaten called, and one by one the servants left. Akhenaten took her hand and led her to her couch. Sitting, he reached for her. "Come onto my lap," he smiled, "and listen carefully. You know that your sister now belongs to Smenkhara?"

"Yes, of course. The women have been gossiping about it. They are saying that the prince has wanted Meritaten for a long time."

"I expect that is true. But I am now without a queen."

"Poor Father! What about Princess Tadukhipa?"

"Kia is very fond of me, but she is only a secondary wife. Would you like to be my queen, Ankhesenpaaten?"

She looked solemnly into his face. "If it will make you happy, Great One."

"Good." He pulled the coronet from her head, and taking her small face between his hands, he kissed her full on the mouth; then he lifted her from his knees and placed her on the couch. "It is hard to make me happy these days," he said. "I am glad that you wish to try."

* * *

Tiye recovered slowly from the illness that had stricken her after Beketaten's funeral and attempted to resume work with Meritaten in the Office of Foreign Correspondence but found she had lost the heart. In any case, dispatches had shrunk to a mere trickle of unimportant information, formal greetings to Pharaoh from the few peaceful nations left in the world, and requests for gold. She knew that she was no longer even nominally in control of any aspect of rule. The events in the palace appalled and frightened her, particularly her son's now obviously deranged behavior, and she was too tired and infirm to make any comment, let alone remonstrate with him. Ay, too, was surprisingly quiescent. She had imagined that he would press for more power for Smenkhara, mobilization of the army, even for the assassination of Egypt's tormented Pharaoh, but the continued drought and famine had sapped his will as surely as it had that of almost every minister, even Horemheb. After disciplining the soldiers at Memphis he had gone north to his natal village of Hnes to visit his parents, and when he returned to Akhetaten, he remained secluded on his estate with Mutnodjme. He might have been plotting revolution, but Tiye no longer cared.

Whispers of rain in Rethennu circulated the palace, of huge crops ready to harvest there, of a bountiful yield in Babylon, while the Nile became poisonous with rotting fish and its steep brown banks thick with frogs. Talk began of the river itself being a plague, for those unfortunate enough to topple into it or children tempted to cool themselves in its stagnant oiliness immediately developed rashes, scabs, and blisters that led to fever and inevitable death.

But Akhetaten continued to cling to the last shreds of its once shining dream. In an Egypt whose suffering had long passed the boundary of human endurance, it was still blessed. Food was scarce but sufficient. The court sheltered behind the comfortable trappings of ritual and protocol. Akhenaten spent his days in the temple with Smenkhara, groaning and imploring pity from the blazing ferocity of the god, and his nights making love to the prince or Ankhesenpaaten. The child was pregnant, a fact that an oblivious court barely recognized and Akhenaten himself could take no joy in. The fertility of his sun family mocked him. Though the business of government had almost slowed to a halt as ministers and courtiers abandoned their duties, the routines of their servants remained unchanged. Pharaoh, his family, and the hundreds of nobles who inhabited the palace still required domestic care.

No underling was busier than Huya, who had been spending less time on his responsibilities in the harem than he should have, for the empress, increasingly frail, took up most of his energy. Although he generally left his duties to his assistant, today he had inspected the nurseries himself and now stood before Pharaoh, who was barely awake. Beside him Smenkhara still slept, breathing heavily and muttering. Akhenaten held a finger to his lips.

"Do not wake him," he hissed. "He has not been asleep long. What do you want, Huya?"

Huya bent and spoke in a low voice. "Majesty, I think you had better come to the nursery. Nefertiti's little daughters are very sick. I have sent your physicians to them."

He could scarcely meet the frightened eyes peering into his own.

"All of them? Is it fever?"

"I am not sure. Certainly they are full of fever, but they seem to be bruised, also."

Akhenaten was struggling to rise. "No more!" he whispered fiercely. "I cannot bear it. What have I done that these things should be visited on me? Even a god cannot suffer indefinitely."

Huya tried to compose himself. "Majesty, may I suggest that you order their mother to come at once?"

Akhenaten was now standing, leaning against his night table, his eyes swollen from heat and lack of sleep, traces of kohl and henna smudging his body. "No," he said. "I do not want to see her again. Order my body slaves to come and dress me."

"Pharaoh," Huya said gently, "they are dying."

The grotesque figure slumped. One hand was pressed tightly against his eyes, as though trying to force back the pain. Akhenaten nodded once. Immediately Huya went out, sending the body slaves in as he went. He had already informed Tiye, but she had merely thinned her lips and looked away. While Pharaoh was being dressed, Huya ordered the King's Own Herald to the north palace and returned to the nursery.

By the time Pharaoh arrived, the youngest, Sotpe-en-Ra, was already dead. "It was as though she was decomposing even before the breath left her," a frightened physician whispered to Huya. "This is a most virulent plague. Do not let Pharaoh see the body."

But Akhenaten did not ask to see her. The other two girls had been placed in an adjoining room, which he hesitantly entered. The odor of corruption hung in the unmoving air. No servants were tending the tossing, unconsciously crying princesses. The tiring women clustered by the door, their noses hidden in their linens, and the physicians and their assistants stood by helplessly. Nefer-neferu-Aten-ta-sherit began to plead for water, and after a moment Pharaoh himself picked up a cup and went to the couch. Swiftly one of the physicians moved forward to raise the lolling head, but the delirious girl thrashed the cup away and went on moaning. Large black weals had appeared on her neck, and Akhenaten, gingerly pulling down the sheet, saw them on her breasts also. He let the linen fall and stood there, hands hanging loosely at his sides, and retched.

Nefertiti swept into the nurseries two hours later, but by then all three princesses were dead. At the sudden flurry of whispers and movement by the door, Akhenaten turned and, seeing who it was, began to weep as he fell toward her. "Nefertiti," he gasped, "I have missed you so, I am desolate, help me..." But she pushed past him grim-faced. The attendants stared at her. She had been absent from the palace for so long that for many of them she had begun to acquire the aura of a myth, a tragic, lonely woman living out her days in solitude, but the vigorous queen striding into the room bore no resemblance to the pale creature of their imagination. Nefertiti snatched the sheet from Sotpe-en-Ra's body. After staring down on it for a long time expressionlessly she went through the door into the other room, and those there saw her repeat the action twice. When she had finished, she stalked back to Pharaoh and dropped the stained linen at his feet. "You killed my children," she said.

Akhenaten put out a hand. "I feel pain also," he whimpered.

She struck it away. "You keep me from them for four years, and then you kill them!" She was white with grief and rage. "Every child dead in Egypt should be laid at your feet. Do you know what the people are calling you, Majesty? The criminal of Akhetaten, and your mother a whore. Between you, you have brought down the curse of the gods on this doomed country! Do you repent? No!" She clenched both fists and began to pound them together. "You pile evil upon evil. Meketaten, Meritaten, and now your brother in your bed! I demand to see Ankhesenpaaten!"

The company gaped at her, their eyes turning to Pharaoh in expectation of seeing the royal uraeus on his forehead spit flame at the blaspheming queen. But Akhenaten had wrapped his arms around himself and was crooning quietly, and as they watched, he slumped to the floor and began to rock himself back and forth. After one contemptuous glance Nefertiti strode out, her own attendants running after her.

Ankhesenpaaten, who was sitting in her room listening to her lute player sing, jumped up in shock as her mother appeared in the doorway, and with a glad cry rushed to meet her. Enfolding her daughter, Nefertiti covered the dark head with kisses. Ankhesenpaaten stepped away, eyes shining.

"Mother! Has he released you? Are you coming back to the palace? Look!" Hurrying to the table, she snatched up a scroll. "The Babylonian king, Burnaburiash, wrote to Pharaoh, calling me Lady of Thy House and promising to send me seal rings made of lapis lazuli! I am really a queen now!"

Nefertiti looked at the cobra rising from the thin gold circlet on her daughter's brow. Her glance traveled down, to the soft swell beneath the transparent linen of the girl's gown. She turned on her heel and left without a word.

During the ride back to the north palace, Nefertiti sat stiffly behind the closed curtains of the litter, so consumed with shock and rage that she was unaware of her surroundings. Not until she had been carried through the thick gate in the wall that separated her home from the south city and her bearers began to lift her up the long flight of steps leading to the palace entrance did she come to herself. For fear of weeping she had not trusted herself to speak to the men who carried her away from the royal palace, and she could only wave them away once they had set her down before her door. With her retinue following she walked into the cool half-light of her hall and then, turning, found her voice.

"Leave me alone, all of you. Go to your quarters. I do not want to hear or see anyone for several hours."

Within moments she was alone. She began to wander the vast, quiet rooms of the palace, arms tightly folded, her grief demanding movement, as though by pacing she could step away from the pain. Gradually her thoughts became calmer, and the anger that had kept her tears at bay began to fade. In the end she went into her hall and, casting herself on a chair, put her hands to her face and wept.

That night she was still sitting at the window of her darkened hall, drinking moodily and gazing out on her ruined terraces, lit feebly by the light of a waning moon, when her herald cleared his throat politely behind her. Still in the grip of bitterness and anger, she turned impatiently. "I had not realized it was so dark," she said. "Have the lamps lit. What do you want?"

"Your father waits without, Majesty."

Nefertiti's feathered eyebrows rose. "It is amazing that he has remembered he even has a daughter," she snapped sarcastically. "Show him in." The man bowed and left, motioning the servants to light the lamps. They began to move quietly about the room with tapers. Nefertiti waited, half-turned on her chair, her cup on the sill. Presently Ay bowed and approached, holding a child by the hand.

"This is not a pleasure," she said coldly as they came to a halt. "I have received no help from you, Fanbearer. You may expect no hospitality from me."

"I ask none," Ay wheezed. "You are right, Majesty, and I know it is no use getting down on my knees and begging forgiveness."

"Even if you could get down," Nefertiti smiled frostily. "You have aged terribly, Father."

"I know. My breath is short, but my girth is not. Listen to me, Daughter. You could now move back into the palace if you wished. Akhenaten would not summon the courage to object. He is a broken man."

"No, thank you. Not after what I have endured today."

"That is what I thought. Then grant me a favor." He pushed the boy forward. "Take Tutankhaten under your protection."

Nefertiti turned her full attention to the prince, assessing him slowly. "Explain," she ordered, but the cold tone had gone out of her voice, and she kept her eyes on Tutankhaten. "Prince, if you go into the passage, you will find my steward. He has a small store of honey secreted away, and if you order him, he will let you dip your finger in it."

"Oh?" The boy smiled uncertainly. "That will be nice, but I really want to go home."

Ay bent. "Highness, you cannot. I will send your toys and

your servants tomorrow, and I will visit you often." Tutankhaten
sighed ostentatiously and went out. Nefertiti waved her father
to a chair. "I do not think that Pharaoh has long to live," he
said breathily, "and Smenkhara will be a useless successor. He
is weak, greedy, and ignorant. But he is not altogether a fool.
If he thought Egypt was anxious to take the crown away from
him and give it to his half brother, I have no doubt he would
murder the boy."

"Is Egypt anxious?"

"She is becoming so. Smenkhara resembles his brother more
every day and makes no attempt to use his influence with
Pharaoh in any productive way. Tutankhaten will be safe here.
You guard yourself well."

Nefertiti raised her cup and drank reflectively, her unwaver-
ing gaze on Ay's face. "I see. And if the time should come
when the Double Crown is placed on his head, who will be
his empress, who his regent?"

"You can put the disk and plumes on your head if you wish.
I will be regent."

"Ah. And what will Horemheb do?"

"He will be making war in Syria."

Nefertiti laughed abruptly and sat forward. "Does he know
about this? Does Tiye?"

"I have discussed it with him. But Tiye is old, Nefertiti.
Afer Beketaten's death and the news of Tia-Ha's passing, she
began to draw into herself. She is often ill and wants to talk
of nothing but the past. I will outlive her."

"You speak of such things so callously, yet she has always
been in your heart, your friend as well as your sister and goddess.
I think it is your ambition that has outlasted hers. How strange."

"I am offering you another chance at active rule, a return
to power, this time as empress."

"Providing I obey the regent-to-be."

"Of course."

A slow smile spread over Nefertiti's still lovely features.
"There are many unforeseen forks in this road you describe so
glibly as wide and straight. And do not forget that assuredly I
shall be present at your funeral, my father." She relaxed again,
folding back into the chair, her fingers curling around the cup.
"I will keep the boy. He can entertain me. But what will Tiye
say when you tell her I have her precious prince?"

Ay got to his feet with difficulty. "I do not think I will tell her. She has no more interest in her children. They have brought her nothing but grief. She will not miss him. No one will. All at the palace are wrapped in their own miseries."

"So am I. You are dismissed, Fanbearer. Put liniment on that chest of yours. It might free your breathing."

He bowed and went out into the night.

Tiye turned on her side and, pulling the cushions lower, lay gazing into the duskiness of her bedchamber. At the far side of the room Piha sat cross-legged on her sleeping mat, haloed in the light from the one lamp by her knee, her head bent over her sewing. Behind her the shadows caused by her small movements glided softly on the wall, and the tune she was humming under her breath was the only sound in the quiet room. Tiye, watching her, envied her contentment. In a while, Tiye knew, she would roll up the linen tidily and come to the couch to enquire if there was anything her mistress needed, but until then she remained wrapped in her task. The day had been uneventful but for the report that had come from the palace, telling Tiye that Pharaoh had been shut in his apartment for four days, refusing food and drink, sitting on the floor of his bedchamber and often failing to recognize the worried servants around him. Tiye, still weak from the attack of fever, could summon no real concern for her son. She had done all she could for Egypt and for him and would no longer allow herself to care.

She had begun to doze when she heard a commotion in the passage outside and opened her eyes in time to see Piha lay aside her work and go to the door, already opening. Her brother stepped through, motioned Piha to wait in the corridor, and before Tiye had finished struggling to a sitting position, he was beside the couch. He did not bow. "Tiye . . ." he began, but seeing the extreme agitation in his face, she interrupted, "Bring the lamp and set it on this table." She was fully awake now, watching him, alarmed, as he did as he was bid. His hands were shaking, and the flame quivered in his grip as he placed the lamp where she had indicated. She nodded for him to speak.

"Pharaoh has just given an order to all his heralds," he said hoarsely, "and threatened them with execution if it is not carried out immediately. They are to go to every city, every temple, even to the small country shrines, taking stonemasons with them, and chisel out, destroy . . ." He faltered, pressing his trembling palms together. "Destroy the name of Amunhotep

III and all his titles wherever they may be found." He swallowed. "They must even go into the quarries where there might be unfinished inscriptions."

Tiye drew back on the couch. "But why?" she whispered.

Ay slumped onto the couch by her feet. "He says that Amunhotep is not dead, that even though he lies beautified in his tomb, he still sails in the Holy Barque, where his presence is an affront to the Aten. He believes that is why the god has cursed Egypt with so much misery and doubted his own devotion. If a name remains, a ka may live." His eyes sought her own. "He is deliberately killing his father. May the gods grant he dies soon! He has unleashed powerful forces of evil in Egypt. Ma'at is extinguished."

Tiye, who had never before seen him lose his sense of reasonable detachment, felt the scrabbles of panic in her stomach. "The blame is not his alone," she said with difficulty. "It is mine also. How blithely I went to his bed! I do not believe the curse will be lifted until I die." Suddenly she began to laugh, a harsh, mirthless sound. "Do you realize that the Son of Hapu was right after all?" she went on. "Doubly right. Akhenaten has grown up to murder both fathers, human *and* divine. I should have let him be killed. I should have listened to the Son of Hapu, but I was proud, and jealous of his power over my husband. But I have paid." Anguish dried her throat. "I know what the people call me now."

Ay was beginning to recover. "The heralds cannot possibly find every inscription," he replied gently, reaching for her hand. "You wear Osiris Amunhotep's name on your fingers every day, carved into your rings. Do not despair, Tiye. We make what decisions we can, with whatever wisdom we can summon at the time, and what more can be asked of us?" He leaned over and kissed her, but she turned away.

"You no longer reveal your decisions to me," she grated, "and you do not bring me comfort. You have become a stranger, Fanbearer. Do what you must. I care for nothing anymore." But in spite of her words she clung to him when he rose to leave, and had to fight to swallow her tears.

After he had gone she rose, forcing her stiff limbs to carry her across the room to the large chest in which her most precious valuables were stored. Pausing a moment to listen to Piha talking with the guard at the door, she lifted the lid. The Declaration of Innocence lay where she had placed it, on its bed of unstarched linen. Carrying it back to the couch, she unrolled it, reading it slowly, tracing with her finger her name and the long list of titles she herself had written so many years earlier. When she had finished, she wrapped it tightly, weighing it for a moment in both hands before calling sharply. Piha came running.

"Take this to the kitchens and put it on the fire," Tiye said. "Stand by it until it is fully consumed." The servant nodded. Tiye dismissed her and leaned back on the pillows with a sigh. *I do not deserve the declaration*, she thought, *and it is beneath me to try to deceive the gods. Either I am one with them, needing no justification, or I am not. Whatever happens, I am ready.*

She slept deeply in spite of the heat and the next day felt well enough to walk through the house, but the experience depressed her. She had never felt at home there. Now, as she went from room to richly furnished room, her eye caught the vibrant wall paintings of ducks crouched in tangled river growth, wet grapes bursting on the vines, fish threading through sparkling blue water, so much lush beauty. But with a slight movement of her head, she suddenly found herself looking out at the real world. The cracked, baking earth, lifeless skeletons of trees, and the near-waterless ravine where the river trickled made her feel like a moving mirage without real substance. Even her own name sounded odd when she whispered it. She returned to the sanctuary of her bedchamber gratefully.

But that night she could not sleep. After enduring several hours of the sound of the fans she irritably sent the bearers away and lay listening to the silence. No sound rose from the river. No slap of oars or crack of sail, no singing of fishermen after the night catches, no subdued laughter of lovers in the reed marshes. There was no ferment of insect life either, for the garden was dead. Only the sad howling of a jackal somewhere high in the eastern cliffs came echoing drearily across the valley. Piha snored gently, invisible in her dark corner. A dry, tired moon cast gray light onto the floor. Tiye had ordered the hangings left raised on the window. As the hours glided slowly by, she half-sat, half-lay on the couch, pillows at her back, hands loose on the sheet, her long, waving hair damp with sweat, her breathing quiet.

She knew that she was waiting for something, and when she caught a tiny flicker of movement out of the corner of her eye, she was not surprised. She merely turned her head and lay relaxed, looking into the dimness. At first she thought she had been mistaken, for after that one movement the room seemed to sink once more into immobility, but presently a long, thin shape undulated across the shaft of moonlight lying on the tiling, moving from the window to the door. Tiye's heart began to pound. She sat up. Afer the plague of snakes the year before, no milk was left in dishes on the floor. Something else had attracted this one. The promise of coolness, perhaps. A tiled corner in which to curl up, away from the earth outside that retained the furnace heat of the day. Leaning on one elbow, she tried to follow its progress. *I should immediately summon the guard*, she thought. *It might be poisonous. Piha might be in danger.* But something prevented her from calling out.

A sense of inevitability began to steal over her, a calm that gradually stilled her frantic heartbeat and relaxed the fingers that had bunched around the rumpled sheet. The snake would disappear through the crack under the door, or it would not. It would find Piha, or it would not. It would turn toward her, or ignore . . . She felt a gentle tug on the bedclothes under her hand and froze. Then slowly, so slowly, a dark head began to appear over the edge of the couch, swaying slightly. The breath caught in Tiye's throat. Higher it rose, until it was almost on a level with her face, a slim column of menace. Still she felt no fear, but then her elbow inadvertently slipped, and she drew back. At the sudden movement a frill and then a dark clouded hood opened, and she realized that she was staring at a cobra. There was not enough light to see any color on the creature, but a glitter of moonlight flashed in the shiny eyes.

Suddenly Tiye knew that it was this for which she had been waiting. Cobras were almost unknown as far south as Thebes and almost as rare here in Akhetaten, as they preferred the fertile Delta land. But the Delta was a wasteland, and this magic symbol of a pharoah's power must have come hunting. *No, not hunting*, Tiye thought, once again perfectly calm, her eyes riveted on the coldly majestic creature. *It is too much to believe that it is here in my room through chance alone. It has come for me.* Tentatively she moved a hand. The snake continued to sway gently, its hood quivering, and Tiye could have sworn that she saw its forked tongue flick quickly out. A patience in its stance communicated itself to her. *It will wait until I am ready*, she reflected. *Defender of Kings, Wazt, Lady of*

*Spells, you come clothed in power to weave about me the last
great spell of all.*

The realization brought first a panic. No, Tiye thought frantically. *I am not ready to die!* But her reaction was only one
of instinct, for close on its heels came a wave of relief. *I am
tired of life. I carry a load of guilt and sorrow that can only
grow heavier as the days go by. Everyone I have loved is gone
but for my son, and it were better for him if he had died a long
time ago. My love has only brought him agony. Egypt is destroyed. I inhabit this rotting body like a shadow imprisoned
in a catafalque. It is time to face the gods.* The cobra continued
to stare at her, a living emblem of all she had worshiped, all
her first husband had so gloriously upheld, all her son ought
to have been. Sighing, she offered her hand. "Strike, then,"
she whispered. "I am ready." For a brief second she touched
its skin, dry and cool. Turning her palm upward, she presented
her wrist. She was smiling.

The snake struck. She saw a flash of light on tiny, sharp
fangs before they were buried deep in her flesh. Involuntarily
she recoiled, dragging the cobra with her, biting her tongue to
keep from crying out, but then she felt its weight leave her. *I
should rouse someone*, she thought. *No one will wish to kill it
because it is holy, but it might do harm elsewhere.* She felt her
wrist, cradled her arm against her breast, and lay back. Slowly
her gaze wandered the room, taking comfort from familiar
things, Piha's small movements, moonlight now climbing the
far wall, the cry of a night-hunting hawk. Peacefully the minutes slid by. Blisters began to swell under the skin of her wrist,
painful to touch.

After an hour Tiye felt her heart begin to palpitate, and she
tried to breathe deeply, once more fighting a momentary terror.
All at once, as nausea grabbed her, she jerked forward and
vomited and then lay back gasping. She had expected it and
was prepared, but the gods were merciful, and it did not come
again. She would have dozed but for the erratic flutter of her
heart. She did her best to keep still. As dawn approached, it
became harder to draw breath, and in the end she was sitting
upright, forcing air into her lungs with all her strength, eyes
wide but no longer seeing. She had no last coherent thought.
There was only a lingering awareness of the sheet sticking to
her drenched limbs, and the unbearable pain in her heart.

Ay came from his post at Pharaoh's door as soon as Huya summoned him. He stood looking down on the small, dainty figure with its wealth of reddish-brown hair tousled over the pillow. Death had smoothed the imperious face, returning to it a little of the fragility of youth. The full mouth was parted slightly in a smile of self-satisfaction. Under the half-closed lids the blue eyes caught the daylight with the hint of a mocking glitter. Lifting the limp arm folded above the sheet, he turned it over. The punctures were clearly visible, surrounded by purple, swollen flesh. Piha was sobbing behind him. "I heard nothing, lord, nothing at all! I would have saved her if I could. I am a wicked servant!"

"Oh, be silent!" he snapped, not turning. "No one will blame you, Piha. Close the door and tell the sem-priests to wait. When Pharaoh comes, you may let him in." He squatted by the couch and searched the immobile face for a long time. He was not certain what he was looking for, but slowly an odd conviction took hold of him. Glancing covertly over his shoulder, he saw Piha busy at the other end of the room. Huya was gazing out the window. Ay drew a short knife from his belt and quickly and silently cut one curling lock of hair, concealing it in his linen. "Very little in your life took place that was not under your direct control," he whispered into the brown ear. "I do not believe in this so-called accident. May your name live forever, dear Tiye." Swiftly he kissed the unresponsive lips and let himself out into the passage.

He was about to close the doors when Akhenaten came running, hard on the heels of the herald calling his titles. All waiting went to the floor. Pharaoh gripped his fanbearer's arm. "It is not true!" he shouted. "Tell me it is not! I want to see her!" Before Ay could answer, he pushed through the doors. Ay stepped to pull them closed before Akhenaten's terrible wailing began, but Pharaoh's agonized howls pursued him long after he had slipped through Tiye's entrance hall and walked back with his escort across the Royal Road.

Ay longed for the comfort of Tey's presence, but before he could snatch a precious hour in the tranquility of his own estate, he had an errand to perform. He no longer drove a chariot. He was carried by his most trusted soldiers in a covered litter to the north palace, enduring the ferocious heat of a summer noon without the shade that used to give travelers some respite along the broad road that joined palace to central city. At the wall,

Nefertiti's guards knew him and let him through. Leaving the litter, he was led within by Meryra. Even in such stultifying heat the north palace was so vast that draughts played continually through its lofty rooms, and the sweat began to cool on Ay's skin as he walked.

Nefertiti was talking to her women and greeted her father with polite indifference. Ay asked that Tutankhaten be brought to him and turned to stare moodily out the window while he waited. Nefertiti said nothing. When the boy came running over the tiled floor with a glad smile, she waved her women away. Ay bent slowly and hugged him.

"It is good to see you again, Prince. Are you happy here?"

"Yes," Tutankhaten replied. "I did not think I would be, but I am. I can do what I like, when I like. The queen plays with me often."

Ay smiled inwardly. The queen had wasted no time getting into the boy's good graces. "I want you to listen to me very carefully," he said, holding Tutankhaten's eye and speaking as clearly as he could. "Your mother is dead. It is right that you should grieve for her, but she would not want you to mourn very much. From now on, Queen Nefertiti is your mother."

Nefertiti stifled a cry, and her hands flew to her cheeks.

Tutankhaten's trusting face turned from one to the other. "Has my mother gone to the Aten?" he asked, manfully trying to still the quiver in his voice.

Ay smiled reassuringly. "Of course she has. Her justification is assured, and she is happy now. I have brought you a lock of her hair." He drew it out and placed it on the boy's palm. "You must go immediately and put it in a very safe place. A little box with a tight lid would be best. Guard it carefully. Regard it as a solemn talisman, a lucky amulet. You must promise me you will never give it away."

Tutankhaten's fingers curled around it. Ay caught Nefertiti's startled glance. "Is it true?" she whispered, and Ay hushed her with a quick frown.

"I will put it with my brother Osiris Thothmes' bow, that she gave me," Tutankhaten said, awed.

"You had better do it now," Ay urged. "Not a single hair must fall to the ground. You will understand better when you are older." The boy nodded and ran out, holding his clenched fist solemnly before him. Nefertiti swung to her father.

"Is it true? If it is, the gods will fail to recognize her!"

Ay did not miss the faintly malicious tone. "No one will ever know for certain," he said heavily, "but I think so. She did not seek the cobra, but surely she could have called for help and did not."

"I think I will attend the funeral," Nefertiti finished, smiling as she ushered her father to the door.

Ay turned with her, wondering as he left whether in giving the lock of hair to Tutankhaten he was giving his own luck away. The hair of a suicide brought great good fortune to the one who owned it.

23

SEVENTY DAYS LATER TIYE WAS LAID TO REST IN THE TOMB her son had prepared for her in the cliffs behind Akhetaten. It was the beginning of Athyr. The river ought to have begun to rise some weeks before, but the high banks remained and Tiye's funeral proceeded under the gaze of every courtier in the city. Nefertiti, surrounded by her guards, sat under a canopy at a short distance from the crowd and watched her husband. His voice could be heard clearly over the murmur of Meryra. In between bouts of loud weeping he knelt in the sand, scooping it up in both hands and placing it on his head. At times he stood with his arms wrapped around Ankhesenpaaten, his face buried in her shoulder, his body shaking with sobs, and when he was not crying or anointing himself with sand, he was kissing and fondling her. She bore it with expressionless fortitude, her hands resting protectively on her swollen belly, her eyes carefully avoiding those of the gathering.

Near the end of the ceremony Akhenaten strode to the coffin and, laying his arm along the top, began talking to the corpse and laughing fondly. Smenkhara and Meritaten, seated side by side, held hands and looked at their laps. Ay and Horemheb exchanged glances. Pharaoh's hysterical child's voice multiplied against the rocks and went shrieking over the sand like the senseless babble of many demons.

There were no flowers to lay on the body when at last it was carried inside the dark tomb. One by one the family placed artificial sprays made of gold, silver, and jewels while Akhenaten leaned over the coffin and fingered the offerings, his head cocked on one side, whispering to himself, his eyes unnaturally bright.

Few waited to see the tomb sealed. Meryra and the priests were left to do the work alone while the courtiers scattered. Nefertiti took Tutankhaten back to the north palace without speaking to anyone. Smenkhara and Meritaten, surrounded by their hangers-on, retired to their private quarters. Akhenaten, still clinging to his daughter, was gently ushered into a litter and taken to his couch. Only Ay remained, sitting beneath his canopy, breathing harshly and watching the sign of the Disk being pressed into the clay that had been plastered over the knots in the tomb's doors. When that was accomplished, he ordered himself carried to Tiye's house and, together with a weeping Huya, walked slowly through the empty rooms. Piha, red-eyed and monosyllabic, was directing the slaves, who were sweeping and washing. Ay went to the cosmetics table and fingered the last flotsam of his sister's life. An empty alabaster kohl pot, small blue beads scattered from some broken necklet, a copper mirror lying half out of its case with Tiye's fingerprints still showing clearly on the polished metal. He lifted it and stared at his reflection before sighing and handing it to Huya as a gift. At last he went out into the blazing red evening to seek his wife's unspoken comfort.

That same week Meritaten-ta-sherit, Akhenaten's little princess by his daughter Meritaten, fell ill. Meritaten had her removed to her own quarters and sat over her, holding her hand and singing soothingly while the two-year-old cried and tossed. But it soon became obvious that Meritaten-ta-sherit was sick of the same virulent fever that had carried off Nefertiti's three younger daughters. Smenkhara hovered about the sickroom uneasily, trying clumsily to comfort Meritaten but unable to evince any sympathy for the little girl who represented for him Pharaoh's lecherous theft of his most precious prize. He was almost relieved when he was summoned to Pharaoh's bedchamber.

Akhenaten was sprawled naked on his couch and, when Smenkhara bowed, held out a shaking hand. Smenkhara took it, swiftly scanning the yellow face, his spirits sinking as he saw that for once Pharaoh was lucid. Since Tiye's funeral, Akhenaten's days had been one fit of vomiting and weeping after another. His hard-pressed servants had done their best to keep him fed and bathed and had tried to close their ears to his babbling. Horemheb had come on Parennefer's request but had been unable to calm him, and a terrified Ankhesenpaaten had tearfully refused to answer Akhenaten's incoherent summons. He slept little, falling at odd times into a motionless slumber from which he would jerk awake an hour or two later, prayers already on his lips, his body at once restless. But on this evening he was quieter, his eyes bloodshot but calm. He pulled Smenkhara down beside him.

"Nefer-neferu-Aten, beloved," he whispered, his arms going around the prince, his body already pressed convulsively against Smenkhara's. "Kiss me. You walk across the room like a vision of my younger self. I see the power of the Disk pulsing in your loins and beaming from your mouth."

"Do you know that your daughter's daughter is dying, Pharaoh?" Smenkhara murmured against the thick lips. He stifled Akhenaten's reply, grinding his mouth against his brother's with a cruel, perverse pleasure, forcing the thin shoulders back against the mattress with both remorseless hands. Akhenaten began to whimper, but Smenkhara knew from experience that this was an expression of lust, not a reaction to his words. "You do not care at the moment, do you, my god? Well, I do not care, either. Shall I kiss you again?" He looked directly into the puffed eyes, himself full of a fierce hatred, driven from his customary passive sullenness by Akhenaten's transparent physical need of him. Akhenaten stared back eagerly, nodding faintly, his hands behind Smenkhara's head, pulling him down. Smenkhara's lips brushed the other's, but before he could go further, the doors burst open, and Panhesy rushed in, falling on his knees beside the couch. He was trembling with excitement. Smenkhara pushed himself away from Akhenaten and sat up. "What is it?"

"Highness, Majesty, the nilometers are showing a small rise in the level of the river! Isis is crying!"

Smenkhara stared at him, a great gush of warmth spreading through his chest. "How small a rise?"

Panhesy indicated a height of about that of a finger.

Akhenaten had groped for Smenkhara's waist and was clinging to him. "The curse is lifted, the god is appeased," he said brokenly. "Later I will go to the temple and give thanks, but now . . . Smenkhara, where are you going? Stay with me, I beg!" But Smenkhara had torn himself free of his brother's grip and was running out the door before he could be ordered to remain. He pelted along the corridors, aware of the smiling faces that sped by him in a blur, the arms raised in thanksgiving, the voices shouting, weeping happily, singing prayers. Behind him his Followers, sandal bearer, herald, and steward tumbled after. Rushing past the guards at the entrance to Meritaten's apartments, he went to the doors of her chamber and burst within.

"Majesty, Isis is crying!" he yelled but came to an abrupt halt. Meritaten did not even look up. She sat with head hanging, both hands clasping the limp fingers of her daughter. Meritaten-ta-sherit was dead.

The preparations for yet another royal funeral went almost unnoticed as the city's entire attention was riveted on the notched stone markers sunk at regular intervals along the banks of the river. The rhythms of the day and night ceased to have meaning. While Akhenaten's daughter was bound and her coffins hastily prepared, crowds sat or lay beside the river under the shade of improvised shelters, occasionally breaking into song or dance but more often quietly tense, their eyes never straying far from the surface of the still fouled, stinking water. Peddlers displaying cheap baubles suitable for offerings of thanksgiving moved among them, doing a brisk trade. Wine sellers quickly cleared their stocks. The city became happily drunk, and the streets were full of weaving, laughing people. At night torches were lit. No one went home. In the palace, only Meritaten mourned quietly for her daughter. The courtiers threw large parties, the guests staggering from the ruins of one to the fresh wine and new musicians of another. Mutnodjme had an enormous raft hurriedly built, garlanded with white ribbons, and tethered to Horemheb's water steps. She had also ordered that a marked board be nailed to one of the supports, and her dwarfs took turns clambering down to the water to call up the readings. At each new inch gained, a cheer went up, and the crowd packed on the gently rocking raft raised their cups to Isis, who had relented. All over Egypt, men stood gazing at the slowly filling banks in a stupefied wonder, like souls in the dark horror of the Duat suddenly finding themselves given a second chance at life. Egypt rose from death on the miraculous, silent swelling of the dark current.

Meritaten-ta-sherit's funeral was almost forgotten in the tumult of rejoicing. Smenkhara stood with his arm around Meritaten as the rites were performed and the little coffin was carried so pitifully easily into the darkness. Pharaoh attended but sat in silence, nodding occasionally or rocking briefly, and no one knew whether he was truly aware of what was happening to his child.

At the end of Khoyak, when the Nile began to brim over and cover the thirsty fields, Ankhesenpaaten gave birth to a girl. The nobles crowding the bedchamber to witness for Egypt were still in a festive mood, and there was much joking and laughter as they sat on the floor gambling or playing board games while the little princess cried and strained. Her labor was almost as long as Meketaten's had been, and when it was over, she was too weak to acknowledge Ay's congratulations or Meritaten's kiss. Akhenaten, though he had been notified that the birth was imminent, did not attend it, and Ankhesenpaaten's servants were secretly relieved.

Pharaoh devoted himself, when he was not in the grip of his madness, to Smenkhara. He had turned the young man into an amulet, a lucky charm, clinging to him both emotionally and physically as his health deteriorated. He ordered the prince to move into a small suite of rooms adjacent to the royal apartments. Smenkhara complied, hoping that his brother would then feel safer and relinquish the stranglehold that was driving the prince mad, but Pharaoh only clung to him more tightly. Ankhesenpaaten was still too unwell to share the royal bed, even if Akhenaten had desired her. Like his father before him, he seemed to draw a kind of mysterious power from the young man's body. Smenkhara nursed his shame, appearing with Pharaoh draped over him at the Window of Appearances when the king made his increasingly infrequent progresses to the temple but otherwise hiding in the half-light of his cramped quarters, snarling and striking out at anyone who approached him. Meritaten had come to him once, but he had cursed even her with such venom that she had retreated in tears. The fellahin might be scraping together what seed they had left, the trees might be flushing with a green that had not been seen in nearly three years, the shadufs might once more be pouring glittering wet life onto the withered royal lawns, but at the heart of Egypt there still lay a cankerous darkness.

Horemheb pushed past Smenkhara's guards with a sharp word, slammed the heavy cedar doors closed behind him, and bowed perfunctorily at the prince's back. Smenkhara was standing at the window with his arms folded, staring out past the roofed and pillared walkway at the sunlit private garden beyond. Although the room was warm, he was swathed in thick white linen that he was clutching tightly to himself. He gave no sign that he had heard someone enter. Horemheb waited for a moment and then said politely, "Highness."

"Get out, Commander."

Horemheb came up to him and bowed again. "Your forgiveness, Highness, but I cannot leave until I have obtained your seal on this document."

Smenkhara's eyes flicked to it and away again. "You will leave immediately and take it with you."

Thoughtfully Horemheb's eyes traveled the sulky, swollen mouth, the faint purple mark of a fading bruise on the tall neck, the tension of the fingers buried in the creased linen. He stepped forward, interposing himself between the prince and the window, and Smenkhara backed away.

"Pharaoh will not live forever," he said gently. He would have continued, but Smenkhara's face suddenly twisted into a grimace of spite.

"How dare you pity me!" he hissed. "Me, a prince of the blood and heir to the throne! I will make him have you disciplined, soldier!"

Horemheb was unmoved by the insult. "I do not pity you, Fledgling," he responded dryly. "It is time to prepare for a new administration."

"If you have come to rub yourself against me like a fawning cat, you can go and play with yourself." He used a particularly obscene expression, but Horemheb refused to be drawn.

"This is an order for the immediate mobilization of the army," he said sharply, lifting the scroll. "I want you to give your official approval, Highness, if there is to be anything left of Egypt for you to rule."

"I don't give a damn for Egypt."

"I know that. But you do want the Double Crown, and if you are clever, my cooperation."

"Threats?" Smenkhara sneered. "Really, Commander, if I lift a finger, I can have you speared and tossed into the Nile."

"I do not think you can, prince," Horemheb said softly. "In any event, it is to your advantage to gain my confidence. Your mother wanted the throne for you, and if you are to secure it, you need me."

Color flamed in Smenkhara's sun-starved cheeks. "Your impudence is unforgivable, Horemheb! I have secured it already!"

"Not quite. Your half brother continues to grow under the protection of Queen Nefertiti. If the succession was a matter of blood alone, his claim would be stronger than yours."

Smenkhara's eyes narrowed. "Are you daring to tell me," he said quietly, "that unless I do what you want, you will transfer your allegiance to the bastard son of an illegal coupling? My father was Amunhotep III, the greatest pharaoh Egypt has ever seen. No claim is greater than mine."

"Highness, I do not think that the claims of blood will have much validity when Pharaoh dies. The Treasury is empty, the administration atrophied through disuse and the corruption of too much bribery, the country as a whole almost irremediably impoverished. Power will go to the fittest, not to the man whose blood is purest. You must be seen to be strong enough to deserve the throne. I loved and admired your father, and your mother was my goddess. Help me to help you."

Smenkhara studied his face. "Your eyes are lying," he said. His fingers went to the bruise on his neck, and he rubbed it absently. "If you want to help me, kill my brother."

"That is not necessary. I am convinced he is dying. We can issue what edicts we like, and he will not interfere. His days are a murky succession of dreams and nightmares. He has lost touch with the world."

"You would not be so sure of that if it was you he kissed and fondled with such monumental lust." Smenkhara's voice shook. "I thought you were his friend. I cannot trust you."

"That does not matter. I do not trust you, either."

"You speak blasphemy. What of Ay?"

Horemheb smiled. "The fanbearer is very old."

"Gods, you are disgusting." Smenkhara jerked away. There was wine by the couch, and he poured for himself and drank deeply, wiping his mouth with the back of his hand. "Give me the scroll. Mobilization?"

"And war." Horemheb stepped from the window and, handing the document to Smenkhara, spoke urgently into the young man's face. "I have been proud of my country, Prince. When I was a young boy growing up in Hnes, my father taught me to serve the gods, honor Pharaoh, and give thanks every day for the privilege of being born an Egyptian. All men envy us, he told me, because Egypt is prosperous, and her laws are just. I did not need to take his word alone." He drew back and, going to the window, leaned wearily against the casing. "He worked hard, but our life was good. Our land produced well, and even after paying our portion each year to Pharaoh's tax collectors there was usually enough grain for my father to barter in exchange for a trinket or two for my mother. Hnes was a happy place. Even the poorest peasants did not need to beg. I wish Your Highness could see my natal town now." He turned his gaze toward the garden. "It is destitute. I send gold to the local priest to be distributed, but the people have become coarsened by privation, and though gold will fill their bellies, it will not buy them back their dignity." He had begun to speak too loudly and now paused, softening his voice. "As a child I was not aware that Hnes lies very close to the border. No one thought much about it. But now Hnes is full of fear. How terrible are those words! Egyptian citizens on Egyptian soil, never knowing when they might wake to find their village full of foreign soldiers! The shame of it!" Suddenly he swung to regard Smenkhara again. "I was never like the other boys in Hnes," he said. "I always knew fate had great things in store for me. I was clever and full of ambition, but above all I burned to serve my country and the god upon the Horus Throne whose benevolent omnipotence enabled me and my family to go to our pallets each night without hunger and sleep without anxiety."

"This is a pretty story," Smenkhara interjected, "but my patience is wearing thin. Everyone knows you are a commoner and rose through the ranks. Get to the point."

Horemheb stiffened. "The point is this," he replied evenly. "I still love Egypt and revere the dignity of her god ruler. I desire above all to see both restored to the place Ma'at has decreed for them. I have watched the disintegration of all that every true Egyptian holds dear. There is still time, a little, to reverse the tide of misfortune that swept over us when your brother ascended the throne, if you, Prince, will only support me. The immediate stabilization of Syria is imperative as a first move. I intend to march the army into our erstwhile dependency and begin a war of recovery."

Smenkhara watched him with a half-smile of speculation. "The clever and ambitious little boy has become a clever and ambitious man," he said coolly. "I have no doubt that your protestations of selfless love for your country have some truth to them, but I would also wager all the gold I have that you will not go into Syria with the army yourself." He went to the lighted candle by the couch and held sealing wax over it. "If you did, you might return to find more shifts in the balance of power at court than you could control. Eh, Commander?" Deftly he dripped the wax onto the edges of the scroll and, removing his ring, pressed the heir's seal into it. "There." He threw it at Horemheb. "Spill all the Egyptian blood you want. Just keep your war away from Akhetaten."

Pharaoh's voice suddenly broke into the small silence that followed. "Smenkhara!" he called shrilly. "Where are you?"

Smenkhara raised his plucked eyebrows. "My royal lover bleats for me," he said. "I wonder what my mother would have had to say about it if she had lived." Horemheb did not answer but stood turning the scroll in his hand, his face expressionless. Envy suddenly marred Smenkhara's handsome face as he looked at Horemheb, and he spat on the floor. "Get out," he whispered. "I am cleaner in the sight of the gods than you, soldier." Akhenaten called again, his voice a shriek of distress. Horemheb bowed and left.

Several days later the rumor of Smenkhara's concession to Horemheb reached Ay's ears. Anxiously he tried to obtain an audience with the prince himself, wanting to ascertain the extent of any influence he might have with his nephew, but Smenkhara had isolated himself in his three small rooms and refused to see anyone. Ay sent a servant to locate Horemheb and, several hours after being turned away from the prince's door, was told that the commander was in the office of the Scribe of Recruits. Calling for his litter, Ay was carried beyond the palace to the site where Pharaoh's ministers had used to conduct the business of government. Most of the rooms were empty, but Ay met several scribes carrying their palettes and scrolls coming out of the headquarters of military conscription. Pushing open the door, he entered.

Horemheb was sitting alone, behind an overflowing desk, the remains of a hurried meal before him. He rose as Ay crossed the floor, and the two men bowed to each other. Horemheb sank back onto his chair and invited Ay to do the same. Ay pulled a stool closer to the desk.

"I came to hear you confirm or deny the rumor that Smenkhara gave you permission to begin a campaign," Ay began. "And if he did, why was I not consulted? I am, after all, the Fanbearer on the Right Hand."

"I would have told you before long," Horemheb answered apologetically, "but I did not want Pharaoh to learn of my intentions prematurely, perhaps during one of his periods of lucidity, and countermand my orders. It does not matter now. They went out to the divisional commanders yesterday."

"You mean," Ay protested hotly, "that you did not acquaint me with your plans for fear I would have immediately told Pharaoh. Of course I would have! What you have done is sacrilege, Horemheb."

Horemheb's fist came down on the desk. "Someone had to do something!" he answered forcefully. "Yes, I have been sacrilegious, and I am guilt-stricken because of it, but I am sick of inaction, sick of giving unheeded advice, sick of the same worn discussions with you that go around in circles. It is not treason!" He grimaced, and his angry gaze dropped to his clenched fingers.

"I did not say it was," Ay put in after a moment, "but it is a decision taken hastily, without due consideration. You have allowed your desperation to triumph over your good sense, Commander. How many divisions are involved?"

"Four are on their way to Memphis for victualing, and they will cross the border soon."

"Are they ready to fight?" Ay waited for an answer, but Horemheb was silent, still looking at his hand, which was now pressed against the smooth wood of the table. "Are they?" Ay urged, now on his feet and leaning toward Horemheb. "You know as well as I that most of our troops have seen no action in more than forty years. They need three months of mock battle drill, time to toughen, to recover from the famine, to learn what they face from the Khatti and the desert! If they are defeated, it will hasten an invasion of Egypt!"

Horemheb's head came up, and he glared at Ay. "You have always been more full of words than actions," he said, "and

what have words accomplished? Nothing! Besides, it has been
years since you retired from active involvement with the cavalry
to become fully the courtier. You do not know what you are
talking about."

"Perhaps not," Ay responded sharply, "but your officers
must have advised caution."

"I did not consult them." Horemheb rose and gave Ay a
brief smile. "I am the Supreme Commander of all the Forces
of His Majesty, and I say the army is ready to go to war. Do
not worry." He came around the desk and put his arm lightly
across Ay's shoulders. "We have been through too much together to cease trusting each other, Fanbearer. I will share the
information in the dispatches that come for me from the front,
I promise."

"Do not patronize me, Horemheb," Ay said, moving away,
still angry. "I have more sympathy with you than you think,
but I beg you to remember that it is I who must stand outside
Pharaoh's chamber watching and listening to the disintegration
of a man I swore long ago to honor and protect. For those of
us in constant attendance on him it is very painful."

"I do remember it," Horemheb answered gently. "I, too,
owe much to Pharaoh, but surely we both owe Egypt more."

Ay pondered Horemheb's words as he was carried back to
the palace, and they made him feel all at once very lonely. He
would have liked to go straight to Tiye's house to discuss the
situation with her, but that pleasure would never come again.
Missing her was a constant dull ache that intensified each night
when he presided at the feasts in Akhenaten's place, for her
granddaughter Ankhesenpaaten, as Great Royal Wife, now sat
beside him in the place where once the empress had looked
out over the company with her impassive blue eyes.

Although Akhenaten himself showed no interest in his latest
daughter, Ankhesenpaaten-ta-sherit, Ay felt sorry for his young
queen and often sent his steward to the nursery to enquire after
the baby's health. It was not good. She did not feed well and
slept too much. On one occasion when he had summoned the
energy to go himself, he found Ankhesenpaaten herself there,
sitting on the floor with her daughter in her lap. At her nod he
approached, bowing. Ankhesenpaaten smiled wanly and, gathering up the baby, held it out to him as trustingly as if it were
a broken doll.

"There is something wrong with her, Grandfather," she said.

"See how limp her right leg is, how weak her arms. The nurses tell me she does not cry, she only whimpers."

Ay took the baby gently, looking at the pallid, thin face that was so startlingly like its father's, expecting Ankhesenpaaten to say, "Can you make it better?" as his own daughters had once done. "Majesty," he said gravely, "I think you must be prepared to lose your daughter. The physicians do not know what is wrong, and neither do I. You must love her while you can."

Ankhesenpaaten solemnly took her back and began to rock her. "When I was very young, my father used to tell us that we would never be ill, and that dying would be easy for us," she said. "My daughter is dying, and he is dying, too, isn't he?" Her eyes filled with tears, and she hugged the baby to her breast. "The courtiers call him evil names, and the common people say he is a criminal, but he is my father, and I love him. They should not speak of Pharaoh like that. Now he is sick, and they have all abandoned him, but you will not, Fanbearer?"

Ay squatted beside her. "I will not, dearest Majesty." He put an arm around her. "Do you miss your mother?"

"Yes, and so does he. When we are in bed together, he sometimes calls me Nefertiti."

Full of pity, Ay kissed her soft cheek. "When the time comes, would you like to live with her in the north palace?"

Her head went down. "I think so. If you will visit me often."

They talked for a while longer, and Ay returned to Pharaoh's apartments. *It would be wise to move the little queen*, he thought. *Smenkhara will be pharaoh, but if he does not rule well, there will be many eyes turning to Tutankhaten, including mine. I have the little prince's confidence, and Ankhesenpaaten trusts me. Horemheb would do well to cultivate Tutankhaten's trust if he wishes to remain high in power.*

The seasons of sowing and growing intoxicated that year as never before. Courtiers who had held their noses at the sight of a cow and had had carpets carried with them in case they might be compelled to place their feet on muddy ground could now be found standing knee deep in the slim green spears of the crops on the west bank, awed by the burst of glorious fecundity they had not believed could be so precious. The sight of banks of vivid blooms in the gardens brought forth admiring exclamations. Each breath of the damp, fragrant air was a miracle.

As the green fields turned slowly golden, and the pleasant warmth of winter began to give way to summer's breathless heat, the first harvest in three years began. But the man who had taken such a delight in the changing seasons and the things of the earth lay on his couch oblivious, living out his last fantasies. Akhenaten was dying. The few faithful servants remaining to him, Ay and Horemheb among them, watched the final disintegration of his mind and the accelerated weakening of his body. Akhenaten still had fits of agitation that culminated in weakening convulsions, but they became fewer as the days went by. He seemed to be entering a world whose inner reality remained a mystery to the watchers. The atmosphere in the quiet room became filled with expectancy, making the men who saw to Pharaoh's physical needs lower their voices. Sometimes Pharaoh paced up and down, stopping to speak perfectly clearly. Once he halted before Horemheb and, staring straight into his eyes said, "But I have spent my life in doing all that the god commanded. I am not ashamed. I cannot say it would have been better had I not been born."

"Of course not, Majesty," Horemheb replied before he realized that Akhenaten was not addressing him and indeed, had not seen him at all.

But before long Akhenaten had become too weak to walk. He lay propped up on the couch, his hands folded on the sheet, scarcely moving. He refused food, though he sometimes drank water, continuing quite clearly the dialogue that had by now been proceeding for many days. Ay was forcibly reminded of the early days of the Teaching, when the prince would gather the young men of the court around him and speak with an authority he exhibited at no other time. But he was visibly sinking, his breathing increasingly shallow, his body thinning, and his face acquiring the transparency of impending death.

Toward the end of a long day when he had lain quietly, alternately sleeping and waking only to whisper unintelligibly to himself, Akhenaten became restless and began to cry, calling agitatedly for his mother. Ay and Horemheb exchanged glances.

"Should we bring Meritaten, or send for Nefertiti?" Horemheb whispered. "Nefertiti has refused to come, but we might try again."

Ay shook his head. "Find Tadukhipa," he decided. "She

has always been devoted to him. Let Meritaten and Ankhesenpaaten in if they wish."

The sound of a door closing made him turn his head. Smenkhara had come through the entrance to his apartment and was
leaning against the wall just inside, arms folded, eyes on the
figure on the couch. Horemheb went out and spoke to the
herald. While they waited, they watched Meryra move quietly
around the couch, describing slow circles with the incense
holder as he murmured. Akhenaten's eyes did not follow him.

Tadukhipa had never lost her air of shy hesitancy. In spite
of the fact that she was a Royal Wife and a princess in her
own right, she answered the men's obeisances with little bows
before moving to the couch and perching on the stool that had
been set for her. Taking one of Pharaoh's hands, she raised it
and kissed the fingers lovingly. Akhenaten's head rolled toward
her on the pillow, and she wiped the tears away.

"Your hands are so warm, Mother," he whispered. "I asked
Kheruef to light the braziers, but I am still cold. They were
going to murder me. I know it now. No one cares about me
but you."

"I will always love you, my dear lord."

"Will you? But words are blown away and vanish into the
mists of time." The whisper trailed away and he fought for
breath. "It does not matter," he went on after a while, his eyes
opening and closing drowsily. "You are here, and I can feel
safe. Do you remember the night at Memphis when the moon
was full and the air was warm and we lay in the hunting skiff
pretending to count the stars? No, you would not remember,
but I do."

"Hush, Akhenaten," Tadukhipa soothed. "Do not talk. You
must save your strength."

He lapsed into silence, breathing lightly and erratically, and
tears of fatigue and sadness began to flow again. Then, suddenly, he wrenched his hand from her grip and struggled up.

"I have tried to do that which is good in the sight of the
god!" he called. "I have tried so hard!" Frightened, Tadukhipa
rose and eased him onto the pillows. For a moment he resisted
and then sank back. His eyes opened wide, all at once fully
aware, and stared at her with surprise. "Little Kia!" he said.
"Did I send for you? Forgive me, I cannot talk to you now, I
am too tired. I think I will sleep."

His eyes dropped shut. Three times the frail, sunken chest

rose and fell and then was quietly still. Tadukhipa turned, and Horemheb came running to the couch. Bending over the king, he listened for a heartbeat but soon straightened. "Horus is dead," he said. "Let his daughters in if they wish to come now." He took his place by Ay as Meritaten and Ankhesen-paaten burst into tears and fled past them, falling by the quiet corpse.

Smenkhara watched impassively, his arms still folded. He did not move even when those in the room turned from the misshapen body to fall at his feet and press their lips against them. The dutiful wails of the women began to float through the windows as the word spread. "Take off his seal ring and give it to me," Smenkhara ordered curtly. Ay obeyed, and Smenkhara rolled it speculatively about on his palm before sliding it onto his finger. "I am going back to my own quarters until these are ready," he went on conversationally. "Clean them well, Panhesy. Meritaten, come here." She got up and joined him. Roughly he snatched up her linen and wiped her face. "Those are the last tears you will shed for your father," he said. "Do you understand? I am hungry. We will eat in the garden." Mutely she followed him through the line of bent heads and outstretched arms. Ay met Horemheb's glance and raised his eyebrows. The new order had begun.

BOOK
THREE

BOOK
THREE

24

NEFERTITI PACED THE GLOOMY LENGTH OF HER BEDCHAMBER, arms folded over the ribbons that held the white cloak under her full breasts, head down. It was full night. One small lamp burned on the table by the couch, casting a pool of yellow light that did little to dispel the shadows around it. The even breathing of the sleeping women, lost in deep unconsciousness at the far end of the room on their pallets, punctuated the warm, still air. Occasionally she would stop, gazing through the dimness at the giant silver reliefs that paraded around the walls, likenesses of herself in kilt and sun crown, decked with ankhs and sphinxes, striding arrogantly over an Egypt bent in homage. Sometimes her absent steps took her to the window, and looking out, she saw her terraces, once again lush with life but now drained of color under a waning moon, tumbling down to the glinting, full river. Her eyes wandered the peaceful scene but hardly saw it. Her fingers uncurled and gently ran over the stone sill without feeling the smooth, breeze-cooled ashlar.

He was dead, he was dead. She said his name in a whisper, not with the grief of love lost but in a kind of angry puzzlement. He had been her route to the power she had exercised in Akhetaten, the father of her children, the strange man who had shared her bed, who had prompted in her both the exasperated affection of a mother for a wayward child and the contempt of a woman for a man who had lacked the rough straightforwardness of the phantom ruler who had inhabited her childhood dreams. In spite of her exalted position she had not gained the empress's crown, for which she had risked the murder of her cousin Sitamun. In spite of those daydreams of girlhood she had not found love. Her life had been a long struggle against the compromises she had been forced to accept. Her extraor-

dinary beauty had been a blunted weapon. As long as Akhenaten had lived, there was a chance that this exile, partly
self-imposed through pride and fear of yet another humiliation,
might end in complete justification, but now he had gone to
whatever god would accept him, and she was permanently
relegated to the honorable but impotent position of dowager
queen. Smenkhara, another cousin, would rule. True, his wife
was her daughter, but between Nefertiti and any influence she
might have with the royal couple stood the Fanbearer on the
Right Hand and the Supreme Commander of All the Forces of
His Majesty, two men whose slow rise to power had been
carefully consolidated at every stage, and who would clearly
not allow her to pursue any independent policies.

Then there was Tutankhaten. Nefertiti was acutely aware of
his presence, blissfully asleep here in her own domain, an eight-
year-old boy whose claim to the throne was as strong as Smenkhara's. *I could marry him myself*, she thought as her feet
carried her soundlessly over the cool tiles, *but I would need
strong men behind me, men who could neutralize my father's
and Horemheb's power. Ay is planning the abandonment of my
city, while Horemheb's arm reaches out for control through
the army. If I married Tutankhaten, Father and Horemheb
would do their best to make sure that I continued to wear only
the queen's crown and walked behind my little husband while
they administered the country. But I am thirty-five years old.
I have a right to rule. And Egypt is ripe for the picking. I want
to pluck it. I want to return to the royal palace in the full
panoply of empress and take at last what is mine. Tiye did it,
and so can I. But how? I grow old here. One day follows the
next like the monotonous dripping of water in the clock. Without
the help of a strong man I can do nothing. Where is there such
a man? No courtier will help me. Amun's men are too weak
and demoralized. Horemheb has the army.* She paused to place
both hands over her burning eyes, a panic rising in her as she
saw herself slowly forgotten, a silent, shadowy figure moving
quietly through the years in a beautiful prison while outside
the shape of history changed and changed again without her.
No! she thought, leaning against the window. *I would rather
kill myself. Tiye was clever. She saw the end, she had done it
all, there was nothing more, and she seized the moment, but
surely I have not yet reached the end of my life. Not at thirty-
five! Shall I marry little Tutankhaten and take the gamble? I*

would lose. I have too many enemies who would ally themselves with Smenkhara. A strong man, a prince . . .

All at once a solution presented itself to her, and its daring made her scalp prickle. She flung away from the window, all weariness gone. *Oh, never!* she thought breathlessly. *I would be risking my very life if it were discovered. Besides, there is not enough time. The period of mourning for Akhenaten has begun, and there are only sixty-nine days left before his successor must perform the Opening of the Mouth.* But the idea grew, and she caught herself smiling into the darkness. *I will,* she thought excitedly. *It is worth a try. The alternative is widowhood and the trappings of power without its sting for the rest of my life. At one blow I can circumvent my father and Horemheb, disinherit Smenkhara, and keep Tutankhaten forever a prince. I am not too old to have children, sons . . . But time is so short.*

She ran to the doors and pulled them open. Her guard sprang to attention, and her herald rose from the stool where he had been dozing. "Bring my scribe at once," she snapped, "and the captain of my household guards. Hurry!" She closed the door and went to a chair, weak with fear, and pouring water, she gulped it down. Summoning up her courage, she went out to her reception rooms, dismissing the guards at the doors. When her captain and scribe bowed before her, she was standing stiffly at the foot of her throne, her heart leaping wildly.

"Have you enough light?" she demanded. The scribe sank cross-legged before her and nodded, dipping his pen in the ink and waiting. "Then take this letter." She was whispering, her throat constricted with excitement. "To His Majesty King Suppiluliumas, Lord of the Khatti. You know his titles; put them in. Then say, 'My husband is dead, and I have no son. People say that your sons are fully grown. If you will send me one of your sons, he will become my husband, for I do not wish to take one of my subjects to make him into my husband.' What is 'Queen' in Akkadian?"

"Dahamunzu."

"Then sign it 'Dahamunzu.' What are you staring at?" Both men's eyes were fixed on her in dumb astonishment. "I know exactly what I am doing. If Suppiluliumas does what I ask, the threat from the Khatti will be over. You may speak, Captain."

"But, Majesty, they are our enemies! A Khatti on the Horus Throne?"

"Yes." She was recovering her composure now that the feverish words had left her mouth. "Think! A marriage that will forever end the possibility of invasion. The foreign prince will have no real power in Egypt, for I will hold it." Suddenly aware of her trembling limbs, she sank onto the throne. "I do not have to explain myself to you. I command simply that you do what you are told. Take the scroll to Boghaz-keuoi yourself, telling no one along the way what your mission is. But be careful at Memphis—Horemheb has many troops there watching the river traffic and patrolling the desert road into Syria. If you are questioned, tell them you are carrying orders to May from the Fledgling Smenkhara."

"But, Majesty," the man persisted, still livid with shock, "our army marches on the Khatti even now. I could find myself in the middle of a battle that Egypt might win!"

I do not want Egypt to win, Nefertiti found herself thinking coldly. *Such a victory would make Horemheb the most dangerous man in the country.* "I do not think our forces have yet met the Khatti," she replied. "And even if they have, and are winning, the negotiations I am opening will simply ensure our stability. Leave tonight. How long is the trip to Boghaz-keuoi?"

"At least three weeks, Majesty."

Apprehension twisted in Nefertiti's stomach. *No,* she thought. *I must not begin to count the days, not yet, or I shall go mad.* "Do your best to make it less. Take gold to bribe the Apiru in Sinai and to buy horses from them. Take an escort, but not so large that you are conspicuous. If you succeed in this, soldier, I will reward you with a fortune and a much higher commission in my service. You, scribe, your tongue will be cut out and your hands crushed if you breathe one word of tonight's work. Do you understand?" He nodded, holding up the scroll, and she pressed her seal into the warm wax and thrust the document at the captain. "Commandeer what transport you need. You already have that authority."

Before he had finished bowing, she had left the room, still trembling. Sliding beneath her sheets, she drew them to her chin and closed her eyes. Sleep did not come easily. She imagined the captain making his way to the wharf where her vessels were tethered, speaking to her overseer in the torch-lit darkness, entering one of her boats. Determinedly she cast about for other, more soothing thoughts. Events had been set in motion, and all she could do was wait.

Horemheb had also set certain events in motion, but unlike Nefertiti, he made no attempt to divert himself from their outcome. As the period of mourning for Pharaoh began, a time when traditionally only the most pressing official acts were performed and the tempo of court life slowed, he retired to his estate to ponder the ramifications of his order to mobilize the army and the probable course Smenkhara's administration might take. He had already begun to receive dispatches from his officers as the army flowed slowly into southern Syria, and had passed them on to Ay, as he had promised. He longed to be in the field with the soldiers, knowing that they respected him not only because he was a capable commander but also because he was not above sharing the hardships of active duty with them: the bad food, rough sleeping conditions, and exhausting marches that were the lot of the serving soldier. Morale would be lower with his absence. The officers would be saying among themselves that the commander had stayed safely at Akhetaten because he had little faith in a successful outcome to the coming engagement with the Khatti, no matter what excuses he had given them.

But he did not dare to leave the city until Smenkhara had been crowned, for in spite of his words to Ay regarding the trust and friendship between them, their relationship was rapidly cooling. Ay did not believe that Egypt's salvation lay with the military. Indeed, he viewed the possible rise of a powerful officer elite with suspicion. Accustomed all his life to dealing with crises through diplomacy and indirect control, he saw the decline of the empire and the threat from Suppiluliumas as a failure on the part of Akhenaten to maintain proper diplomatic relations with the rest of the world and the solution as a return to communication through envoys and ambassadors. Horemheb fervently disagreed and knew that he must remain close to the new pharaoh to press his arguments for an escalating war in the event that Ay managed to ingratiate himself with Smenkhara. There was no indication that the prince cared for either of them, but Horemheb wanted to take no chances.

As he walked his gardens with Mutnodjme, sat beside her as they ate the evening meal together on the quiet terrace to watch the moon rise, talked to her easily of the day-to-day

concerns of the state, he thought over his audience with Smenkhara and his later conversation with Ay, anxiously asking
himself time and again whether what he had done was truly in
the interest of his country or the result of a purely personal
frustration. Either way, there was no going back.

He was sitting under the shade of the sycamores that surrounded his small lake one afternoon, watching his wife swim
effortlessly back and forth, when the daily dispatch was brought
to him. Thanking the herald and dismissing him, he broke the
seal. The scroll was unusually long, and when he had read it,
he began it again, perusing it slowly. Then he dropped it into
his white lap and stared at it thoughtfully. He was unaware that
Mutnodjme had swum up to him until he felt a cool touch and
came to himself with a start. She was leaning on the marble
rim that surrounded the water, her chin resting on her folded
hands, squinting up at him.

"You look pensive," she said. "Or are you merely stupefied
with the heat? It is becoming difficult for me to tell these days.
Perhaps you are in love."

He smiled. "I am sorry, Mutnodjme. I have been very preoccupied since I have been at home."

"So I have noticed." With one lithe movement she pulled
herself onto the stone. A servant came running, towel held out,
and with arms raised Mutnodjme allowed herself to be dried
and then sank to the mat beside Horemheb's chair and began
to unpin her youth lock. "If I had known just how preoccupied
you were going to be lately, I would not have canceled two
boating parties and a trip north just to be with you." She combed
through the long tresses of waving hair with her fingers and
lay back on one elbow. "I see that another dispatch has arrived.
Is anything wrong?"

With a sigh he laid the scroll in the grass and lowered himself
beside her. Her brown hip was cool against his arm. "Many
of the soldiers are sick with fever at Urusalim," he said, "but
that is not the worst problem the officers are facing. According
to our scouts, not only are the Khatti advancing south but the
Assyrians are halfway to northern Syria. If I order the army to
continue north, it may have to fight them first, before the
Khatti. If I order it to wait, and the Khatti and the Assyrians
fight, Egypt will have to meet whatever army is victorious."

Mutnodjme nodded. "I suppose the Assyrians are trying to
invade Amki again. Every time there has been a dispute be-

tween the great powers, they have taken advantage of the confusion to try and wrest Amki from us. But now that the Khatti have taken our little dependency, the Assyrians may well intend to fight them. Poor Amki. What will you do, Horemheb? Order your officers to wait where they are and let the Khatti and the Assyrians batter at one another?"

"If the army keeps moving, it will first have to retake Amki, before Suppuluiumas can arrive to defend it." He began to stroke her leg, but his thoughts were far away. "Frankly, Mutnodjme, I am afraid that Ay was right. The army is sluggish and untried and would not be capable of the swift maneuvering that would be necessary to retake Amki and then turn to face the Khatti or Assyria. I think I will order the men to proceed a little way, into Rethennu, and then wait."

She sat up, swiveling to face him. "Horemheb, what will you do if Egypt suffers a defeat?" she asked quietly. "The blow to your credibility at court would be so great that any chance you might have had to advise Smenkhara would be gone."

He pushed the torrent of damp hair out of the way and kissed her. "I will face one anxiety at a time," he replied. "Now I must go into the house and dictate a letter to my second-in-command." He retrieved the scroll and got to his feet. "Perhaps you should visit friends tonight or go across the river and spend the evening with your parents. I know I am not very good company, Mutnodjme."

She laughed. "I do not think I could be bothered to get dressed and painted. I will order a picnic for us here, by the lake. Go away, Horemheb. I want to swim again."

As he walked away, he heard a splash behind him as she dove into the water. *What* will *I do if Egypt is defeated?* he asked himself as he gained the coolness of the entrance hall. He did not want to consider an answer.

Akhetaten observed the period of mourning for Pharaoh quietly. The harvest was gathered, and all settled to endure the barren heat of high summer. Small crowds still gathered in the blazing forecourt of the Aten temple while Meryra performed the rites in the sanctuary, but the stately gestures and chants lacked animation. The man who had stood between the Aten and the people, who had ordered that every prayer must be directed to him for interpretation to the god, was dead. The city, too, seemed bereft of its essence. It had been built for one purpose, as a vast shrine to contain the living embodiment of the god, its existence the result of Akhenaten's struggle to give his visions reality. His presence had validated it; its unity rested in the worship its citizens gave to him and the Aten. But now that presence had gone, and already the small Aten altars on almost every street corner were joined by shrines to the deities beloved by the commoners so that they would be worshiped equally with the dead pharaoh's god. The feeling of sudden rootlessness in the city was more than the usual hiatus between administrations. The invisible foundations of Akhetaten were trembling.

Within the confines of the palace, however, most courtiers performed their morning and evening devotions to the Aten as usual. Their continuation of prayers to the god was not only a matter of familiarity, but also of expediency: the heir had not yet indicated whether his divinity would spring from Amun or the Aten.

Smenkhara seemed to care for neither. He and Meritaten spent the breathless days constantly together, striving to recapture their first joy in each other, but it came only fleetingly. They wooed it with a sometimes embarrassed deliberation by recalling all the bright memories of childhood they had shared, but the love that had bound them belonged to the innocence of that youth, a fragile emotion that had not withstood the depredations they had both suffered at Akhenaten's hands. The strength of their past had made deep bonds between them that nothing could break, but not the fully realized union of a mature love.

The air of aimless dislocation that hung over city and palace did not infect Nefertiti. In spite of her determination to fill the intervening days with diversions, she found herself waking each morning from a plague of nightmares, with muscles already stiff from apprehension and body bathed in sweat. Many times she cursed herself for an act she imagined as dangerously precipitate, but more often she gazed into a future that would otherwise be as predictable as the sunrise and was glad she had carried out her plan. During the long, searing days she sat drinking and looking out over the drooping vegetation of the terraces, her eyes eventually aching as they scanned the river for her captain's craft, for any new activity down on her docks. At night she watched Tutankhaten prepare for bed, walked in the gardens, lay on her couch while her male dancers wove their stately steps with finger cymbals clashing and flowers around their naked waists, but under the flush of sexual titillation the young servants caused her there was always the cold fear. Her captain had been intercepted, and her father and Horemheb were playing with her before she was arrested. Suppiluliumas had casually had him put to death and forgotten about her. He had become lost in the desert and died of thirst. The steady drip of the water clock was a continual irritation. She carried the pain of anxiety under her breastbone and could eat only sparingly, without pleasure.

Her father visited her twice, spending several hours with Tutankhaten before settling himself in her company and taking the wine and pastries she brusquely offered. She tried to treat him with politeness but could not conceal her preoccupation. Though she enquired after the health of her daughters and listened patiently to him talk of Horemheb's increasing brusqueness, she knew she had not concealed her anxiety, for he left with a puzzled air. She did not care and turned to her station at the window with relief.

Six weeks almost to the day after the captain had left, Nefertiti was woken from a light sleep by her steward Meryra and started up, already fully awake.

"He is back," Meryra whispered. "Shall I have him wait in the audience hall?"

"No. Get rid of my women." She pushed back the sheet and rose, both hands against the fluttering of her heart. "Bring him here immediately." He bowed and retreated into the shadows. Nefertiti lit the night lamp with her own hands, and, groping for her sleeping gown, slipped it over her head. She could hardly control her shaking fingers. *I should be bathed and dressed, put a wig on and be painted*, she thought. *I did not ask Meryra if the captain was alone. Oh, gods, I am afraid!*

Tensely she waited through the moments before the captain entered, and then she watched him kneel and prostrate himself, crawling to kiss her bare feet before answering her choked command to rise. "Where is he?" she managed. "Have you brought a prince. What happened?"

"Great One, I am no diplomat," he said in a low voice. "I did not know with what words to validate the scroll. Suppiluliumas does not believe it is genuine. He thinks that Egypt simply wants a hostage. He has sent his own steward back with me to ascertain the truth. It was not easy, evading Horemheb's

patrols on the border and having to sail past Memphis at night.
We are both very tired."

Bitter anger filled Nefertiti. "Didn't you impress on the
Khatti the urgency of this thing? I must have a prince before
Akhenaten's funeral, or all is lost! Where is this steward?"

The captain bowed himself to the door. Nefertiti watched
as a tall shadow detached itself from the night and emerged
into the faint lamplight. "I am Khattusaziti, Chamberlain to
Suppiluliumas the Mighty," a soft, deep voice said. "Are you
Dahamunzu Nefertiti?"

"I am."

He bowed slightly, and for a moment they considered each
other. *I suppose he is a brave man,* Nefertiti thought, looking
up into the leathery face almost hidden by a beard and long,
well-oiled black hair. *He does not know that I am not part of
some larger conspiracy, or that at any moment he may lose his
head. And what a head! Do all the vile Asiatics breed warriors
like this?*

"My king believed that you were dead," he said at last.
"The seal on the scroll matched imprints on other correspondence, but your ring could have been used by anyone."

"My husband did his best to kill me without touching my
body," she said acidly. "He obliterated every inscription of my
name he could find, but as you can see, I am far from dead."

She removed her seal ring and handed it to him. He peered
at it and laid it back on the extended palm. "In that case,
Majesty, why are you negotiating with my lord in this secretive
way? You say you have no sons. My king doubts that this is
true. But if it is, then who is to be pharaoh, and why do you
want to try to set a Khatti on the throne?"

She indicated that he should sit and herself sank onto the
couch. "Captain, have refreshments brought," she called, and
then she met the foreigner's eyes. "My husband's brother will
take the Double Crown if my plan fails. He is useless. If he
knew I had opened correspondence with your master, he would
arrest me. Egypt will lose a war with your people, with Smenkhara at the helm. But if you give me a Khatti prince there
will be no need for the wastage of lives and gold a full-scale
confrontation between our nations would mean. Egypt will
become a Khatti vassal, responsible for her own internal affairs
but paying tribute to Suppiluliumas."

"What guarantee is there that your enemies will not simply

kill him as soon as he arrives? I presume you will want him backed up with Khatti soldiers?"

Nefertiti was glad that the food she had ordered was now being quietly set out before them. She had not anticipated the complications her plan might bring. All at once chilled and wishing she were not sitting here under the sharp scrutiny of an enemy whose sheer vitality overawed her, she forced a smile. "Only Commander Horemheb is capable of resisting. Smenkhara will sulk, but all will be grateful that the Khatti threat to Egypt has been dealt with." Surprise followed by something she suspected was derision flitted across his eyes. She raised her cup, and immediately he reached for his.

"If my lord entrusts a son to the dubious goodwill of Egypt, he will want to see your pledges backed up by the presence of Khatti soldiers in Akhetaten. A pharaoh is only as powerful as his support."

"That may be true of the rulers of your country, but not in Egypt. A pharaoh, once crowned, is a god, and his sacredness cannot be lightly threatened."

He smiled, showing crooked white teeth that gleamed in the dimness, and again an expression resembling mild contempt wrinkled the battered face. "A Khatti as a god? What an exalted prospect! Simply because he was a god your people endured the incompetence of your dead husband?"

She was offended by the familiarity of his tone. "An ignorant foreigner cannot be expected to understand the subtleties of Ma'at," she said coldly. "That is something I will teach the prince your master must send."

"That I *do* understand." The humility in his voice was faintly mocking. "I will return to my lord and tell him of your intentions."

"Leave now, tonight." She stood, and politely he rose also. "Precious time has been wasted by Suppiluliumas's mistrust. If I do not have a husband within a month, we will all be groveling to Smenkhara, and once he is crowned, only his death would release the throne for another. Meryra will show you to a room where you can sleep for an hour while I dictate another message to your king, and I will send an ambassador with you this time. You are dismissed."

He inclined his leonine head and turned away, but as if a thought had suddenly struck him, he swung back. "May I have permission to speak once more?" he asked with quick servility.

She nodded. "It occurs to me that Egypt's messengers may not travel as fast as the queen's spies. Therefore the queen may not know that my lord has repulsed the Egyptian army and has completely occupied Amki. There was no great slaughter but a wondrous scattering. Sleep well, Majesty."

He slipped out of the circle of weak light, and she knew he had gone only by the sound of the doors closing quietly. Meryra had come in and was waiting for further orders. Nefertiti realized that her head was aching intolerably, and her hands were pressed to both burning cheeks. She forced them away. Egypt defeated. She knew that she was glad, for Horemheb would be weakened, and all Egyptians would be grateful to her for averting the invasion that otherwise would surely follow. But under the relief of her thoughts was a burden of shame and sadness in her heart, wounded pride for her country and a flood of blind anger at her dead husband, who had betrayed them all. Turning her back on her patient steward, she quelled a ridiculous impulse to cry. *Egypt is nothing but a herd of beasts with dumb eyes turned to their rulers for direction*, she reminded herself. *Surely such beasts will put their safety above any intangible love for mere soil and water!* She fought down the pain and was at last able to face Meryra calmly. "Precious time has been wasted," she said. "Now there must be no mistakes. I need an ambassador, Meryra, someone who loved my husband and is devoted to me, someone who does not look forward to the prospect of being ruled by a pharaoh whose allegiance to the Aten is questionable. Such a man might be persuaded to act for me and keep his counsel if it is put to him that the Khatti worship the sun and a Khatti pharaoh would be better than an Amun man."

"Your Majesty might offer him some more concrete reward for his endeavors, also," Meryra replied politely. "The promise of a position as the new pharaoh's Eyes and Ears perhaps, and a substantial quantity of gold. Hani might be suitable. Since Osiris Akhenaten ceased to make use of the diplomats, many of them have been idle and unpaid. Hani has always been a worrier with ambitions. Such a combination might well suit Your Majesty's purpose."

"Remind me to reward you also, Meryra," she said. "Very well. Hani will do. Make the offer of preferment to him first so as to make his mouth water, then tell him what he must do, then threaten him, but very gently. We do not want to frighten him into running to Ay. If he balks, or appears too eager, have him killed at once. Rouse him and send him with Khattusaziti, and do not let him speak to anyone. Now I will dictate a new scroll to Suppiluliumas. Take the dictation yourself." Meryra took up palette and pen and sank to the floor by the lamp as Nefertiti began. "Start with his titles as before. Then say, 'Your chamberlain Khattusaziti reports to me that you thought me dead and that you do not believe that I have no son. Why do you accuse me of having deceived you? He who was my husband is dead, and I have no son. If I had a son, would I indeed write abroad to publish the distress of myself and my country? Be assured that I have written to no other country, but only to you. Everyone believes that you have many sons. Give me one in order that he may be my husband and reign in Egypt!'" She wanted to say more, to pour more than her bitterness and pride onto the papyrus, but she fell silent and, after waiting to seal the scroll, waved Meryra out. The empty room was redolent with the gray despondency of the hour before dawn. With the weariness of an old habit despised but impossible to break, she dragged a chair to the window, although it still showed her only darkness.

25

HOREMHEB ROSE AS AY CAME INTO THE ROOM, HIS HAND already out in an apologetic greeting, his eyes indicating the chair set for the fanbearer. The antechamber was airless and dark but for the one lamp Horemheb had himself lighted and carried in from his bedchamber. Ay advanced slowly, still drugged with a heavy, restless sleep, trying to gather his wits for whatever this strange request might bring, yet for the present aware only of his laboring breath. He held the commander's lean fingers briefly before lowering himself into the proffered seat and wiping the sweat from his face. His eyes burned; his mouth felt dry and foul. His mind was full of the nightmare he had been having when his steward had shaken him awake, and the terror of it still quickened his heartbeat. The same dream came to him often these nights, sometimes jerking him awake to reach for Tey's reassuring body but more often lasting until the first grayness of dawn, leaving him exhausted and frightened.

"There is water if you need it," Horemheb said quietly, himself taking a chair. "Forgive me for disturbing you in the middle of the night, Fanbearer, but this could not wait, and although you and I have seen little of each other lately, I did not want to act alone on a matter of such gravity."

Surprised, Ay studied the commander. Horemheb was naked in the heat. His shoulder-length black hair straggled stickily against his brown neck. Without paint, his face was open to Ay's gaze, still handsome, now tensely alert, making Ay feel old, flabby, and sick. *I shall die before you*, Ay thought. *I knew it but had not really considered it before. I think I have always envied you, my imperious son-in-law.* "Tell me," he said tersely.

Horemheb handed him a scroll and pushed the lamp toward him. At any other time Ay might have considered the gesture an insult to his failing powers, but tonight he simply unrolled the papyrus and began to read.

Once finished, he did not need to look at it again. Carefully he let it roll up, placed it on the table, and then folded his hands, feeling Horemheb's steady gaze on him. For a long time he could not move, but finally he had composed himself enough to look up and meet the commander's eyes. "How did you come by this scroll?" he asked shakily.

"May sent it to me from the fort that guards the desert road into southern Syria," Horemheb replied, himself immobile as he regarded Ay. "A small company passed through from Egypt, one of our ambassadors and a foreigner who said he was a Canaanite envoy on his way home to Askalon to help arrange a sale of grain to us, but May became suspicious and had the ambassador's belongings searched while the two travelers were resting." He pointed at the roll of papyrus on the table. "The original of that was in the man's pouch. May did not know whether to detain the company, or whether we at court were involved with your daughter's help in some complex negotiation with the Khatti, so he let them proceed. It is as well for us that May followed his intuition."

Shocked and sick at heart, Ay dropped his gaze. "This is

not a royal woman seeking to fill the emptiness of her bed with a lover," he ventured. "This is my daughter, a queen of Egypt, engaged secretly in deepest treason with an enemy." He knew he must not ask Horemheb what should be done, and thus put himself in the position of an underling. The first advantage had been the commander's, and Ay must not strengthen it. "Nefertiti has always been in love with position and power but lacking the means to retain what she did acquire," he offered in the steadiest voice he could. "But I cannot believe her capable of perceiving this plot as cold-blooded treason. Surely all she saw was a desperate chance to regain an active role in government."

"I agree," Horemheb said. "But I am surprised that she was capable of conceiving such a plan at all, and having taken it, Ay. If May had not had his wits about him, if her ambassador had passed unseen . . ."

"But he did not," Ay cut in, still battling the emotion that threatened to disarm him. *My daughter. My own flesh, willing to hand over the whole of Egypt in one moment at a time when the country is in agony. Does she feel any remorse? Did she battle any shame?*

"No, he did not," Horemheb reiterated slowly. "So we must decide what to do. I am particularly shocked because the queen cannot have known the outcome of the battle with Suppiluliumas when she began to make her overtures. She cannot therefore even be excused by the justification that this was Egypt's only chance for peace after defeat. It is nothing but the most ruthless bid for power."

"Such self-righteousness, from a man with his own glance straying to the Double Crown!" Ay snapped, stung into an irrational defense of his daughter, for whom, he had already been forced to acknowledge, there was no defense. "I know you well, Horemheb, as you know me. If the opportunity came your way, you would take it, wouldn't you?"

"I am tired of seeing the might of Egypt passing and passing again into hands not worthy or capable of controlling it!" Horemheb shouted back. "Years ago I should have risked all to depose Akhenaten and find a faithful son of Amun to place on the throne, as you should. We, too, are traitors for letting the greatest empire in the world die slowly while we argued the validity of the Aten's right to rule Egypt through your nephew!" Horemheb sat back, breathing hard, and Ay scanned him slowly.

"You think you are safe in revealing yourself to me tonight

because I am old, and you believe my day is over," he said softly. "But you are wrong, Commander, so be prudent in what you say. Your own position has never been more precarious. Your bid for influence over Smenkhara through a successful war did not work." He wanted a drink of water but would not reach for the jug. "But you did not ask me to come to air our personal grievances. We must solve this dilemma."

"It is no dilemma." Horemheb had retreated, leaning back into the shadows so his face was in darkness. "She deserves execution."

"Whether she deserves it or not, we cannot kill her. The credibility and veneration accorded to royalty has never been weaker. Egypt is weary of its ruler's selfishness and is crying out for reassurance. If a queen is put under the knife, that credibility will be destroyed. How can a goddess be executed by her worshipers? The common people must never be allowed to ask themselves that question. Besides, Horemheb, Nefertiti is no Tiye. She is not entirely responsible for actions whose consequences she did not foresee."

"So speaks the doting father!" Horemheb sneered. "She could have saved Egypt long ago, when Akhenaten adored and trusted her, but she was too selfish and stupid to try. She deserves death. But you are right when you speak of political necessity. Therefore I suggest that we send to May, ordering him to lie in wait for this prince just over the border and kill him and all with him when he appears."

"Providing Suppiluliumas cooperates." Despondently Ay had come to realize in the course of their conversation that Horemheb need not have consulted him at all. He could have made the excuse that it was primarily a military matter and dealt with it himself, presenting Ay later with a remedy already applied. Pulling the water toward him, he drank deeply. *I wonder how long it will be*, he thought darkly, *before Horemheb realizes that Nefertiti could be killed secretly and some innocuous story spread for the benefit of the peasants. She has been living quietly in the north palace for so long that many must believe her already dead.*

"Oh, he will," Horemheb replied emphatically. "Whatever doubts he may have, he will not neglect an opportunity for a bloodless victory. He has loomed over Egypt for so long that we have begun to imbue him with the attributes of a god, but he is not without weaknesses. Yes, he sent our army fleeing, but if our soldiers had been even slightly better prepared, the story would have been different. One day we will defeat him."

"But we cannot dream of one day. We must consider the next hour," Ay reminded him dryly. "Does Smenkhara know of this?" *It was a foolish question*, Ay thought even as he asked it. *Of course Horemheb would have gone straight to the prince for permission to act, and Smenkhara must have insisted that the commander confer with me. Otherwise*, Ay thought, *I might never have known of this*.

"Yes," Horemheb answered. "He has graciously consented to wait while we deliberate, and, of course, if we had disagreed on a plan of action, he would have had the last word. Shall we go to him?"

Ay pulled himself out of the chair and stood for a moment to allow his heartbeat to slow before following Horemheb from the room.

Smenkhara, like Horemheb, was naked but for a sweat-stained blue ribbon bound around his forehead and a small turquoise Eye of Horus hanging on a thin gold chain around his neck. He was slumped on the throne in his reception room, cushions under him, one heel hooked high on the edge of the gilt seat, one pale arm resting on a raised knee. They knelt before him and rose, waiting for him to speak. In here there were many lamps, and Smenkhara did not seem to mind the added heat or their throat-catching perfume.

"Well, Uncle," he said caustically, "my royal cousin has outdone herself in foolishness this time. Is there any reason why she should not be killed or exiled? Perhaps we could send her to the Khatti, seeing that she seems to have such a desire for their company."

It was a personal accusation, and Ay prepared to answer, but surprisingly Horemheb said quickly, "Highness, nothing would be served by the queen's death. The fanbearer and I propose that sentries be posted in northern Syria and a small accident arranged for the foreigner who will surely come. If we are clever, even Suppiluliumas will not be able to accuse Egypt directly of the murder."

"Nothing would be served?" Smenkhara cut in violently, his voice rising, the languid hand hanging from his knee suddenly clenching. "My mother promised me the Double Crown. She promised! I deserve it. It is mine by right of blood, and Nefertiti would have taken it from me!"

Curiously Ay watched the color rise quickly in the long face, the shallow chest heave with emotion. He did not dare to meet Horemheb's eye, but he knew the commander was also keenly aware of the faint echo of Akhenaten. For the first time in many months a moment of mutual understanding passed between the two men, and as though the prince had sensed it, he ran a hand quickly and almost defensively over his shaven skull.

"I suppose it does not matter," he went on more calmly. "In a short time Akhenaten will be buried, and I will be Pharaoh, with Meritaten as my queen. What can my cousin do then?" He leaned forward slightly and stared coldly at the two men. "You both realize that if you ambush the foreigner, you must be sure to kill every member of his entourage, including any of Nefertiti's messengers. Otherwise word will get back to Suppiluliumas."

Horemheb nodded. "Your Highness can leave the details to me."

Smenkhara shot a shrewd glance at his uncle. "Does the fanbearer have any objections?"

Ay bowed. "None, Fledgling."

Smenkhara uncurled, stood, and without another look at them strode into the shadows. Ay let out a long breath. Horemheb was smiling at him quizzically. "It is like stepping back ten years, is it not?" he remarked.

"Use the cavalry, Commander," Ay said, ignoring Horemheb's comment, "and disguise the men as desert Apiru. The Khatti prince's escort will doubtless be mounted, and we want no mistakes. Everyone knows how dangerous the desert road has become. We may just succeed with it."

"A good idea." Horemheb's eyes cleared in a flash. "Do you want copies of my directives to May?"

"No. Only send me word when it is all over." Ay managed a sketchy, polite bow before turning and walking slowly away. He had never been so weary.

The period of mourning for Akhenaten was drawing to a close. Day after day Nefertiti sat by the window in silence, searching the hot silver surface of the river flowing below, watching the flicker of the torches she had ordered to be set along the banks at night. She woke each dawn after brief and troubled sleeps with bloodshot, itching eyes and hands already shaking with an anxiety she could no longer control. She could not bear to be addressed and would answer with sharp words or tears that inflamed her eyes even more. Her physician prescribed an ointment that gummed her lashes together and caused her to sit hour upon hour whisking at the flies attracted by its strong odor, but at least it cooled her eyes and afforded her some relief. She at last forced herself away from the damning window, lying instead on her couch in a darkened room. No one came near her. Even Tutankhaten, a placid and biddable boy, had grown weary of her screams and the sting of her fist and kept to his own apartments and the peace of the empty gardens. Nefertiti tasted her own loneliness and found it bitter.

On the morning of her husband's funeral she found the strength to sit at her cosmetics table to be painted. With vanity she laid aside the ointment in order to wear kohl, but her face had to be washed and washed again, so badly did her eyes water. There was still time for the Khatti prince to arrive. Anything could have happened to him, to Hani: lame horses, a detour to avoid discovery, illness, perhaps. They might even now be approaching Akhetaten. At the thought she opened her eyes, and her cosmetician stifled an exclamation of annoyance and reached for a damp cloth. Smenkhara would not become divine until tomorrow. There were still hours, and any hour could bring deliverance. The heavy wig was lowered onto her head. The gold net set with lapis lazuli followed, attached carefully onto the coronet to which a hooded cobra, which she was allowed to wear, having once been a queen, was hooked. Behind her stood her tiring women, waiting to dress her in the blue sheath of mourning, the golden sandals, the diaphanous short blue cloak. Outside under the blazing sun her barge nudged the water steps whose every fleck of color, every angle, was now as familiar to her as her own face. "I must have wine if I am to get through this day," she gasped, feeling her eyes begin to run again, and immediately a servant knelt with a silver goblet. She drank quickly, without pleasure. *I began this torment*, she thought, *but I cannot end it*. Turning her face to the cosmetician, she waited for the man to wipe away the streaks of kohl from her cheeks. When it was time to depart, she found she could not walk without the unobtrusive support of her attendants.

Nefertiti kept her litter curtains closed during the walk to the place on the eastern edge of the city where the funeral

procession was forming. Though she could hear the cries of
her heralds and guards clearing a way for her through the
crowds gathered on either side of the Royal Road in the hope
of catching a glimpse of her, she had no wish to satisfy their
curiosity or see the acres of buildings and gardens that had
once represented so much happiness to her. Once away from
the center of the city, however, the noise of the populace died
away, and she looped back the hangings, shielding her eyes
against the glare of sun on the sand. The Overseer of Protocol
approached her, bowing and indicating to her bearers the position behind the coffin that she was to occupy. As she was
carried forward, Meritaten and Ankhesenpaaten detached themselves from their retinue. The litter halted. Nefertiti leaned out
hesitantly, and her daughters knelt, both in tears, to embrace
her. Briefly she held them close, and then, signaling her steward
that she was ready to proceed, she withdrew, once more pulling
the curtains closed. She had no wish to watch her husband's
body being dragged across the sand toward the barren, rocky
gully he had selected for his tomb. Behind her she could hear
Meritaten and Ankhesenpaaten sobbing and farther back the
formal ululations of the mourners, but her own eyes were dry.
She would find no more tears for Akhenaten. They had all
been shed long ago.

Akhenaten had composed the burial rite himself, with all
the joy in his god and appreciation for beauty of which he had
been capable. The words Meryra intoned, the steps prescribed
for the dancers, the music floating in the still air, all combined
to impress upon those present both the grandeur and the pathos
of the era that was now ended. Even the many enemies of
Akhenaten among the courtiers forgot for a while that they
were entombing a pharaoh who had led them all along the path
of his delusion, and remembered only that he had been a man
of honesty.

During the ceremonies Nefertiti sat under a canopy, turning
occasionally to the surreptitious ministrations of her cosmetician, trying to hide the agitation of her hands. In spite of her
determination to be still, she could not prevent herself from
glancing often to the place where the gully opened out into
desert, and beyond that, unseen, the river. But the sand shimmered in the heat, the rock shook, and there was no sign of
any messenger.

Smenkhara stepped forward to Open the Mouth. It was the

most solemn moment of any funeral, and all eyes ought to have been fixed on the heir, but Nefertiti became increasingly aware that the stares of the company were directed at her. *It is not so, it is my imagination*, she tried to tell herself. But glancing over the crowd from under lowered lids, she found her father gazing at her with the sleepy regard that had always indicated speculative thought, and beside him, Horemheb's eyes met hers coldly and steadily. Panic rose in her throat, acrid and dry, and she became frantic for wine. Tearing her gaze away, she looked to the ceremony just as Smenkhara handed the sacred knife to Meryra and turned, and he, too, seemed to fix her with an accusatory stare. Suddenly she felt as though every eye was on her, piercing her, hostile and condemning. Sweat began to stream down her face. Casting her eyes downward, she strove to ignore them. Pain struck under her breastbone, and she clutched at herself, suppressing a groan. *I must show nothing*, she told herself dimly through the panic. *If I flee I will give them an excuse to despise me all the more.* But even as the thought entered her mind, she found herself swaying to her feet. "What are you staring at, you sacrilegious peasants?" she shouted. "I am a queen! Avert your eyes!"

Meryra stopped singing, and the rite faltered. Now, indeed, she saw, every eye had turned to her in blank astonishment. Tears blurred her vision. Nefertiti felt a hand close firmly over her arm.

"Be quiet, Majesty," her half sister's voice breathed close to her ear. "Do you want them to think you are mad? Is this grief or illness?"

Nefertiti shrank from Mutnodjme's touch, but then another hand gently touched her shoulder, and without opening her eyes Nefertiti knew it was Tey. "I want to go home," she whispered into the shocked silence. Mutnodjme glanced at her husband. Horemheb nodded once and then curtly bade Meryra continue. Quickly Mutnodjme and Tey helped Nefertiti to her litter through the whispering throng. Out of the corner of her eye Nefertiti glimpsed Tutankhaten, resplendent in glinting jaspers and snowy linen, his black youth lock plaited and wound with blue ribbons, watching her with curiosity. Ankhesenpaaten took a step toward her mother, but Ay restrained her. Meritaten, face puckered with worry, remained at Smenkhara's side.

"Take a massage and lie down," Tey said soothingly to Nefertiti as she held open the curtains of the litter for her. "I will go into the tomb with your flowers. Your isolation is foolish, Majesty. Come to your father's house this evening. The mourning is over. We will have music and dancing, and then you will feel better."

Nefertiti dabbed at her cheeks and looked away. "I do not feel well enough," she said stiffly, furious with herself for her lapse and bitter with embarrassment at her loss of dignity. "Perhaps later, Tey."

Tey bowed good-naturedly and let the curtains fall. The litter started off. Nefertiti heard the chanting resume and then gradually fade as her bearers left the cliff and veered toward the city. Full of shame, she curled on the cushions with her face in her hands. The Khatti prince had not come. Akhenaten was buried. She had failed in her bid to salvage something of her life, and hot tears flowed through her fingers.

Just after sunset Nefertiti's steward announced her father. She had returned to the north palace and had gone immediately to her couch, having it moved so that she could lie bolstered with pillows and look out the window, even though a reason for vigilance no longer existed. She was listlessly playing with her rings in the soft pink light of evening when Ay greeted her, coming to stand beside the bed. He bowed, breathing heavily, and she indicated that he might sit.

"I used to run up those steps to the terrace," he wheezed, "but today I had them carry me in my litter. Time is cruel, Majesty."

She glanced at him sharply, but his scarlet, perspiring face was bland. "If you have come to enquire after my welfare, I am better," she said. "It was the heat, and my grief."

"Ah." He nodded understandingly. "That is unfortunate, but do not fret over it, Nefertiti. Everyone knows how devoted you were to Osiris Akhenaten, even though he did not treat you well."

Again she gave him a keen look, and this time saw his half-smile. "He would be wounded to hear you call him an Osiris one," she smiled back. "I am generous enough, Father, to hope that the Aten gives him the rewards he deserved."

"Perhaps the Aten will try, but perhaps the other gods will be enraged at the fate your husband brought upon Egypt and will not allow Akhenaten's divinity to bring him blessedness."

She leaned back and closed her eyes, resisting the desire to

rub them. "Can I have them bring you anything?" she murmured. "It is so good to have grapes again, and pomegranates,
and the melons are huge this year. My granaries are full. So
strange, a funeral at the time of harvest."

"No food, thank you, Majesty."

She heard a hesitation in his voice and, opening her eyes,
rolled her head towards him on the pillow. "You did not come
to enquire after my health or discuss the harvest," she said.
"What is it, Father?"

Ay leaned into the last shaft of red light that lay across the
couch. "May I dismiss your women?"

"Of course."

He gave a command, and the servants gathered up the games
and trinkets that had been amusing them and filed out. When
they had gone, Ay sat quietly for a moment, fingers pyramided
under his chin, and Nefertiti, watching his eyes half-close in
thought, was suddenly tense. Then his hands loosened.

"I am going to take Tutankhaten away from the north palace," he said. "As the only male left of Amunhotep's line he
should be receiving the education and training proper to his
station."

"I see," she replied slowly, still watching his face. "But is
it not too early yet to assume that Smenkhara and my daughter
will not produce a son? They are young. They could have many
children. Any son of theirs would inherit the throne."

Ay sighed. "I cannot wait to see what the future will bring.
I must prepare now for any eventuality. If Smenkhara had come
to power in a different age, when Egypt was strong and her
administration sure, his character would not matter. But he is
spoiled, angry, and weak. He will do nothing to bring order
out of the governmental chaos your husband left. He is fawned
upon by young men who want wealth but no responsibility."
He paused, and Nefertiti realized that twilight now filled the
room, and her father's features were becoming indistinct. "The
hope of salvation for Egypt that was kindled when your husband
died will not last long when this country sees that Smenkhara
is not able to rule and has no ministers left who could form an
effective administration. In times like these the jackals gather,
the assassins, the power-hungry, the ambitious without scru-
ples. If Smenkhara dies or is murdered, there must be a clear
successor."

Nefertiti began to sift the rings that lay scattered on her

sheets. "I see that you have given this much thought," she said dryly. "What makes you think that Tutankhaten will be acceptable to Egypt? He is, after all, a living reminder of the curse my aunt brought about by her marriage to her son." She peered at him, wanting to read his expression but seeing nothing now but the gray oval of his face.

"I will make sure that he is raised in the traditional manner, as a servant of Amun, a lover of the true gods of Egypt, a respecter of Amun's servants at Karnak. If anything happens to Smenkhara, Tutankhaten will represent Ma'at, the ancient rightness of things, a return to a healthy and prosperous Egypt."

Nefertiti turned and looked out the window. Far below, on the dock where her barge was tied, the torches flared orange, their reflections broken into shards against the rippling surface of the Nile. "And what of Horemheb?" she asked softly. "He is the one you fear, is he not? You are afraid that he will dominate Smenkhara, and then perhaps the little prince, and one day you will wake to find him regent, a man who all his life had relied on his great ambition to realize his fortune. Do you think if he tastes real power, he will be satisfied with a regent's place behind the throne?"

Ay now sat entirely in darkness, and the only indication that she had been heard was the quickened pace of his breathing. After a while he said, "Horemheb loves Egypt. He has always felt that he owes his country a debt. I do not yet know to what lengths he would go to pay it. Certainly his childlike faith in a pharaoh's omnipotence has been shaken."

"Are you not afraid to be so frank with me?" Nefertiti pushed the rings aside and swung her legs over the edge of the couch. She felt her knee brush her father's. "I am a queen. I have ruled, and my daughter Meritaten has not. What if I should go to Horemheb and offer him marriage? He could easily divorce Mutnodjme, or make her second wife. I have the people's sympathy. I am the poor queen banished by a heartless husband. Together we could depose and exile Smenkhara." She did not know why she was so certain that Ay was smiling into the darkness.

"My dear Nefertiti," he answered, an edge of humor to his voice that confirmed her impression. "I admire your tenacity. I pity you because your life has been full of suffering, and I love you because you were once my little girl, running through the gardens at Akhmin, but I do not really trust you. Do you think I would be speaking so openly to you tonight if I believed Horemheb would even listen to you?" He unexpectedly groped for her hand, and startled, Nefertiti responded to his touch. His fingers were dry and very warm. "Forgive me for what I am about to tell you, Majesty, if you can. Horemheb and I, and Smenkhara, too, have known of your plot to bring a Khatti prince to Akhetaten ever since your ambassador was intercepted at the border by May. To Horemheb you are a traitor."

Nefertiti went cold with shock. Tearing her hand from Ay's, she sprang to her feet, and ran to the door. "Lights!" she screamed, and servants hurried in with the lamps that had already been lit and stood in the passage, placing them around the room before bowing themselves out again. Now she could see Ay, half-turned on his chair, looking at her with his face twisted in concern and apology. "You knew and you did not tell me!" she shouted at him, rigid with pain. "You let me go on suffering, you let me believe, hope—even today I still hoped . . ." She swallowed. "I would never have presumed you to have so much cruelty in you."

"By then it was too late to halt your plot," he said. "It was simpler to have Prince Zennanza waylaid and killed in such a way that Suppiluliumas would believe the Apiru responsible. Now you see why Horemheb will have nothing to do with you."

"So my request was answered." She could feel tears of humiliation begin, already pricking agonizingly against her sore lids. "Suppiluliumas sent him. Prince Zennanza." She walked to the couch and sank down, arranging her linens over her knees with small, formal gestures, not looking at Ay. "By all means, take Tutankhaten away," she finished in a low voice. "Then there will be no need for me ever to speak to you again."

He rose and bowed. "I defended you before Horemheb," he said. "In spite of everything, I am your father, and you have my loyalty. But, Nefertiti, it is time for you to accept the lot life has cast for you, and be at peace. I will send for Tutankhaten in the morning." He waited, and when she did not acknowledge either his bow or his words, he turned away, and the door closed quietly behind him.

It was almost midnight by the time Ay walked wearily up his water steps and, escorted by his bodyguards, made his way through the rustling dark garden and into his house. He had been quite safe in revealing his thoughts to Nefertiti tonight, he knew. She had no resources left with which to insinuate herself into the good graces of anyone influential at court, and it was certain that Horemheb would have nothing whatever to do with her. *He does not trust me anymore either*, Ay thought as he dismissed his men, entered his bedchamber, and brusquely ordered his body servants to undress him. *Our opinions on how to restore this country to order have always differed, but now the divergence between us is growing rapidly and may develop into complete rivalry. I hope not. At the moment he is confused and unsure of how he wishes to proceed, but whatever happens, I must not allow him to gain an ascendancy over Tutankhaten. I must remain actively at court, waiting upon Smenkhara, keeping Tutankhaten visible, trying to contain Horemheb's impatience.*

He stood with his head back and his eyes half-closed, surrendering to the soothing, respectful touch of the men who came and went with perfumed water, soft fresh linen, quivering fans. His bedside lamp was lit, the others extinguished. His staff bowed a good-night. He lay in the hot room, tired but unable to rest, thinking of the murder of the foreign prince that he had sanctioned. Smenkhara had already forgotten about it, and Horemheb had regarded it as a military necessity. *We could have simply captured him and sent him home to his father*, he thought. *Suppiluliumas might have regarded such a move as a weakness, but it might have prevented a further deterioration in the relations between our two countries.*

He was beginning to doze when he sensed the opening of the door and, propping himself on an elbow, saw his wife come into the lamplight. Tey was clutching a saffron cloak under her chin. She was barefoot, and her gray hair was pushed back haphazardly from her high forehead. In the gentle light the wrinkles of her face were invisible.

"It is so late I thought you would be asleep." He smiled, patting the couch.

Tey sat, pursing her lips. "I heard you come in," she answered. "I was waiting up for you." Characteristically she did not ask him where he had been. She had never pried into his mind or his actions, and her very indifference had kept him close to her. "I wanted you to know immediately that a message came from the palace after you left. Ankhesenpaaten's little baby has died."

Ay sighed. "Poor princess. Her doll has been taken away from her. I must go to her in the morning."

"Kia has taken her to her apartments for a while. Akhenaten's holy sun family is stricken one by one. The curse seems to linger."

"Perhaps." He knew by the tone of her voice, the way she was chewing her lip, that there was more. "Go on, beloved."

"Ay, I am going home to Akhmin tomorrow. The servants can pack up my belongings and bring them later. You have done all you can to make me happy here, but I can no longer bear the feeling of doom that hangs over the city. Akhetaten is finished. The dream has ended."

He did not smile at her choice of words. The city was indeed a dream, but the dreamer was dead. "Would you stay if I begged you?"

"No." She took his hand. "Much has changed between us, Ay. The love can never change, but there is a difference between the kind of marriage we once had, you and me apart and yet joined, and what our marriage has become. I am an Egyptian wife, not a barbarian's chattel, a concubine to be used. You bring me your body, but it has been a long time since I knew your thoughts. You are no longer as recognizable to me as you once were. Since Tiye died, you have shut yourself up. I am lonely in a way I have never been before, and the work I have done here is no good. At Akhmin I will work, I will get dirty again, I will be content."

He lifted her hand to his mouth, desolate yet knowing that she spoke the truth. "I have to stay. I am needed. I am sorry," he whispered. "I should have asked for your help, Tey."

"But you did not, and besides, I do not think I could have given you any. My presence alone has not been enough to make you content. So I bid you farewell, my husband. Come to Akhmin as you used to in the old days, unexpectedly, because you wanted to."

"I will indeed visit you, Tey," he said huskily, "and will, of course, see to your every need."

She leaned across and kissed him lightly, but he was too proud to pull her down beside him. Long after she had gone, the fragrance of her perfume lingered on his skin, on the sheet where she had sat, and he did not forbid the flood of memories that washed over him with cruel force, leaving a homesickness he knew would not blunt with time.

26

IN THE WEEKS THAT FOLLOWED SMENKHARA'S CORONATION Ay found his thoughts turning often to Tey's last words to him. The dream of Akhetaten was not quite over. The characters who peopled it clung to its shreds as though they were afraid that waking would cause them to vanish. Outside the city, Egypt tottered and grappled with the lingering aftermath of the famine, the lack of officials to run efficiently an administration that had virtually disappeared, the rise of crimes of looting and violence, but inside Akhetaten, all was still orderly and pleasant.

"What is it that holds them to Akhetaten like dying men sitting before an empty granary?" Ay asked Horemheb once in an outburst of frustration. The two men had come to an uneasy, unspoken truce when it became evident that both were going to be powerless under the new regime.

Horemheb had shrugged phlegmatically. "The fear of what is beyond," he had answered. "Only Akhetaten has not changed. Everyone in the city is afraid to travel, to see what has happened to Egypt, what Thebes has now become." He smiled grimly at Ay. "Smenkhara knows he is not capable of ruling, yet he is terrified to delegate the needed authority to others. He knows he is not worthy to be pharaoh, and that makes him even more afraid and angry. Have you taken a clear look at our pharaoh, Fanbearer?" Ay shook his head. "Then I suggest you do so. When you have decided that something must be done, come to my house."

Ay decided to ignore the challenge in the commander's eyes. He hoped he would never be forced into a partnership of necessity with Horemheb. He was afraid of being made privy to designs that might require him to abrogate his belief in the untouchability of a pharaoh's person. But the need for such a compromise was remote, for he was spending an increasing amount of time with Tutankhaten. The prince had dutifully and indifferently moved into the palace, where he was largely ignored by Smenkhara. To many of the courtiers he was an embarrassment, a reminder of the brief madness that had overtaken Egypt's royalty and which was best forgotten, but to some the sacred blood in his veins made him worth wooing. The times were uncertain, and perhaps the little prince might become pharaoh. Ay himself would listen as the boy recited his studies, watch him at his prayers and in his chariot, play board games with him, and tell him stories of his mother. The prince had taken to wearing the lock of his mother's red-brown hair around his neck, safe in a tiny gold chest, and Ay often had to wonder whether Tutankhaten was as guileless as he appeared. Perhaps he knew that he needed the powerful spell of that luck, always with him. Ay deliberately cultivated his trust and was happy to see him enjoying Ankhesenpaaten's company. The orphaned boy and the friendless princess liked each other. Ay knew that the possibilities were there, waiting for a ruthless hand to manipulate them.

Smenkhara and Meritaten showed no signs of producing an heir. Though they were inseparable, sleeping, eating, and playing together, engaged in a constant round of pleasures, they were like two flighty children to whom the realm of adult responsibilities was unknown. Yet there was about them an air of melancholy, a darkness pressing on the fringes of their days and nights that must be held at bay at any cost. Their laughter was shrill and forced, their infrequent silences charged with fear. Smenkhara's cheerfulness could turn at any time into sullen rages, and Meritaten's to tears.

Although no longer a fanbearer except in name, Ay was often summoned by his nephew to give advice, and while it was never taken, he nevertheless missed no opportunity to remind his nephew of what was expected of him. The problem immediately facing the country, and one causing Ay the greatest concern, was that of the supply of gold. The Treasury was disgracefully and dangerously empty, yet monuments had to be paid for, the peasants kept marginally alive if they were to go on producing food and working at building projects, and foreign dignitaries housed and entertained. Embassies began to return to a city that was still ethereally beautiful, a court that still strove to be the most sumptuous in the world, and to a young pharaoh and his queen who played the part of arrogant godhead. But they came without tribute and left without treaties, for Egypt had nothing left with which to bargain. Horemheb fought to keep the Nubian gold routes open, but wealth from that source alone would not fill the Treasury. Increasingly the caravans that used to disgorge a profusion of exotic and costly things over the country were going on to Babylon and the Khatti, and the ships that had once crossed the Great Green Sea, fearful of pirates and knowing that Egypt would no longer protect them, took their cargoes elsewhere. Nor could Pharaoh call upon temple treasuries, for his brother had impoverished them all.

Forced to find an expedient way to meet the country's debts, Smenkhara began to sell abroad grain from the granaries, which were once again filling. None of his young friends who were now members of the new administration attempted to remonstrate with him over this rash move for fear of losing the favors he showered on them, and it was finally Ay who requested audience a few days before the beginning of Khoyak. Akhet, the season of flooding, was almost over, and the weather had cooled. Men looked to Peret and the sowing with lighter hearts.

Smenkhara greeted his uncle's obeisance with obvious relief. When Ay entered, he had been pacing desultorily around the echoing reception hall, pecking at the sweetmeats set on tables here and there and flicking at the insects that filled the moist air while his attendants trailed after him. He stood still while Ay kissed his hennaed feet and then mounted the steps of the throne. Flinging himself down, he indicated the ebony stool below. Ay sat, and with barely audible sighs the attendants sank onto cushions on the floor.

"I hate Akhet," Smenkhara said. "Half of it is too hot to do anything, and the other half is too wet. Nothing but sheets of water to look at, and the river running too swiftly for barging. Everyone else goes hunting behind the city, but I do not enjoy killing animals. When I was younger, I would long for the river to sink, because then the fishing would be tremendous, but of course now that I am pharaoh, I am forbidden to catch them or eat them. Akhenaten did, but then for him there was no Hapi in the Nile to be offended."

"Your Majesty could always go boating on one of the lakes, or wander through Maru-Aten."

"No, I can't. Today I had to sit here and listen to the Aten priests whine."

Ah, Ay thought. *There is the cause of this pouting.* "Would Your Majesty care to tell me what they wanted?"

"If you like." Smenkhara tugged at one swinging golden earring. "Offerings are becoming scarce. Fewer worshipers go to the temple, and the street shrines are being defaced. In a word, Uncle, they do not have enough to do, and they are becoming bored."

"What did Your Majesty tell them?"

"To go and have some fun."

Ay watched the long, red-nailed fingers pull and worry at the earring. "Has Your Majesty considered closing some of the smaller Aten temples and sending the priests out into the countryside to reopen and repair the houses of other gods?"

Smenkhara stared at him. "Are you mad? Who is going to keep them alive while they pretend to work? And besides, priests do not like to get their hands dirty."

"They would have no choice. They could be supported by this coming summer's produce from the holdings in the Delta that had belonged to Amun."

Smenkhara laughed. "So you wish me to return to Amun his land? Certainly not. My fellahin are even now waiting for the flood to abate so that they can begin sowing that land for me. I need the crops."

Many times Ay had wished to bring to Pharaoh's attention a matter of great urgency, but a more suitable moment than this had not arisen before. The talk of Amun gave him an opening. "Great Horus," Ay said urgently, "it is time to send an official embassy to Maya in Thebes granting him permission to reopen Karnak, and stewards to the palace there to see what must be done to make it habitable again. You do not know the temper of your people. Believe me——"

Smenkhara raised a hand. The smile had disappeared from his face. "I have already done as you wished, and made a great fuss about hollowing a tomb in the western hills at Thebes. I have ostentatiously said my prayers at the Amun shrine here in the palace. I have even appointed Pwah"—he waved at a young man dressed in priestly white behind him—"as Scribe of the Offerings of Amun in the Mansion of Ankheperura. My mansion. Mine. I have no intention of handing back any land to Amun and impoverishing myself. Nor do I intend to leave Akhetaten. For years I waited in Thebes, in an empty palace with my stubborn mother, longing for Meritaten, miserable,

while here the music and dancing never stopped. I despise
Thebes. If it was noisy and dirty then, it will be doubly so
now. Speak of something else!" His voice had risen, and the
curved shoulders draped in gold hunched with anger.

Horemheb's words came back to Ay, and as he watched his
nephew, he realized with a chill that he was, for the first time,
taking a clear look at Pharaoh. *When did it begin?* he thought
despairingly. *When did the gods decree a curse on Egypt? When
Tiye bedded with her son? Or much earlier, when she moved
to prevent his murder against the express order of the oracle?*
Smenkhara's thighs were spread, filling the throne under his
scarlet linen. His belly, though he was still young, had begun
to sag. "Majesty," Ay managed, though he felt suddenly weak,
"at least send the Vizier of the South to Thebes to tell the
people that they may once more worship as they choose."

Smenkhara jerked his head. "Nakht-pa-Aten! Do you want
to go to Thebes and tell the people this thing?"

The vizier crawled to him, touching the royal foot with his
forehead. "I believe it to be unnecessary, Holy One. The people
have always worshiped as they chose, in secret."

"But they must be told publicly, they must be reassured, or
else . . ." Ay had come to his feet. Smenkhara leaned down at
him.

"Or else what, Uncle? Are you going to threaten me as
Horemheb did when I was still a prince? I gave him his way
then, but I swore to myself I would never again hear a word
he said. If you have finished, you may go."

"There is one more thing, with your permission." Ay knew
he ought not to stir Smenkhara's anger further, but he was
determined to discuss the matter that had brought him here
initially. "This matter of selling our grain to foreigners. From
ancient days, Pharaoh has stored grain against times of famine.
Your predecessors emptied the granaries in exchange for gold,
and when famine struck many starved. Egypt is still recovering
from the drought, and is still vulnerable. I beg you, Horus,
keep the grain!"

"Oh, leave me in peace." Smenkhara glowered at Ay. "You
are a meddlesome old man. Let Egypt starve, I do not care.
The land belongs to me, as well as everything that grows in it
or lives on it. I am master and god." Sullenly he evaded Ay's
eye. "You seem to take a delight in making me angry, Uncle.
You lack the respect due to me as pharaoh. You are no longer

THE TWELFTH TRANSFORMING 407

welcome at court." It was an immediate dismissal. Ay made
his prostration and left.

Sitting rigid on the deck of his barge while his sailors struggled to pull him across the swiftly flowing river, Ay grew aware
of the perfume of Akhetaten drifting around him, made more
languorous by the humidity in the air. Flowers, budding trees,
a hint of incense, wove with the stench of muddy water, Egypt's
most ancient odor. Laughter and the faint tinkle of finger cymbals reached his ears, and on the receding bank he caught a
glimpse of brown limbs and white linen as a group of young
men and women ran under the palms. *He has a daunting likeness to his brother, but there is much of Tiye in him as well*,
Ay thought, *and that is why I have some sympathy for him.
He will do nothing to bind up Egypt's wounds, but neither will
he harm her further. That is some comfort.*

Walking through the cool passages of his house, he fancied
that he heard Tey's laughter coming from her apartment, and
he stopped and turned toward the sound before he realized it
was only a servant girl cleaning and gossiping. He accepted
that it was his fault that she had gone, but he had never needed
her more.

He did not try to sleep that night but sat in his bedchamber
in a woolen cloak, watching the pattern of fire and darkness
the brazier made on the ceiling. Several times he was on the
point of summoning his steward and dictating a message to
Horemheb, but each time he changed his mind. It was impossible. He knew what Horemheb wanted him to do, wanted to
implicate him in, wanted his support for, and he could not
consent. *I am too much a man of reflection, not action*, he
thought, *to murder again, too traditional an Egyptian to contemplate the killing of a young man who is now a god. To
become Horemheb's accomplice in this thing would also be to
place myself forever under his thumb. Let him bear the responsibility, and let him bear it alone.*

He took a lamp to his cosmetics table and, lifting his copper
hand mirror, gazed at himself. *You are a stupid old man*, he
thought, critically appraising the black pouches under rheumy
eyes, the rough, sun-weathered, loose skin, the deeply furrowed forehead and dry, knobbed, shaven scalp. *Give up, retire, go home to Akhmin*. But he knew he could not, not yet.
Not as long as members of his bloodline survived to perpetuate
the power they had fought for generations to acquire. He had

a duty to Tutankhaten, and to his granddaughter Ankhesen-paaten. He smiled grimly into the mirror. "You lie to yourself, stupid old man," he whispered. "You hope that Horemheb will do the unthinkable and thus you will be enabled to rule as regent behind Tutankhaten, if death does not claim you first."

Hearing of Ay's unsuccessful and humiliating audience with Smenkhara, Horemheb expected an offer of complete coop-eration to arrive at any moment from Pharaoh's uncle, but the days passed with no communication from him. In spite of the rivalry between the two men, Horemheb respected Ay's polit-ical acumen, and in the dead hours at his own house, when he lay without sleeping in the silence, he wondered why Ay did not want to act. Was there some consideration that he had overlooked? Some reason, not obvious to his own straightfor-ward, military mind but clear to Ay with his diplomatic think-ing, why the murder of Pharaoh would not be expedient? Horemheb tried to imagine every result of such a plot. He did not lack support, and although he knew that he was not in favor at court, neither were any of Akhenaten's men, with a few exceptions. It was the army, finally, that mattered. He had questioned his officers closely. Some of the soldiers' faith in him had been shaken because of their rout at Suppiluliumas's hands, but it seemed unlikely that they would not support him if he reached for the crown.

Reflectively he tried to remember when the idea of himself as pharaoh had taken shape in his mind. When the empress had died, and with her Egypt's belief in the absolute authority that had always been accorded to royalty? When he had threat-ened Pharaoh, then a prince, with so little, so very little, and been believed? Or had it happened many years earlier, when he had looked at a pharaoh and for the first time seen only an uncertain, tortured Egyptian, dependent on him, a mere captain at the time, for friendship?

He knew that for Ay, a return to security in Egypt had to begin with the reinstatement of Amun as lord and a slow re-establishing of diplomatic relations with what was left of the empire. But he himself disagreed. An immediate priority was the securing of the borders against the Khatti, another attempt to regain Egypt's Syrian dependencies, the stabilization of Nu-bia, and only then a turning to the internal problems of the country, which would take a very long time to correct. There was no time to wait for Ay to try his way. He seemed to have no sense of urgency regarding the threat of a Khatti invasion that might begin tomorrow and would mean the death of Egyptian sovereignty forever. Then considerations such as the preservation of Pharaoh's divinity and Amun's rightful place as Egypt's major deity would be meaningless. *Save Egypt first,* he thought as he tossed restlessly beside a quietly slumbering Mutnodjme, *even if it means destroying the mighty dynasty that began with Smenkhara's god ancestor Thothmes I, hentis ago, when the Hyksos were driven from this soil. The greatest obstacle to safety is Smenkhara himself, repository of all hereditary authority. He must be removed. But if I kill him, Tutankhaten will come to the throne, and behind him stands Ay, adamantly refusing any military solution to our troubles. Would anything have been gained by murder? Would Ay be more amenable with Smenkhara gone?* They were questions whose answers would not become clear until action had been taken.

Am I prepared to damn myself before the gods by such an act? he wondered as night after night the dead hours stood still. *Surely they know that I would have served my king all my life if he had been worthy. But he was not. Neither is Smenkhara. But an Egyptian does not serve his pharaoh because that pharaoh is worthy to be served,* he reminded himself. *He surrenders his allegiance to the unchanging spark of the god within the man, to that immortal essence passing unblemished from king to king. Yet Akhenaten broke that thread. Does it exist anymore? I do not know.*

For many days he struggled with himself. Mutnodjme and her friends went north, to Djarukha and the Delta, to celebrate the completion of the sowing. He stood in his chariot behind the city, watching his troops go through their drill with the sun sparkling on the thousands of polished spears and filtering through the choking dust. Often, listening to the spies he had placed long ago in Ay's household give their reports, he had to fight a desire to go to the fanbearer, confess his agony, ask the older man's advice. He knew that it was only a need to show his hand, to somehow rid himself of the constant ache of guilt for an act he had not yet committed. Briefly he considered approaching Nefertiti with an offer of marriage but discarded the idea with the contempt it deserved. The dowager queen had long ago been discredited in his eyes.

On the morning of the first day of Phamenat he woke with

his decision made. Calmly he allowed his servants to dress
him, ate some dried figs, and rode out to the parade ground.
Since the army's ignominious defeat he had ordered regular
maneuvers, forced marches, and mock battles for the soldiers.
This morning he sat under a canopy and watched critically as
the Shock Troops ran obstacle courses in the chariots. The day
was pleasantly warm, with a light breeze, the sky a cornflower
blue, and the sheltering semicircle of cliffs cast cool shadows
over the sand, but Horemheb brooded, blind to the freshness
around him. When the drenched, exhausted troops wheeled in
the direction of the stables, he summoned his favorite general
under the canopy. Nakht-Min bowed and sank to the carpet,
pulling off his blue linen helmet and using it to mop his face.

"I am still not satisfied with the men from the Division of
Splendor of the Aten," he said, nodding his thanks as Horemheb
pushed wine toward him. "They seem to think that, as they
are an elite, it is beneath them to have to learn to drive chariots
as well as being able to fight. I have pointed out that charioteers
get killed in alarming numbers, and who will handle the horses
for the proud idiots then? Ah, well. We all had to learn."

"We did indeed." Horemheb smiled. "And most of us still
bear the scars of that learning." He waited until the young man
had drained his cup, then said, "Nakht-Min, I want you to send
to Tjel for me. I need the services of a Medjay assassin."

Nakht-Min nodded calmly. He knew from whom any ad-
vancement would come. "There are many of our desert police
much closer," he objected. "Mahu could bring one quickly from
the Sinai."

"No. I am not in a hurry, and I want a man who has seen
fairly constant action and who, moreover, has never been anywhere near Akhetaten. I want him brought to my house, not
quartered in the barracks. How long?"

Nakht-Min considered. "Tjel is our farthest outpost on the
Asiatic border. A month, perhaps. Some of the Medjay are
Apiru mercenaries. Do you want a foreigner?"

"Yes," Horemheb said slowly. "A foreigner would be very
good. Needless to say, this is a private matter."

"I understand."

Horemheb knew that Nakht-Min never needed to have an
instruction repeated. He changed the subject immediately and,
after some minutes of light conversation, dismissed him.

Horemheb ate and slept better in the weeks that followed

and at times even forgot that he had set his plan in motion. He was disciplined enough to wait calmly for whatever fate would send him. Mutnodjme returned pale and satiated from the Delta, kissed him wanly, and scarcely stirred from her couch for four days. He held a boating party for his senior officers. He prayed to the local god of his natal village of Hnes, and to Amun also.

He was not surprised when, sitting in his garden in the dusk one evening in the first week of Pharmuti, he saw his steward bowing Nakht-Min and a stranger in his direction. The Medjay was much as he had expected, a tall, long-haired man whose flowing thick robes doubtless hid a body without any excess flesh. Pharaoh Amunhotep III had used just such an individual to murder Aziru's father. Horemheb wished, not for the first time, that the entire Egyptian army could be composed of Medjay. He welcomed them and had food and wine presented, talked of the border forts and their welfare, and then rose to escort Nakht-Min to the water steps. Returning to his guest, he attempted a little more conversation before showing him to his quarters and warning him to remain in them and to speak to no one. The man did not demur.

Now it is a matter of luck, Horemheb told himself as he went to his bedchamber. *I know where Smenkhara will sleep tomorrow night. I know the hour he likes to retire, and how many Followers guard him, for it was I myself who appointed and deployed them. I can do no more.*

In the morning he gave Nakht-Min further instructions under the rattle of drums and the shouted orders of the drill officers. "Bring two of your own personal staff to my garden tonight," he said. "The Medjay will come up from the water steps toward the entrance. Kill him before he reaches the house, but be very careful. Remember, he is himself trained to strike and survive. If you are not seen, weigh him with rocks and cast him into the river. If one of my servants discoveres you, you can say you were coming to receive orders and caught an intruder in the garden." His voice lost its crisp, authoritative tone. "Do you believe, Nakht-Min, that I love and serve Egypt?"

"Of course," the general replied, meeting the commander's eyes. "I know how to do my duty."

Horemheb met with the Medjay in the afternoon. Mutnodjme, unaware of an alien presence on the estate, had taken her bodyguards and gone into the city, and the house was quiet. "I hope you have not been bored," Horemheb offered, walking across the sun-dappled tiles and seating himself by the couch on which the man lay, his arms behind his head. The Medjay turned a brown, thin face to the Egyptian and smiled.

"Bored, no," he said in gutteral Egyptian. "But it has been a long time since I have slept on a mattress between sheets of real linen. I could not rest. I rolled in my cloak and slept on the floor."

Horemheb was sorry to find himself liking the man. "We are now going to get into my boat," he said, "and I will show you where to go tonight. How you get there later is up to you, but my barge will be waiting to bring you back again. I want you to kill a man, without rope or knife."

The black eyes went on regarding him quietly. "Of course you do, but you have gone to much trouble," he said. "Why not poison?"

"Because poison leaves traces, and the cause of death is then in no doubt. There will be suspicion toward me afterward, but toward others also. Do not strangle him."

"Very well. You will pay me."

"In gold, tomorrow. If there is a woman with him, kill her also."

The man shrugged. "I am an admirer of women," he replied. "Such a waste. More gold."

"If you wish. It does not matter." Horemheb struggled against a sudden fit of nausea, and with it came a reckless urge to order the assassin to murder them all, Tutankhaten, Ankhesenpaaten, sweep away the whole royal brood so that their blood might wash the country clean at last. But he quickly recognized the urge as one of panic's faces and controlled himself.

"Does Pharaoh know what you have asked of me?" the Medjay enquired casually.

Horemheb shook his head. "No, and he never will. Come. I do not want to arrive back at the same time as my wife."

He poled the man out into the current himself, standing off well away from any eye on the bank that might recognize him, and rowed them past the edge of the south city until they were level with Manu-Aten. Once there, he described the pavilion in the trees, the times of the guard changes, the arrangement of the rooms. As he spoke, he was uncomfortably aware of the man's slowly narrowing gaze, the rapid conjecture taking place, but he knew that the Medjay were trained to give their allegiance only to their superior officers. Most of them knew

nothing of Egypt but the border itself, and the idea of serving
a god they would never see had no interest for them. Their
independence was both a threat and a strength to Egypt, and
every Egyptian commander knew it and respected their peculiar
place in the ranks of the army. As Horemheb turned the skiff
around, he asked the man to repeat what he had been told, and
he did so without much trouble. There was nothing more to be
done then but to return to the house and wait for nightfall.

Smenkhara went to his couch early that evening, lying awake
for a while to listen to the wind in the trees that crowded against
the pavilion walls. He had never shared Meritaten's distaste
for Maru-Aten, and the ownership of it filled him with a proprietary pleasure. He had grown to hate his brother but grudgingly recognized Maru-Aten as an achievement that transcended
the pharaoh's weakness. Akhetaten had loved the natural world
with a passion and realized that love in the creation of the
summer palace. For Smenkhara it had a quality of purity that
he could no longer find within himself. He knew that his brother
had corrupted both him and Meritaten, that they had already
died with their youth, but here, where there was the scent of
lotus and the murmur of clear water, he could still pretend that
one day they would both be healed.

But tonight he did not sleep long. Soon he woke and lay
frowning into the darkness, and although the warmth of the
braziers made him drowsy and he dozed again, he drifted awake
only an hour later, burdened with a sourceless anxiety. Shadows
moved across the window. Birds called sleepily. His bodyguards stepped to and fro, black shapes of reassurance. As they
had so often lately, his thoughts turned to his mother, the blue
cold glitter of her eyes when he had irritated her, the feel of
her arms around him on the few occasions when there had been
tenderness between them. He fancied that he could smell the
heavy musk of her perfume. *She never really loved me*, he
thought, turning over and pulling the sheet across his shoulder.
*The only man who commanded her affection was my father.
What was he like, the god whom people speak of with such
awe?* Smenkhara did not really care, for in the end they had
all used and betrayed him, his father, his mother, his grotesque
brother. Yet in the defenseless hours of darkness they often
assumed more human proportions in his mind, catching him
off guard and softening the wall of loneliness that protected

him. He wished he had commanded Meritaten to sleep with
him tonight. He would have liked the warmth of another body
beside him. Listening to the sighs and mutters of his manservant, unconscious at the far end of the room, he almost
called out but mentally shrugged and changed his mind. The
man would not give him what he neded. Nor could Meritaten,
or the pliant young men he occasionally coaxed to his bed. He
slept again.

He did not wake when the soft-footed Medjay slipped through
the window and crouched beside the couch. He was standing
by the river in the shade of a date palm, watching himself
loosely asleep at the foot of the palm in the heat of a summer
afternoon, and though he could not see through the trees, he
knew he was somewhere on the Malkatta estate. With a dawning relief he saw his sleeping self begin to smile, and the smile
grew wider and tighter until the painted mouth strained and
split.There was no blood, and he saw that his other self did
not wake. A great sense of well-being expanded in him, and
though he knew he was dreaming, he was able to recognize
the good omen. Something he was afraid of would be explained
by the god. *I will make offerings to Amun in the morning*, he
said to his dream self. *I must run and tell my mother*.

He did not wake when the Medjay eased the pillow from
under his head and gathered up a portion of the sheet. The man
worked without haste. He hesitated once, with the handful and
sheet poised over Smenkhara's parted mouth and the young
man's warm breath on his fingers. It was not a moment of
indecision, but rather, a summoning of his strength. The eyes
flared open as he rammed the sheet into the mouth and pushed
the pillow over the face. This was the most dangerous moment.
The dying man's smothered grunts might rouse the servants,
or the flailing limbs make too much noise. The Medjay sat
astride Smenkhara's chest, imprisoning the jerking arms so that
the nails could not draw blood. He did not like to kill this way;
it took too long. He kept his weight on the pillow, his knees
against the frenetic arms until the resistance grew weaker and
finally ceased. He had just replaced the pillow under the lolling
head and pulled the sheet out of the mouth when a sleepy voice
asked, "Majesty, did you call me?" Quickly the Medjay drew
the eyelids shut and slid down beside the couch, but the servant
did not come. He sensed him sitting up, listening, but after a
minute he lay down again with a sigh. Still the Medjay did not

stir. The night was thinning. Ra was in the last House of his transforming.

At last he rose and, bending over Smenkhara's body, inspected it carefully. The young man was dead. The Medjay stood loosely, considering, and only when he had made a firm decision did he slide through the window and give himself up to the shadows. He had killed a god, and he knew it. Even if the servant's query had not confirmed his own suspicions, he would have thought twice about returning to the commander's house. He glided out of Maru-Aten, away from the river and into the dark desert toward the sheltering cliffs.

Smenkhara's death, while a shock to the courtiers, who had seen pharaohs succumb only at advanced ages or after recognizable illnesses, followed so closely upon other royal tragedies that the stir it caused was soon dissipated. But the more superstitious among the city dwellers whispered among one another darkly that the young man's fate could not have been averted. The curse brought upon Egypt's ruling family and its unhappy subjects by Osiris Akhenaten and his mother had yet to run its course, and the anger of the gods, once roused, was difficult to appease. Some supernatural agent had struck Pharaoh, for was it not significant that the royal physicians could find no mark on the king's body, though the face was swollen and discolored? In homes and market places, the gossip was furtive and apprehensive.

Horemheb's spies brought him news of the indifference of the court and the frightened conjecture of the city. The talk did not alarm him, for the fingers of accusation were pointed at the gods, not at living men. After a brief exchange with Nakht-Min, who had waited all night in the commander's garden for a man who had not appeared, he realized that his second victim had run, but it did not matter. The Medjay would keep his own counsel. Horemheb did what was expected of him. He ordered Smenkhara's manservant severely whipped and dismissed, and reprimanded the Followers who had heard and seen nothing. Neither his actions nor his words invited suspicion.

Only two people believed they knew the truth about Smenkhara's death. Ay had stood beside Horemheb in the light of early dawn, looking down at Pharaoh's sprawled corpse while Meritaten screamed and sobbed at its feet and the manservant lay prostrate and trembling before the crowd of courtiers and priests who thronged the room.

"You should have killed Tutankhaten, too," he said to Horemheb in a low voice under cover of the noise and confusion. "Now if you want the crown, you will have to wait. Your judgment was impaired, Commander."

"I have bloodied my hands for you also," Horemheb replied softly. "You did not have the courage to do it yourself. Look at him!" He motioned toward the stiffening corpse. "He was worth nothing. Egypt is in crisis, and the gods give us that! We have suffered enough. Believe me, Ay, I am not a traitor. The crown will of course go to Tutankhaten as the legitimate heir."

"You have no choice," Ay responded, drawing Horemheb away from the couch. "Another royal death would point the finger of accusation directly at you. I would not be suspect. Am I not the uncle of both gods? If you had struck at them together, it would still have been seen as divine displeasure, given the present climate of superstitious awe in Akhetaten. Do you not fear the gods, Horemheb?"

"Yes, old friend, I fear them," Horemheb said slowly, the ghost of a smile flitting across his mouth, "but it is Amun and Ra and Khonsu that I fear, not the febrile god of what is left of his insane dynasty. There has been no true pharaoh in Egypt since Osiris Amunhotep." He leaned closer to Ay, and his voice dropped even further. "I see your new confidence. Tutankhaten loves and reveres you. Enjoy the rebirth of your power. If you use it for Egypt, you will be left in peace."

Ay's retort remained unspoken, for a silence fell as the doors were opened, and those present pulled their garments close to their bodies and looked away as the sem-priests entered. The clinging stench of death moved with them wherever they went, and even those among them who were privileged to handle the bodies of gods were regarded as unclean. They filed into the room with heads lowered, and one by one the company slipped hurriedly away behind them. Pwah and the other Amun priests waited with censers to purify the room when they had taken Smenkhara away.

Only Meritaten disregarded their presence. Huddled by the couch, she clung to her husband's feet with both hands, her face buried against them, while the men from the House of the Dead stood away awkwardly from her. Horemheb nodded at her attendants. Reverently they lifted her to her feet. "Servants of Ma'at," Horemheb said suddenly to the sem-priests, "the god you are about to touch appears to be male, and thus you would beautify him with both arms lying at his sides. But this Horus was in fact female, lover of Osiris Akhenaten. Therefore he would wish to be laid in his coffin in the pose of a woman, with right arm extended but with the left folded across the breast, so that he may be recognized as a woman in the next world. Do you understand?"

The men nodded, not daring to defile the room with their breath. Ay glanced at Meritaten. Though she was no longer weeping, sobs continued to shake her, and her large gray eyes were fixed on Horemheb in horror. Before she could speak, he again nodded, and her women led her away.

"I do not think it is necessary to hold the corpse for five days before releasing it to the House of the Dead, do you?" Horemheb asked, turning to Ay. "Even though Smenkhara was more woman than man, I cannot imagine any lustful sem-priest wanting to defile him before he begins to rot."

Ay barely managed to answer. "I must go immediately and cleanse myself," he muttered, turning to the door. He did not know whether it was the taint of the sem-priests' presence he frantically wished to purify himself of, or Horemheb's inexplicable ferocity.

The court at Akhetaten was prepared to accept Smenkhara's death at the hands of the gods and so did not urge that the matter be investigated further. However, Horemheb found himself threatened, not by the revelations of the assassin or by his general Nakht-Min, but by the agony of a queen. Accusations tumbled from Meritaten as though the words might ease her bereavement, yet the words themselves only made her feel it all the more keenly. She allowed no one to comfort her. Ay was denied admittance to her apartments. Ankhesenpaaten, still grieving for her daughter, would go to her sister and sit dumbly for hours while Meritaten drank and wept, calling down every curse she knew on Horemheb and his household.

Horemheb waited for the storm to abate, but Pakhons went by, the harvest began, and Meritaten became even more unstable. Her tears had stopped, but the recriminations went on, increasingly voiced in public. Horemheb saw the doubts in the eyes of those around him and realized that Meritaten must be silenced. Nothing could be proved against him, but the constant flow of the queen's vicious words inevitably shook the confidence of those who were sympathetic to him. Above all, Tutankhaten, though he encountered Horemheb only on formal occasions, was beginning to look at the Supreme Commander of All the Forces of His Majesty with speculative eyes.

For weeks Horemheb hesitated to take any action against Meritaten, torn between pity for her and an instinct for his own preservation. He began to avoid most formal feasts which Tutankhaten attended but could not absent himself from them entirely for fear of drawing too much attention to his behavior. Therefore one evening toward the end of the period of mourning he was present when Tutankhaten and his entourage were dining in Akhenaten's vast banqueting hall. The little heir sat on the dais with Ay at his side, his half sister Ankhesenpaaten on his left. She had given Tutankhaten a new pet, a gosling whose green fluff had only just been replaced by sleek white feathers.

"You will soon be the incarnation of Amun-Ra, the Great Cackler," she had told him. "The goose is the symbol of your sacredness." Tonight the goose held all their attention. The boy had had a thick gold collar made for it, and it squatted on the table between them, snatching the morsels of food they offered and hissing balefully at every servant who came near. *It is good to hear them laughing*, Ay thought. *Malkatta used to be drunk with laughter. How sad and wary we have all become!*

His glance strayed to Horemheb, toying with his food, his blue-ribboned head down while Mutnodjme whispered in his ear. Ay found his heart warming as he looked at his younger daughter. In spite of the life of indolent dissipation she led, time had dealt kindly with her, and at thirty-five she was still surrounded by the clusters of admiring young charioteers that had begun to bore her in her late twenties. Tonight the youth lock she still wore was braided, bound up against her skull and hung with silver bells. Her eye paint was silver, and the arm pushed loosely through her husband's was heavy with silver amulets. She had mixed silver dust with her lip henna, so that her teeth seemed faintly yellow, her skin sallow, her eyes yellow-tinged. As with every fashion she affected, it bordered on the bizarre but somehow fascinated rather than repelled. The sight of her pausing in whatever flow of spicy words she was pouring at Horemheb to take the lobe of his ear between sharp teeth filled Ay with a sudden longing for the days of his vigorous youth, now long past. *What right does she have to remain untouched?* he thought. *Why have the gods spared her when the rest of us were led young and innocent into the dark passages of necessity to emerge maimed and sullied?*

She sensed his stare and looked up, smiling, but he did not return the smile, for all at once a hush had fallen. Ay followed the eyes of the crowd to the rear of the hall. Meritaten was stepping out of the shadows where night seeped between the pillars. She swayed forward, leaving the support of the stone. A hot draught caught her white pleated linens and sent them billowing before her, and her black, uncombed hair whipped about her unpainted face. Her feet were bare. In one hand she clutched the queen's cobra coronet, while the other held a goblet of wine. Uncertainly the assembly went down before her as she picked her way between tables with exaggerated care. When she reached the dais, she bowed to Tutankhaten, and the gesture took her forward. Collapsing onto a step, she sat rocking for a moment, the attendants who had followed her hesitating, their fearful eyes on Ay. Ankhesenpaaten snatched up the goose and cuddled it as if for protection. Tutankhaten leaned toward his uncle. "Shall I order a table brought for her, or have them take her away?" he whispered. "She looks as though she were going to be sick." Ay hesitated. Meritaten placed the goblet on the step beside her and, taking the coronet in both hands, set it on her brow. The Followers looked to Horemheb, who began to rise, but his small movement brought Meritaten's head around.

"You courtiers do not seem to care with what demon you dine," she said thickly, rising. "All of you know what the Supreme Commander did. His presence here sours your wine and poisons your meat, yet you talk and laugh as though it does not matter. O King-to-be," she addressed Tutankhaten without taking her eyes off Horemheb, "whose hands will curl invisible around your own when you lift the crook, flail, and scimitar? We have become an accursed people!" Her voice had risen, echoing against the dark ceiling, and as she spoke, she lifted her naked arms, the fists clenched.

Horemheb stood and walked calmly to her side. "Majesty, you need to sleep," he said soothingly. "You are distressed."

Turning her disfigured face up to his, she began to cry. Her legs were splayed to keep her balance. She smelled of wine, of unwashed skin and undried tears, but the glinting cobra on her forehead gave her dignity. "Distressed?" she said harshly.

"My heart has been torn out, and you dare to stand before me and mouth such blasphemy? I wonder what thoughts fill your wife when she lies in the arms of a god-killer? My arms are empty. Empty!" Tears choked her, and Horemheb caught her as she slipped toward the floor. At his sharp order her women supported her and led her away, her sobs growing fainter.

No one in the hall dared to look about, and the only sound was the soft clucking of the goose as it nibbled at Ankhesen-paaten's jasper earring. Tutankhaten had gone very white. At last he rose, and at the movement the frozen company sprang to life, prostrating themselves before him as he left the dais with his entourage and disappeared through the nearer doors. For appearances' sake Horemheb stayed a little longer, drinking and talking with Nakht-Min and the other officers whose tables were pulled close to his own, all the while feeling the overt glances of the courtiers. Finally he rose and, bidding his wife and friends good-night, plunged into the dark passages leading to the queen's apartments.

Meritaten's bodyguards politely tried to refuse him entrance. As their superior he could have brushed them aside, but he talked to them patiently and sensibly, aware of their irrational fear, and in the end they let him pass. At the doors to her bedchamber her herald and steward again barred his way. Resignedly he waited while the steward went to enquire if he should be admitted. Horemheb expected to be refused but found himself soon ushered into the apartments that had been Nefertiti's. She still haunted the room. Her image smiled haughtily from the walls, beautiful and regal beneath the sun crown's height. Her golden hands, heavy with rings, still made offerings to the Aten while her husband held the ankh, symbol of life, to her smiling lips and the Aten itself touched her with its rays. Already those things belonged to an unfathomable past. Horemheb paced slowly to the imposing couch with its golden disk, its sphinx-lined frame, its clawed feet. The small figure dwarfed in its depth watched him advance. He bowed. "Why did you let me in?" he asked.

"You have no respect for me as your queen," she answered wearily. "If you had, you would have waited for me to speak first. But I am still queen of Egypt until Tutankhaten is crowned. I do not know why I let you in. I do not think I could have prevented you anyway, murderer."

She sounded stronger, more lucid, and Horemheb thought

that she must have vomited the wine. "Majesty, you know that your father destroyed Smenkhara long before I," he said quietly. "I did not have to come to you tonight. I do not have to justify myself to you. You were his wife. You know better than I how like your father he was becoming. He knew it, too."

"It was no reason to kill him." She lay very still, pale hands loose on the sheets, her cheeks wet, and Horemheb realized all at once that she was no longer a young woman. In his mind she had remained the girl who had welcomed Smenkhara to Akhetaten, the steady, smiling daughter of the Aten. She looked up at him with contempt. "You may not have to justify yourself to me, Horemheb, but be assured that the Aten has already judged you. Smenkhara would have done anything you told him to, as long as we were left alone." Her voice quivered. "But you took away the only chance for happiness we had."

"It was too late," he cut in brutally. "And you know that, too, Majesty. Smenkhara resisted me. He resisted Ay, as well. He wanted to be left alone in a time when Egypt needs the healing power of a god." Unbidden he sat on the edge of the couch. "In a few days he will be buried. I give you a choice, Meritaten. I do not want to harm you. You may close your mouth and live here in peace. Men's memories are short. If you will not be silent, I will have you exiled."

"Egypt is already wounded beyond all healing when a mere noble may threaten a goddess and go unpunished," she whispered. "Have you thought of that, Commander? In spite of the power you slowly gather to yourself, the gulf between you and me can never be bridged. You believe that it matters to me whether I go on living or not, but in that respect your threats are meaningless. I do not care. That makes me dangerous, doesn't it?"

The pathetic challenge moved him. Taking her cold hand, he said, "In the beginning, Majesty, I was your father's friend. We all were. We longed for change. Osiris Amunhotep had reigned too long. But your father fell under a strange spell and brought us all to ruin. We have become people who do what has to be done and do not question the morality of our acts. That is what your father has done to us. Your god-husband was no different. I wish you could understand."

She did not withdraw her hand, but it lay in his lifelessly. "You have become evil, and you do not yet know it," she said brokenly, her face turned away. "I do not even have a child to keep his memory bright before me as the years go by."

He sighed and rose. "I am sorry. Akhetaten has become the grave of hopes for us all. Only in the next world can all wounds be healed."

"You hypocrite. May your words burn your throat and sear your lying lips." She gestured violently, and he bowed and walked quickly to the doors. Her speech, he reflected, was worthy of her mother. Her curse stayed with him, a tiny spot of coldness in his heart.

Mutnodjme was not asleep when at last he wearily closed his doors. She was lying on his couch in her sleeping robe, her face freshly scrubbed, watching the acrobatics of her dwarfs. As Horemheb entered, they bobbed to him and went scuttling out.

"I thought you would be shut in your own apartments tonight," he said as his body servant held back the sheets and he gratefully slid beside his wife. The man bowed himself out, and the glimmering light he held was gradually replaced by a bar of moonlight, dusky in the darkness. Mutnodjme shifted beside Horemheb, and her voice came warm and close out of the dimness. "Love is a surprising thing," she said. "Hathor not only looks like a cow, I sometimes think she has the mind of one. We, her devotees, wander blindly after her, moo moo, long after the sharper delights Bast has to offer have begun to pall. Little of the roughly honest young general I married remains, Horemheb. You are still the most handsome man in Egypt, but what I see behind those black eyes of yours is not very attractive. I suppose I do not divorce you because you pay my terrible debts."

For answer he pulled her against him and kissed her, profoundly grateful for this lazy, infuriating woman the dead empress had forced upon him. *As long as I have Mutnodjme*, he thought, *I know the gods have not yet condemned me.*

27

SMENKHARA'S BODY WAS TAKEN SOUTH TO THEBES FOR BUR-
ial in the tomb prepared for him there. It rode the sluggish
current of the summer river, curtained from profane eyes in
the cabin of *Kha-em-Ma'at* and attended by the priest Pwah
and a silent, steadily drinking Meritaten. Tutankhaten, Ankhesenpaaten, and Ay followed, and the members of the court
were strung out behind in their own boats. The harvest was
over. Egypt lay parched under the weight of a fiery sky, and
it seemed to those who drifted slowly on the sullen brown
breast of the Nile that they had left a haven of lush safety only
to journey through the dangers of a hostile land. No mourners
stood on the bank to wail with outstretched arms as the funeral
procession floated by. The brittle, choked vegetation that formed
a narrow barrier between water and fields shimmered, empty
of human life in the heat. Villages seemed deserted. Oxen stood
motionless under the thin shade of dusty palms, and donkeys
cooled themselves, heads down, in the shallows, but no ragged
village boys herded them. Crocodiles lay baking on the sand-
banks.

As the hours passed, an apprehensive silence began to cloak
the flotilla. Tutankhaten sat on a folding traveling chair under
an awning, staring incredulously as his birthright slid by him.
"Egypt is ugly," he said angrily to Ay beside him. "Why does
everyone tell me how beautiful it is?"

"Highness, it is high summer, that is all," he objected quietly, realizing that the boy could not remember ever having
been anywhere but the cultivated loveliness of Akhetaten. "Soon
Isis will cry, and the land will become a lake, and when the
waters sink, Egypt will be beautiful again."

"It is not just that," Tutankhaten responded. "Egypt is . . .
is derelict." The prince had relished the difficult word and was
smiling at his mastery, and Ay admitted to himself painfully
that the boy's precocious assessment was correct. They were

now sailing past a small temple, and he could see that one of its pillars had collapsed and the others were leaning wearily outward. Brown grass almost obscured the paving of the forecourt. It was not the first of such ruins. He had seen linen hung to dry in sacred places, the remains of fires blackening sanctuaries, crude peasant children's toys scattered around battered images of local gods. *The task is too large*, he thought, his heart fluttering erratically with the heat and his sudden fear. *Egypt is dead. I did not want to see this. None of us did. I am afraid to consider the state of Thebes.*

They berthed for one night at Akhmin, and Ay was carried on his litter to visit Tey. Walking through the garden toward the sprawling house made him feel like a ka stepping back in time, and he fully expected to see Tiye come running out of the portico's shade with Anen at her heels. The experience filled him with dread. Those years, so far away now, buried under a lifetime, held memories more vivid to him than those more recent visits, when he had come here from Malkatta as a vigorous, arrogant man to escape briefly the demands of his energetic sister. Tey greeted him with sleepy delight. He spent the evening talking to her of what he had seen on the river but was finally forced to acknowledge in the course of their conversation that he was no different from the men and women with whom he was sharing this journey, that somewhere, somehow, he, too, had succumbed to the dream and did not really want to wake.

Thebes was at first a relief, a gleam of ancient permanence. Though the company docked at the Malkatta water steps, it was obvious even from a distance that the city on the east bank, though now shrunken and with many dilapidated buildings on its outskirts, had not physically changed very much. Everywhere Ay looked, his eyes fell on something familiar: the configuration of the small islands in the middle of the Nile, the sharp soar of Karnak's towers against the deep blue of the noon sky, the thin pall of friendly dust over everything. The warehouses at the water's edge were tumbledown, many without roofs, and most of the unloading docks had disappeared completely, but it was Thebes, and Ay felt an oppression leave him. Even the crowds shoving and cursing one another made him smile before his barge swung to the west bank, away from them. They seemed neither hostile nor welcoming but were simply greedy for a spectacle which they had been denied for years.

Nonetheless Malkatta was a ruin. The canal up which kings had floated was choked with silt, the water steps slimed with green river growth, the fountains dry, the mighty lake now no more than a puddle of brackish water. An aging Maya and a dozen Amun priests threw themselves at Tutankhaten's feet, calling him Majesty, many of them in tears, but Ay looked beyond them to the imposing forest of white pillars that fronted Amunhotep's palace. The door to the women's garden hung from one twisted hinge. The lawn had reverted to sand. Many trees had already died, and many more lay uprooted over the weed-choked flower beds. *The servants left behind to tend the empty rooms, forgotten and unpaid, must have gone long ago,* Ay thought, *and only a fear of the dead has kept the Theban citizens from looting everything.*

With Tutankhaten by his side and the priests trailing eagerly behind, Ay walked into the reception hall. In spite of the dryness of the air, a smell of mold and disuse assailed his nostrils. The floor stirred with dead leaves and unidentifiable dry refuse. Steadily Ay crossed the room, past the throne baldachin whose frieze of cobras and sphinxes still gleamed gold, and through the great doors at the rear. As he walked, the memories woke and whispered at his back, swirling murmurous in the dust at his heels, so that by the time he entered Amunhotep's bedchamber, he could hardly bear their mute demands. Here the force of Pharaoh's great personality still lingered. Bes still gyrated, fat and lustful, around the walls, and grapes still hung, their paint unfaded, from the vines entwined around the wooden pillars.

"Do I have to sleep here?" Tutankhaten protested. "There are bat droppings over everything."

"No, Highness," Ay replied thickly. "I suggest that you stay on the barge. We must now return to Karnak and sacrifice to Amun."

Tutankhaten grimaced but made no demur, returning eagerly to the comforts of the boat. He was poled to the temple water steps, where another group of priests hailed him almost hysterically and covered his feet with kisses. Karnak, too, had suffered. Animals scampered out of their way as the party proceeded through the forecourt and under the pylons leading to the inner court. Everywhere Ay looked the name of Amun had been savagely obliterated, the inscriptions now incomplete and meaningless. Empty niches showed where images had once stood. Everything was unkempt, neglected.

"There were enough of us to maintain the upkeep of Karnak," a priest whispered to Ay as they watched Tutankhaten and Maya vanish into the sanctuary, "and after Pharaoh ordered the temples actually closed and the priests dismissed, few dared to come here. Thanks be to Amun, there is a young incarnation who will restore the precepts of Ma'at!"

And how will he do it? Ay wanted to retort sarcastically. *Shall he turn stones into gold?* Yet gladness swept over him as he stood under the canopy in the broiling sun, watching a thin plume of incense rise above the sanctuary wall, and feeling the rejuvenation of his thoughts.

That night Tutankhaten ordered Ay to have his cot set up beside the royal couch, and together they lay behind the curtains while the Followers paced the deck and thronged the bank. Ay knew that Horemheb was sleepless, patrolling his sentries, and was grateful for the commander's vigilance. The buildings of Thebes were in darkness as soon as the sun went down, but dots of orange light flickered along the alleys, furtive and faint. Jackals howled so loudly that Ay could have sworn that they were not out on the desert but prowling the city. Sometimes Ay would doze, only to be jerked awake by drunken shouts and screaming that wafted full-blown across the Nile.

"I will never move back here!" Tutankhaten snorted once in the darkness. "This is no place for a god to dwell! No wonder my father left it."

"It was not thus when your father began to build Akhetaten," Ay replied. "It was the center of the world."

"It is disgusting," Tutankhaten said scornfully, "like the rest of the country. I am a god of poverty."

Wisely Ay did not argue. He was as troubled as Tutankhaten.

Smenkhara's funeral procession, made up only of the family and a few courtiers, was meager. Women had been recruited as mourners from the shrunken harem that had become the only living cell at Malkatta. A few remembered Smenkhara as a baby, but most donned the blue linen and keened and cast soil on their heads without emotion. So many Amun priests were in attendance, thin, ragged men with hope rekindled in their eyes, either walking at the rear of the company or gathered in small groups along the route, that to Ay, mopping the sweat from under his wig and gasping in the heat, it seemed less a ritual of respect and magic for a pharaoh than a ceremony of reassurance for the servants of the god. The thought gave him only a passing twinge of regret. Amun's restoration was infinitely more important than the pitiful remains of an unlucky young man. Slowly the procession wound toward the Valley in West-of-Thebes. Under the wailing of the harem women there was talk and laughter. Ay parted the curtain of his litter in time to see the mighty likeness of the Son of Hapu, and he glanced up at the wide-open, mild stone eyes with a shudder before letting the curtains swing shut. He had been more than a man, after all.

Smenkhara's small tomb was unfinished. He had begun it without much interest, in response to Ay's urging, and had not cared to oversee its progress. Its floor was still rough, its walls uninscribed, and the one coffin prepared for the body stood propped against the rock beside the hole gouged for a door. The rites began hurriedly, without reverence. One by one those present knelt to kiss the foot of the coffin, their forced tears long since dried. Only Meritaten clung to the sarcophagus, hysterical with grief, laying her cheek against the painted wood with swollen eyes closed tightly. After Tutankhaten as heir performed the Opening of the Mouth, the funeral dancers went through their paces without interest. In the end even Ay wished that the hypocritical play might be over.

The coffin was carried into the tiny room and placed inside the golden shrine Akhenaten had presented to his mother. Ay was dreading another outburst from Meritaten, but she stood regally, flowers in her hands, bravely composed. He looked about, and shame stabbed him. He had ordered that funerary equipment for the tomb be selected from the place where the family had for generations stored objects they either wanted to be buried with or thought might be needed at their funerals, and those responsible for filling Smenkhara's tomb had not chosen with much care. Furniture had been simply flung into the tomb and left to lie haphazardly about. A few token weapons bearing Amunhotep III's cartouche, some cups of Tiye's, jewelry belonging to harem children that had died, a canopic chest incised with a name even Ay did not recognize—such were the insults Smenkhara was to carry into the next world, providing the gods wanted him.

Ay's glance lit upon the four magic bricks set hurriedly into the four walls. Bending surreptitiously under cover of Maya's sonorous chants, he hoped he might read Smenkhara's name, but saw that the bricks bore the cartouche of Osiris Akhenaten. *They must have been made*, Ay reflected dismally, *in the years when Akhenaten was still preparing his tomb in Thebes and did not yet mind having his name linked with a god who was not the Aten. What protection from the demons can the name of Akhenaten afford this poor young man?* Meritaten stepped forward to lay her flowers on the coffin before the shrine was closed. Ay moved closer, dropping his eyes to the foot of the coffin so that he might not see Meritaten's tears. There he noticed something crudely inscribed in gold leaf, the lines uneven, the characters scrawled. Intrigued, he went closer. "I breathe thy sweet breath which comes forth from thy mouth," he read. "It is my desire that I may hear thy sweet voice, even the north wind. Give me thy hands. Thou mayest call upon my name eternally, and it shall not fail from thy mouth, my beloved brother, thou being with me to all eternity." Startled and deeply moved, he looked up. Meritaten was watching him, pride and love suddenly transforming her disfigured face, and he smiled weakly and dropped his gaze.

He could hardly bear to sit through the travesty of a funeral feast that had been prepared on carpets before the tomb, but he forced down the food for the sake of Smenkhara's ka. Horemheb and Tutankhaten were discussing the lion hunt that had been planned for the following day. The courtiers and women lounged under their canopies, tossing goose bones onto the sand and flirting with one another. Ankhesenpaaten knelt by her sister, trying to tempt Meritaten with pomegranates and sweet wine, but after the obligatory tasting Meritaten sat with her knees drawn up to her chin under the transparent blue linen, watching the priests seal Smenkhara's tomb. It was with overwhelming relief that Ay rose with the company to return to the barges. He was ashamed of the whole gathering, including himself.

He woke just after dawn, still with a tension in his chest, to find his steward kneeling by the cot in the gray light. The barge was motionless. Behind the damask curtains of the cabin, Tutankhaten was breathing evenly in sleep. Ay sat up slowly, his eyes burning. "What is it?"

"Something has happened in the harem, Fanbearer," the man

said in a low voice. "The commander was roused by the Keeper of the Harem Door, and he asks you to come."

"Very well. Rouse my body servant. If Pharaoh wakes, tell him I will wait upon him as soon as possible."

His sleepy servant dressed him, and taking a Follower, Ay walked the ramp onto the bank and made his way along the canal, through the rotting garden door, and across the harem lawn. It did not look quite so desolate in the early light. The large lake was a dusty bowl, but beyond the main garden and another wall was a small oasis of greenness and order where the harem attendants still cared for the grounds behind the harem. Here the women Akhenaten had not appropriated for himself swam and lazed their way through the uneventful, endless days. Most of them were old or aging, relics from the reign of their master Amunhotep III, supported over the years by funds from Akhetaten. None of them ventured far from her own quarters.

Ay was greeted abstractedly at the door by the keeper and led toward the apartments that had been hurriedly prepared for Meritaten and her sister. Before he reached the rooms, Ankhesenpaaten came running toward him, shrieking. Flinging herself into his astonished arms, she buried her face against his chest. "Meritaten is dead," she sobbed. "They are cutting off her hair!" Even had he not wanted to pause and soothe her, his legs would not have obeyed him. Vividly he saw himself kneeling by Tiye's couch, one hand in her red hair, the other reaching for his knife. Apprehension filled him. He eased his granddaughter's fingers away, forcing himself to treat her gently. "Take her somewhere quiet and give her wine," he ordered the keeper, and ignoring Ankhesenpaaten's screams, he hurried along the passage. The door to Meritaten's bedchamber was open, and a babble of excited women's voices spilled out. He was met by a terrified servant girl who, seeing him enter, threw herself at his feet.

"Do not punish me, Great Lord!" she wept. "The queen would not let me sleep in the room with her! She sent me away!"

Ay's terror erupted. He kicked her aside and roughly forced his way through the crowd of knife-waving women, cursing them as he went. Many of them already waved locks of Meritaten's hair. As he neared the couch, the sweetish stench of blood rose around him, and he was dimly aware that his sandals were sticking to the floor. The women fell back, and Ay came to a halt.

Meritaten lay on her back. At first Ay thought that she had been wearing a soiled sleeping gown but a second later realized that she was covered in blood. The sheet was stained with it, the mattress still wet with it. Blood had poured over her pillow and trickled along her arm onto the floor. Ay had never seen such destruction. But at the center of it was Meritaten's face, brown-smeared yet peaceful. Ay went closer. Half under the couch was the ivory-hilted knife she had used. He glanced at her hands. She had not sawed at her wrists. Squatting, he lifted what remained of her black hair and found the neat, deep cut just below her ear. He could not rise again without placing his hands on the mattress by her pale cheek. A sudden silence had fallen, and Ay turned to see the women slipping out, bowing, as Horemheb came in.

"You should have left a guard in here!" Ay shouted at him. "Look what they have done to her hair!"

"I was only gone a few moments," Horemheb replied. "I brought no men with me, I was not prepared for this, there are only a handful of harem guards on duty, and I ran to make sure that no one left these quarters." With effort he ceased speaking and drew a deep breath. "It might have been murder, you see."

"She was my flesh!" Ay howled at him. "It is the blood of my family soaking this room! This is your doing!"

Horemheb was clearly shaken. "I did not harm her," he protested urgently. "I had no reason."

"You gave her reason." Faintness blurred his vision, and he strove to remain upright. "I hope you are satisfied. She is a suicide. She cannot be beautified. Her ka is lost. She cannot even be buried. Horemheb . . ." Shamefully he began to cry. Horemheb had stepped to his side and taken his elbow when a movement in the doorway caused both men to look up in time to see Tutankhaten's eyes widen and the color leave his face. Ay staggered forward. Horemheb sprang to the boy's side, slamming the doors closed behind them, but it was too late. Tutankhaten turned to the wall and began to retch. No one dared to touch him. When he had finished, he wiped his mouth on his kilt.

"Ankhesenpaaten woke me shrieking," he whispered. "The women who bowed to me as I came had locks of hair in their hands." He put a shaking hand on Ay's arm. "Uncle," he choked, "is that why I wear my mother's hair around my neck?" Defenseless, Ay nodded. Tutankhaten whimpered, but then, aware of the men silently watching, he controlled himself. "I have begun my reign in blood," he said. Taking his hand from Ay's arm, he walked unsteadily away.

Meritaten's body was wrapped in white linen and given to the river. The priests, though sympathetic and eager to please the young god whom they depended on to restore their fortunes, did not dare to bury her. Ay, standing on the bank with the little group that had gathered to cast flowers after the weighted form, knew that he would never forgive Horemheb, or himself. For in spite of the words he had hurled at the commander out of his own shock and anguish as he stood by Meritaten's couch, he knew he must share the responsibility for her death. He had wanted Smenkhara removed in such a way that his principles might remain uncompromised. Coward that he was, he had not been able to put his wishes into practice but had been secretly relieved when Horemheb shouldered the risks he himself was unwilling to face. He had somehow imagined a future free of complications once Smenkhara was gone. The true consequence of Horemheb's act horrified him, and he began to wonder, as he watched Ankhesenpaaten place a comforting arm around Tutankhaten's shoulders and Horemheb step to the river's brink to add his tribute to the others, what further unforeseen events might have been set in motion by the murder in which he was implicated by his desire to be rid of his nephew. He hated the commander for the havoc that had been wrought within the family and for making him confront his guilt, but he also feared the cold place in Horemheb that had enabled him to execute such deeds. *Having escaped retribution*, Ay thought, *will Horemheb grow more confident that he is above the law?* He could hardly bear to be in the man's presence, and as soon as Tutankhaten turned toward the sanctuary of his state barge, Ay fled them all.

At the end of Mesore the court sailed north to Memphis, and on New Year's Day Tutankhaten was crowned king in Egypt with full and ancient ceremony. On Ay's advice he took to himself every traditional pharaonic title—Mighty Bull, the Horus of Gold, Beautiful God, Lord of the Two Lands—and though he had spent no time as high priest in the temple of Ptah, as every heir before him had done, he made his devotions to the creator of the world with exemplary reverence. He did not, however, travel to On. "Later you may worship in the city of Ra," Ay had told him, "but not yet. It is too soon to be seen in the temples of the sun." Tutankhaten did not argue. He was content to enjoy the adoration of priests and people and to preside over the traditional gift giving and feasts.

Nor did he object when, several weeks after the coronation, Ay had a marriage contract drawn up between the young pharaoh and Ankhesenpaaten. The court considered her a good choice. She was popular, kind, and beautiful, and had already proved that she could bear children. From Ay's point of view her attraction lay in the fact that she loved him and would do whatever he asked. *Now there will be no one in any position of power*, Ay thought with relief, *able to be manipulated by Horemheb. If indeed he does dream of taking the crown for himself, it cannot be through the aid of high officials. Only another act of violence would bring it within his grasp, and I do not believe his ambition is so great that he would once again risk his complete undoing.*

With the shadow of the drought still dark in Egyptian minds, all waited anxiously for the Inundation, and there were great celebrations when Isis began to cry at the end of Paophi. But Ay was hardly aware of the beginning of a new season. Since the court's return to Akhetaten from Memphis, he had been busy formulating a policy that would gradually return Egypt to its full glory. Day by day his servants brought him reports on the state of affairs at Karnak, the waning crowds gathering to worship in the Aten temple, the ebb and flow of gold in the Treasury, and he conferred long into each night with representatives from the nomes, who brought to him the hopes of the common people. He oversaw the marriage of Tutankhaten and Ankhesenpaaten, and was delighted when he saw them take pleasure in each other's company. He knew he must be very sure of the direction he wished Pharaoh to take, and not until he had tested every argument possible against his proposal did he request a formal audience with Tutankhaten, asking Pharaoh if Horemheb could be present also.

On a sparkling winter morning he lay before the king to kiss the royal feet and press his lips against Ankhesenpaaten's smooth skin. Horemheb, carefully painted and arrayed in yellow linen, was already there, standing with arms folded in the midst of his attendants and some of his officers. The reception hall was crowded with ministers, nobles, and Pharaoh's young friends. At a word from Tutankhaten, Ay rose. Smiling, the boy indicated a chair at the foot of the throne steps. "You may sit, Uncle," he said. "You, also, Commander. I believe that today I am to be told what to do."

"No, Precious Egg," Ay countered swiftly, meeting his enquiring glance with alarm at the boy's perception. "No man would dare to tell the incarnation what to do. Yet my heart is heavy on behalf of Egypt, and I beg Your Majesty to look kindly on my suggestions."

Horemheb had remained standing, but Ay did not bother to protest. The commander would need every advantage today. Tutankhaten nodded for him to continue. "As Your Majesty doubtless knows, the gulf between the Divinity and the people has never been wider. Your predecessor not only removed himself from Amun's holy city, but he then proceeded to take from his people their gods, their livelihood, and their empire. It is your privilege to restore to them what your father removed." Tutankhaten was listening politely, but Ankhesenpaaten frowned. "Your Majesty has few competent ministers on whom to call," Ay went on carefully. "And I would first point out that the Treasury is depleted. It is impossible at present to do everything I know Your Majesty desires to accomplish." Horemheb had begun to smile, and Ay knew that he had seen the direction his words were taking. "Therefore Your Majesty must decide what tasks are most urgent." He glanced briefly at Horemheb. "The commander will tell you that it is imperative to regain our empire immediately. Truly, it is the shame of every Egyptian that the world no longer bows to us. But such a move would not please your subjects. They would see their young men march away while their village shrines remained a haven for owls and jackals. War would increase their sufferings."

Tutankhaten held up a hand. "Is this indeed what you would propose, Commander?"

Horemheb nodded. "What your uncle says is true, Majesty. I believe that only by regaining the empire can the Treasury be filled and Egypt prosper again. The first, the most important task before you is the occupation of northern Syria, Rethennu, Amki, and Amurru. The princes of those people now pay allegiance to Suppiluliumas. At any moment the Khatti could invade us, and we would be defeated."

"Majesty, if Suppiluliumas were planning to invade Egypt,

I think he would have attempted it by now," Ay cut in quickly. "But Egypt is a long way from Khatti, and Suppiluliumas's own empire is already very extended. I think he does not invade because he knows that as yet he could not hold us. We have time for other things first, things that are more important. If Your Majesty makes war, your gold cannot go into healing Egypt."

"Then what do you suggest?" The clear eyes were regarding him intently.

Ay met their gaze without hesitation. "First, repair Karnak and give Maya the authority to appoint new priests. Let the people see that once again the god who brought prosperity to Egypt is being honored. Then send your architects throughout the country to restore the village shrines. Let the palace at Malkatta be restored, and move back to Thebes."

"But, Ay," Ankhesenpaaten interjected hesitantly, "my father taught us that there was only one god, the Aten Disk. If we forsake that god, we will be punished."

"Dear Majesty," Ay said gently, looking into the earnest young face, "I do not propose that the worship of the Aten be proscribed or its temples closed. Those who wish should be allowed to continue to bring offerings. But the common people have never understood the purity of the Aten and do not feel safe without the protection of the ancient gods. It is time for your husband to be seen as Amun in the land."

"And who will pay for all this running about on behalf of the gods?" Horemheb broke in hotly. "You have said yourself that the Treasury is empty. Such a policy will require a great deal of time. A war to regain the empire will be a quick undertaking, and one with the immediate compensation of booty and tribute!"

"Providing we were victorious," Ay said dryly. For a second their eyes met. Ay knew that Horemheb still suffered from the shame of Egypt's defeat at the hands of the Khatti, and desired to restore his dignity. "If not, the people's hardships would be increased, and any chance to regain our subject lands would be forfeited forever. Egypt would be a Khatti vassal. Do you want to take that risk?"

"Attend!" Tutankhaten snapped, and they both fell silent and turned to him, having almost forgotten his presence. "The commander has a point, Uncle. Restoring the power of the gods will demand time, but also much gold. From where will all the riches come?"

"Out of the coffers of your nobles and princes," Ay replied. He was forced to raise his voice above the indignant murmur that now broke out in the hall. "Your father seized Amun's land in the Delta, his cattle and slaves, to pay for offerings to the Aten. Some was given to those who served the Disk well." He was on shaky ground, not wanting to accuse Akhenaten of paying for friendship before his son. "I propose, Majesty, that you return to Amun his land in the Delta, and enough cattle from the estates of the nobles for the god's servants to start new herds. Give them seed to sow, and take Amun's vineyards away from those who have lately acquired them. In this way Maya and his priests can effect their own recovery."

"And I suppose you want to restore the god's Treasury, also?" Horemheb sneered.

"Partly, yes. The full amount was incalculable, and much of it was used to build this city, but I ask Pharaoh to empty part of the Aten's coffers in behalf of Amun. The priests of the Disk can live directly on the offerings of the faithful. But your restorations should not only involve Amun." He turned to Tutankhaten and a white-faced Ankhesenpaaten. "The plots of land belonging to the local gods were ceded to your father's ministers, Horus. If you return them, you will have earned the love of all your subjects." He stood now and faced the sullen courtiers. "All of you! You know this must be done. You are Egypt's richest men and women, the sons and daughters of Osiris Akhenaten's ministers. If you think to side with Horemheb and thus keep your wealth, you are mistaken. He will take it for his wars. Give to the god who has never failed his people, and in the end you will prosper." Their expressions did not alter, but the muttering died away. He lowered his voice so that only Horemheb and the royal couple could hear. "Commander, you abandoned the empress, Pharaoh's mother, to come to Akhetaten because Osiris Akhenaten gave you the Nubian gold monopoly that had been Amun's. If you return it to Maya's hands, you will hasten the recovery by many months."

"You goatish old hypocrite," Horemheb hissed back. "I was not the only prince who changed face. You also deserted her, your own sister. The Nubian gold was not my only reason for standing beside the Aten's incarnation!"

"Yes, I know." Ay looked up at Tutankhaten. "Your Majesty's tutors admire your quick grasp of learning," he said. "I know that Your Majesty begins to comprehend the problems. I would like to add that it is necessary to stop at once Osiris Smenkhara's policy of selling grain. All trade must cease. We must once more fill the storage granaries, live only from Egypt's own bounty, hoard all we can until we are ready to invite the rest of the world to bring us their goods in exchange for the wealth of a country restored."

Tutankhaten's hand had stolen into his queen's. "Is that all, Uncle?"

"No, Horus." Ay mentally took a deep breath. "I would like you to consider changing your name."

Silence greeted his words, followed by murmurs of outrage. A name was a sacred and magic thing, a protection for the bearer, with power to conjure the help of the god whose own name was woven into it. No child was named without lengthy consultations with oracles and much prayer, a process that was doubly complicated for a pharaoh, an incarnation of the god himself. Tutankhaten's hennaed lips were parted in shock.

"Why do you suggest this?" he managed.

"Because no matter how Your Majesty is seen to honor Amun, the people will hear in your name the name of the Disk, with all the bitter memories it brings. They will not forget, and hence they will not trust you."

"I do not care about the trust of cattle, of slaves!" the boy retorted. "You have been very sacrilegious in your description of my father. He gave me my name. It is a holy name!"

Ay anticipated his fear, but by now he also knew his little nephew well. Tutankhaten would ponder his advice and, better still, would ask Ankhesenpaaten for her opinion. Ay already respected the young queen's judgment. He knelt in apology. "Forgive an old man who loves you," he said.

"Majesty, I beg leave to answer the fanbearer's proposals with arguments of my own!" Horemheb began, but by now Tutankhaten was stirring impatiently on the throne, and his gold-sandaled foot was beginning to swing.

"Not now, Commander," he said. "I am bored with all this talk, and I want to swim. Some other time. You are all dismissed."

"Father is right," Mutnodjme said to Horemheb that night as they sat beside the small ornamental pool in their garden.

The light was fading, and as dusk fell, the fragrance of the flowers intensified. Moths began to flutter in and out of the lamp glow that spilled out between the entrance pillars. The still water of the pool was broken occasionally by the flick and swirl of goldfish that rose to snap at the hovering mosquitoes. Horemheb watched the ripples on the surface that reflected the red and purple of the sunset. "He is not necessarily making a bid for complete power. He has enough control of Pharaoh now. Tutankhaten is a child, with a child's hostility toward you, but that will fade as he grows. Once Egypt stands upright again, his thoughts will turn to war, and Amun will smile on you once more."

He glanced sharply at her, stung by the sarcasm in her voice. She was wrapped in a white woolen cloak, but as the evening had not yet turned chilly, the garment hung loosely from her shoulders and fell away from her naked belly. One foot was tucked up under her brown thigh. "He must at least let me march on Gaza," he replied. "Egypt has held it since the days of mighty Thothmes III, and it is our most important seaport."

"He will, when we have something to trade." She sipped her wine, running her tongue around the rim of the cup. "It is not so bad, Commander, to lose the gold monopoly. We may have to sell a few dozen slaves, though the gods know who can afford to buy any these days, and perhaps close one of our houses. I still have the land deeded to me at Djarukha by the empress. Her old trading connections are in chaos, but if all goes well, that situation will soon be remedied." A burst of laughter came wafting over the wall that separated their private garden from the lawns of Horemheb's concubines, followed by the excited squealing of Mutnodjme's two dwarfs.

"The empress would not be so craven," Horemheb said bitterly. "She would have found a way to strengthen Egypt internally *and* make war."

"I think not. You admired her very much, didn't you, although you betrayed her? I often believe you were a little in love with her yourself."

Horemheb managed a grin. "I was born too soon, Mutnodjme, or too late, I don't know which. I would have made a glorious incarnation."

"Unfortunately your blood lacks the fire of the divine," she retorted.

"Perhaps. But as you are the half sister of a woman who was once a queen, yours contains a little of that rare glow."

They fell silent. The light on the pool faded to a dusky blue, and the shadows of the garden began to blur and emerge into full night. Mutnodjme drained her cup and dropped it into the grass.

"Meritaten's suicide was a terrible thing," she said quietly after a while, "and people will not forget. Be circumspect, my husband, and wait."

He did not answer, nor did he look at her. A constraint grew between them, until Horemheb stood abruptly and shouted for his litter bearers. "I am going to gamble with Nakht-Min," he said and went away.

28

DURING THE FOLLOWING WEEK AY CONTAINED HIS IMPA-tience, knowing that the suggestions he had made to Pharaoh were being discussed with Ankhesenpaaten. On the eighth day he was summoned to hear Tutankhaten's decision. Pharaoh, as Ay surmised he would, agreed to every proposal he had made.

Tutankhaten made him regent, thus giving him a legitimate power that in all his life as courtier, advisor, and royal confidant he had never before held. The position also gave him new vigor. Time could not return to him the stamina of his youth, but he learned to husband his resources and within the confines of his age ruled with wisdom and experience. At his request Pharaoh appointed Horemheb as King's Deputy, an honorary post that would last only until the queen produced an heir but that kept the commander actively at court. Nakht-Min was given the title of Fanbearer on the Right Hand.

Three years were to pass before Malkatta was considered fit for occupation, and in that time Ay worked to bring all his strategies to fruition. Under his careful rule, Egypt began to struggle to her feet. Without compunction he took gold and land that had once belonged to Amun and the other gods and returned it. Maya became a familiar sight at court through his frequent conferences with Pharaoh and the regent. It soon became clear that there were not enough priests left in Egypt to staff the refurbished temples. Ay spoke to the Aten's men, particularly those who had once served Amun but who had defected under Akhenaten, coercing no one but making it clear that there was to be no return to the years of heresy and no priest who wished to live in comfort should believe otherwise.

Maya's new men traveled the nomes, inducting priests from local families and training them in their native villages. Holy dancers were appointed from the palace and their expenses met from Pharaoh's private coffers, which were also used to refashion images of the gods and rehabilitate their sanctuaries. Heralds went into every village, publicly proclaiming the rescinding of Akhenaten's proscription against all gods but the Aten. Aten shrines began to be defaced, and Ay watched anxiously lest a spirit of violent reaction should lead to bloodshed across the country, but though crude epithets calling Akhenaten a criminal and curse-bringer continued to appear on public buildings for many months, the people's indignation soon died.

In a further effort to strengthen his link to Egypt's past, Pharaoh began to emphasize his relationship to Amunhotep III. Ay had already suggested to him that he set his architects and masons to work to finish Amunhotep III's temple at Soleb and inscribe their names together prominently there. On the lions sculpted for the temple he referred to him as his father. Tutankhaten also took upon himself the completion of Amun's southern home in Luxor, a project that had absorbed so much of Amunhotep's interest that it had come to be associated more closely with the dead pharaoh than with Amun himself. Ay had proposed, as tactfully as possible, that Tutankhaten affirm his kinship with Amunhotep III, not wanting to belittle the boy's memories of his father, and if Tutankhaten was hurt, he did not show it. Cheerfully he pored over the plans his craftsmen placed before him, taking a delight in every detail and making many suggestions himself.

With Pharaoh's permission, Ay imposed crushing taxes on the peasants in order to repair Malkatta, build new docks at Thebes, and start renovations in the city. He issued an edict commanding that every noble's crops be assessed at harvest and a portion of grain from their holdings be deposited in the village granaries adjacent to each estate. The wealthy courtiers grumbled, but knew that the end result of such harsh policies would be their ultimate enrichment once the economy was stable.

Despite the stream of ministers to his office every day, Ay was lonely. He dictated voluminous letters to Tey at Akhmin and read her rambling replies many times over. He grew to hate the nights at Akhetaten. Though Pharaoh had begun to host great feasts like those that had awed foreign embassies in Malkatta's days of glory, their gaiety could not dam the dark current of past miseries that waited to flood the many quiet corners of the palace when the guests had departed. Ay slept lightly and often woke at odd hours. While he occasionally summoned his scribe and lay listening to stories, he more often left his quarters and wandered the passages of the palace, sometimes meeting other courtiers disturbed by dreams of blood and sadness.

Ay knew that the curse would linger for as long as the city remained occupied. The deformed young pharaoh from whose mind Akhetaten had sprung cast a stronger spell of madness over it now than he had in life. Ay sometimes caught himself holding his breath as he stood under torchlight in some little-used corner of the palace, waiting in fear for some terrible outburst that never came. Tiye would call to him in the night, and Akhenaten's dead children sobbed in the shadows. The soldiers who guarded the tombs in the cliffs behind the city were already being paid twice their normal salary. *Tiye never liked this place*, Ay thought to himself time and again. *Long before the foundations of Akhetaten were laid, she said that the site was unlucky, the cliffs jealously guarding its virginity.*

But such fancies did not reach Tutankhaten. He was becoming a handsome young man with a cheerful disposition, and although he occasionally betrayed flashes of Tiye's bad temper, those who watched him covertly for any sign of instability saw only a pharaoh who disliked being still, who laughed loudly, who hunted with vigor, and who went to his couch late and reluctantly. He reminded Ay of Thothmes, Tiye's first son, who had blazed so brightly at court. The queen, too, was blooming. Tutankhaten, though still only fourteen in his third year of rule, had precociously consummated his marriage and had already begun to organize his harem, retiring many of his father's older women and taking the younger ones for himself.

Ankhesenpaaten was pregnant, at seventeen reflecting the new spirit of recovery that was slowly infecting the whole court.

Four days before Pharaoh took his final leave of Akhetaten, he sat in full regalia before Maya and a packed hall, the Double Crown on his brow and the crook, flail, and scimitar in his hands, and solemnly dictated the changing of his name. His name had meant Living Image of the Aten, but as he pressed his seal against the scroll he became Tutankhamun, Living Image of Amun. Ankhesenpaaten followed his example, obviously distressed as she heard herself for the first time called Ankhesenamun, Living Through Amun. To her it was a betrayal of her father and the god she had been raised to worship. She sat white and silent as the people roared their approval, her hands protectively caressing her swollen womb, but she knew by now how to keep her sorrow to herself.

On the following day Tutankhamun, Ankhesenamun, and Ay were carried along the Royal Road to the north palace, surrounded by the noise and chaos of the impending move. Carts already piled with household possessions choked the alleys. Domestic animals fluttered and dodged before the royal cavalcade, pursued by frantic naked children. Out of sight, behind the palace's high wall and the gardens that ran down to the river, the shouts and curses of the barge captains could be clearly heard. The river was choked with craft of all sizes, and every available dock was full. Ay knew that the stretch of water that flowed past the secluded estates of the nobles was not much clearer, and that today Horemheb himself was abroad in the city with the local Mazoi, trying to prevent outbreaks of violence in the congested streets and offering protection to the wealthy. Only the precincts of the Aten temple were quiet, the empty forecourt lying burning under Ra's noon fury. The few priests, including Meryra, who had elected to stay were hidden in the sanctuary. Dust hung golden in the air. Clouds of flies hovered everywhere over the deluge of refuse and offal scoured from the emptying homes. Already the pretty Aten shrines that adorned every street corner were bare and soiled, the incense hollows blackened and cold. Dogs panted under the shade they afforded, and sand drifted over the small paved areas before them where the dancers used to sway. Ay, a square of perfumed linen held to his nose, was glad that the queen's litter curtains remained closed. Akhetaten resembled a city threatened by an invading army, its citizens frantic to escape.

The double gates set into the wall that separated the north palace from the rest of the city were closed, but Nefertiti's guards swung them open before the heralds reached them, and the litters passed through. Ay braced himself for the effort his litter bearers must make to mount the long stair and, as the climb began, sat watching the terraces unfold. The grass glistened with water. The flowers massed, rank upon rank of color, and the trees clustered on each terrace draped leaves over the tops of the ones on the level below. There was no dust here, no cacophony, only the gentle tinkle of falling water in the fountains and the gust of flower fragrance carried on the breezes.

The litters were set down, the paving stone hurriedly dampened with milk and wine to receive Pharaoh's holy feet, and the three stepped out. Far below them the Nile ran blue and silver, swirling where it met the pilings of Nefertiti's wharves. Her golden barge flashed as it rocked in the swell of a craft passing swiftly from the north customs house. Ankhesenamun sighed. "Nothing has changed here," she said, her voice wistful.

"I thought I had forgotten it," Pharaoh replied, "but it all comes back to me now. There is the tree I used to climb, and from there I could swing down all the terraces. It was a stiff climb back up, though." His servants waited while he admired the view, the gardens, the long prospect of the river. Ay did not know whether he was giving his queen a moment to collect herself or was insensitively prolonging her anguish, but at last he turned to the steward Meryra's prostrate form by the open enrance. "Get up and lead us to your mistress," he ordered.

Meryra rose and bowed several times. "It is a great honor, Mighty Bull," he said gravely, and they followed him into the welcome coolness of Nefertiti's little kingdom.

The public hall was filled with statues. As Meryra glided ahead, Ay looked about incredulously. Nefertiti gazed at them solemnly as they went, her face formed from the dark oiliness of ebony, the streaked shine of marble, the warmth of sandstone. Some of the works were busts, some merely heads, but the majority were full-size likenesses. Some were very formal, the head wigged and crowned with the cobra or the masculine lines of the sun crown, the stiff body covered in pleated linen to the sandaled feet, the arms rigid at the stone sides. But many were soft and flowing with the curves and arrested movements of life. The artistic genius Akhenaten had clumsily tried to foster had found its flowering here, in one man's hidden tribute to the woman he adored. Every piece portrayed Nefertiti in the fullness of her character. Thothmes had no illusions about her. Together with her sensuality and beauty, the hall breathed her arrogance, her pettiness, her strange defenselessness. *This is my daughter*, Ay thought, dazed. One statue caused them all to pause. Nefertiti, in white limestone, the heaviness of middle age in her thighs and sagging breasts and belly, was bending to one side. In her outstretched hand she held a lotus. She was smiling slightly. Her eyes were closed, and her nostrils flared toward the open bloom. Her own hair fell straight to her shoulders, and she wore a thin circlet that held an ankh above her forehead. Ankhs were strung around her neck and fingers. The whole piece was languorous with the worship of life.

"Gods!" Tutankhamun exclaimed with disgust. "Sculptors are far from being anything more than the servants of better men, but this one is no more than a slave. He would starve before he found a patron." Ay pulled his gaze from the statue and walked on.

The passages leading to the private reception hall were also graced with carvings of Nefertiti, and it seemed that Thothmes was a painter as well, for the walls of the hall itself were brilliant with immense likenesses of her. Here he had kept to traditional modes of expression, but Ay noticed that the flesh had been painted red, the color used for portraying males, and the hair blue, for the lapis lazuli of the gods.

Meryra had led them to where a few chairs were pulled close together at a low table containing refreshments and flowers. As they approached, Nefertiti and the sculptor rose from their seats. Thothmes whispered in Nefertiti's ear, and immediately she knelt and prostrated herself, rising with his help to stand unsmiling with hands clasped before her. She was simply dressed in a soft white sheath that fell from the onyx jewels at her throat in many pleats to the floor. More onyx studded her belt. On each arm she wore thick bracelets. Her wig, too, was simple, a straight black fall of hair to her shoulders, fringed and surmounted by a gold circlet made up of tiny disks. She looked, Ay thought, as though she had stepped out of another age. Her face was heavily painted, but the paint could not obscure the delicate nest of lines around her eyes or the faint grooves in her cheeks. Thothmes was also painted, wigged, and ribboned, but beneath the formality of his attire Ay saw a lean, graceful man with a deep, generous gaze. Ankhesenamun smiled at her mother, but Nefertiti seemed not to notice her. Nor would she meet her father's eye as her glance swept them. Without invitation, Tutankhamun took a chair and said, "It is good to see you again, Nefertiti."

The others sat, Ankhesenamun looking down at her distorted lap, hurt and disappointed.

"Your Majesty has grown a great deal since I saw you last," Nefertiti said, "and you, Father, you are fatter!"

Ay looked at her curiously, for he had, in fact, lost weight since assuming the responsibilities of regent. Her old fire was gone, the restless body strangely calm, her movements studied. At Ay's glance, Thothmes leaned toward Nefertiti with a small proprietary gesture. Ay took Ankhesenamun's hand.

"But, no," he replied. "I have become thinner in the service of my king." He turned to Ankhesenamun with a silencing gesture. "Nefertiti, I am sorry that your daughter could not come today. You were expecting her, but she is not well."

The wide mouth turned down. Nefertiti seemed to be listening, her head on one side, and then she smiled coldly. "You are senile, Regent. Ankhesenpaaten, is your health not good?"

"You are blind, aren't you?" Ay said softly before the girl could answer. "Oh, Nefertiti, such pride! If we had known . . ."

"If you had known," she sneered, her voice thin, "I would have had to endure everyone's pity. Poor Nefertiti, once so powerful, now an aging, blind traitor who cannot take one step without assistance. Let us fling her a little sympathy, though surely the gods do not expect it of us. After all, she sinned and she is being punished!" One hand flitted briefly over her pale face. "No, I am not completely blind. I can distinguish between light and darkness."

The words hung over them. With a cry, Ankhesenamun left her chair and embraced her mother. Nefertiti's arms closed around her.

"You must leave here at once!" Pharaoh exclaimed. "At Malkatta you can have apartments and servants, and my own physicians will attend you. Come with us, Nefertiti."

Her fingers were exploring Ankhesenamun's face. "Malkatta?" she replied quietly. "No, Majesty, it is too late for that. I will not endure the silent laughter of the court behind my back day after day. Here I am still queen. My husband is gone, all my children but one dead, no son of mine sits on the Horus Throne. But at last some measure of peace has come to me. Would you destroy it in order to show your mercy?"

Stung at the condemnation in her voice, Tutankhamun said hotly, "We are not obliged to show you mercy! We listen to the entreaties of our queen!"

Nefertiti set Ankhesenamun gently away from her and nodded. "My husband made me holy," she said. "The city of Akhetaten is a song of praise to the Aten, and to me. It is mine. I will never leave."

"I cannot guarantee your safety once the Mazoi go," Ay reminded her anxiously.

She shrugged. "I have soldiers of my own. Four of my daughters lie here in the rock, Father. I will not desert them."

"Your duty lies with Ankhesenamun, the survivor!"

"Ankhesenamun? Your father would weep to hear the name of that god. As for my duty, Ay, I have done it."

She had allowed the memories to warp, to change shape to fit her own long ambitions and disguise her old frustrations. Here in the north palace, Ay thought, her dreams had taken on a kind of reality. It was a shrine to her, a sanctuary of adoration, and the man sitting quietly beside her with such composure had at last given her the love for which she had always yearned. In her new fulfillment she no longer inspired pity.

For a while they sat on together, talking of innocuous things while Meryra, directed by Thothmes' unobtrusive gestures, served them delicacies. There was no trace of fussy possession in his attitude, no flaunting of ownership. Ay was convinced by the time they rose to leave that Thothmes' love for Nefertiti was honest, unselfish, and steady. He and she prostrated themselves to Tutankhamun and walked with him into the late afternoon sunshine, Nefertiti's hand resting on Thothmes' guiding elbow. At the last moment, as Pharaoh was stepping into his litter, the queen turned back to embrace her mother.

"I will have incense burned before the Son of Hapu for you every day," she said, weeping, "and I will send you many letters."

Nefertiti turned blank gray eyes in the direction of her face. "Give Egypt a son, Ankhesenamun, and do not meddle in things that do not concern you. I love you."

Still sobbing, Ankhesenamun got onto her litter. The last glimpse she had of her mother was of Nefertiti's immobile face, the white linen pressed against her stately body by the wind, and the flash of sunlight on her rings as she reached for Thothmes' hand.

Two days later, in the cool of early morning, Pharaoh and Ankhesenamun sat on the deck of *Kha-em-Ma'at* and were poled away from the palace water steps for the last time. The queen, watching the central city slide past, tried to pretend they were merely on a boating party and in the evening would return home. But the illusion was hard to maintain, for Akhetaten had shut them out. The green palms ranking along the bank rustled in the fresh breeze, the vinehung white walls gleamed in the new sunlight, and flashes of bright color showed through the lush wetness of many trees, yet an atmosphere of incipient decay already hung over the empty homes and deserted gardens. Behind the sealed doors and boarded windows, many rooms were left as they were, the chairs still waiting to be used, the tables laden with vases of wilting flowers, the shuttered bed-chambers still dim with rumpled couches and lamps still warm from the night. There had been both a sudden panic to leave a ghost-haunted, ill-omened place and an uncertainty about the future. Perhaps Pharaoh would not settle at Thebes and would return. Perhaps he would become homesick for the city's beauty and greenness; perhaps the Aten's eclipse would be brief after all and in his maturity Pharaoh would return to his father's god. Regret lingered in the gardens and imbued the quiet streets with nostalgia.

As the royal barge slid past Horemheb's estate, Ankhes-enamun gave a cry and turned to her husband. "Tutankhamun, look! What is happening?"

Naked brown children were leaping into the river from Hor-emheb's white water seeps with shrieks of delight. A woman knelt by his ornamental pool, scouring a pile of coarse linen. Two goats were tethered to the pillars of his entrance hall. The homeless had begun to converge on the city even before all its occupants had left.

Pharaoh watched, fascinated. "I suppose I should order them thrown out," he said. "But today I will be magnanimous. There is no point, in any case. I do not think that we will ever return, and as yet we cannot afford to pay soldiers to police an empty city. The glass and faïence factories are still working. I suppose those peasants want work in them."

Ankhesenamun rose and went to the rail. The ethereal pleasure palace of Maru-Aten was passing, and she thought she caught a glimpse of the shady pavilion beyond the trees. Then it was gone. Into the past. The southern customs house was almost abreast, and the end of the long sweep of high cliffs that had sheltered Akhetaten. Ankhesenamun looked back. The city was a silent mirage of white, green, and gold, dancing on the warm haze, held tenuously to the present only by the umbilical cord of glittering barges strung out behind. Ankhesenamun did not look away until the cliffs and the bending river removed it protectively from her sight.

The flotilla beat its way slowly back to Thebes, bearing with it the bodies of Akhenaten and Tiye, whom Ay had arranged to inter at Thebes. The travelers had begun in good spirits, whiling away the long hours on the river with parties held on deck under the sheltering canopies, but before long the presence of the two imperial coffins and the anxiety about what awaited them at Thebes had sobered the court. Sleep became fitful and troubled. The more impressionable women among the courtiers began to see unfavorable omens, and many felt burdened by a sense of foreboding. It would have been better, they whispered among themselves, to have left the accursed one and his mother-wife to the hot silence of the cliffs. Surely they were bringing with them a taint that would infect Malkatta. It was unlucky to disturb the dead.

Long before Pharaoh's barge nudged the Malkatta water steps, the riverbanks began to be thick with people who lay reverently beneath the palms and then rose to cheer him, and when his captain gave the order that swung the flotilla toward the west, the whole of Thebes could be seen filling the east bank, screaming and jostling in delirious relief. The barges turned into the canal. It had been dredged, the huge lake scoured and filled, the water steps repaired. Flags of blue and white rippled on the wooden flagstaffs before the imposing facade of the palace. As Tutankhamun and his retinue stepped from the ramp, priests in flowing white linen sent clouds of incense pouring to the heavens, and the paving was already sticky with milk and wine. By the portable altar a garlanded bull waited patiently for the slash of Pharaoh's knife.

It was more than a homecoming. It was a return to sanity,

to the immutable ways of Ma'at, and the ceremonies moved
forward with a lighthearted gaiety. The courtiers flooded through
the refurbished palace, laughing and singing. Delicious odors
wafted from the kitchens. In the harem, the new women mingled with the old, their apartments a jumble of belongings
through which their servants picked their way while the women
themselves spilled into the harem gardens and rushed to the
lake. The tumultuous welcome of the Thebans could be heard
fitfully for hours, a rumble of sound coming across the Nile.
Incense columned thickly above Karnak. The feast Tutankhamun presided over that night went on until dawn, a noisy,
music-filled expression of joy and thanksgiving. Pharaoh retired to his apartments just after midnight, falling onto Amunhotep's wide couch and into his dreams almost simultaneously,
and when he awoke as Ra tipped the horizon, Maya and his
acolytes began the Song of Praise outside the door. "Hail Living
Incarnation, rising as Ra in the east! Hail, Divinely Immortal
Source of Egypt's Health."

Later in the day Tutankhamun stood in full panoply in Amun's
dark sanctuary. Before him the god towered, a figure fashioned
by Tutankhamun's own artists and clothed in his own gold.
Dishes of choicest delicacies were set at his feet, and flowers
hung from his neck. Mildly he smiled at his obedient son while
the priests held the censers and Maya, resplendent in the priestly
leopard skin, bowed reverently before him. "The sun of him
who knows Thee not goes down, O Amun!" the temple singers
chanted in the forecourt. "The temple of him who assailed Thee
is in darkness!" There was no mistaking the gloating triumph
in the words. Tutankhamun listened soberly. He had no other
father now but Amun.

When the bodies of Tiye and Akhenaten were placed together in a hurriedly prepared tomb in the Valley in West-of-
Thebes, all watching as the necropolis attendants knotted the
rope across the entrance believed that they were witnessing the
final burial of the past. Mud was smeared over the knots, the
seal of the necropolis pressed into it, and the solemn warnings
against violation and theft intoned. The small ceremony had
been attended only by the royal couple and a handful of chosen
courtiers. As they afterward made their way from the tombs
to their waiting litters, they felt as though a burden had been

lifted. The last impiety of a doomed administration had been redressed.

On the trip back to the palace Ankhesenamun stopped at the Son of Hapu's funerary temple with offerings for the seer and earnest prayers for the recovery of her mother's sight. Ay, watching the delicate royal fingers sift the incense grains onto the holder, thought grimly that the dead noble would feel a spiteful satisfaction in disregarding Ankhesenamun's fervent prayers. He had been thwarted, and as a consequence his terrible prophecies had come true. He would not intercede with the gods for the wife of a prince he had ordered killed so long ago but would relish the full consequences of his royal master's disobedience.

Yet those who had seen the interment of the empress and her son as a sign that all would now be well in Egypt found their hope waning when shortly afterward Ankhesenamun gave birth to a stillborn daughter. The courtiers observed her anguish with knowing smiles. "The royal blood is thin," they whispered to one another. "Her mother gave Egypt only girls, and she is not fertile enough for sons. The gods have grown weary of this effeminate house." Many eyes surreptitiously followed Horemheb's comings and goings through the palace. The King's Deputy was handsome, mature, and capable, a man of action among children and old men, but in the increasingly satisfying life of Malkatta politics were no more than a diversionary topic, soon superseded by less weighty matters.

Horemheb seemed to have resigned himself good-naturedly to his subordinate position. When he was not discharging his duties as King's Deputy, he could be found in the office of the Scribe of Assemblage or mingling with his officers and men in the barracks. Ay would have relieved Horemheb of his control over the Followers of His Majesty if he had dared, but he knew that as the gods were growing strong again, the arguments with which he had bested Horemheb had less authority with every passing year. Ay admitted to himself that he was afraid of the man. Although Egypt had in Tutankhamun a popular young pharaoh of whom everyone approved, a deep and irrevocable change had taken place since the days of Osiris Amunhotep's magnificence, when Pharaoh was numinous with divinity, and behind the stiff formality of sheltering protocol the ruling god, no matter what his human weaknesses, was infallible. Since then, Egypt had suffered a pharaoh who had proven himself to be not only deluded but cosmically criminal, a man against whom the gods themselves had militated, whose painful fallibility had become apparent even to every poverty-stricken peasant.

Without his traditional invulnerability, Pharaoh was no longer untouchable. Had not one of Egypt's rulers already died by violent hands? *It is not*, Ay mused as he discharged his duties through each long day, *that Pharaoh is merely no longer divine. His divinity is now sunk beneath his flesh, and everyone is aware that the flesh will bleed at the touch of a knife. None knows that better than Horemheb. What precisely are his ambitions? Is it the Double Crown that shimmers in his fantasies, or simply the dream of an Egypt presiding once again over a mighty empire? If the empire, then he will be patient, and Tutankhamun has nothing to fear, but if the crown, then he is simply biding his time for an opportunity to strike, and unless he betrays his designs in some way, I will be helpless to prevent a tragedy.*

Later that year a scroll came for Ay from Akhetaten. He unrolled it and read absently, but was then transfixed by its contents. "She is dead," it said. "I woke one morning to find her cold beside me. I have buried her in the cliffs. I leave the north palace, taking with me only that which is mine. Long life and happiness to you, Regent." It was signed Thothmes, sculptor. Ay let the scroll fall onto his desk, and the small sound invoked a flood of memories. Nefertiti as a child, sitting naked at Tey's feet in the garden on a hot summer's day at Akhmin, her hands full of cheap beads, her startled dark eyes turned to him questioningly as he called her. He did not know why that insignificant scene had stayed so vividly in his mind. Nefertiti full of pouts and bad temper, trying to quarrel with Mutnodjme, who could never be bothered to be drawn. Nefertiti high above the heads of her worshipers, coldly beautiful in the sun crown, her red mouth faintly smiling. And now buried quietly, laid secretly in the darkness by a commoner. Ay knew that when he did mourn, it would be for the little girl in the garden.

He picked up the scroll and went to the queen's quarters, waiting while her herald obtained permission for him to enter. Ankhesenamun greeted him cheerfully, draped loosely in a white wrap, her hair wet and disheveled. Her brown skin gleamed with fresh oil.

"Please sit, Grandfather," she invited. "I am just out of my bath. Pharaoh says that I spend more time cleansing myself than a priest. He sent me new earrings this morning. Do you like them?" She held them out, and he nodded, forcing a smile. Her own laugh faded. "Do you bring me bad news?"

For answer he handed her the scroll, watching in silence as she scanned it. She set the papyrus aside and sat abruptly on the edge of the couch, drawing the wrap tightly around her with both hands. "I hate these apartments," she said after a while. "I hated them the moment I stepped through the doors. They are dark and old and smell of past sins. Tutankhamun thinks I like them and is pleased, because the empress Tiye lived here, but I remember only that my mother slept on this couch and walked these floors." Her voice trembled. "I do not sleep well."

"Then for Set's sake tell him! He adores you, Majesty. He will build a new wing for you!"

"It is not new apartments that I need," she said bitterly. "I went to my father's bed when I was eleven years old. I was innocent, Ay, I did not understand. Even the birth of my daughter did not lift the veil from my eyes. What my father did to me, to my sisters, was not against the law of Ma'at for a pharaoh, yet here at Malkatta I suddenly see clearly that it was more than dynastic necessity that impelled him. Knowing that darker thing, I find myself a jaded old woman whose sweet memories have all at once become nothing but lies." Her eyes filled with tears. "Thothmes did not send us word until it was too late to go to her, to mourn, to stand with her! I do not understand!"

Ay made no move to comfort her, knowing that her pride would forbid it.

"I do," he replied. "She was his, not ours. He wanted her to himself until the last. He could not bear the thought of the north palace full of courtiers invading its silence, and I think he was justified. I will ask Pharaoh to build a mortuary temple for her here."

She lifted her chin. "It is not that. Malkatta is a lonely place, and lonelier now knowing she is gone."

He placed an arm along her delicate shoulders. "Ankhesenamun, you are only seventeen years old, already a queen, beautiful and loved. The future is full of promise for all of us. Do not look back."

She turned away. "I cannot help it," she said coldly. "The past will not let me go."

29

ONCE TUTANKHAMUN GAINED HIS MAJORITY, AY RELIN-quished his position as regent, but the relationship with the young king that he had forged in Tutankhamun's infancy remained so strong—Pharaoh consulting Ay on all matters and always taking his advice—that he effectively continued to hold the highest power in Egypt. The courtiers marveled at his longevity, acknowledging it as a mark of favor from the gods whom he had restored to prominence. Yet at the same time their resentment was stirred, for the only way to Pharaoh was through his uncle, and Ay refused to allow him to delegate any authority. Although the various ministers had been reinstated, they were denied independent action, so that while Malkatta had budded, it did not bloom.

Ankhesenamun conceived once more and gave birth to another stillborn girl. She bore her humiliation bravely, aided by the fact that none of Tutankhamun's secondary wives or concubines had been able to conceive at all. But concern over a successor began to dominate the courtiers' conversations. Egypt needed an heir, a promise that Ma'at would go on, that its so recent fragile reestablishment could be made increasingly secure. There were no promising royal princes springing up in the harem, no new generation of Horus-Fledglings on whom the eyes of anxious ministers could rest. Instead, those eyes found themselves drawn to Horemheb, who, still pacing behind Pharaoh as King's Deputy, reminded everyone by his very holding of the office in the place of an heir that the future was a void.

Horemheb was well aware of the speculative glances that followed him. He was also aware that Ay feared him for reasons, Horemheb told himself, that so far had no validity. Egypt had been well served by Tutankhamun, although not in the way that Horemheb himself would have chosen, and he had been content to bow to Ay's assessment of the country's needs and their solution once he saw the process of recovery begin. He had been pleased at his appointment to the position of King's Deputy—even when it became apparent that Ay had urged the appointment on Pharaoh in order to keep an eye on the commander—believing that as such he would have as great an access to Pharaoh as the regent. Because he believed that, given time, Tutankhamun would turn his attention to military matters as Mutnodjme had predicted, he was content.

But as the years passed and Egypt began to regain her strength, Pharaoh would still hear no words from his deputy but those of worship and protocol. Horemheb tried on several occasions to make representations to Tutankhamun on behalf of the army, but any serious suggestion of mobilization on his part had been rejected. With a growing anger, Horemheb began to realize that it was in fact Ay, not Pharaoh, who was consistently blocking any attempt to recover the empire. Ay was looking increasingly to the past, when Egypt had been strongly self-contained, a nation that traded with other nations but had no dreams of conquest, content to hold itself apart in pride from the rest of the world. The regent believed so firmly in the rightness of his own policies and the inadvisability of conquering any territory for many years to come—perhaps forever—that he persisted in binding his young and malleable nephew ever more closely to himself.

Horemheb found some consolation in the thought that by killing Smenkhara he had at least attained one objective, namely, the restoration of Amun and the return of the administration to Thebes. But his hope that a future generation of royal princes would turn its attention to the other desire that lay closest to Horemheb's heart vanished when the queen gave birth to her second stillborn daughter. If there was no heir in the years to come, Tutankhamun would designate some young noble from among the ministers Ay had selected to govern, undoubtedly a man who shared the pacifism Pharaoh had learned from his uncle, and Egypt would remain forever in the position of inferiority to which she had sunk. The thought was insupportable, yet Horemheb was not quite ready to allow the alternative to take shape in his mind until he had made every effort to assure himself that Pharaoh would never agree to consider his advice.

He confronted Tutankhamun as Pharaoh was walking by the

lake on a scorching Mesore evening, going to him over the tired grass. Nakht-Min stood beside the king, the downy white ostrich fan over his shoulder, and Ay shared the shelter of the canopy. Other members of the court elite were following, strolling arm in arm and talking quietly. "Fold the canopy away," Tutankhamun ordered the servants. "Ra nears the horizon, so it is useless now. I shall bathe in a moment." He turned a neutral, heavily-kohled gaze on the deputy. "This is not the time to discuss matters of state policy, Horemheb. It is still too hot to have to think."

Horemheb had made his prostration and now faced Pharaoh determinedly. "Then will Your Majesty grant me an audience tomorrow?"

Tutankhamun sighed and slid onto the chair that had been set behind him, waving his entourage down onto the grass. "No. Tomorrow Nakht-Min and I are going hunting, and then there is the preparation for the New Year's celebration to discuss. Take your problems to my uncle."

Horemheb settled himself cross-legged on the ground and looked at Ay. The sun was setting behind the regent, making his expression difficult to read. "I have done so, Imperial One," he said frostily, "but we talk in circles, the regent and I. I am your deputy, and the commander of your loyal army. My request is small."

"But pressing, I suppose. Well, make it quickly."

Carefully but respectfully Horemheb scanned the handsome face. At nineteen, Tutankhamun had his mother's sensual lips and pleasing nose, and her crisp manners of speech, but his father's large, mild eyes, which seldom betrayed any depth of thought. He would have made a good courtier, pleasant to look at, with a sense of fashion, an ability to get along with everyone, and an adeptness at light conversation. Horemheb thought him immature and blamed Ay for denying him any responsiblity.

"Majesty, I greatly desire your permission to take half a division north and recapture Gaza. As Your Majesty is aware, Egypt is ready once again to open herself to flourishing trade, and we cannot trade in any volume without Gaza. We must have it back."

"Majesty," Ay interrupted, "Horemheb knows full well that the Khatti might interpret an attack on Gaza as a prelude to an offensive on Egypt's part. We are not yet ready for that."

"I am addressing Horus, not you!" Horemheb said hotly.

"Keep out of this, Ay! You think and speak like a drooling old fool." As soon as the words had left his mouth, he regretted them. *I am becoming short-tempered*, he cursed himself angrily. *Is it the arrogance Mutnodjme accuses me of?* He saw a condescending smile split Ay's jowly face. Tutankhamun glanced around briefly at the sudden silence that had fallen. The assembly was listening avidly, hoping for a scandal.

"You do me scant reverence by hurling insults in my sacred presence," Pharaoh said dryly. "I agree with my uncle. It is too soon to think of any military operation. Such a move would reawaken the fears of the people. They are only now learning to trust the beginnings of the new prosperity we are bringing them. War would take it away from them."

"I do not speak of war," Horemheb objected thickly. "The capture of Gaza would be a small, swift foray. That would be the end of it."

"Would it?" Tutankhamun met his eye shrewdly. "I know your desire. I am not prepared to let you fulfill it."

With inner fury, Horemheb knew that the god was once again mouthing Ay's words. "If Your Majesty will not listen to my advice, then at least consult some of your other ministers. They have voices."

The implied criticism stung Tutankhamun. He leaned forward and flicked Horemheb across the cheek with his fly whisk. "Unless you wish to be relieved of your command, you would do well to remove yourself from my sight," he said curtly. "I have never liked you. You are dismissed." The silence was pregnant with the watchers' glee. White with humiliation, Horemheb stood, bowed stiffly, and strode away, head high, the eyes of all burning into his back.

Horemheb spent the rest of the day out on the desert behind the palace, shouting and slashing at the horses as they dragged his chariot through the sand, but his anger had still not abated by nightfall, when he returned to his house. He had not eaten. Pharaoh's casual slash with the fly whisk continued to burn like the vicious stripe of a whip, and Horemheb strode to and fro before Mutnodjme in their bedchamber, his fingers stroking the invisible mark on his cheek.

"My belly aches with them, Mutnodjme, " he said. "My patience is exhausted. Akhenaten, a prince on whom I bestowed my friendship, yet what was he? A criminal. Smenkhara, a twisted depraved brat. Tutankhamun, a toy. He struck me. Me! I do not deserve such a reward for my loyalty."

"You speak of gods," Mutnodjme warned. She was sprawled across the couch on her stomach, naked, her face to the wind catcher.

"Gods," Horemheb sneered. "There has been no god in Egypt since Amunhotep. That puppy hit me!"

"So you said." She rolled languidly onto her back. "But I think it was your pride he struck, not your face. What does it matter? I do not understand this anger, Horemheb. Come and make love to me."

"You are like all women. You think with your genitals," he retorted. "Where is your sympathy?"

Mutnodjme sat up with a sigh, arranging the cushions behind her. "I am afraid for you," she said. "Nothing pleases you anymore. You drink too much, you slap the servants, you shout at everyone. Why? Life is good."

"Life is good? No, Mutnodjme, life is not good. There are thongs around my wrists. I am a prisoner. Did you hear me?" He stared at her and then abruptly flung his cup across the room. It struck a fragile alabaster lamp before smashing into the wall. Pieces of pale stone skidded across the floor, and the oil dripped onto the couch. Mutnodjme did not flinch but regarded him steadily. He was breathing noisily, shoulders hunched, and all at once he came to the couch, falling across it and pulling her under him. "You are wrong," he hissed into her mouth. "This still pleases me." For a moment she endured his kiss, but then coolly she pushed him away and slid off the couch.

"That is not pleasure," she said, "and I do not feel like playing violent games with you tonight, Horemheb. I am going to sleep on the roof. Call a concubine if you wish to hurt someone." Picking up her sleeping gown with one slow gesture, she swayed out.

For a long time Horemheb lay spread-eagled on the couch as Mutnodjme had left him, his eyes open, his face pressed into the sheets, which smelled of her perfume and the cloying miasma of the spilled oil. He was afraid to think. Now and then brief gusts of hot air reached him from the unshuttered mouth of the wind catcher, making him break out anew in sweat. She would be sitting up there, sunk in cushions, drowsy but alert to every caress of the same breeze on her polished skin, her hooded eyes lazily reflecting starlight, her senses open to every movement of the night. Perhaps she was listening to music. Perhaps she had already sent for her nocturnal friends to help her pass the summer night in gambling or gossip, or for just one friend in whose arms the strange, hot poignancy of the darkness might be enhanced. He let himself imagine her with a man up there, the muffled laughter, the whispers, two naked shapes black against the shadow of the wind catcher's funnel, but at last his mind resisted distraction and he found himself cold with those thoughts that must be examined.

Wearily he dragged himself to a sitting position. *Tutankhamun's lack of respect today was not simply the anger of a god toward a subject who had presumed*, he thought. *No. It is a pharaoh's right to treat and dispose of his people in any way he chooses. That flick of the whisk was a symbol of his complete lack of regard for my station and my opinions. I can no longer believe that Pharaoh will ever turn his attention to me so that at last I might be allowed to return Egypt's honor to her. Now I know that, unless I prevent it, I will go to my tomb in Memphis having accomplished nothing for myself or the country I love. Pharaoh will never make war. If he had been allowed to listen to me, I would have gradually gained his trust and cooperation, but the young man has been poisoned against me.* The intensity of his thoughts brought him to his feet, and he wandered to the window, laying his arms along the sill and leaning out over the pale blur of the flower bed below.

I am not a violent man. No matter what Mutnodjme thinks, the necessary cruelties of war have nothing to do with a perverse desire to twist and break, a desire I do not possess, a desire no commander can afford to harbor. Then what do I want? I betrayed the empress for gold, and because I believed that my influence with her son would grow. I murdered Smenkhara to save Egypt from another agony. But killing him brought me no nearer to influence with the Horus Throne. What could? There is no royal blood in my veins that would ensure me the respect and attention of Pharaoh. Ah, but in Mutnodjme's . . . Is that, then, what I really want? The Double Crown on my head? The chance to do with Egypt what I will? He groaned, rubbing his hot palms over his face. *I do not want to kill again, yet surely Amun must look with disdain on the pitiful remnant of his divine family. I am more worthy to be his son than*

Tutankhamun, whose very blood is filthy with the sin of his parents.

Oh, how you can invent justifications, he mocked himself, smiling wanly into the darkness. *What pious nonsense you can conjure! You want to be Pharaoh because you want it, without excuse. Supposing you kill Tutankhamun? It would be easier than last time. The gods have not punished you for what you did. And if I do kill him, will Ay make a bid for the throne? Probably, and I cannot kill both. Courtiers would accept one death but could not turn a blind eye to two. I cannot go on like this, waiting, waiting, wondering what will happen to Egypt when I am dead, Pharaoh gone. Wondering? Knowing. That is what eats at me. Knowing. It would be anarchy, poverty, and bloodshed. Let Tutankhamun have his Anniversary of Appearings next month at New Year. By then I will have devised some sort of a plan, but this time I can trust no one but myself.*

Having cleared his mind, he was suddenly hungry, and calling for a servant, he ordered food and more wine. While he waited for it to be brought, he thought of Mutnodjme. Should he confide in her? It was not necessary. She would know.

The traditional presentation of gifts for that year's New Year celebrations included not only an embassy from Nubia but also ambassadors from Alashia and Babylon, the first foreigners to come seeking renewed trading agreements since Akhenaten's twelfth year of reign. Ay, who had sent tentative embassies to the rulers of those countries months earlier, was overjoyed. The Treasury was opened and gold spent liberally for the first time since Tutankhamun had inherited the confusion his predecessors had left.

Six weeks later, in the middle of Paophi, it was a lighthearted pharaoh who accepted his deputy's invitation to a four-day lion hunt. Horemheb had performed the yearly prostration at his master's feet with due humility. His artificial wreath had been of electrum, its flowers of lapis lazuli. His gift was a new bow ornamented with floral designs and bordered in gold, and an ivory throwing stick inlaid with silver clumps of papyrus. He had been careful not to appear too abject in his adoration. He organized the hunt himself: the invitations to all the ministers, the procuring of dozens of damask tents, the appropriation of chariots and horses from the stables of the Shock Troops, the provision of hordes of slaves to prepare the many baskets of food and serve the wine he had sent for from his Delta estates. Musicians were hired and dancers inspected. His only defeat was Mutnodjme, who refused to go.

"I hate living in tents," she told him. "One ends up eating sand and waking in the morning with aching hips from those traveling couches. If you had invited Pharaoh on a boating journey, that would be different. I will go and visit my mother at Akhmin while the court sweats under thin tents and drinks gritty wine and pretends to enjoy it."

"What will the queen say? She will be your guest."

"No, my husband," she responded lightly. "Ankhesenamun will be your guest. She knows me well. She will understand why I am not there and will doubtless be wishing she was not there either."

"What do you mean?"

"You are gripping me too tightly," she said, and he released her wrist with a murmured apology. "I mean only what I say. Ankhesenamun likes her comfort." She looked at him oddly. "Do not hunt too recklessly, Horemheb. In spite of your foul temper I am rather fond of you." She had left him quickly, as though she knew he wished to be spared a reply. It was quite true what she had said. Everyone knew of her aversion to both hunting and tenting and would not think it strange that she was not in the company. Nevertheless, Horemheb fretted. Her absence might be wrongly interpreted later.

On the day of departure the glittering company poured slowly out into the desert behind the western cliffs, stirring a red dust cloud as it went. Horemheb rode in his chariot beside Pharaoh's own, in a position of honor, outwardly affable and smiling, inwardly tense with anticipation and fear. He had been unable to make a detailed plan and knew he must be prepared to seize whatever opportunity arose. Tutankhamun was in a buoyant mood, talking and laughing under the small canopy Nakht-Min held over him as he handled his chariot with instinctive skill. Ay followed in a litter, and for once he was disregarded. Behind them the court straggled in their own litters, and at the rear the royal bodyguards shepherded the empty chariots and chests of weapons for all those who wished to try their skill later. After a day's easy ride the crowd reached the tents that had already mushroomed over the raked and smoothed sand, where the shrines had also been set up, the kitchens readied, and the bored and uncomfortable slaves waited squatting on the carpets rolling dice.

After the prayers for a safe and successful hunt were said that evening, the gathering gave itself over to food and entertainment. The vibrations of drumbeats and the wail of pipes trembled over the desert. Dancers passed and repassed the twinkling fires as the guests wandered from tent to tent, cups in hand. At Pharaoh's invitation Horemheb went to the royal tent to talk. Ay was absent. For several hours the young king and the morose commander spoke of the past, the present, Tutankhamun's hopes for the future. Horemheb found himself almost liking the vain, impulsive young man but all the same felt no regret for what he had to do. It was too late for that.

He waited through two days of the hunt. He had loosened the pins holding one of the wheels of Tutankhamun's chariot to its axle, knowing it would hold through the rigors of ordinary use, and he did not think Pharaoh would feel the tiny tremors of the loose wheel on the uneven surface of the desert. Only the stress of a fast chase would release it.

Horemheb was resigned to seeing the hunt finish without mishap, if necessary. For two days the men rolled easily along the sand near the rear of the cliffs, sighting nothing on the first day and on the second losing a lion that was glimpsed high in the rocks and then vanished.

But on the third morning a golden beast broke from the jumble of early shadows at the base of the cliffs and streaked across the sand. Tutankhamun had elected, as he often did, to drive himself. With a whoop he pointed and then sent his whip down hard on the flanks of the horses. The chariot sprang forward. Horemheb, his throat suddenly dry, spread his legs and leaned into his own chariot's speed as he fled after Pharaoh. The rest of the hunters, some six or seven courtiers, followed more slowly, for the first kill by tradition must be Pharaoh's. "Break, break," Horemheb muttered between clenched teeth as his eyes narrowed against the warm wind and he felt his kilt flatten against his thighs. Guiding his horses to the right so that he and they should not be blinded by the sand flung up by Tutankhamun's animals, he held his position.

Then his heart leaped into his mouth. One gleaming wheel tottered, fell away from the chariot, and veered off into the sand. He heard the king shout, more in surprise than in fear. The axle hit the ground. Tutankhamun released the reins. A scream of dismay went up behind as his body soared, cart-wheeled, struck the confused horses, which had already jerked to a halt, and fell huddled to the sand. Horemheb glanced behind. He and Pharaoh had had a good lead. Hauling savagely on his own reins, he jumped down and ran, kneeling quickly, his arms and legs liquid with momentary terror. To his astonishment, Tutankhamun opened his eyes. He was lying on his side, his saffron kilt torn, his helmet half off, his breathing shallow. He was merely stunned. At that moment Horemheb might have made the decision to wait, or perhaps to have seen Pharaoh's miraculous preservation as a sign of the god's protection. But a quick glance showed him two things. The ground was littered with small pieces of rock, and lying within reach, glinting malevolently in the sun, was one of the axle pins. He did not hesitate. Already men were running toward him, waving and yelling. Grabbing the pin and a rock, he pushed Tutankhamun onto his stomach. One finger searched for the hollow at the base of the skull, exposed by the dislodged helmet. The angle of the head was not right. He tilted it slightly, placed the point of the golden pin in the hollow, and with a grunt slammed the rock against it. There was brief resistance, and then the pin slid upward. Pharaoh made a tiny sound, like the mewing of a kitten. Cursing in haste, Horemheb wrenched out the pin. A small amount of blood welled slowly, sank, welled again. He rubbed the rock in the blood, pulled the helmet into place, and rolled the body onto its back. He had no time to verify whether Tutankhamun was dead. Dropping the rock and thrusting the pin deep into the sand, he turned. Men were already jumping from their chariots and running forward. Ay's litter bearers were coming at a run. Ay himself was sitting upright, slapping them. "Is the physician here?" Horemheb called, amazed at the steadiness of his voice. "We must get Pharaoh out of the sun. I think he is seriously injured." Ay got down, breathing harshly, pushing through the courtiers to stand frozen, the only sound for a moment his ragged breath. Seeing the trace of blood fresh on Tutankhamun's neck and one shoulder, he nudged the stained rock with one foot, then knelt, placing his ear against Pharaoh's chest.

"He is not injured, he is dead!" he whispered. "It happened so fast. I cannot believe it. You." He pointed a shaking finger at the litter bearers as he rose to his feet. "Put him on my litter.

It is like Prince Thothmes, all those years ago," he said to Horemheb, his voice reedy. "So fast . . ."

Horemheb stepped to him. He himself was pale and unsteady. "We must get to the queen before any of this mob," he managed, his last few words drowned in the flood of wailing that had broken out as the curtains on the litter were closed and the body lifted. "Try to compose yourself, Ay."

Ay nodded. Together they stumbled to Horemheb's chariot and mounted. Guards were unhitching the horses from Tutankhamun's damaged vehicle and examining the axle, which had bent on impact with the ground. Horemheb picked up the reins, and with the small action came a burst of relief. He had done it. Pharaoh was dead.

Word had already reached Ankhesenamun, and as the two men pulled up in front of her tent, she came running out, evading Ay's warning arm, her eyes wide with horror. Falling toward the litter, she tore the curtains open, and then sank to her knees and began to pull at her hair. "Each of his children was cursed!" she sobbed. "And the gods will not be content until I am dead also. I am the last! Tutankhamun, my brother, my love!"

"No, Majesty, it is a foolish fancy," Ay said soothingly as he bent over her. But she refused to be comforted. Long after the litter had disappeared on its way to the House of the Dead, and the silent servants were striking the tents, she continued to kneel on the desert and keen, lifting sand in both hands and letting it trickle over her head. The sight chilled those who were observing her grief. There was something anciently tragic and despairing in the sight of the young queen, her delicate features disfigured, her long black hair dusted with sand and blowing out on the hot noon wind, kneeling and rocking while behind her the cliffs shimmered brown in the haze and above, the dry deep blue sky spread, endlessly immense. Her cries seemed to encompass all the tears shed by the members of her doomed family, yet every god was turning his back upon that wild beseeching.

As the seventy days of mourning began, Egypt's shock gave way to widespread grief. Tutankhamun's peaceful reforms had won him the veneration of all citizens, and they had begun to feel secure under his administration. Now that security had been snatched away, and their sorrow was mingled with apprehension for the future. At Malkatta the courtiers withdrew, stunned, to their apartments. Only Ay, with an uneasiness he could not define, questioned the physician who had reverently examined the body.

"He was tossed against the sharp rock with tremendous force," the man said in answer to Ay's query. "There was a deep hole just above the neck. How tragic that he should have been struck in the spot, though I cannot understand why Horus died so quickly. A blow to the temple would have been a more likely cause of immediate death."

It was obvious that since Pharaoh had already been dead when he was carried back to the palace, the physician had not examined the body as carefully as he would have if Tutankhamun had survived his injury, and his answer did not satisfy Ay. The fanbearer kept returning to the picture of Horemheb bent over Pharaoh, sheltering the body from view, but told himself that his suspicion was fanciful. Ay dreamed that moment, worried at it in his mind as the days of mourning passed, and the longer he considered the matter, the stronger a curious conviction grew. If Tutankhamun had not struck the commander with the fly whisk that day, perhaps he would not have died.

But more pressing matters demanded Ay's attention. Tutankhamun, confident with youth, had given no thought to a successor. Ay and Maya spent long, troubled hours in consultation with each other and the viziers of the south and north.

"It does not matter whom we choose," he said. "We all know that Horemheb looms over these deliberations. At all costs he must not be allowed the crown. Amun does not want his new wealth channeled into war, and neither do the people. The army is Horemheb's to command, and I fear he will use it to take the throne if we cannot make a decision. But would he do so if the crown had already passed to someone else? That is the question."

No pharaoh would wish to rule by force, without the support of Karnak, Ay thought. *Not yet, not with the awful memories of Amun's rejection still so fresh. Any incarnation not having Maya's blessing would fear a curse, an oracle's accusing finger, a revolt fueled by priests. Even Horemheb.* Ay cleared his throat. "I propose the crown for myself," he suggested. "You all know that under my hand Egypt has flourished. Amun has nothing to fear from me. I am an old man with few years left, yet behind me is a record of faithfulness to every pharaoh since my sister married the great Amunhotep." He had deliberately chosen to remind them of his close relationship with his brother-in-law. He watched carefully as they considered his plan. He knew what they were thinking. Proudly he lifted his head. "At least it will give you time to cast about for a suitable heir," he said. "You are an old man yourself, Maya. You remember the empress well. Neither you nor I will live much longer. The wind that blew so much weary misfortune on Egypt is almost spent. A new age is almost upon us. We must preserve what we can. Stand behind me, and let me be deified."

The anxious, tired eyes slipped over and away from him, and finally Maya knelt to kiss his feet. The homage brought no surge of exultation to Ay. His thoughts were full of Tutankhamun's bright face, Smenkhara's sullen helplessness, Akhenaten's agonized search for his truth. He was inheriting a crown that would place an invisible weight of disillusionment and decay on his brow.

That night, after several hours spent drawing up a marriage contract in the company of his scribe and the two viziers, Ay walked through the quiet palace to Ankhesenamun's apartments. He could not explain the vague sense of urgency that was forcing him, now that the decision was made, to see it implemented. He only knew that tonight his granddaughter must become his wife, the seals affixed, the heralds sent out. Already the inhabitants of Malkatta had learned what was to come, and the bows he received from those he chanced to meet in the shadowed corridors were exaggeratedly subservient. Filled with sudden abhorrence, he ignored them.

Outside Ankhesenamun's cedar doors her steward greeted him politely, warned him that the queen was receiving no one, and disappeared into the room. When he returned, it was to bow Ay within. Ankhesenamun rose from the chair by the couch and inclined her head to him as he reverenced her. She stood very straight in the white linen gown that fell gracefully to the floor, her hands loose at her sides. She was unpainted, her hair undressed, her arms and fingers bare of adornment. She had been weeping, and her eyes were swollen, but the tears had dried. Her glance went to the scroll in his hand and then to his face.

"Tell me your business and then leave," she said flatly. "You are the regent, Ay. Can you not spare me any state problems?"

"Not this one, I fear, dear Majesty," he replied, advancing

through the incense smoke curling from her shrine. "You see, I am no longer regent." Her tired gaze registered no surprise. As gently as he could, Ay told her the decision that had been made, and why. Then he held out the scroll. "I need your seal on this marriage contract, and your titles and signature. It will, of course, be a marriage in name only, Ankhesenamun, so that I am legitimized. I am far too old to consider bedding a twenty-two-year-old woman."

Listlessly she took it, unrolled it, and read. "You know as well as I do that I have no choice in the matter," she said tonelessly. "But I do not care very much. All my life I have been a bauble passed from hand to hand. Your palm will feel no different. I should not have expected the gods to allow me any happiness with Tutankhamun." Her voice broke on his name, but she quickly mastered it. Going to the table, she took a pen, dipped it in ink, and laboriously wrote out her name and titles. Heating wax and allowing a few drops to fall, she took the ring lying beside the lamp and pressed it into the scroll. "There." She threw it at Ay. "I hope Egypt is pleased. Tey will not be."

"It will make little difference to her, or to you, Majesty. You have my word."

"Please go away, Prince." She turned her back on him.

Prince, he thought, startled. *Why, so I am, now.* The ludicrousness of the title bestowed so easily on an old man brought a rush of heat to his face. He bowed to her stiff shoulders and went out.

Rounding the corner of the passage, he almost ran into Horemheb. "Where are you going?" he blurted, caught off guard.

Horemheb raised his eyebrows under the white and black striped helmet. "I am on my way to offer my condolences to the queen, of course."

A dreadful suspicion grew in Ay. "She is seeing no one but me tonight. Surely Mutnodjme could more suitably express your sorrow."

"Perhaps." The dark eyes held a hint of fleeting amusement. "In any event, dear father-in-law, I see you have reached the goal before me. I have just heard the news that you are to become a god. My felicitations." There was nothing now but acceptance and a measure of warmth in Horemheb's face, and

Ay's suspicions suddenly became a certainty. He leaned against the wall, feeling faint.

"Of course, of course," he said dully. "You have been too clever for me, Commander. You did kill Tutankhamun out there on the desert."

Horemheb glanced swiftly around. The passage was empty. He stepped closer to Ay. "You are right. I did, and it is good that you know, Prince. Remember it well. And do not think that you can have me quietly disposed of. You can prove nothing against me. There is not a hand in Egypt that will be lifted against me now. Think." His fingers went to the scar on the square chin. His restless black eyes wandered Ay's face almost sympathetically. "Only I now stand between your rule and the chaos that will follow your death. Every lover of this country knows it. I am safer even than you."

"And you will not touch me, will you?" Ay said slowly. "You do not need to. I will die in peace, this year, next year, and you will mount the throne at your leisure." His lip curled. "A common soldier!"

Horemheb smiled tightly into the rheumy eyes. "I am justified before the gods. The impious ones are all dead, and I am waiting to sweep Egypt clean of every vestige of their accursed presence. Long life and prosperity to you, Majesty." He bowed and, turning on his heel, walked slowly away. He was voicing the desire of a court weary of irresponsible rule, of death and calamity, and Ay knew it. It was the hardest truth he had ever faced.

When Horemheb returned to his house, Mutnodjme was asleep. He did not wake her. Lowering himself onto the chair by the couch, he sat alternately watching her quiet breathing and dozing lightly. At dawn there was a stirring. Doors were flung open, fires stirred in the kitchens, morning prayers sung by Horemheb's priest in the house chapel. But Mutnodjme slumbered on until the steward knocked on the door and entered with a tray of fruit and bread. Horemheb took the tray himself, waiting until his wife had groggily pulled herself to a sitting position before setting it across her knees and returning to the chair.

Mutnodjme yawned, sat staring into space with sleep-swollen eyes, ran a tentative tongue over her teeth, and grimaced. She sipped the cool water that had been drawn for her from the large jug that had been left to stand all night in the passage.

Horemheb waited. At last she nodded, and he got up and raised the window hangings. A gush of scentless morning air poured into the room, together with sparkling light and the clamor of birds. Mutnodjme blinked and turned her head away.

"I fell asleep waiting for you," she said. "I am sorry."

"It does not matter." He took the chair again, folding his arms, watching her pick through the fruit with the dainty, absent gestures he knew so well while she began to revive like a wilted flower under a sprinkling of water. He had frightened and annoyed her of late, he knew, yet with characteristic patience and courage she had refused to be threatened. He did not know why he still loved her. It was more than the indolent, animal sensuality that surrounded her every move. Perhaps it was her self-absorption, the indifference to all but her own needs, which created an aura of self-sufficiency around her that both men and women mistakenly perceived as a challenge. "Mutnodjme, are you fully awake now?" he asked. "Will you take in what I have to say?"

"Do you have to be serious at this hour?" She pushed the tray away and leaned back, giving him a lopsided smile. "I prefer to discuss business in the evening."

"This is not business. I want you to notify the servants to start packing. After Tutankhamun's funeral we are moving to the estate at Memphis."

"Why?"

"For two reasons. Ay is to be pharaoh, and I want to remove myself completely from his attention. He called me a common soldier last night. Well, so I am, in spite of my wealth and titles, and I will behave like one. I will tour the border, drill the northern divisions, and in my spare time see to my crops and herds and entertain the local nomarchs. The Delta is, after all, the place where my ancestors settled."

"It sounds distressingly boring." She looked at him speculatively. "Are you afraid of my father?"

"No. If he is the statesman I think he is, he knows he dare not touch me."

"Then you want to cultivate actively the support of the officers who seldom see you. Are you plotting a civil war, Horemheb?"

He laughed, startled. "Again, no. It is true that I want the army to know more about its commander than his name, but it is also time for a temporary retirement. Mutnodjme, would you like to be a queen?"

She gaped at him and then exploded into hoarse laughter. "No, thank you, dearest brother! The queen's crown would not sit well on my youth lock, and besides, the penalties for a goddess's infidelities are very severe. Though I doubt that I shall find diverting lovers in the provinces. Are you going to declare our estates a separate kingdom?"

Unwillingly he smiled at her mirth. "I should not have said queen," he corrected himself. "I mean empress. I am very serious, Mutnodjme."

Her laughter died. "I understood your reasons for killing poor Smenkhara," she said soberly, "though the aftermath was terrible. I believe that you also have the blood of Tutankhamun on your hands, though I will never ask you outright if you were responsible. You are twice a god-killer, Horemheb. If you kill again, I will be forced to divorce you, take all that is mine, and retire to Akhmin or Djarukha. Ay is my father. I could not turn a blind eye to his murder."

"I have always been a hard man," he replied, "but I am not wantonly cruel. I swear by Amun that I will not harm your father. There is no need."

"No, I suppose there is not. But if there were, you would not hesitate, would you?"

He tentatively shook his head. "If the choice was forced upon me, I do not know. But I think I would decide to hold you to me above all else."

"You have that deceptively innocent look in your eyes," she retorted. "In any event, you are safe from such a decision because my father is very old. You need say no more. I understand it all."

He got up, kissed her briefly on the forehead, and went to the door. Pausing, he turned back, his face lit by a mischievousness she had not seen in years. "It is time you shaved off your youth lock, anyway," he teased. "There is so much gray in it."

"And you, my vain commander, should stop spending a fortune on face paint and accept your wrinkles! Please tell them to heat the water for my bath as you go out."

He knew that he could trust her, had known it before he obliquely asked, but his heart suddenly lightened as he walked out between the sun-splashed pillars of his portico and into the freshness of the morning. They would go north and settle in the shabby, rambling house outside Memphis he had begun to build while he was still a captain. He would attend to his unfinished tomb at Saqqara, walk the canals beside his fields, argue tactics with his officers in the cool, sweet Memphis evenings, perhaps even rediscover some of the simple pleasures he had enjoyed before ambition robbed him of their joy. It would not be enough, he knew that. It had never been enough. But for the time being he would be content.

30

THE KEEPER OF THE ROYAL REGALIA KNELT TO RECEIVE THE crook, flail, and scimitar and reverently kissed them before laying them carefully in their golden chest. Bent almost double, the cosmetician mounted the steps of the throne and, murmuring an apology, patted the sweat from the god's face and gently retouched the black kohl around the eyes. The great hall slowly filled with richly clad courtiers, ambassadors, ministers, and governors, exhausted by the long morning of ceremonies. At the foot of the dais steps the contingent of Followers stood stiffly, their watchful eyes scanning the hall, and the heralds with white staffs in their hands waited patiently before calling all to prostrate themselves. The sandal bearer knelt patiently with the empty box on the tiles before him. To right and left of the throne the fanbearers held the quivering white symbols of Pharaoh's inalienable right to every protection, and before it, resplendent in the leopard skin, a crabbed and aging Maya held incense over the throng.

Conversation in the hall was desultory, expectant, the painted eyes of the assembly glancing frequently at the dais. Horemheb let them wait. Turning, he smiled at Mutnodjme, stiff with jewels and gold-shot linen, the horned disk and plumes of the empress's crown gleaming dully above her forehead. With one red-hennaed palm he cupped her chin, his rings glinting, and her wide lips parted in an answering smile. He had insisted that she receive the empress's crown during the ceremony, not because the empire had as yet been won back, but as a sign to the privileged assembly that it would be. He dropped his hand and beckoned Nakht-Min. The fanbearer bent.

"Your Majesty desires?"

"Today is the time of beginnings," Horemheb said. "Old ministers are dismissed, new ones appointed, nobles created, rewards bestowed. It is my divine will that you be relieved of the position of Fanbearer on the Right Hand, Nakht-Min." Nakht-Min struggled to hide his shock. It was the most coveted task in Egypt and led inevitably to the position of Eyes and Ears of the King or the King's Own Scribe. Horemheb watched his effort at self-control with an inward smile. "As your Majesty wishes," the man managed. Horemheb laughed.

"I have another task for you, General. Did your four years under Pharaoh Osiris Ay cause you to forget what you really are?"

Nakht-Min's face cleared. "No, indeed, Great Horus."

"Good. I want you to take command of the army. Three divisions are massed in the Delta. It is time to push into southern Syria. That is the first directive of my reign. I am about to make young Rameses Vizier of the South, but I want him as your second-in-command for the present. The position of vizier is to keep him happy. He is a good soldier." He brushed aside Nakht-Min's thanks, his gaze going thoughtfully to the rear of the hall, where the curious foreign embassies were massed, here in Memphis to test the waters of a new administration. Horemheb noted the dark visage of the Khatti ambassador sent by their new ruler, the son of Suppiluliumas, Mursilis. He smiled to himself. Mursilis was about to receive more than polite greetings from Egypt. He spoke to Nakht-Min again. "Let your last task as fanbearer be to command my architects to design a triumphal pylon for me at Thebes. Nefertiti's temple at Karnak shall be torn down to provide the building blocks. Akhenaten's Karnak temple will be completely razed as well, and you may let it be known that any man needing stone for his monuments may use whatever he pleases from the dead city of Akhetaten without punishment." He waved at the heralds, who immediately lifted their staffs and began to shout his titles, and the people went down on their faces.

Horemheb surveyed the worshiping crowd with quiet satisfaction. *Thus I will wipe their memory from the face of the earth*, he thought, *and the gods will forgive me everything. Tomorrow we return to Malkatta, and a new day will dawn for Egypt. I will take the empress Tiye from the polluting atmosphere of her son and place her in the sanctity of her true husband's tomb. And Akhenaten? Him I will burn, like the purifying fire of his Aten. My will is the law, for at last I have become a god.* He felt Mutnodjme's hand brush his own and came to himself. The people had risen and were waiting patiently. It was time to begin. Horemheb felt the Double Crown heavy on his brow. He cleared his throat.

"Maya, stand forth!" he commanded. "Hear my desire for the House of Amun. . . ."

ABOUT THE AUTHOR

PAULINE GEDGE was born in Auckland, New Zealand. She spent part of her childhood in Oxfordshire, England, and now lives with her two sons in Alberta, Canada. Her previous novels are *Child of the Morning* (1977), *The Eagle and the Raven* (1978), and *Stargate* (1982).